WINGS OF FIRE

THE DARK SECRET
THE GRAPHIC NOVEL

For Oscar and Beatrice, two of the most awesome
people ever — we feel so lucky to have you as friends!
—T.T.S.

For Ruby and Gabby, who I hope will always
let me know if my art's any good
—M.H.

Story and text copyright © 2021 by Tui T. Sutherland
Adaptation by Barry Deutsch and Rachel Swirsky
Map and border design © 2012 by Mike Schley
Art by Mike Holmes © 2021 by Scholastic Inc.

Library of Congress Control Number Available

ISBN 978-1-338-34422-6 (hardcover)
ISBN 978-1-338-34421-9 (paperback)

10 9 8 7 6 5 4 3 2 1   21 22 23 24 25

Printed in China   62
First edition, January 2021
Edited by Amanda Maciel
Coloring by Maarta Laiho
Lettering by E.K. Weaver
Creative Director: Phil Falco
Publisher: David Saylor

WINGS OF FIRE

THE DARK SECRET
THE GRAPHIC NOVEL

BY TUI T. SUTHERLAND

ADAPTED BY BARRY DEUTSCH
AND RACHEL SWIRSKY

ART BY MIKE HOLMES
COLOR BY MAARTA LAIHO

AN IMPRINT OF
SCHOLASTIC

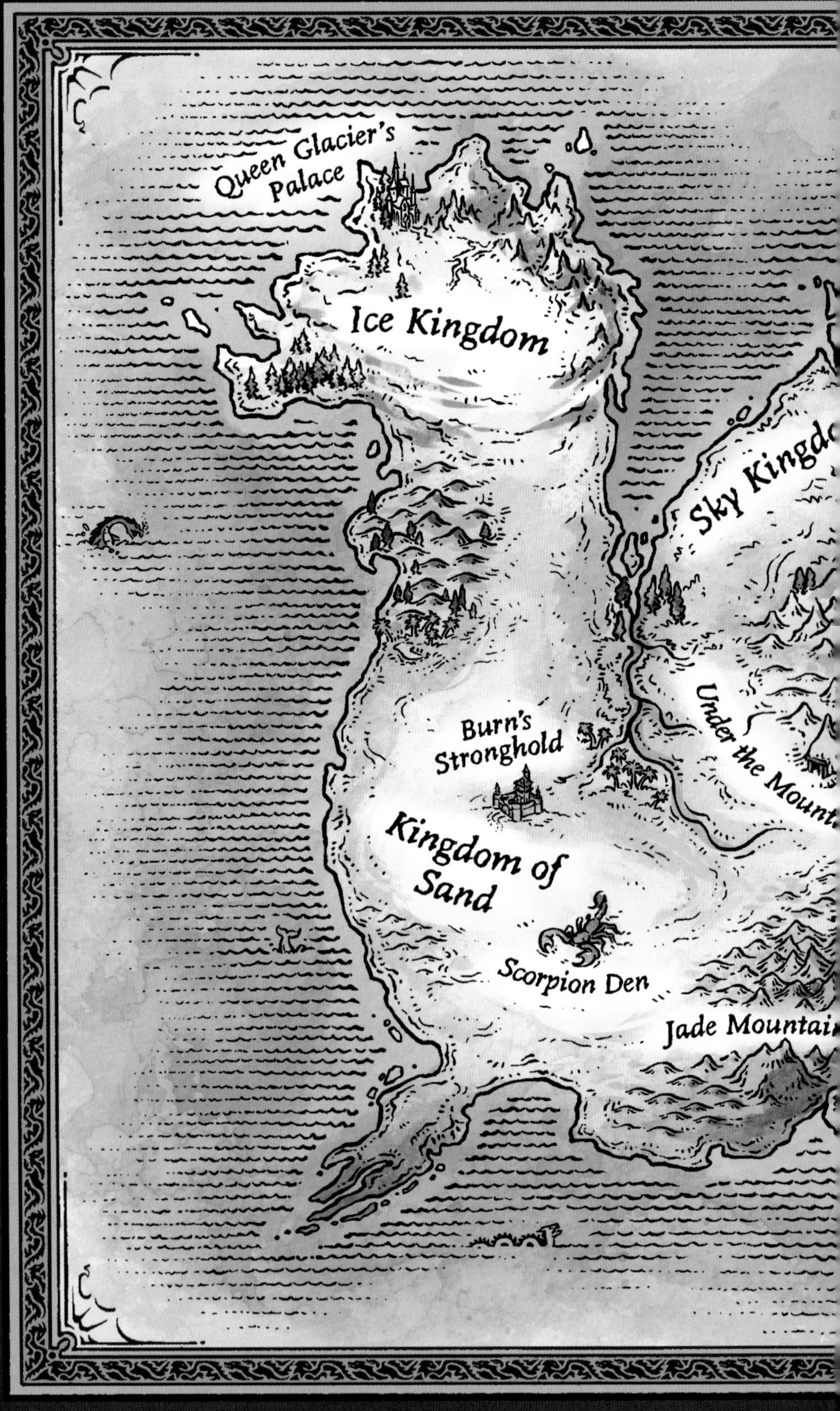

Queen Glacier's Palace
Ice Kingdom
Sky Kingd
Under the Mount
Burn's Stronghold
Kingdom of Sand
Scorpion Den
Jade Mountai

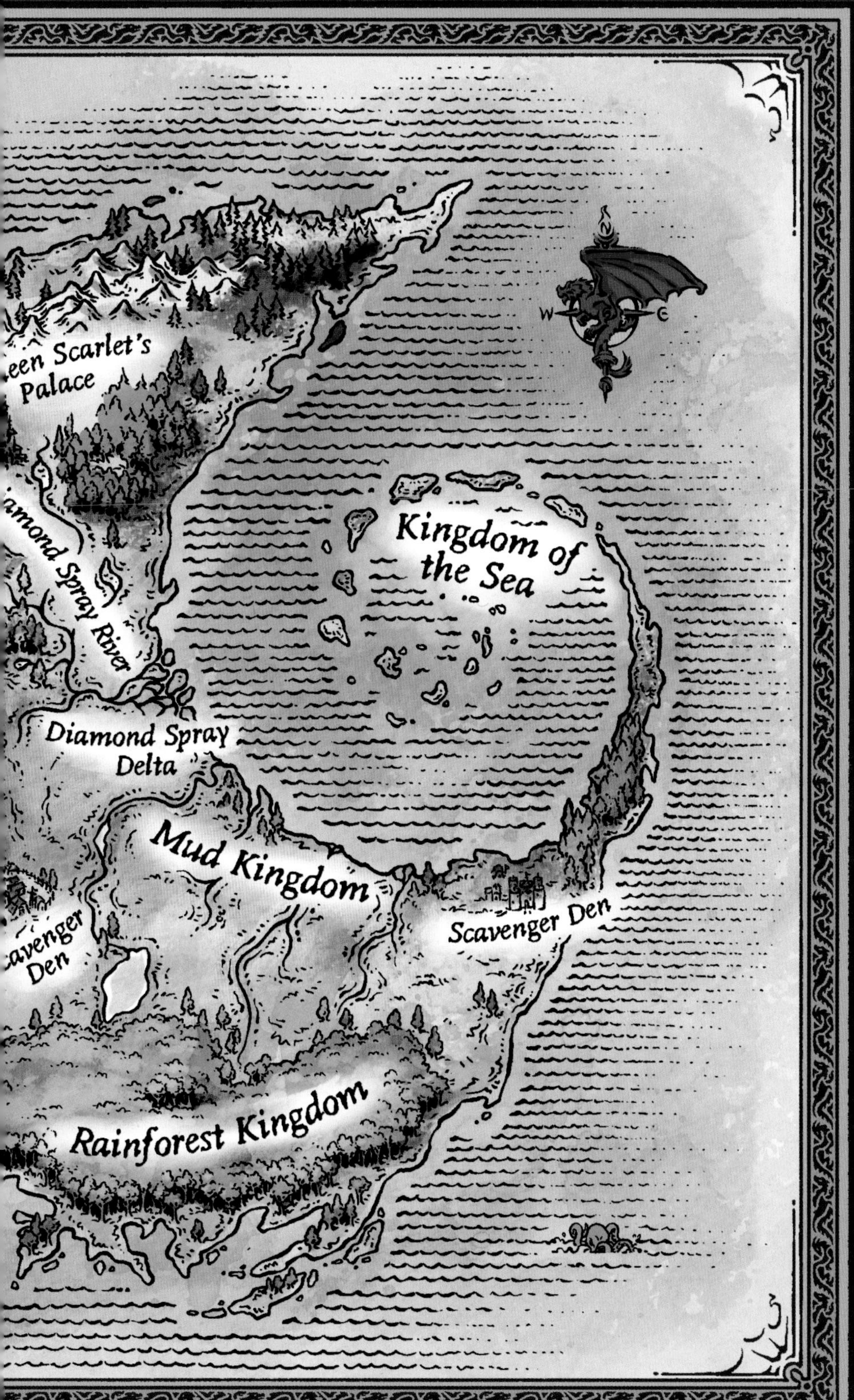

een Scarlet's
Palace
amond Spray River
Diamond Spray
Delta
Kingdom of
the Sea
Mud Kingdom
cavenger
Den
Scavenger Den
Rainforest Kingdom
W

THE DARK SECRET

THE DRAGONET
PROPHECY

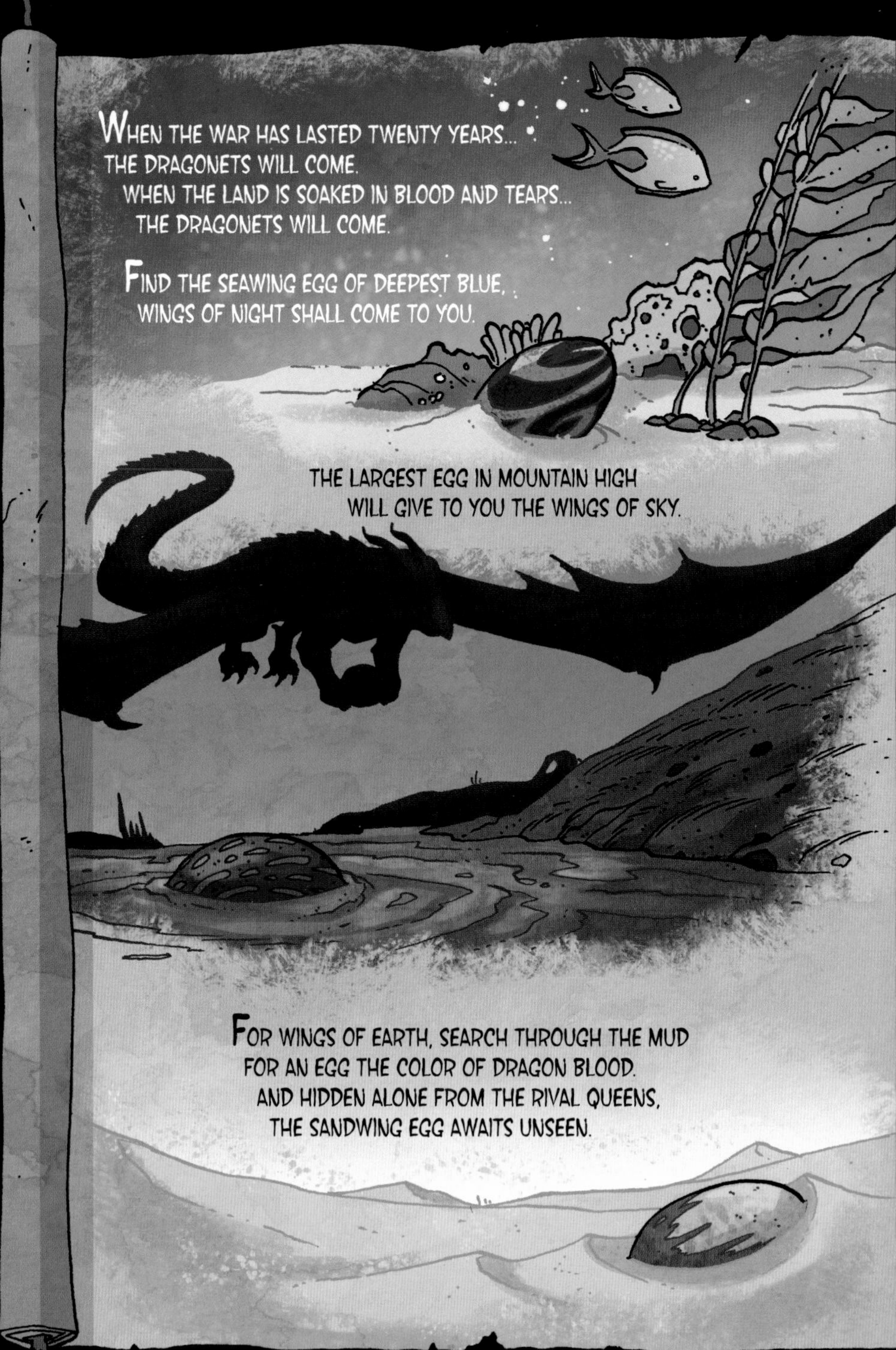
WHEN THE WAR HAS LASTED TWENTY YEARS...
THE DRAGONETS WILL COME.
WHEN THE LAND IS SOAKED IN BLOOD AND TEARS...
THE DRAGONETS WILL COME.
FIND THE SEAWING EGG OF DEEPEST BLUE,
WINGS OF NIGHT SHALL COME TO YOU.
THE LARGEST EGG IN MOUNTAIN HIGH
WILL GIVE TO YOU THE WINGS OF SKY.
FOR WINGS OF EARTH, SEARCH THROUGH THE MUD
FOR AN EGG THE COLOR OF DRAGON BLOOD.
AND HIDDEN ALONE FROM THE RIVAL QUEENS,
THE SANDWING EGG AWAITS UNSEEN.

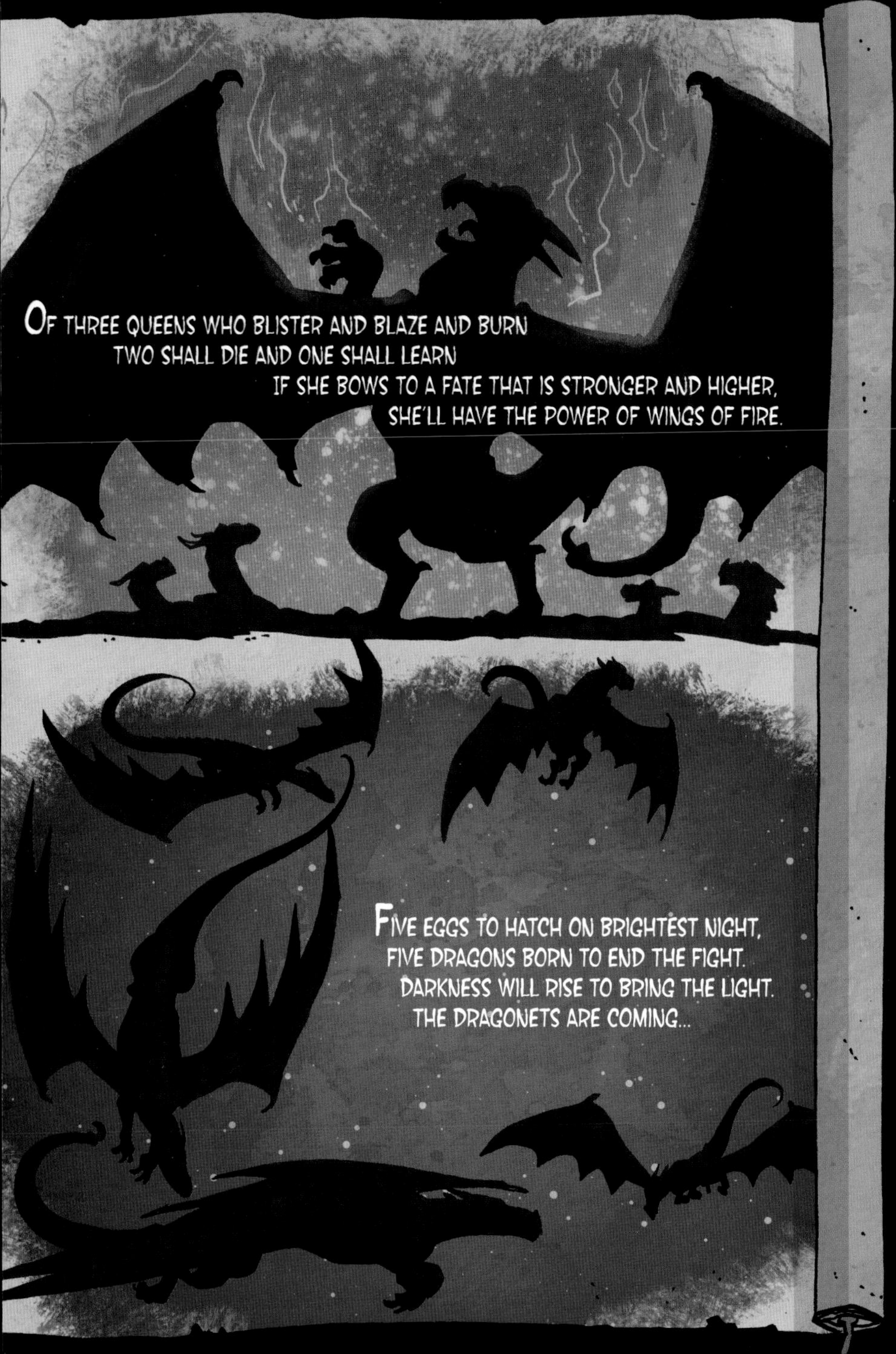
OF THREE QUEENS WHO BLISTER AND BLAZE AND BURN
TWO SHALL DIE AND ONE SHALL LEARN
IF SHE BOWS TO A FATE THAT IS STRONGER AND HIGHER,
SHE'LL HAVE THE POWER OF WINGS OF FIRE.
FIVE EGGS TO HATCH ON BRIGHTEST NIGHT,
FIVE DRAGONS BORN TO END THE FIGHT.
DARKNESS WILL RISE TO BRING THE LIGHT.
THE DRAGONETS ARE COMING...

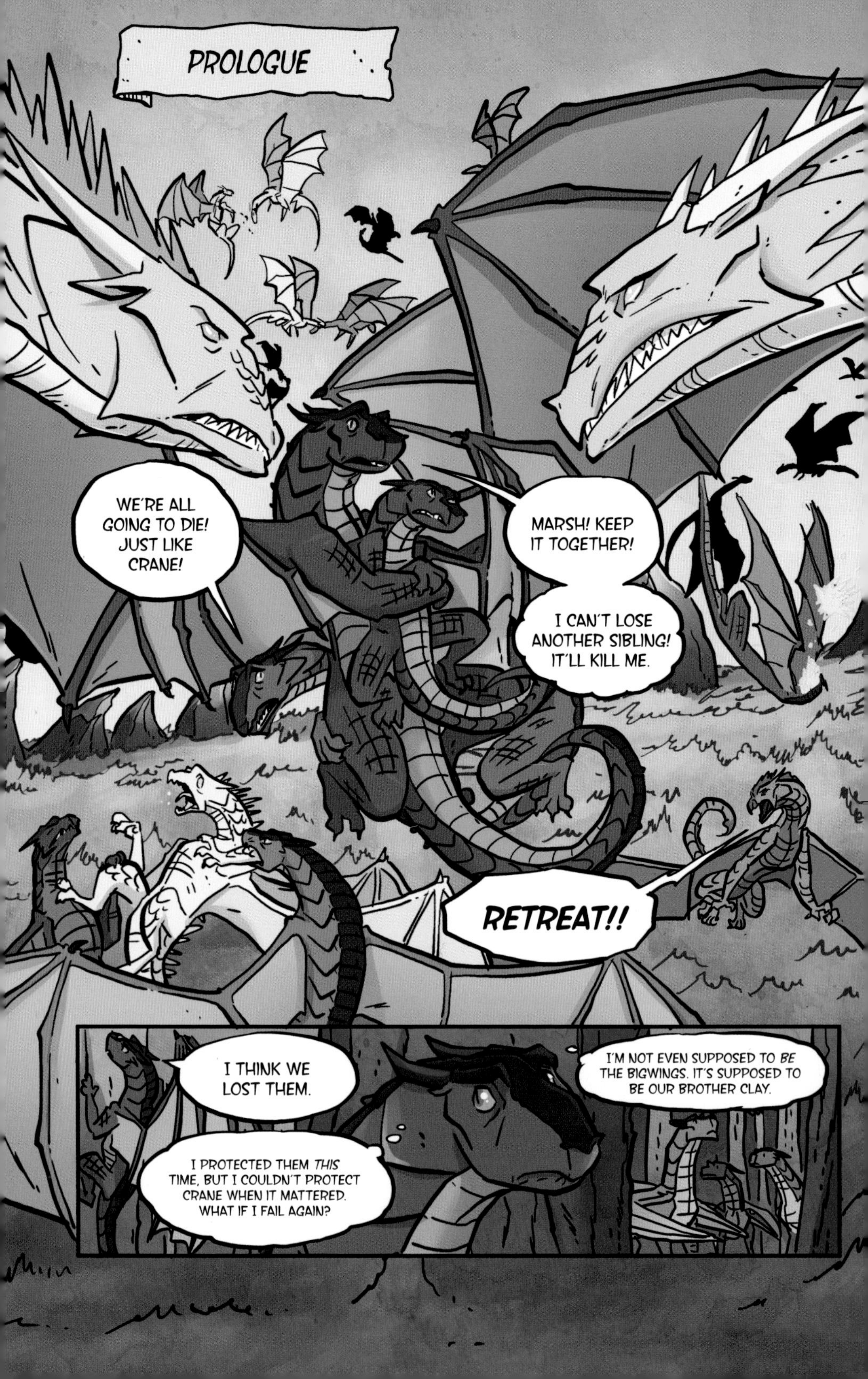
PROLOGUE
WE'RE ALL GOING TO DIE! JUST LIKE CRANE!
MARSH! KEEP IT TOGETHER!
I CAN'T LOSE ANOTHER SIBLING! IT'LL KILL ME.
RETREAT!!
I THINK WE LOST THEM.
I'M NOT EVEN SUPPOSED TO *BE* THE BIGWINGS. IT'S SUPPOSED TO BE OUR BROTHER CLAY.
I PROTECTED THEM *THIS* TIME, BUT I COULDN'T PROTECT CRANE WHEN IT MATTERED. WHAT IF I FAIL AGAIN?

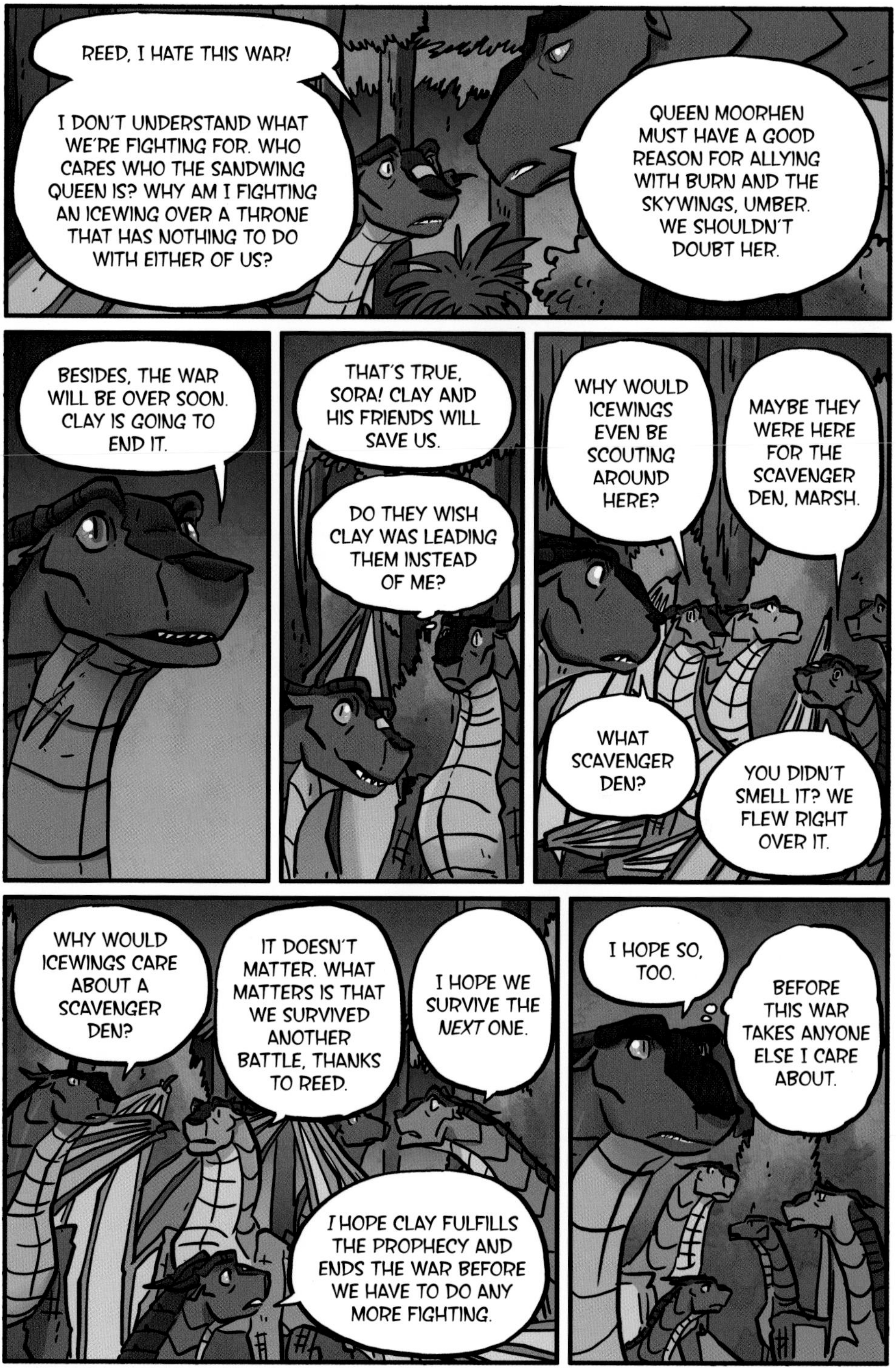
REED, I HATE THIS WAR!
I DON'T UNDERSTAND WHAT WE'RE FIGHTING FOR. WHO CARES WHO THE SANDWING QUEEN IS? WHY AM I FIGHTING AN ICEWING OVER A THRONE THAT HAS NOTHING TO DO WITH EITHER OF US?
QUEEN MOORHEN MUST HAVE A GOOD REASON FOR ALLYING WITH BURN AND THE SKYWINGS, UMBER. WE SHOULDN'T DOUBT HER.
BESIDES, THE WAR WILL BE OVER SOON. CLAY IS GOING TO END IT.
THAT'S TRUE, SORA! CLAY AND HIS FRIENDS WILL SAVE US.
DO THEY WISH CLAY WAS LEADING THEM INSTEAD OF ME?
WHY WOULD ICEWINGS EVEN BE SCOUTING AROUND HERE?
MAYBE THEY WERE HERE FOR THE SCAVENGER DEN, MARSH.
WHAT SCAVENGER DEN?
YOU DIDN'T SMELL IT? WE FLEW RIGHT OVER IT.
WHY WOULD ICEWINGS CARE ABOUT A SCAVENGER DEN?
IT DOESN'T MATTER. WHAT MATTERS IS THAT WE SURVIVED ANOTHER BATTLE, THANKS TO REED.
I HOPE WE SURVIVE THE *NEXT* ONE.
I HOPE CLAY FULFILLS THE PROPHECY AND ENDS THE WAR BEFORE WE HAVE TO DO ANY MORE FIGHTING.
I HOPE SO, TOO.
BEFORE THIS WAR TAKES ANYONE ELSE I CARE ABOUT.

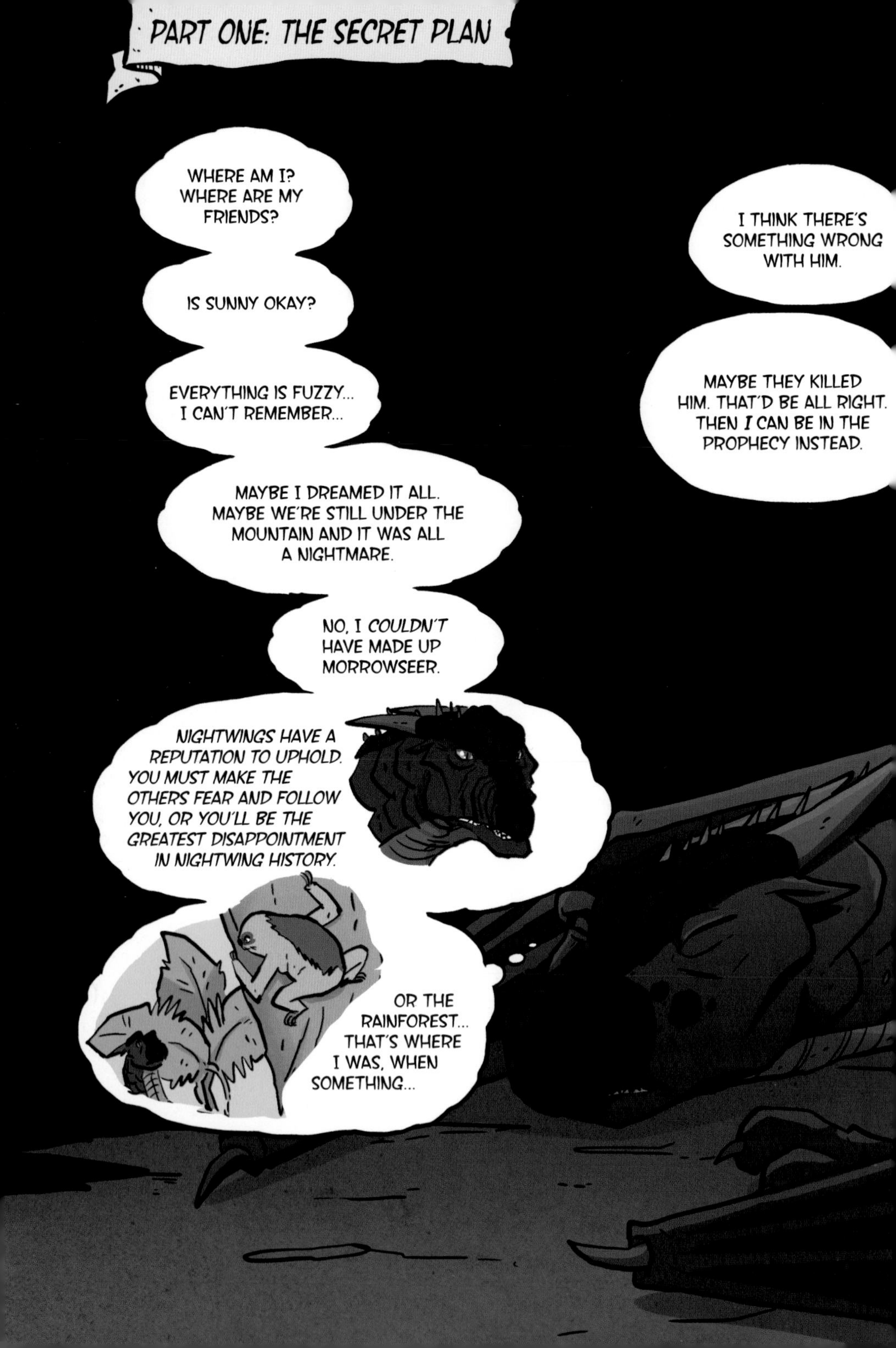
PART ONE: THE SECRET PLAN
WHERE AM I? WHERE ARE MY FRIENDS?
IS SUNNY OKAY?
EVERYTHING IS FUZZY... I CAN'T REMEMBER...
MAYBE I DREAMED IT ALL. MAYBE WE'RE STILL UNDER THE MOUNTAIN AND IT WAS ALL A NIGHTMARE.
NO, I *COULDN'T* HAVE MADE UP MORROWSEER.
NIGHTWINGS HAVE A REPUTATION TO UPHOLD. YOU MUST MAKE THE OTHERS FEAR AND FOLLOW YOU, OR YOU'LL BE THE GREATEST DISAPPOINTMENT IN NIGHTWING HISTORY.
OR THE RAINFOREST... THAT'S WHERE I WAS, WHEN SOMETHING...
I THINK THERE'S SOMETHING WRONG WITH HIM.
MAYBE THEY KILLED HIM. THAT'D BE ALL RIGHT. THEN *I* CAN BE IN THE PROPHECY INSTEAD.

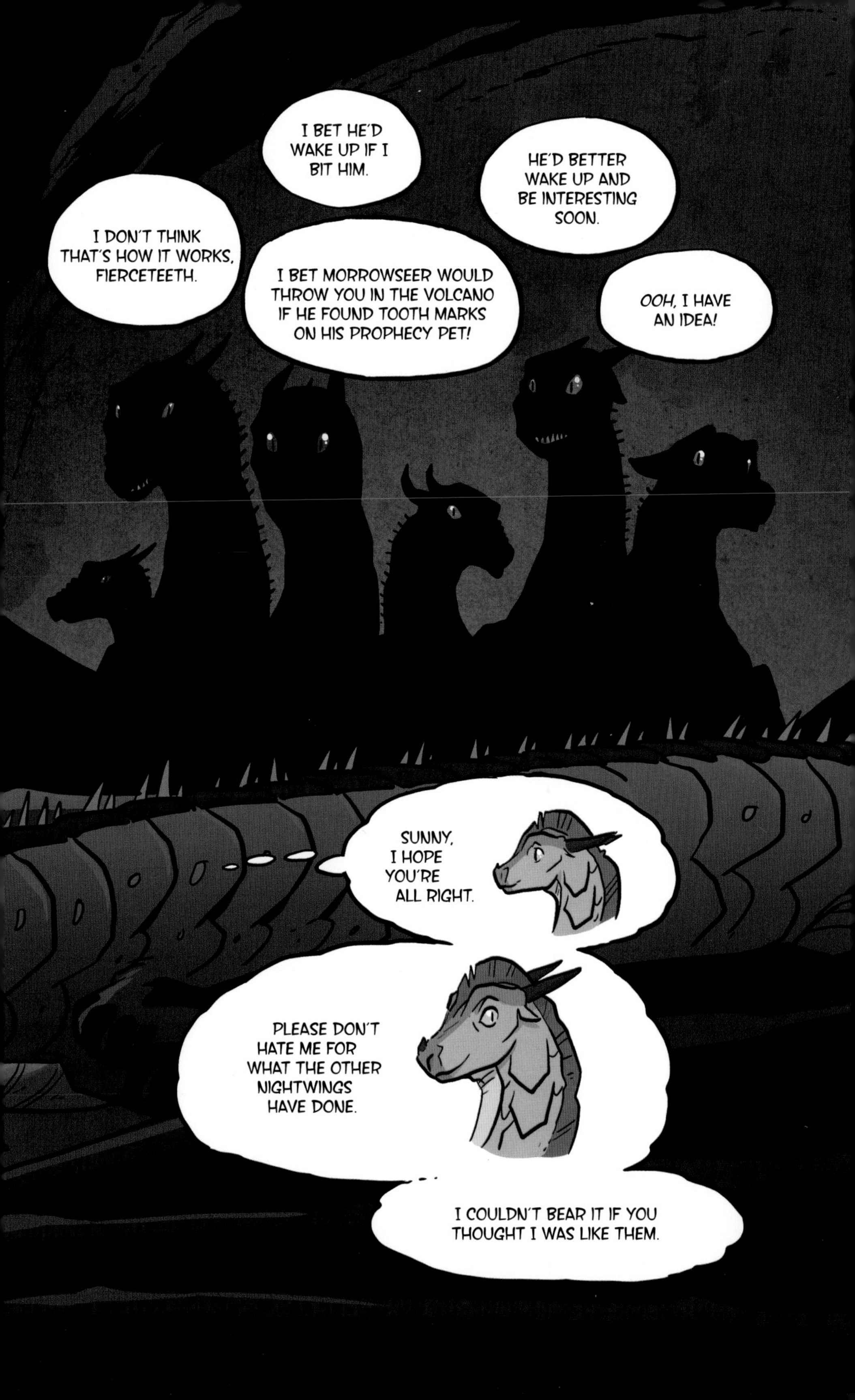
I BET HE'D WAKE UP IF I BIT HIM.
HE'D BETTER WAKE UP AND BE INTERESTING SOON.
I DON'T THINK THAT'S HOW IT WORKS, FIERCETEETH.
I BET MORROWSEER WOULD THROW YOU IN THE VOLCANO IF HE FOUND TOOTH MARKS ON HIS PROPHECY PET!
OOH, I HAVE AN IDEA!
SUNNY, I HOPE YOU'RE ALL RIGHT.
PLEASE DON'T HATE ME FOR WHAT THE OTHER NIGHTWINGS HAVE DONE.
I COULDN'T BEAR IT IF YOU THOUGHT I WAS LIKE THEM.

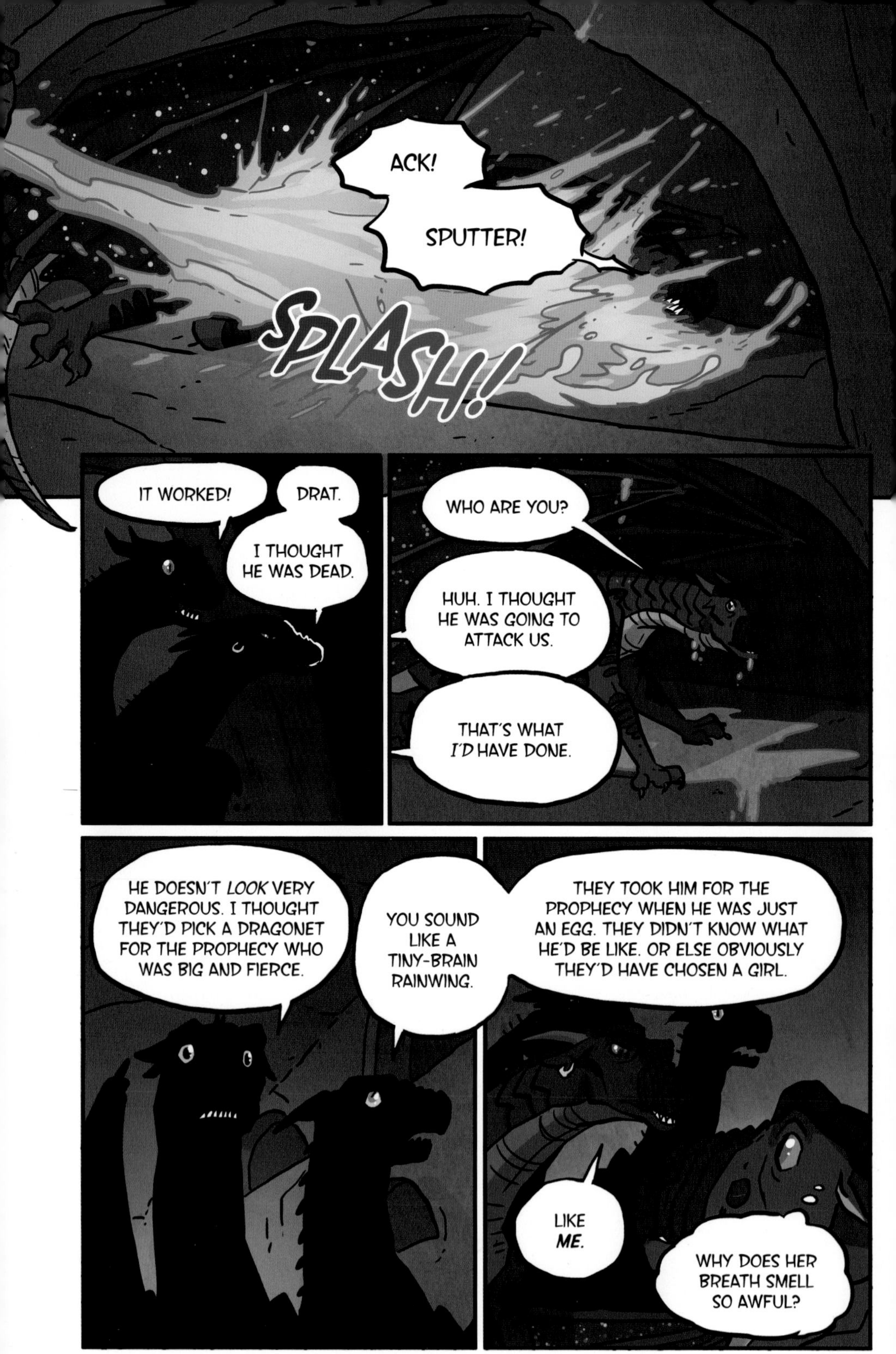
ACK!
SPUTTER!
SPLASH!
IT WORKED!
DRAT.
I THOUGHT HE WAS DEAD.
WHO ARE YOU?
HUH. I THOUGHT HE WAS GOING TO ATTACK US.
THAT'S WHAT *I'D* HAVE DONE.
HE DOESN'T *LOOK* VERY DANGEROUS. I THOUGHT THEY'D PICK A DRAGONET FOR THE PROPHECY WHO WAS BIG AND FIERCE.
YOU SOUND LIKE A TINY-BRAIN RAINWING.
THEY TOOK HIM FOR THE PROPHECY WHEN HE WAS JUST AN EGG. THEY DIDN'T KNOW WHAT HE'D BE LIKE. OR ELSE OBVIOUSLY THEY'D HAVE CHOSEN A GIRL.
LIKE *ME.*
WHY DOES HER BREATH SMELL SO AWFUL?

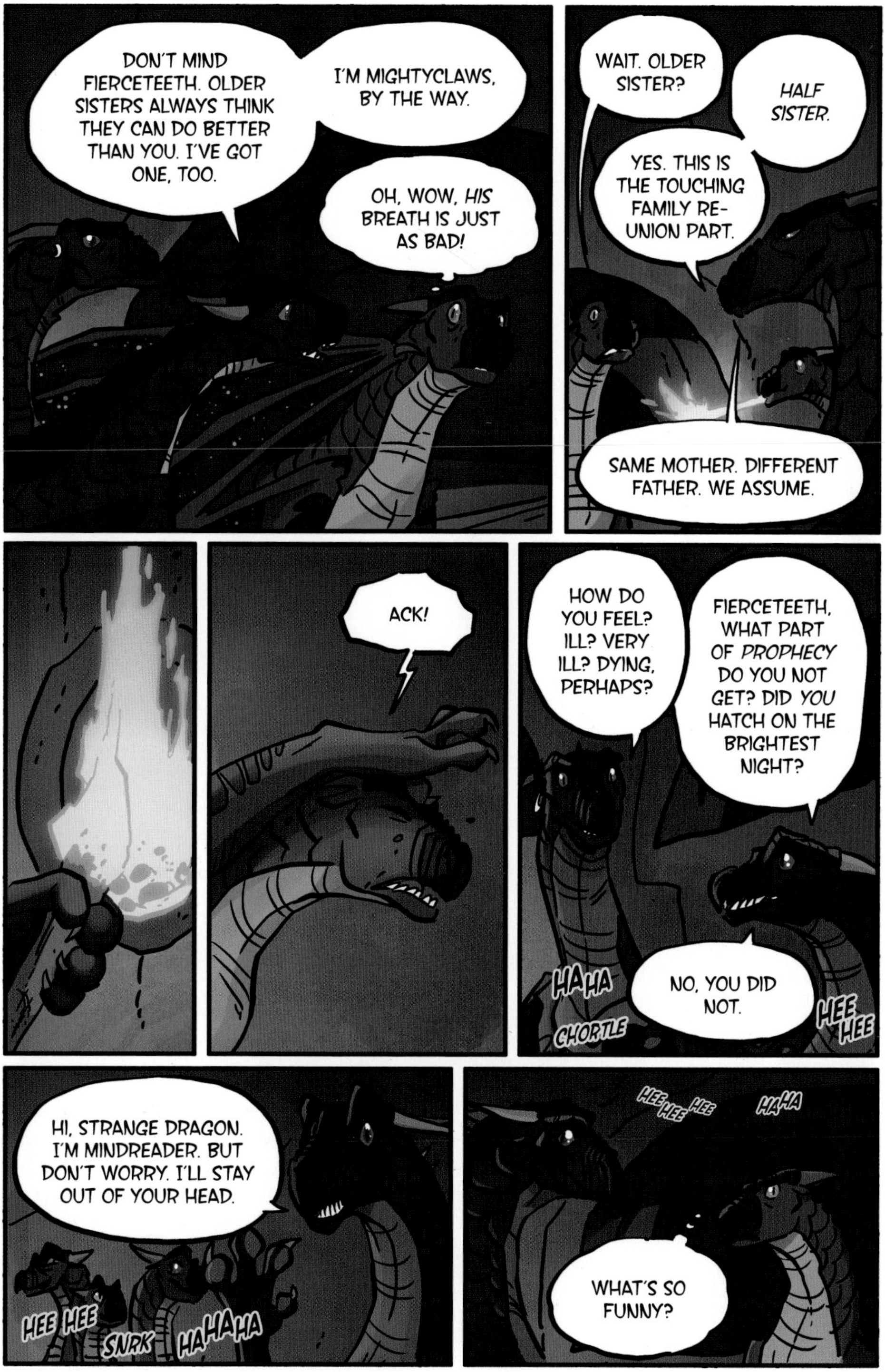
DON'T MIND FIERCETEETH. OLDER SISTERS ALWAYS THINK THEY CAN DO BETTER THAN YOU. I'VE GOT ONE, TOO.
I'M MIGHTYCLAWS, BY THE WAY.
OH, WOW, *HIS* BREATH IS JUST AS BAD!
WAIT. OLDER SISTER?
HALF SISTER.
YES. THIS IS THE TOUCHING FAMILY RE-UNION PART.
SAME MOTHER. DIFFERENT FATHER. WE ASSUME.
ACK!
HOW DO YOU FEEL? ILL? VERY ILL? DYING, PERHAPS?
FIERCETEETH, WHAT PART OF *PROPHECY* DO YOU NOT GET? DID *YOU* HATCH ON THE BRIGHTEST NIGHT?
HAHA
CHORTLE
NO, YOU DID NOT.
HEE HEE
HI, STRANGE DRAGON. I'M MINDREADER. BUT DON'T WORRY. I'LL STAY OUT OF YOUR HEAD.
HEE HEE
SNRK
HAHAHA
HEE HEE HEE
HAHA
WHAT'S SO FUNNY?

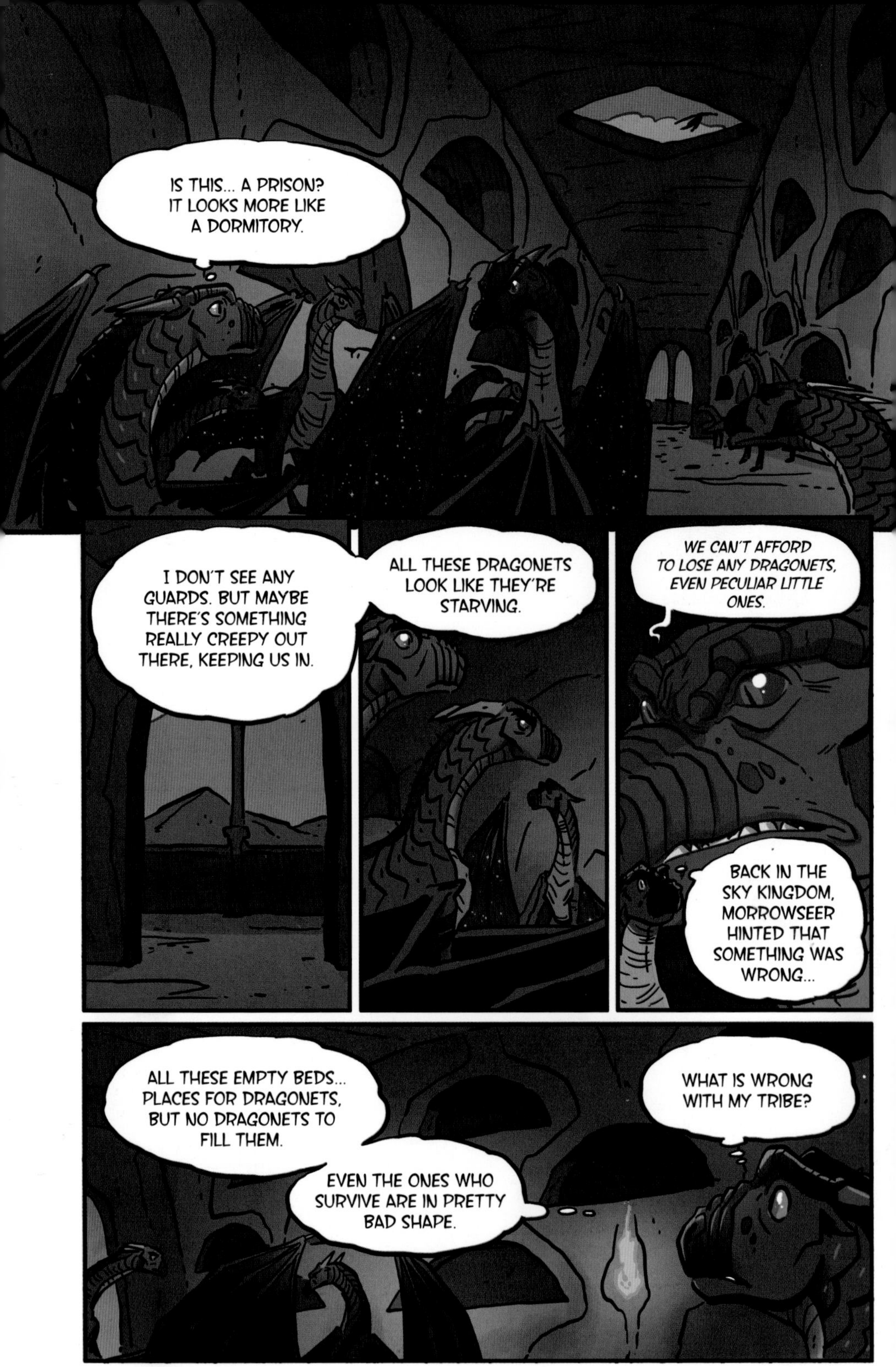
IS THIS... A PRISON? IT LOOKS MORE LIKE A DORMITORY.
I DON'T SEE ANY GUARDS. BUT MAYBE THERE'S SOMETHING REALLY CREEPY OUT THERE, KEEPING US IN.
ALL THESE DRAGONETS LOOK LIKE THEY'RE STARVING.
WE CAN'T AFFORD TO LOSE ANY DRAGONETS, EVEN PECULIAR LITTLE ONES.
BACK IN THE SKY KINGDOM, MORROWSEER HINTED THAT SOMETHING WAS WRONG...
ALL THESE EMPTY BEDS... PLACES FOR DRAGONETS, BUT NO DRAGONETS TO FILL THEM.
EVEN THE ONES WHO SURVIVE ARE IN PRETTY BAD SHAPE.
WHAT IS WRONG WITH MY TRIBE?

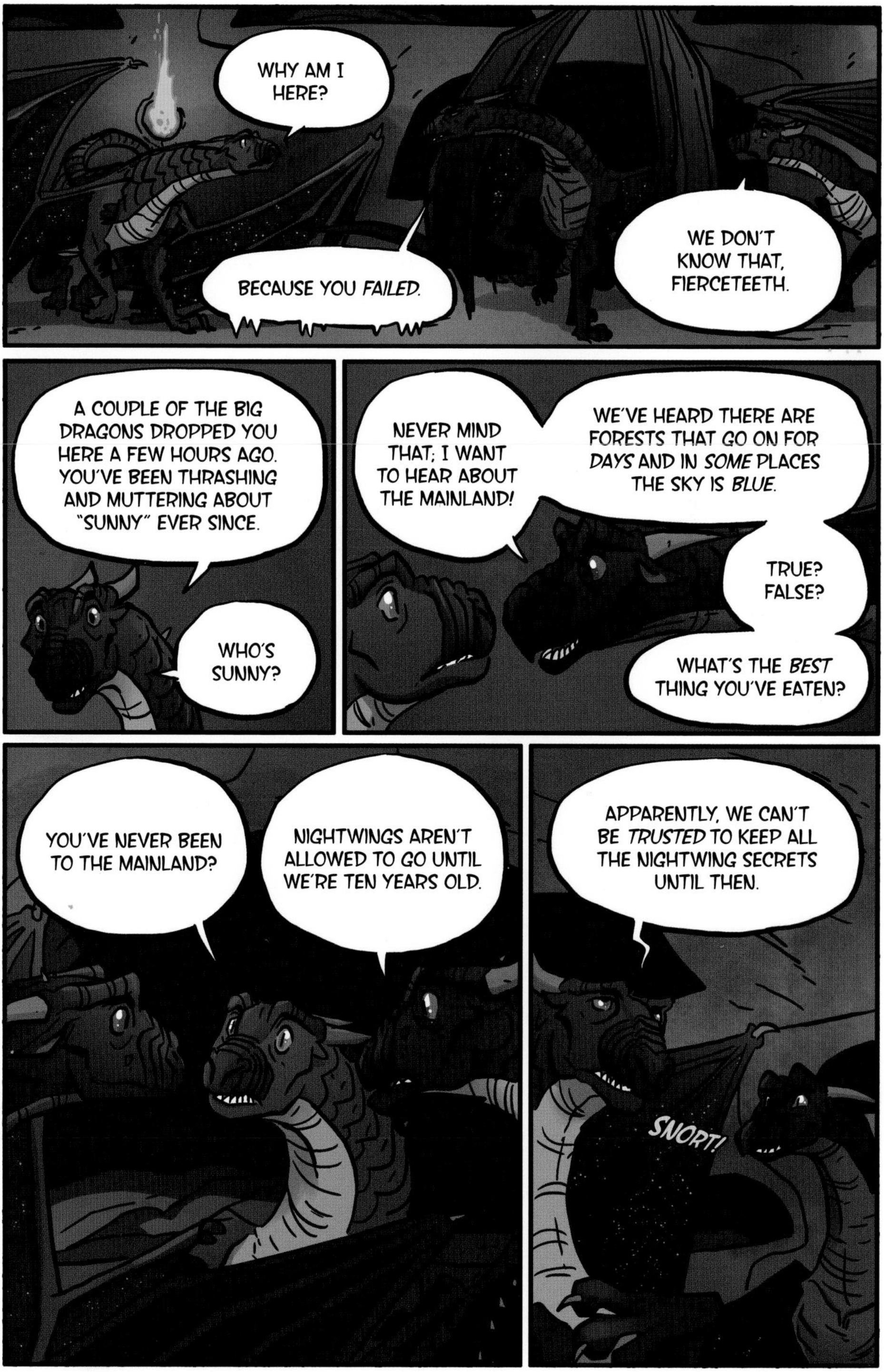
WHY AM I HERE?
BECAUSE YOU *FAILED.*
WE DON'T KNOW THAT, FIERCETEETH.
A COUPLE OF THE BIG DRAGONS DROPPED YOU HERE A FEW HOURS AGO. YOU'VE BEEN THRASHING AND MUTTERING ABOUT "SUNNY" EVER SINCE.
WHO'S SUNNY?
NEVER MIND THAT; I WANT TO HEAR ABOUT THE MAINLAND!
WE'VE HEARD THERE ARE FORESTS THAT GO ON FOR *DAYS* AND IN *SOME* PLACES THE SKY IS *BLUE.*
TRUE? FALSE?
WHAT'S THE *BEST* THING YOU'VE EATEN?
YOU'VE NEVER BEEN TO THE MAINLAND?
NIGHTWINGS AREN'T ALLOWED TO GO UNTIL WE'RE TEN YEARS OLD.
APPARENTLY, WE CAN'T BE *TRUSTED* TO KEEP ALL THE NIGHTWING SECRETS UNTIL THEN.
SNORT!

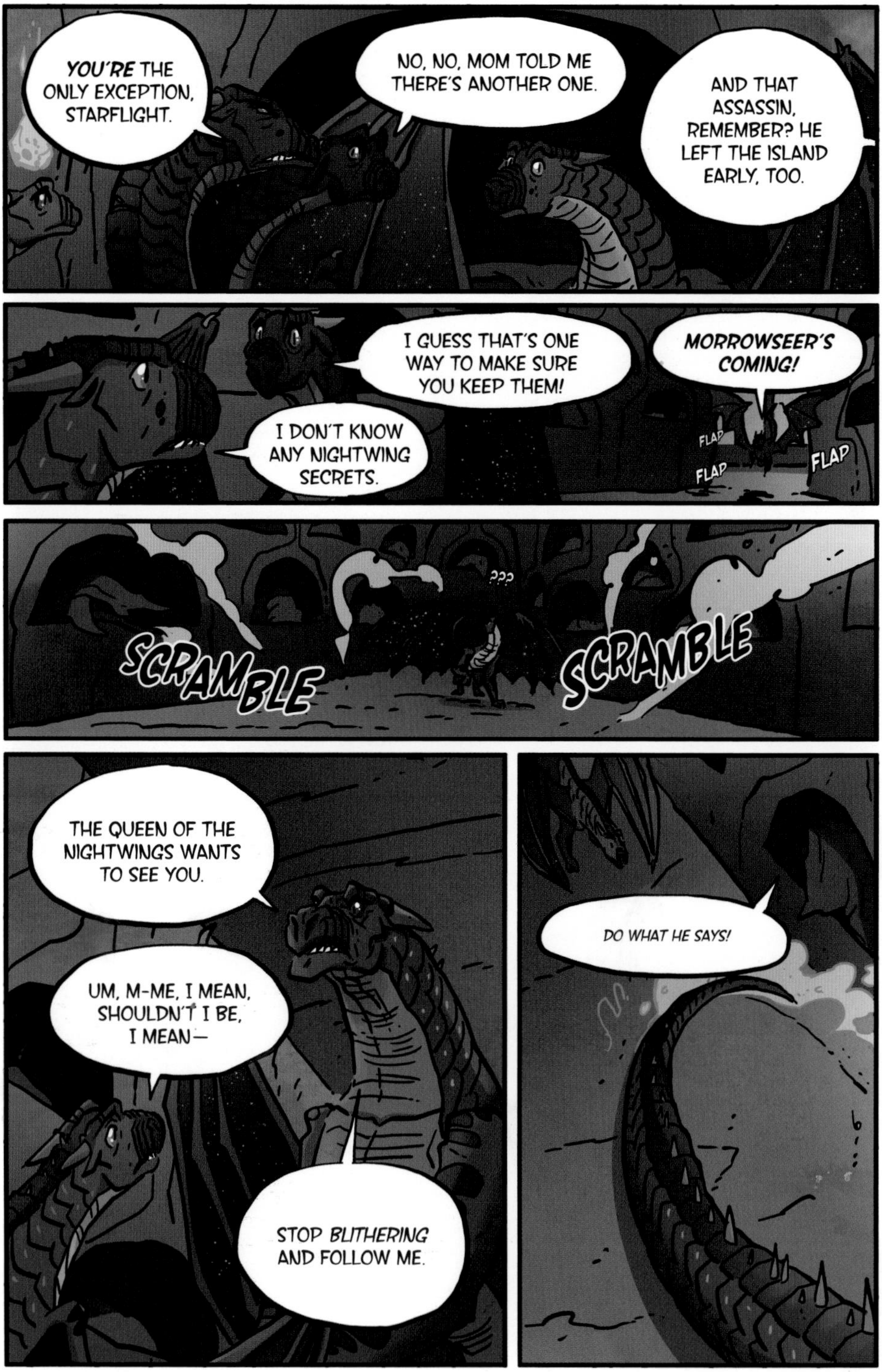
YOU'RE THE ONLY EXCEPTION, STARFLIGHT.
NO, NO, MOM TOLD ME THERE'S ANOTHER ONE.
AND THAT ASSASSIN, REMEMBER? HE LEFT THE ISLAND EARLY, TOO.
I DON'T KNOW ANY NIGHTWING SECRETS.
I GUESS THAT'S ONE WAY TO MAKE SURE YOU KEEP THEM!
MORROWSEER'S COMING!
FLAP
FLAP
FLAP
SCRAMBLE
???
SCRAMBLE
THE QUEEN OF THE NIGHTWINGS WANTS TO SEE YOU.
UM, M-ME, I MEAN, SHOULDN'T I BE, I MEAN—
STOP BLITHERING AND FOLLOW ME.
DO WHAT HE SAYS!

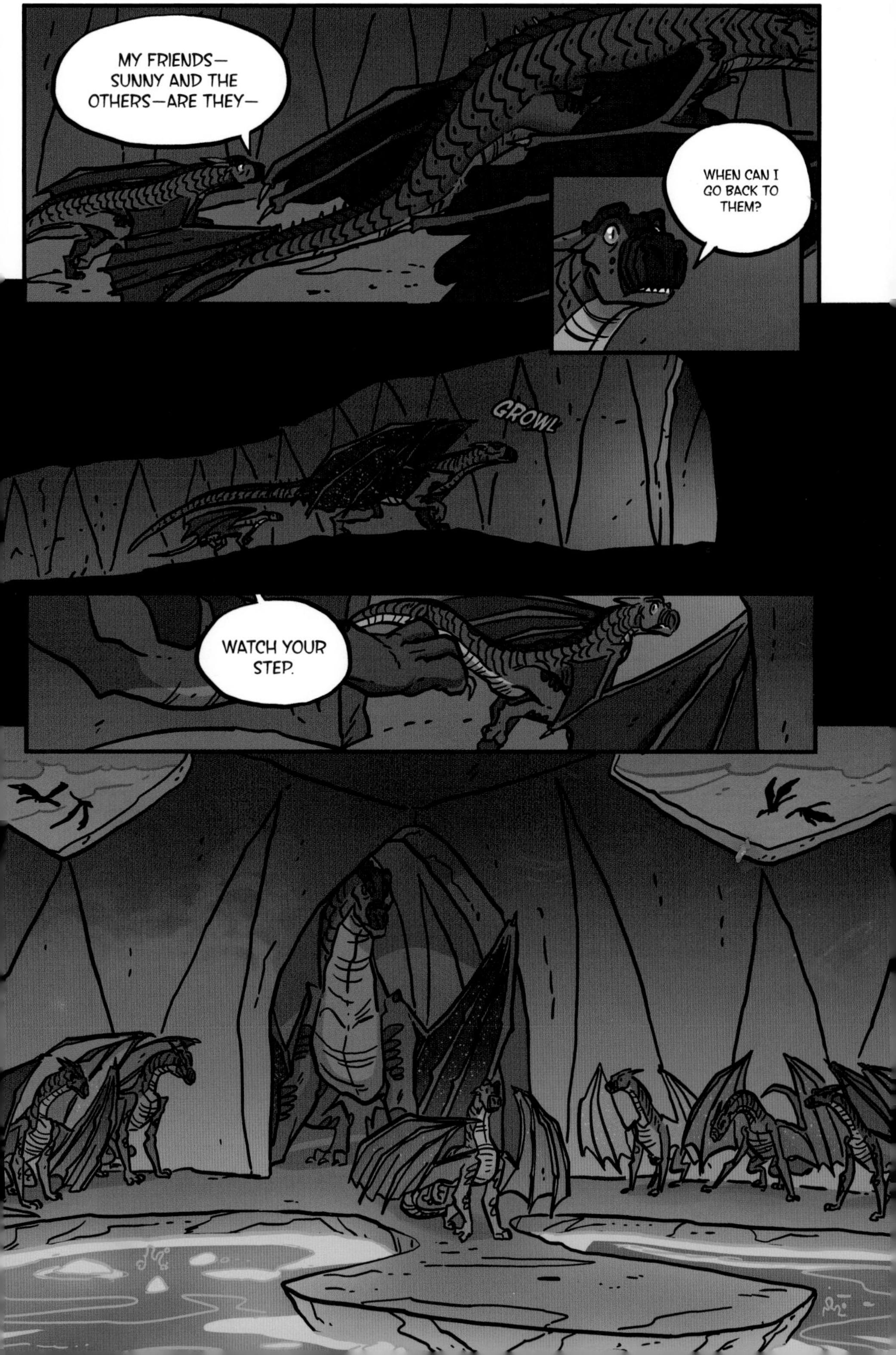
MY FRIENDS—SUNNY AND THE OTHERS—ARE THEY—
WHEN CAN I GO BACK TO THEM?
GROWL
WATCH YOUR STEP.

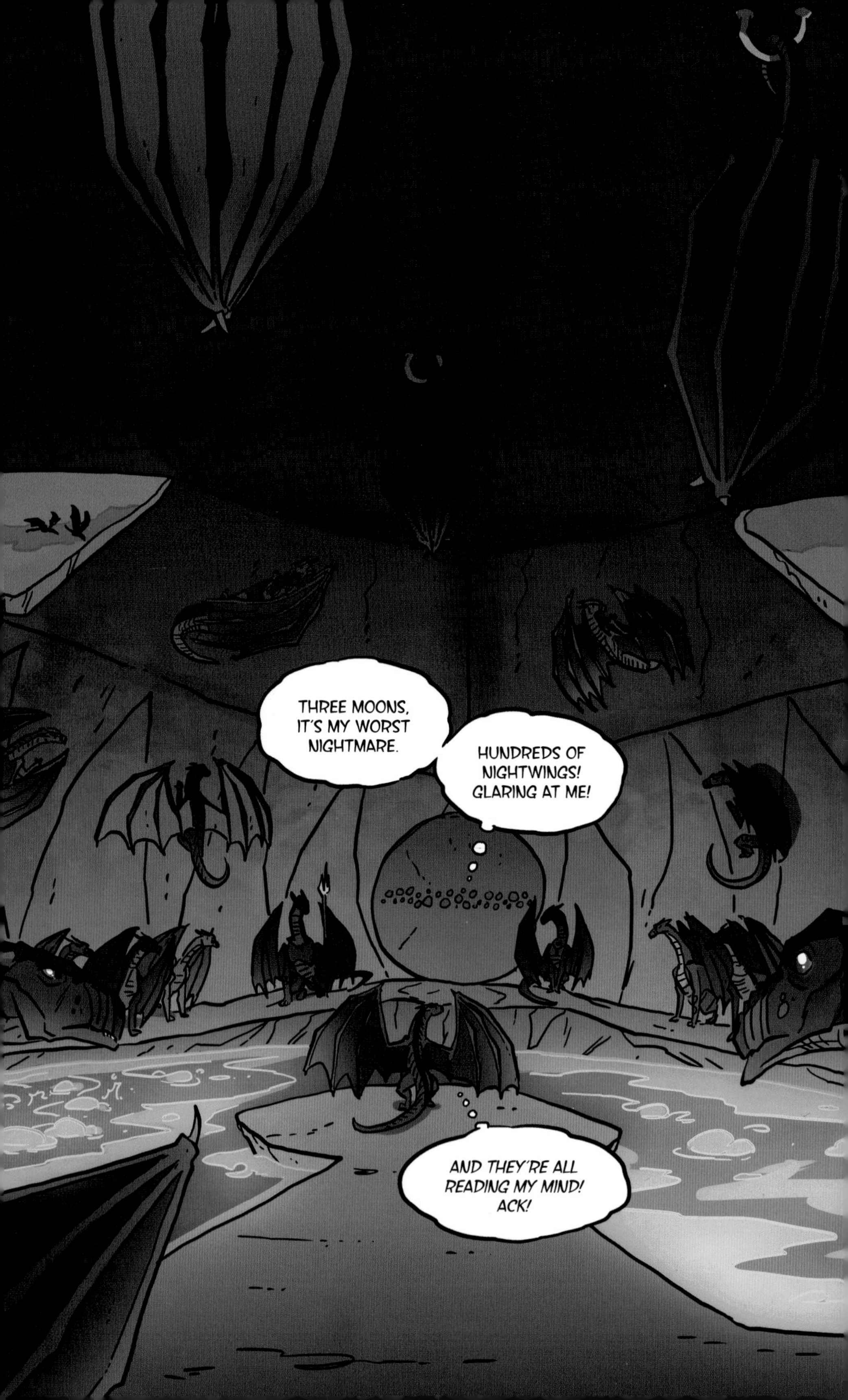
THREE MOONS, IT'S MY WORST NIGHTMARE.
HUNDREDS OF NIGHTWINGS! GLARING AT ME!
AND THEY'RE ALL READING MY MIND! ACK!

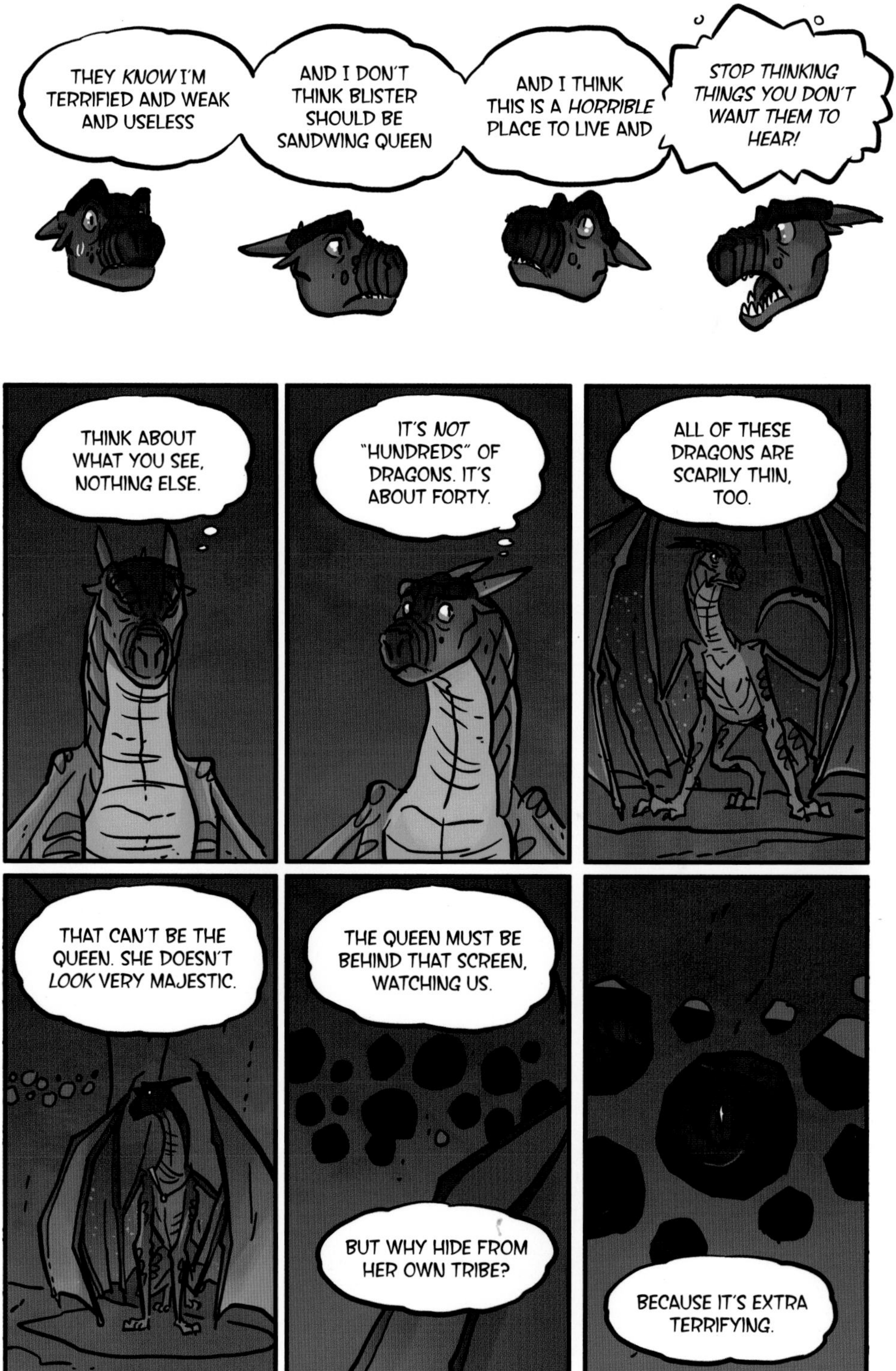
THEY *KNOW* I'M TERRIFIED AND WEAK AND USELESS
AND I DON'T THINK BLISTER SHOULD BE SANDWING QUEEN
AND I THINK THIS IS A *HORRIBLE* PLACE TO LIVE AND
STOP THINKING THINGS YOU DON'T WANT THEM TO HEAR!
THINK ABOUT WHAT YOU SEE, NOTHING ELSE.
IT'S *NOT* "HUNDREDS" OF DRAGONS. IT'S ABOUT FORTY.
ALL OF THESE DRAGONS ARE SCARILY THIN, TOO.
THAT CAN'T BE THE QUEEN. SHE DOESN'T *LOOK* VERY MAJESTIC.
THE QUEEN MUST BE BEHIND THAT SCREEN, WATCHING US.
BUT WHY HIDE FROM HER OWN TRIBE?
BECAUSE IT'S EXTRA TERRIFYING.

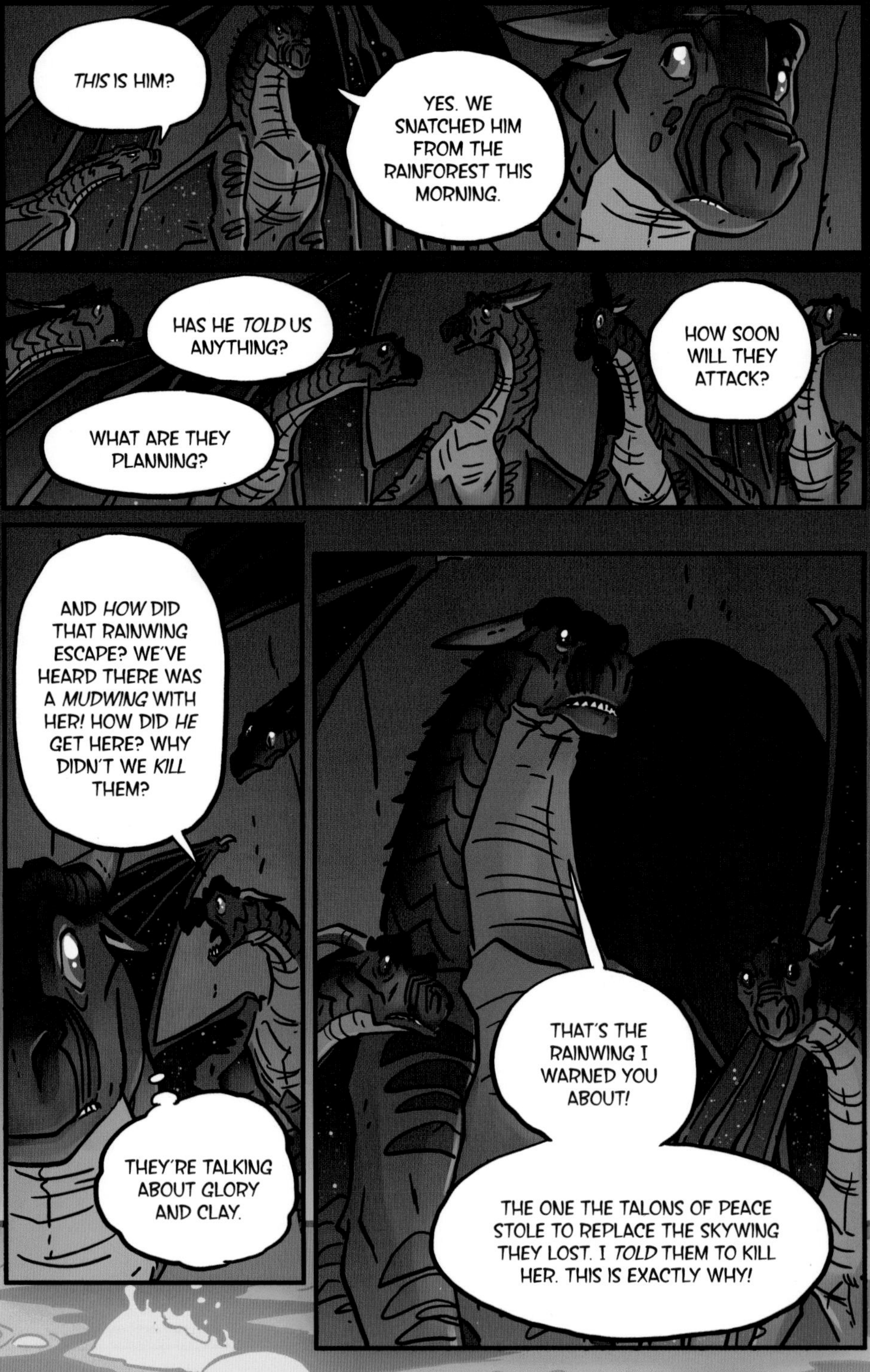
THIS IS HIM?
YES. WE SNATCHED HIM FROM THE RAINFOREST THIS MORNING.
HAS HE TOLD US ANYTHING?
WHAT ARE THEY PLANNING?
HOW SOON WILL THEY ATTACK?
AND HOW DID THAT RAINWING ESCAPE? WE'VE HEARD THERE WAS A MUDWING WITH HER! HOW DID HE GET HERE? WHY DIDN'T WE KILL THEM?
THEY'RE TALKING ABOUT GLORY AND CLAY.
THAT'S THE RAINWING I WARNED YOU ABOUT!
THE ONE THE TALONS OF PEACE STOLE TO REPLACE THE SKYWING THEY LOST. I TOLD THEM TO KILL HER. THIS IS EXACTLY WHY!

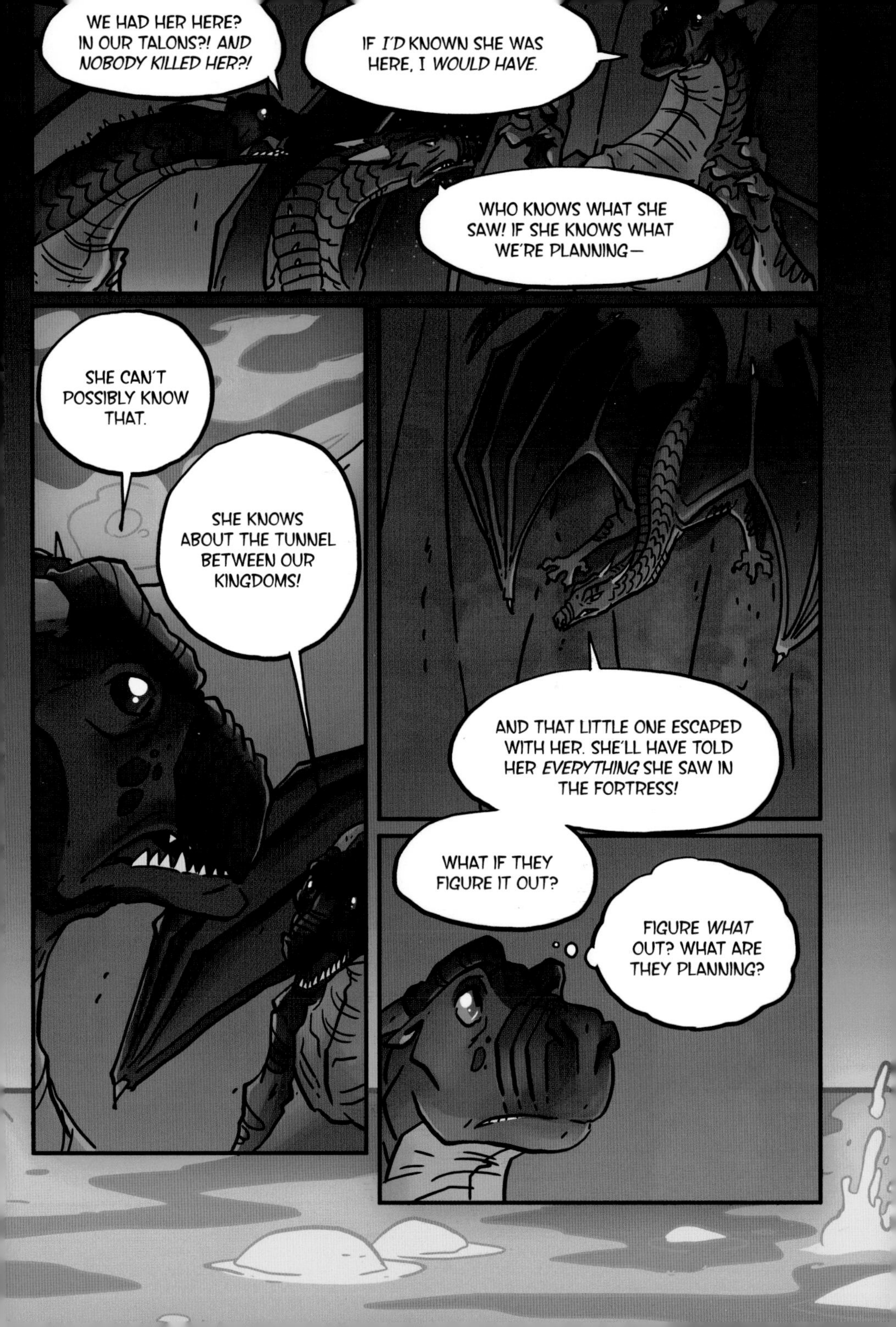
WE HAD HER HERE? IN OUR TALONS?! AND NOBODY KILLED HER?!
IF I'D KNOWN SHE WAS HERE, I WOULD HAVE.
WHO KNOWS WHAT SHE SAW! IF SHE KNOWS WHAT WE'RE PLANNING—
SHE CAN'T POSSIBLY KNOW THAT.
SHE KNOWS ABOUT THE TUNNEL BETWEEN OUR KINGDOMS!
AND THAT LITTLE ONE ESCAPED WITH HER. SHE'LL HAVE TOLD HER EVERYTHING SHE SAW IN THE FORTRESS!
WHAT IF THEY FIGURE IT OUT?
FIGURE WHAT OUT? WHAT ARE THEY PLANNING?

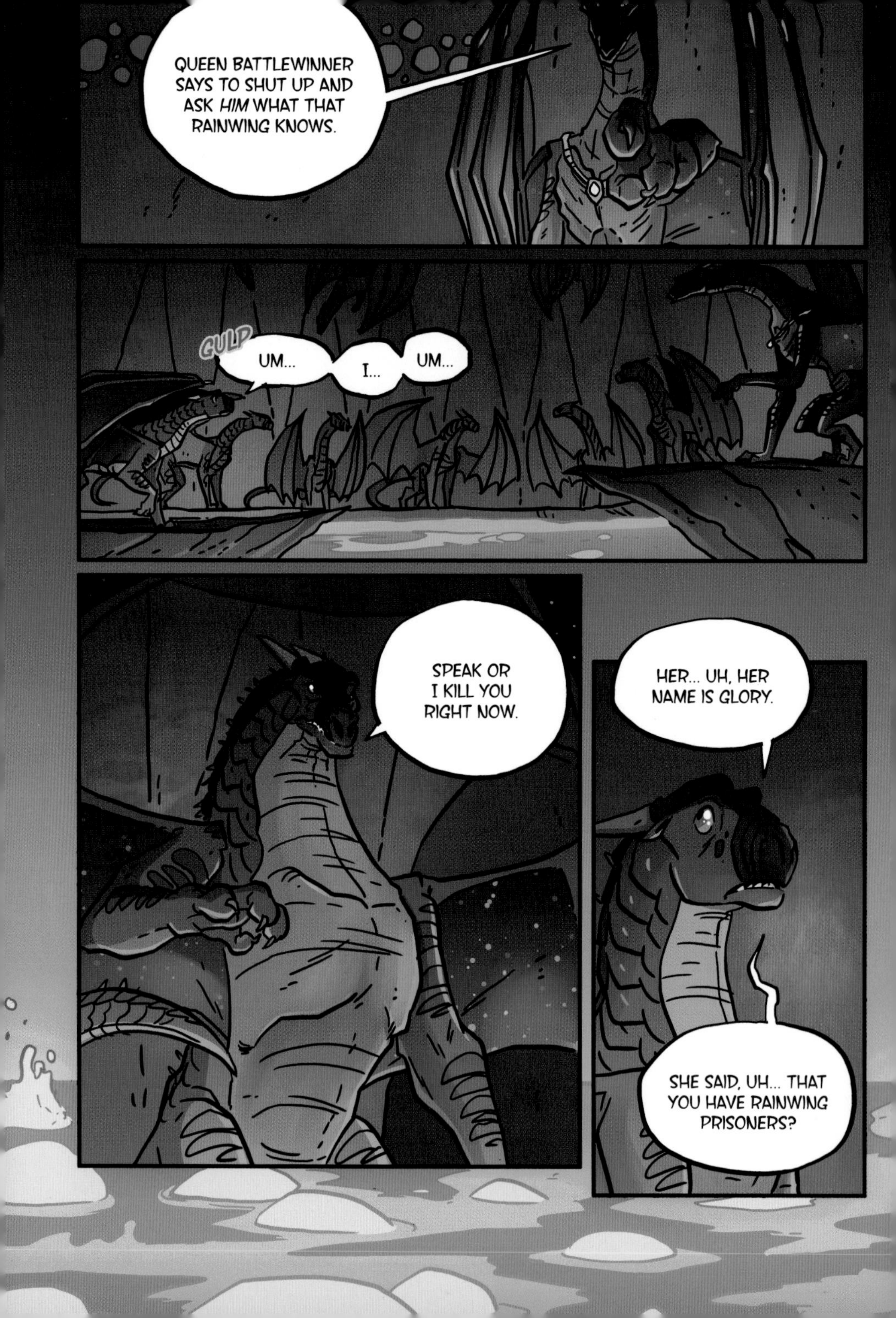
QUEEN BATTLEWINNER SAYS TO SHUT UP AND ASK *HIM* WHAT THAT RAINWING KNOWS.
GULP
UM...
I...
UM...
SPEAK OR I KILL YOU RIGHT NOW.
HER... UH, HER NAME IS GLORY.
SHE SAID, UH... THAT YOU HAVE RAINWING PRISONERS?

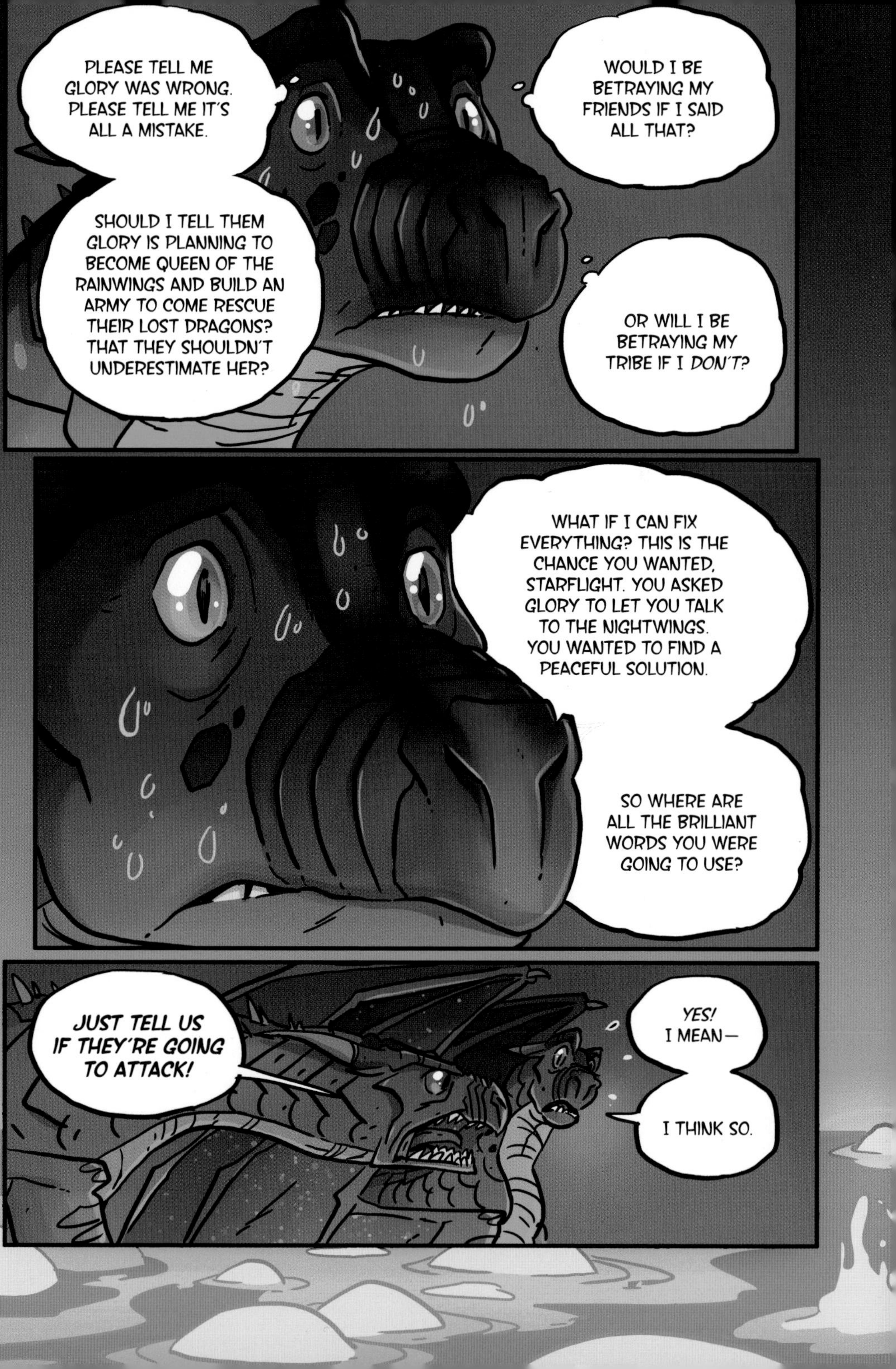
PLEASE TELL ME GLORY WAS WRONG. PLEASE TELL ME IT'S ALL A MISTAKE.
WOULD I BE BETRAYING MY FRIENDS IF I SAID ALL THAT?
SHOULD I TELL THEM GLORY IS PLANNING TO BECOME QUEEN OF THE RAINWINGS AND BUILD AN ARMY TO COME RESCUE THEIR LOST DRAGONS? THAT THEY SHOULDN'T UNDERESTIMATE HER?
OR WILL I BE BETRAYING MY TRIBE IF I *DON'T*?
WHAT IF I CAN FIX EVERYTHING? THIS IS THE CHANCE YOU WANTED, STARFLIGHT. YOU ASKED GLORY TO LET YOU TALK TO THE NIGHTWINGS. YOU WANTED TO FIND A PEACEFUL SOLUTION.
SO WHERE ARE ALL THE BRILLIANT WORDS YOU WERE GOING TO USE?
JUST TELL US IF THEY'RE GOING TO ATTACK!
YES! I MEAN—
I THINK SO.

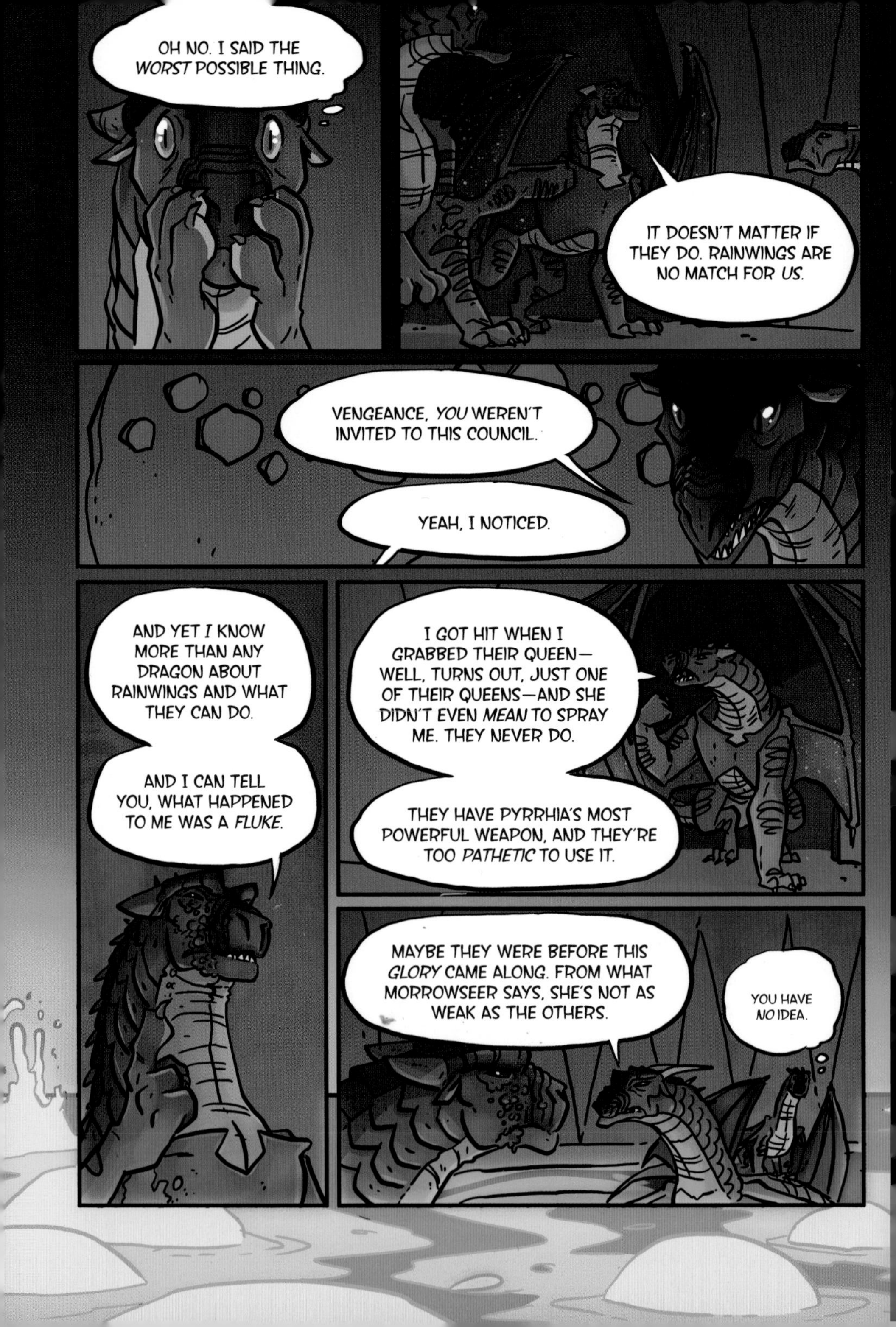

OH NO. I SAID THE *WORST* POSSIBLE THING.
IT DOESN'T MATTER IF THEY DO. RAINWINGS ARE NO MATCH FOR *US*.
VENGEANCE, *YOU* WEREN'T INVITED TO THIS COUNCIL.
YEAH, I NOTICED.
AND YET *I* KNOW MORE THAN ANY DRAGON ABOUT RAINWINGS AND WHAT THEY CAN DO.
AND I CAN TELL YOU, WHAT HAPPENED TO ME WAS A *FLUKE*.
I GOT HIT WHEN I GRABBED THEIR QUEEN—WELL, TURNS OUT, JUST ONE OF THEIR QUEENS—AND SHE DIDN'T EVEN *MEAN* TO SPRAY ME. THEY NEVER DO.
THEY HAVE PYRRHIA'S MOST POWERFUL WEAPON, AND THEY'RE TOO *PATHETIC* TO USE IT.
MAYBE THEY WERE BEFORE THIS *GLORY* CAME ALONG. FROM WHAT MORROWSEER SAYS, SHE'S NOT AS WEAK AS THE OTHERS.
YOU HAVE *NO* IDEA.

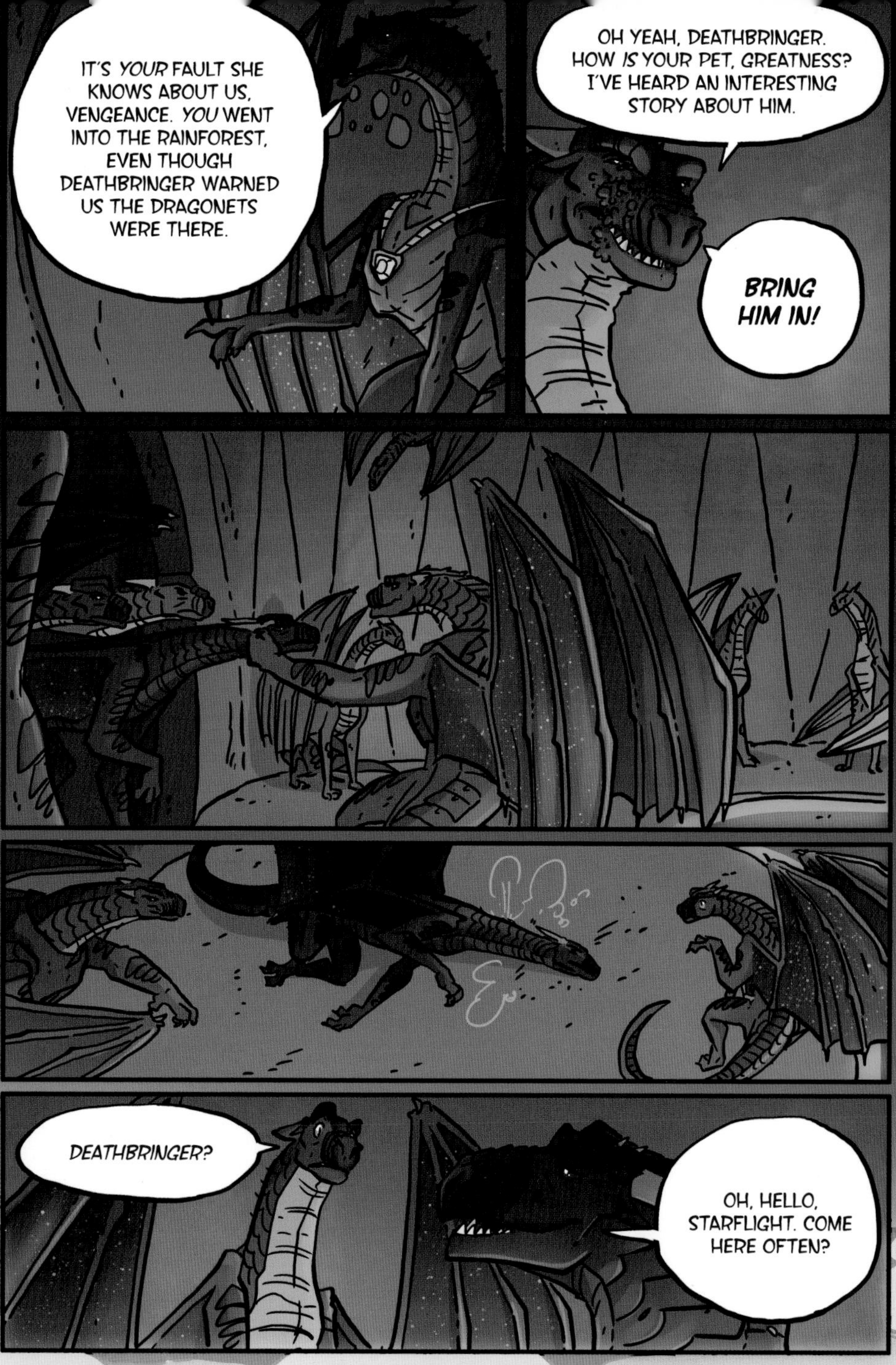
IT'S YOUR FAULT SHE KNOWS ABOUT US, VENGEANCE. YOU WENT INTO THE RAINFOREST, EVEN THOUGH DEATHBRINGER WARNED US THE DRAGONETS WERE THERE.
OH YEAH, DEATHBRINGER. HOW IS YOUR PET, GREATNESS? I'VE HEARD AN INTERESTING STORY ABOUT HIM.
BRING HIM IN!
DEATHBRINGER?
OH, HELLO, STARFLIGHT. COME HERE OFTEN?

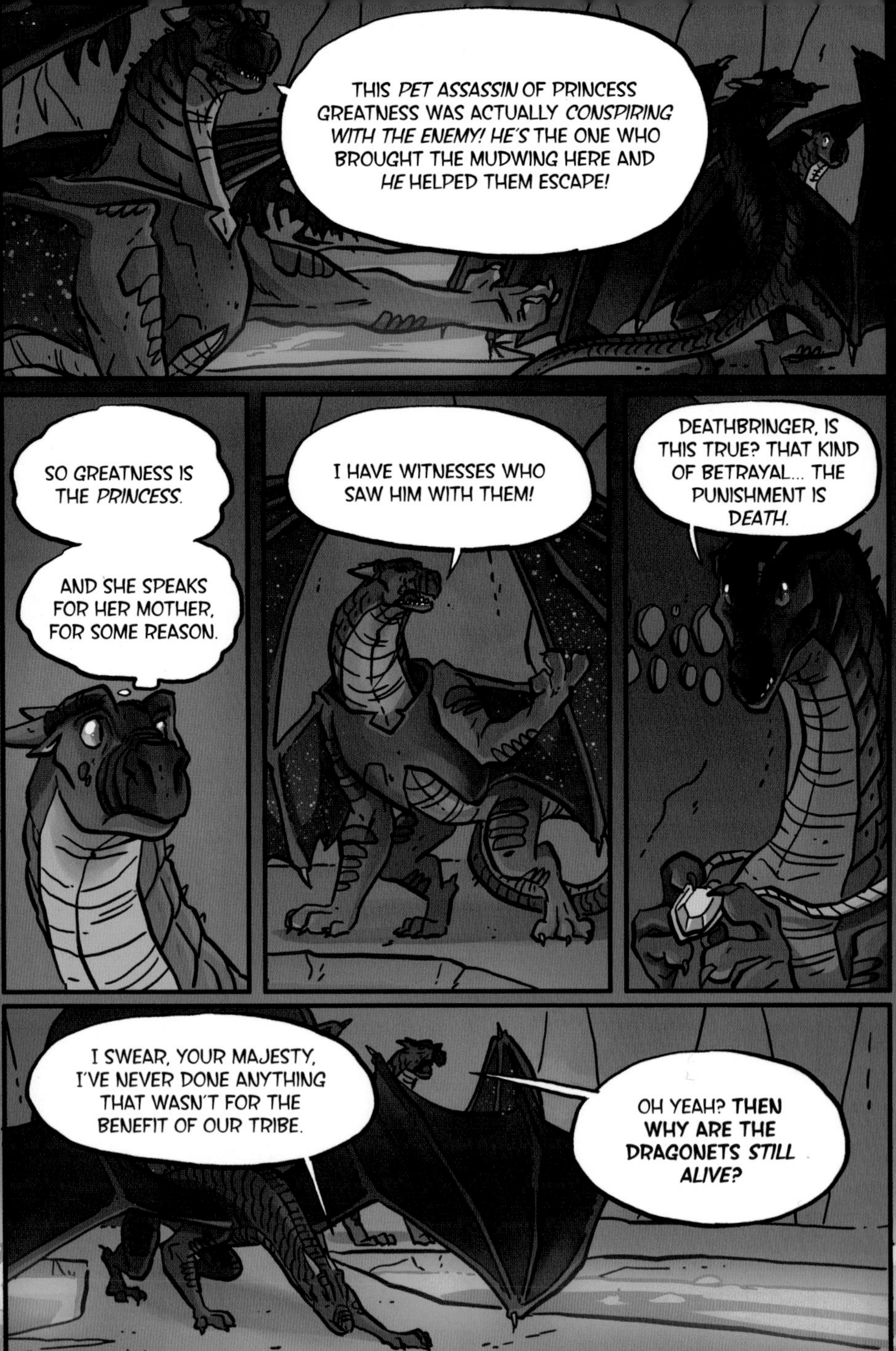
THIS *PET ASSASSIN* OF PRINCESS GREATNESS WAS ACTUALLY *CONSPIRING WITH THE ENEMY! HE'S* THE ONE WHO BROUGHT THE MUDWING HERE AND *HE* HELPED THEM ESCAPE!
SO GREATNESS IS THE *PRINCESS*.
AND SHE SPEAKS FOR HER MOTHER, FOR SOME REASON.
I HAVE WITNESSES WHO SAW HIM WITH THEM!
DEATHBRINGER, IS THIS TRUE? THAT KIND OF BETRAYAL... THE PUNISHMENT IS *DEATH*.
I SWEAR, YOUR MAJESTY, I'VE NEVER DONE ANYTHING THAT WASN'T FOR THE BENEFIT OF OUR TRIBE.
OH YEAH? **THEN WHY ARE THE DRAGONETS *STILL ALIVE*?**

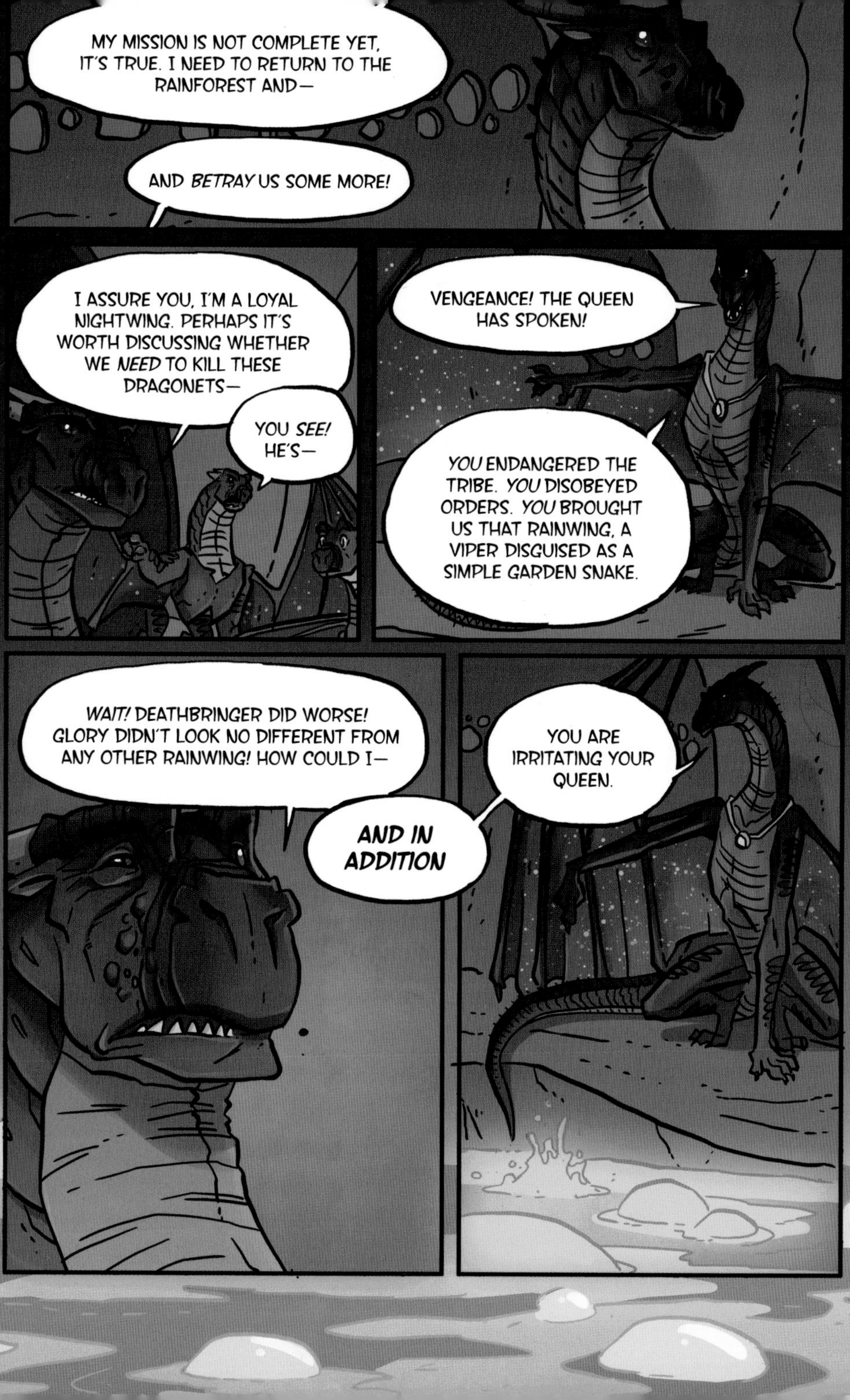
MY MISSION IS NOT COMPLETE YET, IT'S TRUE. I NEED TO RETURN TO THE RAINFOREST AND—
AND *BETRAY* US SOME MORE!
I ASSURE YOU, I'M A LOYAL NIGHTWING. PERHAPS IT'S WORTH DISCUSSING WHETHER WE *NEED* TO KILL THESE DRAGONETS—
YOU *SEE!* HE'S—
VENGEANCE! THE QUEEN HAS SPOKEN!
YOU ENDANGERED THE TRIBE. *YOU* DISOBEYED ORDERS. *YOU* BROUGHT US THAT RAINWING, A VIPER DISGUISED AS A SIMPLE GARDEN SNAKE.
WAIT! DEATHBRINGER DID WORSE! GLORY DIDN'T LOOK NO DIFFERENT FROM ANY OTHER RAINWING! HOW COULD I—
YOU ARE IRRITATING YOUR QUEEN.
AND IN ADDITION

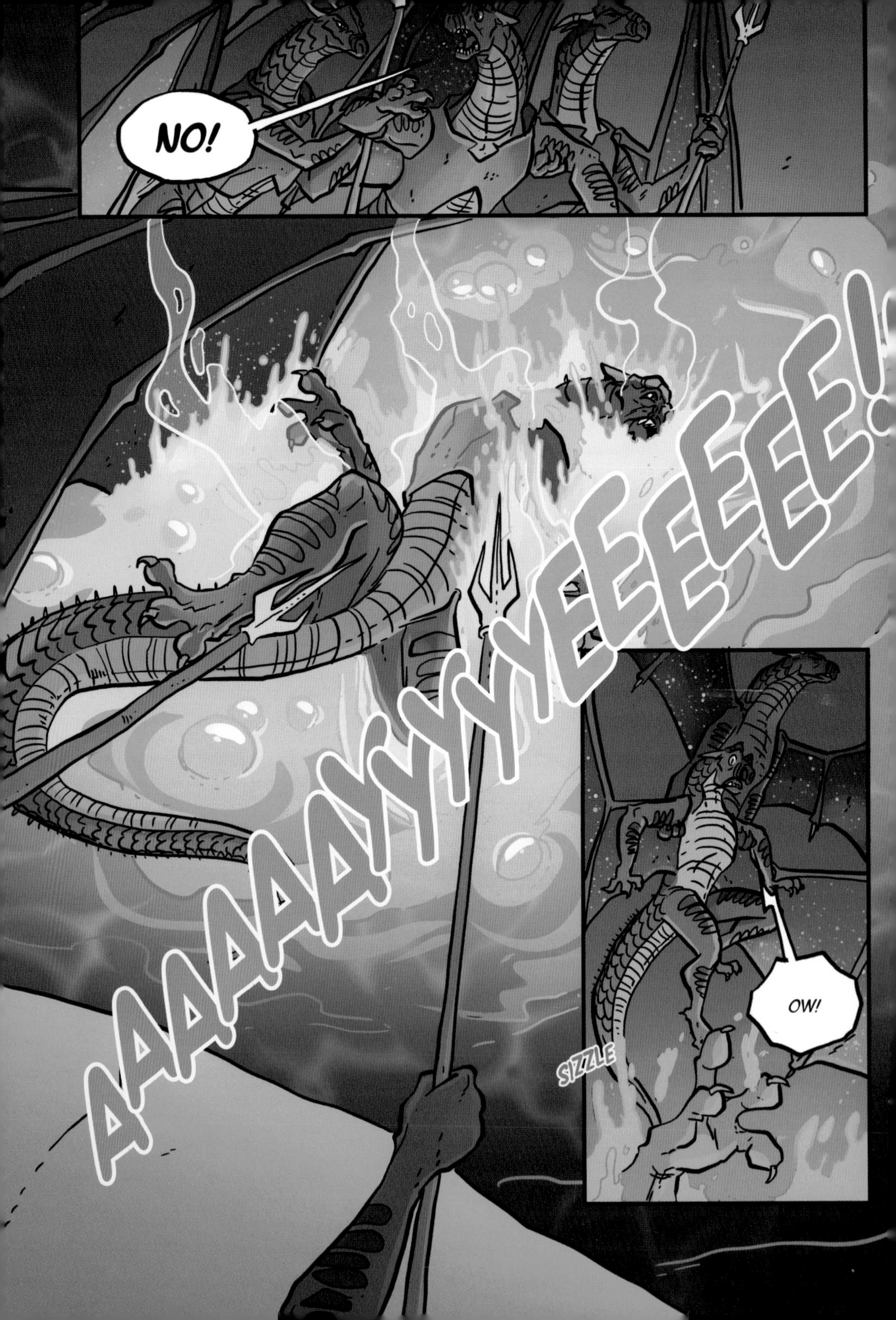
NO!
AAAAAAYYYYYEEEEEEE!!
SIZZLE
OW!

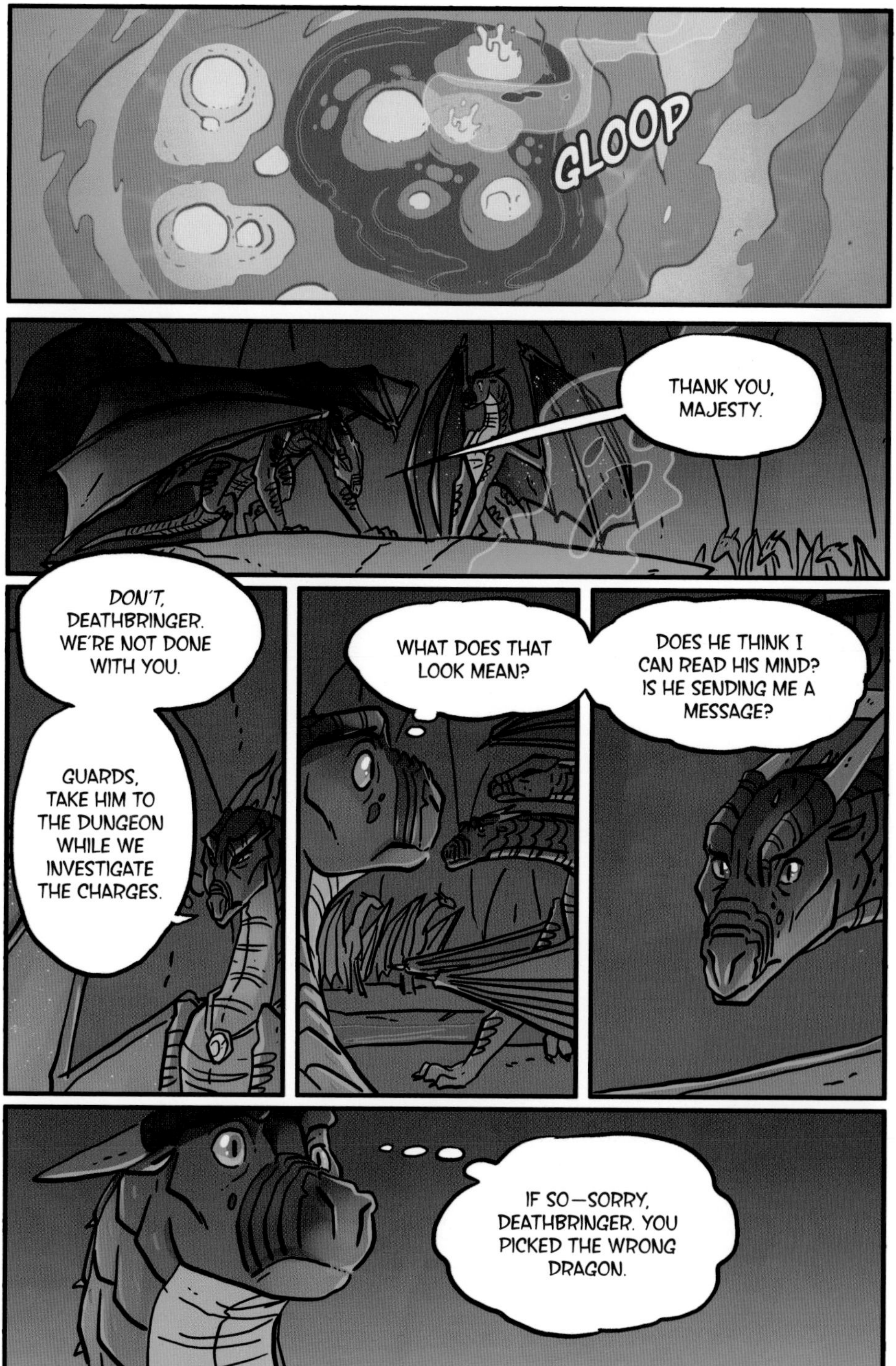
GLOOP
THANK YOU, MAJESTY.
DON'T, DEATHBRINGER. WE'RE NOT DONE WITH YOU.
GUARDS, TAKE HIM TO THE DUNGEON WHILE WE INVESTIGATE THE CHARGES.
WHAT DOES THAT LOOK MEAN?
DOES HE THINK I CAN READ HIS MIND? IS HE SENDING ME A MESSAGE?
IF SO—SORRY, DEATHBRINGER. YOU PICKED THE WRONG DRAGON.

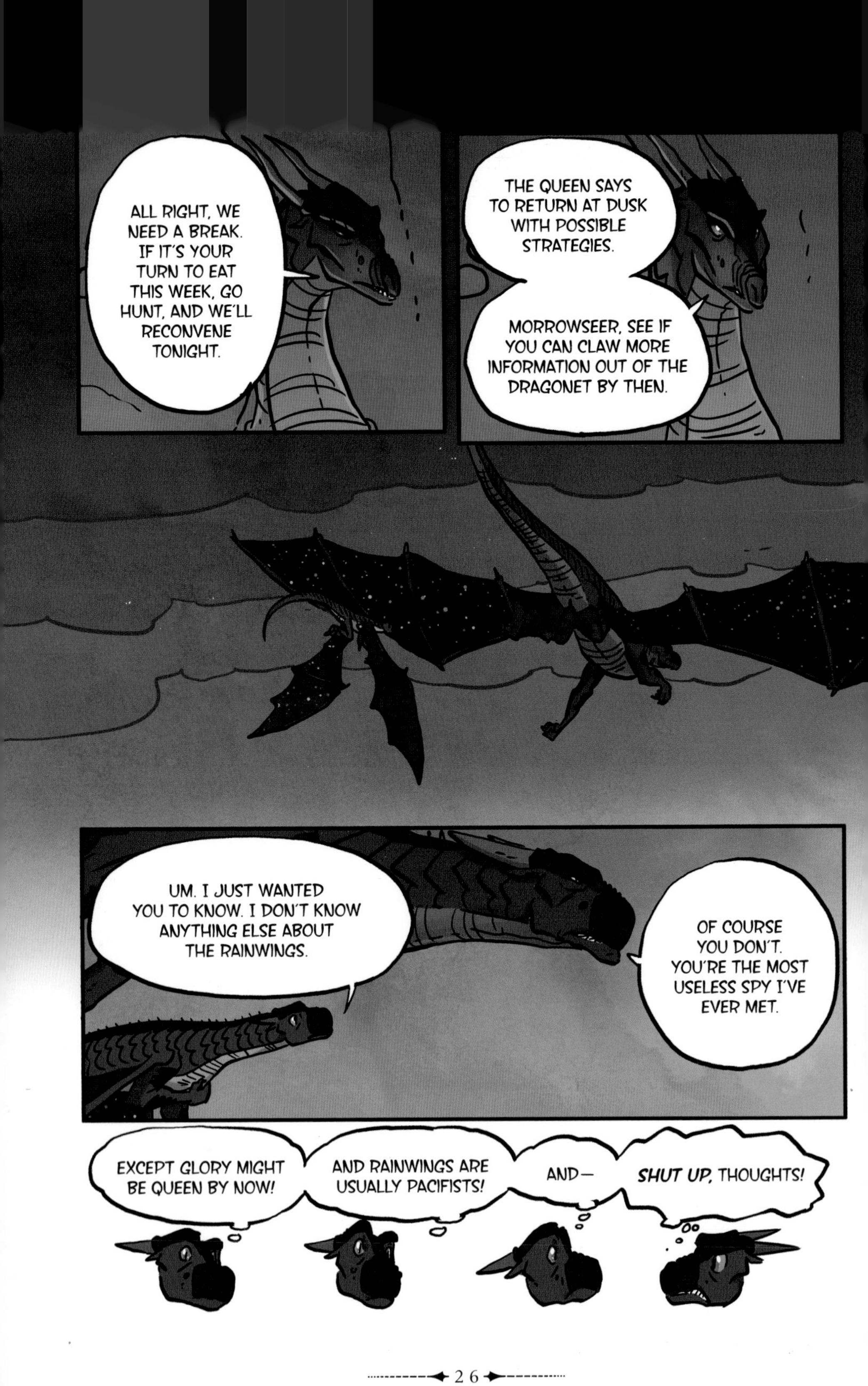

ALL RIGHT, WE NEED A BREAK. IF IT'S YOUR TURN TO EAT THIS WEEK, GO HUNT, AND WE'LL RECONVENE TONIGHT.
THE QUEEN SAYS TO RETURN AT DUSK WITH POSSIBLE STRATEGIES.
MORROWSEER, SEE IF YOU CAN CLAW MORE INFORMATION OUT OF THE DRAGONET BY THEN.
UM. I JUST WANTED YOU TO KNOW. I DON'T KNOW ANYTHING ELSE ABOUT THE RAINWINGS.
OF COURSE YOU DON'T. YOU'RE THE MOST USELESS SPY I'VE EVER MET.
EXCEPT GLORY MIGHT BE QUEEN BY NOW!
AND RAINWINGS ARE USUALLY PACIFISTS!
AND—
SHUT UP, THOUGHTS!

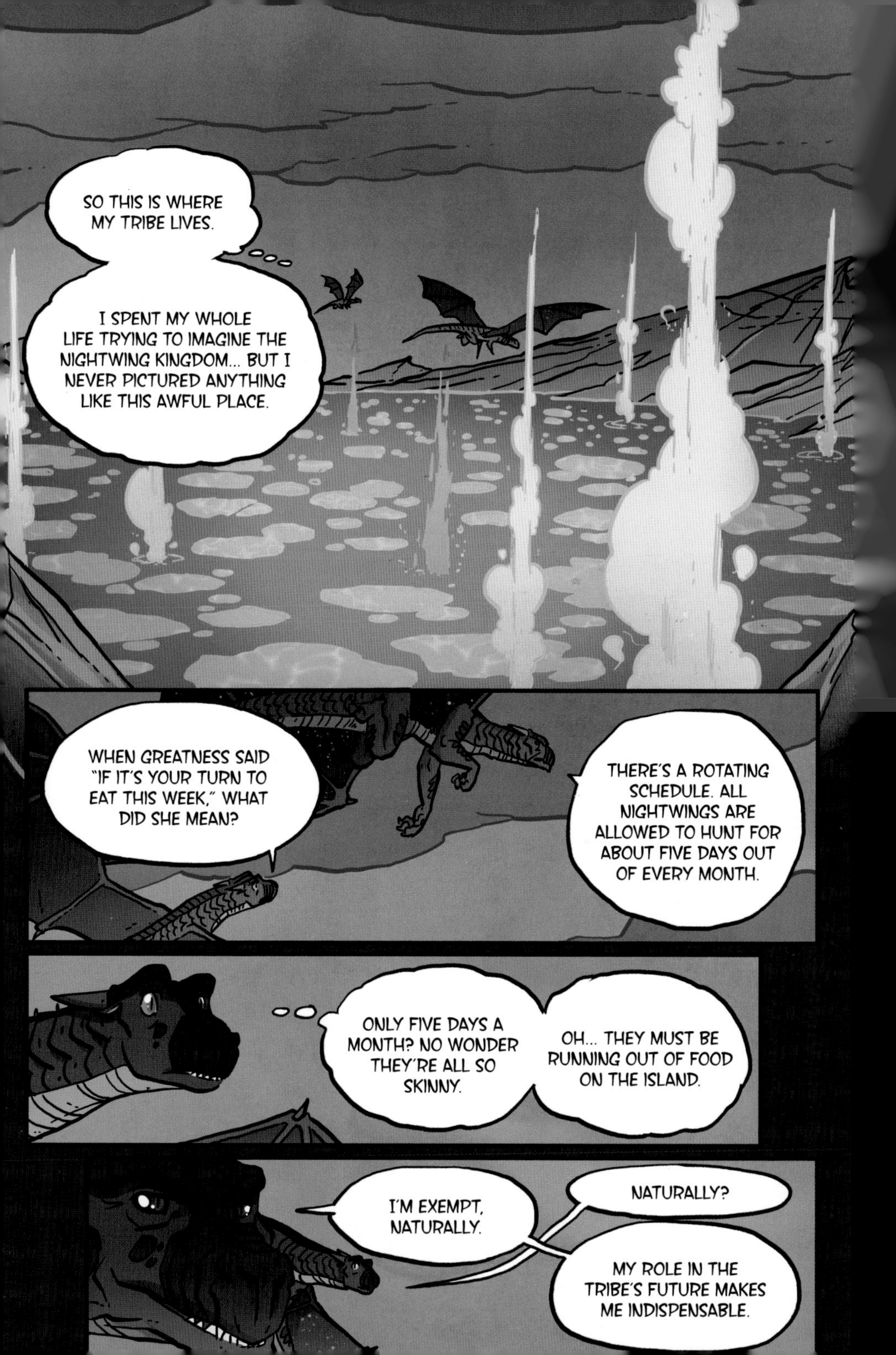
SO THIS IS WHERE MY TRIBE LIVES.
I SPENT MY WHOLE LIFE TRYING TO IMAGINE THE NIGHTWING KINGDOM... BUT I NEVER PICTURED ANYTHING LIKE THIS AWFUL PLACE.
WHEN GREATNESS SAID "IF IT'S YOUR TURN TO EAT THIS WEEK," WHAT DID SHE MEAN?
THERE'S A ROTATING SCHEDULE. ALL NIGHTWINGS ARE ALLOWED TO HUNT FOR ABOUT FIVE DAYS OUT OF EVERY MONTH.
ONLY FIVE DAYS A MONTH? NO WONDER THEY'RE ALL SO SKINNY.
OH... THEY MUST BE RUNNING OUT OF FOOD ON THE ISLAND.
I'M EXEMPT, NATURALLY.
NATURALLY?
MY ROLE IN THE TRIBE'S FUTURE MAKES ME INDISPENSABLE.

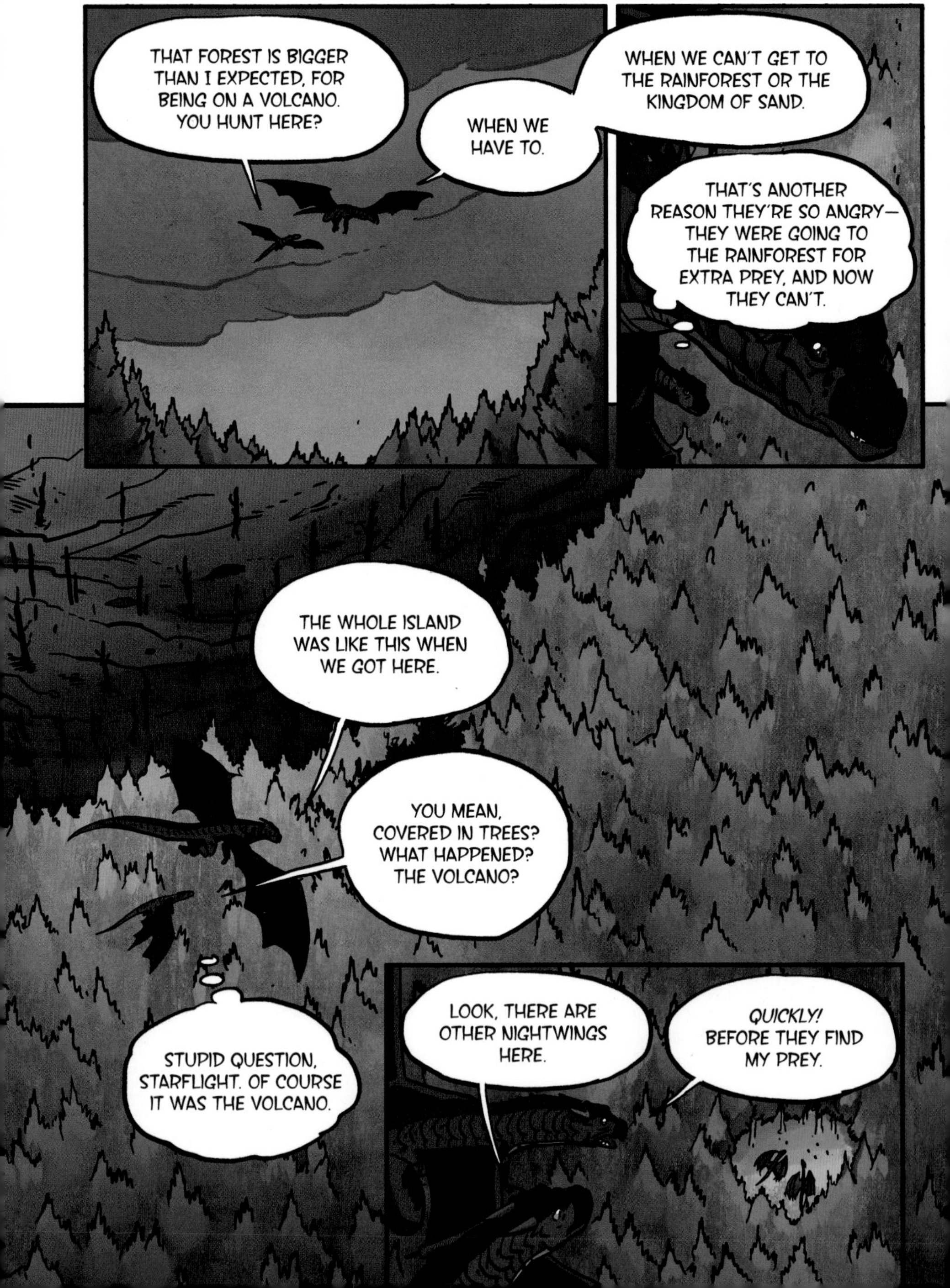
THAT FOREST IS BIGGER THAN I EXPECTED, FOR BEING ON A VOLCANO. YOU HUNT HERE?
WHEN WE HAVE TO.
WHEN WE CAN'T GET TO THE RAINFOREST OR THE KINGDOM OF SAND.
THAT'S ANOTHER REASON THEY'RE SO ANGRY— THEY WERE GOING TO THE RAINFOREST FOR EXTRA PREY, AND NOW THEY CAN'T.
THE WHOLE ISLAND WAS LIKE THIS WHEN WE GOT HERE.
YOU MEAN, COVERED IN TREES? WHAT HAPPENED? THE VOLCANO?
STUPID QUESTION, STARFLIGHT. OF COURSE IT WAS THE VOLCANO.
LOOK, THERE ARE OTHER NIGHTWINGS HERE.
QUICKLY! BEFORE THEY FIND MY PREY.

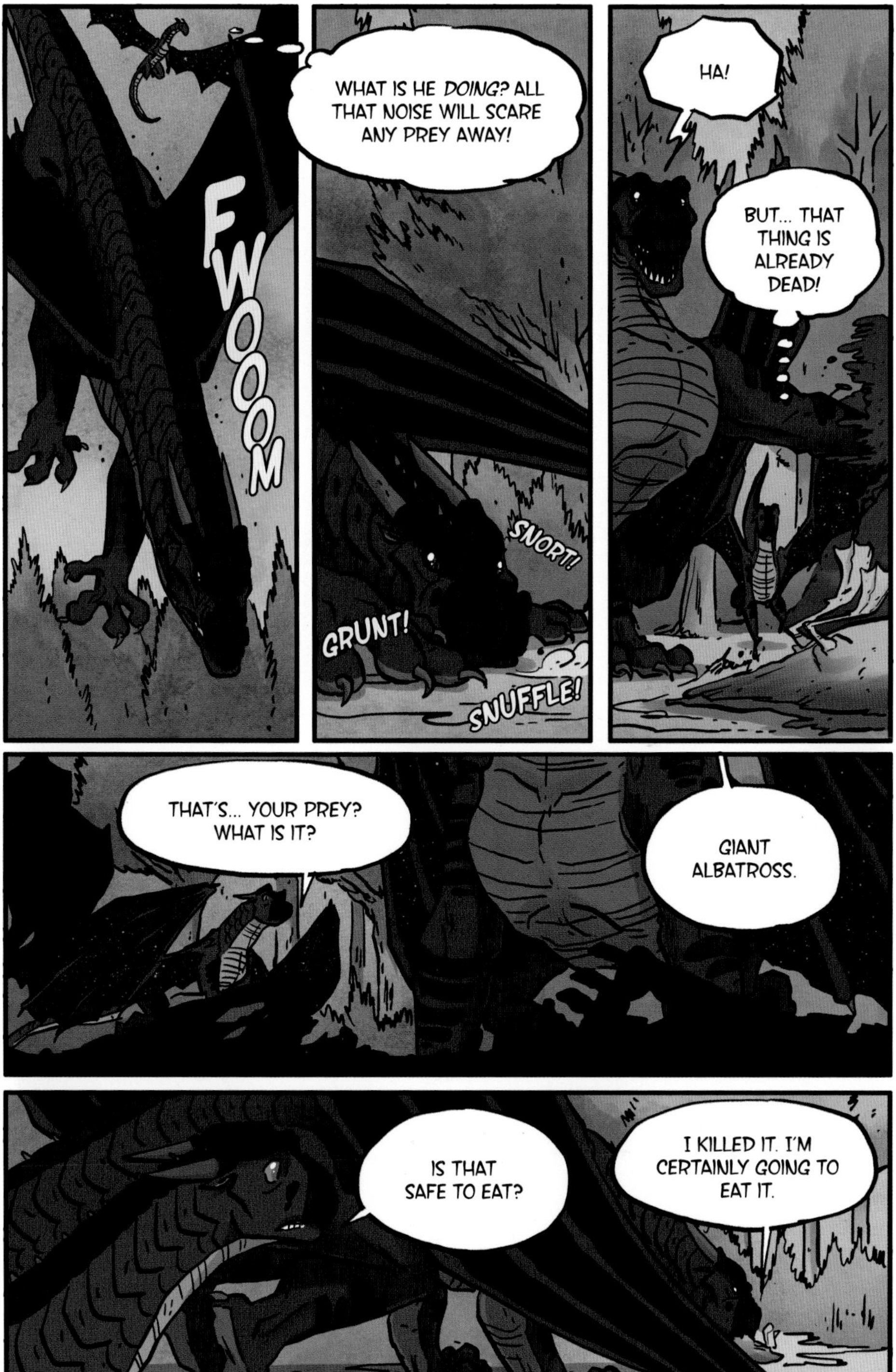
FWOOOM
WHAT IS HE *DOING?* ALL THAT NOISE WILL SCARE ANY PREY AWAY!
SNORT!
GRUNT!
SNUFFLE!
HA!
BUT... THAT THING IS ALREADY DEAD!
THAT'S... YOUR PREY? WHAT IS IT?
GIANT ALBATROSS.
IS THAT SAFE TO EAT?
I KILLED IT. I'M CERTAINLY GOING TO EAT IT.

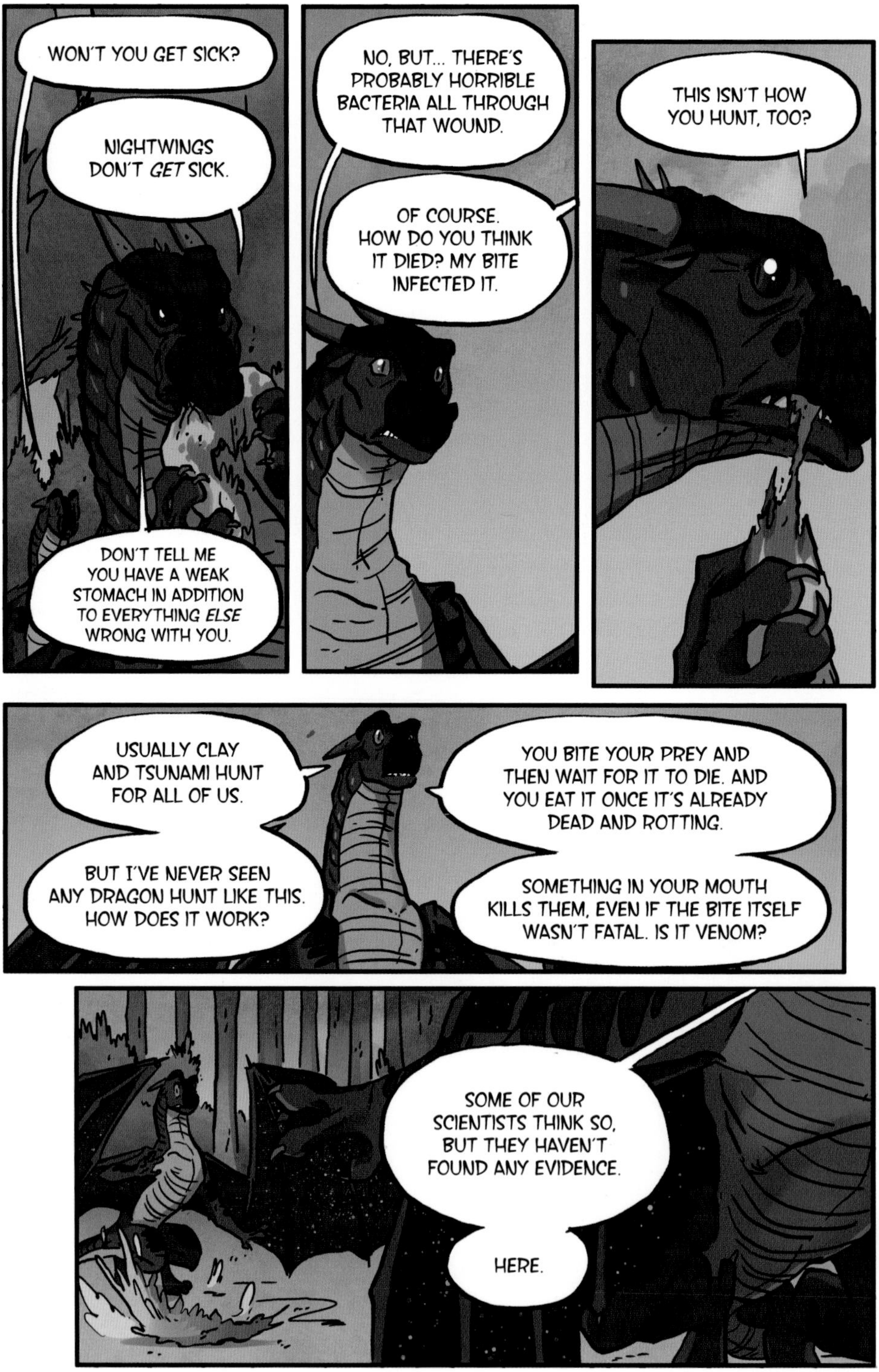
WON'T YOU GET SICK?
NIGHTWINGS DON'T *GET* SICK.
DON'T TELL ME YOU HAVE A WEAK STOMACH IN ADDITION TO EVERYTHING *ELSE* WRONG WITH YOU.
NO, BUT... THERE'S PROBABLY HORRIBLE BACTERIA ALL THROUGH THAT WOUND.
OF COURSE. HOW DO YOU THINK IT DIED? MY BITE INFECTED IT.
THIS ISN'T HOW YOU HUNT, TOO?
USUALLY CLAY AND TSUNAMI HUNT FOR ALL OF US.
BUT I'VE NEVER SEEN ANY DRAGON HUNT LIKE THIS. HOW DOES IT WORK?
YOU BITE YOUR PREY AND THEN WAIT FOR IT TO DIE. AND YOU EAT IT ONCE IT'S ALREADY DEAD AND ROTTING.
SOMETHING IN YOUR MOUTH KILLS THEM, EVEN IF THE BITE ITSELF WASN'T FATAL. IS IT VENOM?
SOME OF OUR SCIENTISTS THINK SO, BUT THEY HAVEN'T FOUND ANY EVIDENCE.
HERE.

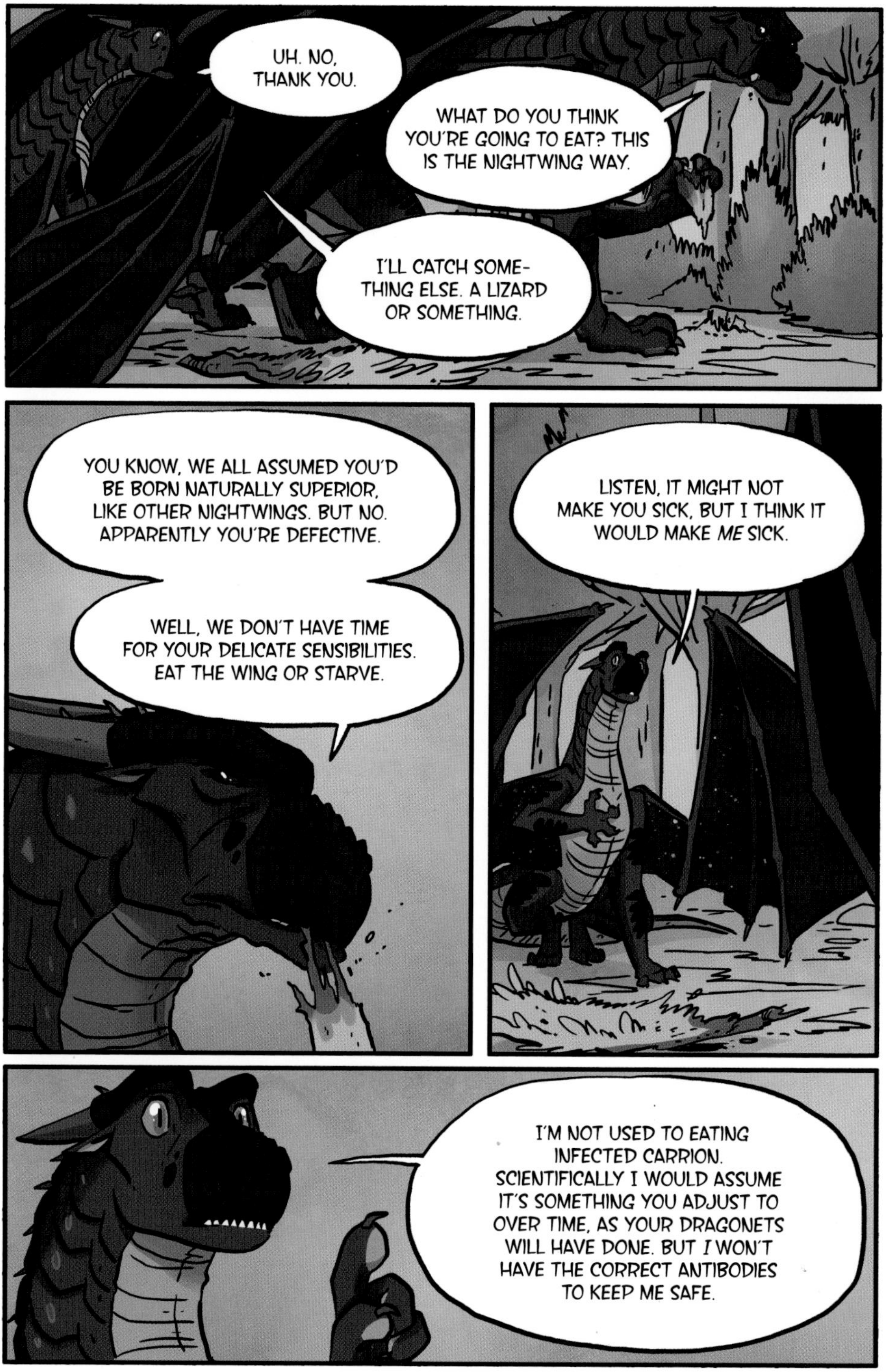
UH. NO, THANK YOU.
WHAT DO YOU THINK YOU'RE GOING TO EAT? THIS IS THE NIGHTWING WAY.
I'LL CATCH SOME-THING ELSE. A LIZARD OR SOMETHING.
YOU KNOW, WE ALL ASSUMED YOU'D BE BORN NATURALLY SUPERIOR, LIKE OTHER NIGHTWINGS. BUT NO. APPARENTLY YOU'RE DEFECTIVE.
WELL, WE DON'T HAVE TIME FOR YOUR DELICATE SENSIBILITIES. EAT THE WING OR STARVE.
LISTEN, IT MIGHT NOT MAKE YOU SICK, BUT I THINK IT WOULD MAKE *ME* SICK.
I'M NOT USED TO EATING INFECTED CARRION. SCIENTIFICALLY I WOULD ASSUME IT'S SOMETHING YOU ADJUST TO OVER TIME, AS YOUR DRAGONETS WILL HAVE DONE. BUT *I* WON'T HAVE THE CORRECT ANTIBODIES TO KEEP ME SAFE.

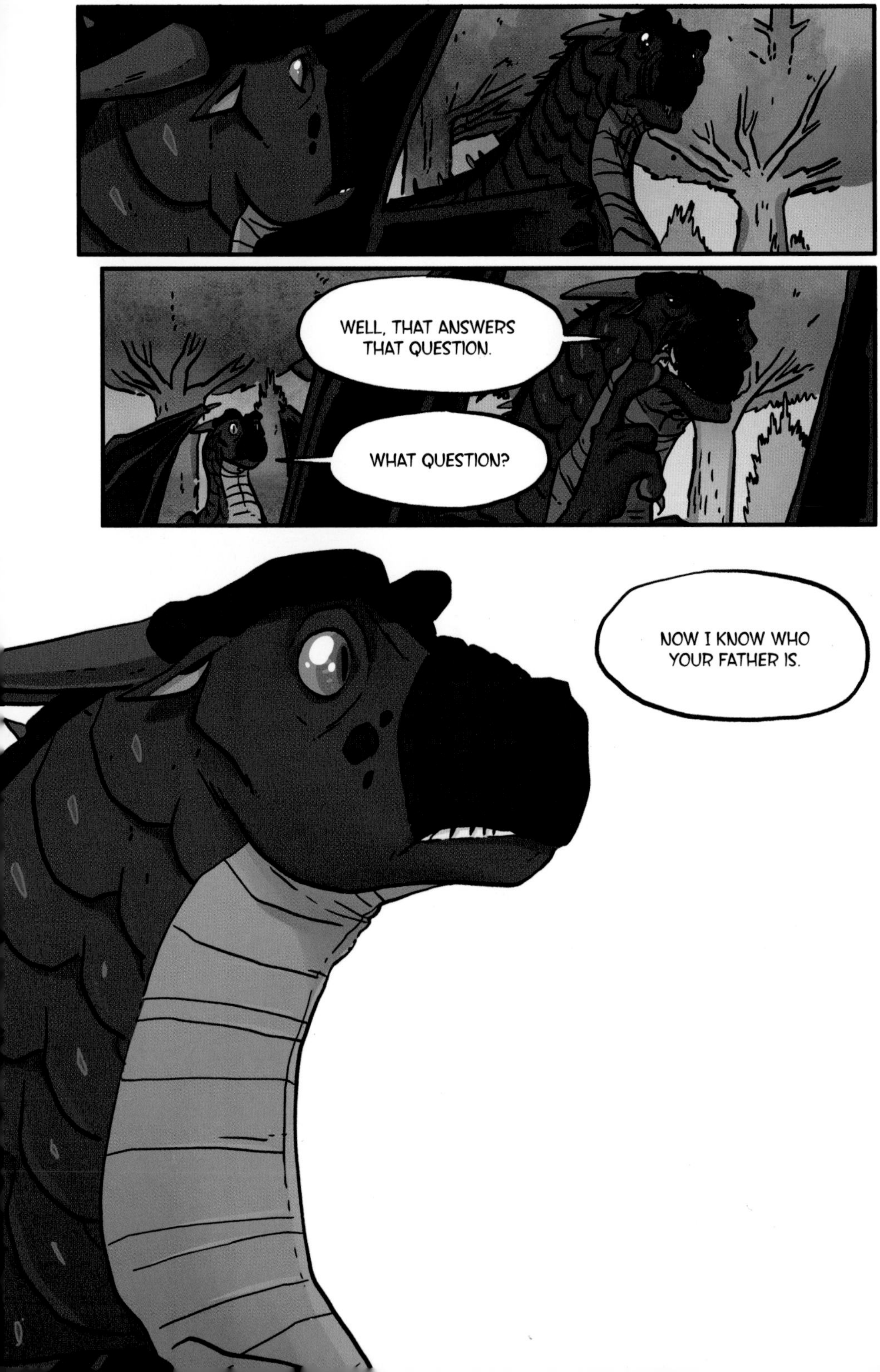
WELL, THAT ANSWERS THAT QUESTION.
WHAT QUESTION?
NOW I KNOW WHO YOUR FATHER IS.

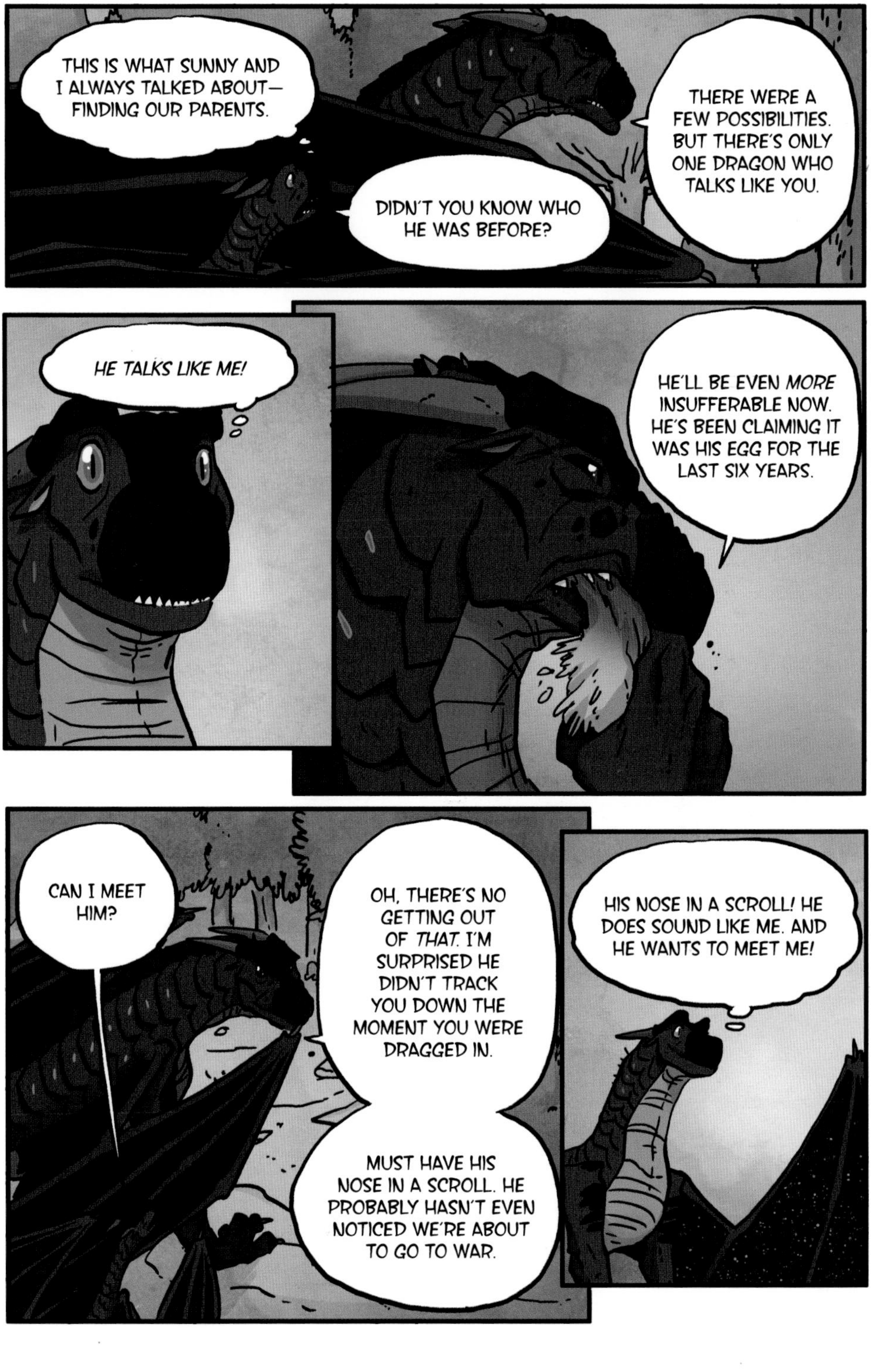
THIS IS WHAT SUNNY AND I ALWAYS TALKED ABOUT—FINDING OUR PARENTS.
DIDN'T YOU KNOW WHO HE WAS BEFORE?
THERE WERE A FEW POSSIBILITIES. BUT THERE'S ONLY ONE DRAGON WHO TALKS LIKE YOU.
HE TALKS LIKE ME!
HE'LL BE EVEN *MORE* INSUFFERABLE NOW. HE'S BEEN CLAIMING IT WAS HIS EGG FOR THE LAST SIX YEARS.
CAN I MEET HIM?
OH, THERE'S NO GETTING OUT OF *THAT.* I'M SURPRISED HE DIDN'T TRACK YOU DOWN THE MOMENT YOU WERE DRAGGED IN.
MUST HAVE HIS NOSE IN A SCROLL. HE PROBABLY HASN'T EVEN NOTICED WE'RE ABOUT TO GO TO WAR.
HIS NOSE IN A SCROLL! HE DOES SOUND LIKE ME. AND HE WANTS TO MEET ME!

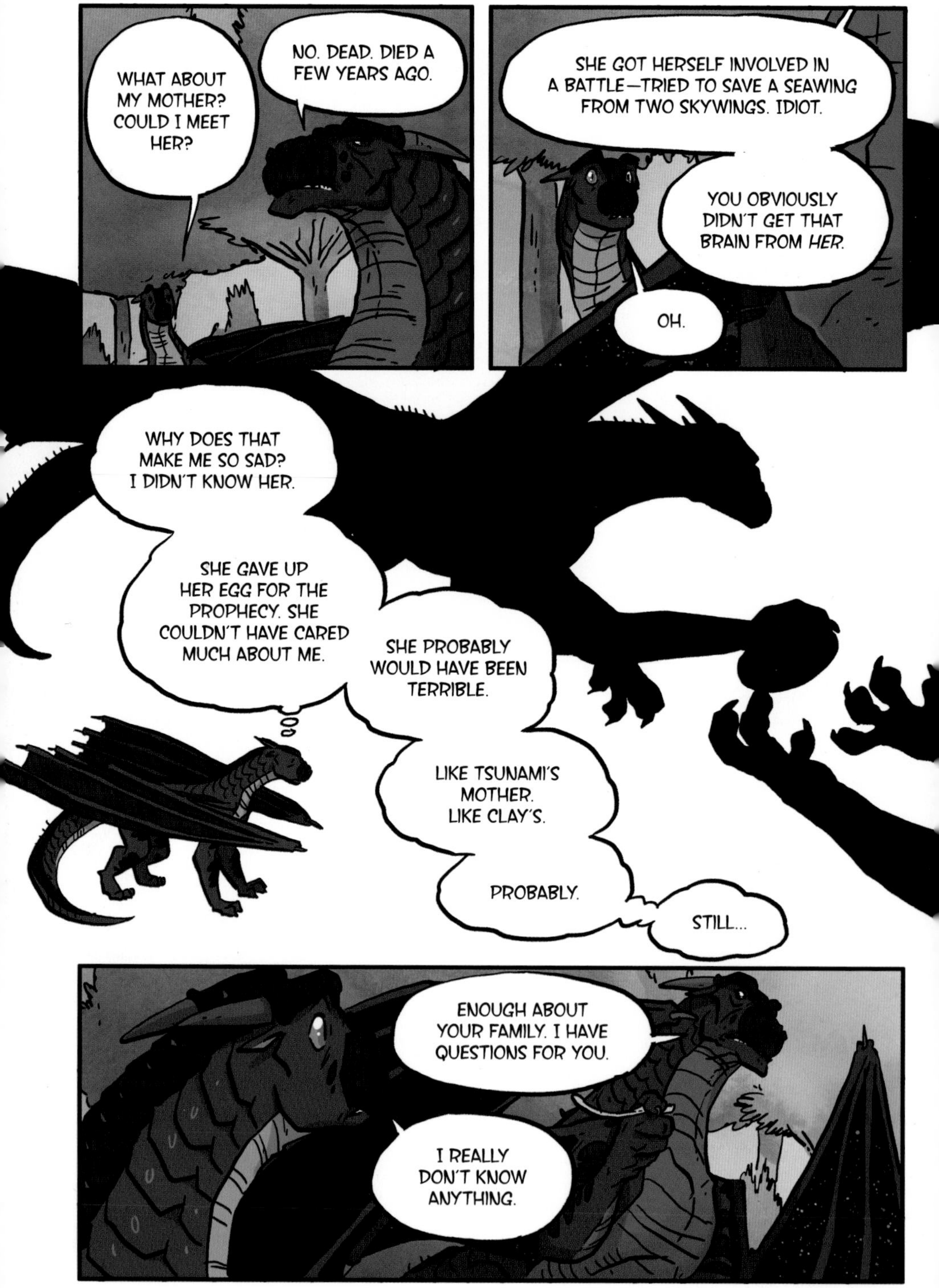
WHAT ABOUT MY MOTHER? COULD I MEET HER?
NO. DEAD. DIED A FEW YEARS AGO.
SHE GOT HERSELF INVOLVED IN A BATTLE—TRIED TO SAVE A SEAWING FROM TWO SKYWINGS. IDIOT.
YOU OBVIOUSLY DIDN'T GET THAT BRAIN FROM *HER*.
OH.
WHY DOES THAT MAKE ME SO SAD? I DIDN'T KNOW HER.
SHE GAVE UP HER EGG FOR THE PROPHECY. SHE COULDN'T HAVE CARED MUCH ABOUT ME.
SHE PROBABLY WOULD HAVE BEEN TERRIBLE.
LIKE TSUNAMI'S MOTHER. LIKE CLAY'S.
PROBABLY.
STILL...
ENOUGH ABOUT YOUR FAMILY. I HAVE QUESTIONS FOR YOU.
I REALLY DON'T KNOW ANYTHING.

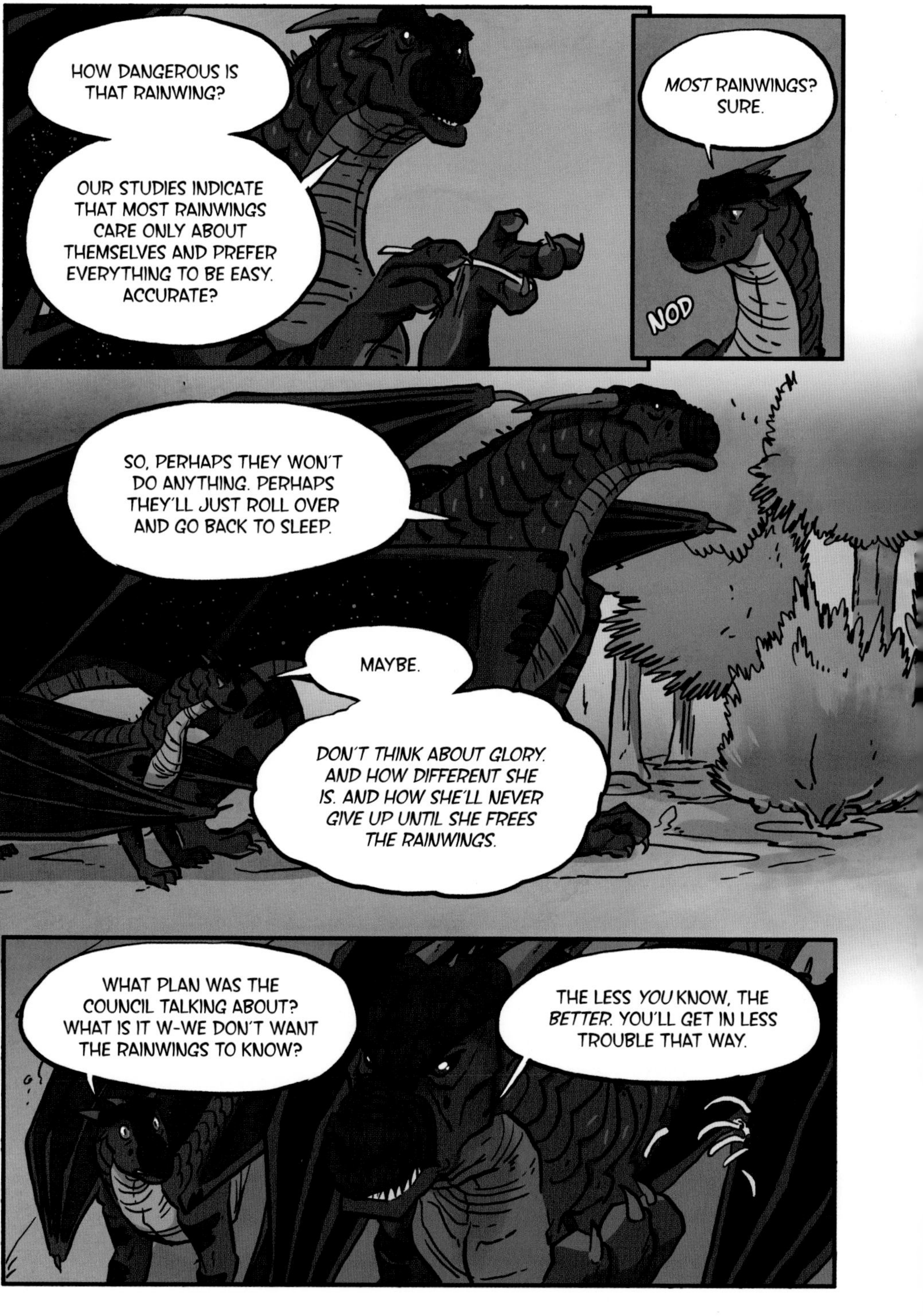
HOW DANGEROUS IS THAT RAINWING?
OUR STUDIES INDICATE THAT MOST RAINWINGS CARE ONLY ABOUT THEMSELVES AND PREFER EVERYTHING TO BE EASY. ACCURATE?
MOST RAINWINGS? SURE.
NOD
SO, PERHAPS THEY WON'T DO ANYTHING. PERHAPS THEY'LL JUST ROLL OVER AND GO BACK TO SLEEP.
MAYBE.
DON'T THINK ABOUT GLORY. AND HOW DIFFERENT SHE IS. AND HOW SHE'LL NEVER GIVE UP UNTIL SHE FREES THE RAINWINGS.
WHAT PLAN WAS THE COUNCIL TALKING ABOUT? WHAT IS IT W-WE DON'T WANT THE RAINWINGS TO KNOW?
THE LESS *YOU* KNOW, THE *BETTER*. YOU'LL GET IN LESS TROUBLE THAT WAY.

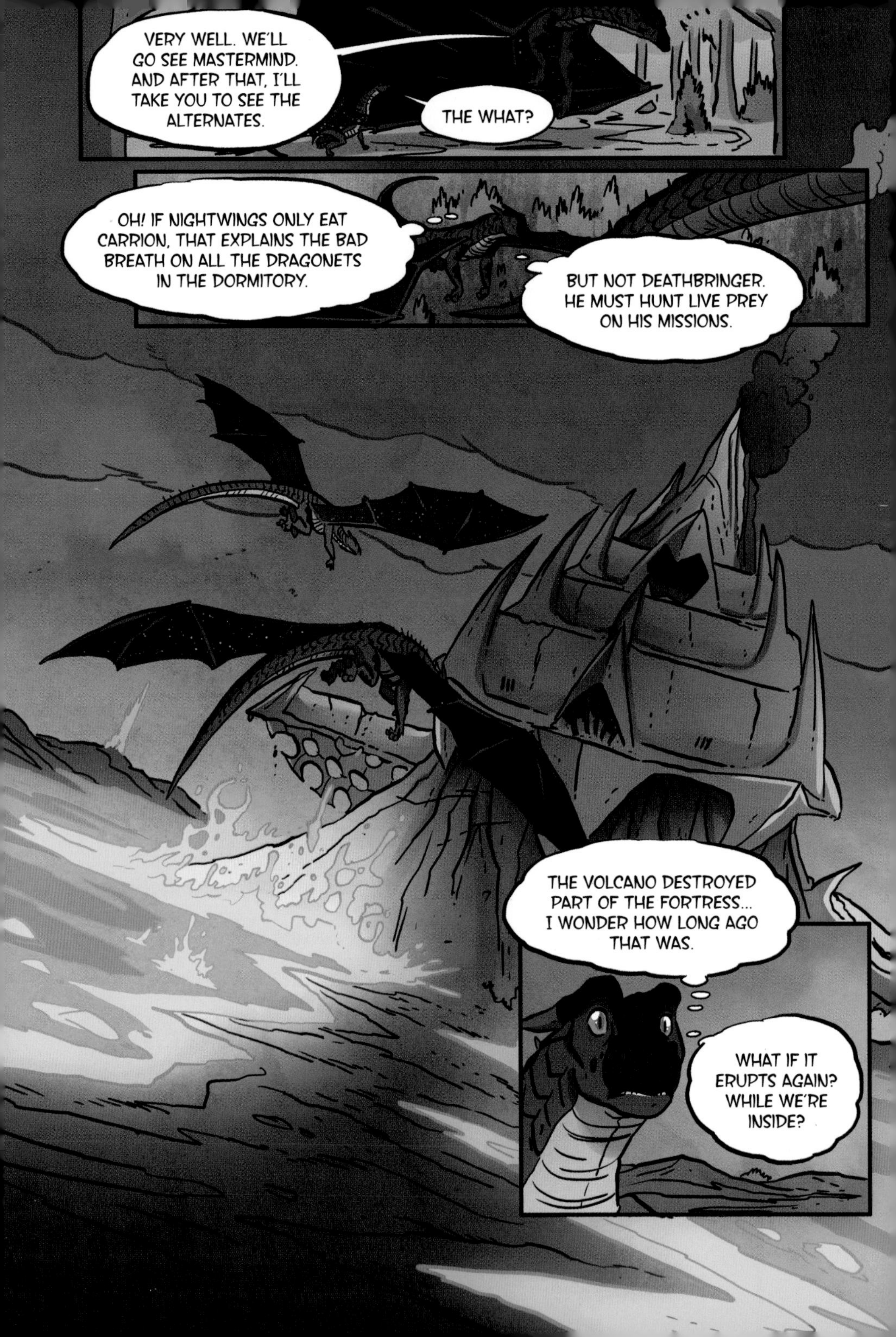
VERY WELL. WE'LL GO SEE MASTERMIND. AND AFTER THAT, I'LL TAKE YOU TO SEE THE ALTERNATES.
THE WHAT?
OH! IF NIGHTWINGS ONLY EAT CARRION, THAT EXPLAINS THE BAD BREATH ON ALL THE DRAGONETS IN THE DORMITORY.
BUT NOT DEATHBRINGER. HE MUST HUNT LIVE PREY ON HIS MISSIONS.
THE VOLCANO DESTROYED PART OF THE FORTRESS... I WONDER HOW LONG AGO THAT WAS.
WHAT IF IT ERUPTS AGAIN? WHILE WE'RE INSIDE?

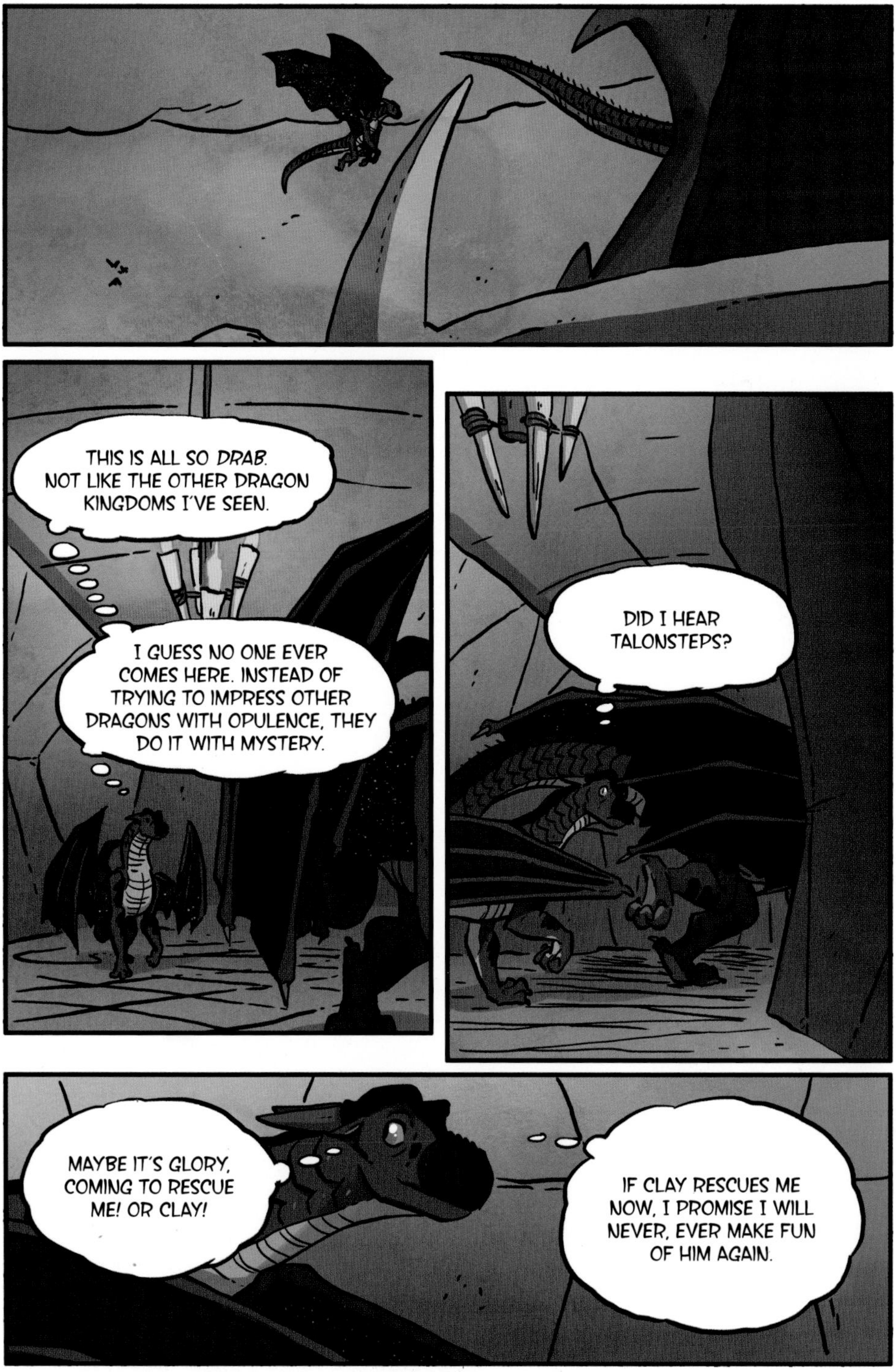
THIS IS ALL SO *DRAB*. NOT LIKE THE OTHER DRAGON KINGDOMS I'VE SEEN.
I GUESS NO ONE EVER COMES HERE. INSTEAD OF TRYING TO IMPRESS OTHER DRAGONS WITH OPULENCE, THEY DO IT WITH MYSTERY.
DID I HEAR TALONSTEPS?
MAYBE IT'S GLORY, COMING TO RESCUE ME! OR CLAY!
IF CLAY RESCUES ME NOW, I PROMISE I WILL NEVER, EVER MAKE FUN OF HIM AGAIN.

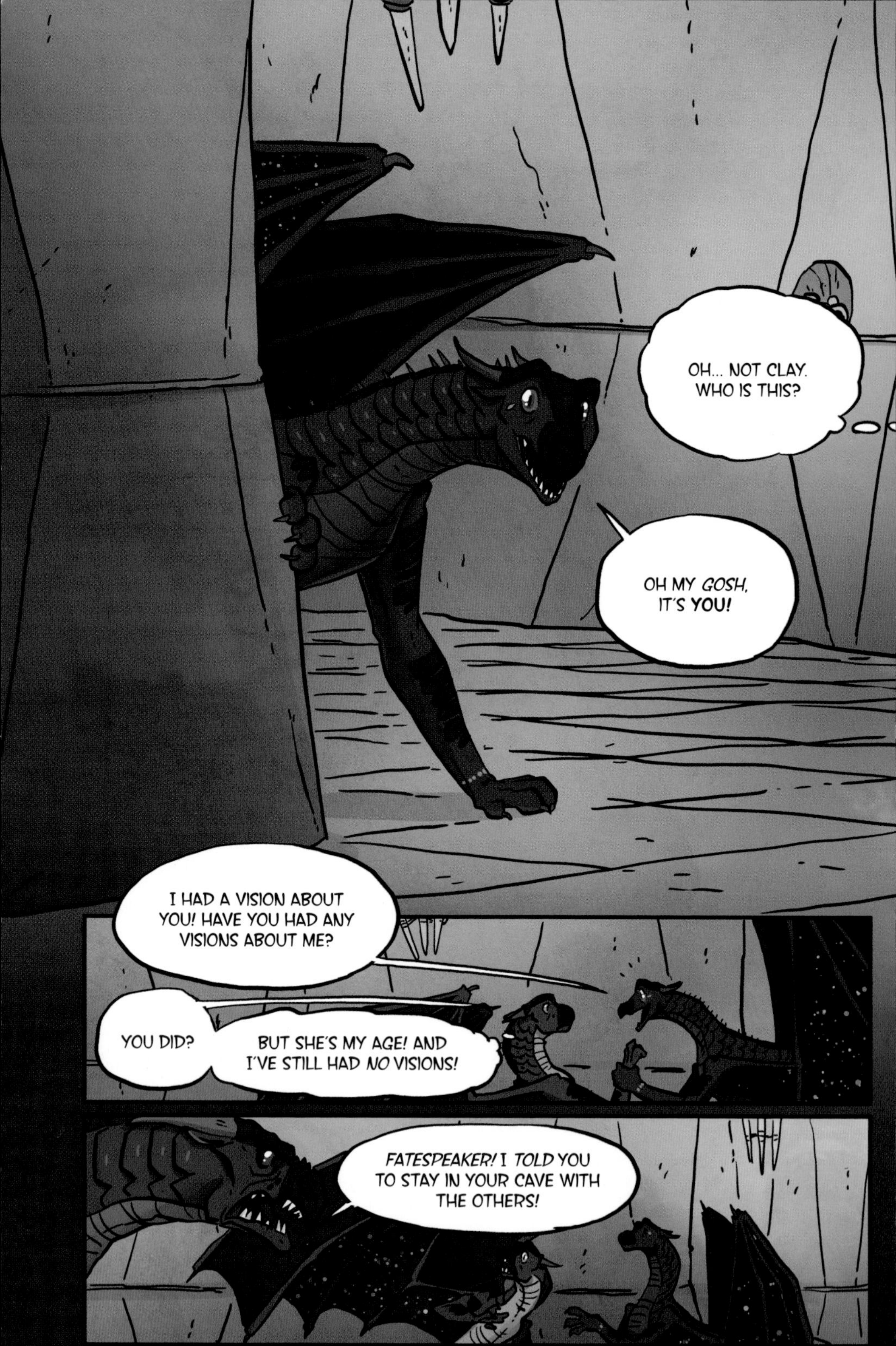
OH... NOT CLAY. WHO IS THIS?
OH MY *GOSH*, IT'S **YOU!**
I HAD A VISION ABOUT YOU! HAVE YOU HAD ANY VISIONS ABOUT ME?
YOU DID?
BUT SHE'S MY AGE! AND I'VE STILL HAD *NO* VISIONS!
FATESPEAKER! I *TOLD* YOU TO STAY IN YOUR CAVE WITH THE OTHERS!

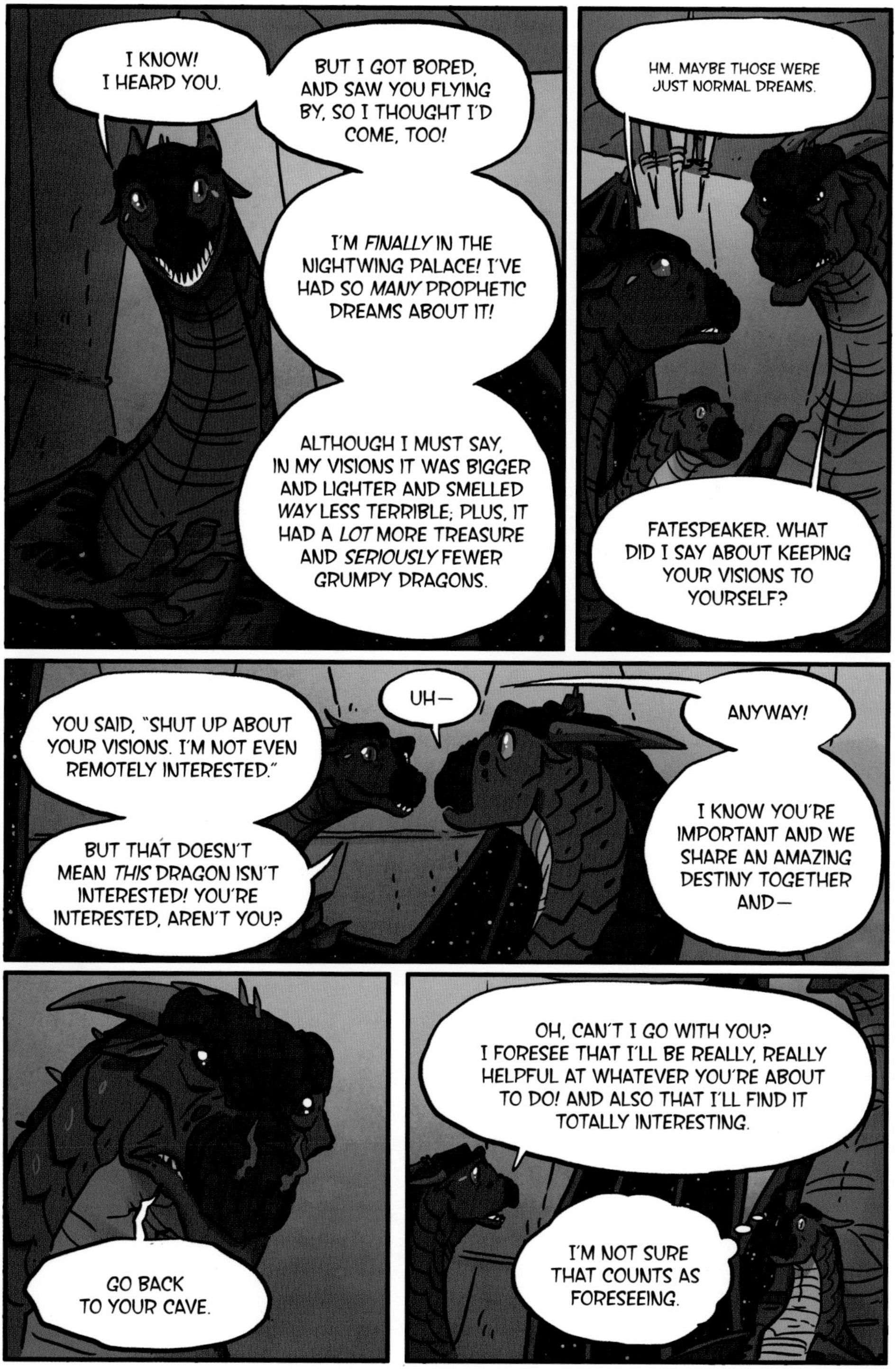
I KNOW! I HEARD YOU.
BUT I GOT BORED, AND SAW YOU FLYING BY, SO I THOUGHT I'D COME, TOO!
I'M *FINALLY* IN THE NIGHTWING PALACE! I'VE HAD SO *MANY* PROPHETIC DREAMS ABOUT IT!
ALTHOUGH I MUST SAY, IN MY VISIONS IT WAS BIGGER AND LIGHTER AND SMELLED *WAY* LESS TERRIBLE; PLUS, IT HAD A *LOT* MORE TREASURE AND *SERIOUSLY* FEWER GRUMPY DRAGONS.
HM. MAYBE THOSE WERE JUST NORMAL DREAMS.
FATESPEAKER. WHAT DID I SAY ABOUT KEEPING YOUR VISIONS TO YOURSELF?
YOU SAID, "SHUT UP ABOUT YOUR VISIONS. I'M NOT EVEN REMOTELY INTERESTED."
BUT THAT DOESN'T MEAN *THIS* DRAGON ISN'T INTERESTED! YOU'RE INTERESTED, AREN'T YOU?
UH—
ANYWAY!
I KNOW YOU'RE IMPORTANT AND WE SHARE AN AMAZING DESTINY TOGETHER AND—
GO BACK TO YOUR CAVE.
OH, CAN'T I GO WITH YOU? I FORESEE THAT I'LL BE REALLY, REALLY HELPFUL AT WHATEVER YOU'RE ABOUT TO DO! AND ALSO THAT I'LL FIND IT TOTALLY INTERESTING.
I'M NOT SURE THAT COUNTS AS FORESEEING.

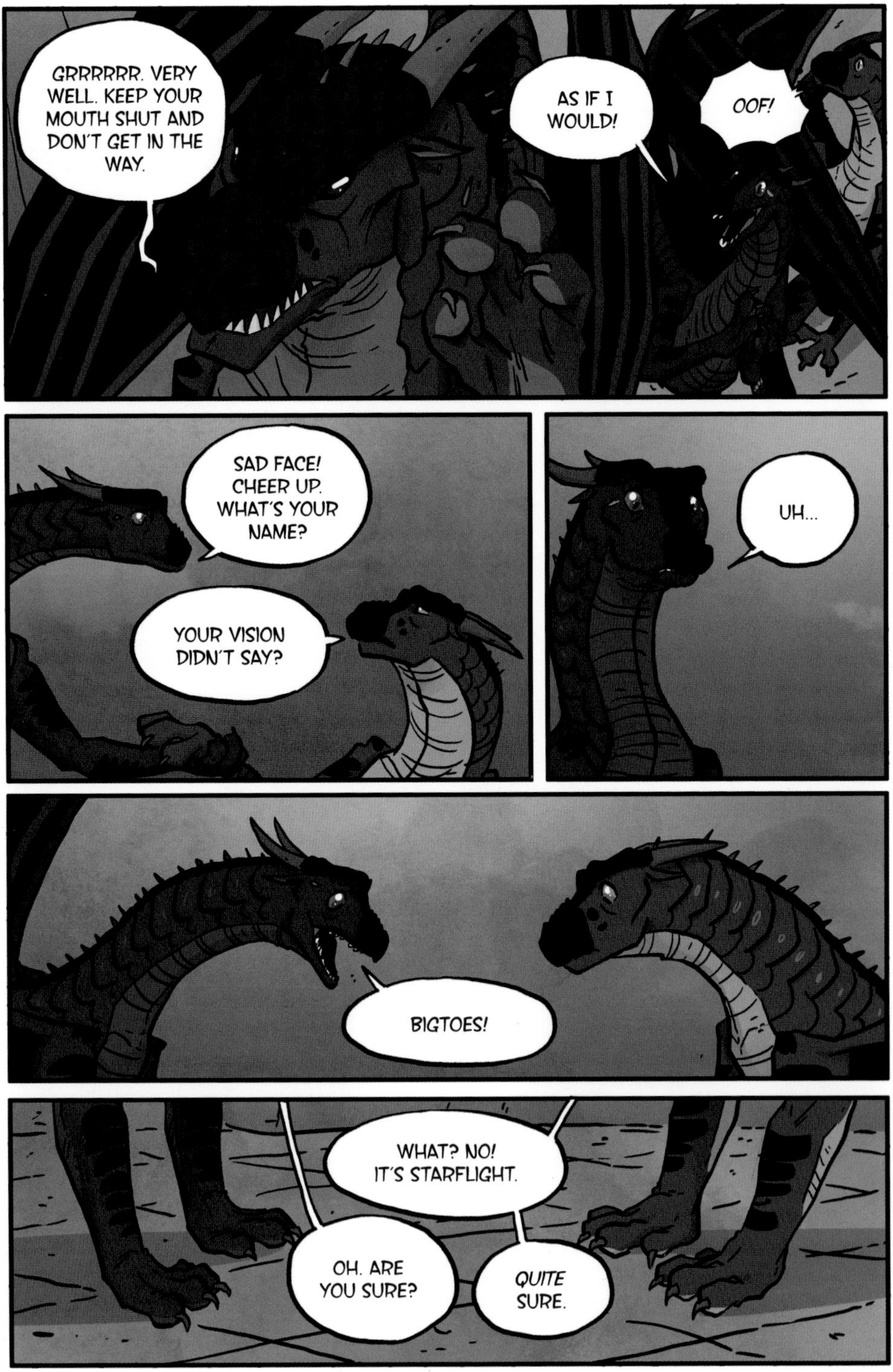
GRRRRRR. VERY WELL. KEEP YOUR MOUTH SHUT AND DON'T GET IN THE WAY.
AS IF I WOULD!
OOF!
SAD FACE! CHEER UP. WHAT'S YOUR NAME?
YOUR VISION DIDN'T SAY?
UH...
BIGTOES!
WHAT? NO! IT'S STARFLIGHT.
OH. ARE YOU SURE?
QUITE SURE.

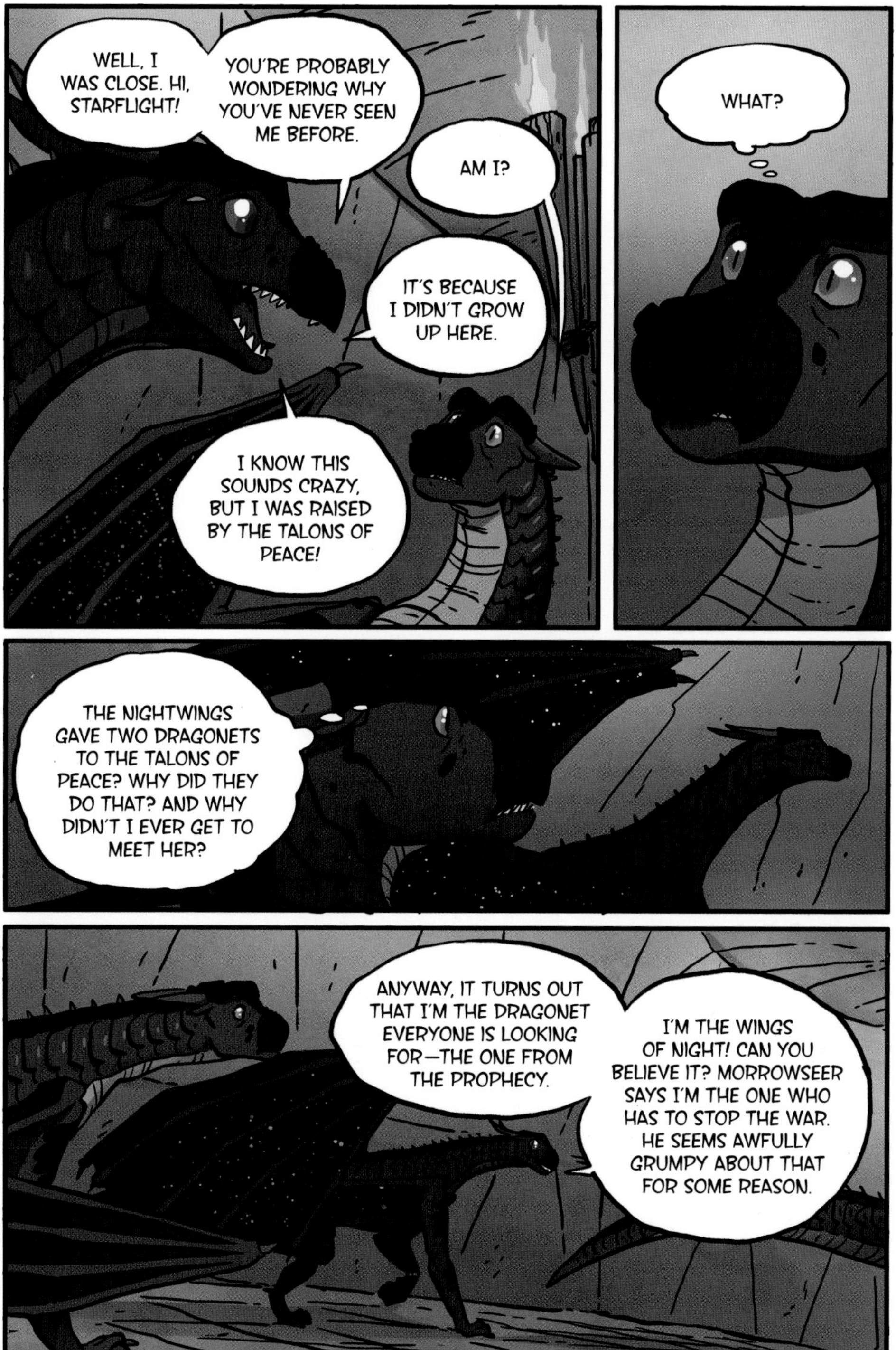
WELL, I WAS CLOSE. HI, STARFLIGHT!
YOU'RE PROBABLY WONDERING WHY YOU'VE NEVER SEEN ME BEFORE.
AM I?
IT'S BECAUSE I DIDN'T GROW UP HERE.
I KNOW THIS SOUNDS CRAZY, BUT I WAS RAISED BY THE TALONS OF PEACE!
WHAT?
THE NIGHTWINGS GAVE TWO DRAGONETS TO THE TALONS OF PEACE? WHY DID THEY DO THAT? AND WHY DIDN'T I EVER GET TO MEET HER?
ANYWAY, IT TURNS OUT THAT I'M THE DRAGONET EVERYONE IS LOOKING FOR—THE ONE FROM THE PROPHECY.
I'M THE WINGS OF NIGHT! CAN YOU BELIEVE IT? MORROWSEER SAYS I'M THE ONE WHO HAS TO STOP THE WAR. HE SEEMS AWFULLY GRUMPY ABOUT THAT FOR SOME REASON.

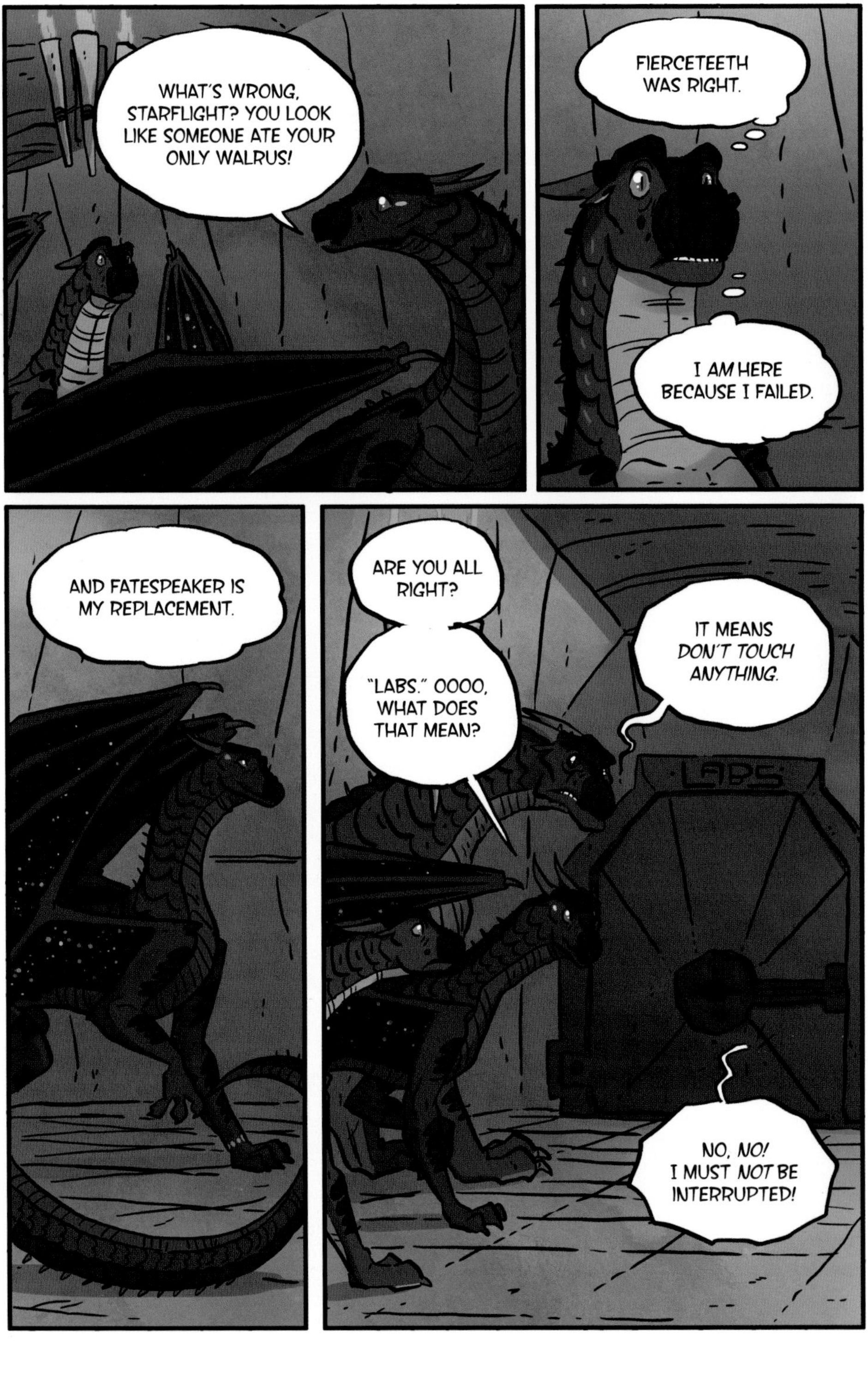
WHAT'S WRONG, STARFLIGHT? YOU LOOK LIKE SOMEONE ATE YOUR ONLY WALRUS!
FIERCETEETH WAS RIGHT.
I *AM* HERE BECAUSE I FAILED.
AND FATESPEAKER IS MY REPLACEMENT.
ARE YOU ALL RIGHT?
"LABS." OOOO, WHAT DOES THAT MEAN?
IT MEANS *DON'T TOUCH ANYTHING.*
LABS
NO, *NO!* I MUST *NOT* BE INTERRUPTED!

PLEASE LEAVE! THIS EXPERIMENT IS AT A *CRITICAL JUNCTURE!* AND PRINCESS GREATNESS SAYS I MIGHT BE SHUT DOWN *AT ANY MOMENT!*

MASTERMIND, IT SEEMS YOU WERE CORRECT. THE DRAGONET FROM FARSIGHT'S EGG WAS INDEED YOUR SON. I HAVE BROUGHT HIM HERE TO MEET YOU.

MY SON?

THREE MOONS. I HAVE A *SON.*

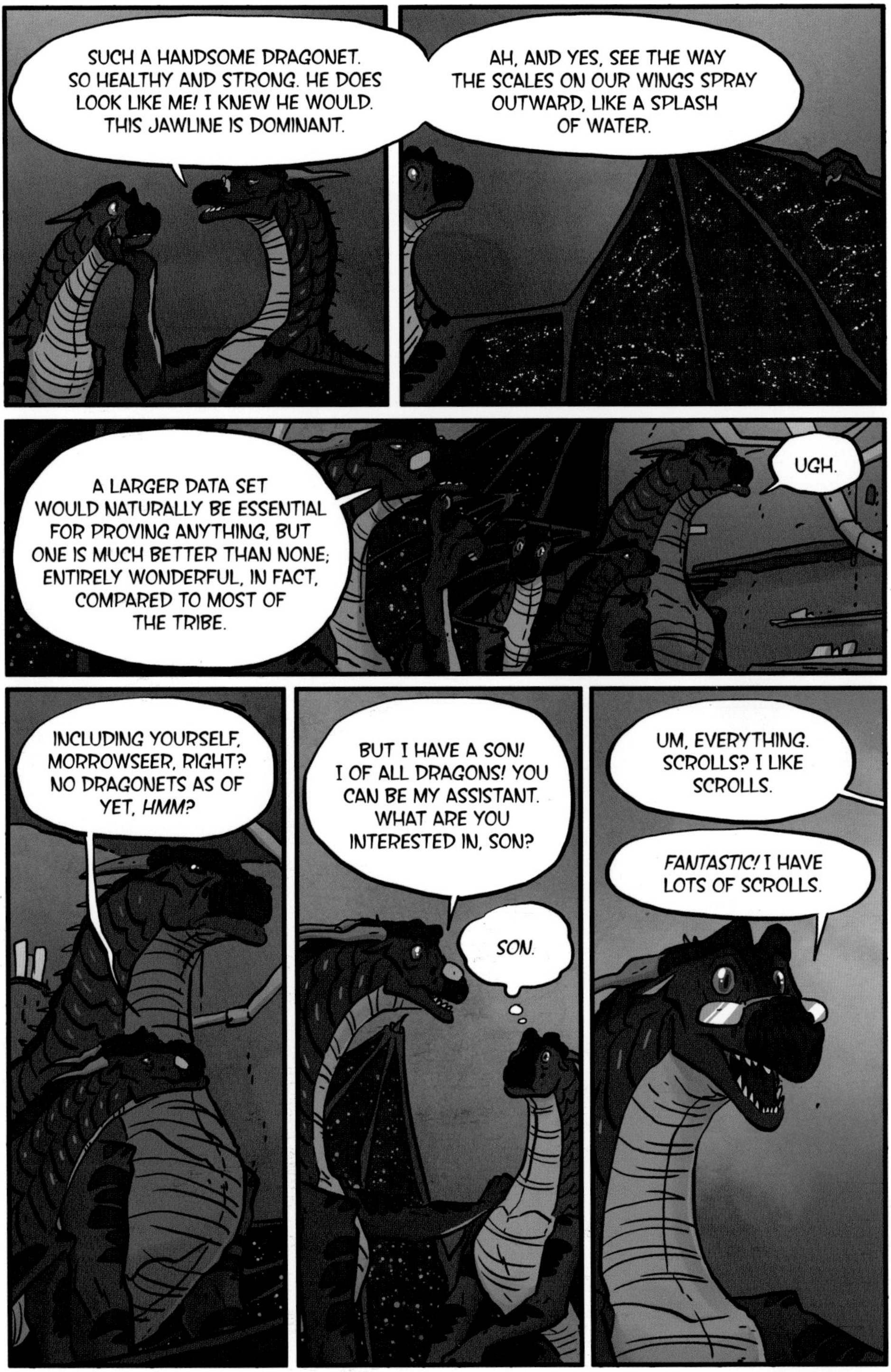
SUCH A HANDSOME DRAGONET. SO HEALTHY AND STRONG. HE DOES LOOK LIKE ME! I KNEW HE WOULD. THIS JAWLINE IS DOMINANT.
AH, AND YES, SEE THE WAY THE SCALES ON OUR WINGS SPRAY OUTWARD, LIKE A SPLASH OF WATER.
A LARGER DATA SET WOULD NATURALLY BE ESSENTIAL FOR PROVING ANYTHING, BUT ONE IS MUCH BETTER THAN NONE; ENTIRELY WONDERFUL, IN FACT, COMPARED TO MOST OF THE TRIBE.
UGH.
INCLUDING YOURSELF, MORROWSEER, RIGHT? NO DRAGONETS AS OF YET, *HMM?*
BUT I HAVE A SON! I OF ALL DRAGONS! YOU CAN BE MY ASSISTANT. WHAT ARE YOU INTERESTED IN, SON?
SON.
UM, EVERYTHING. SCROLLS? I LIKE SCROLLS.
FANTASTIC! I HAVE LOTS OF SCROLLS.

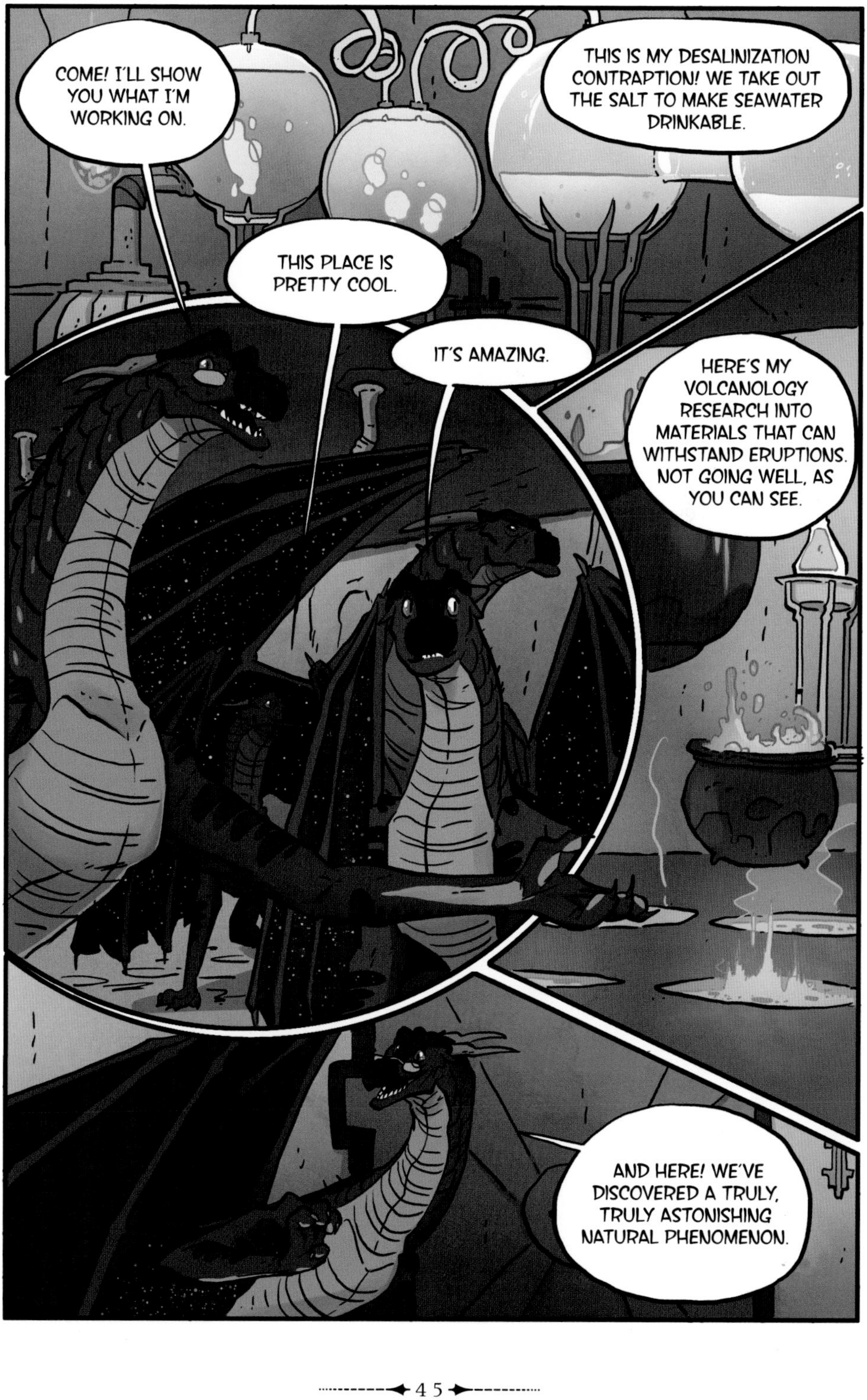
COME! I'LL SHOW YOU WHAT I'M WORKING ON.
THIS IS MY DESALINIZATION CONTRAPTION! WE TAKE OUT THE SALT TO MAKE SEAWATER DRINKABLE.
THIS PLACE IS PRETTY COOL.
IT'S AMAZING.
HERE'S MY VOLCANOLOGY RESEARCH INTO MATERIALS THAT CAN WITHSTAND ERUPTIONS. NOT GOING WELL, AS YOU CAN SEE.
AND HERE! WE'VE DISCOVERED A TRULY, TRULY ASTONISHING NATURAL PHENOMENON.

OUR UNDERSTANDING OF THIS BIOLOGICAL ANOMALY IS SO NEW THAT WE HAVEN'T EVEN PUT IT IN ANY SCROLLS. IT TURNS OUT ONE TRIBE OF DRAGONS HAS EVOLVED AN UNUSUAL DEFENSE MECHANISM. YOU'LL NEVER GUESS WHICH ONE!

OH NO.

RAINWINGS!

RAINWINGS?

YES! THEY CAN SHOOT *VENOM* FROM THEIR *FANGS!* LET ME SHOW YOU.

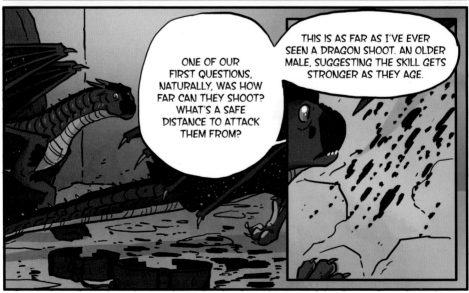

ONE OF OUR FIRST QUESTIONS, NATURALLY, WAS HOW FAR CAN THEY SHOOT? WHAT'S A SAFE DISTANCE TO ATTACK THEM FROM?

THIS IS AS FAR AS I'VE EVER SEEN A DRAGON SHOOT. AN OLDER MALE, SUGGESTING THE SKILL GETS STRONGER AS THEY AGE.

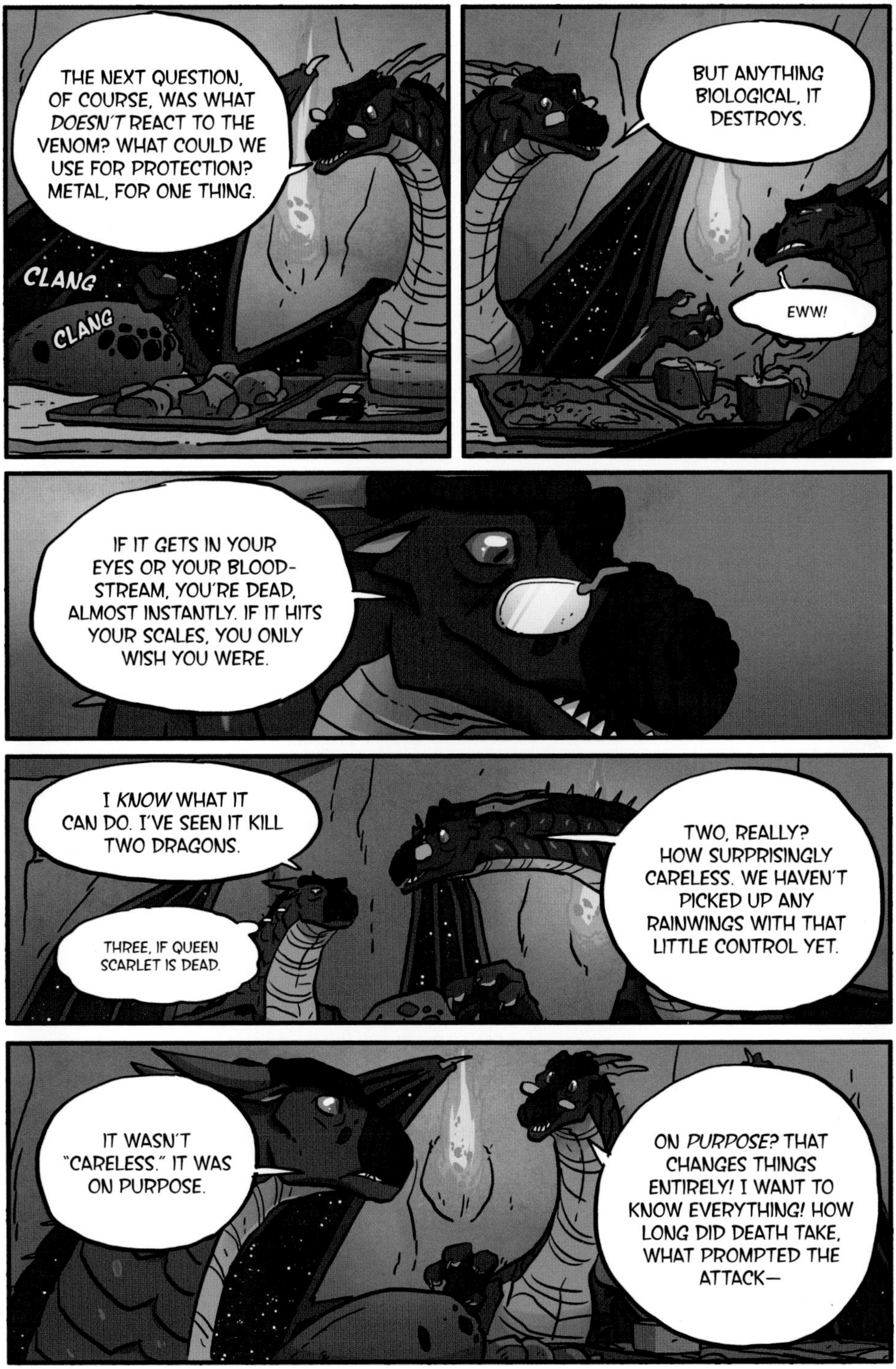
THE NEXT QUESTION, OF COURSE, WAS WHAT *DOESN'T* REACT TO THE VENOM? WHAT COULD WE USE FOR PROTECTION? METAL, FOR ONE THING.
CLANG
CLANG
BUT ANYTHING BIOLOGICAL, IT DESTROYS.
EWW!
IF IT GETS IN YOUR EYES OR YOUR BLOOD-STREAM, YOU'RE DEAD, ALMOST INSTANTLY. IF IT HITS YOUR SCALES, YOU ONLY WISH YOU WERE.
I *KNOW* WHAT IT CAN DO. I'VE SEEN IT KILL TWO DRAGONS.
THREE, IF QUEEN SCARLET IS DEAD.
TWO, REALLY? HOW SURPRISINGLY CARELESS. WE HAVEN'T PICKED UP ANY RAINWINGS WITH THAT LITTLE CONTROL YET.
IT WASN'T "CARELESS." IT WAS ON PURPOSE.
ON *PURPOSE*? THAT CHANGES THINGS ENTIRELY! I WANT TO KNOW EVERYTHING! HOW LONG DID DEATH TAKE, WHAT PROMPTED THE ATTACK—

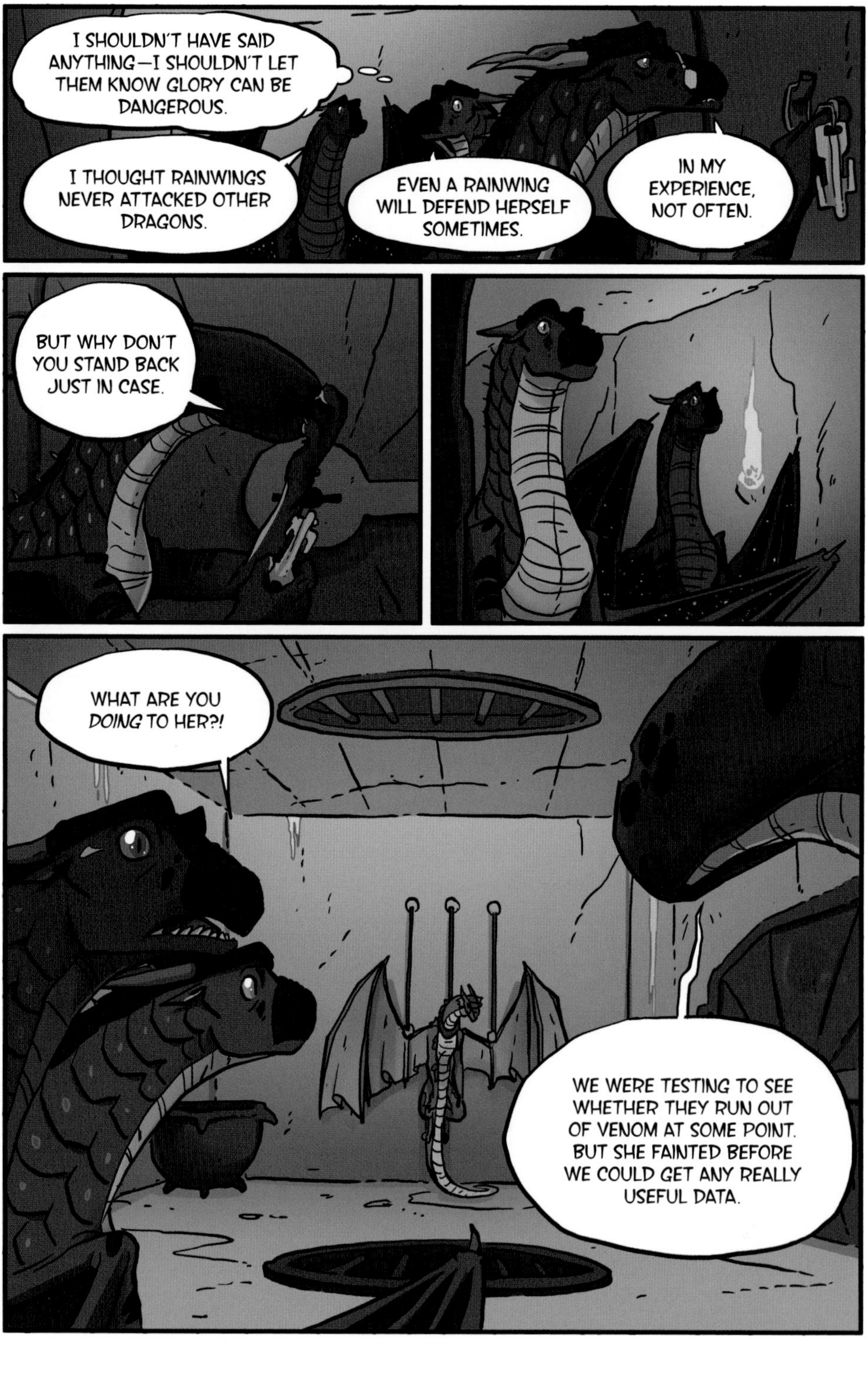
I SHOULDN'T HAVE SAID ANYTHING—I SHOULDN'T LET THEM KNOW GLORY CAN BE DANGEROUS.
I THOUGHT RAINWINGS NEVER ATTACKED OTHER DRAGONS.
EVEN A RAINWING WILL DEFEND HERSELF SOMETIMES.
IN MY EXPERIENCE, NOT OFTEN.
BUT WHY DON'T YOU STAND BACK JUST IN CASE.
WHAT ARE YOU *DOING* TO HER?!
WE WERE TESTING TO SEE WHETHER THEY RUN OUT OF VENOM AT SOME POINT. BUT SHE FAINTED BEFORE WE COULD GET ANY REALLY USEFUL DATA.

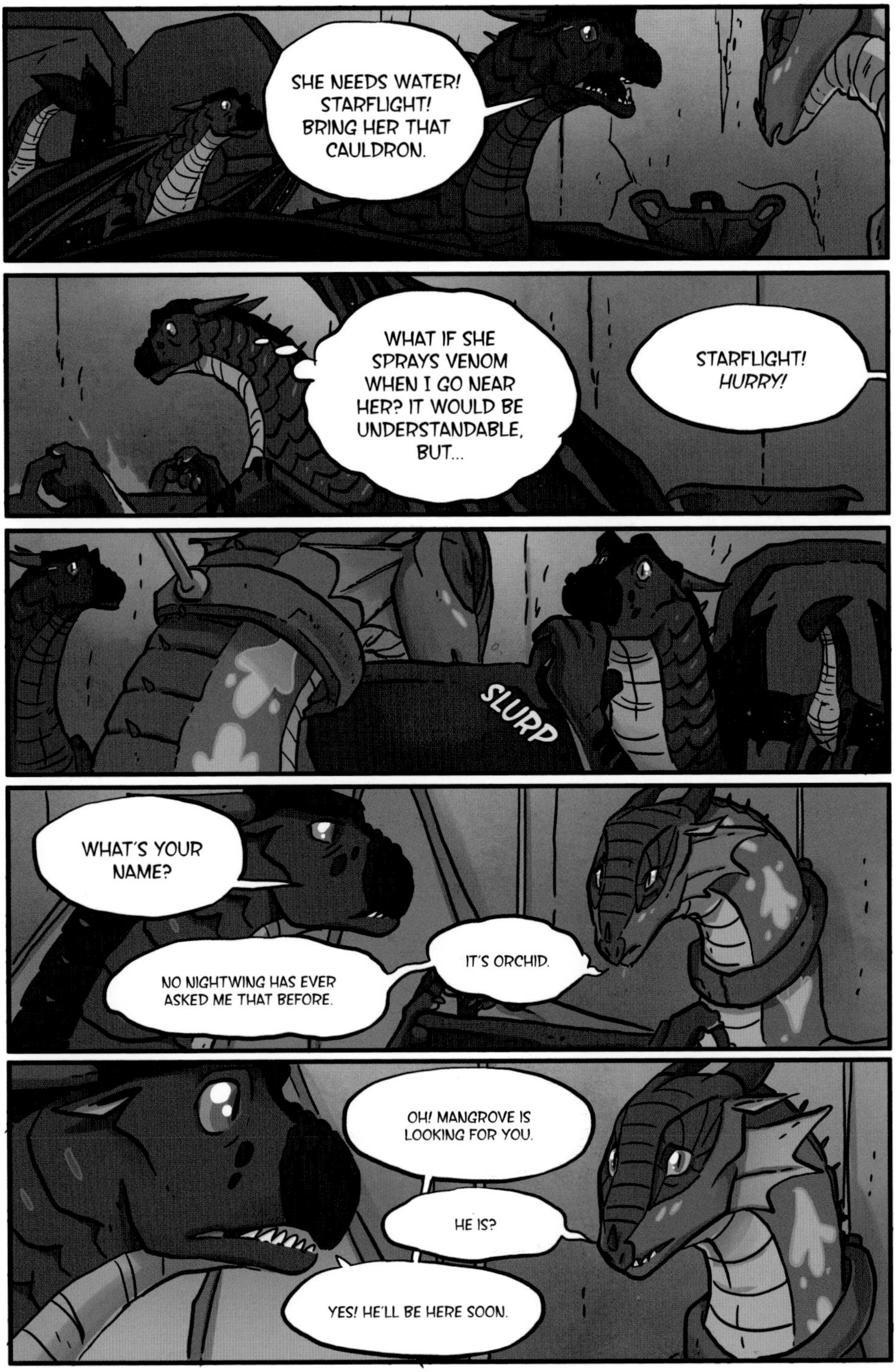
SHE NEEDS WATER! STARFLIGHT! BRING HER THAT CAULDRON.
WHAT IF SHE SPRAYS VENOM WHEN I GO NEAR HER? IT WOULD BE UNDERSTANDABLE, BUT...
STARFLIGHT! *HURRY!*
SLURP
WHAT'S YOUR NAME?
IT'S ORCHID.
NO NIGHTWING HAS EVER ASKED ME THAT BEFORE.
OH! MANGROVE IS LOOKING FOR YOU.
HE IS?
YES! HE'LL BE HERE SOON.

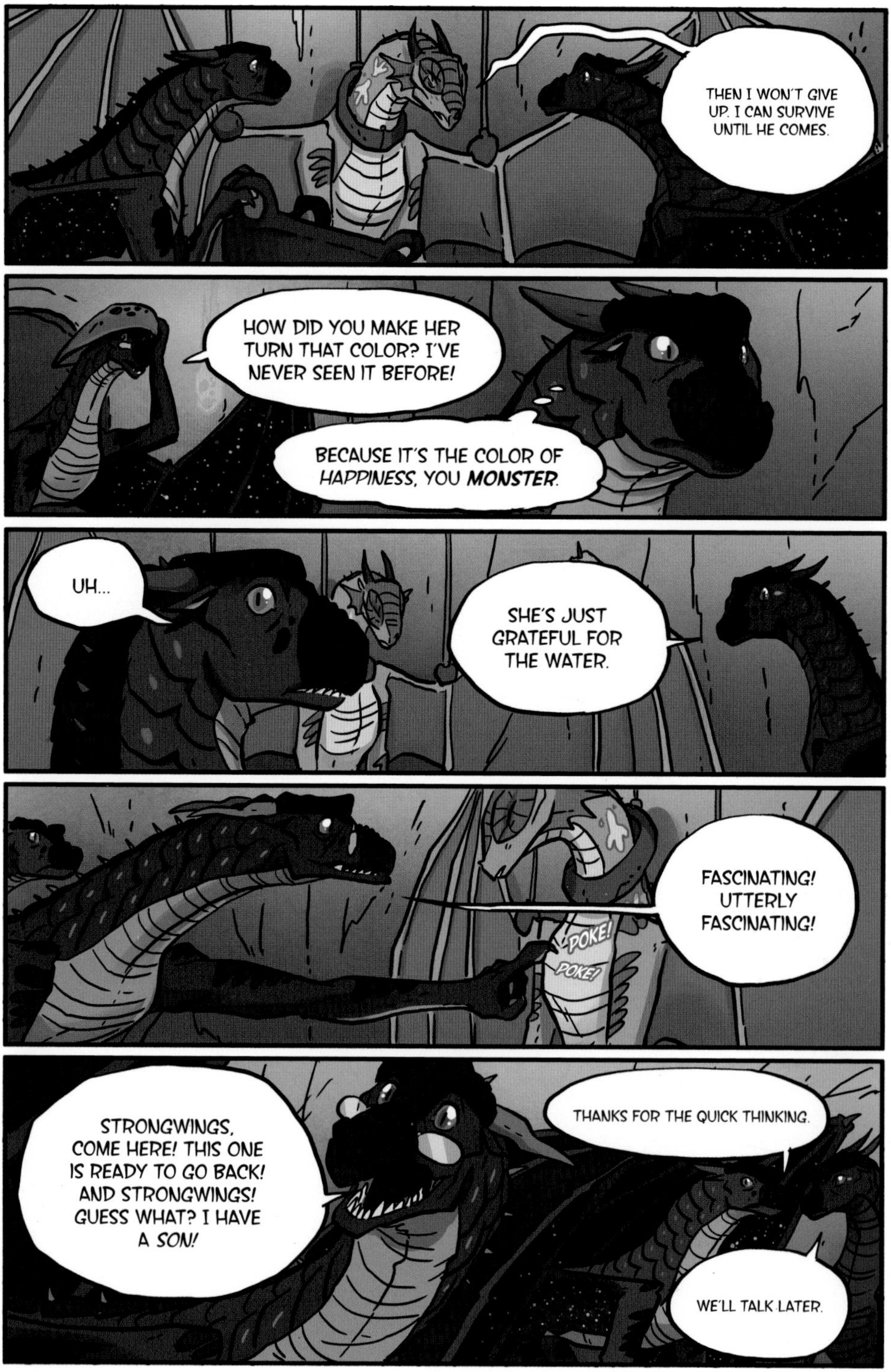
THEN I WON'T GIVE UP. I CAN SURVIVE UNTIL HE COMES.
HOW DID YOU MAKE HER TURN THAT COLOR? I'VE NEVER SEEN IT BEFORE!
BECAUSE IT'S THE COLOR OF *HAPPINESS*, YOU ***MONSTER***.
UH...
SHE'S JUST GRATEFUL FOR THE WATER.
FASCINATING! UTTERLY FASCINATING!
POKE!
POKE!
STRONGWINGS, COME HERE! THIS ONE IS READY TO GO BACK! AND STRONGWINGS! GUESS WHAT? I HAVE A *SON*!
THANKS FOR THE QUICK THINKING.
WE'LL TALK LATER.

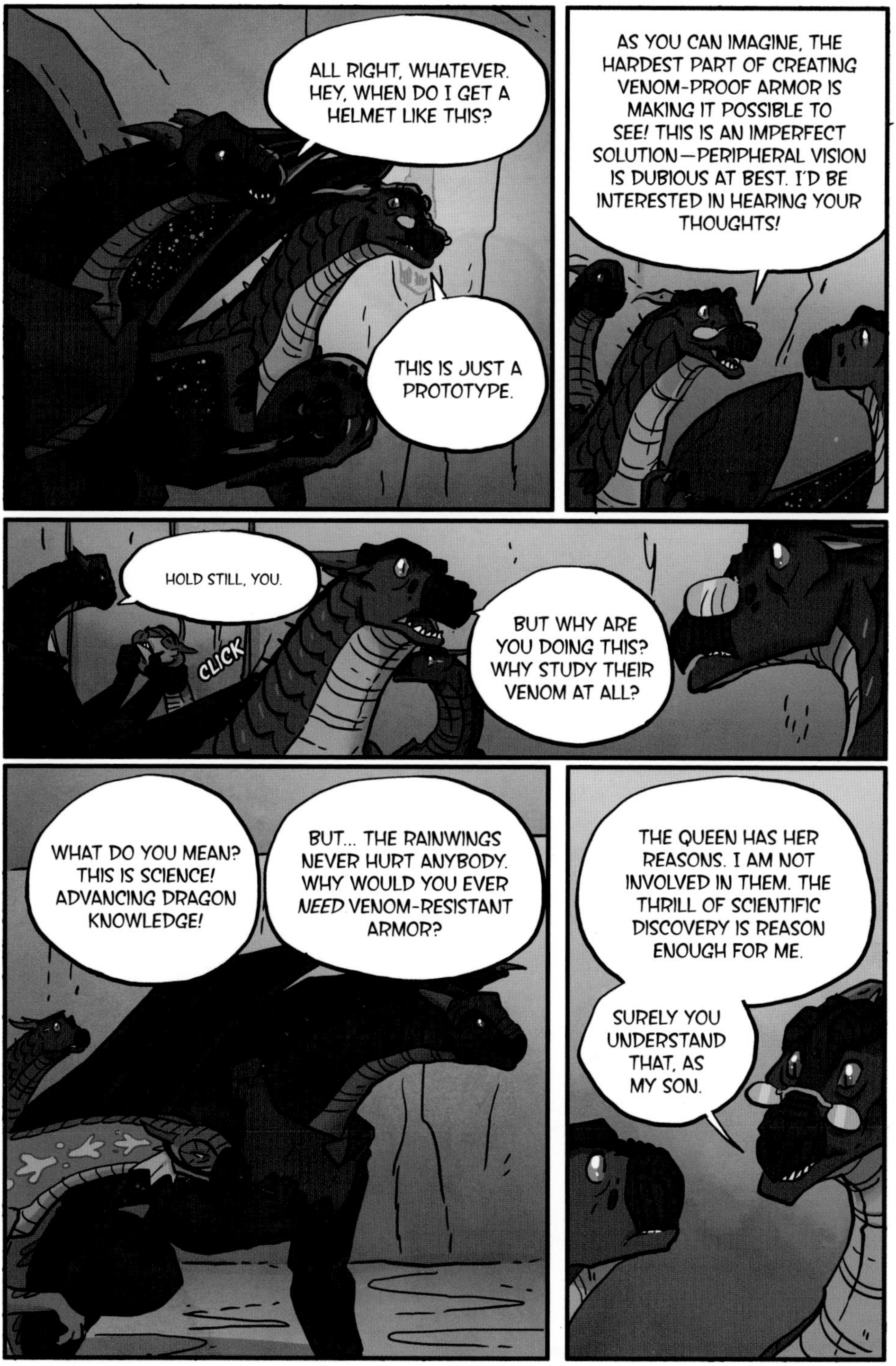
ALL RIGHT, WHATEVER. HEY, WHEN DO I GET A HELMET LIKE THIS?
THIS IS JUST A PROTOTYPE.
AS YOU CAN IMAGINE, THE HARDEST PART OF CREATING VENOM-PROOF ARMOR IS MAKING IT POSSIBLE TO SEE! THIS IS AN IMPERFECT SOLUTION—PERIPHERAL VISION IS DUBIOUS AT BEST. I'D BE INTERESTED IN HEARING YOUR THOUGHTS!
HOLD STILL, YOU.
CLICK
BUT WHY ARE YOU DOING THIS? WHY STUDY THEIR VENOM AT ALL?
WHAT DO YOU MEAN? THIS IS SCIENCE! ADVANCING DRAGON KNOWLEDGE!
BUT... THE RAINWINGS NEVER HURT ANYBODY. WHY WOULD YOU EVER *NEED* VENOM-RESISTANT ARMOR?
THE QUEEN HAS HER REASONS. I AM NOT INVOLVED IN THEM. THE THRILL OF SCIENTIFIC DISCOVERY IS REASON ENOUGH FOR ME.
SURELY YOU UNDERSTAND THAT, AS MY SON.

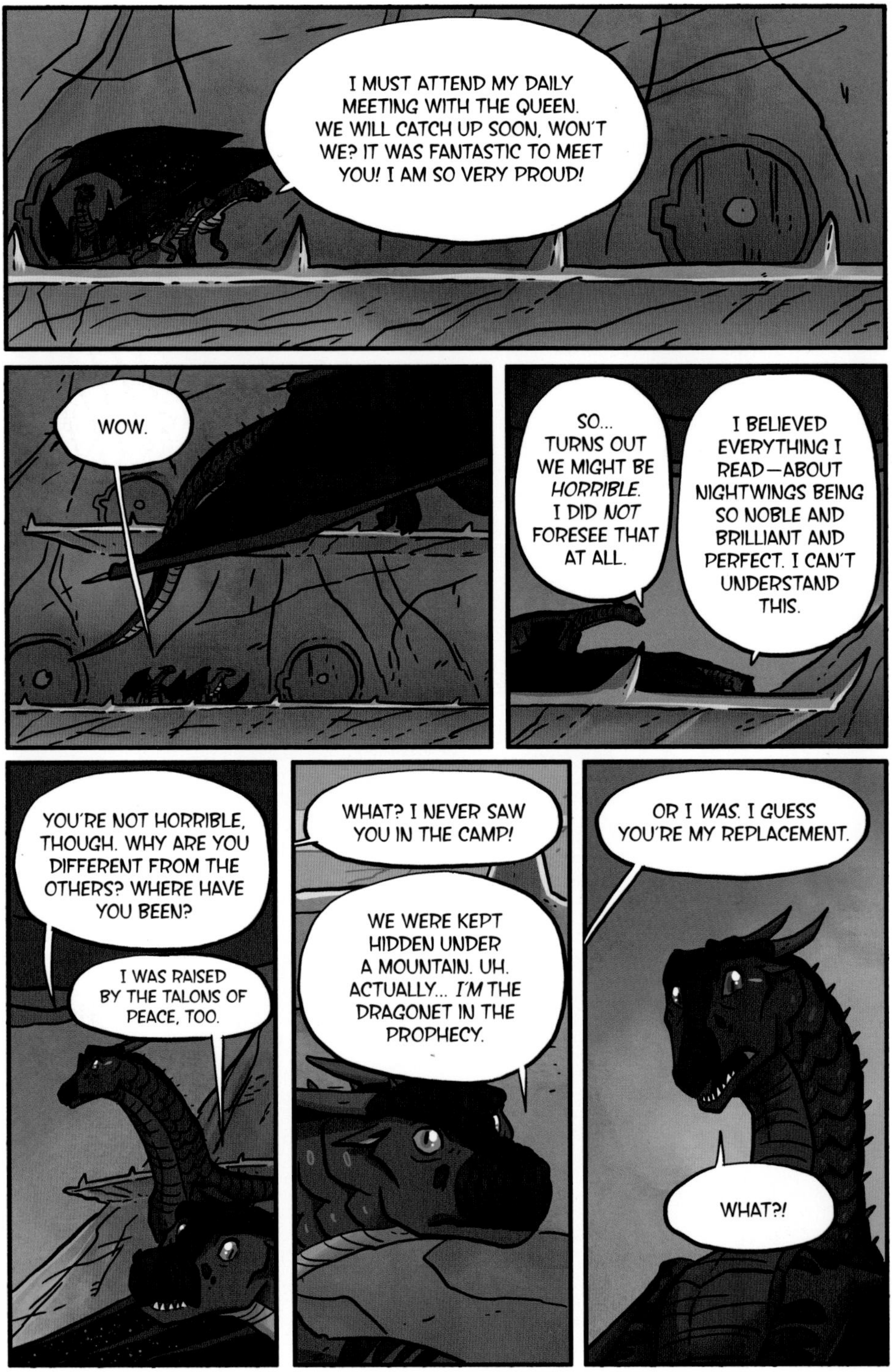
I MUST ATTEND MY DAILY MEETING WITH THE QUEEN. WE WILL CATCH UP SOON, WON'T WE? IT WAS FANTASTIC TO MEET YOU! I AM SO VERY PROUD!
WOW.
SO... TURNS OUT WE MIGHT BE *HORRIBLE*. I DID *NOT* FORESEE THAT AT ALL.
I BELIEVED EVERYTHING I READ—ABOUT NIGHTWINGS BEING SO NOBLE AND BRILLIANT AND PERFECT. I CAN'T UNDERSTAND THIS.
YOU'RE NOT HORRIBLE, THOUGH. WHY ARE YOU DIFFERENT FROM THE OTHERS? WHERE HAVE YOU BEEN?
I WAS RAISED BY THE TALONS OF PEACE, TOO.
WHAT? I NEVER SAW YOU IN THE CAMP!
WE WERE KEPT HIDDEN UNDER A MOUNTAIN. UH. ACTUALLY... *I'M* THE DRAGONET IN THE PROPHECY.
OR I *WAS*. I GUESS YOU'RE MY REPLACEMENT.
WHAT?!

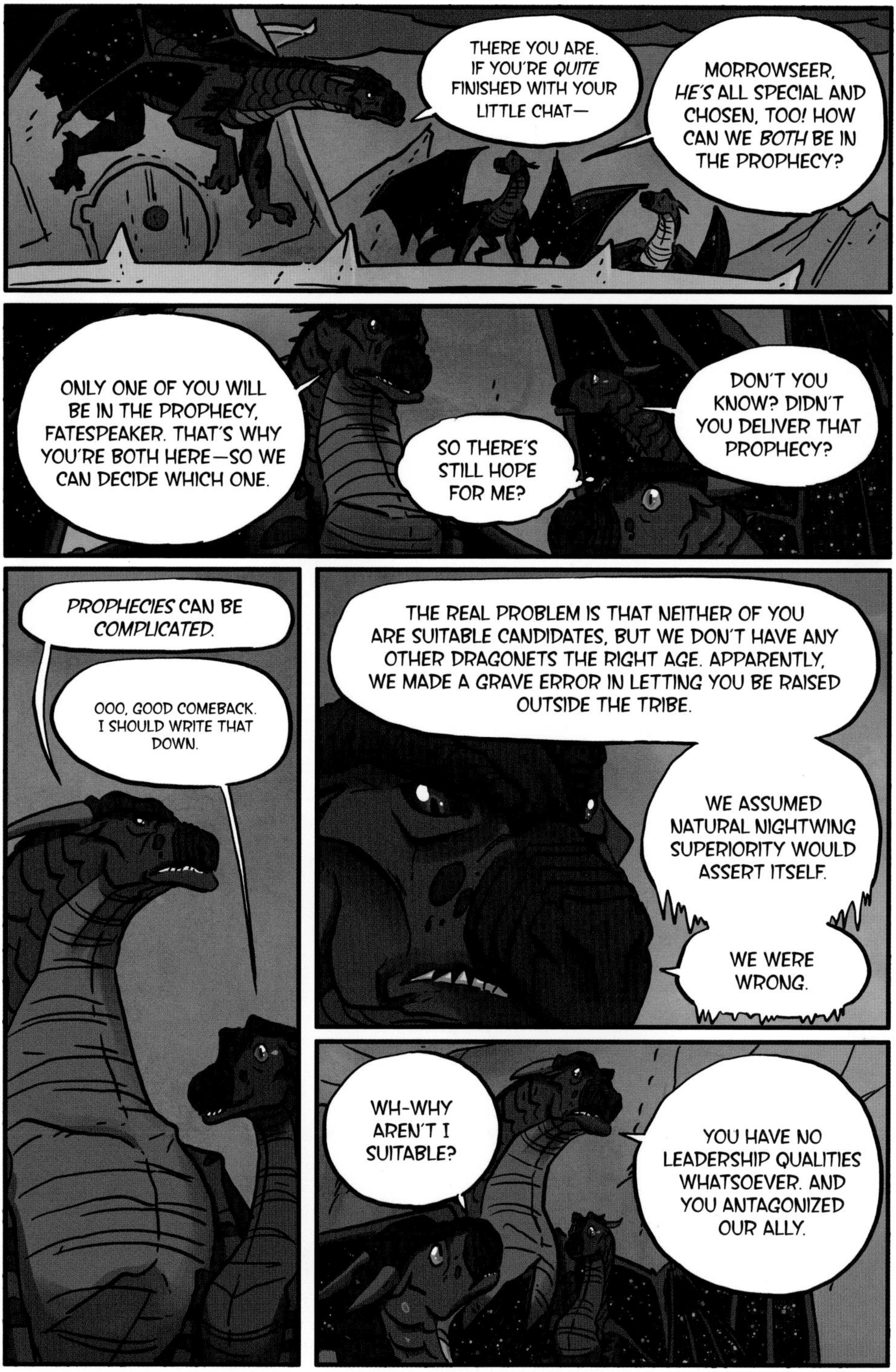
THERE YOU ARE. IF YOU'RE *QUITE* FINISHED WITH YOUR LITTLE CHAT—
MORROWSEER, *HE'S* ALL SPECIAL AND CHOSEN, TOO! HOW CAN WE *BOTH* BE IN THE PROPHECY?
ONLY ONE OF YOU WILL BE IN THE PROPHECY, FATESPEAKER. THAT'S WHY YOU'RE BOTH HERE—SO WE CAN DECIDE WHICH ONE.
SO THERE'S STILL HOPE FOR ME?
DON'T YOU KNOW? DIDN'T YOU DELIVER THAT PROPHECY?
PROPHECIES CAN BE *COMPLICATED.*
OOO, GOOD COMEBACK. I SHOULD WRITE THAT DOWN.
THE REAL PROBLEM IS THAT NEITHER OF YOU ARE SUITABLE CANDIDATES, BUT WE DON'T HAVE ANY OTHER DRAGONETS THE RIGHT AGE. APPARENTLY, WE MADE A GRAVE ERROR IN LETTING YOU BE RAISED OUTSIDE THE TRIBE.
WE ASSUMED NATURAL NIGHTWING SUPERIORITY WOULD ASSERT ITSELF.
WE WERE WRONG.
WH-WHY AREN'T I SUITABLE?
YOU HAVE NO LEADERSHIP QUALITIES WHATSOEVER. AND YOU ANTAGONIZED OUR ALLY.

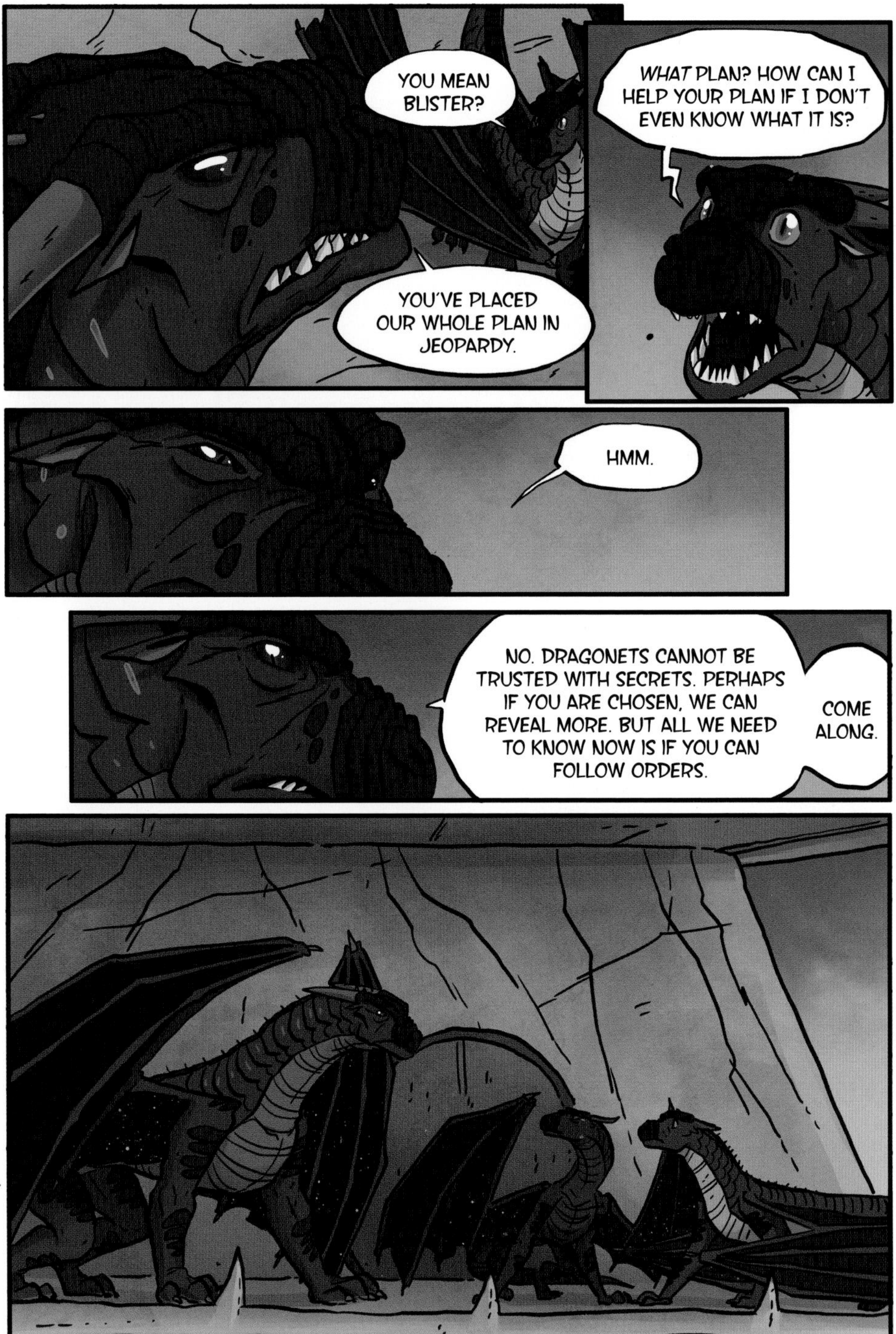
YOU MEAN BLISTER?
YOU'VE PLACED OUR WHOLE PLAN IN JEOPARDY.
WHAT PLAN? HOW CAN I HELP YOUR PLAN IF I DON'T EVEN KNOW WHAT IT IS?
HMM.
NO. DRAGONETS CANNOT BE TRUSTED WITH SECRETS. PERHAPS IF YOU ARE CHOSEN, WE CAN REVEAL MORE. BUT ALL WE NEED TO KNOW NOW IS IF YOU CAN FOLLOW ORDERS.
COME ALONG.

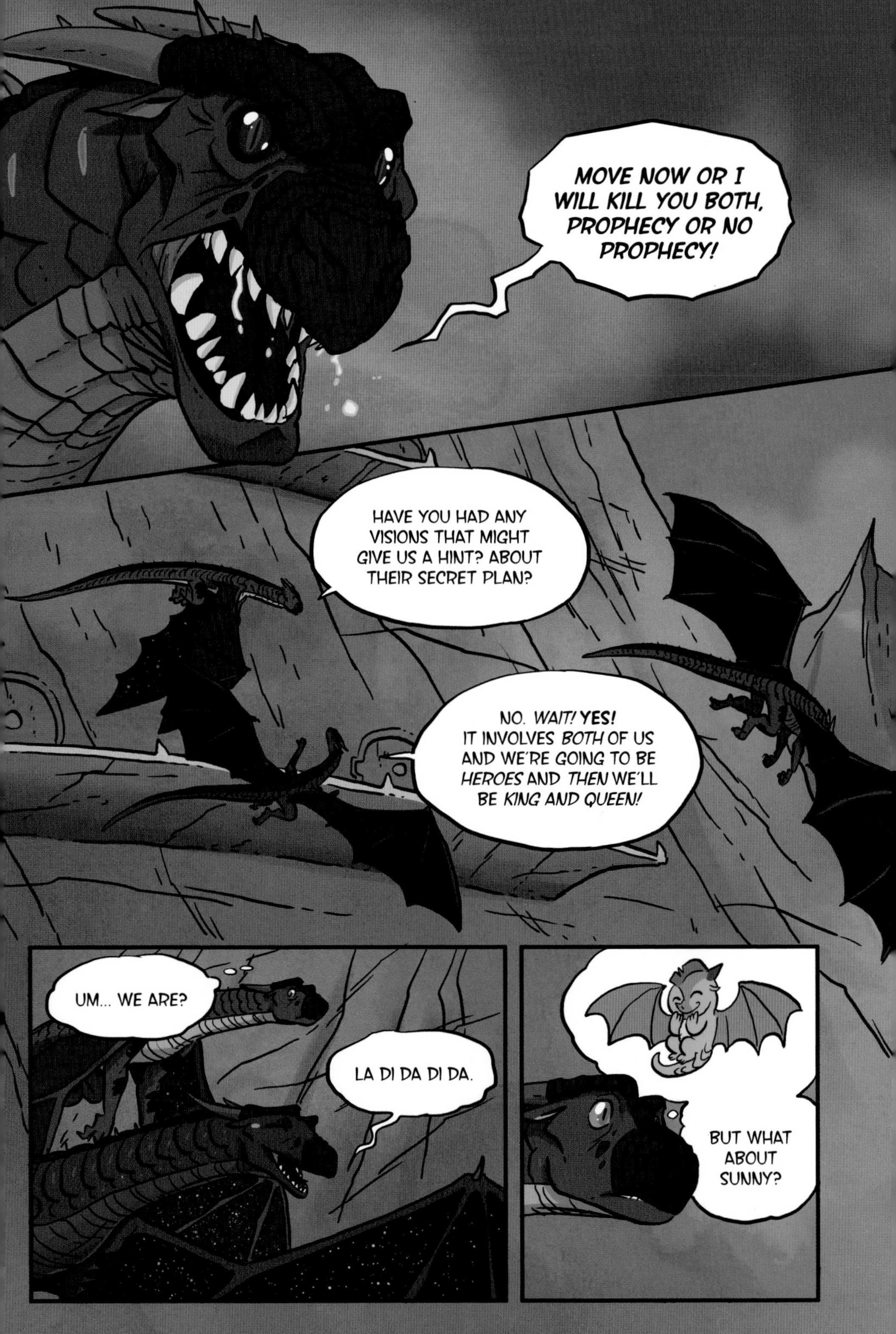
MOVE NOW OR I WILL KILL YOU BOTH, PROPHECY OR NO PROPHECY!
HAVE YOU HAD ANY VISIONS THAT MIGHT GIVE US A HINT? ABOUT THEIR SECRET PLAN?
NO. *WAIT!* **YES!** IT INVOLVES *BOTH* OF US AND WE'RE GOING TO BE *HEROES* AND *THEN* WE'LL BE *KING AND QUEEN!*
UM... WE ARE?
LA DI DA DI DA.
BUT WHAT ABOUT SUNNY?

WHY ARE THEY TORTURING THE RAINWINGS? I CAN FIGURE THIS OUT.

MAYBE THEY WANT TO USE RAINWING VENOM THEMSELVES? THEY'RE ON QUEEN BLISTER'S SIDE. MAYBE THEY'LL USE RAINWING VENOM TO FIGHT FOR HER?

BUT WHY WOULD THEY JOIN NOW, EIGHTEEN YEARS INTO THE WAR?

PERHAPS BLISTER PROMISED THE NIGHTWINGS SOMETHING, THE WAY BLAZE IS GIVING UP TERRITORY TO THE ICEWINGS IN EXCHANGE FOR THEIR HELP.

TERRITORY!
MORE THAN ANYTHING, THE NIGHTWINGS NEED A NEW HOME. THE ISLAND IS A *HORRIBLE* PLACE TO LIVE, AND THE VOLCANO IS EXTREMELY DANGEROUS.

MASTERMIND'S EXPERIMENTS ARE ALL ABOUT HOW TO DEFEND AGAINST RAINWING VENOM BECAUSE *THE NIGHTWINGS ARE PLANNING TO INVADE THE RAINFOREST!*

THINK, STARFLIGHT, THINK!

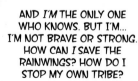

THAT'S WHAT BLISTER PROMISED THEM. IF THE NIGHTWINGS HELP BLISTER WIN THE WAR, BLISTER WILL USE HER ARMIES AND MAGIC TUNNEL FROM THE DESERT TO HELP THE NIGHTWINGS DESTROY THE RAINWINGS.

AND *I'M* THE ONLY ONE WHO KNOWS. BUT I'M... I'M NOT BRAVE OR STRONG. HOW CAN *I* SAVE THE RAINWINGS? HOW DO I STOP MY OWN TRIBE?

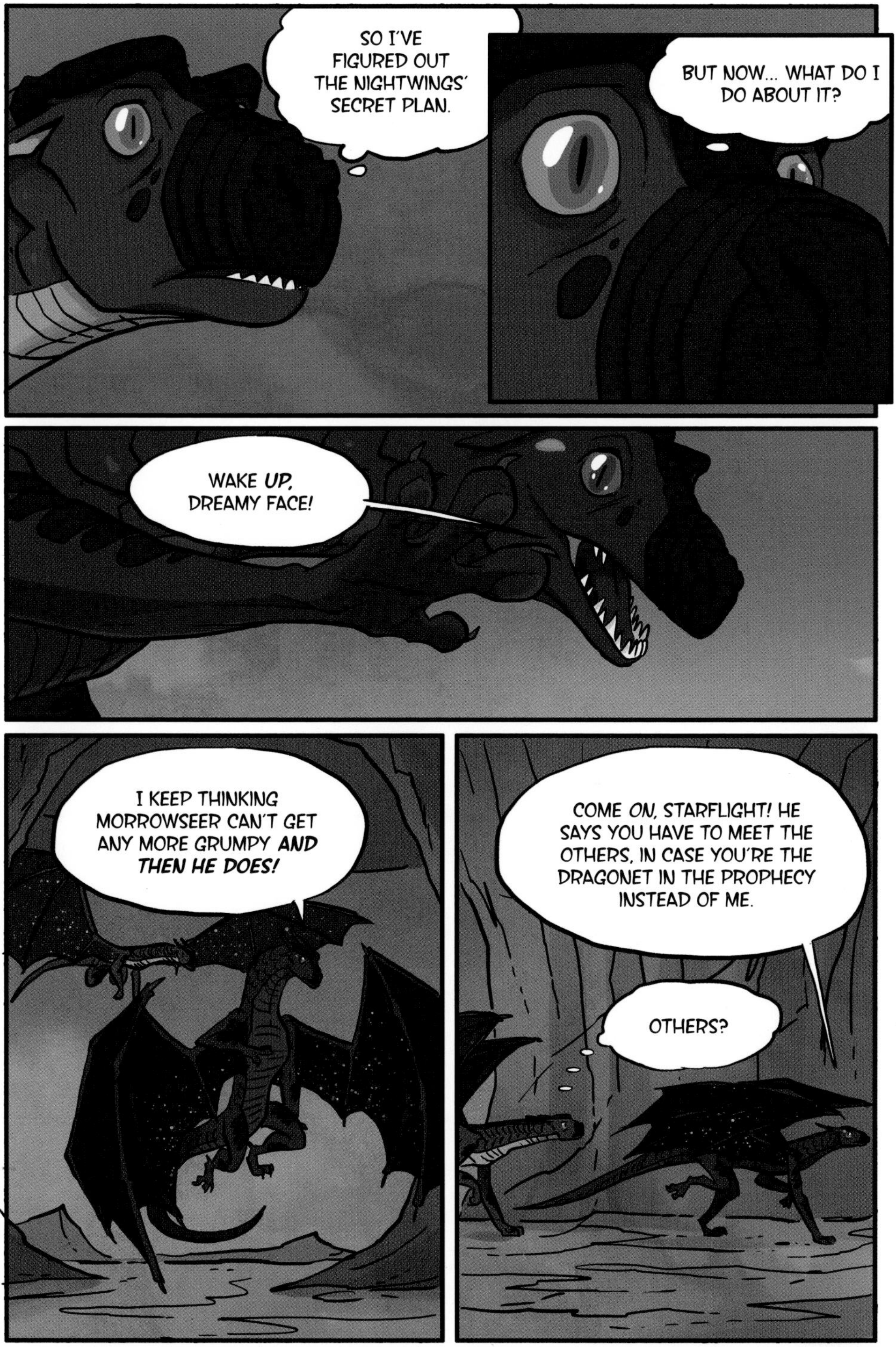
SO I'VE FIGURED OUT THE NIGHTWINGS' SECRET PLAN.
BUT NOW... WHAT DO I DO ABOUT IT?
WAKE *UP*, DREAMY FACE!
I KEEP THINKING MORROWSEER CAN'T GET ANY MORE GRUMPY ***AND THEN HE DOES!***
COME *ON*, STARFLIGHT! HE SAYS YOU HAVE TO MEET THE OTHERS, IN CASE YOU'RE THE DRAGONET IN THE PROPHECY INSTEAD OF ME.
OTHERS?

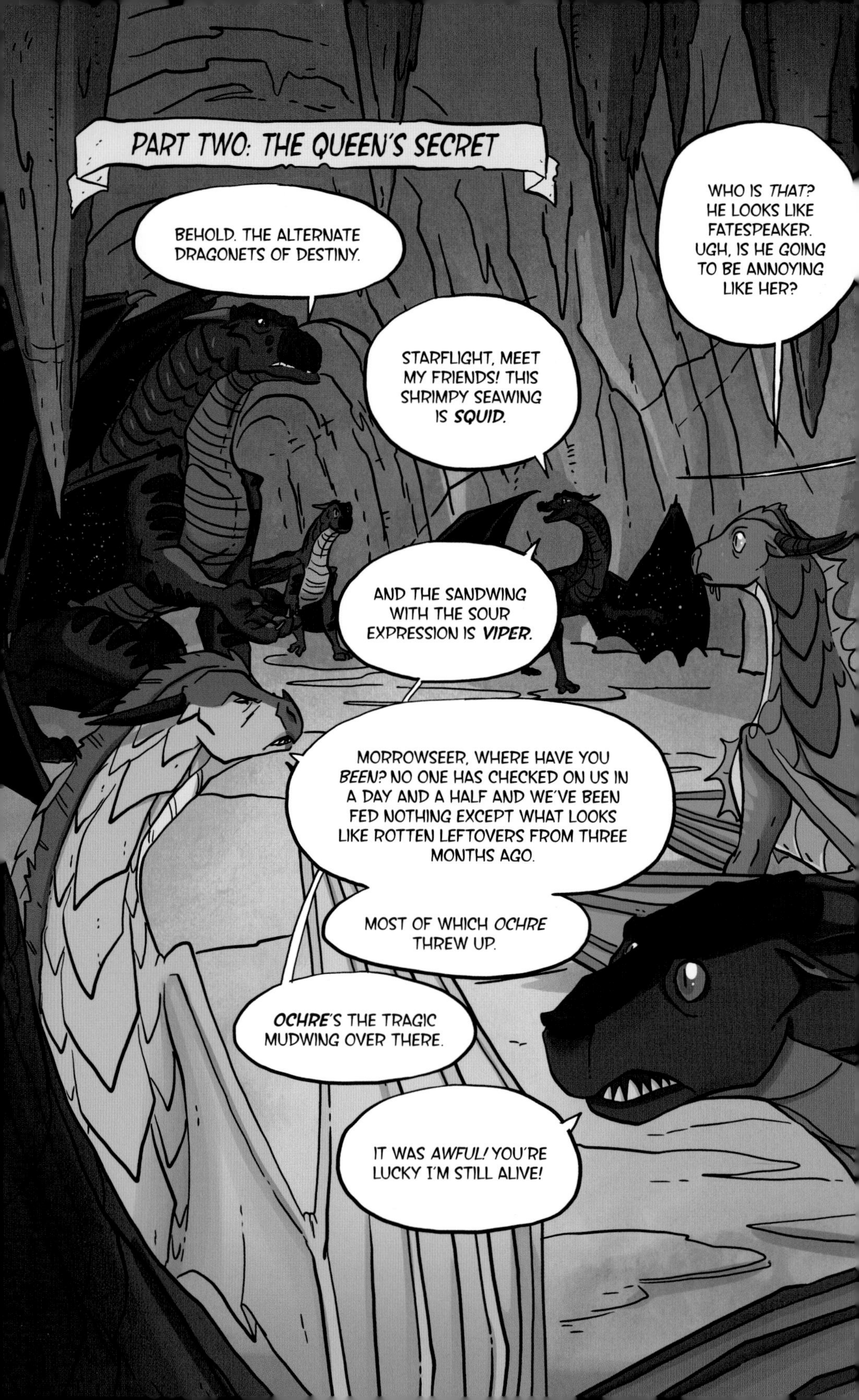
PART TWO: THE QUEEN'S SECRET
BEHOLD. THE ALTERNATE DRAGONETS OF DESTINY.
WHO IS THAT? HE LOOKS LIKE FATESPEAKER. UGH, IS HE GOING TO BE ANNOYING LIKE HER?
STARFLIGHT, MEET MY FRIENDS! THIS SHRIMPY SEAWING IS SQUID.
AND THE SANDWING WITH THE SOUR EXPRESSION IS VIPER.
MORROWSEER, WHERE HAVE YOU BEEN? NO ONE HAS CHECKED ON US IN A DAY AND A HALF AND WE'VE BEEN FED NOTHING EXCEPT WHAT LOOKS LIKE ROTTEN LEFTOVERS FROM THREE MONTHS AGO.
MOST OF WHICH OCHRE THREW UP.
OCHRE'S THE TRAGIC MUDWING OVER THERE.
IT WAS AWFUL! YOU'RE LUCKY I'M STILL ALIVE!

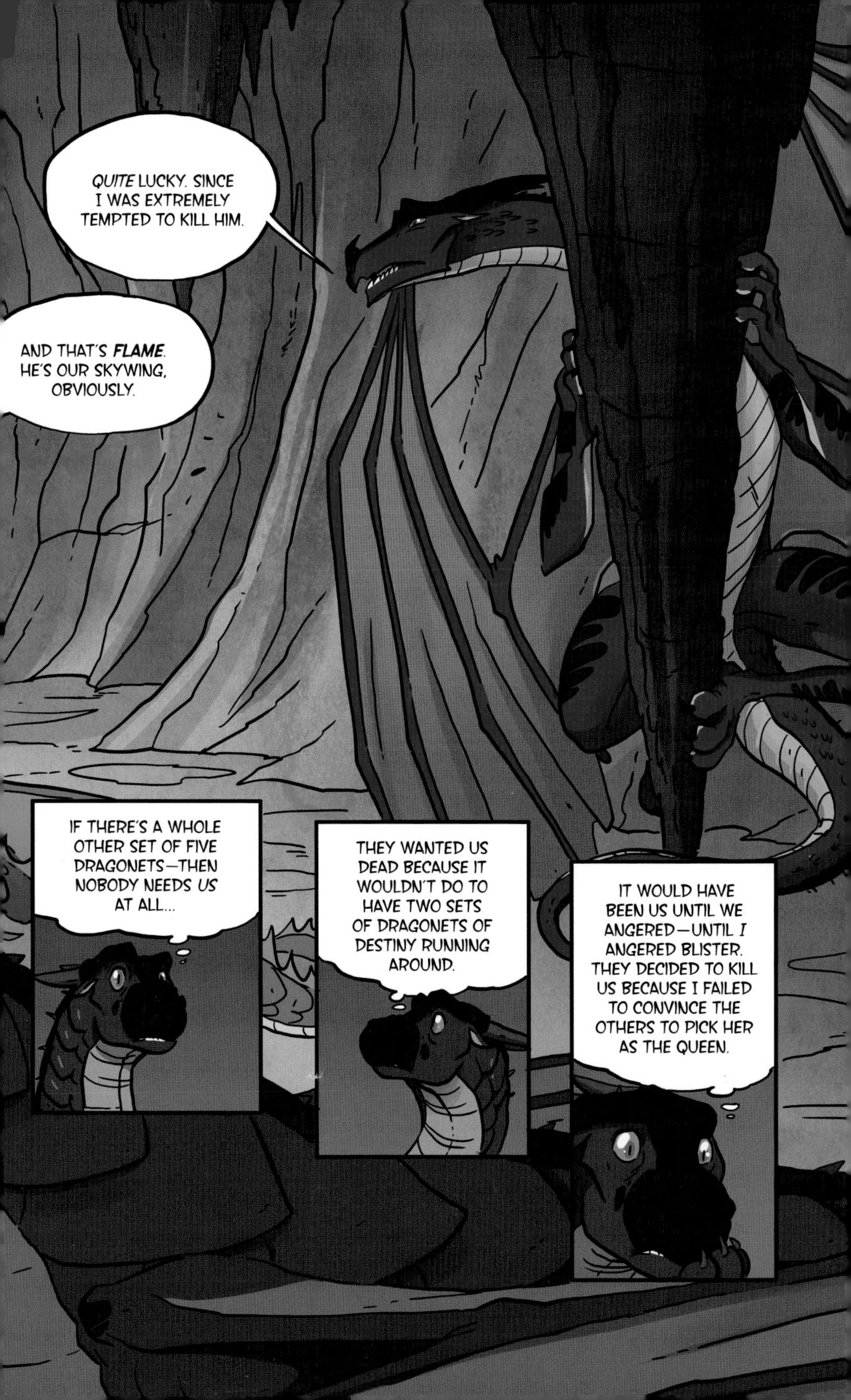
QUITE LUCKY. SINCE I WAS EXTREMELY TEMPTED TO KILL HIM.
AND THAT'S ***FLAME***. HE'S OUR SKYWING, OBVIOUSLY.
IF THERE'S A WHOLE OTHER SET OF FIVE DRAGONETS—THEN NOBODY NEEDS *US* AT ALL...
THEY WANTED US DEAD BECAUSE IT WOULDN'T DO TO HAVE TWO SETS OF DRAGONETS OF DESTINY RUNNING AROUND.
IT WOULD HAVE BEEN US UNTIL WE ANGERED—UNTIL *I* ANGERED BLISTER. THEY DECIDED TO KILL US BECAUSE I FAILED TO CONVINCE THE OTHERS TO PICK HER AS THE QUEEN.

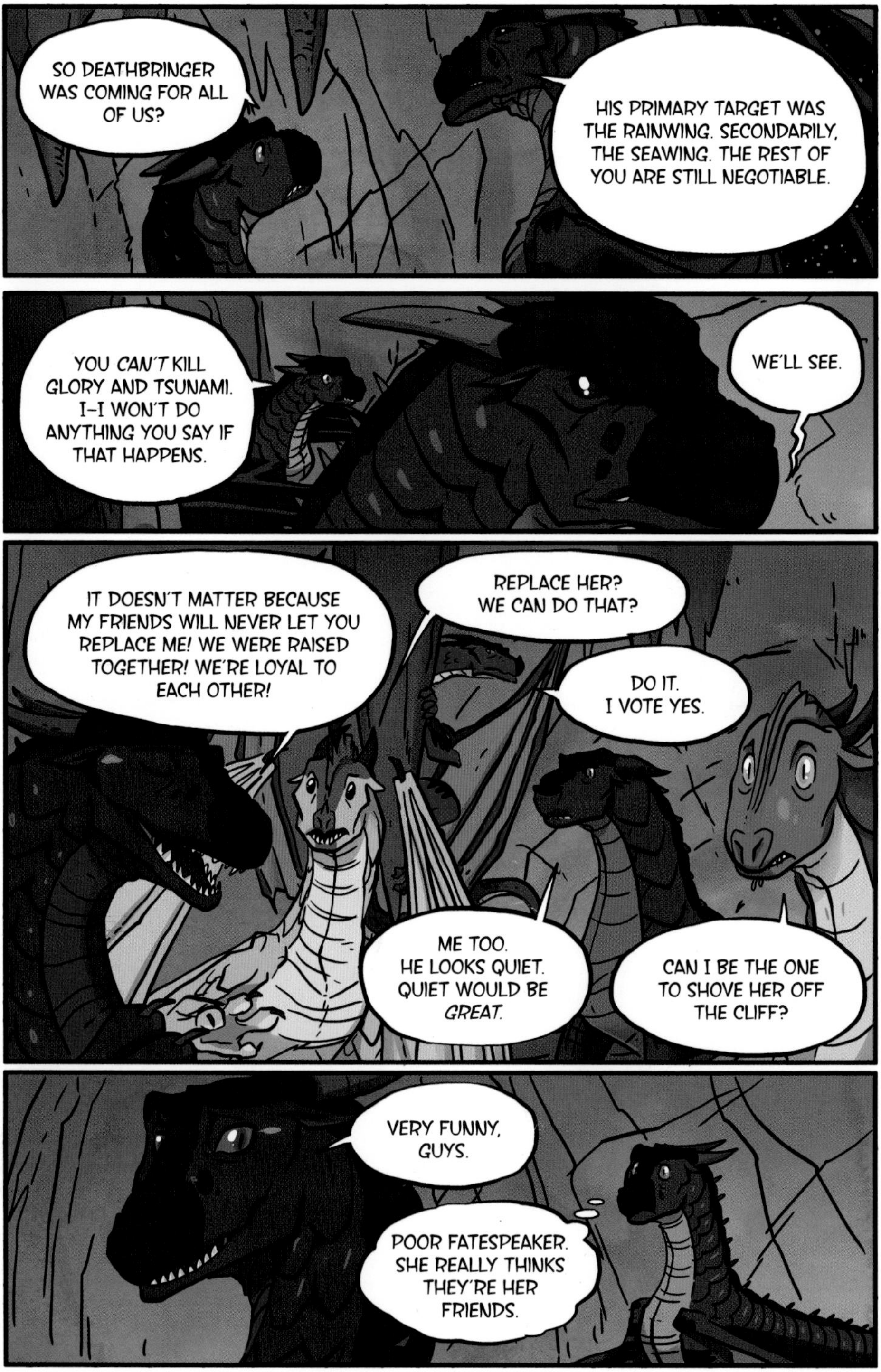
SO DEATHBRINGER WAS COMING FOR ALL OF US?
HIS PRIMARY TARGET WAS THE RAINWING. SECONDARILY, THE SEAWING. THE REST OF YOU ARE STILL NEGOTIABLE.
YOU *CAN'T* KILL GLORY AND TSUNAMI. I–I WON'T DO ANYTHING YOU SAY IF THAT HAPPENS.
WE'LL SEE.
IT DOESN'T MATTER BECAUSE MY FRIENDS WILL NEVER LET YOU REPLACE ME! WE WERE RAISED TOGETHER! WE'RE LOYAL TO EACH OTHER!
REPLACE HER? WE CAN DO THAT?
DO IT. I VOTE YES.
ME TOO. HE LOOKS QUIET. QUIET WOULD BE *GREAT*.
CAN I BE THE ONE TO SHOVE HER OFF THE CLIFF?
VERY FUNNY, GUYS.
POOR FATESPEAKER. SHE REALLY THINKS THEY'RE HER FRIENDS.

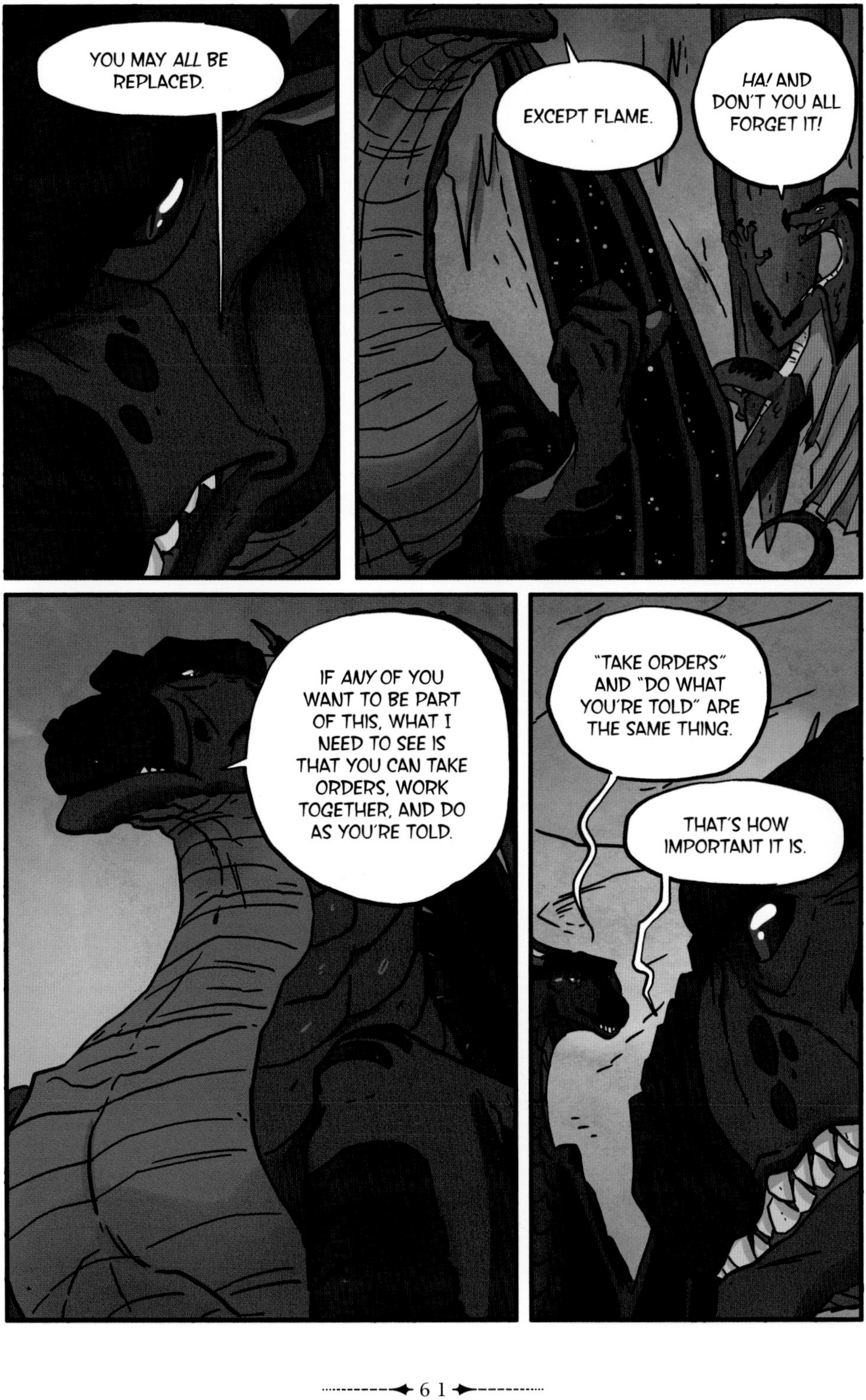
YOU MAY *ALL* BE REPLACED.
EXCEPT FLAME.
HA! AND DON'T YOU ALL FORGET IT!
IF *ANY* OF YOU WANT TO BE PART OF THIS, WHAT I NEED TO SEE IS THAT YOU CAN TAKE ORDERS, WORK TOGETHER, AND DO AS YOU'RE TOLD.
"TAKE ORDERS" AND "DO WHAT YOU'RE TOLD" ARE THE SAME THING.
THAT'S HOW IMPORTANT IT IS.

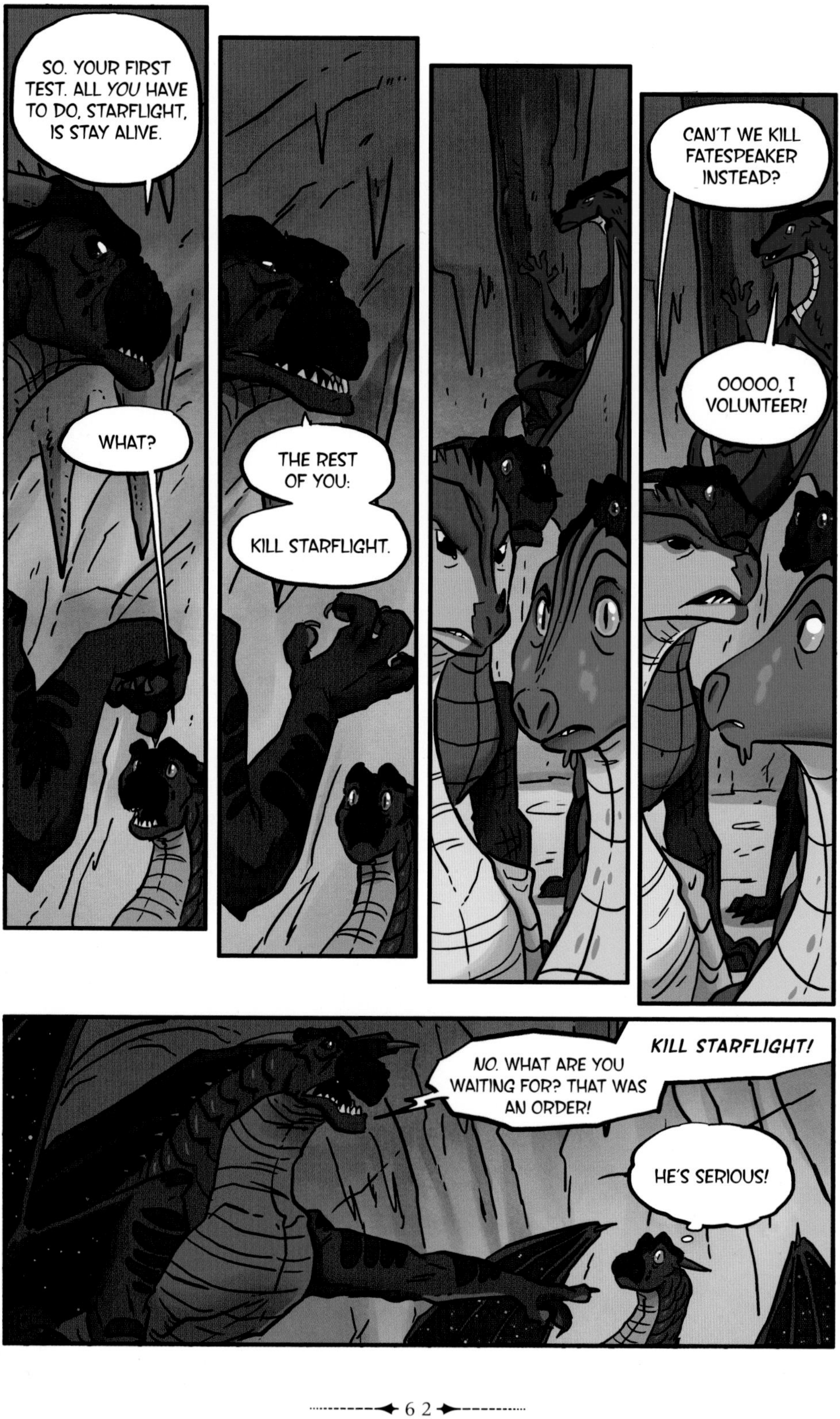
SO. YOUR FIRST TEST. ALL *YOU* HAVE TO DO, STARFLIGHT, IS STAY ALIVE.
WHAT?
THE REST OF YOU:
KILL STARFLIGHT.
CAN'T WE KILL FATESPEAKER INSTEAD?
OOOOO, I VOLUNTEER!
NO. WHAT ARE YOU WAITING FOR? THAT WAS AN ORDER!
KILL STARFLIGHT!
HE'S SERIOUS!

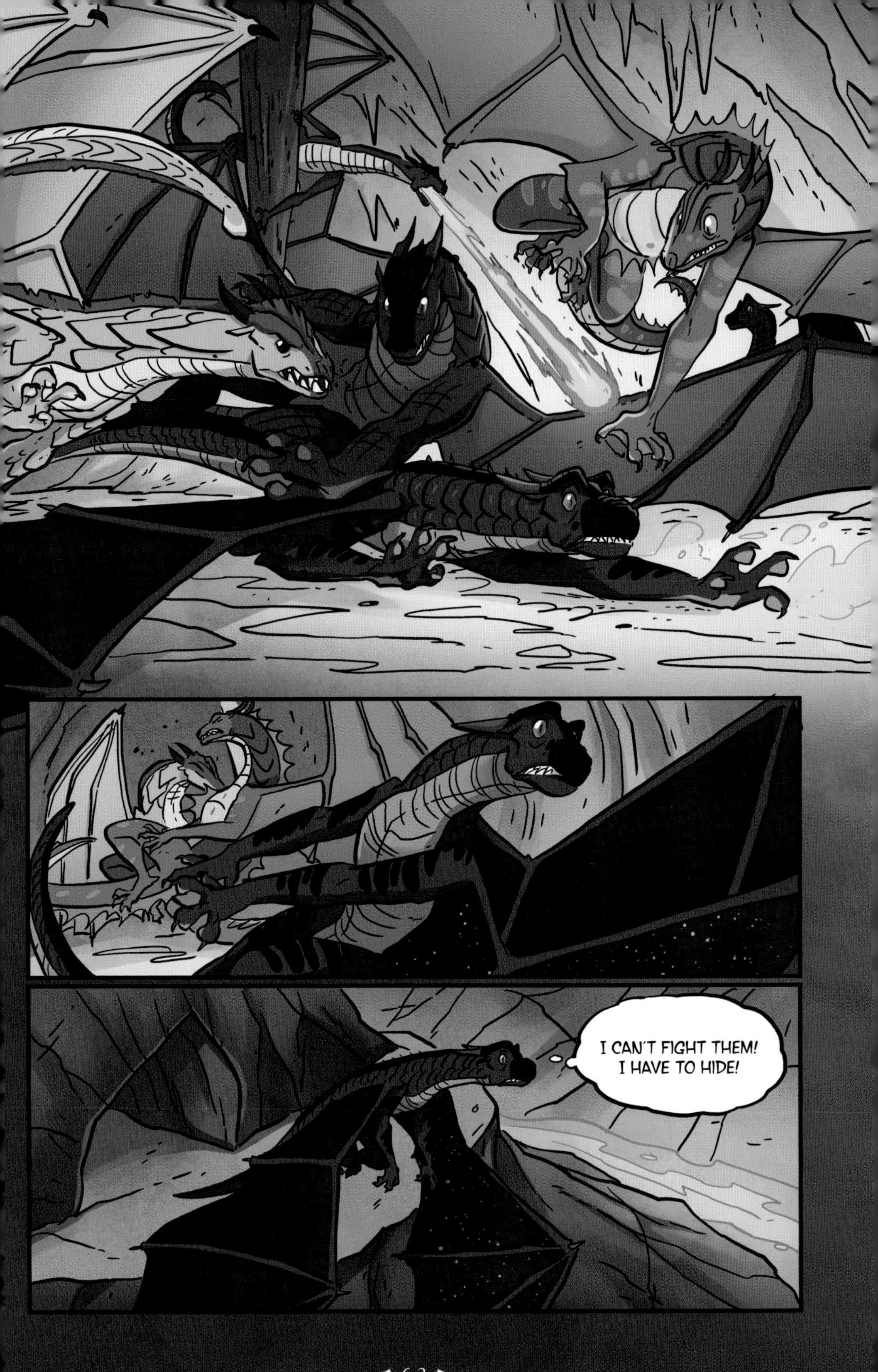
I CAN'T FIGHT THEM!
I HAVE TO HIDE!

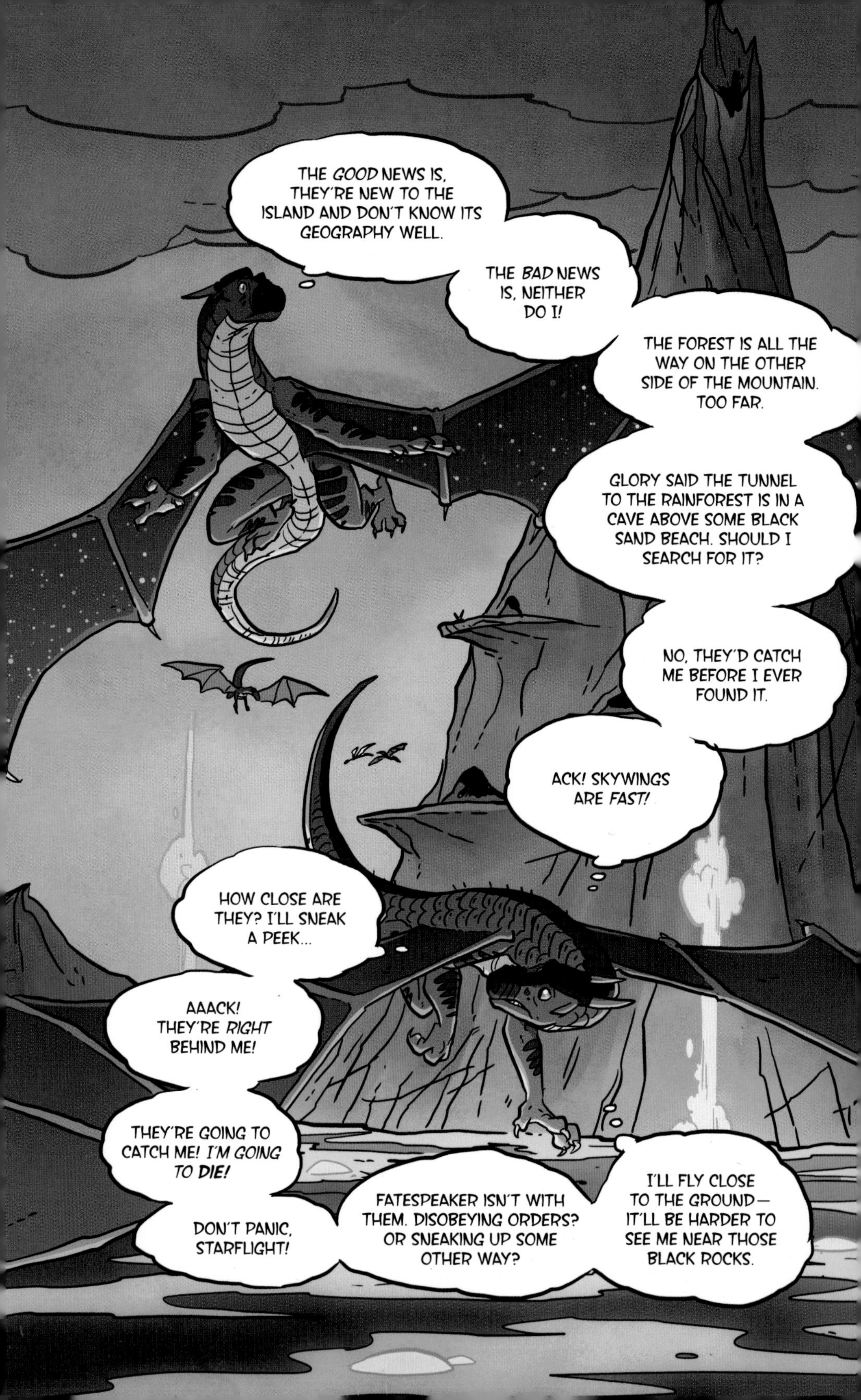
THE *GOOD* NEWS IS, THEY'RE NEW TO THE ISLAND AND DON'T KNOW ITS GEOGRAPHY WELL.
THE *BAD* NEWS IS, NEITHER DO I!
THE FOREST IS ALL THE WAY ON THE OTHER SIDE OF THE MOUNTAIN. TOO FAR.
GLORY SAID THE TUNNEL TO THE RAINFOREST IS IN A CAVE ABOVE SOME BLACK SAND BEACH. SHOULD I SEARCH FOR IT?
NO, THEY'D CATCH ME BEFORE I EVER FOUND IT.
ACK! SKYWINGS ARE *FAST!*
HOW CLOSE ARE THEY? I'LL SNEAK A PEEK...
AAACK! THEY'RE *RIGHT* BEHIND ME!
THEY'RE GOING TO CATCH ME! *I'M GOING TO **DIE!***
DON'T PANIC, STARFLIGHT!
FATESPEAKER ISN'T WITH THEM. DISOBEYING ORDERS? OR SNEAKING UP SOME OTHER WAY?
I'LL FLY CLOSE TO THE GROUND— IT'LL BE HARDER TO SEE ME NEAR THOSE BLACK ROCKS.

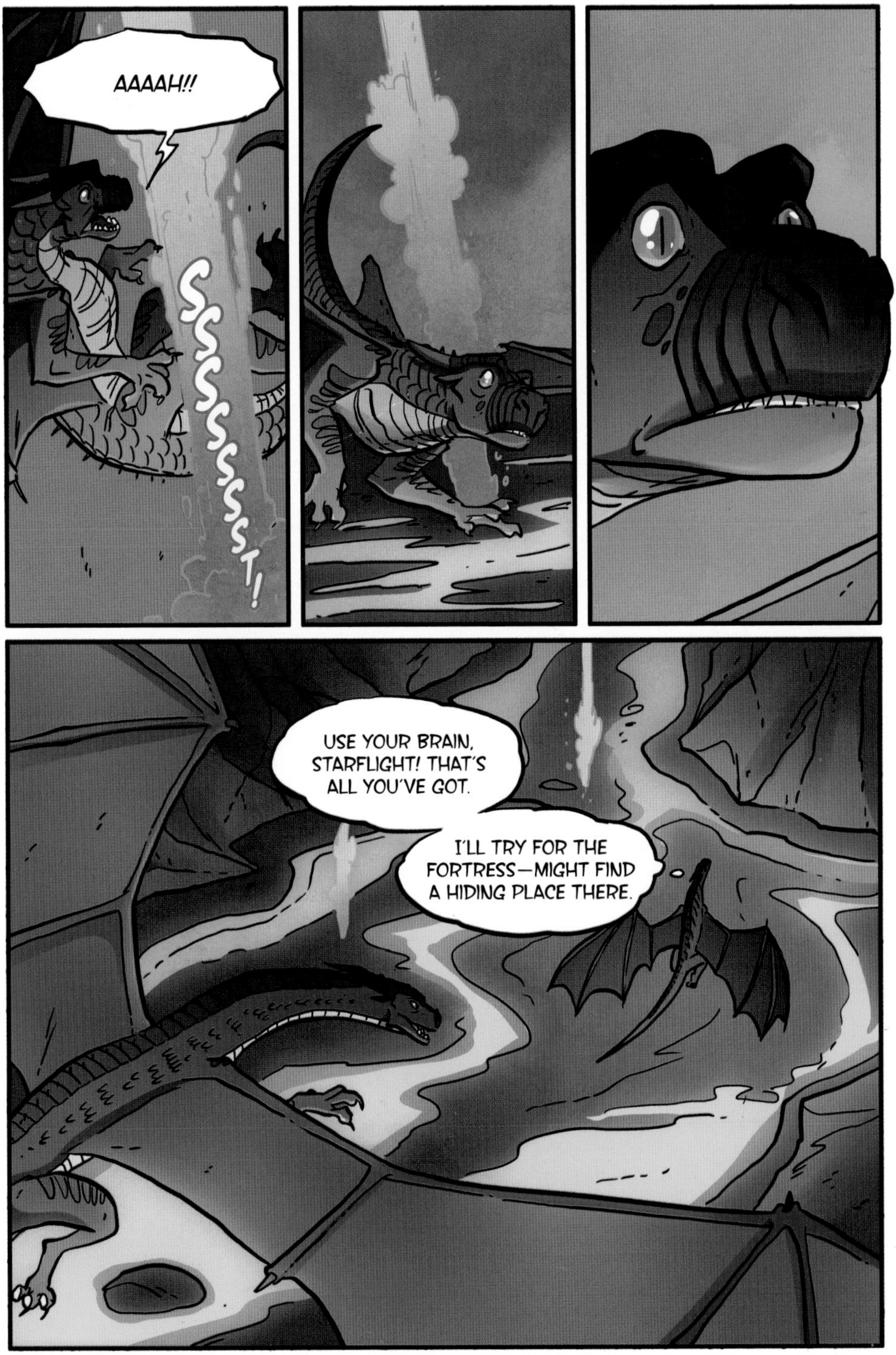
AAAAH!!
SSSSSSSST!
USE YOUR BRAIN, STARFLIGHT! THAT'S ALL YOU'VE GOT.
I'LL TRY FOR THE FORTRESS—MIGHT FIND A HIDING PLACE THERE.

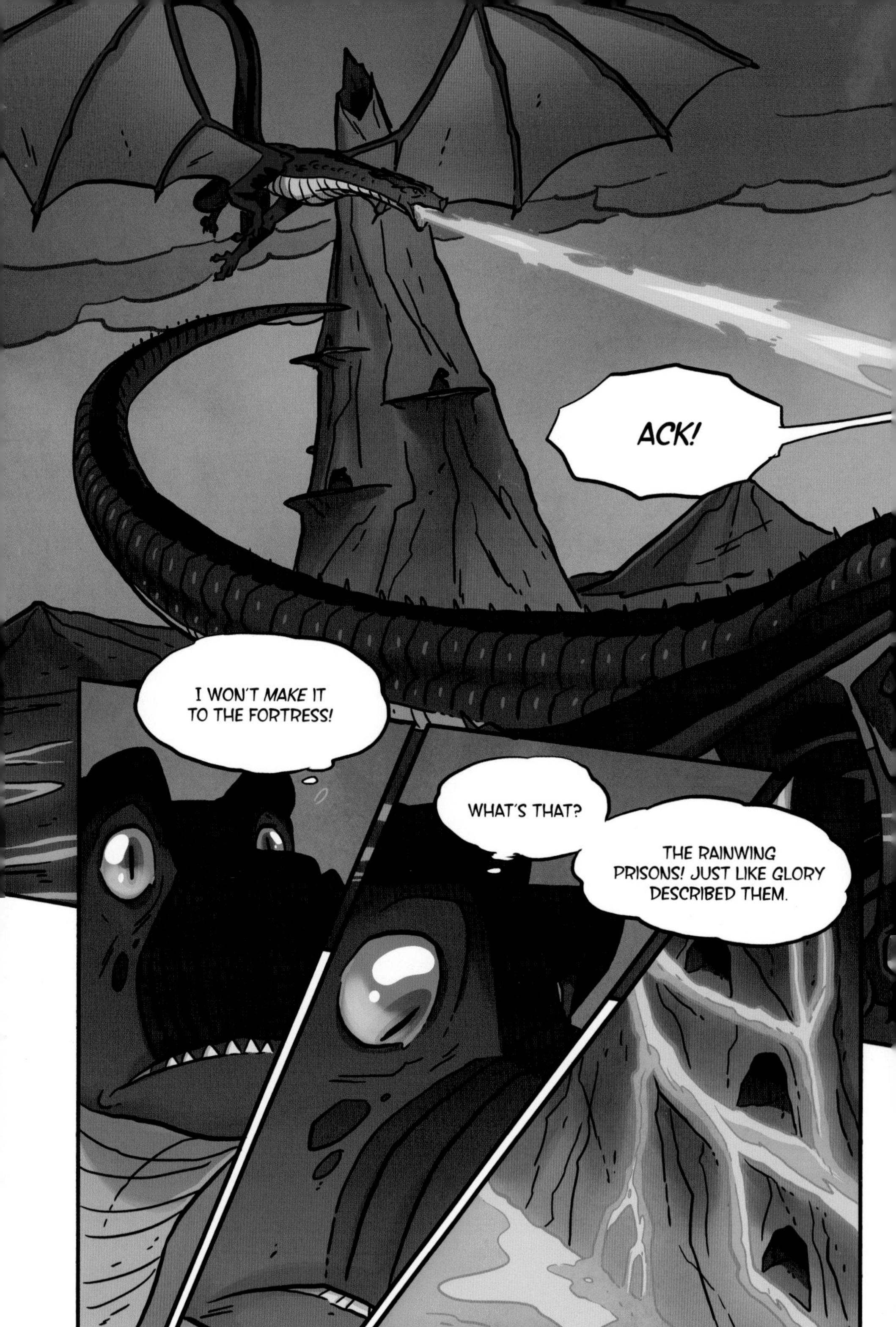
ACK!
I WON'T *MAKE* IT TO THE FORTRESS!
WHAT'S THAT?
THE RAINWING PRISONS! JUST LIKE GLORY DESCRIBED THEM.

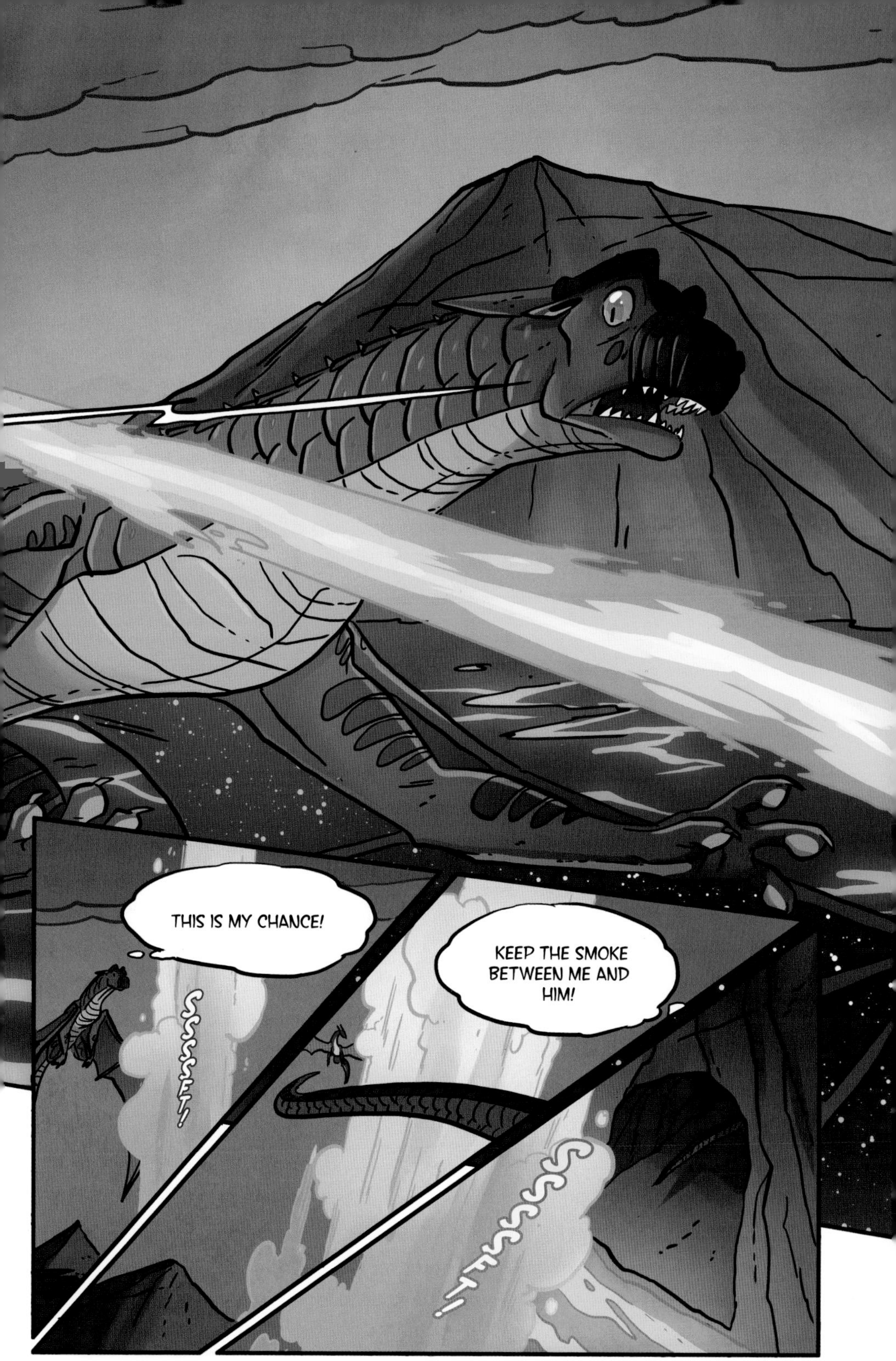
THIS IS MY CHANCE!
SSSSSFT!
KEEP THE SMOKE BETWEEN ME AND HIM!
SSSSSSFT!

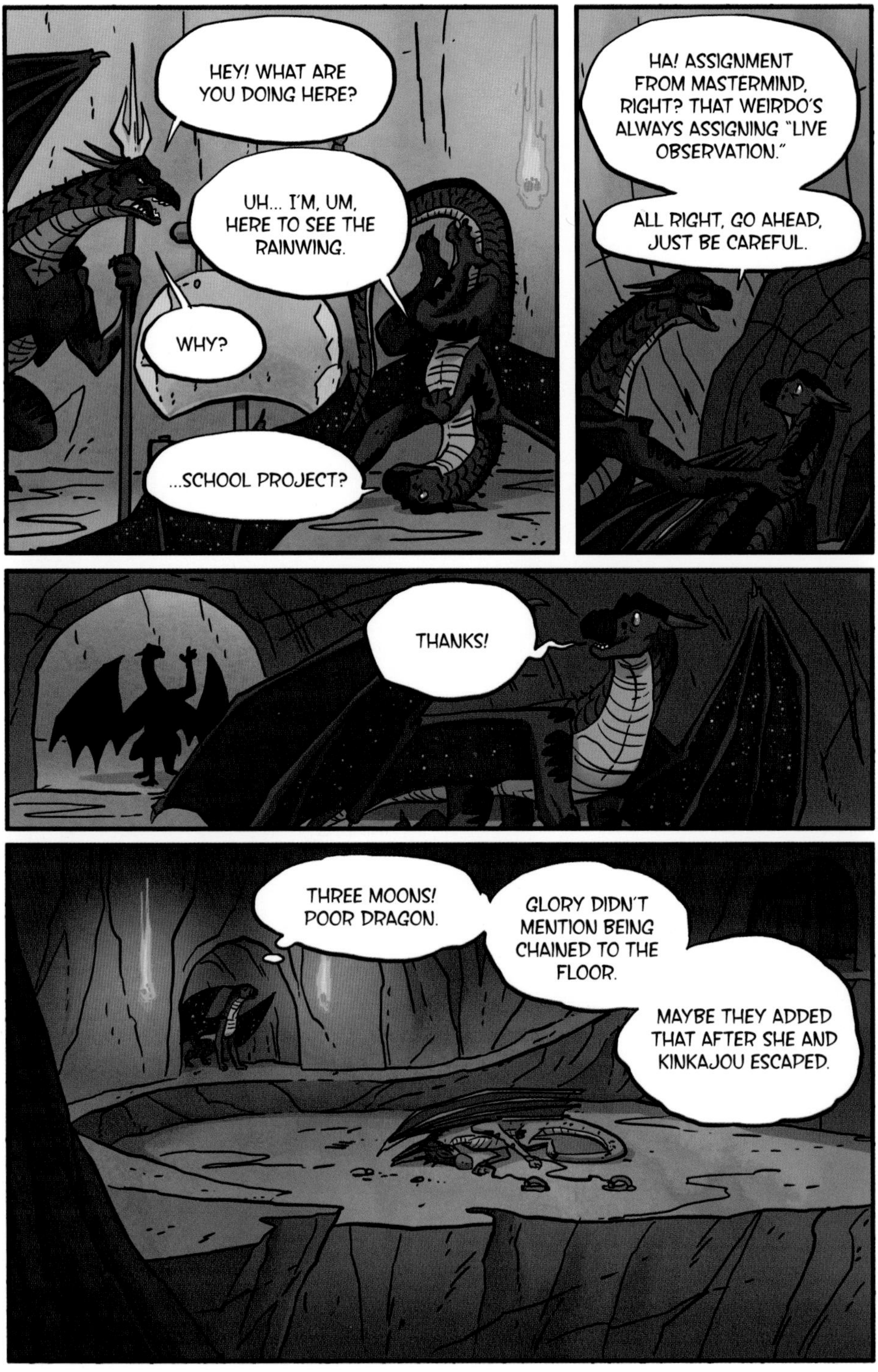
HEY! WHAT ARE YOU DOING HERE?
UH... I'M, UM, HERE TO SEE THE RAINWING.
WHY?
...SCHOOL PROJECT?
HA! ASSIGNMENT FROM MASTERMIND, RIGHT? THAT WEIRDO'S ALWAYS ASSIGNING "LIVE OBSERVATION."
ALL RIGHT, GO AHEAD, JUST BE CAREFUL.
THANKS!
THREE MOONS! POOR DRAGON.
GLORY DIDN'T MENTION BEING CHAINED TO THE FLOOR.
MAYBE THEY ADDED THAT AFTER SHE AND KINKAJOU ESCAPED.

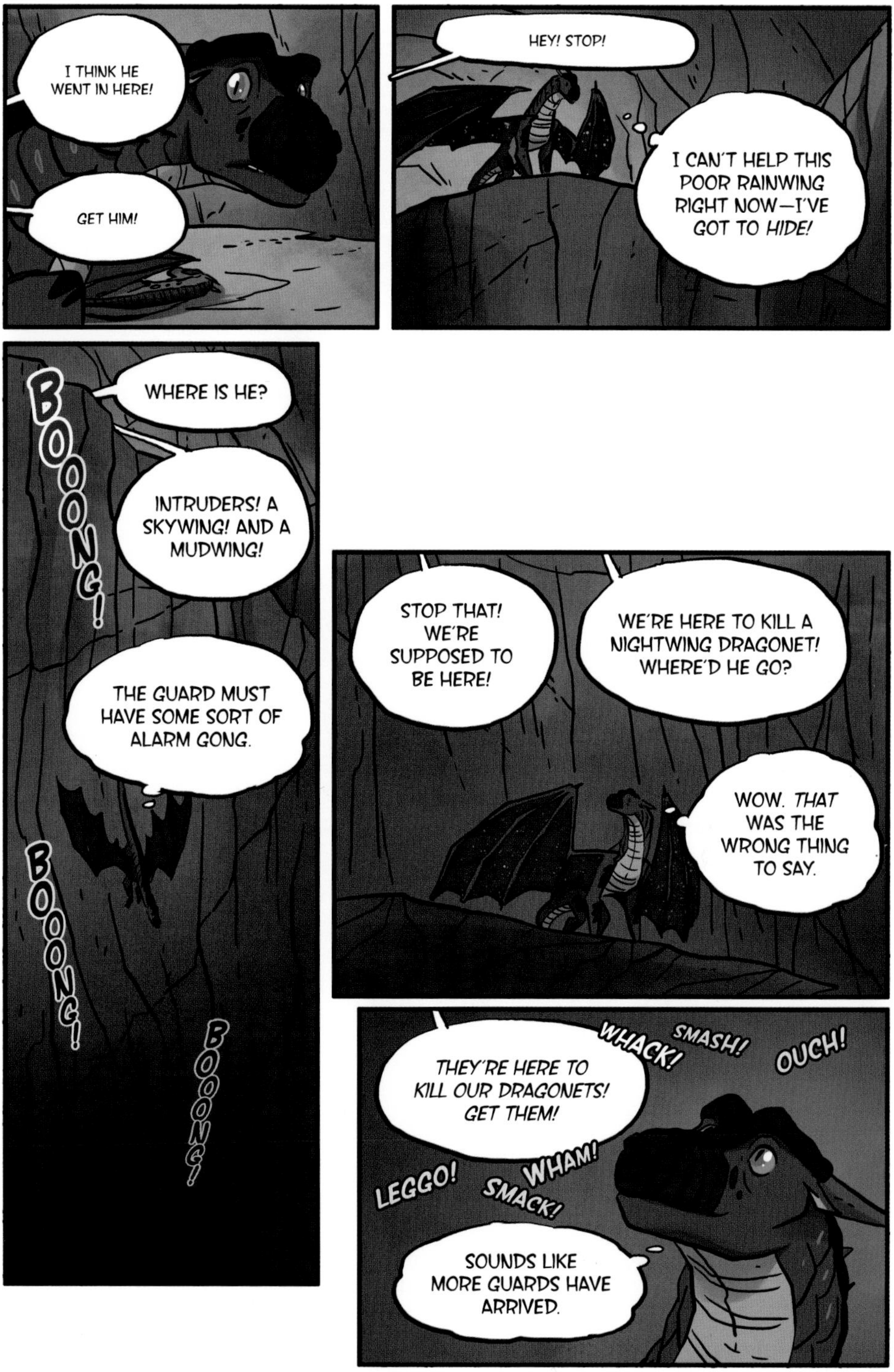
I THINK HE WENT IN HERE!
GET HIM!
HEY! STOP!
I CAN'T HELP THIS POOR RAINWING RIGHT NOW—I'VE GOT TO *HIDE!*
WHERE IS HE?
BOOOONG!
INTRUDERS! A SKYWING! AND A MUDWING!
THE GUARD MUST HAVE SOME SORT OF ALARM GONG.
BOOOONG!
BOOOONG!
STOP THAT! WE'RE SUPPOSED TO BE HERE!
WE'RE HERE TO KILL A NIGHTWING DRAGONET! WHERE'D HE GO?
WOW. *THAT* WAS THE WRONG THING TO SAY.
THEY'RE HERE TO KILL OUR DRAGONETS! GET THEM!
WHACK!
SMASH!
OUCH!
LEGGO!
WHAM!
SMACK!
SOUNDS LIKE MORE GUARDS HAVE ARRIVED.

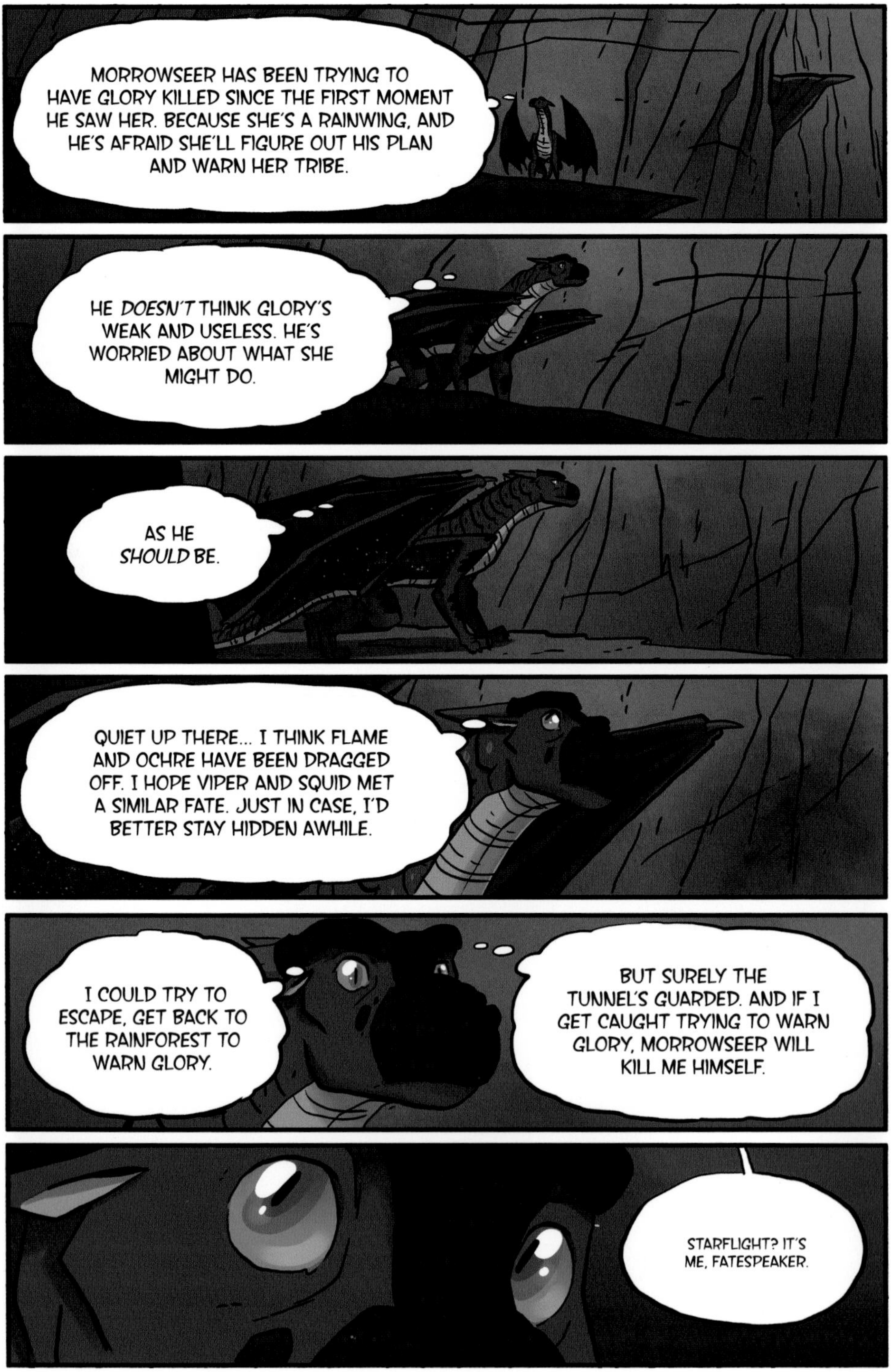
MORROWSEER HAS BEEN TRYING TO HAVE GLORY KILLED SINCE THE FIRST MOMENT HE SAW HER. BECAUSE SHE'S A RAINWING, AND HE'S AFRAID SHE'LL FIGURE OUT HIS PLAN AND WARN HER TRIBE.
HE *DOESN'T* THINK GLORY'S WEAK AND USELESS. HE'S WORRIED ABOUT WHAT SHE MIGHT DO.
AS HE *SHOULD* BE.
QUIET UP THERE... I THINK FLAME AND OCHRE HAVE BEEN DRAGGED OFF. I HOPE VIPER AND SQUID MET A SIMILAR FATE. JUST IN CASE, I'D BETTER STAY HIDDEN AWHILE.
I COULD TRY TO ESCAPE, GET BACK TO THE RAINFOREST TO WARN GLORY.
BUT SURELY THE TUNNEL'S GUARDED. AND IF I GET CAUGHT TRYING TO WARN GLORY, MORROWSEER WILL KILL ME HIMSELF.
STARFLIGHT? IT'S ME, FATESPEAKER.

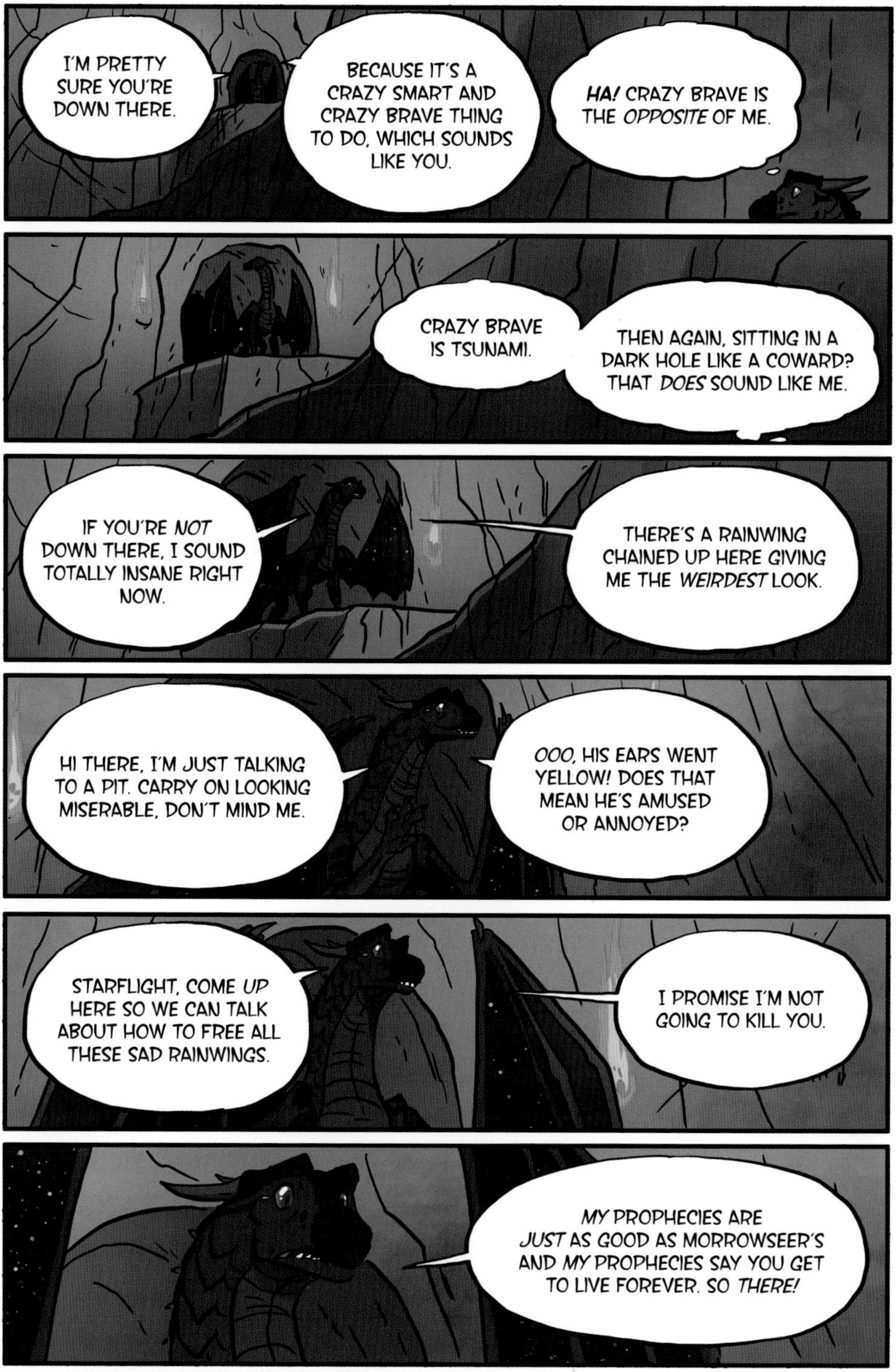
I'M PRETTY SURE YOU'RE DOWN THERE.
BECAUSE IT'S A CRAZY SMART AND CRAZY BRAVE THING TO DO, WHICH SOUNDS LIKE YOU.
HA! CRAZY BRAVE IS THE *OPPOSITE* OF ME.
CRAZY BRAVE IS TSUNAMI.
THEN AGAIN, SITTING IN A DARK HOLE LIKE A COWARD? THAT *DOES* SOUND LIKE ME.
IF YOU'RE *NOT* DOWN THERE, I SOUND TOTALLY INSANE RIGHT NOW.
THERE'S A RAINWING CHAINED UP HERE GIVING ME THE *WEIRDEST* LOOK.
HI THERE, I'M JUST TALKING TO A PIT. CARRY ON LOOKING MISERABLE, DON'T MIND ME.
OOO, HIS EARS WENT YELLOW! DOES THAT MEAN HE'S AMUSED OR ANNOYED?
STARFLIGHT, COME *UP* HERE SO WE CAN TALK ABOUT HOW TO FREE ALL THESE SAD RAINWINGS.
I PROMISE I'M NOT GOING TO KILL YOU.
MY PROPHECIES ARE *JUST* AS GOOD AS MORROWSEER'S AND *MY* PROPHECIES SAY YOU GET TO LIVE FOREVER. SO *THERE!*

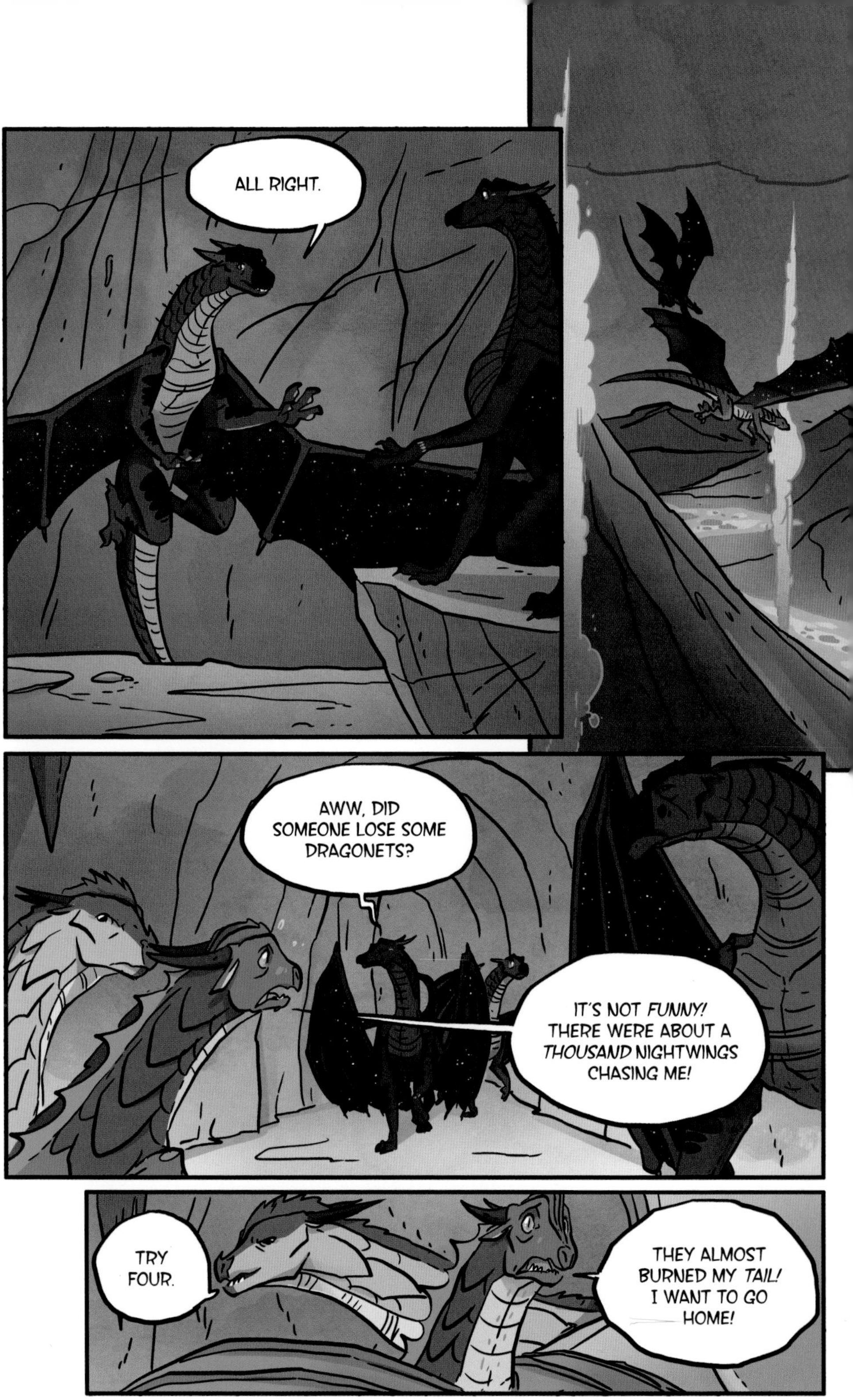
ALL RIGHT.
AWW, DID SOMEONE LOSE SOME DRAGONETS?
IT'S NOT *FUNNY!* THERE WERE ABOUT A *THOUSAND* NIGHTWINGS CHASING ME!
TRY FOUR.
THEY ALMOST BURNED MY *TAIL!* I WANT TO GO HOME!

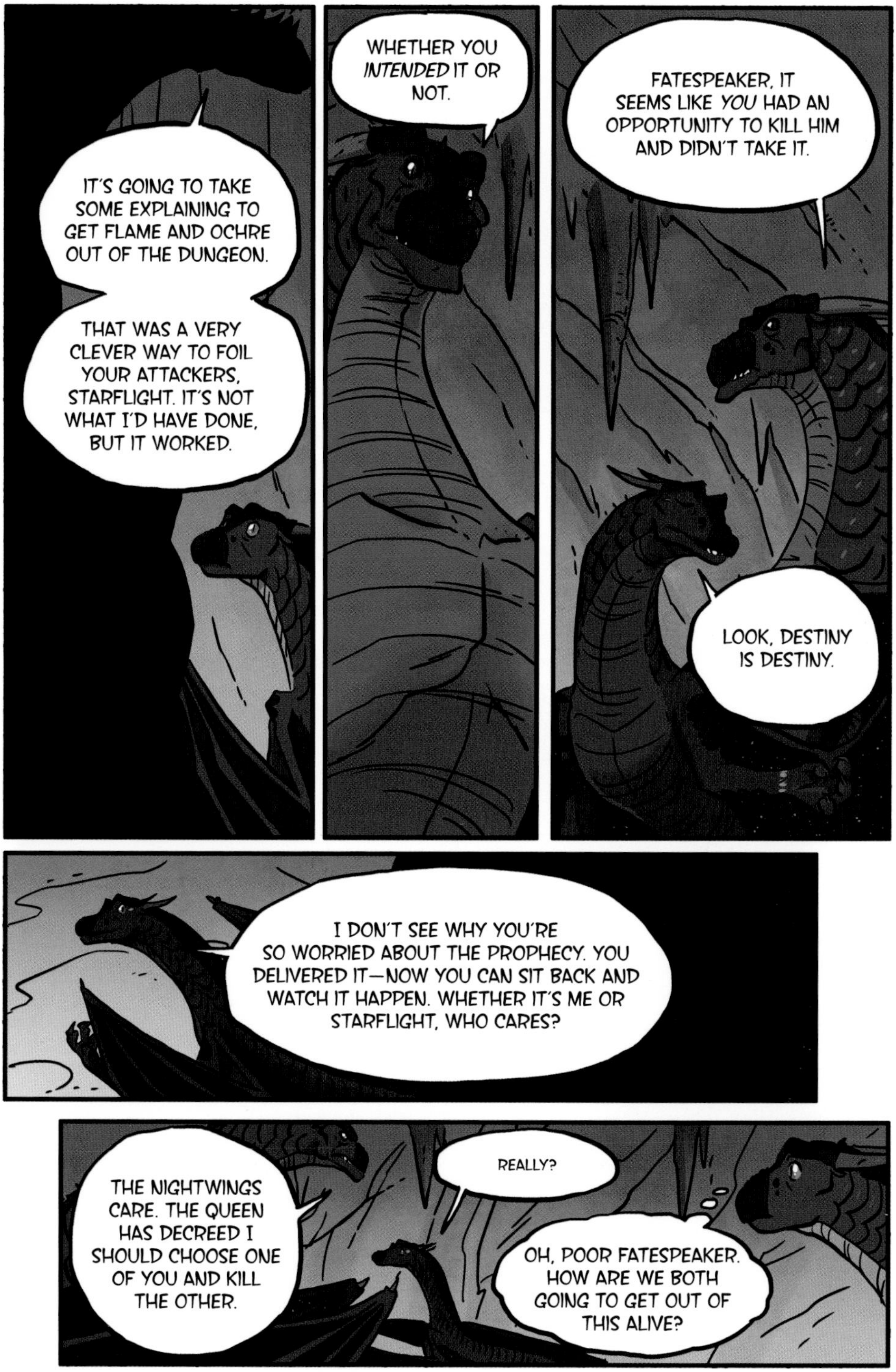
IT'S GOING TO TAKE SOME EXPLAINING TO GET FLAME AND OCHRE OUT OF THE DUNGEON.
THAT WAS A VERY CLEVER WAY TO FOIL YOUR ATTACKERS, STARFLIGHT. IT'S NOT WHAT I'D HAVE DONE, BUT IT WORKED.
WHETHER YOU *INTENDED* IT OR NOT.
FATESPEAKER, IT SEEMS LIKE *YOU* HAD AN OPPORTUNITY TO KILL HIM AND DIDN'T TAKE IT.
LOOK, DESTINY IS DESTINY.
I DON'T SEE WHY YOU'RE SO WORRIED ABOUT THE PROPHECY. YOU DELIVERED IT—NOW YOU CAN SIT BACK AND WATCH IT HAPPEN. WHETHER IT'S ME OR STARFLIGHT, WHO CARES?
THE NIGHTWINGS CARE. THE QUEEN HAS DECREED I SHOULD CHOOSE ONE OF YOU AND KILL THE OTHER.
REALLY?
OH, POOR FATESPEAKER. HOW ARE WE BOTH GOING TO GET OUT OF THIS ALIVE?

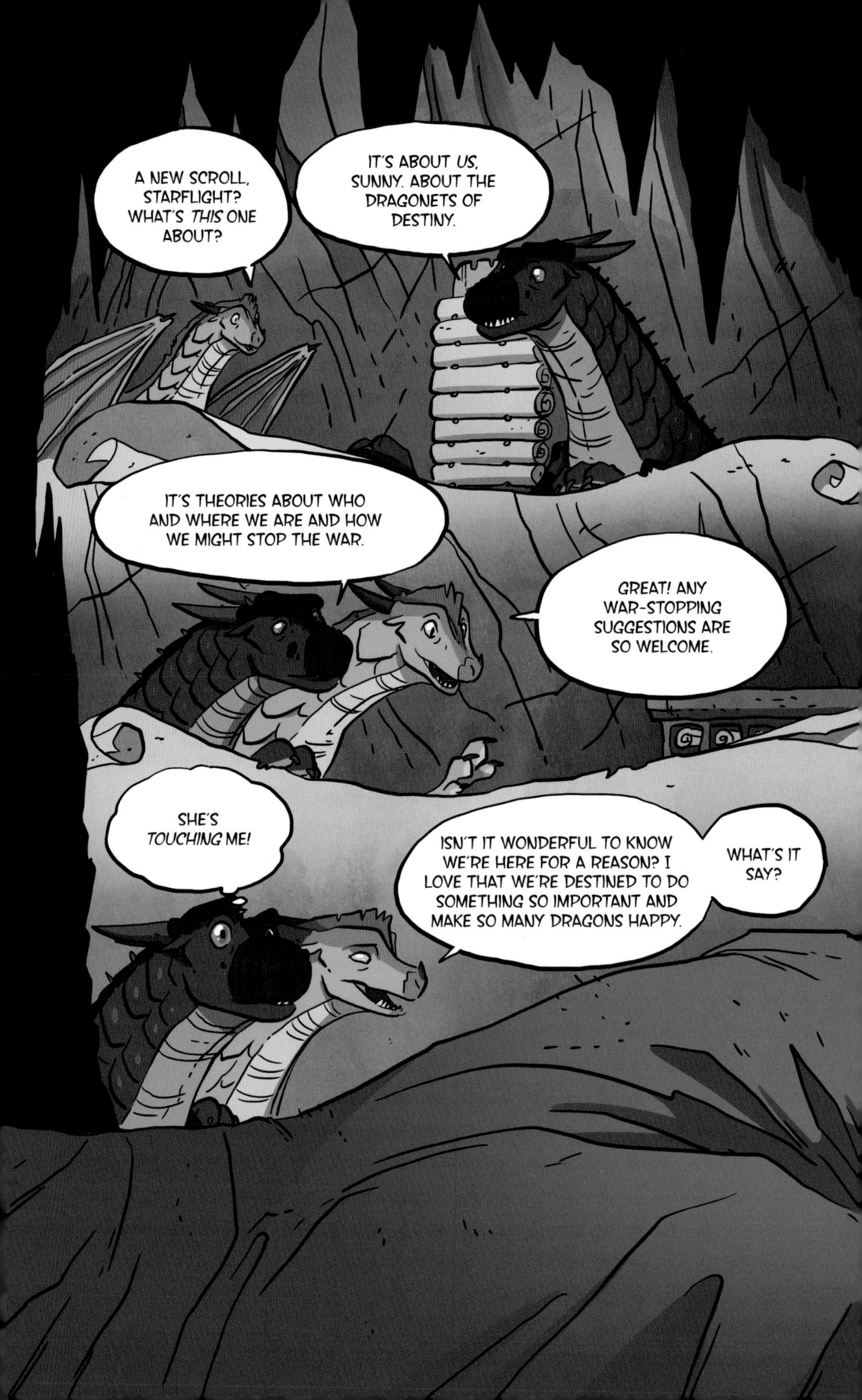
A NEW SCROLL, STARFLIGHT? WHAT'S *THIS* ONE ABOUT?
IT'S ABOUT *US*, SUNNY. ABOUT THE DRAGONETS OF DESTINY.
IT'S THEORIES ABOUT WHO AND WHERE WE ARE AND HOW WE MIGHT STOP THE WAR.
GREAT! ANY WAR-STOPPING SUGGESTIONS ARE SO WELCOME.
SHE'S *TOUCHING* ME!
ISN'T IT WONDERFUL TO KNOW WE'RE HERE FOR A REASON? I LOVE THAT WE'RE DESTINED TO DO SOMETHING SO IMPORTANT AND MAKE SO MANY DRAGONS HAPPY.
WHAT'S IT SAY?

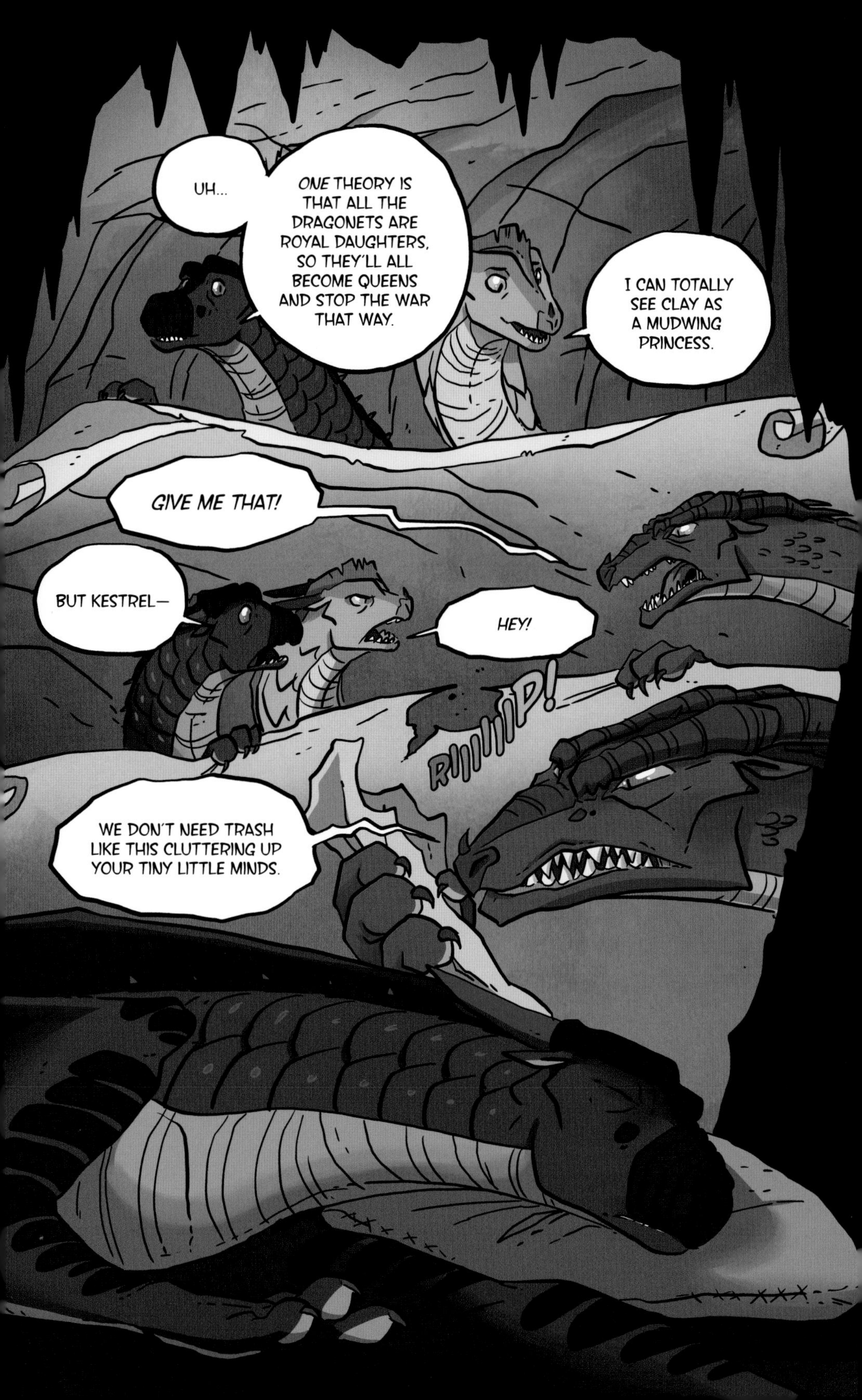
UH...
ONE THEORY IS THAT ALL THE DRAGONETS ARE ROYAL DAUGHTERS, SO THEY'LL ALL BECOME QUEENS AND STOP THE WAR THAT WAY.
I CAN TOTALLY SEE CLAY AS A MUDWING PRINCESS.
GIVE ME THAT!
BUT KESTREL—
HEY!
RIIIIIIP!
WE DON'T NEED TRASH LIKE THIS CLUTTERING UP YOUR TINY LITTLE MINDS.

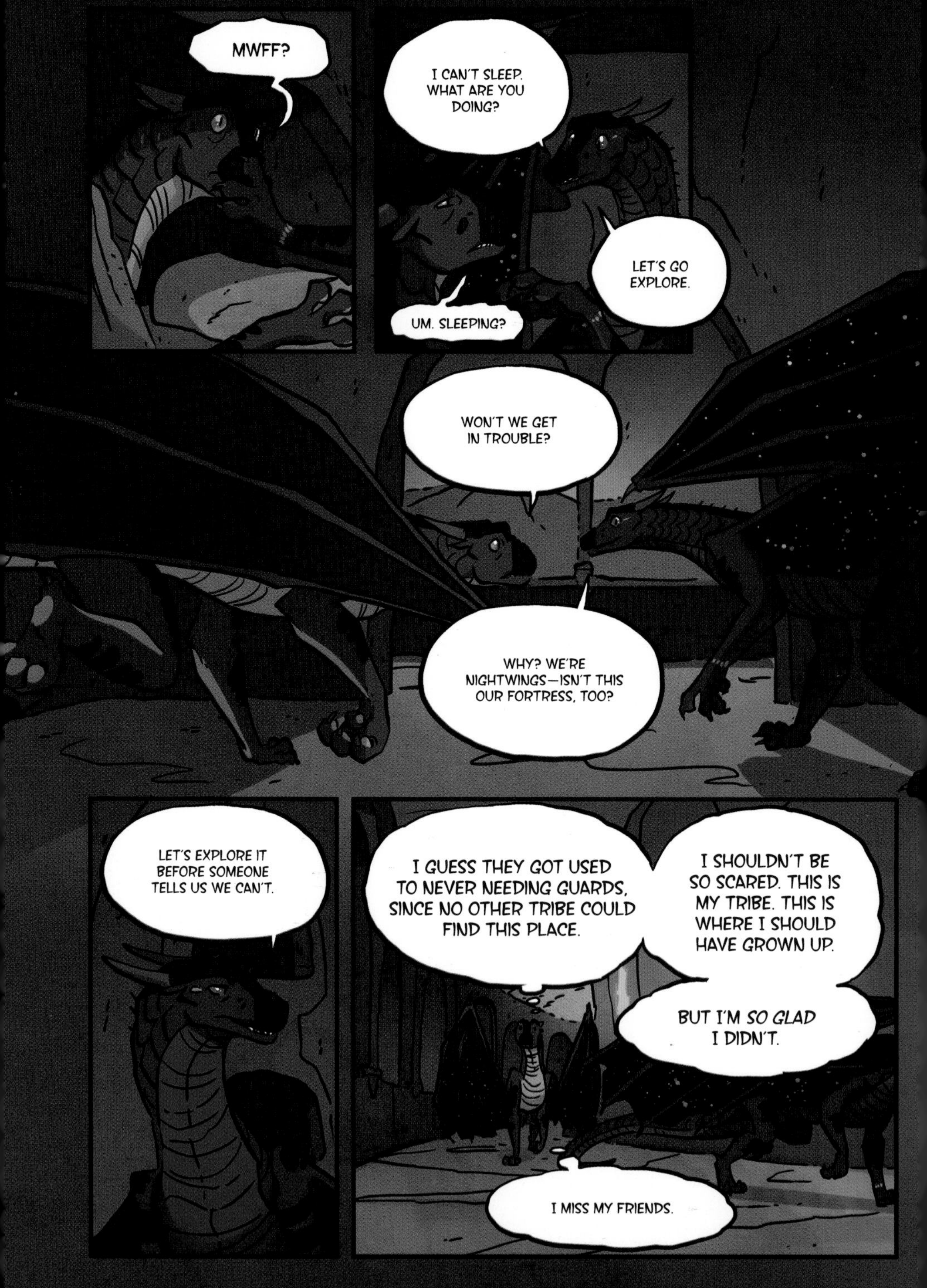
MWFF?
I CAN'T SLEEP. WHAT ARE YOU DOING?
UM. SLEEPING?
LET'S GO EXPLORE.
WON'T WE GET IN TROUBLE?
WHY? WE'RE NIGHTWINGS—ISN'T THIS OUR FORTRESS, TOO?
LET'S EXPLORE IT BEFORE SOMEONE TELLS US WE CAN'T.
I GUESS THEY GOT USED TO NEVER NEEDING GUARDS, SINCE NO OTHER TRIBE COULD FIND THIS PLACE.
I SHOULDN'T BE SO SCARED. THIS IS MY TRIBE. THIS IS WHERE I SHOULD HAVE GROWN UP.
BUT I'M *SO GLAD* I DIDN'T.
I MISS MY FRIENDS.

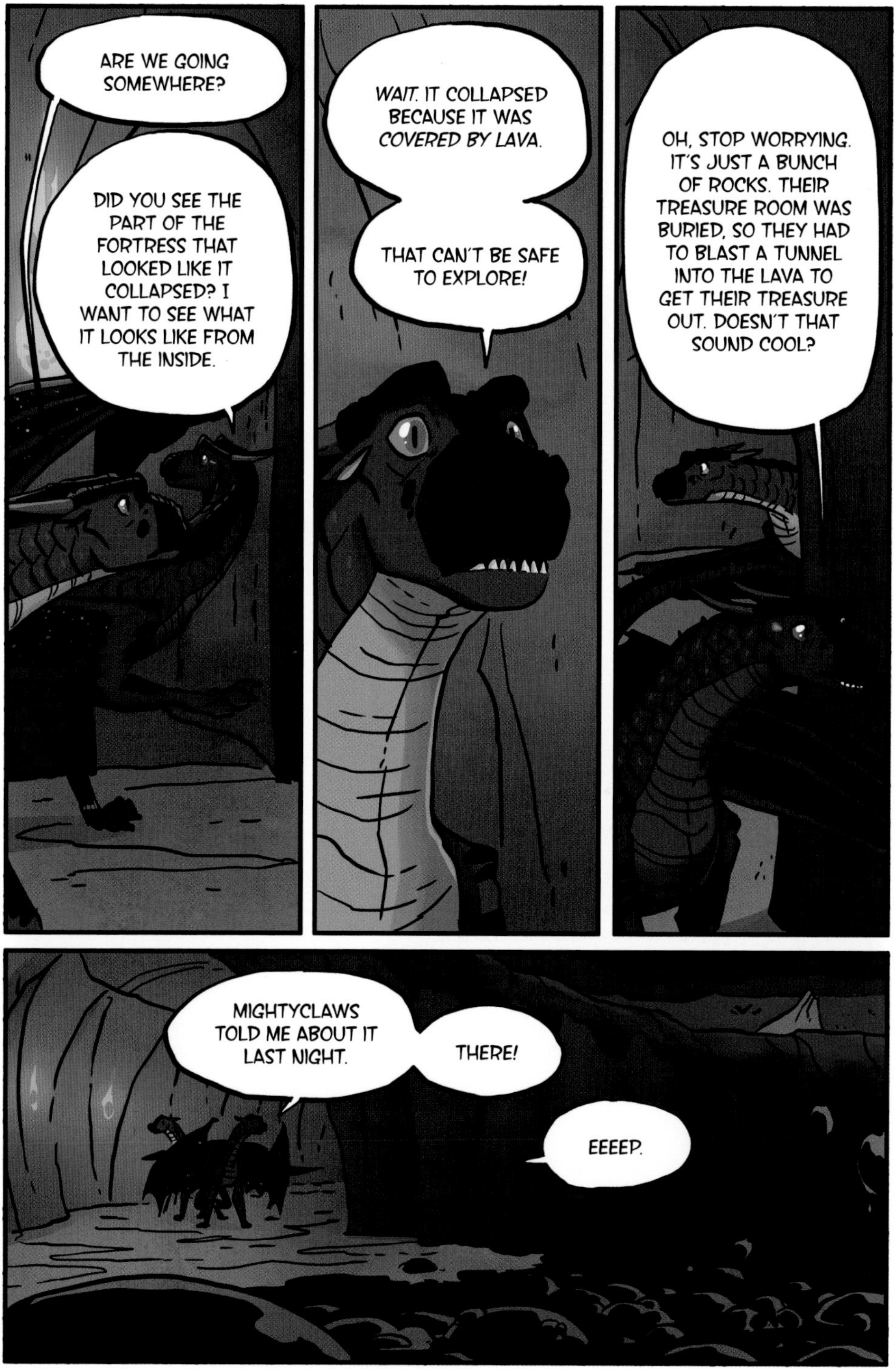
ARE WE GOING SOMEWHERE?
DID YOU SEE THE PART OF THE FORTRESS THAT LOOKED LIKE IT COLLAPSED? I WANT TO SEE WHAT IT LOOKS LIKE FROM THE INSIDE.
WAIT. IT COLLAPSED BECAUSE IT WAS COVERED BY LAVA.
THAT CAN'T BE SAFE TO EXPLORE!
OH, STOP WORRYING. IT'S JUST A BUNCH OF ROCKS. THEIR TREASURE ROOM WAS BURIED, SO THEY HAD TO BLAST A TUNNEL INTO THE LAVA TO GET THEIR TREASURE OUT. DOESN'T THAT SOUND COOL?
MIGHTYCLAWS TOLD ME ABOUT IT LAST NIGHT.
THERE!
EEEEP.

COME ON!

I THINK WE'LL NEED THIS.

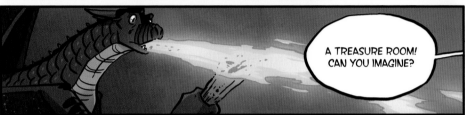

A TREASURE ROOM! CAN YOU IMAGINE?

WON'T THE TREASURE ROOM BE EMPTY?

EMPTY AND *FASCINATING!* I'VE NEVER EVEN SEEN *ANY* TREASURE BEFORE.

I'VE BEEN TO THE SKY KINGDOM AND THE KINGDOM OF THE SEA, AND I SAW ENOUGH TREASURE THERE TO KNOW THAT TREASURE DOESN'T MAKE YOU A GOOD QUEEN, OR A HAPPY TRIBE.

I THOUGHT I READ THAT QUEEN CORAL *WAS* A GOOD QUEEN.

WELL, KEEP IN MIND SHE PROBABLY WROTE THOSE SCROLLS HERSELF.

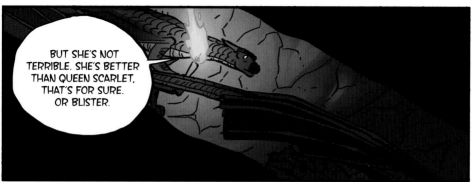

BUT SHE'S NOT TERRIBLE. SHE'S BETTER THAN QUEEN SCARLET, THAT'S FOR SURE. OR BLISTER.

I BET THE SANDWINGS WOULD BE HAPPIER IF THEY COULD FIND THE TREASURE THAT SCAVENGER STOLE, THOUGH.

MAYBE. THERE WERE SOME FAMOUS PIECES TAKEN—AND RUMOR HAS IT THAT SOME OF THAT TREASURE WAS MAGICKED BY AN ANIMUS.

THOSE PIECES WOULD BE LEFT WITH SOME SORT OF POWER—LIKE A NECKLACE THAT CAN MAKE YOU INVISIBLE.

OR A STATUE THAT KILLS HEIRS TO THE SEAWING THRONE.

STARFLIGHT...

THIS LOOKS LIKE THE PLACE.

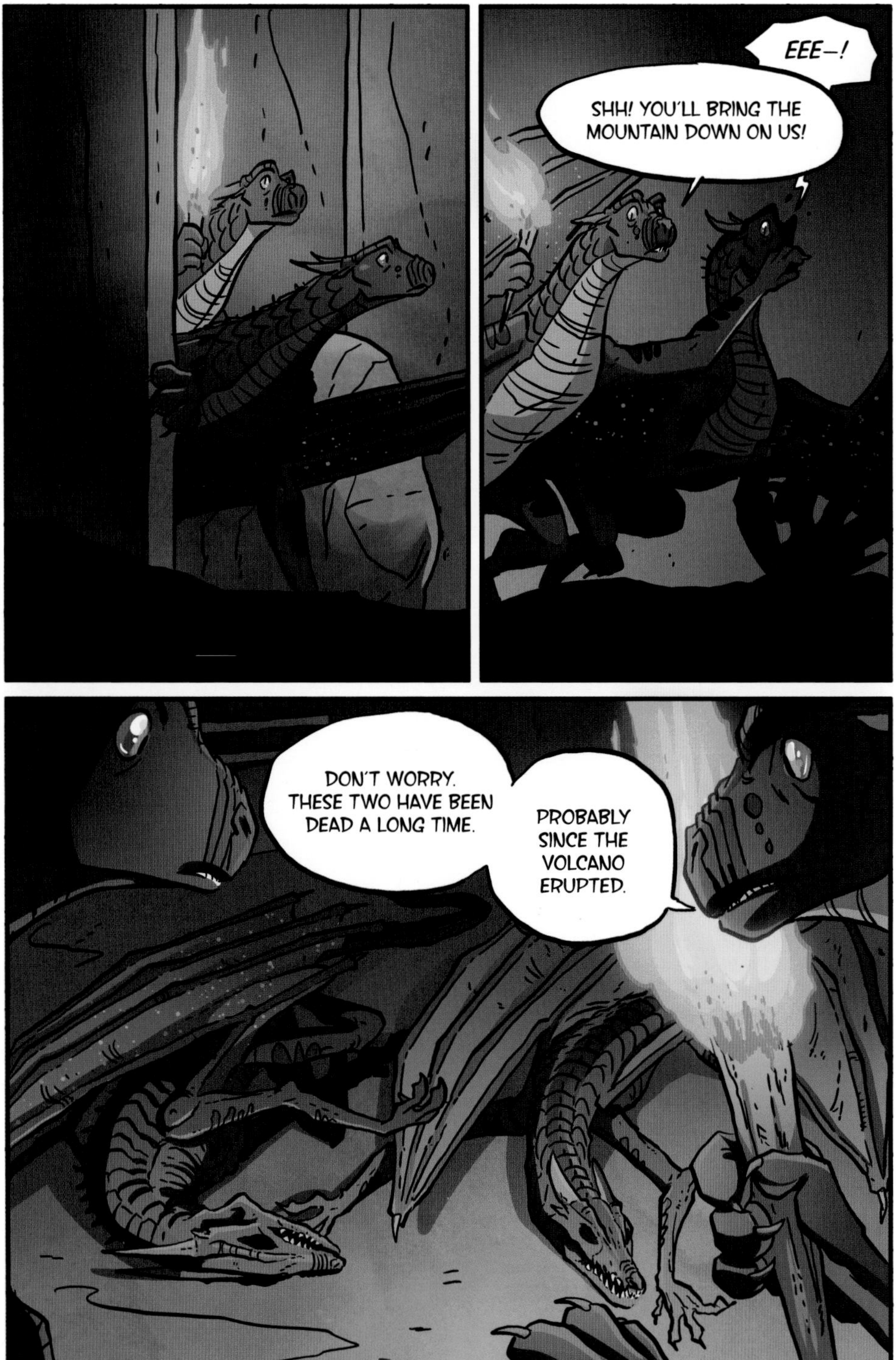
EEE–!
SHH! YOU'LL BRING THE MOUNTAIN DOWN ON US!
DON'T WORRY. THESE TWO HAVE BEEN DEAD A LONG TIME.
PROBABLY SINCE THE VOLCANO ERUPTED.

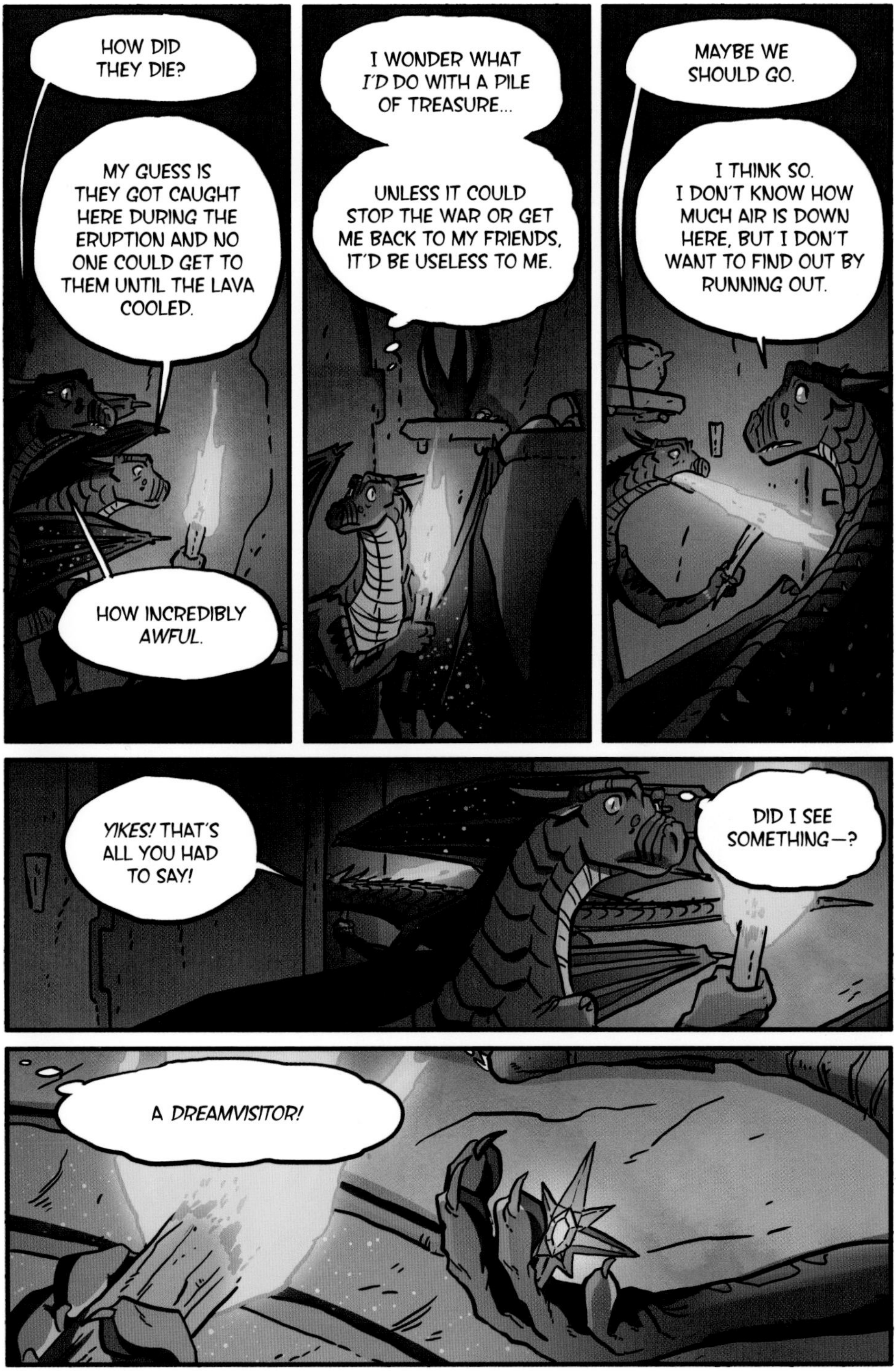
HOW DID THEY DIE?
MY GUESS IS THEY GOT CAUGHT HERE DURING THE ERUPTION AND NO ONE COULD GET TO THEM UNTIL THE LAVA COOLED.
HOW INCREDIBLY *AWFUL*.
I WONDER WHAT *I'D* DO WITH A PILE OF TREASURE...
UNLESS IT COULD STOP THE WAR OR GET ME BACK TO MY FRIENDS, IT'D BE USELESS TO ME.
MAYBE WE SHOULD GO.
I THINK SO. I DON'T KNOW HOW MUCH AIR IS DOWN HERE, BUT I DON'T WANT TO FIND OUT BY RUNNING OUT.
YIKES! THAT'S ALL YOU HAD TO SAY!
DID I SEE SOMETHING—?
A *DREAMVISITOR!*

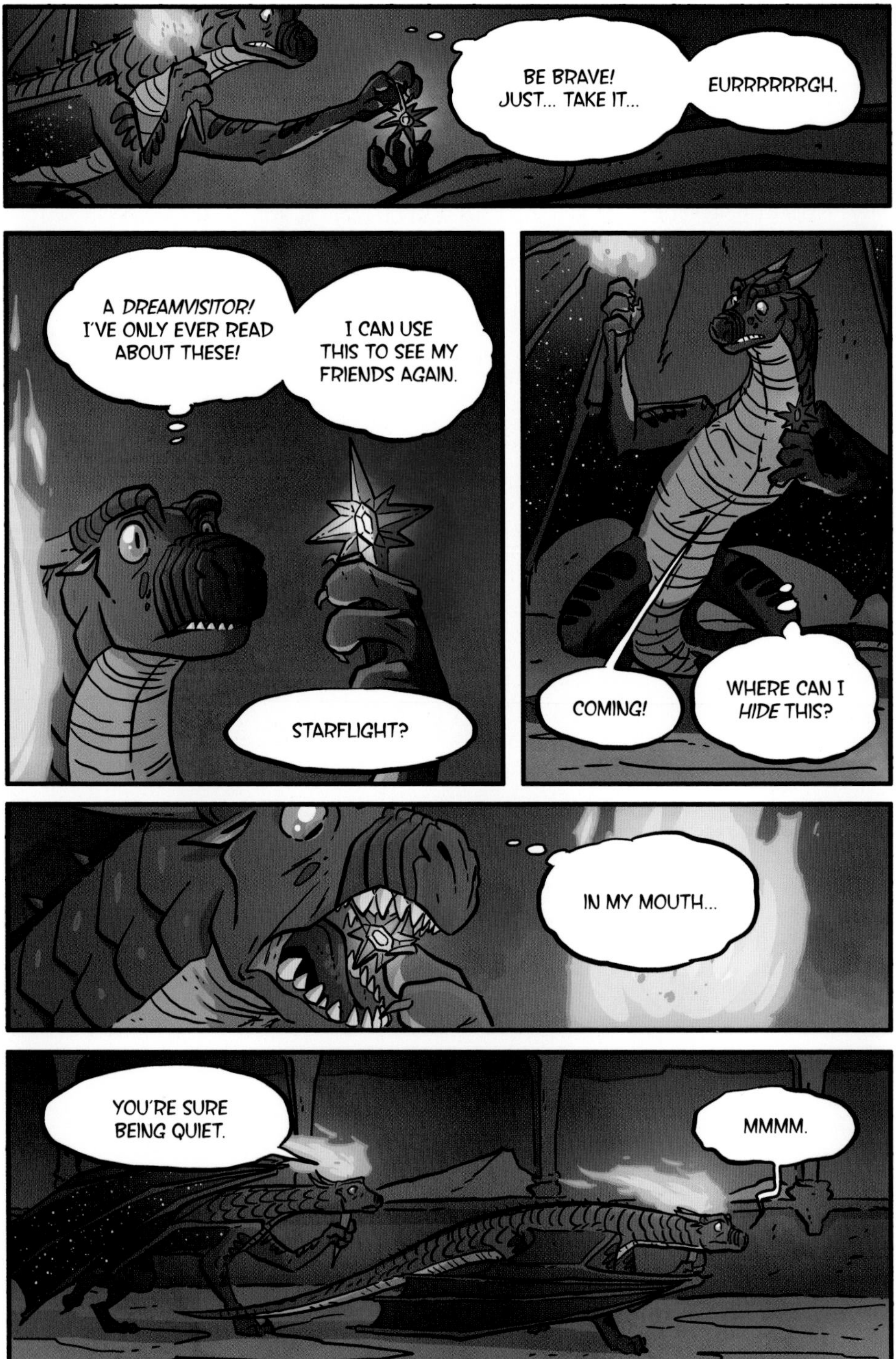
BE BRAVE! JUST... TAKE IT...
EURRRRRRGH.
A *DREAMVISITOR!* I'VE ONLY EVER READ ABOUT THESE!
I CAN USE THIS TO SEE MY FRIENDS AGAIN.
STARFLIGHT?
COMING!
WHERE CAN I *HIDE* THIS?
IN MY MOUTH...
YOU'RE SURE BEING QUIET.
MMMM.

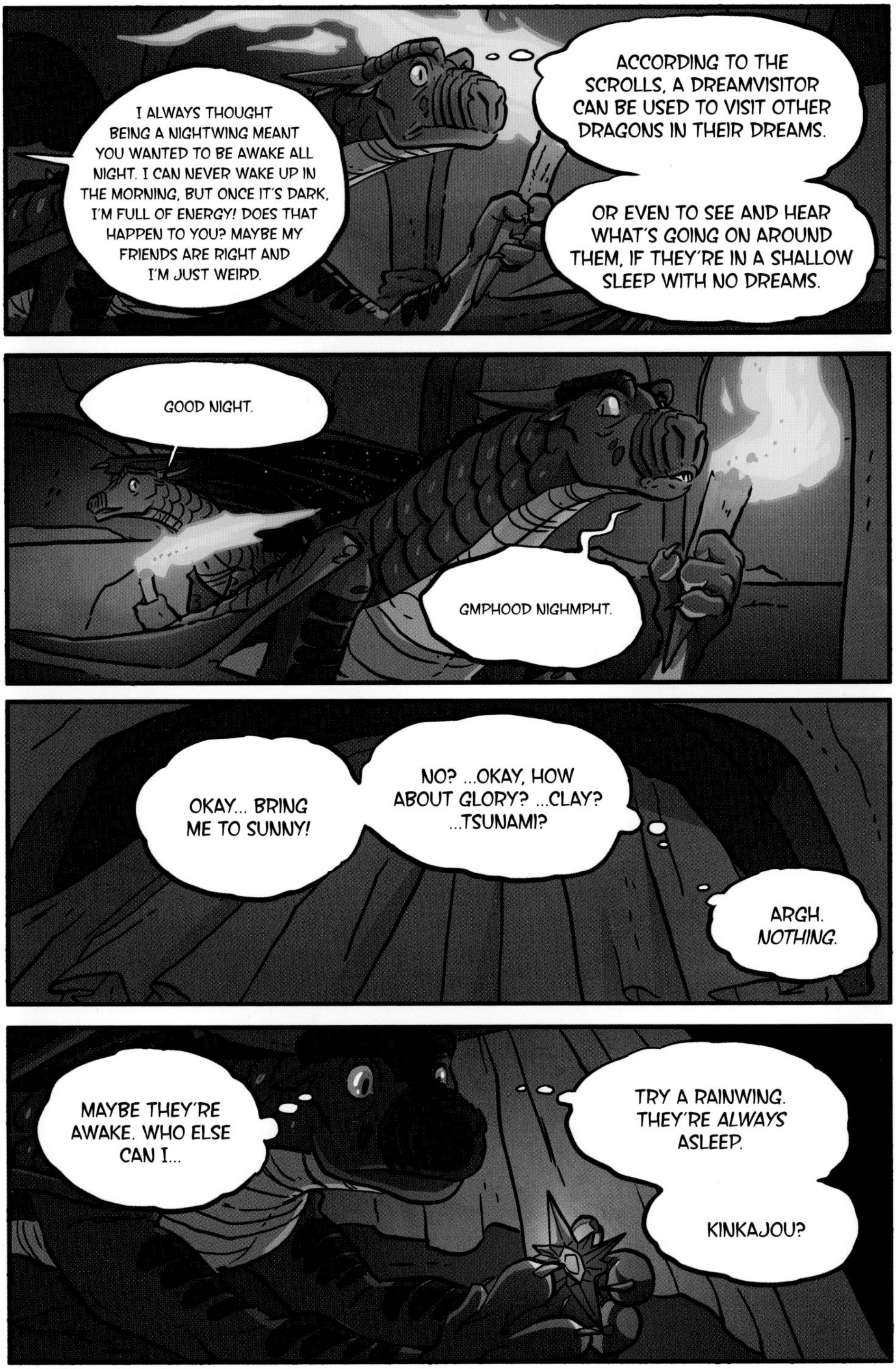
ACCORDING TO THE SCROLLS, A DREAMVISITOR CAN BE USED TO VISIT OTHER DRAGONS IN THEIR DREAMS.
OR EVEN TO SEE AND HEAR WHAT'S GOING ON AROUND THEM, IF THEY'RE IN A SHALLOW SLEEP WITH NO DREAMS.
I ALWAYS THOUGHT BEING A NIGHTWING MEANT YOU WANTED TO BE AWAKE ALL NIGHT. I CAN NEVER WAKE UP IN THE MORNING, BUT ONCE IT'S DARK, I'M FULL OF ENERGY! DOES THAT HAPPEN TO YOU? MAYBE MY FRIENDS ARE RIGHT AND I'M JUST WEIRD.
GOOD NIGHT.
GMPHOOD NIGHMPHT.
OKAY... BRING ME TO SUNNY!
NO? ...OKAY, HOW ABOUT GLORY? ...CLAY? ...TSUNAMI?
ARGH. *NOTHING.*
MAYBE THEY'RE AWAKE. WHO ELSE CAN I...
TRY A RAINWING. THEY'RE *ALWAYS* ASLEEP.
KINKAJOU?

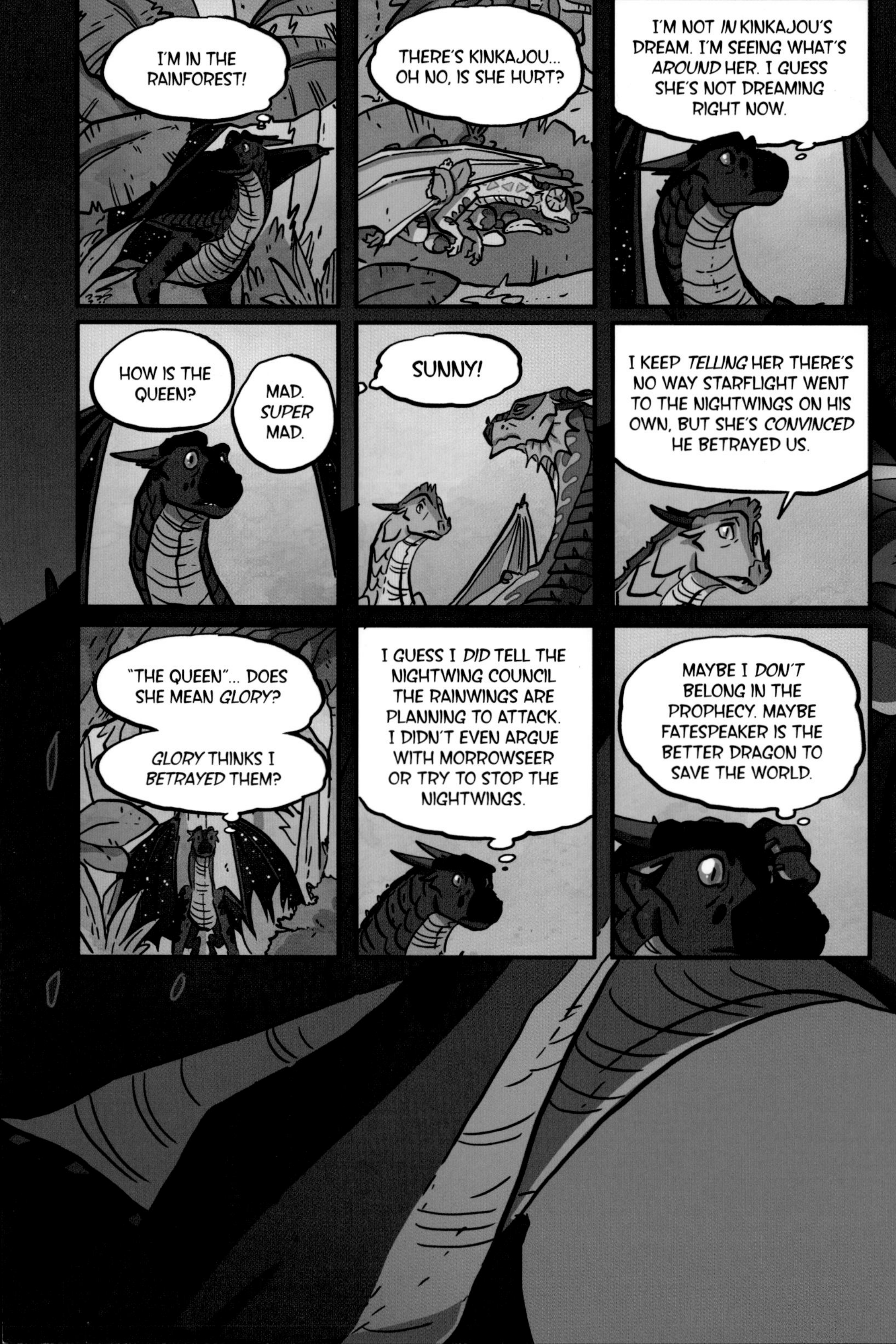
I'M IN THE RAINFOREST!
THERE'S KINKAJOU... OH NO, IS SHE HURT?
I'M NOT *IN* KINKAJOU'S DREAM. I'M SEEING WHAT'S *AROUND* HER. I GUESS SHE'S NOT DREAMING RIGHT NOW.
HOW IS THE QUEEN?
MAD. *SUPER* MAD.
SUNNY!
I KEEP *TELLING* HER THERE'S NO WAY STARFLIGHT WENT TO THE NIGHTWINGS ON HIS OWN, BUT SHE'S *CONVINCED* HE BETRAYED US.
"THE QUEEN"... DOES SHE MEAN *GLORY*?
GLORY THINKS I *BETRAYED* THEM?
I GUESS I *DID* TELL THE NIGHTWING COUNCIL THE RAINWINGS ARE PLANNING TO ATTACK. I DIDN'T EVEN ARGUE WITH MORROWSEER OR TRY TO STOP THE NIGHTWINGS.
MAYBE I *DON'T* BELONG IN THE PROPHECY. MAYBE FATESPEAKER IS THE BETTER DRAGON TO SAVE THE WORLD.

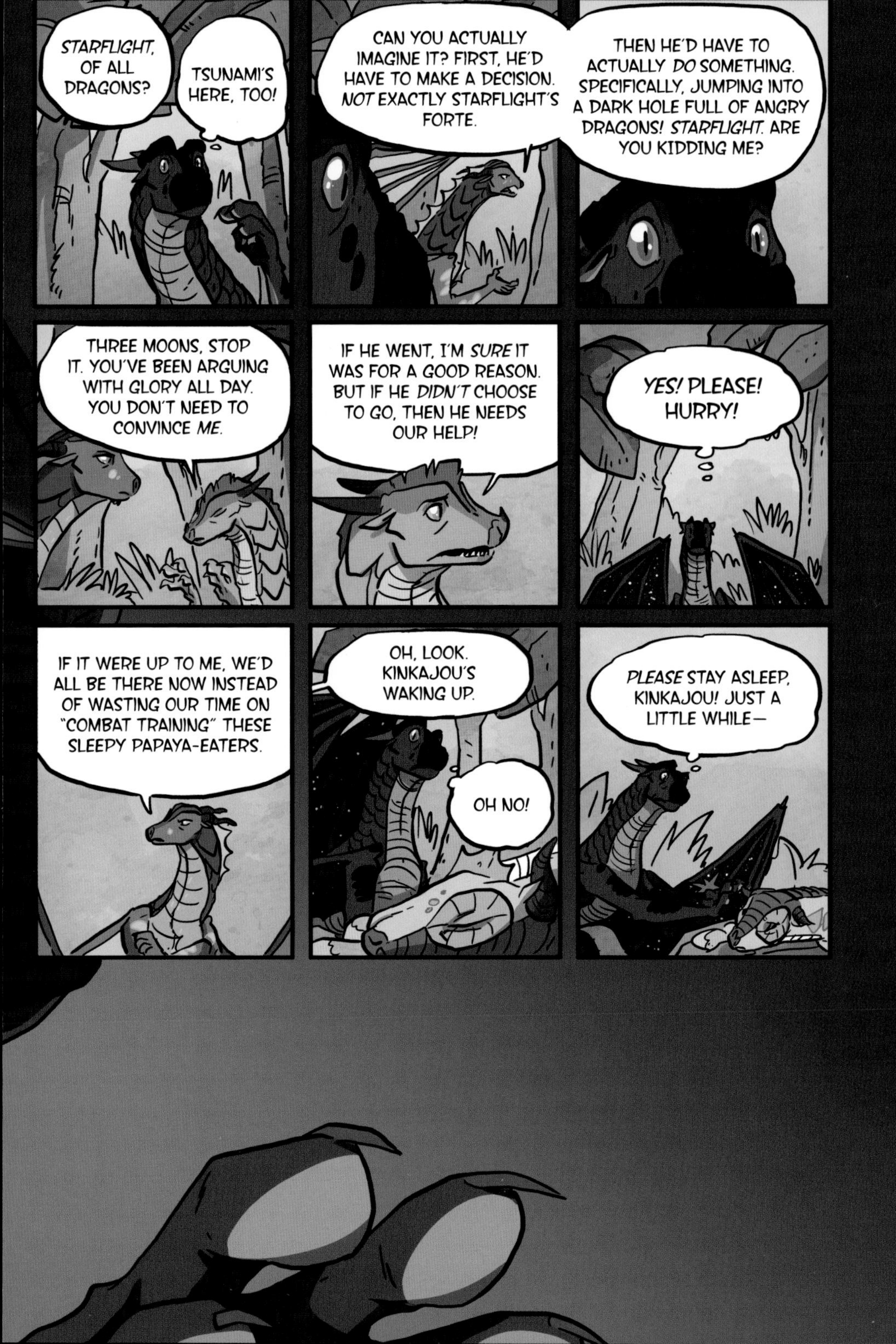
STARFLIGHT, OF ALL DRAGONS?
TSUNAMI'S HERE, TOO!
CAN YOU ACTUALLY IMAGINE IT? FIRST, HE'D HAVE TO MAKE A DECISION. NOT EXACTLY STARFLIGHT'S FORTE.
THEN HE'D HAVE TO ACTUALLY DO SOMETHING. SPECIFICALLY, JUMPING INTO A DARK HOLE FULL OF ANGRY DRAGONS! STARFLIGHT. ARE YOU KIDDING ME?
THREE MOONS, STOP IT. YOU'VE BEEN ARGUING WITH GLORY ALL DAY. YOU DON'T NEED TO CONVINCE ME.
IF HE WENT, I'M SURE IT WAS FOR A GOOD REASON. BUT IF HE DIDN'T CHOOSE TO GO, THEN HE NEEDS OUR HELP!
YES! PLEASE! HURRY!
IF IT WERE UP TO ME, WE'D ALL BE THERE NOW INSTEAD OF WASTING OUR TIME ON "COMBAT TRAINING" THESE SLEEPY PAPAYA-EATERS.
OH, LOOK. KINKAJOU'S WAKING UP.
OH NO!
PLEASE STAY ASLEEP, KINKAJOU! JUST A LITTLE WHILE—

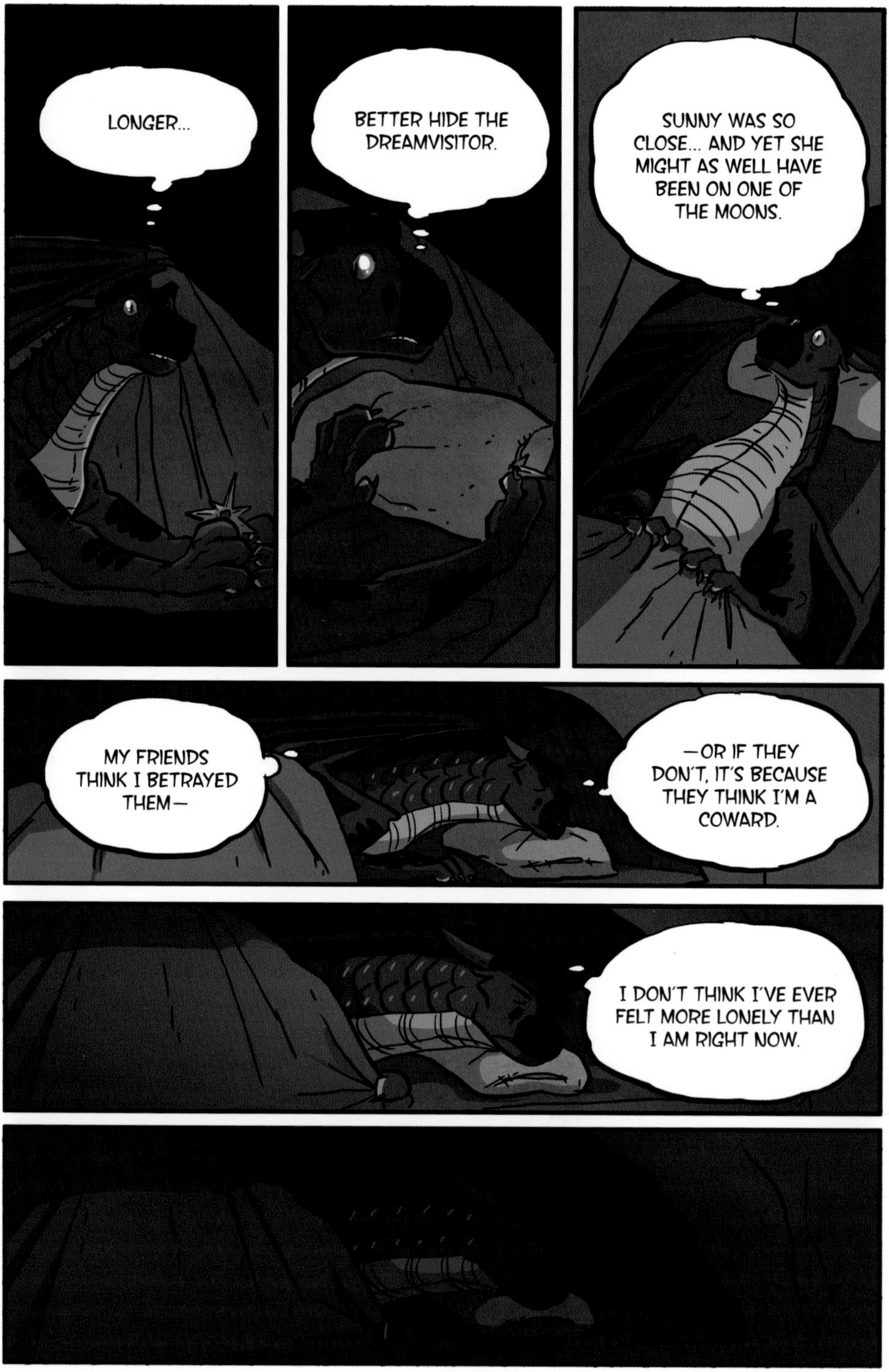
LONGER...
BETTER HIDE THE DREAMVISITOR.
SUNNY WAS SO CLOSE... AND YET SHE MIGHT AS WELL HAVE BEEN ON ONE OF THE MOONS.
MY FRIENDS THINK I BETRAYED THEM—
—OR IF THEY DON'T, IT'S BECAUSE THEY THINK I'M A COWARD.
I DON'T THINK I'VE EVER FELT MORE LONELY THAN I AM RIGHT NOW.

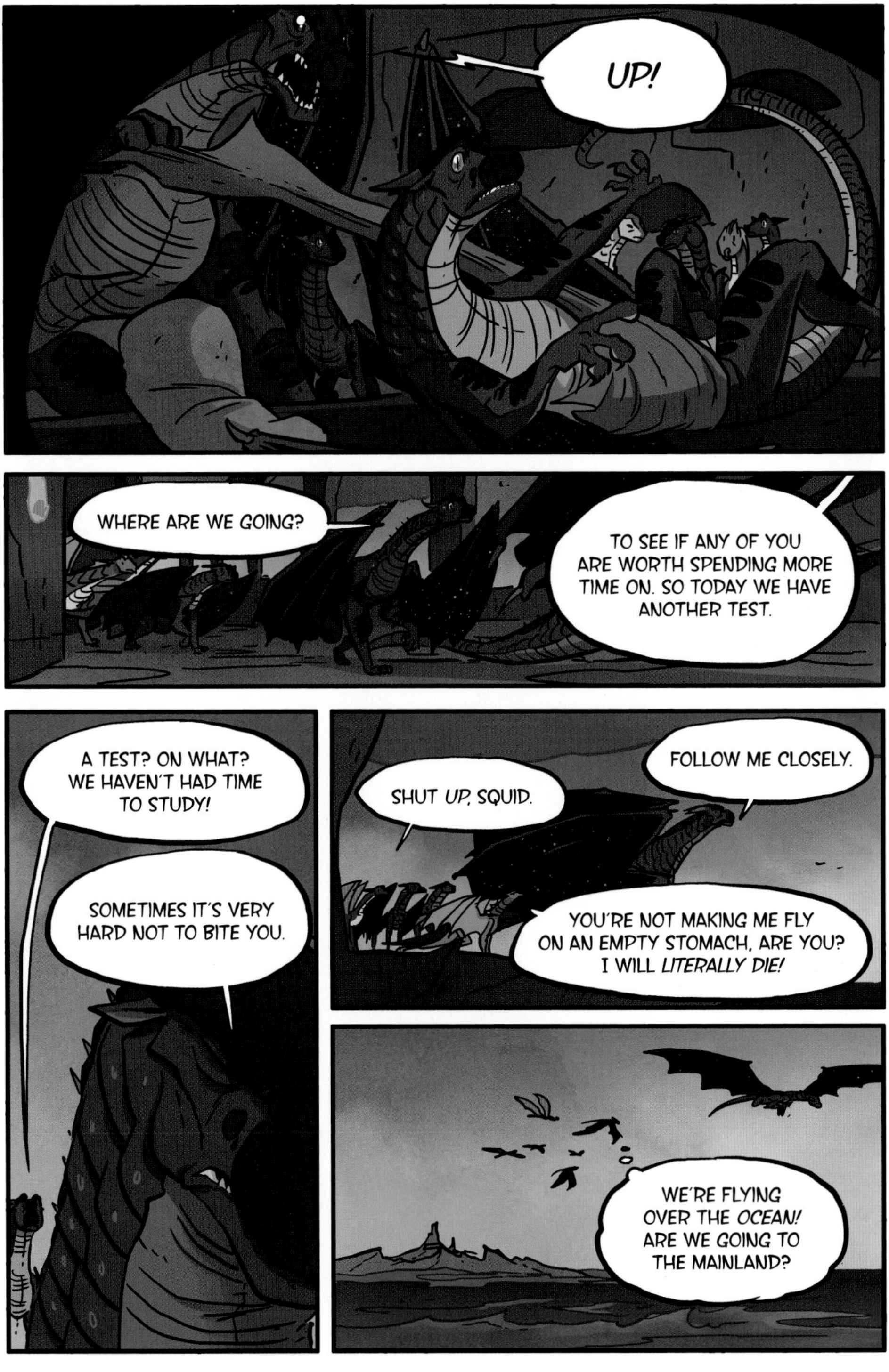
UP!
WHERE ARE WE GOING?
TO SEE IF ANY OF YOU ARE WORTH SPENDING MORE TIME ON. SO TODAY WE HAVE ANOTHER TEST.
A TEST? ON WHAT? WE HAVEN'T HAD TIME TO STUDY!
SOMETIMES IT'S VERY HARD NOT TO BITE YOU.
SHUT *UP*, SQUID.
FOLLOW ME CLOSELY.
YOU'RE NOT MAKING ME FLY ON AN EMPTY STOMACH, ARE YOU? I WILL *LITERALLY DIE!*
WE'RE FLYING OVER THE *OCEAN!* ARE WE GOING TO THE MAINLAND?

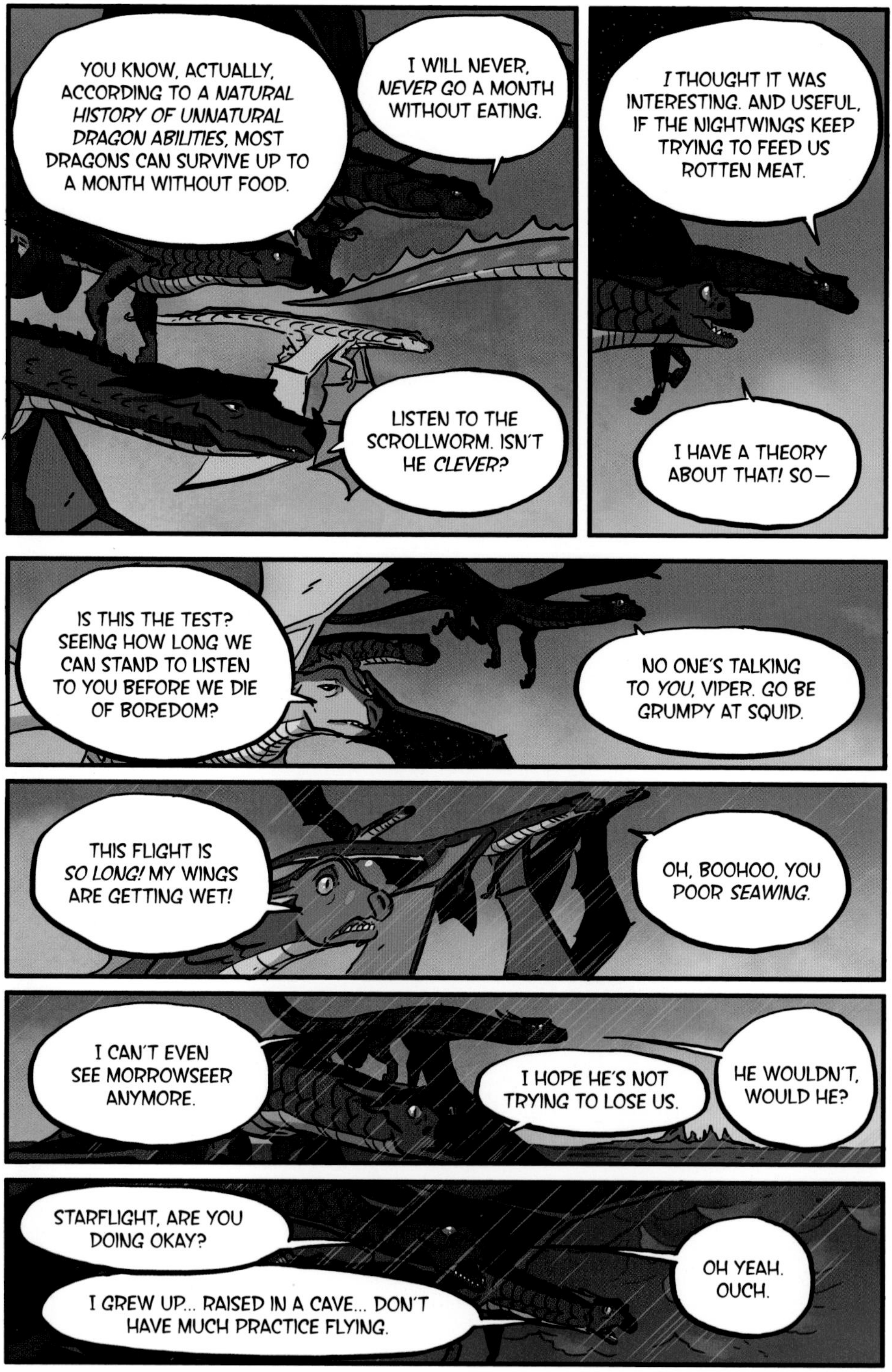
YOU KNOW, ACTUALLY, ACCORDING TO A *NATURAL HISTORY OF UNNATURAL DRAGON ABILITIES*, MOST DRAGONS CAN SURVIVE UP TO A MONTH WITHOUT FOOD.
I WILL NEVER, *NEVER* GO A MONTH WITHOUT EATING.
LISTEN TO THE SCROLLWORM. ISN'T HE *CLEVER?*
I THOUGHT IT WAS INTERESTING. AND USEFUL, IF THE NIGHTWINGS KEEP TRYING TO FEED US ROTTEN MEAT.
I HAVE A THEORY ABOUT THAT! SO—
IS THIS THE TEST? SEEING HOW LONG WE CAN STAND TO LISTEN TO YOU BEFORE WE DIE OF BOREDOM?
NO ONE'S TALKING TO *YOU*, VIPER. GO BE GRUMPY AT SQUID.
THIS FLIGHT IS *SO LONG!* MY WINGS ARE GETTING WET!
OH, BOOHOO, YOU POOR *SEAWING*.
I CAN'T EVEN SEE MORROWSEER ANYMORE.
I HOPE HE'S NOT TRYING TO LOSE US.
HE WOULDN'T, WOULD HE?
STARFLIGHT, ARE YOU DOING OKAY?
I GREW UP... RAISED IN A CAVE... DON'T HAVE MUCH PRACTICE FLYING.
OH YEAH. OUCH.

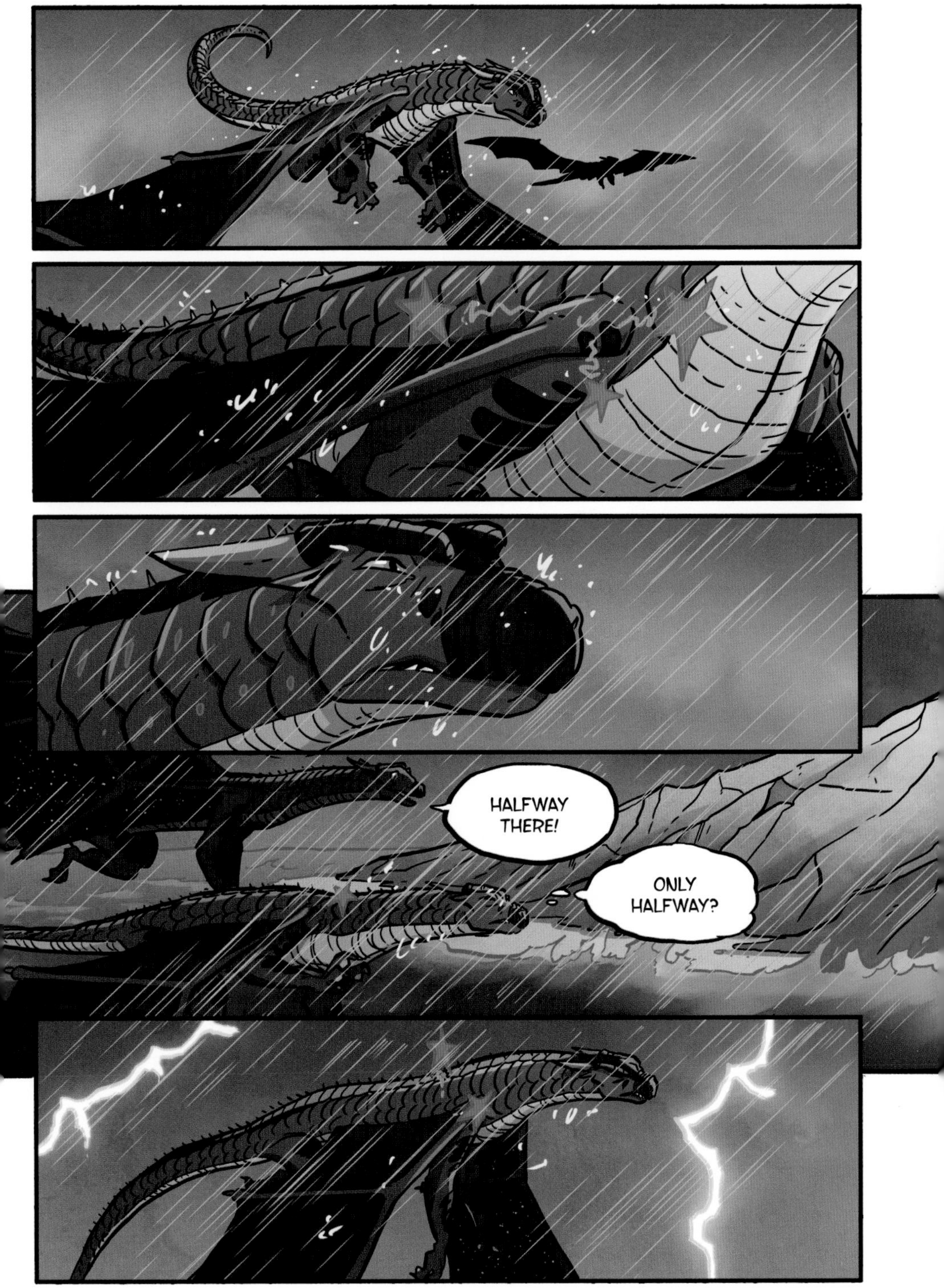
HALFWAY THERE!
ONLY HALFWAY?

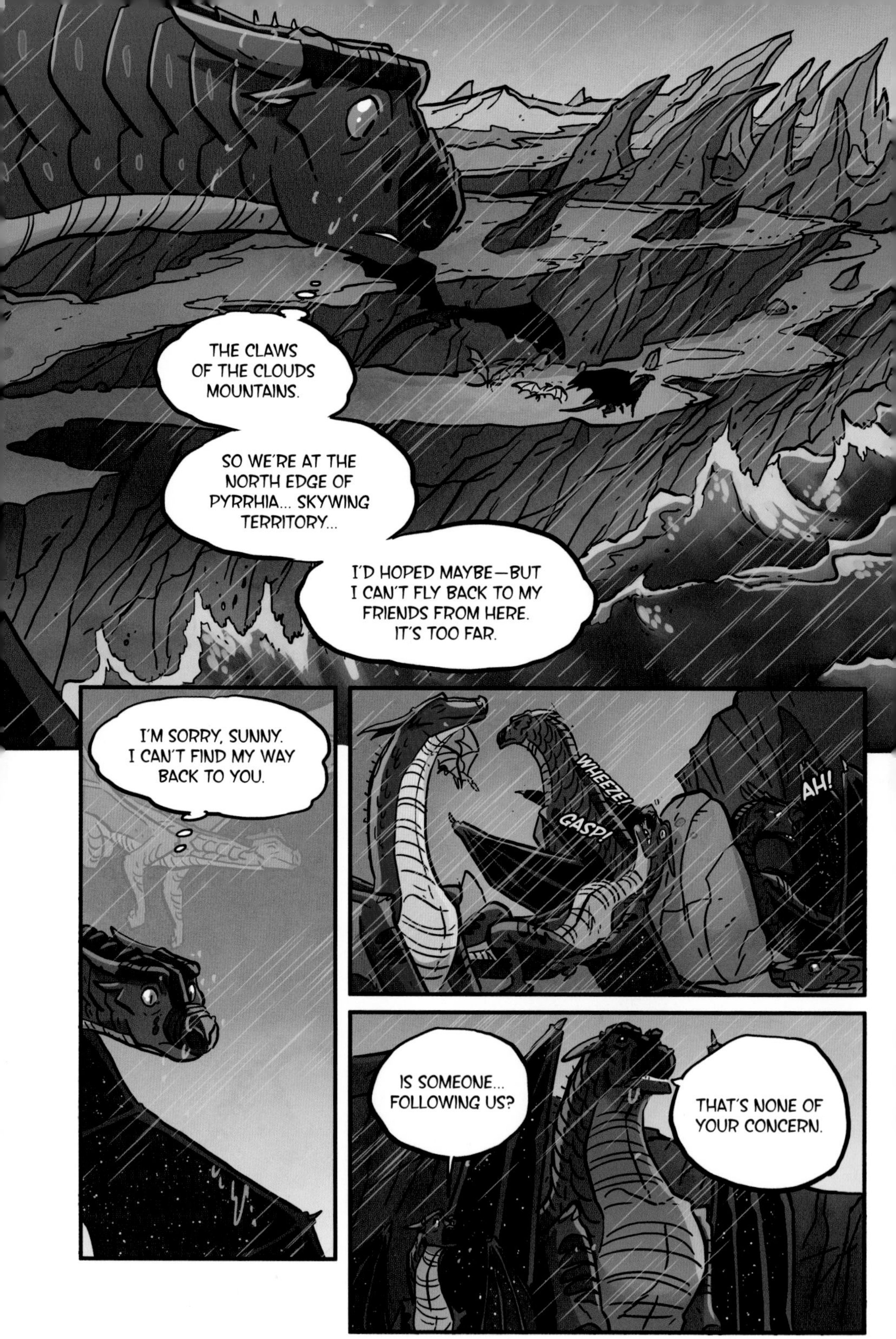
THE CLAWS OF THE CLOUDS MOUNTAINS.
SO WE'RE AT THE NORTH EDGE OF PYRRHIA... SKYWING TERRITORY...
I'D HOPED MAYBE—BUT I CAN'T FLY BACK TO MY FRIENDS FROM HERE. IT'S TOO FAR.
I'M SORRY, SUNNY. I CAN'T FIND MY WAY BACK TO YOU.
WHEEZE!
GASP!
AH!
IS SOMEONE... FOLLOWING US?
THAT'S NONE OF YOUR CONCERN.

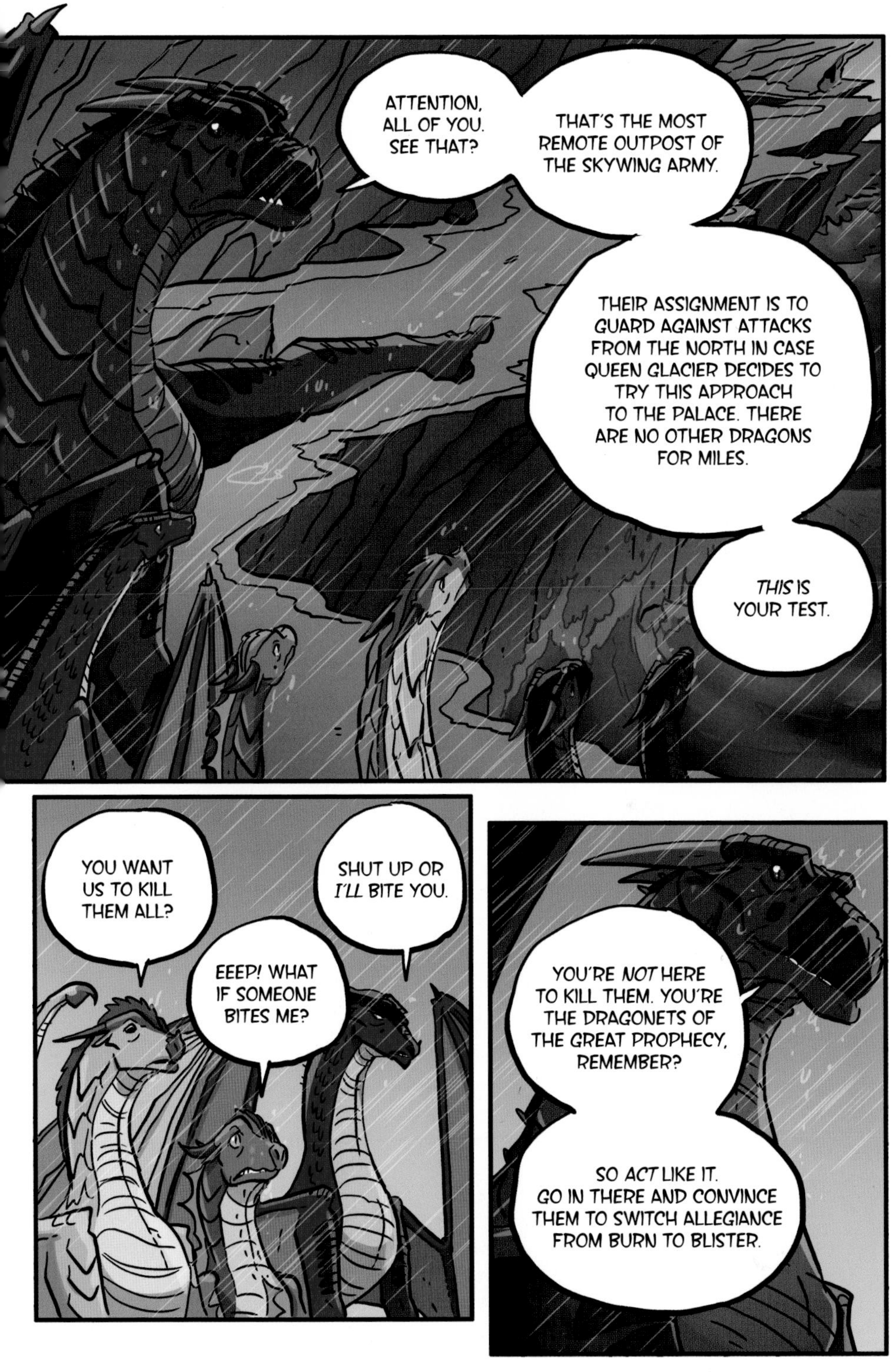
ATTENTION, ALL OF YOU. SEE THAT?
THAT'S THE MOST REMOTE OUTPOST OF THE SKYWING ARMY.
THEIR ASSIGNMENT IS TO GUARD AGAINST ATTACKS FROM THE NORTH IN CASE QUEEN GLACIER DECIDES TO TRY THIS APPROACH TO THE PALACE. THERE ARE NO OTHER DRAGONS FOR MILES.
THIS IS YOUR TEST.
YOU WANT US TO KILL THEM ALL?
SHUT UP OR *I'LL* BITE YOU.
EEEP! WHAT IF SOMEONE BITES ME?
YOU'RE *NOT* HERE TO KILL THEM. YOU'RE THE DRAGONETS OF THE GREAT PROPHECY, REMEMBER?
SO *ACT* LIKE IT. GO IN THERE AND CONVINCE THEM TO SWITCH ALLEGIANCE FROM BURN TO BLISTER.

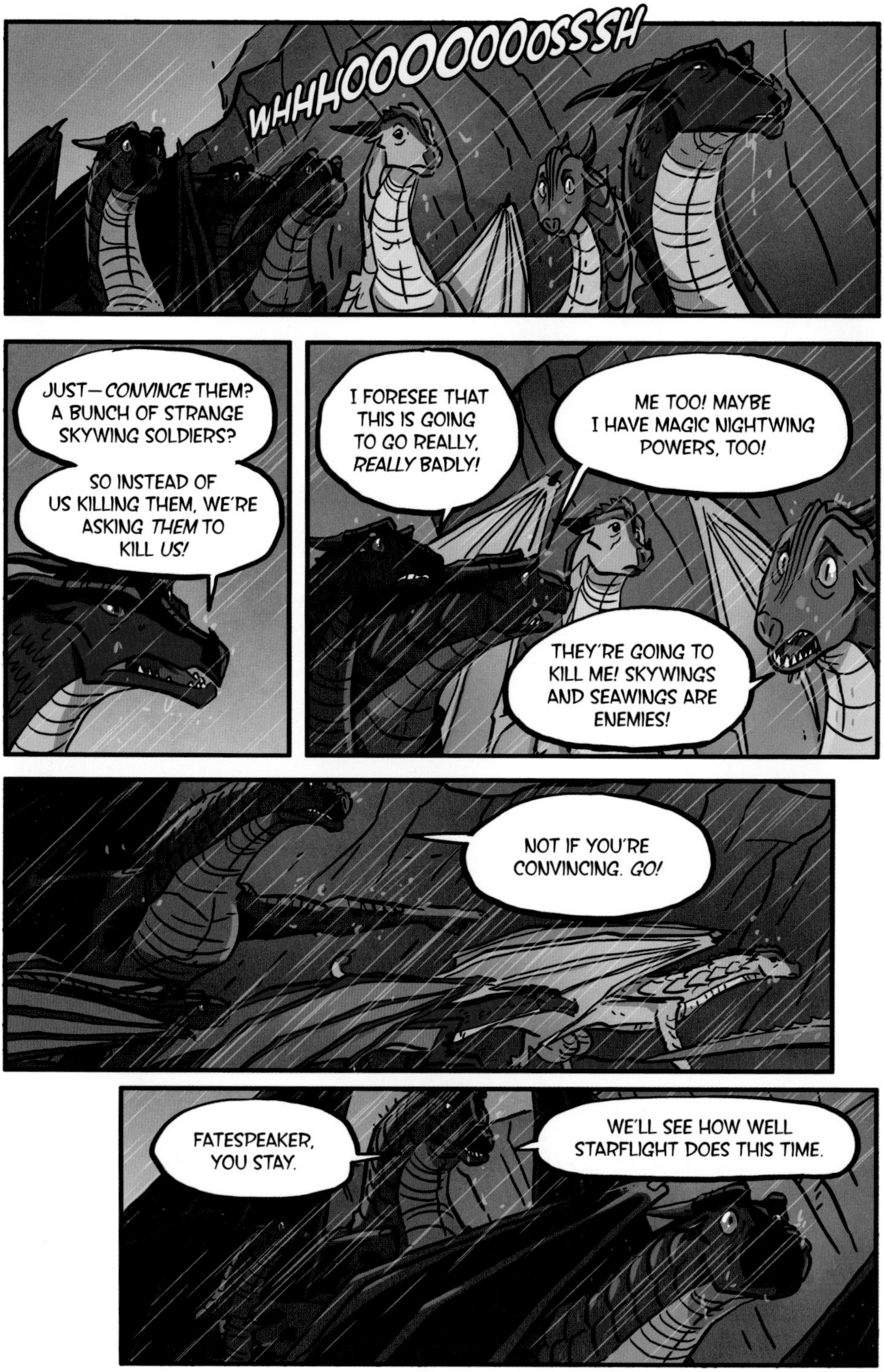
WHHHOOOOOOOOSSSH
JUST—*CONVINCE* THEM? A BUNCH OF STRANGE SKYWING SOLDIERS?
SO INSTEAD OF US KILLING THEM, WE'RE ASKING *THEM* TO KILL *US!*
I FORESEE THAT THIS IS GOING TO GO REALLY, *REALLY* BADLY!
ME TOO! MAYBE I HAVE MAGIC NIGHTWING POWERS, TOO!
THEY'RE GOING TO KILL ME! SKYWINGS AND SEAWINGS ARE ENEMIES!
NOT IF YOU'RE CONVINCING. *GO!*
FATESPEAKER, YOU STAY.
WE'LL SEE HOW WELL STARFLIGHT DOES THIS TIME.

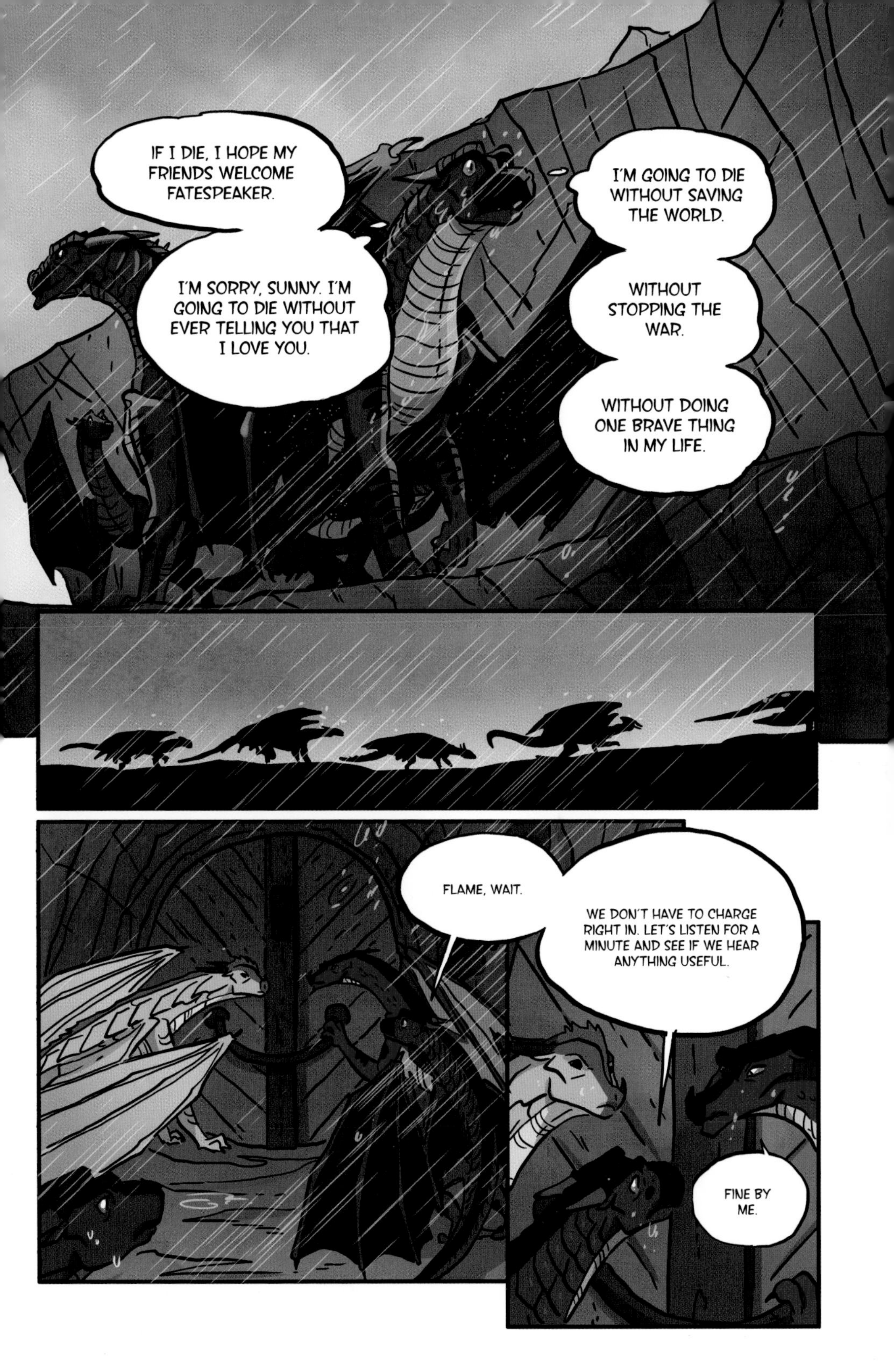
IF I DIE, I HOPE MY FRIENDS WELCOME FATESPEAKER.
I'M SORRY, SUNNY. I'M GOING TO DIE WITHOUT EVER TELLING YOU THAT I LOVE YOU.
I'M GOING TO DIE WITHOUT SAVING THE WORLD.
WITHOUT STOPPING THE WAR.
WITHOUT DOING ONE BRAVE THING IN MY LIFE.
FLAME, WAIT.
WE DON'T HAVE TO CHARGE RIGHT IN. LET'S LISTEN FOR A MINUTE AND SEE IF WE HEAR ANYTHING USEFUL.
FINE BY ME.

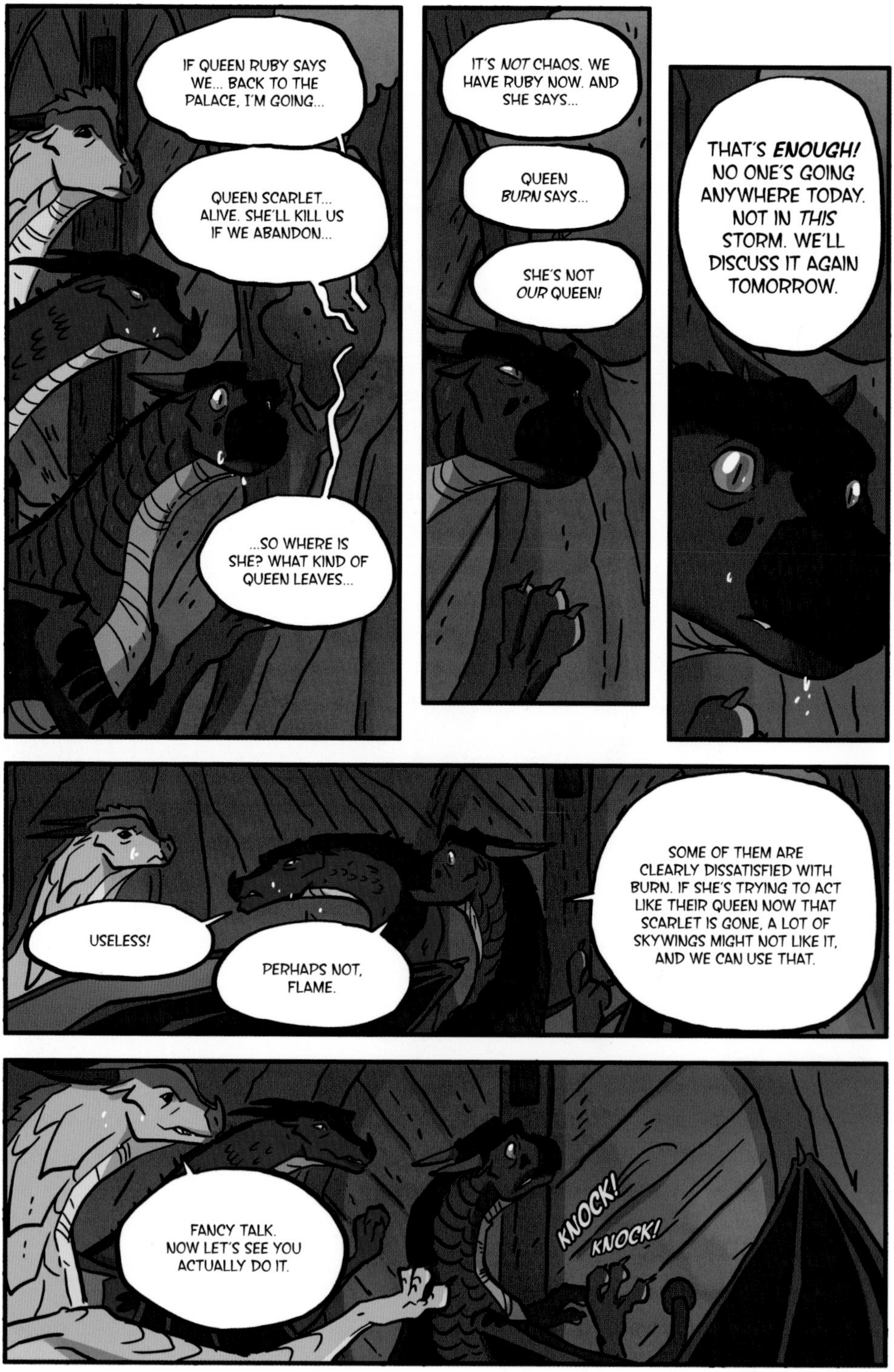
IF QUEEN RUBY SAYS WE... BACK TO THE PALACE, I'M GOING...
QUEEN SCARLET... ALIVE. SHE'LL KILL US IF WE ABANDON...
...SO WHERE IS SHE? WHAT KIND OF QUEEN LEAVES...
IT'S *NOT* CHAOS. WE HAVE RUBY NOW. AND SHE SAYS...
QUEEN *BURN* SAYS...
SHE'S NOT *OUR* QUEEN!
THAT'S ***ENOUGH!*** NO ONE'S GOING ANYWHERE TODAY. NOT IN *THIS* STORM. WE'LL DISCUSS IT AGAIN TOMORROW.
USELESS!
PERHAPS NOT, FLAME.
SOME OF THEM ARE CLEARLY DISSATISFIED WITH BURN. IF SHE'S TRYING TO ACT LIKE THEIR QUEEN NOW THAT SCARLET IS GONE, A LOT OF SKYWINGS MIGHT NOT LIKE IT, AND WE CAN USE THAT.
FANCY TALK. NOW LET'S SEE YOU ACTUALLY DO IT.
KNOCK!
KNOCK!

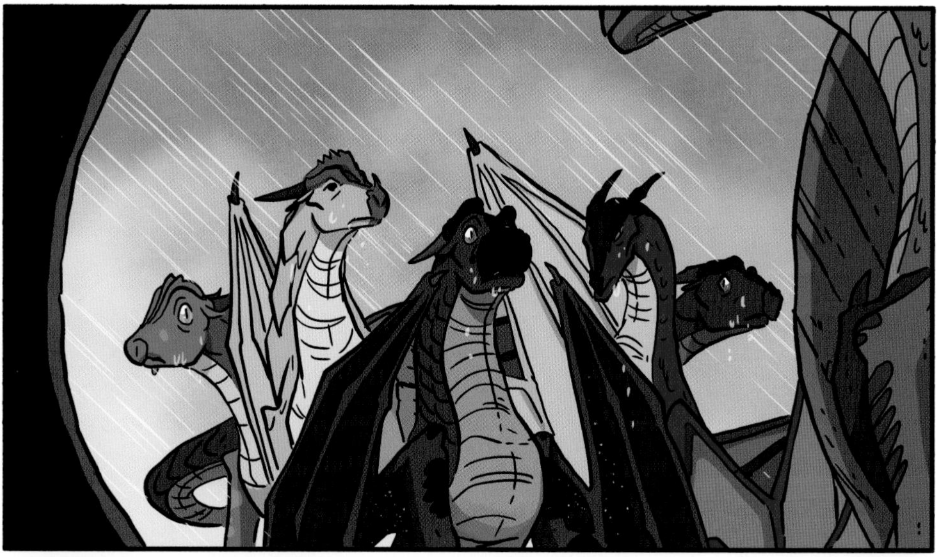

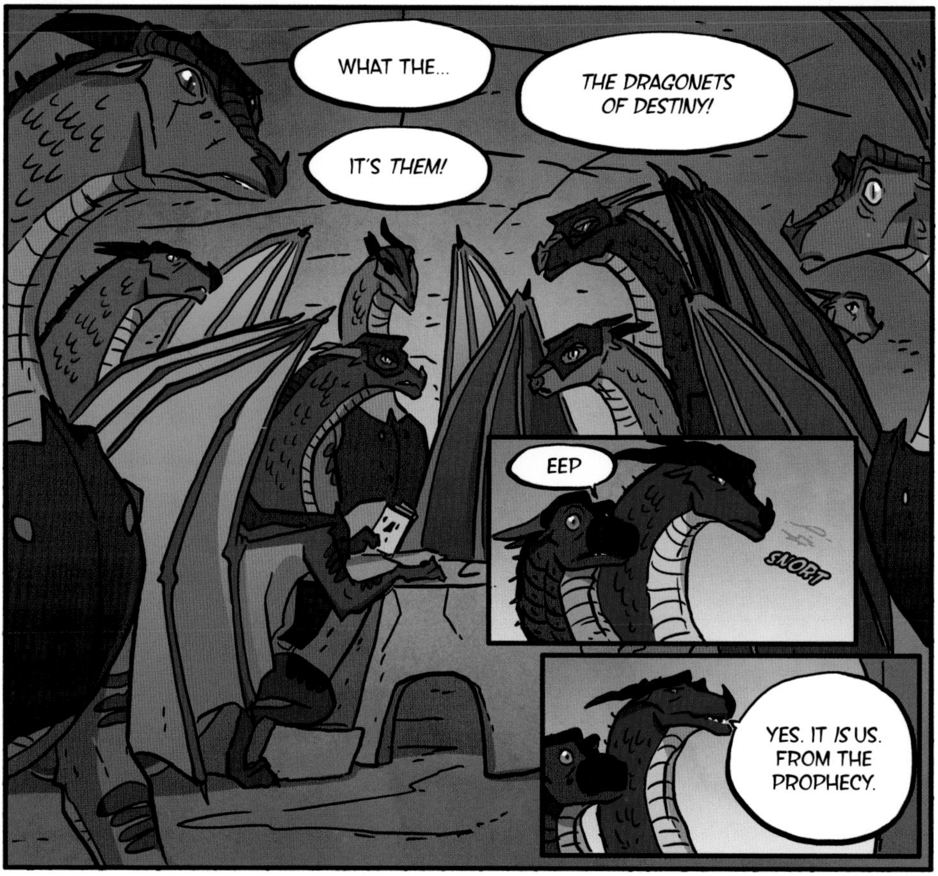
WHAT THE...
THE DRAGONETS OF DESTINY!
IT'S THEM!
EEP
SNORT
YES. IT IS US. FROM THE PROPHECY.

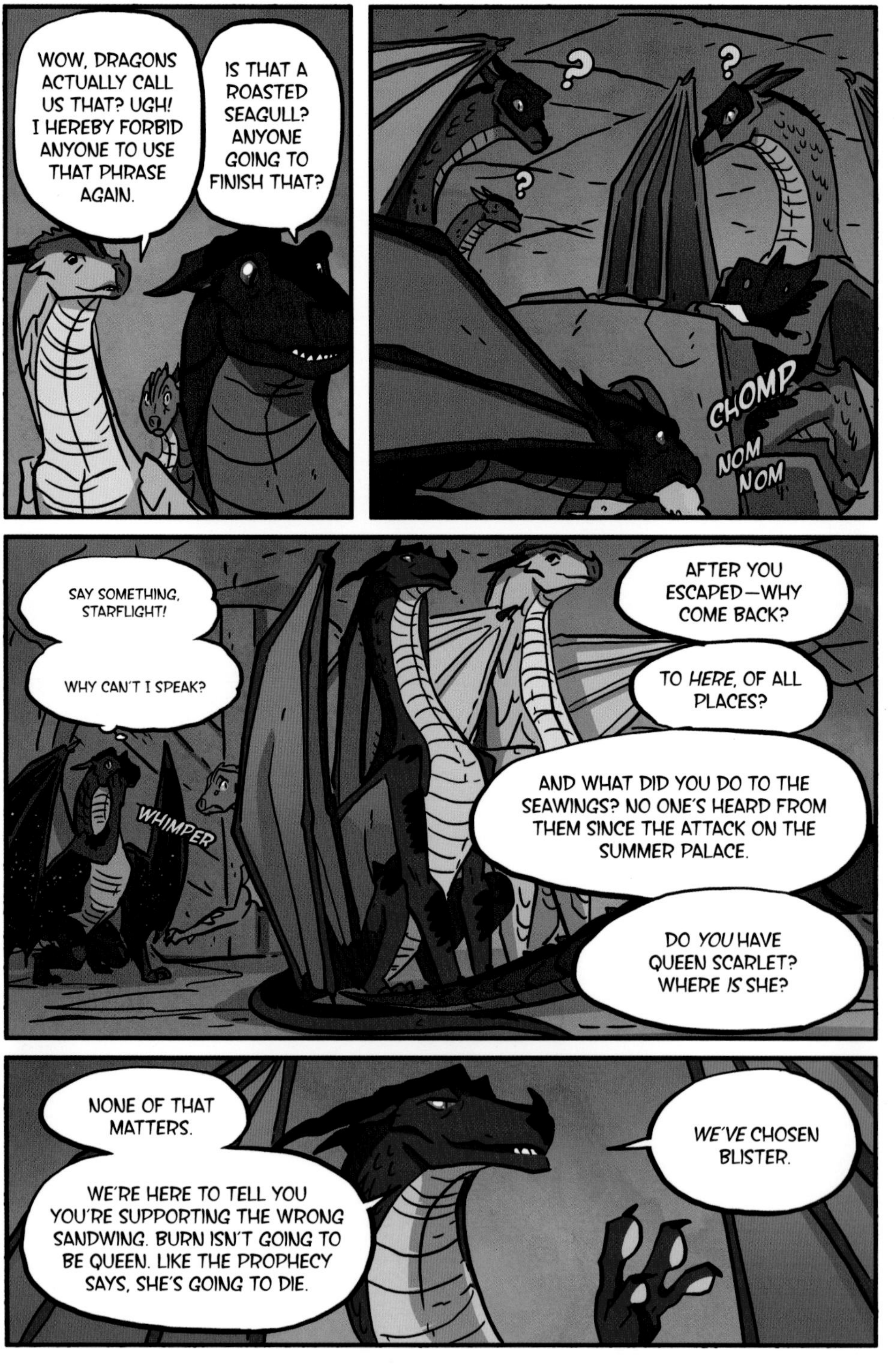
WOW, DRAGONS ACTUALLY CALL US THAT? UGH! I HEREBY FORBID ANYONE TO USE THAT PHRASE AGAIN.
IS THAT A ROASTED SEAGULL? ANYONE GOING TO FINISH THAT?
? ? ?
CHOMP
NOM NOM
SAY SOMETHING, STARFLIGHT!
WHY CAN'T I SPEAK?
WHIMPER
AFTER YOU ESCAPED—WHY COME BACK?
TO *HERE*, OF ALL PLACES?
AND WHAT DID YOU DO TO THE SEAWINGS? NO ONE'S HEARD FROM THEM SINCE THE ATTACK ON THE SUMMER PALACE.
DO *YOU* HAVE QUEEN SCARLET? WHERE *IS* SHE?
NONE OF THAT MATTERS.
WE'RE HERE TO TELL YOU YOU'RE SUPPORTING THE WRONG SANDWING. BURN ISN'T GOING TO BE QUEEN. LIKE THE PROPHECY SAYS, SHE'S GOING TO DIE.
WE'VE CHOSEN BLISTER.

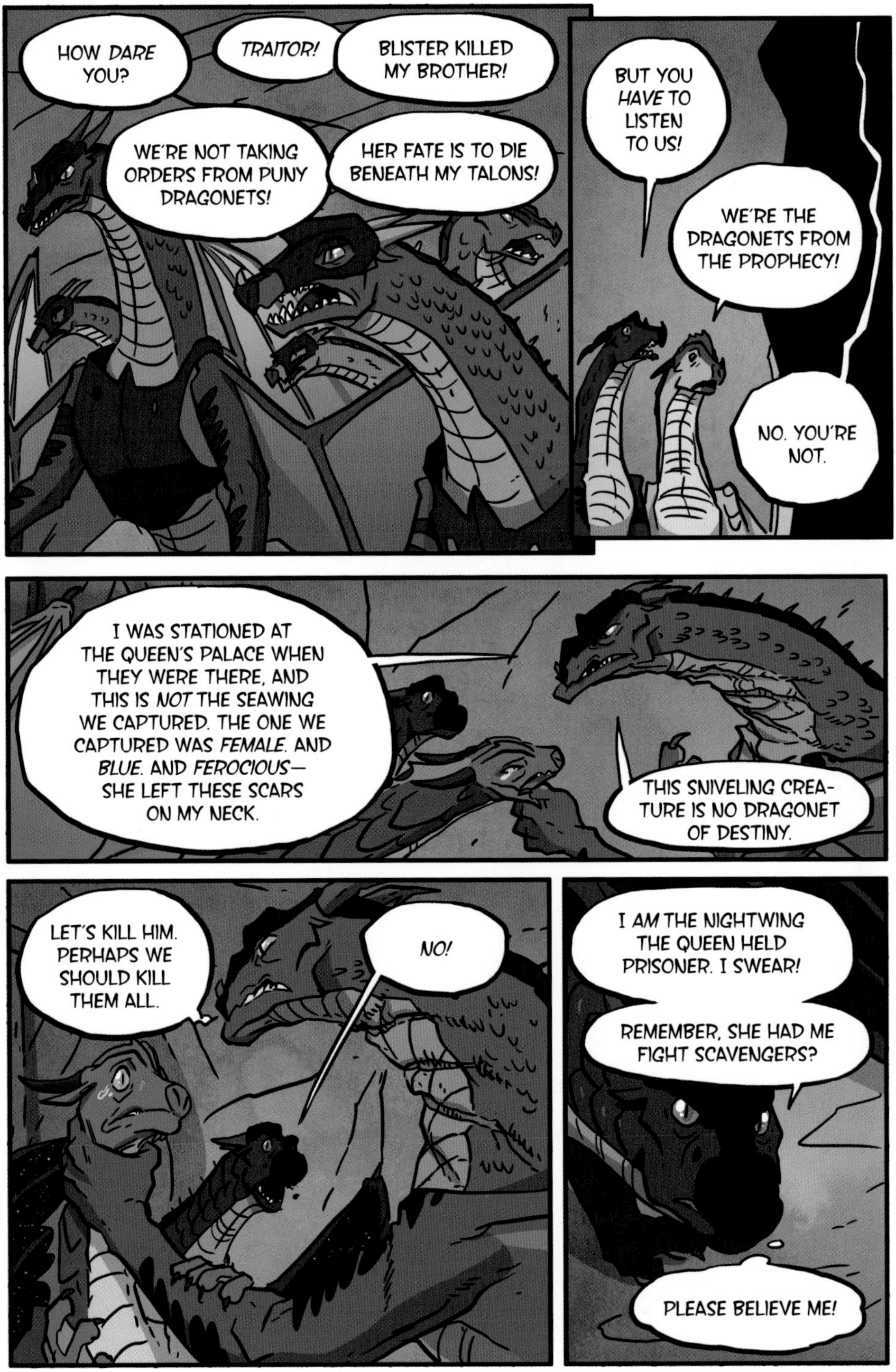
HOW *DARE* YOU?
TRAITOR!
BLISTER KILLED MY BROTHER!
WE'RE NOT TAKING ORDERS FROM PUNY DRAGONETS!
HER FATE IS TO DIE BENEATH MY TALONS!
BUT YOU *HAVE* TO LISTEN TO US!
WE'RE THE DRAGONETS FROM THE PROPHECY!
NO. YOU'RE NOT.
I WAS STATIONED AT THE QUEEN'S PALACE WHEN THEY WERE THERE, AND THIS IS *NOT* THE SEAWING WE CAPTURED. THE ONE WE CAPTURED WAS *FEMALE*. AND *BLUE*. AND *FEROCIOUS*—SHE LEFT THESE SCARS ON MY NECK.
THIS SNIVELING CREATURE IS NO DRAGONET OF DESTINY.
LET'S KILL HIM. PERHAPS WE SHOULD KILL THEM ALL.
NO!
I *AM* THE NIGHTWING THE QUEEN HELD PRISONER. I SWEAR!
REMEMBER, SHE HAD ME FIGHT SCAVENGERS?
PLEASE BELIEVE ME!

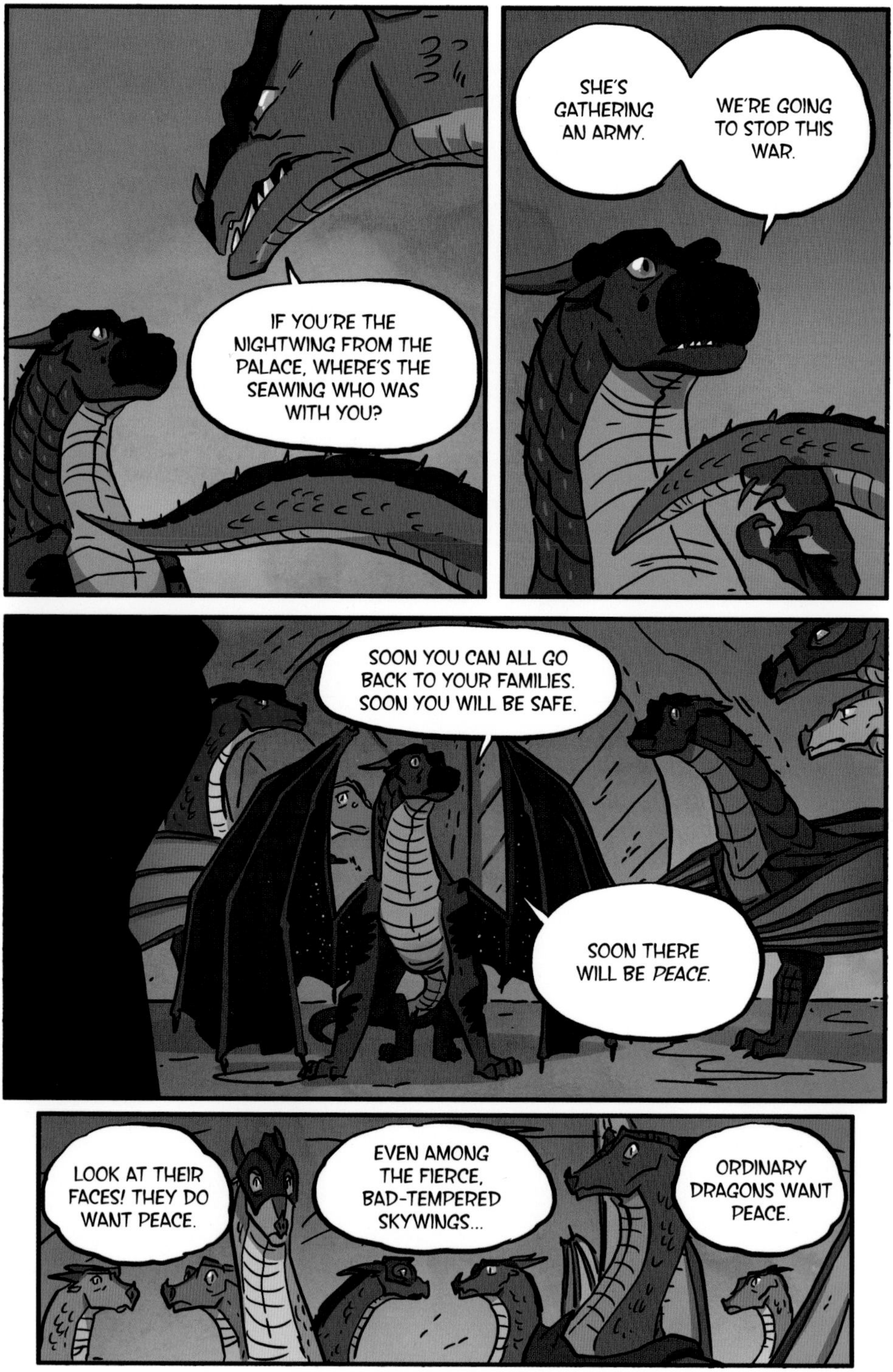

IF YOU'RE THE NIGHTWING FROM THE PALACE, WHERE'S THE SEAWING WHO WAS WITH YOU?
SHE'S GATHERING AN ARMY.
WE'RE GOING TO STOP THIS WAR.
SOON YOU CAN ALL GO BACK TO YOUR FAMILIES. SOON YOU WILL BE SAFE.
SOON THERE WILL BE *PEACE*.
LOOK AT THEIR FACES! THEY DO WANT PEACE.
EVEN AMONG THE FIERCE, BAD-TEMPERED SKYWINGS...
ORDINARY DRAGONS WANT PEACE.

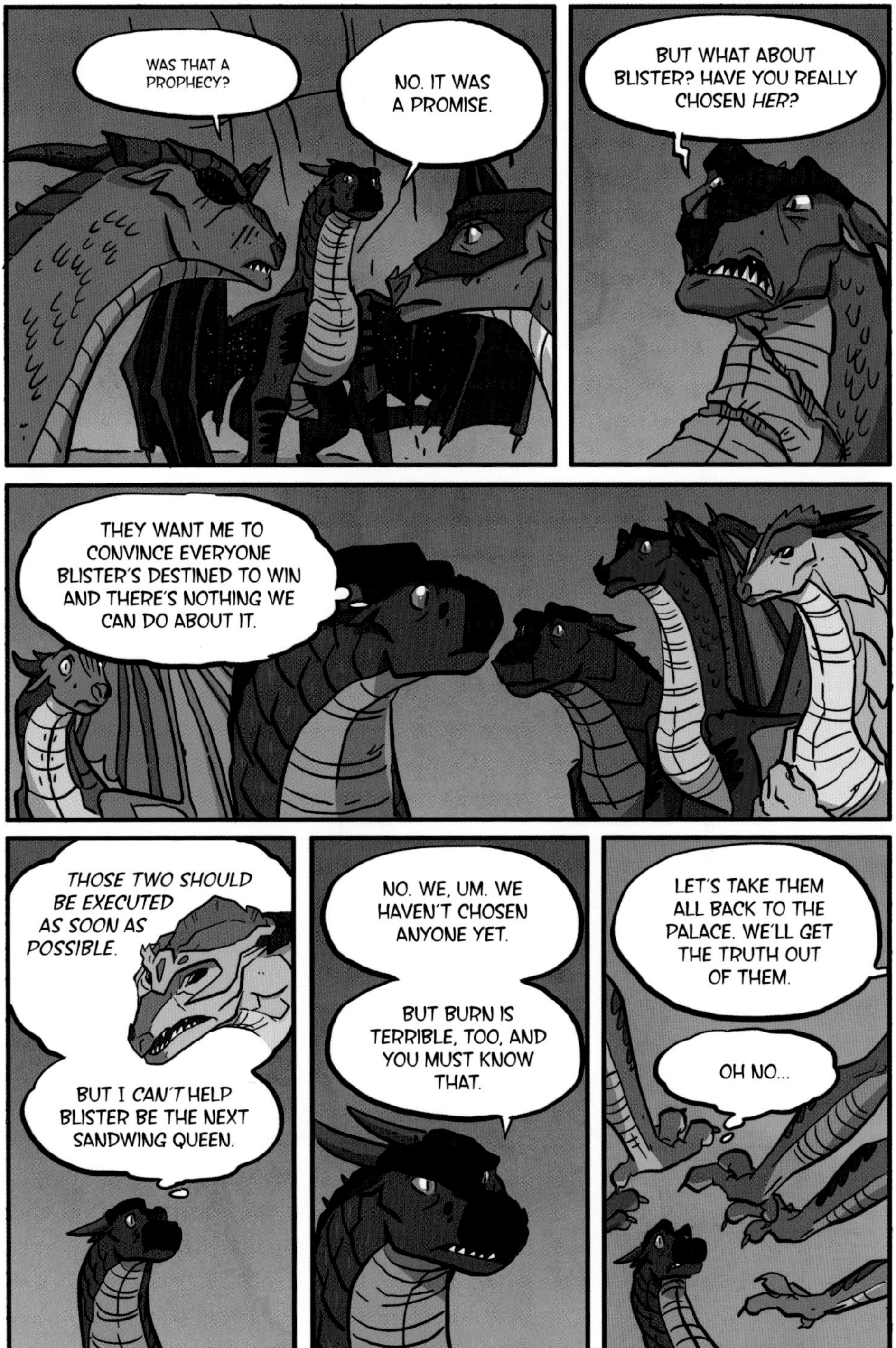
WAS THAT A PROPHECY?
NO. IT WAS A PROMISE.
BUT WHAT ABOUT BLISTER? HAVE YOU REALLY CHOSEN *HER*?
THEY WANT ME TO CONVINCE EVERYONE BLISTER'S DESTINED TO WIN AND THERE'S NOTHING WE CAN DO ABOUT IT.
THOSE TWO SHOULD BE EXECUTED AS SOON AS POSSIBLE.
BUT I *CAN'T* HELP BLISTER BE THE NEXT SANDWING QUEEN.
NO. WE, UM. WE HAVEN'T CHOSEN ANYONE YET.
BUT BURN IS TERRIBLE, TOO, AND YOU MUST KNOW THAT.
LET'S TAKE THEM ALL BACK TO THE PALACE. WE'LL GET THE TRUTH OUT OF THEM.
OH NO...

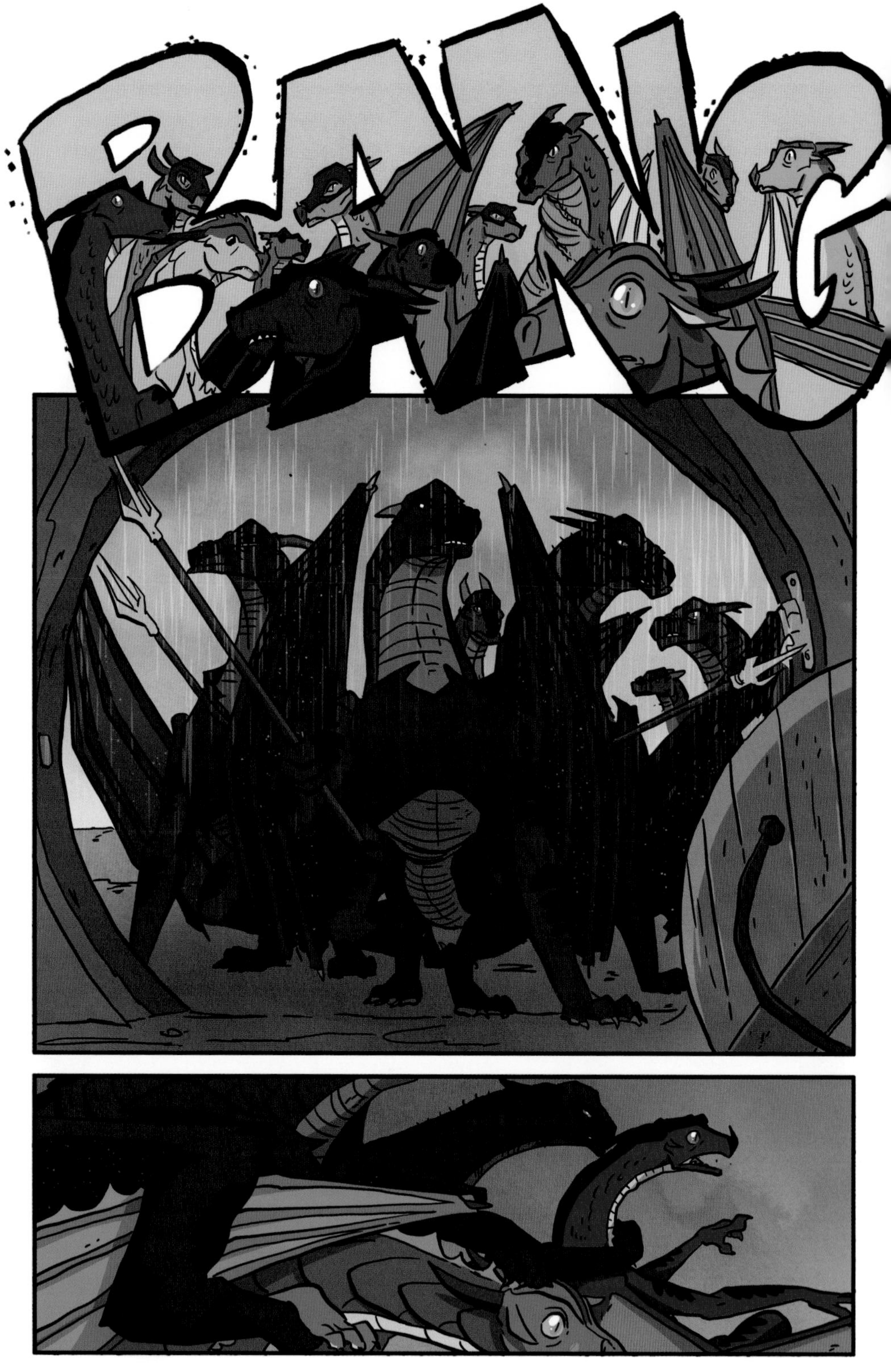
BANG

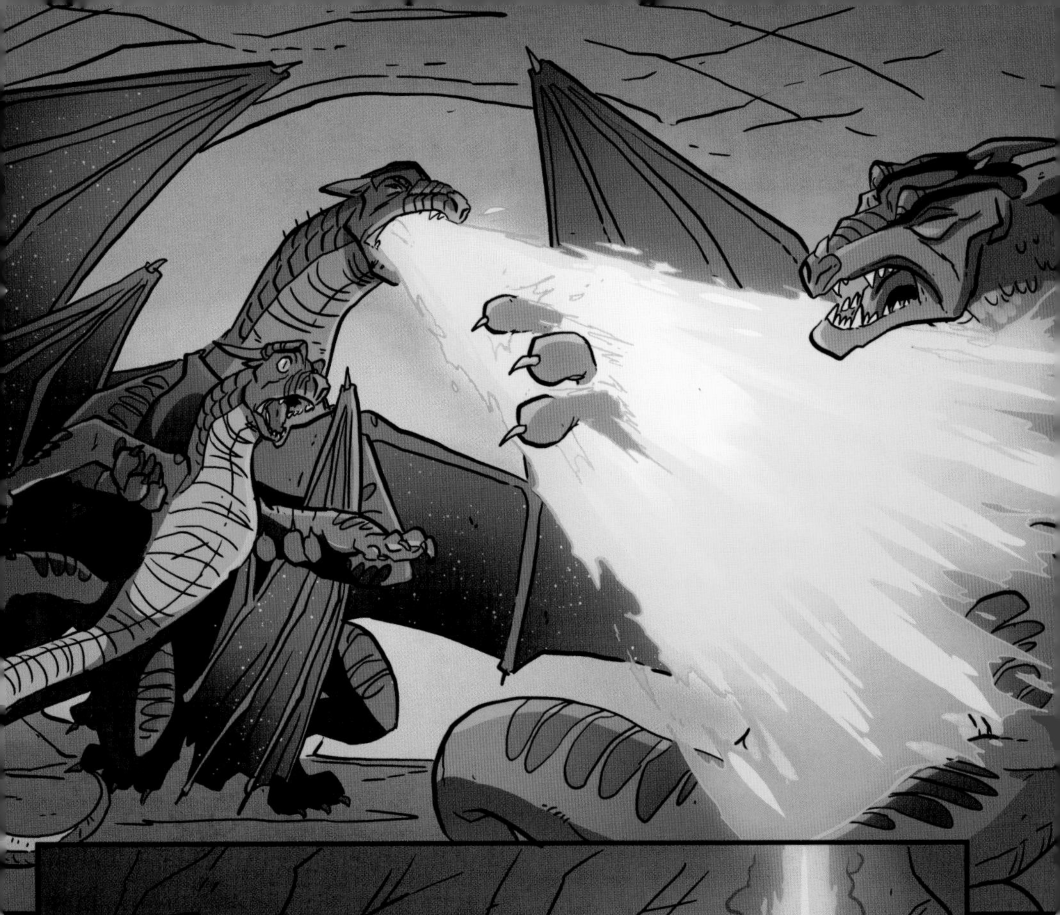

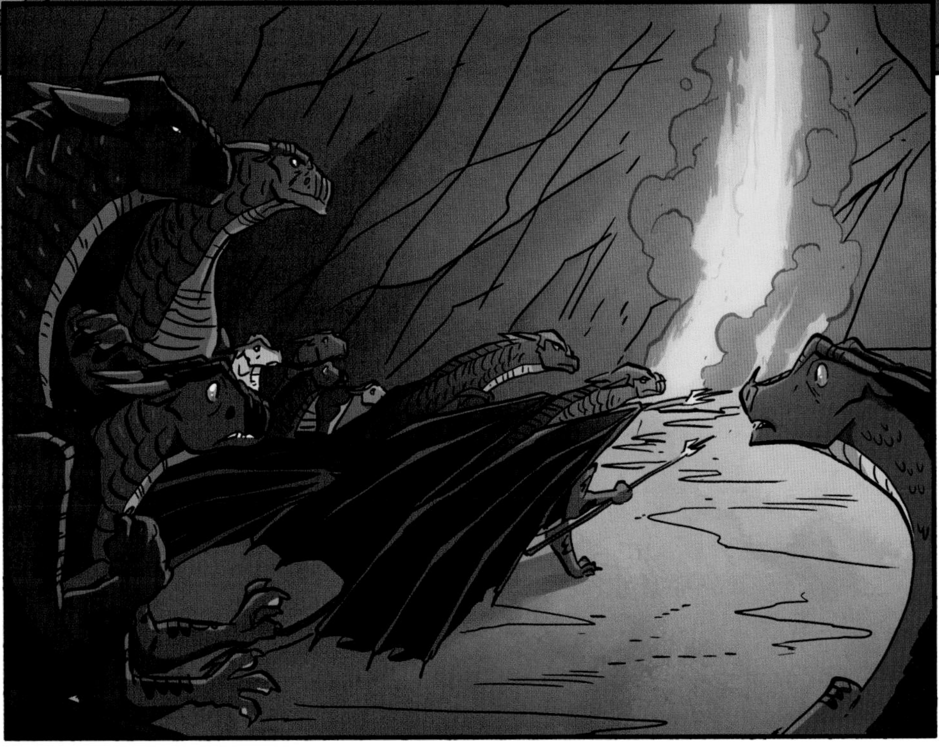

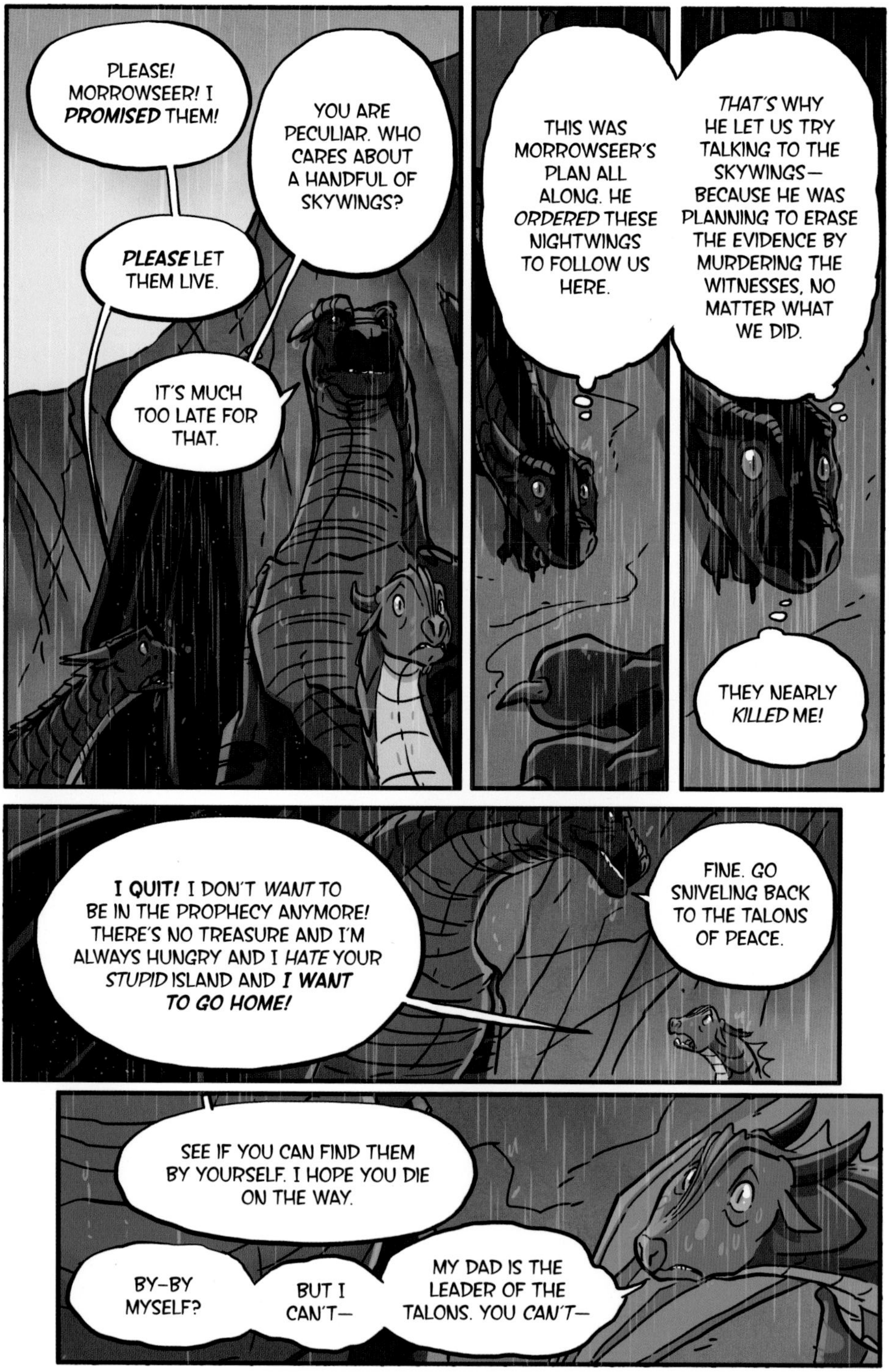
PLEASE! MORROWSEER! I ***PROMISED*** THEM!
YOU ARE PECULIAR. WHO CARES ABOUT A HANDFUL OF SKYWINGS?
PLEASE LET THEM LIVE.
IT'S MUCH TOO LATE FOR THAT.
THIS WAS MORROWSEER'S PLAN ALL ALONG. HE *ORDERED* THESE NIGHTWINGS TO FOLLOW US HERE.
THAT'S WHY HE LET US TRY TALKING TO THE SKYWINGS— BECAUSE HE WAS PLANNING TO ERASE THE EVIDENCE BY MURDERING THE WITNESSES, NO MATTER WHAT WE DID.
THEY NEARLY *KILLED* ME!
I QUIT! I DON'T *WANT* TO BE IN THE PROPHECY ANYMORE! THERE'S NO TREASURE AND I'M ALWAYS HUNGRY AND I *HATE* YOUR *STUPID* ISLAND AND ***I WANT TO GO HOME!***
FINE. GO SNIVELING BACK TO THE TALONS OF PEACE.
SEE IF YOU CAN FIND THEM BY YOURSELF. I HOPE YOU DIE ON THE WAY.
BY—BY MYSELF?
BUT I CAN'T—
MY DAD IS THE LEADER OF THE TALONS. YOU *CAN'T*—

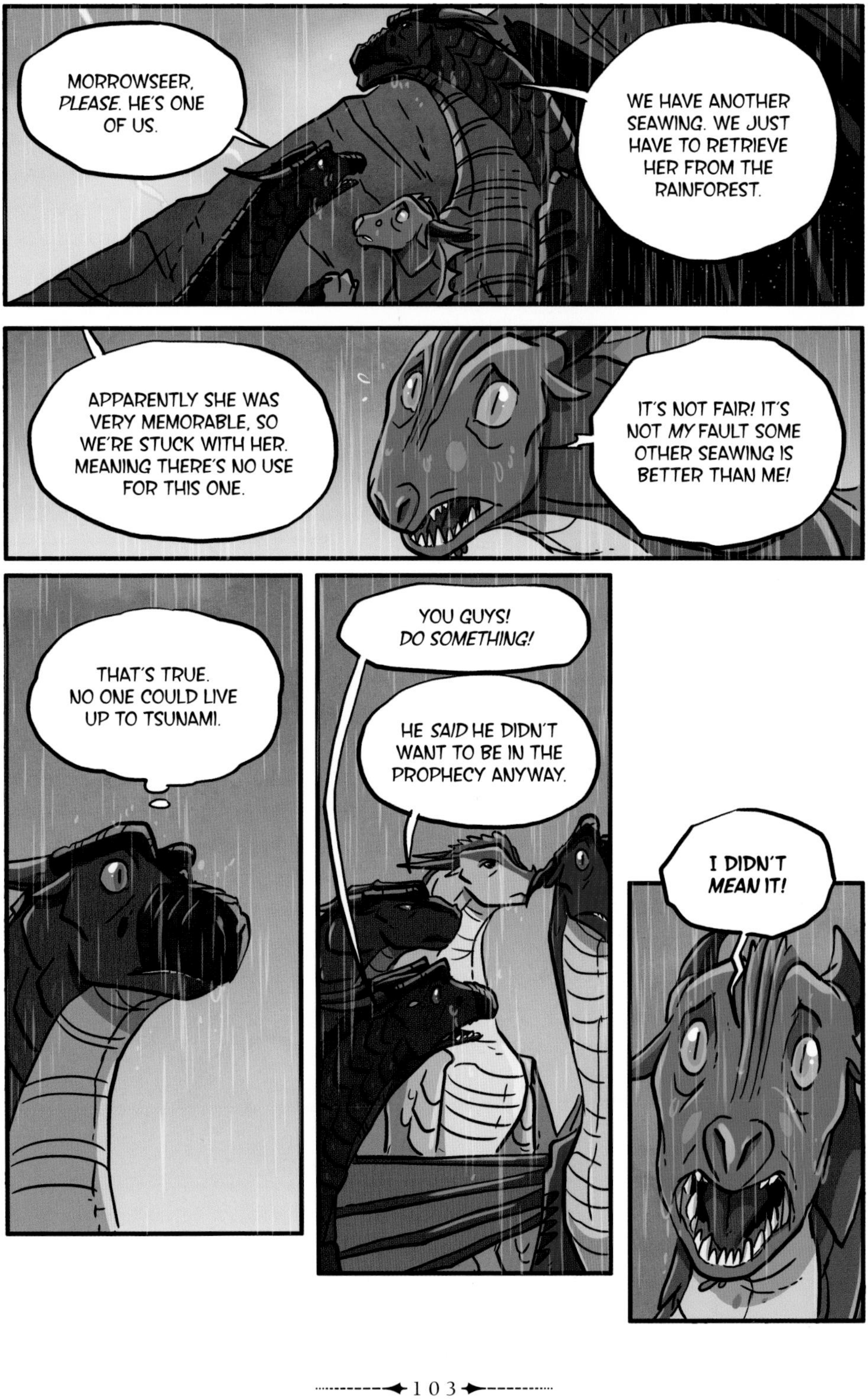
MORROWSEER, PLEASE. HE'S ONE OF US.
WE HAVE ANOTHER SEAWING. WE JUST HAVE TO RETRIEVE HER FROM THE RAINFOREST.
APPARENTLY SHE WAS VERY MEMORABLE, SO WE'RE STUCK WITH HER. MEANING THERE'S NO USE FOR THIS ONE.
IT'S NOT FAIR! IT'S NOT MY FAULT SOME OTHER SEAWING IS BETTER THAN ME!
THAT'S TRUE. NO ONE COULD LIVE UP TO TSUNAMI.
YOU GUYS! DO SOMETHING!
HE SAID HE DIDN'T WANT TO BE IN THE PROPHECY ANYWAY.
I DIDN'T MEAN IT!

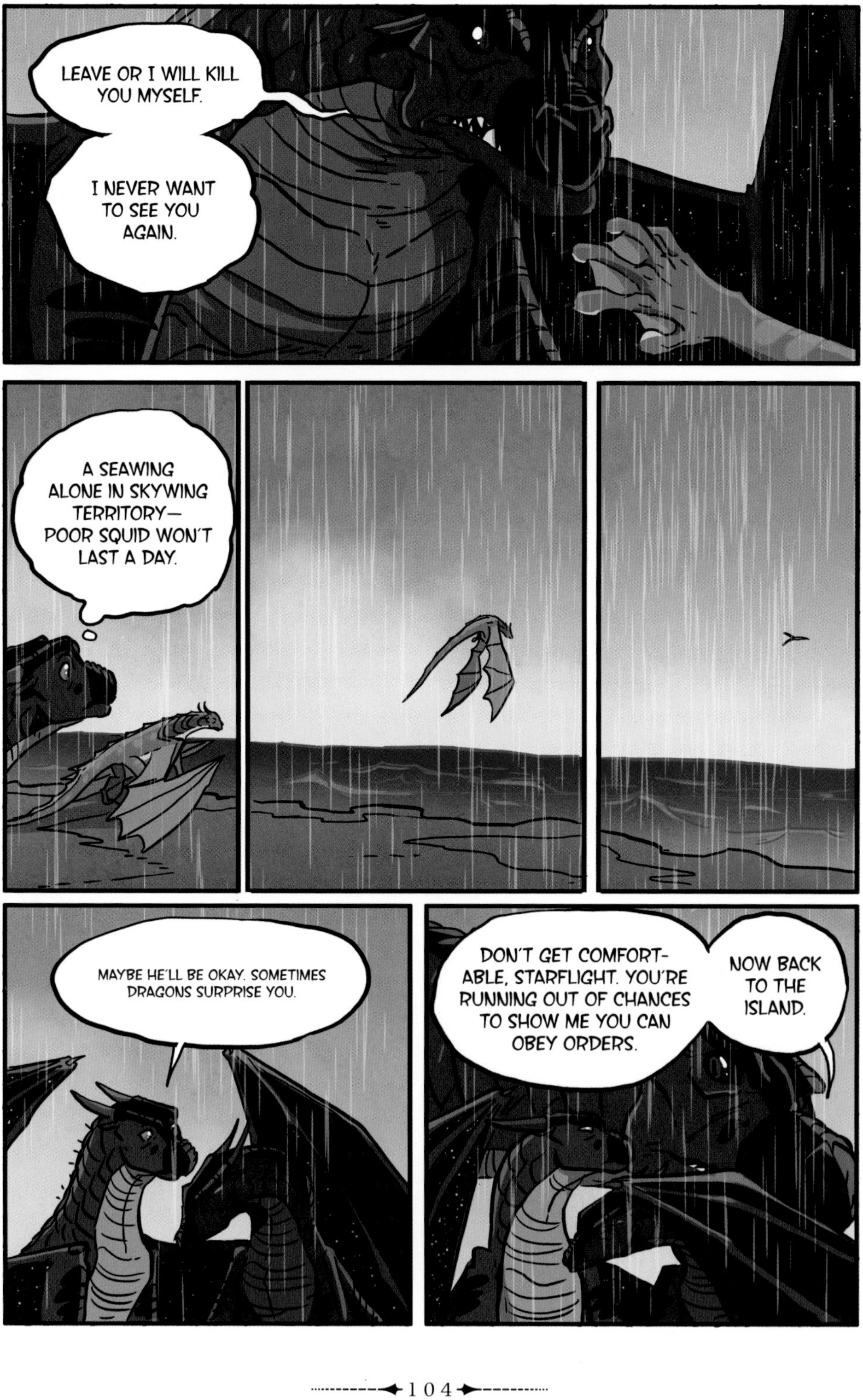
LEAVE OR I WILL KILL YOU MYSELF.
I NEVER WANT TO SEE YOU AGAIN.
A SEAWING ALONE IN SKYWING TERRITORY— POOR SQUID WON'T LAST A DAY.
MAYBE HE'LL BE OKAY. SOMETIMES DRAGONS SURPRISE YOU.
DON'T GET COMFORT-ABLE, STARFLIGHT. YOU'RE RUNNING OUT OF CHANCES TO SHOW ME YOU CAN OBEY ORDERS.
NOW BACK TO THE ISLAND.

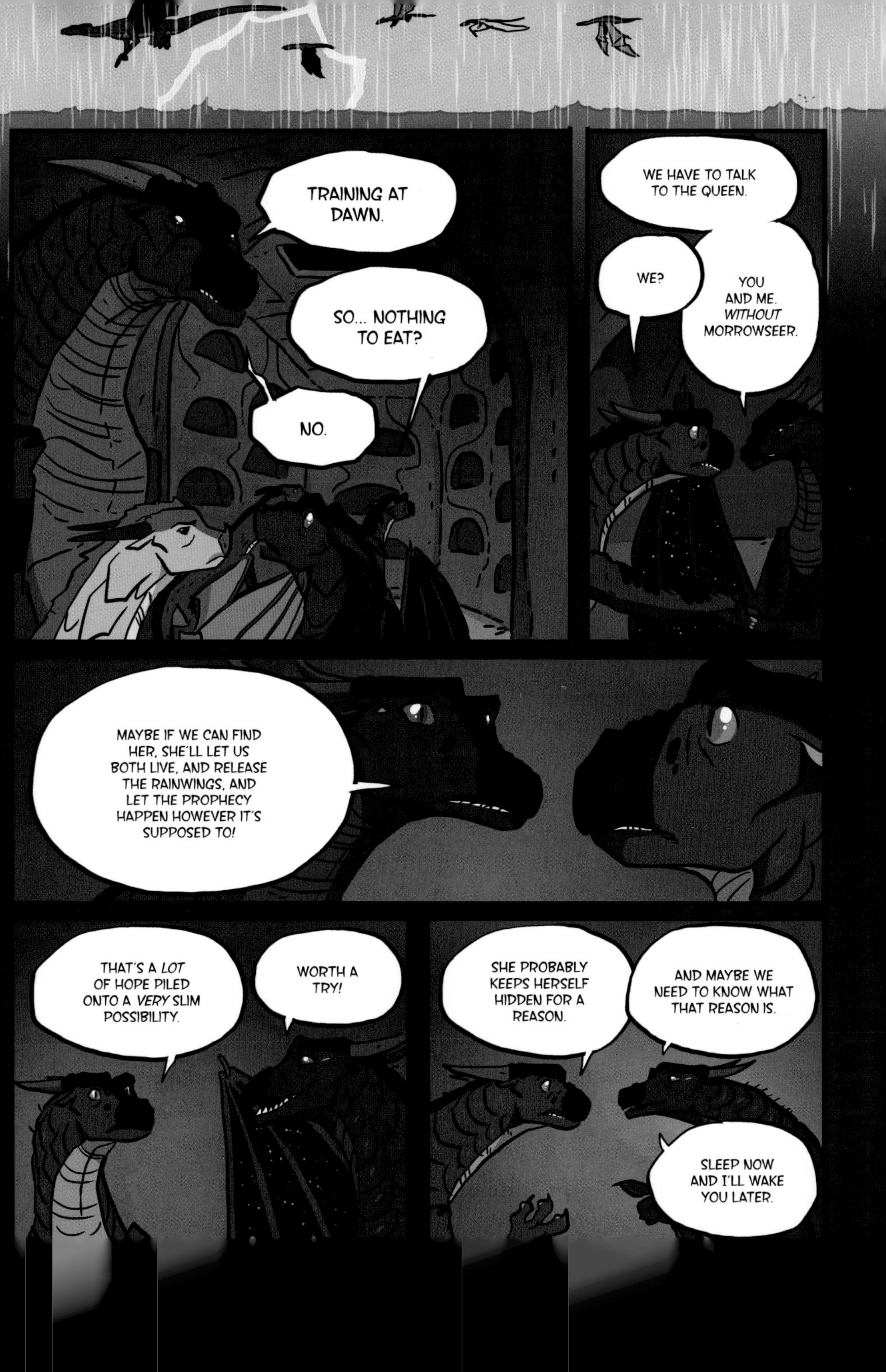

TRAINING AT DAWN.
SO... NOTHING TO EAT?
NO.
WE HAVE TO TALK TO THE QUEEN.
WE?
YOU AND ME. *WITHOUT* MORROWSEER.
MAYBE IF WE CAN FIND HER, SHE'LL LET US BOTH LIVE, AND RELEASE THE RAINWINGS, AND LET THE PROPHECY HAPPEN HOWEVER IT'S SUPPOSED TO!
THAT'S A *LOT* OF HOPE PILED ONTO A *VERY* SLIM POSSIBILITY.
WORTH A TRY!
SHE PROBABLY KEEPS HERSELF HIDDEN FOR A REASON.
AND MAYBE WE NEED TO KNOW WHAT THAT REASON IS.
SLEEP NOW AND I'LL WAKE YOU LATER.

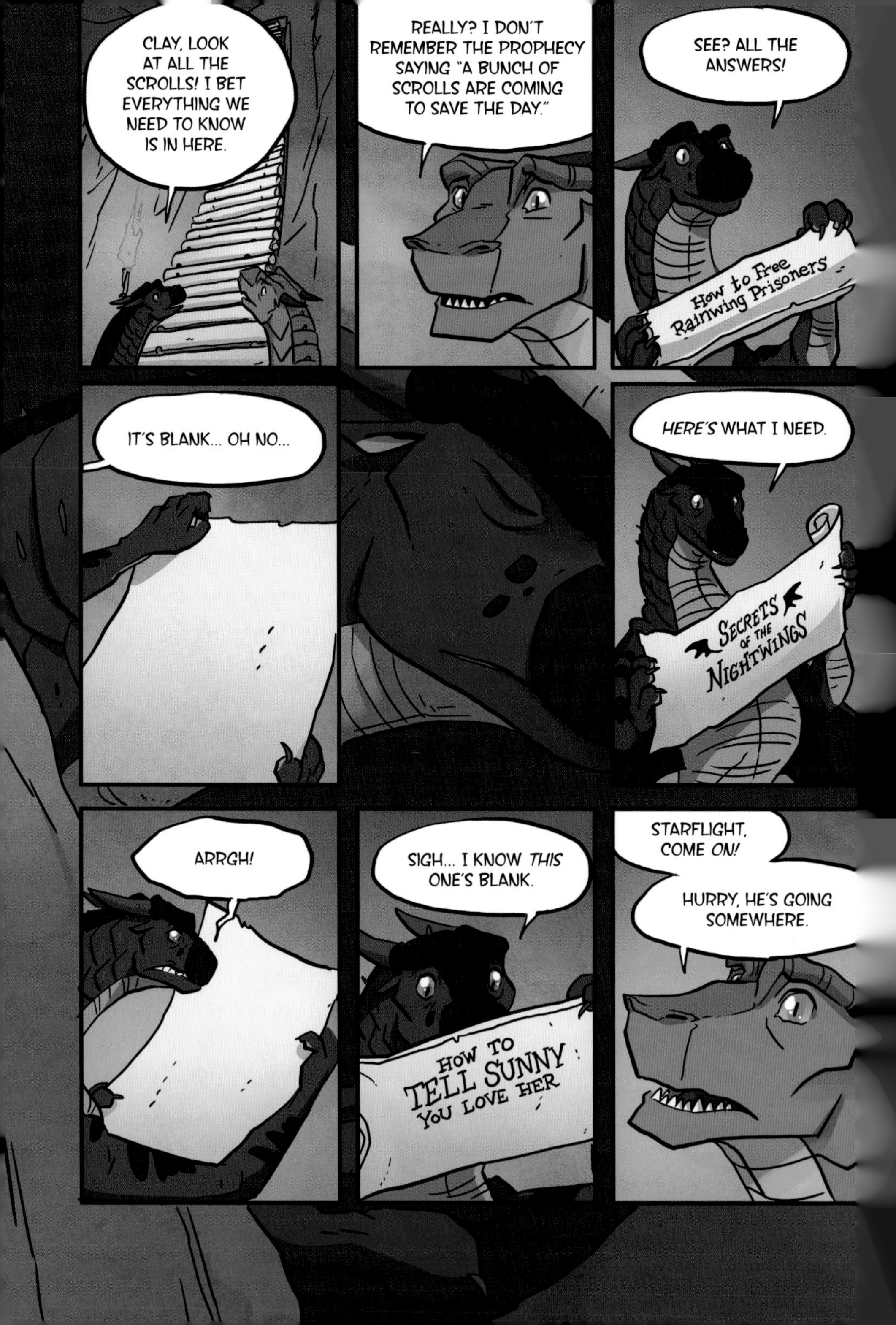
CLAY, LOOK AT ALL THE SCROLLS! I BET EVERYTHING WE NEED TO KNOW IS IN HERE.
REALLY? I DON'T REMEMBER THE PROPHECY SAYING "A BUNCH OF SCROLLS ARE COMING TO SAVE THE DAY."
SEE? ALL THE ANSWERS!
How to Free Rainwing Prisoners
IT'S BLANK... OH NO...
HERE'S WHAT I NEED.
SECRETS OF THE NIGHTWINGS
ARRGH!
SIGH... I KNOW *THIS* ONE'S BLANK.
HOW TO TELL SUNNY YOU LOVE HER
STARFLIGHT, COME *ON!*
HURRY, HE'S GOING SOMEWHERE.

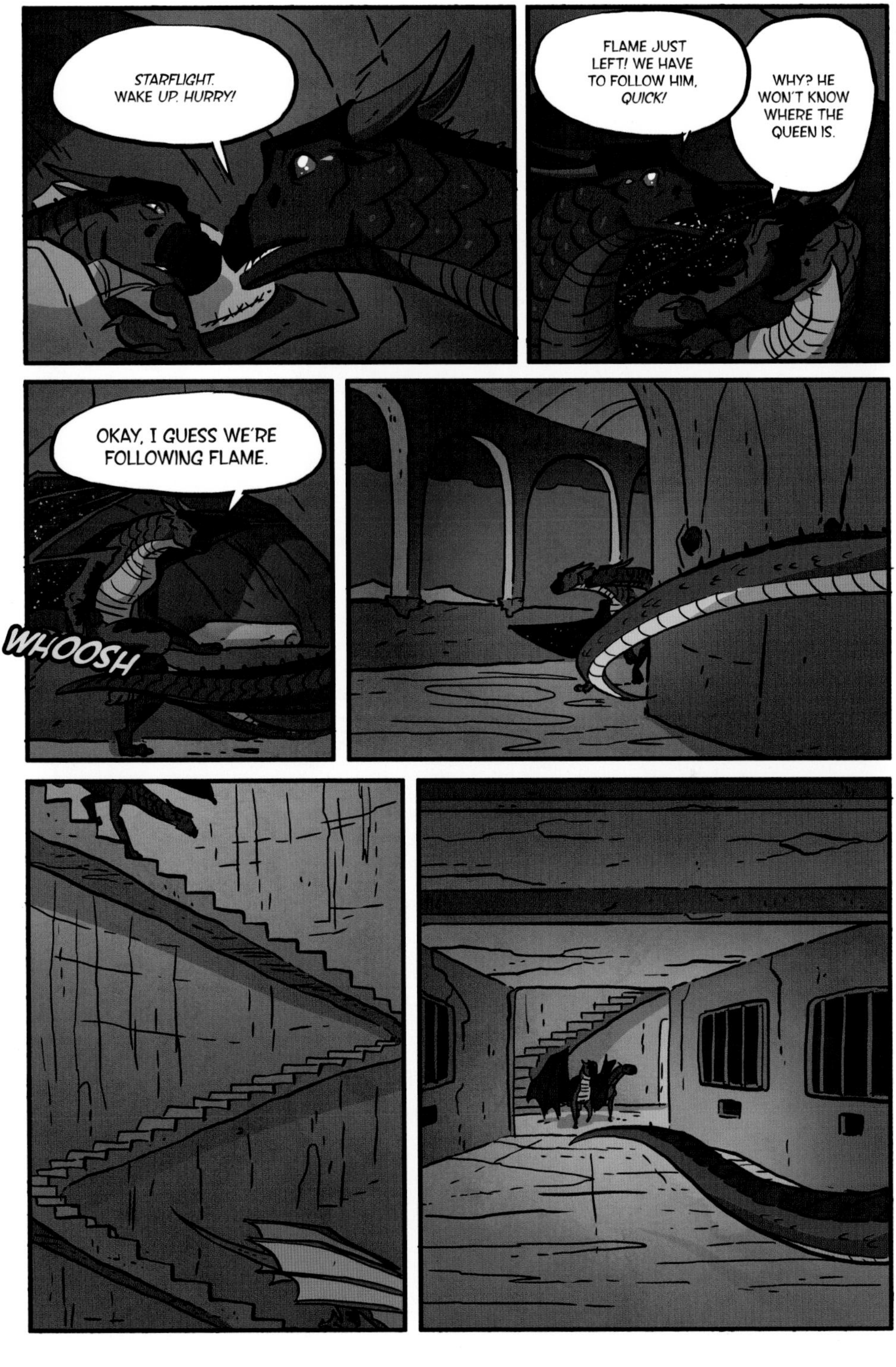
STARFLIGHT. WAKE UP. HURRY!
FLAME JUST LEFT! WE HAVE TO FOLLOW HIM, QUICK!
WHY? HE WON'T KNOW WHERE THE QUEEN IS.
OKAY, I GUESS WE'RE FOLLOWING FLAME.
WHOOSH

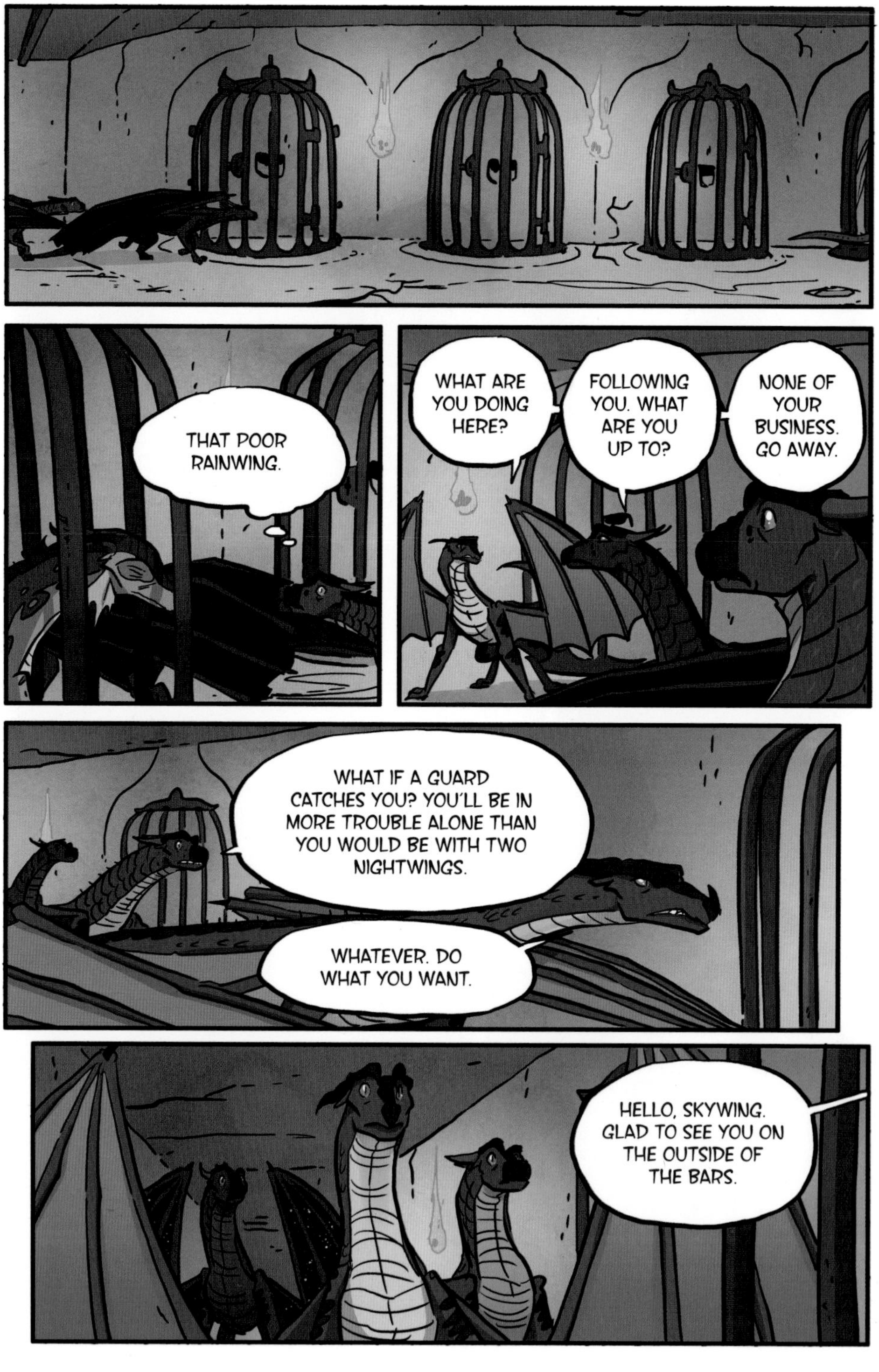
THAT POOR RAINWING.
WHAT ARE YOU DOING HERE?
FOLLOWING YOU. WHAT ARE YOU UP TO?
NONE OF YOUR BUSINESS. GO AWAY.
WHAT IF A GUARD CATCHES YOU? YOU'LL BE IN MORE TROUBLE ALONE THAN YOU WOULD BE WITH TWO NIGHTWINGS.
WHATEVER. DO WHAT YOU WANT.
HELLO, SKYWING. GLAD TO SEE YOU ON THE OUTSIDE OF THE BARS.

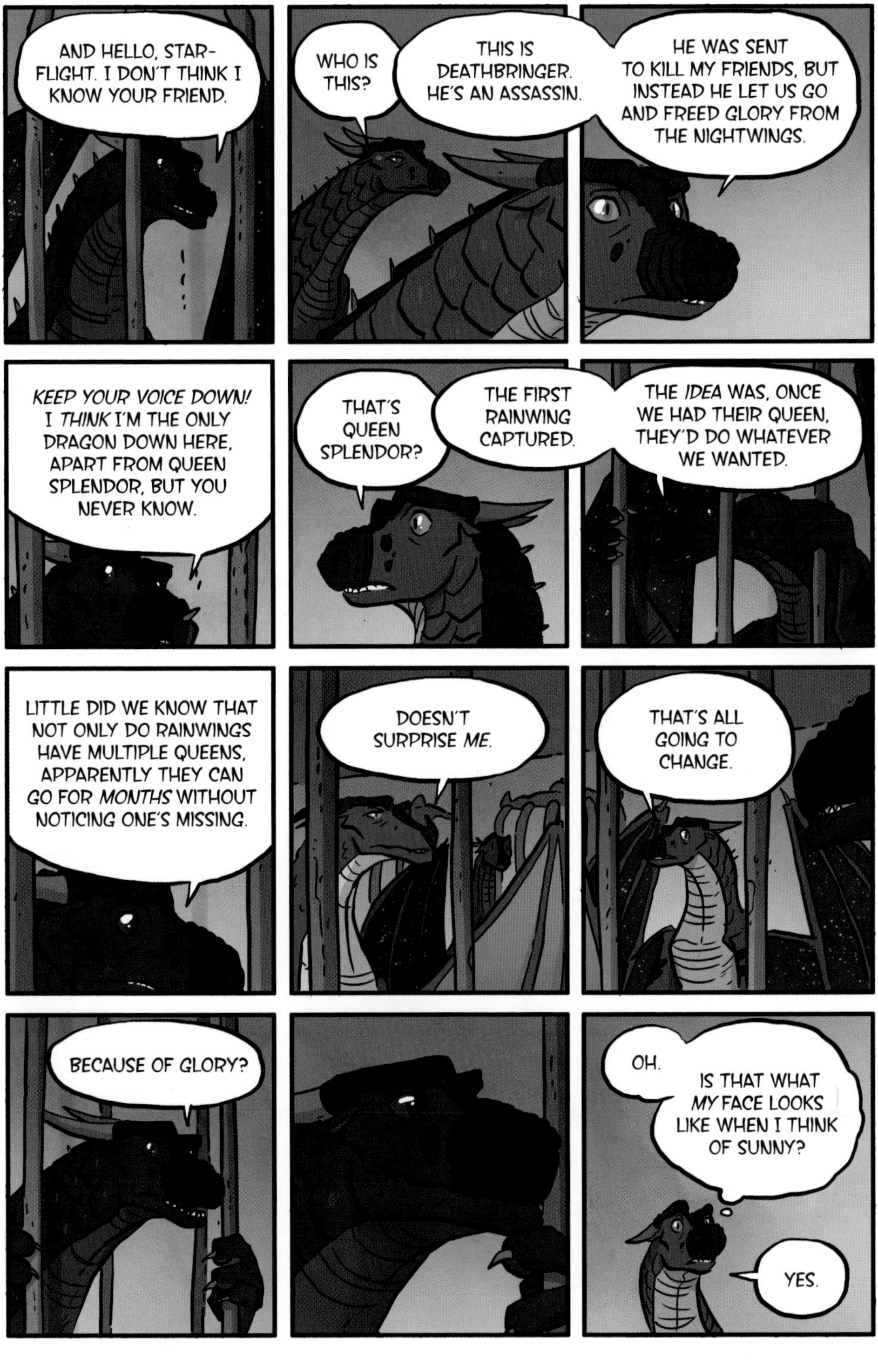
AND HELLO, STARFLIGHT. I DON'T THINK I KNOW YOUR FRIEND.
WHO IS THIS?
THIS IS DEATHBRINGER. HE'S AN ASSASSIN.
HE WAS SENT TO KILL MY FRIENDS, BUT INSTEAD HE LET US GO AND FREED GLORY FROM THE NIGHTWINGS.
KEEP YOUR VOICE DOWN! I *THINK* I'M THE ONLY DRAGON DOWN HERE, APART FROM QUEEN SPLENDOR, BUT YOU NEVER KNOW.
THAT'S QUEEN SPLENDOR?
THE FIRST RAINWING CAPTURED.
THE *IDEA* WAS, ONCE WE HAD THEIR QUEEN, THEY'D DO WHATEVER WE WANTED.
LITTLE DID WE KNOW THAT NOT ONLY DO RAINWINGS HAVE MULTIPLE QUEENS, APPARENTLY THEY CAN GO FOR *MONTHS* WITHOUT NOTICING ONE'S MISSING.
DOESN'T SURPRISE *ME*.
THAT'S ALL GOING TO CHANGE.
BECAUSE OF GLORY?
OH.
IS THAT WHAT *MY* FACE LOOKS LIKE WHEN I THINK OF SUNNY?
YES.

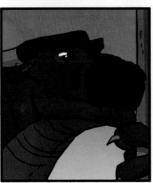

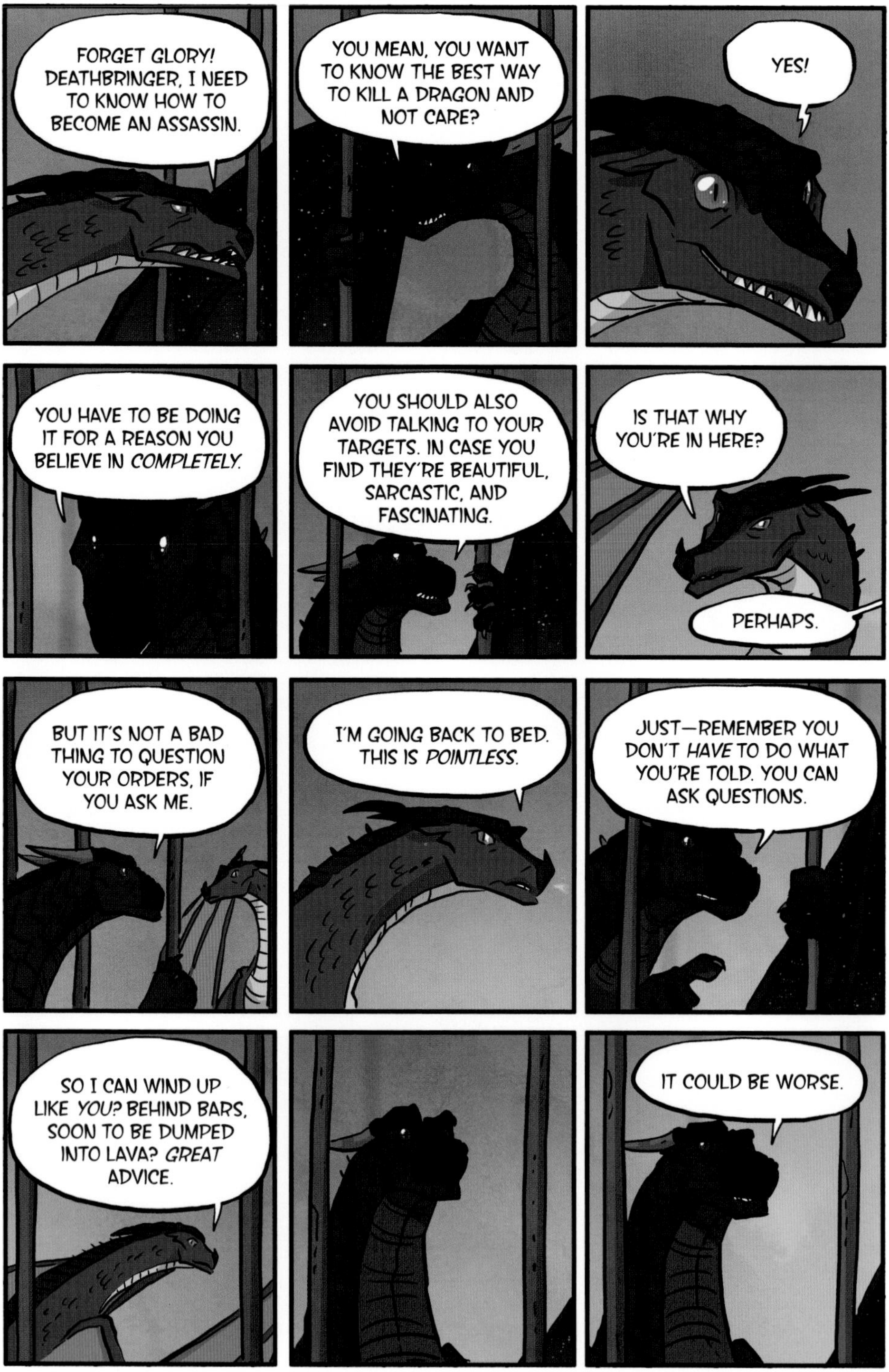
FORGET GLORY! DEATHBRINGER, I NEED TO KNOW HOW TO BECOME AN ASSASSIN.
YOU MEAN, YOU WANT TO KNOW THE BEST WAY TO KILL A DRAGON AND NOT CARE?
YES!
YOU HAVE TO BE DOING IT FOR A REASON YOU BELIEVE IN *COMPLETELY.*
YOU SHOULD ALSO AVOID TALKING TO YOUR TARGETS. IN CASE YOU FIND THEY'RE BEAUTIFUL, SARCASTIC, AND FASCINATING.
IS THAT WHY YOU'RE IN HERE?
PERHAPS.
BUT IT'S NOT A BAD THING TO QUESTION YOUR ORDERS, IF YOU ASK ME.
I'M GOING BACK TO BED. THIS IS *POINTLESS.*
JUST—REMEMBER YOU DON'T *HAVE* TO DO WHAT YOU'RE TOLD. YOU CAN ASK QUESTIONS.
SO I CAN WIND UP LIKE *YOU?* BEHIND BARS, SOON TO BE DUMPED INTO LAVA? *GREAT* ADVICE.
IT COULD BE WORSE.

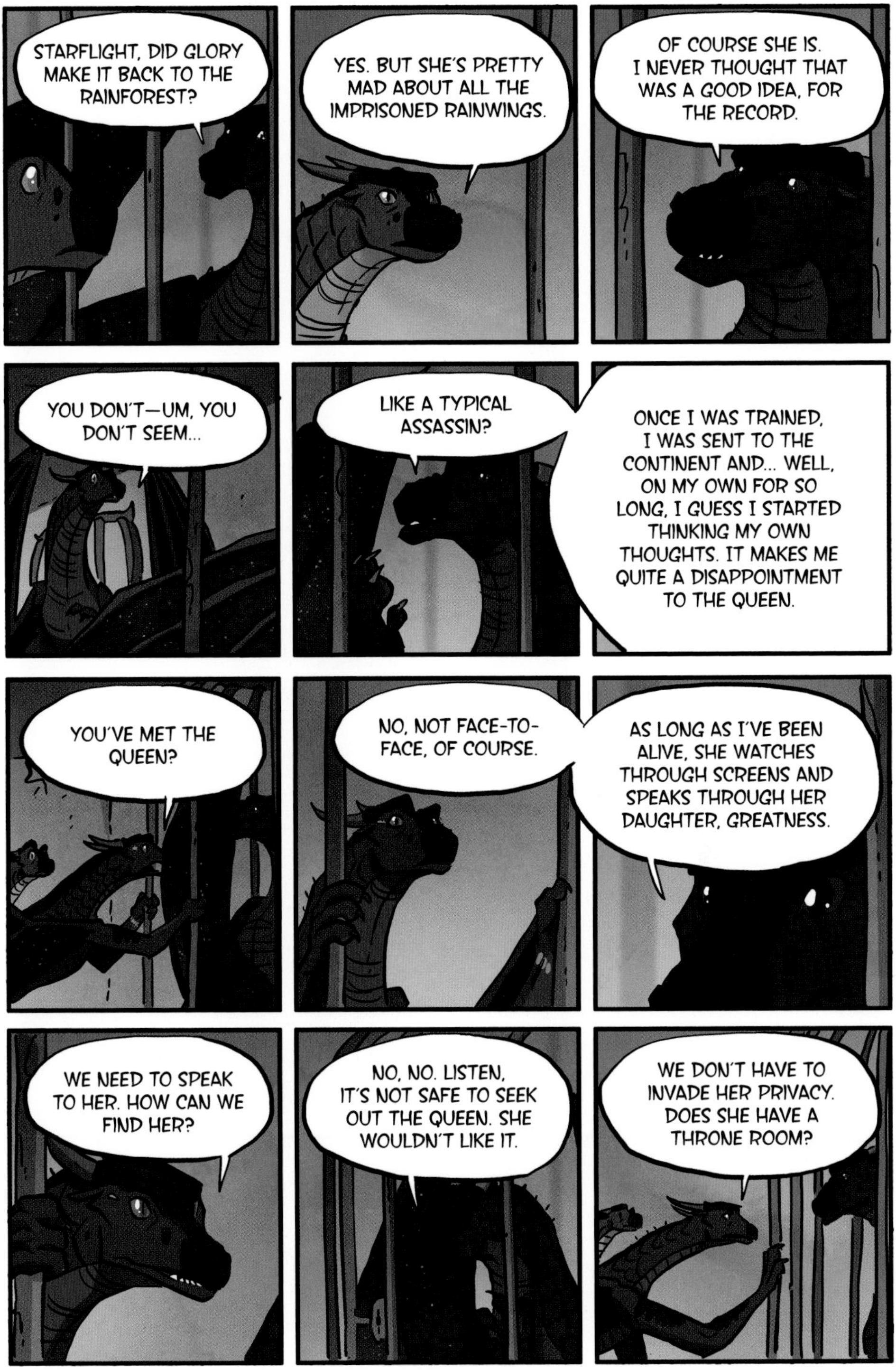
STARFLIGHT, DID GLORY MAKE IT BACK TO THE RAINFOREST?
YES. BUT SHE'S PRETTY MAD ABOUT ALL THE IMPRISONED RAINWINGS.
OF COURSE SHE IS. I NEVER THOUGHT THAT WAS A GOOD IDEA, FOR THE RECORD.
YOU DON'T—UM, YOU DON'T SEEM...
LIKE A TYPICAL ASSASSIN?
ONCE I WAS TRAINED, I WAS SENT TO THE CONTINENT AND... WELL, ON MY OWN FOR SO LONG, I GUESS I STARTED THINKING MY OWN THOUGHTS. IT MAKES ME QUITE A DISAPPOINTMENT TO THE QUEEN.
YOU'VE MET THE QUEEN?
NO, NOT FACE-TO-FACE, OF COURSE.
AS LONG AS I'VE BEEN ALIVE, SHE WATCHES THROUGH SCREENS AND SPEAKS THROUGH HER DAUGHTER, GREATNESS.
WE NEED TO SPEAK TO HER. HOW CAN WE FIND HER?
NO, NO. LISTEN, IT'S NOT SAFE TO SEEK OUT THE QUEEN. SHE WOULDN'T LIKE IT.
WE DON'T HAVE TO INVADE HER PRIVACY. DOES SHE HAVE A THRONE ROOM?

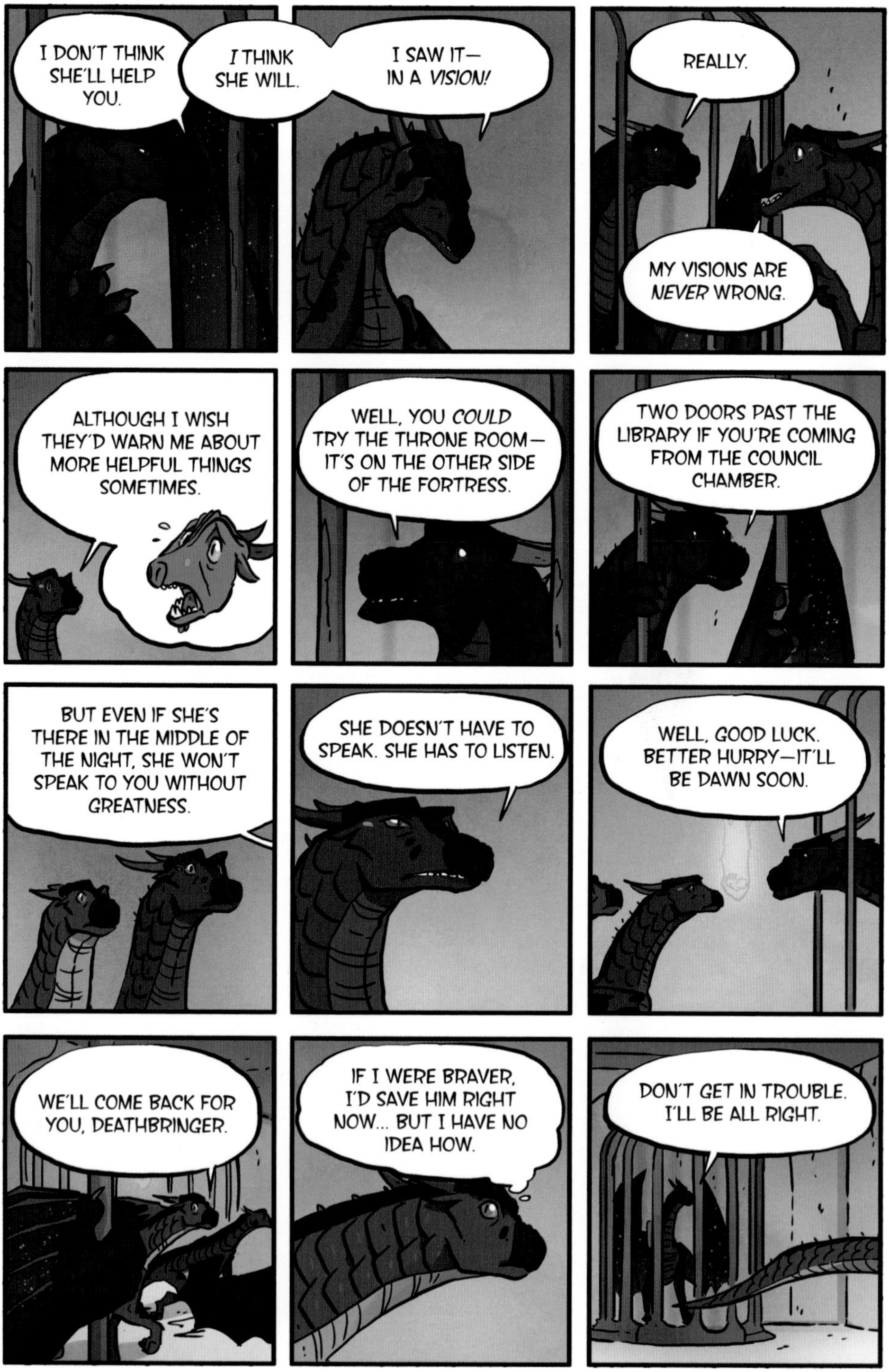
I DON'T THINK SHE'LL HELP YOU.
I THINK SHE WILL.
I SAW IT— IN A *VISION!*
REALLY.
MY VISIONS ARE *NEVER* WRONG.
ALTHOUGH I WISH THEY'D WARN ME ABOUT MORE HELPFUL THINGS SOMETIMES.
WELL, YOU *COULD* TRY THE THRONE ROOM— IT'S ON THE OTHER SIDE OF THE FORTRESS.
TWO DOORS PAST THE LIBRARY IF YOU'RE COMING FROM THE COUNCIL CHAMBER.
BUT EVEN IF SHE'S THERE IN THE MIDDLE OF THE NIGHT, SHE WON'T SPEAK TO YOU WITHOUT GREATNESS.
SHE DOESN'T HAVE TO SPEAK. SHE HAS TO LISTEN.
WELL, GOOD LUCK. BETTER HURRY—IT'LL BE DAWN SOON.
WE'LL COME BACK FOR YOU, DEATHBRINGER.
IF I WERE BRAVER, I'D SAVE HIM RIGHT NOW... BUT I HAVE NO IDEA HOW.
DON'T GET IN TROUBLE. I'LL BE ALL RIGHT.

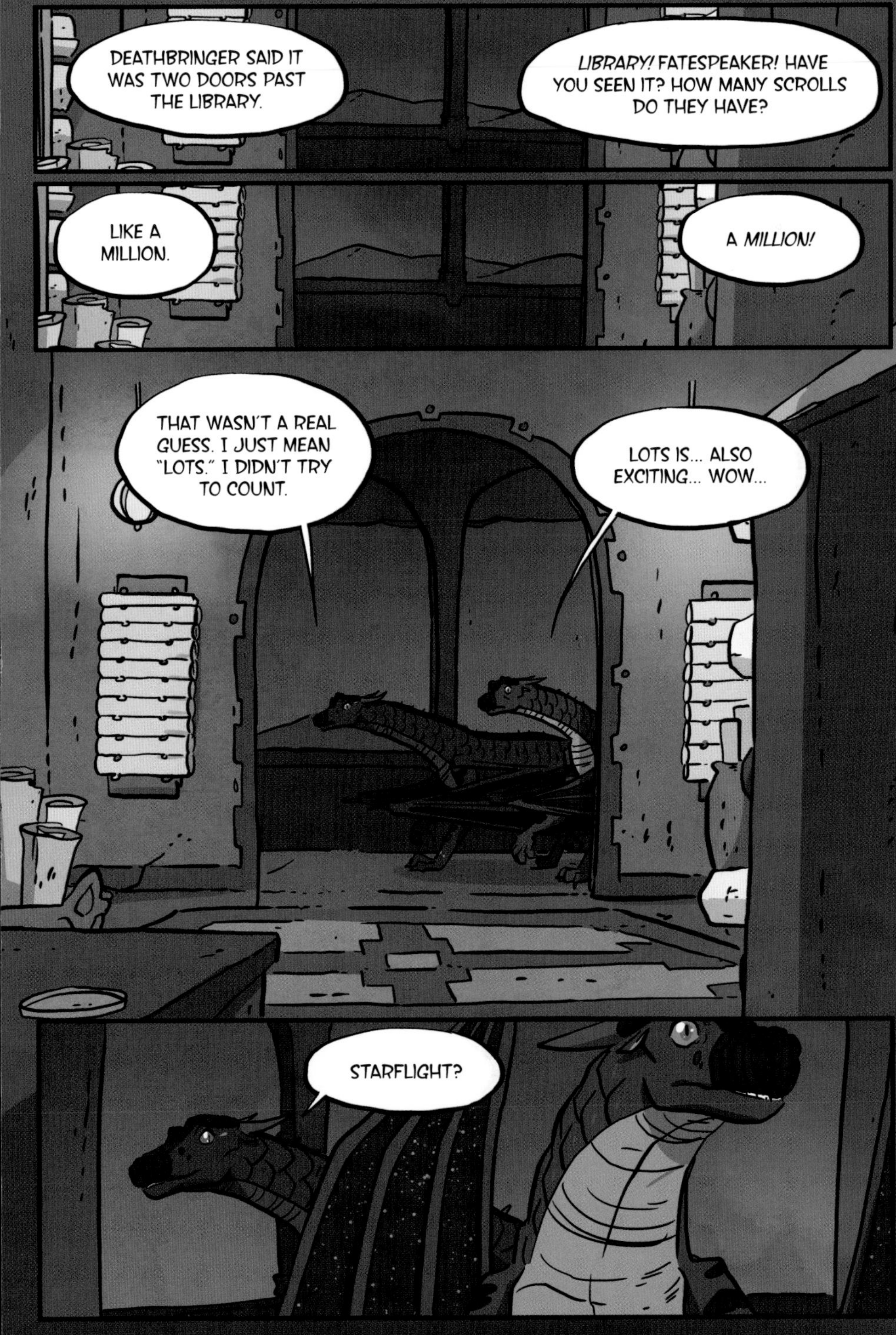
DEATHBRINGER SAID IT WAS TWO DOORS PAST THE LIBRARY.
LIBRARY! FATESPEAKER! HAVE YOU SEEN IT? HOW MANY SCROLLS DO THEY HAVE?
LIKE A MILLION.
A *MILLION!*
THAT WASN'T A REAL GUESS. I JUST MEAN "LOTS." I DIDN'T TRY TO COUNT.
LOTS IS... ALSO EXCITING... WOW...
STARFLIGHT?

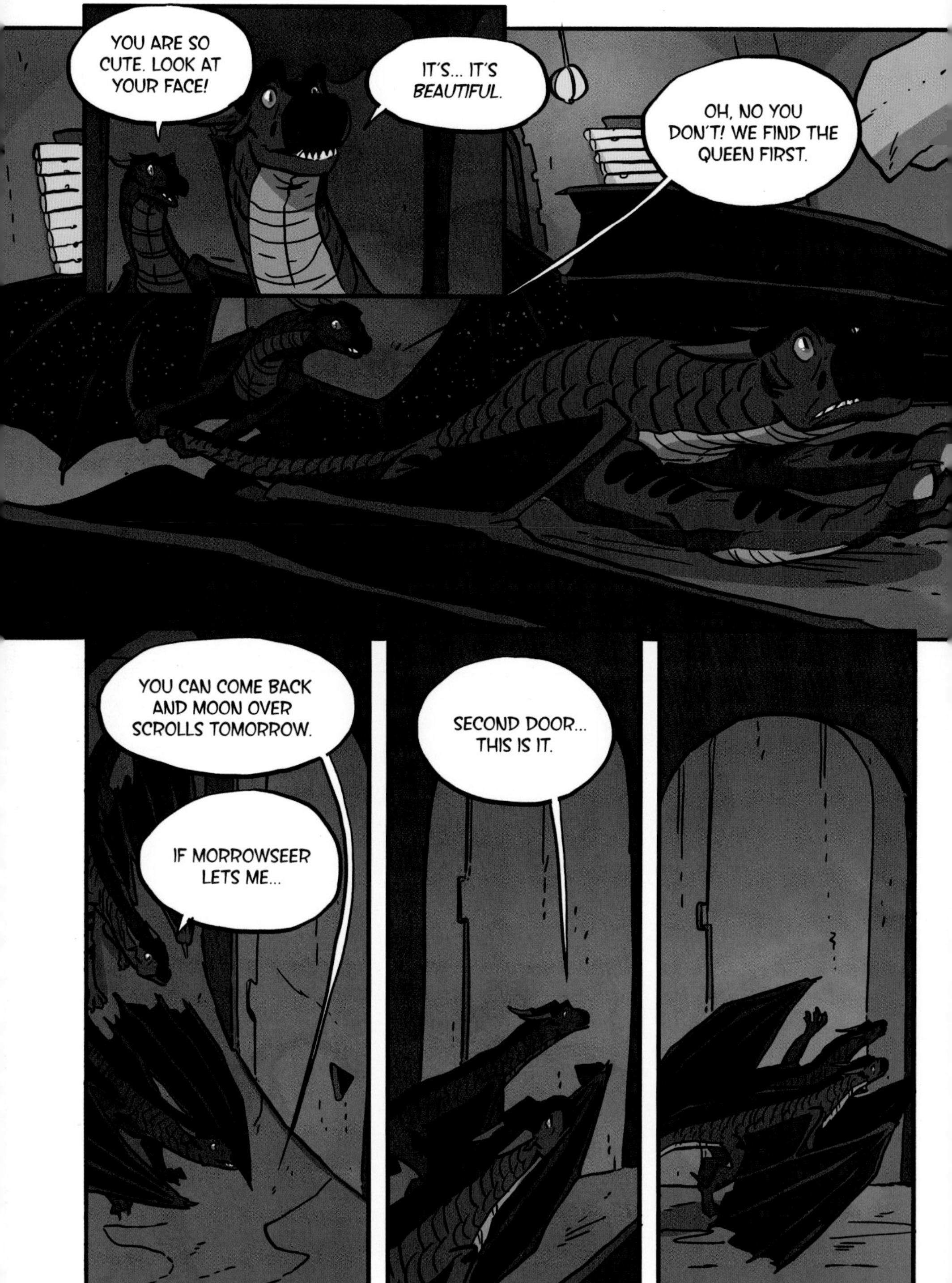
YOU ARE SO CUTE. LOOK AT YOUR FACE!
IT'S... IT'S *BEAUTIFUL.*
OH, NO YOU DON'T! WE FIND THE QUEEN FIRST.
YOU CAN COME BACK AND MOON OVER SCROLLS TOMORROW.
IF MORROWSEER LETS ME...
SECOND DOOR... THIS IS IT.

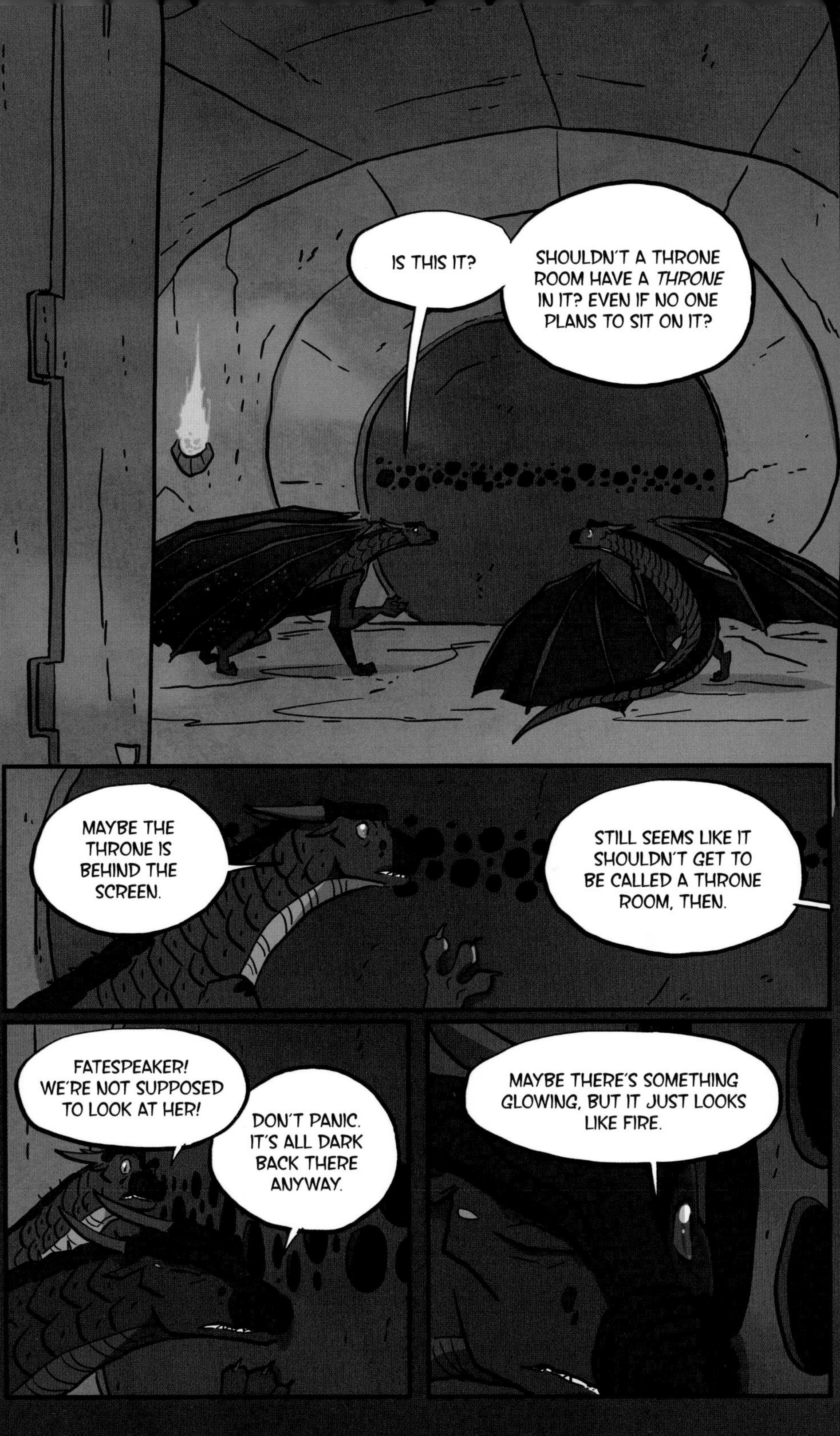
IS THIS IT?
SHOULDN'T A THRONE ROOM HAVE A *THRONE* IN IT? EVEN IF NO ONE PLANS TO SIT ON IT?
MAYBE THE THRONE IS BEHIND THE SCREEN.
STILL SEEMS LIKE IT SHOULDN'T GET TO BE CALLED A THRONE ROOM, THEN.
FATESPEAKER! WE'RE NOT SUPPOSED TO LOOK AT HER!
DON'T PANIC. IT'S ALL DARK BACK THERE ANYWAY.
MAYBE THERE'S SOMETHING GLOWING, BUT IT JUST LOOKS LIKE FIRE.

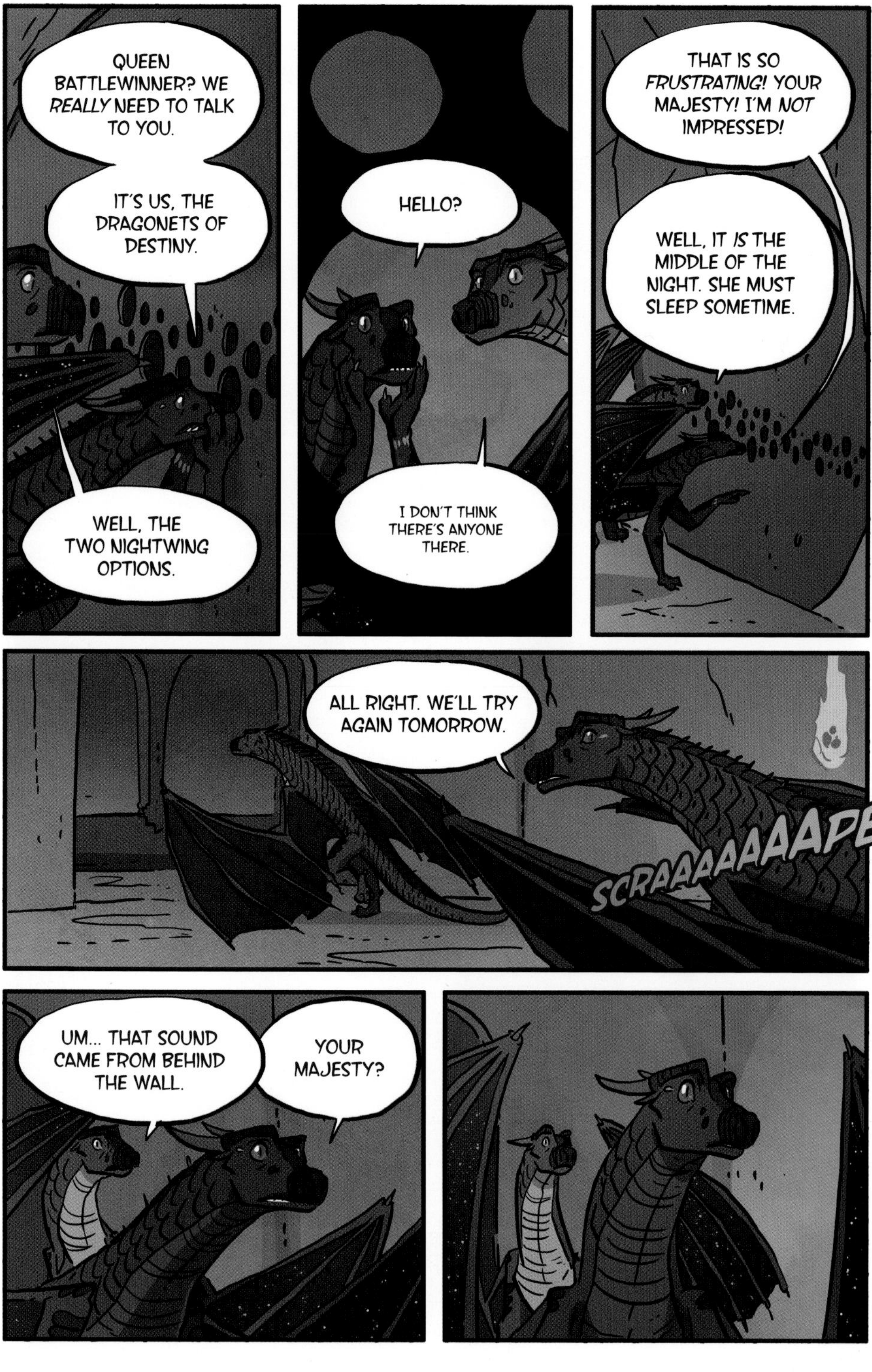
QUEEN BATTLEWINNER? WE *REALLY* NEED TO TALK TO YOU.
IT'S US, THE DRAGONETS OF DESTINY.
WELL, THE TWO NIGHTWING OPTIONS.
HELLO?
I DON'T THINK THERE'S ANYONE THERE.
THAT IS SO *FRUSTRATING!* YOUR MAJESTY! I'M *NOT* IMPRESSED!
WELL, IT *IS* THE MIDDLE OF THE NIGHT. SHE MUST SLEEP SOMETIME.
ALL RIGHT. WE'LL TRY AGAIN TOMORROW.
SCRAAAAAAAAPE
UM... THAT SOUND CAME FROM BEHIND THE WALL.
YOUR MAJESTY?

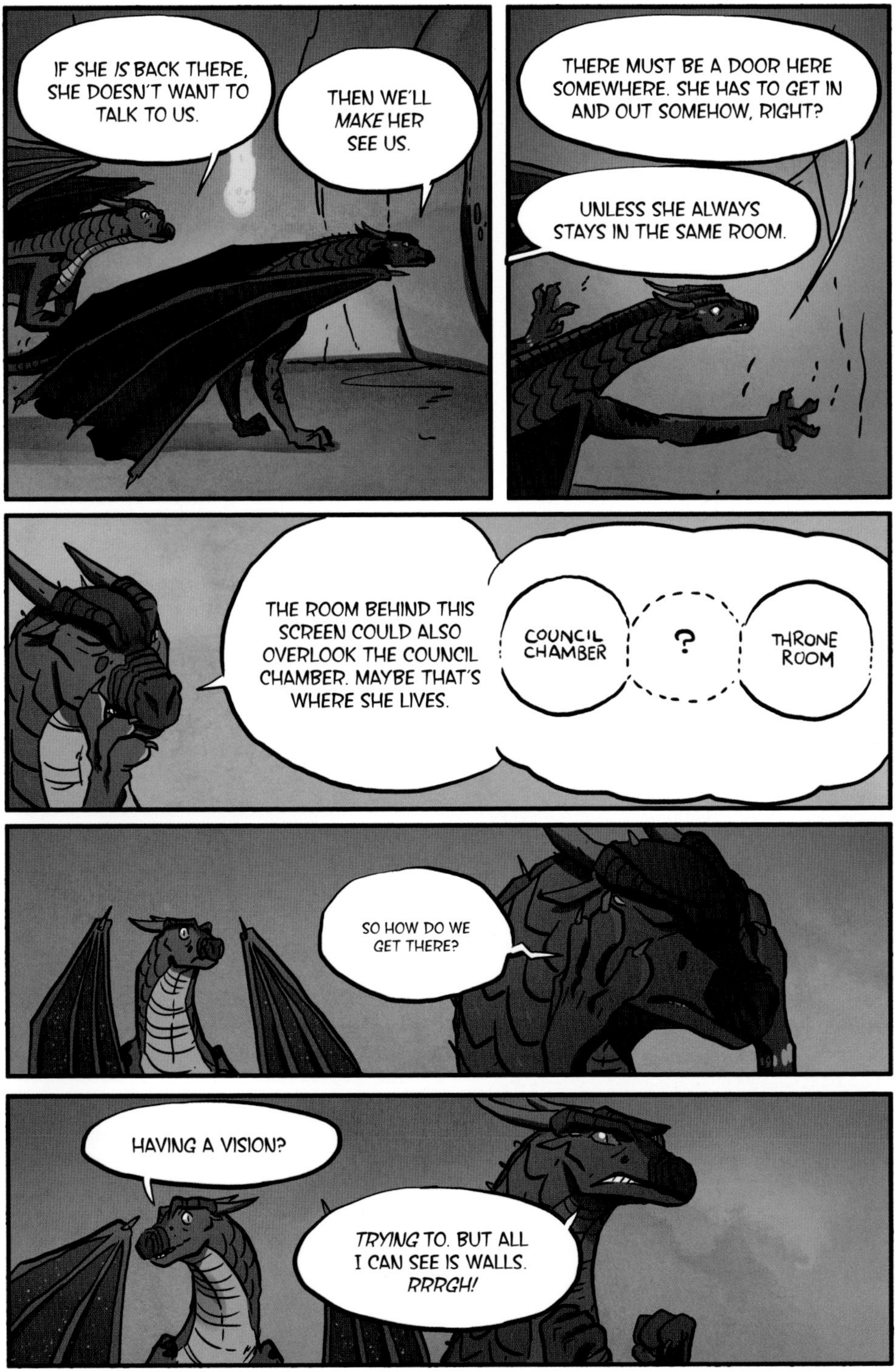
IF SHE IS BACK THERE, SHE DOESN'T WANT TO TALK TO US.
THEN WE'LL MAKE HER SEE US.
THERE MUST BE A DOOR HERE SOMEWHERE. SHE HAS TO GET IN AND OUT SOMEHOW, RIGHT?
UNLESS SHE ALWAYS STAYS IN THE SAME ROOM.
THE ROOM BEHIND THIS SCREEN COULD ALSO OVERLOOK THE COUNCIL CHAMBER. MAYBE THAT'S WHERE SHE LIVES.
COUNCIL CHAMBER
?
THRONE ROOM
SO HOW DO WE GET THERE?
HAVING A VISION?
TRYING TO. BUT ALL I CAN SEE IS WALLS. RRRGH!

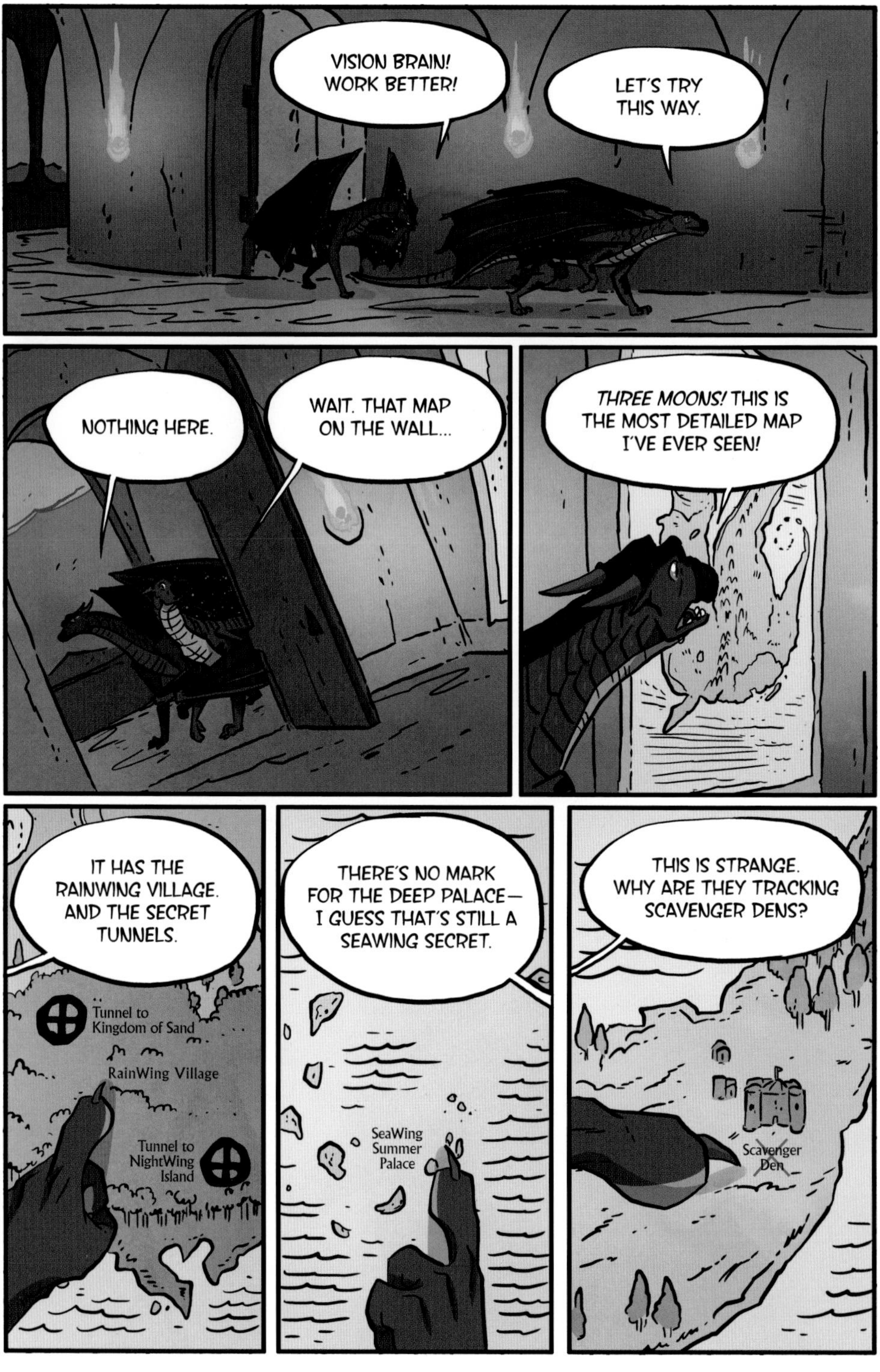
VISION BRAIN! WORK BETTER!
LET'S TRY THIS WAY.
NOTHING HERE.
WAIT. THAT MAP ON THE WALL...
THREE MOONS! THIS IS THE MOST DETAILED MAP I'VE EVER SEEN!
IT HAS THE RAINWING VILLAGE. AND THE SECRET TUNNELS.
Tunnel to Kingdom of Sand
RainWing Village
Tunnel to NightWing Island
THERE'S NO MARK FOR THE DEEP PALACE— I GUESS THAT'S STILL A SEAWING SECRET.
SeaWing Summer Palace
THIS IS STRANGE. WHY ARE THEY TRACKING SCAVENGER DENS?
Scavenger Den

THEY'RE ALL OVER THE MAP. THERE'S EVEN ONE IN THE ICE KINGDOM.

SCAVENGERS? LIKE THE ONE WHO KILLED QUEEN OASIS AND STARTED THE WAR IN THE FIRST PLACE?

EXACTLY.

SO THESE DENS—THAT'S WHERE THEY LIVE?

I GUESS. I HAVE NO IDEA WHY THE NIGHTWINGS WOULD BE INTERESTED IN THEM.

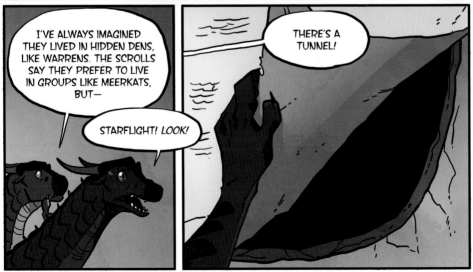

I'VE ALWAYS IMAGINED THEY LIVED IN HIDDEN DENS, LIKE WARRENS. THE SCROLLS SAY THEY PREFER TO LIVE IN GROUPS LIKE MEERKATS, BUT—

STARFLIGHT! *LOOK!*

THERE'S A TUNNEL!

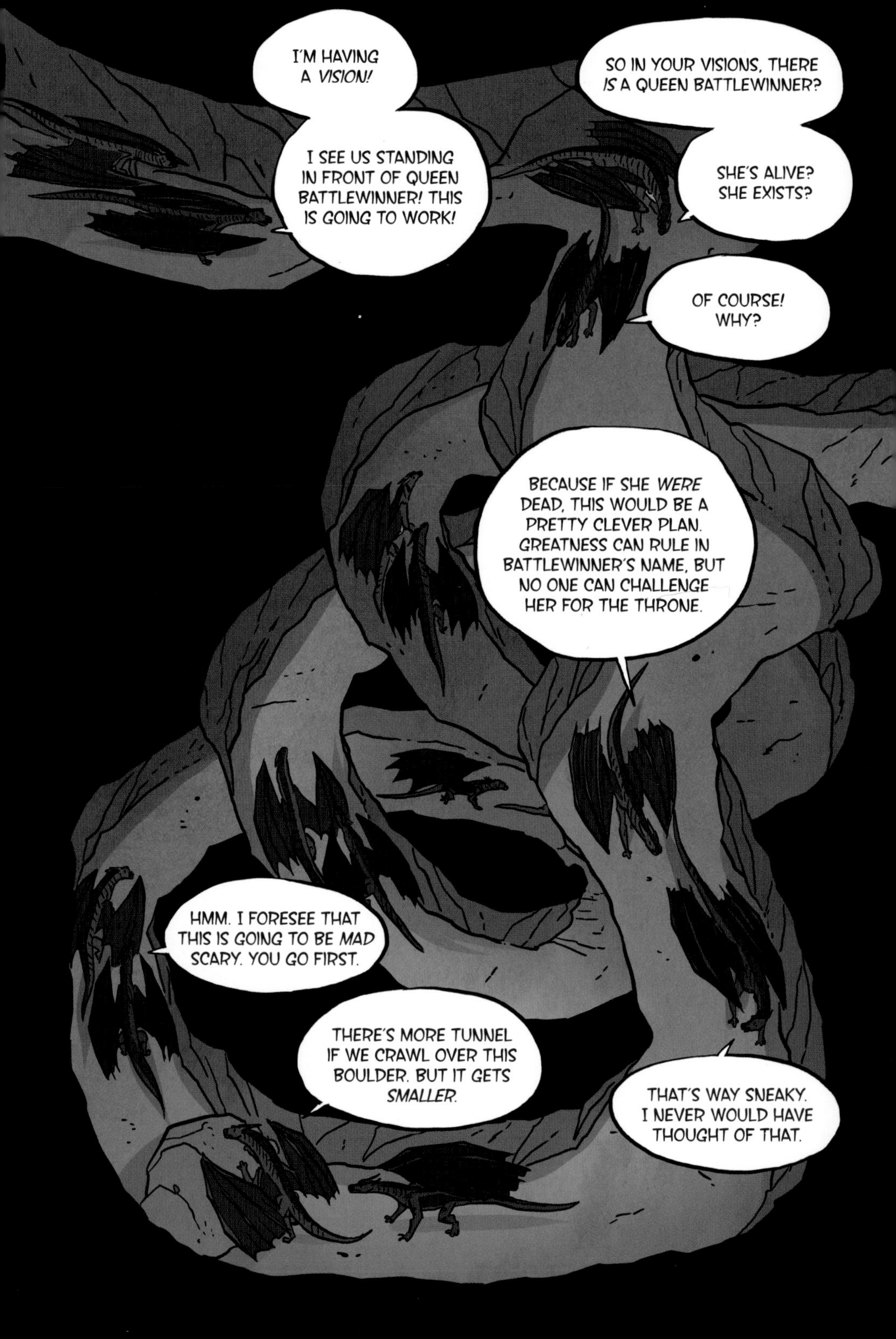
I'M HAVING A *VISION!*
I SEE US STANDING IN FRONT OF QUEEN BATTLEWINNER! THIS IS GOING TO WORK!
SO IN YOUR VISIONS, THERE *IS* A QUEEN BATTLEWINNER?
SHE'S ALIVE? SHE EXISTS?
OF COURSE! WHY?
BECAUSE IF SHE *WERE* DEAD, THIS WOULD BE A PRETTY CLEVER PLAN. GREATNESS CAN RULE IN BATTLEWINNER'S NAME, BUT NO ONE CAN CHALLENGE HER FOR THE THRONE.
HMM. I FORESEE THAT THIS IS GOING TO BE *MAD* SCARY. YOU GO FIRST.
THAT'S WAY SNEAKY. I NEVER WOULD HAVE THOUGHT OF THAT.
THERE'S MORE TUNNEL IF WE CRAWL OVER THIS BOULDER. BUT IT GETS *SMALLER.*

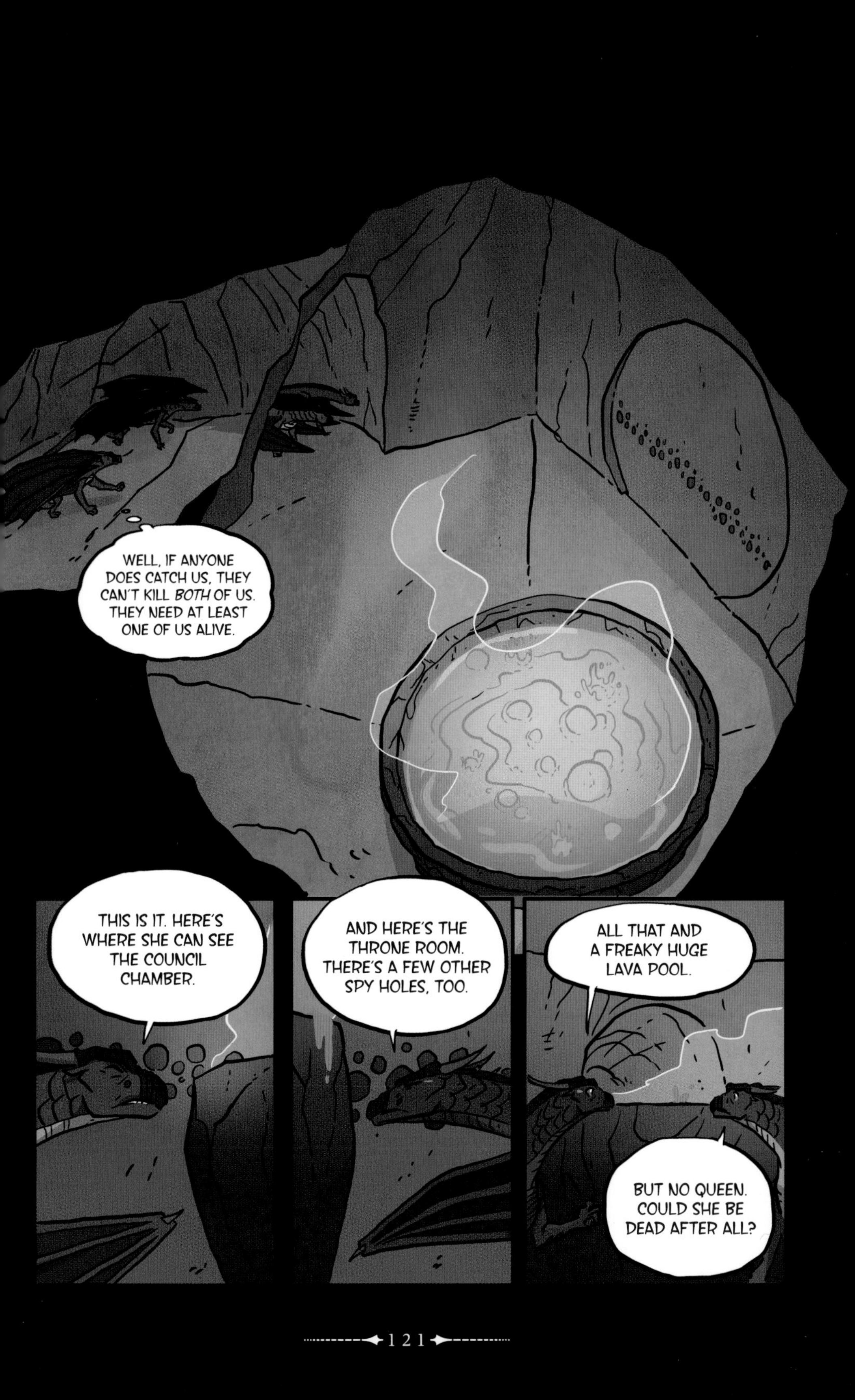
WELL, IF ANYONE DOES CATCH US, THEY CAN'T KILL *BOTH* OF US. THEY NEED AT LEAST ONE OF US ALIVE.
THIS IS IT. HERE'S WHERE SHE CAN SEE THE COUNCIL CHAMBER.
AND HERE'S THE THRONE ROOM. THERE'S A FEW OTHER SPY HOLES, TOO.
ALL THAT AND A FREAKY HUGE LAVA POOL.
BUT NO QUEEN. COULD SHE BE DEAD AFTER ALL?

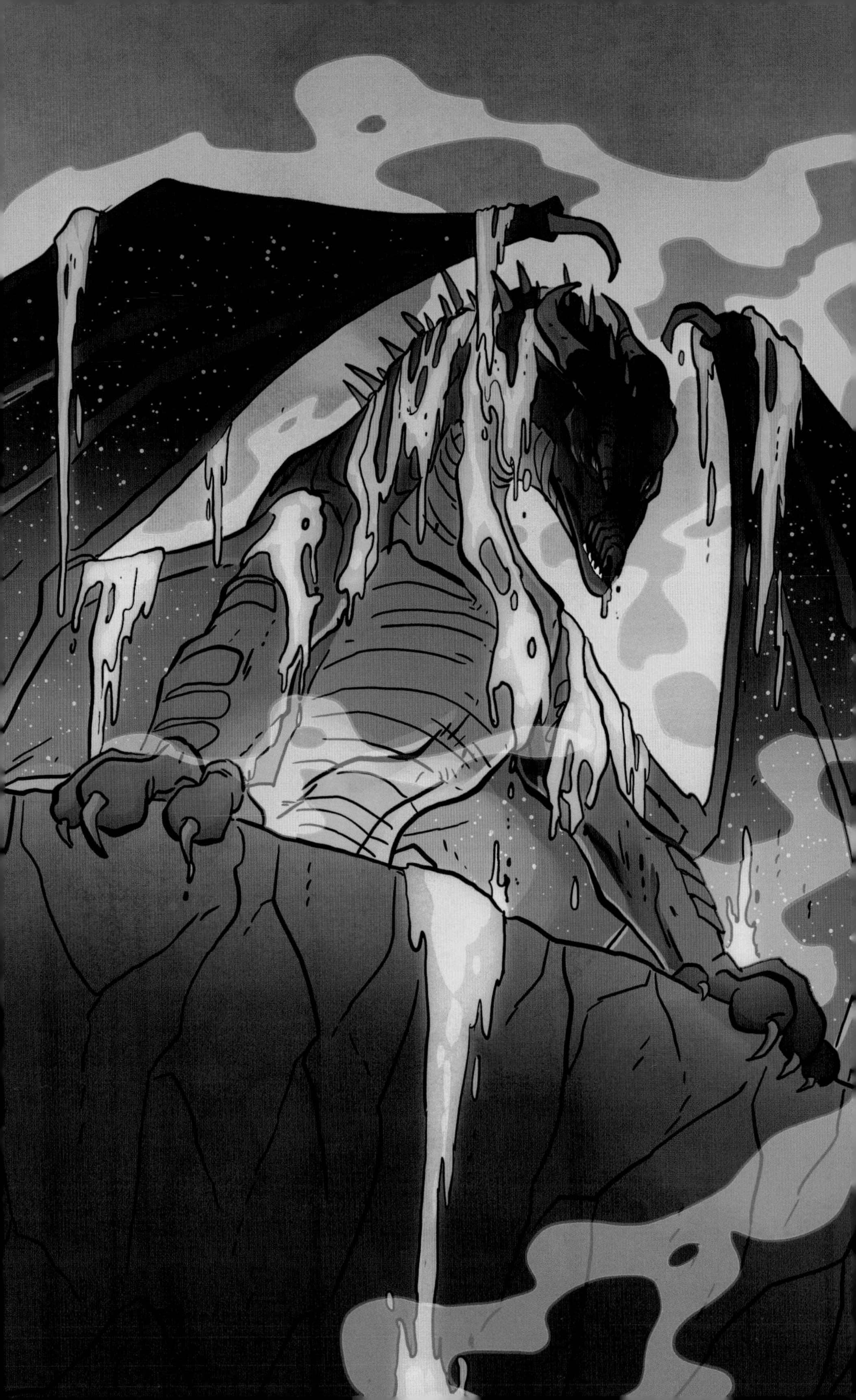

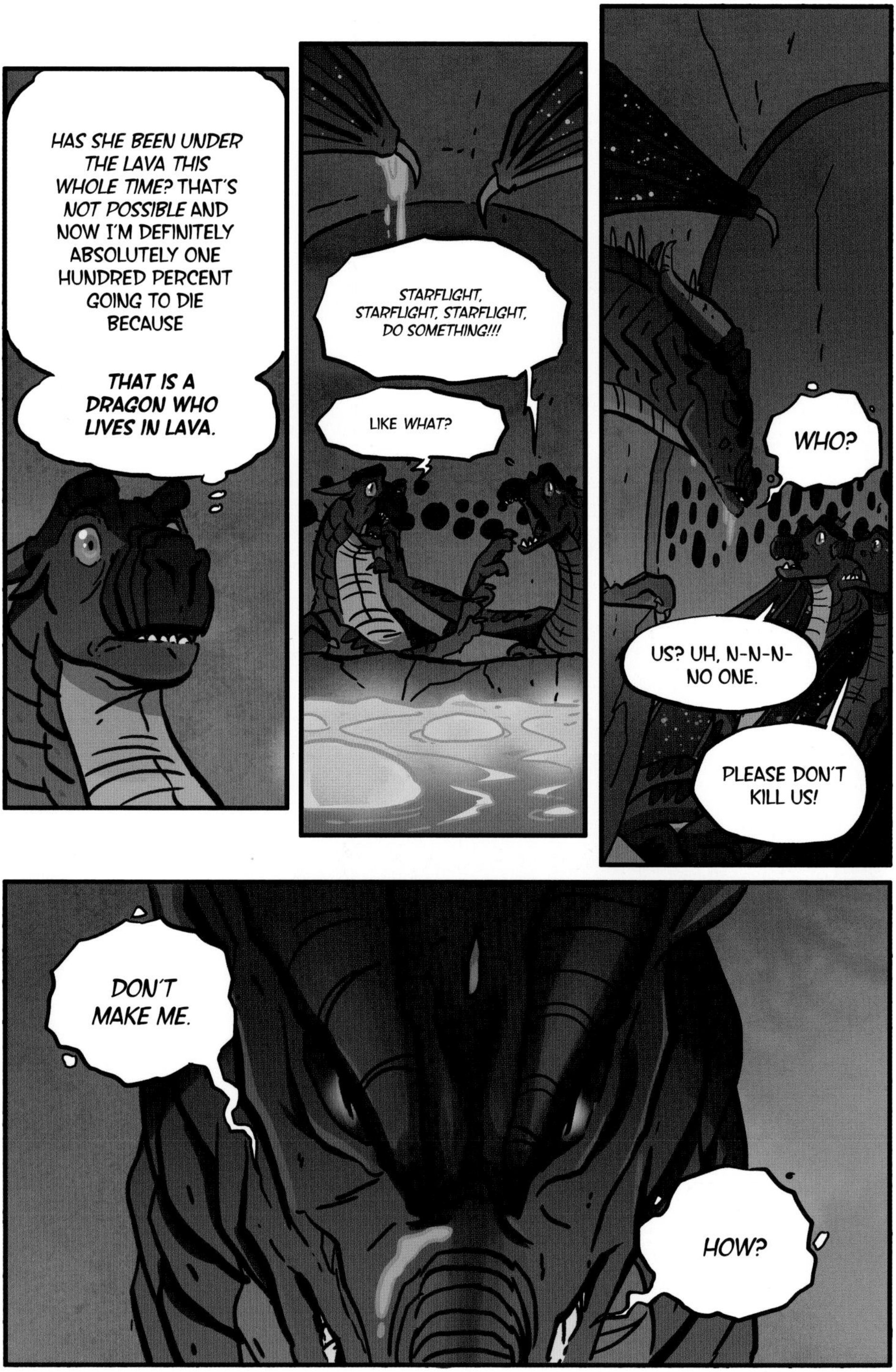

HAS SHE BEEN UNDER THE LAVA THIS WHOLE TIME? THAT'S NOT POSSIBLE AND NOW I'M DEFINITELY ABSOLUTELY ONE HUNDRED PERCENT GOING TO DIE BECAUSE
THAT IS A DRAGON WHO LIVES IN LAVA.
STARFLIGHT, STARFLIGHT, STARFLIGHT, DO SOMETHING!!!
LIKE WHAT?
WHO?
US? UH, N-N-N-NO ONE.
PLEASE DON'T KILL US!
DON'T MAKE ME.
HOW?

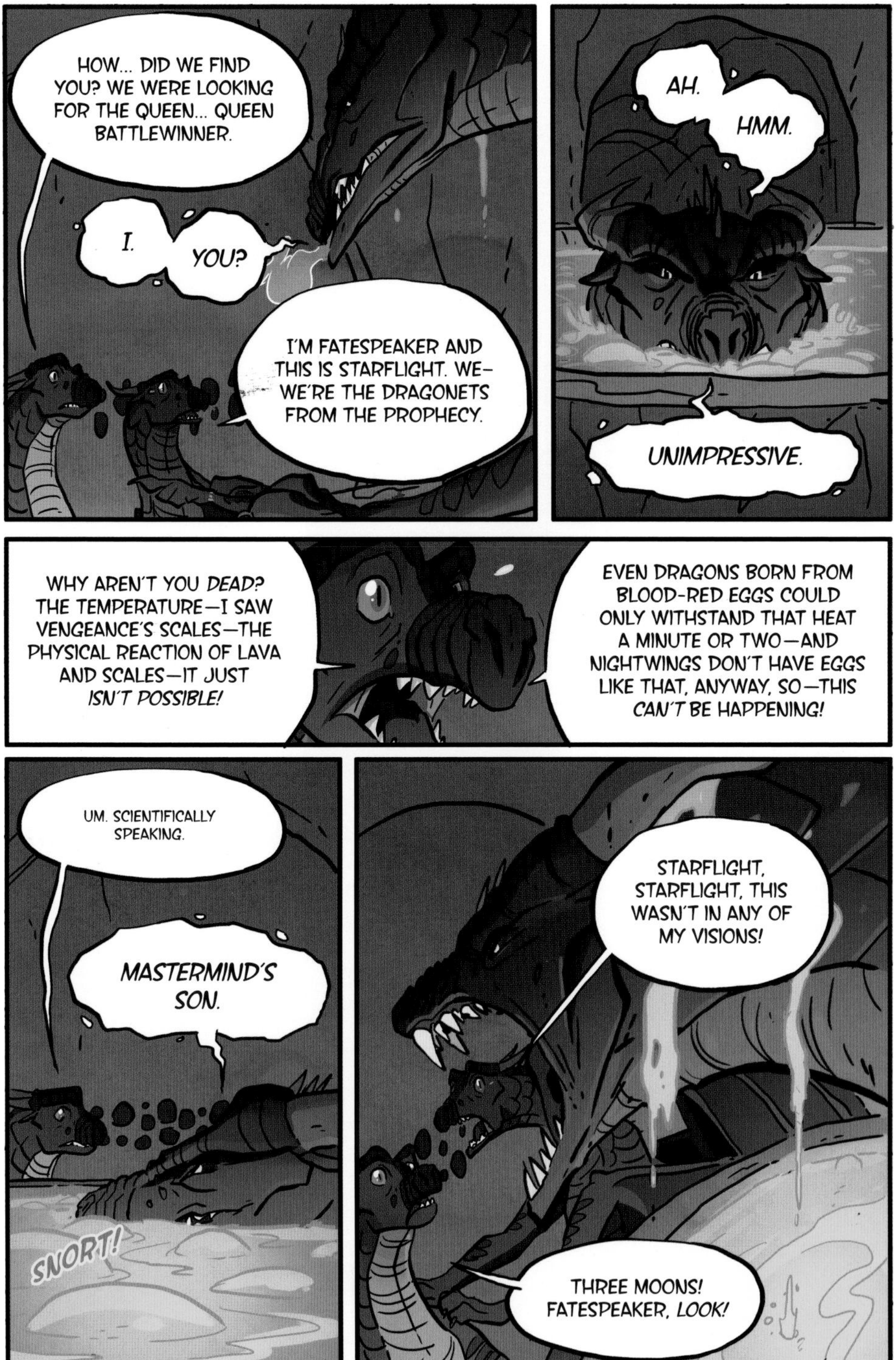
HOW... DID WE FIND YOU? WE WERE LOOKING FOR THE QUEEN... QUEEN BATTLEWINNER.
I.
YOU?
I'M FATESPEAKER AND THIS IS STARFLIGHT. WE—WE'RE THE DRAGONETS FROM THE PROPHECY.
AH.
HMM.
UNIMPRESSIVE.
WHY AREN'T YOU DEAD? THE TEMPERATURE—I SAW VENGEANCE'S SCALES—THE PHYSICAL REACTION OF LAVA AND SCALES—IT JUST ISN'T POSSIBLE!
EVEN DRAGONS BORN FROM BLOOD-RED EGGS COULD ONLY WITHSTAND THAT HEAT A MINUTE OR TWO—AND NIGHTWINGS DON'T HAVE EGGS LIKE THAT, ANYWAY, SO—THIS CAN'T BE HAPPENING!
UM. SCIENTIFICALLY SPEAKING.
MASTERMIND'S SON.
SNORT!
STARFLIGHT, STARFLIGHT, THIS WASN'T IN ANY OF MY VISIONS!
THREE MOONS! FATESPEAKER, LOOK!

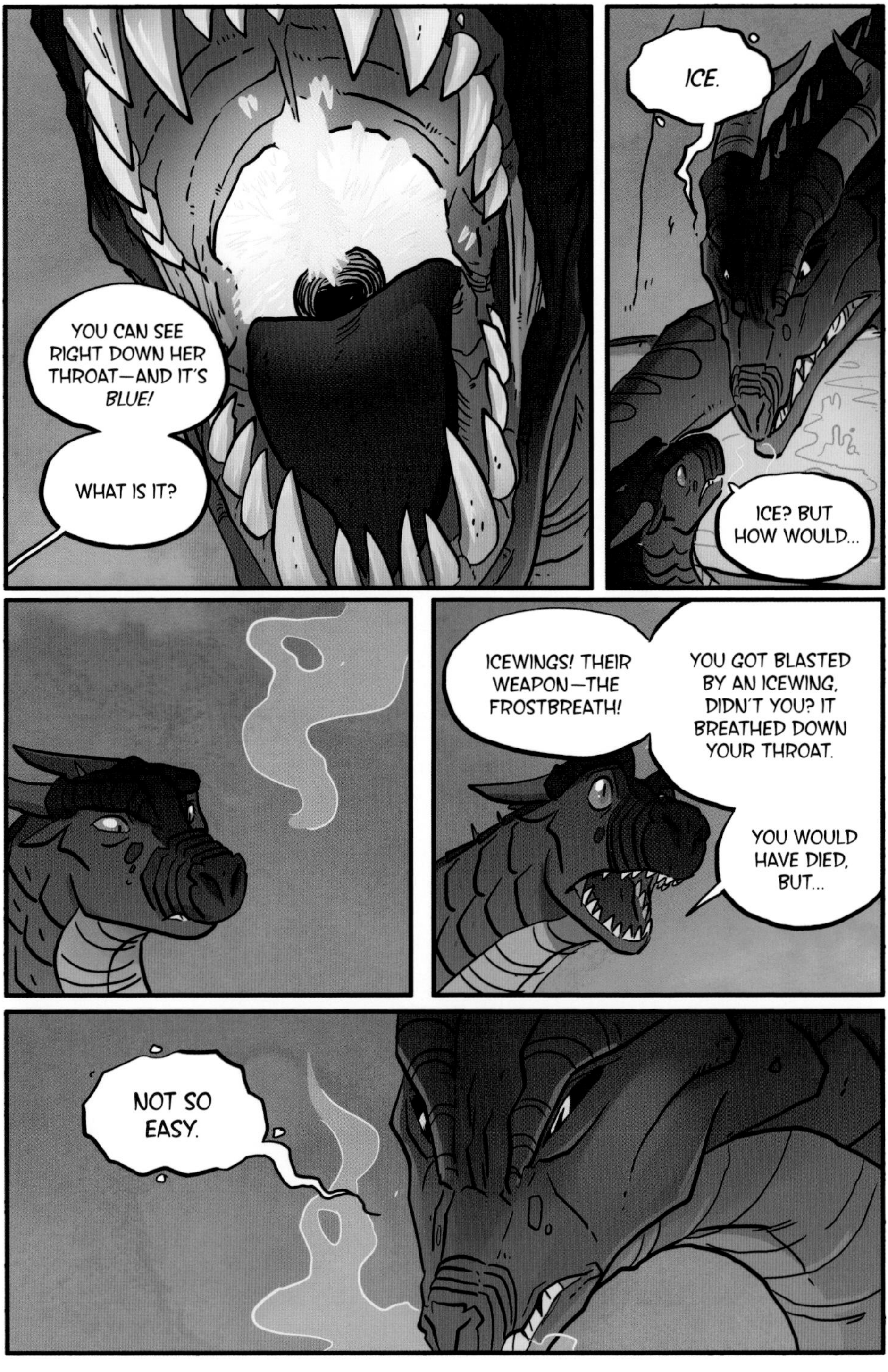
YOU CAN SEE RIGHT DOWN HER THROAT—AND IT'S *BLUE!*
WHAT IS IT?
ICE.
ICE? BUT HOW WOULD...
ICEWINGS! THEIR WEAPON—THE FROSTBREATH!
YOU GOT BLASTED BY AN ICEWING, DIDN'T YOU? IT BREATHED DOWN YOUR THROAT.
YOU WOULD HAVE DIED, BUT...
NOT SO EASY.

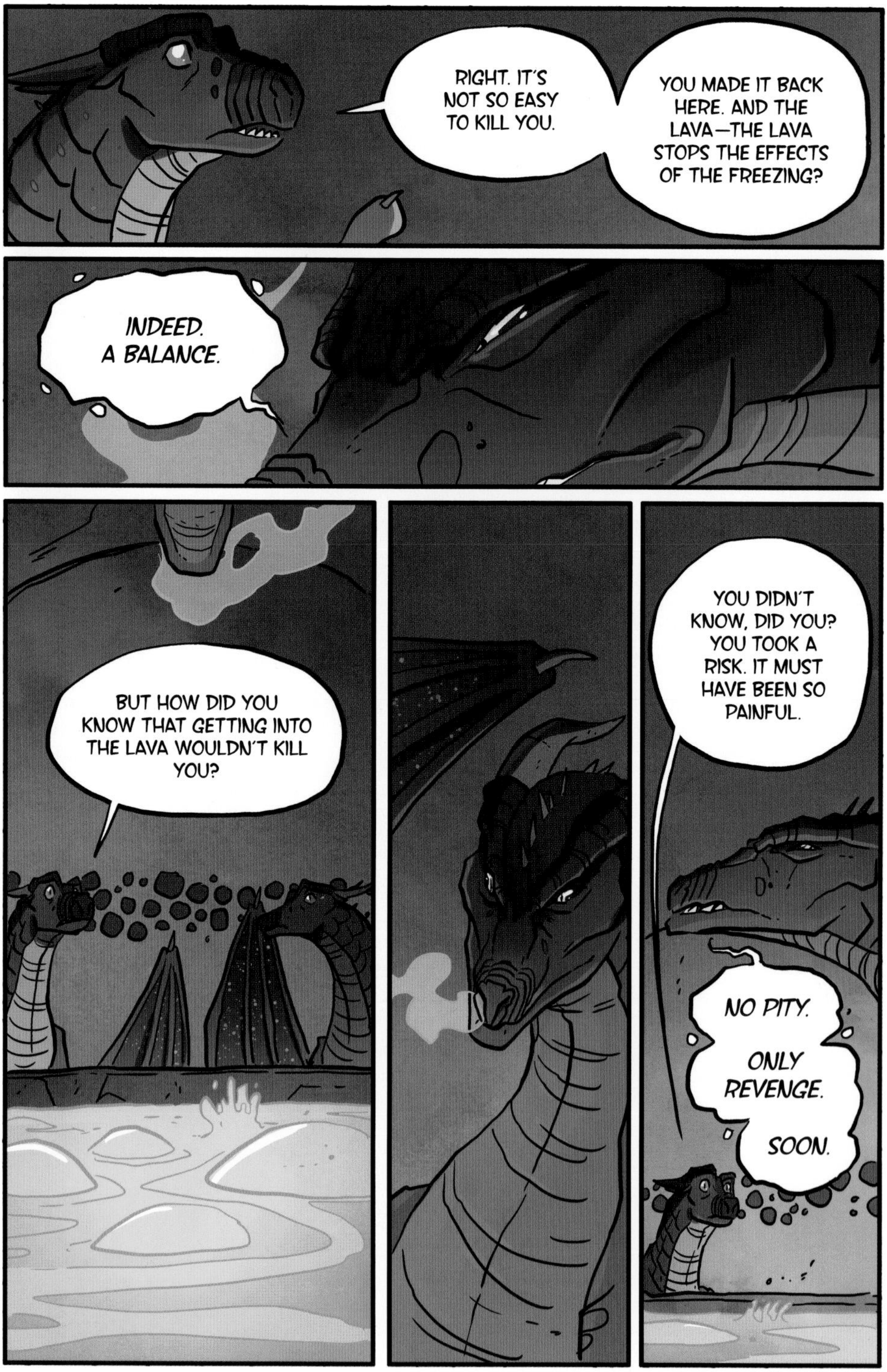

RIGHT. IT'S NOT SO EASY TO KILL YOU.
YOU MADE IT BACK HERE. AND THE LAVA—THE LAVA STOPS THE EFFECTS OF THE FREEZING?
INDEED. A BALANCE.
BUT HOW DID YOU KNOW THAT GETTING INTO THE LAVA WOULDN'T KILL YOU?
YOU DIDN'T KNOW, DID YOU? YOU TOOK A RISK. IT MUST HAVE BEEN SO PAINFUL.
NO PITY.
ONLY REVENGE.
SOON.

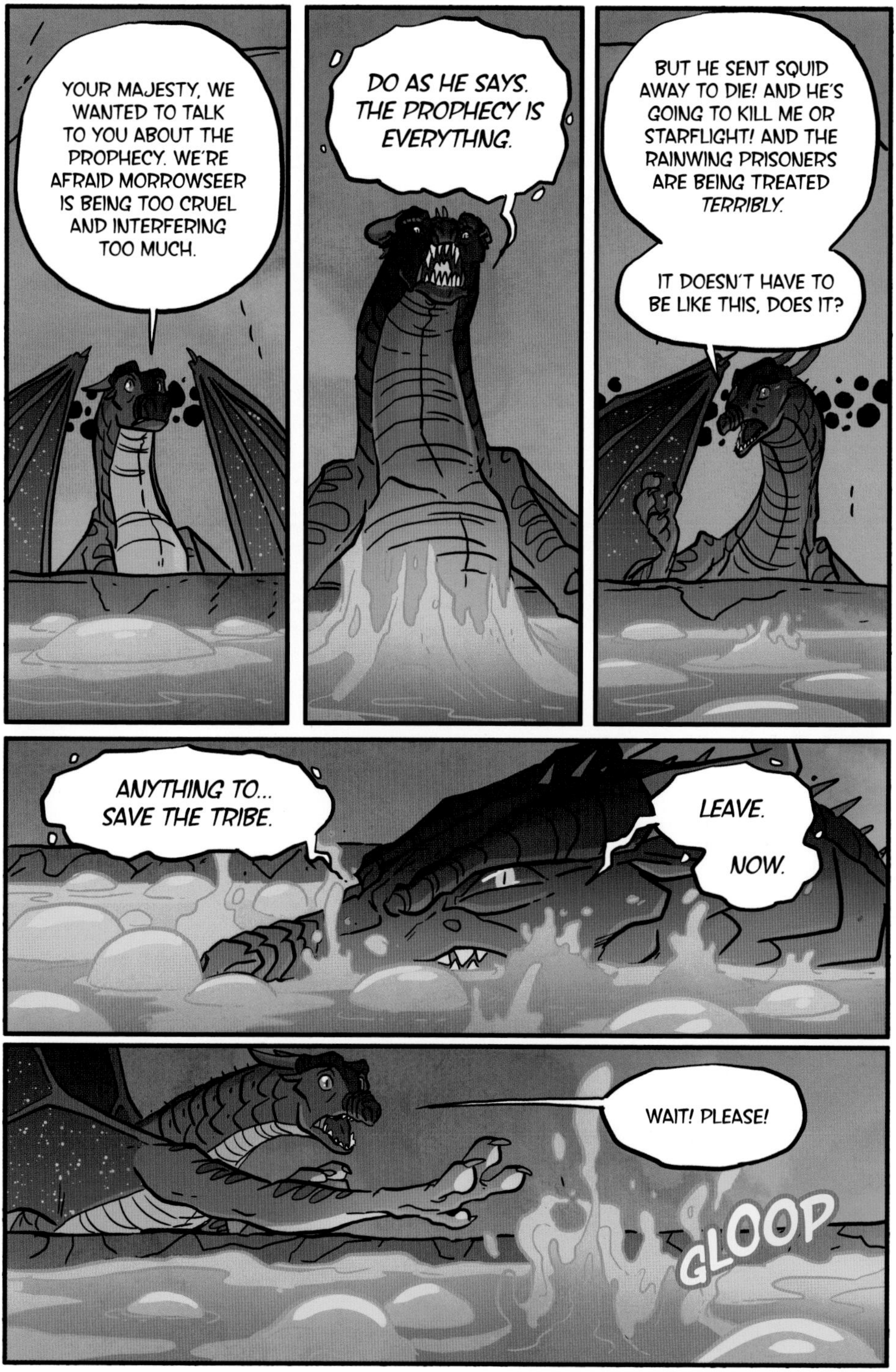
YOUR MAJESTY, WE WANTED TO TALK TO YOU ABOUT THE PROPHECY. WE'RE AFRAID MORROWSEER IS BEING TOO CRUEL AND INTERFERING TOO MUCH.
DO AS HE SAYS. THE PROPHECY IS EVERYTHNG.
BUT HE SENT SQUID AWAY TO DIE! AND HE'S GOING TO KILL ME OR STARFLIGHT! AND THE RAINWING PRISONERS ARE BEING TREATED *TERRIBLY.*
IT DOESN'T HAVE TO BE LIKE THIS, DOES IT?
ANYTHING TO... SAVE THE TRIBE.
LEAVE.
NOW.
WAIT! PLEASE!
GLOOP

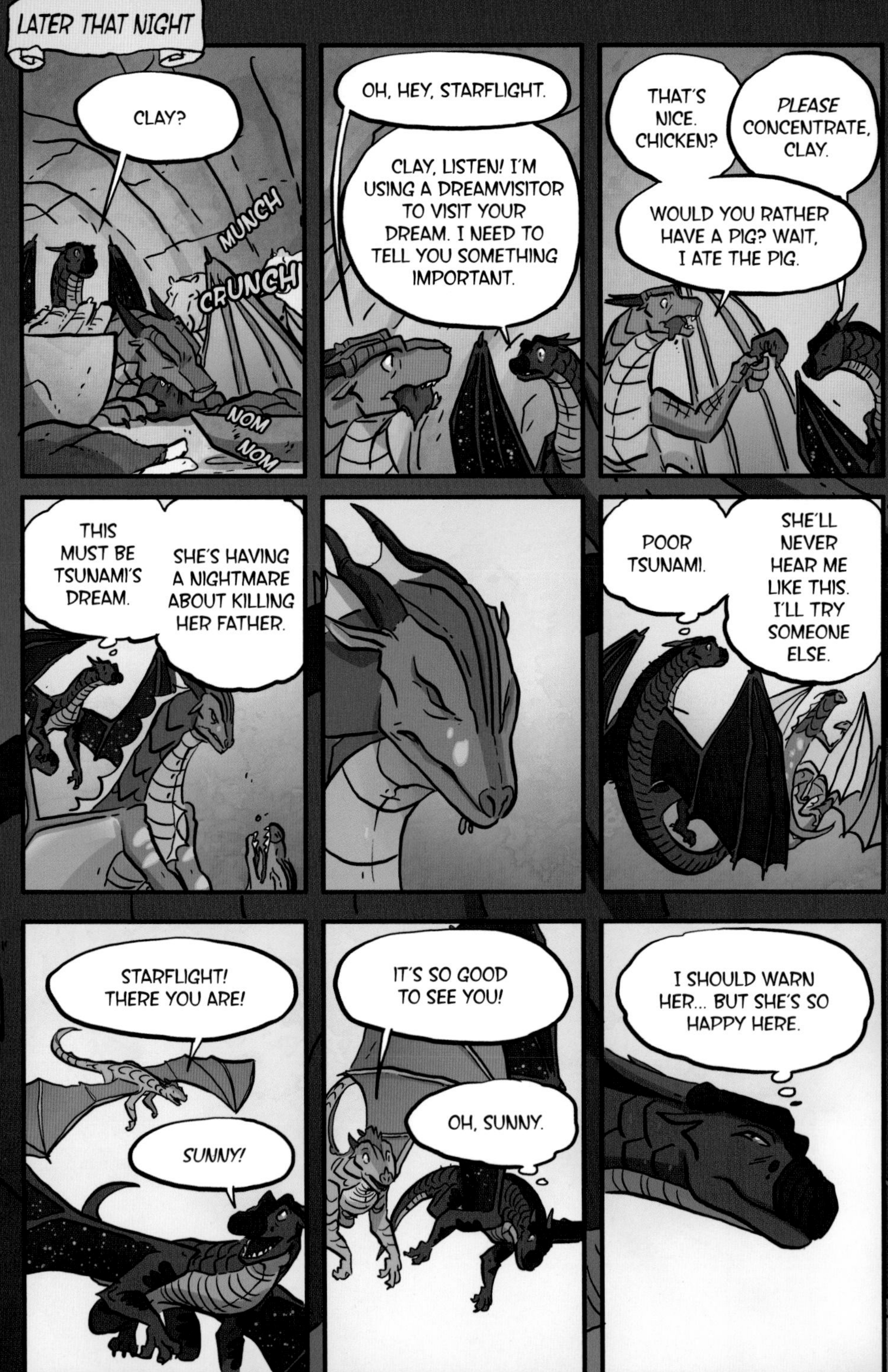
LATER THAT NIGHT
CLAY?
MUNCH
CRUNCH
NOM
NOM
OH, HEY, STARFLIGHT.
CLAY, LISTEN! I'M USING A DREAMVISITOR TO VISIT YOUR DREAM. I NEED TO TELL YOU SOMETHING IMPORTANT.
THAT'S NICE. CHICKEN?
PLEASE CONCENTRATE, CLAY.
WOULD YOU RATHER HAVE A PIG? WAIT, I ATE THE PIG.
THIS MUST BE TSUNAMI'S DREAM.
SHE'S HAVING A NIGHTMARE ABOUT KILLING HER FATHER.
POOR TSUNAMI.
SHE'LL NEVER HEAR ME LIKE THIS. I'LL TRY SOMEONE ELSE.
STARFLIGHT! THERE YOU ARE!
SUNNY!
IT'S SO GOOD TO SEE YOU!
OH, SUNNY.
I SHOULD WARN HER... BUT SHE'S SO HAPPY HERE.

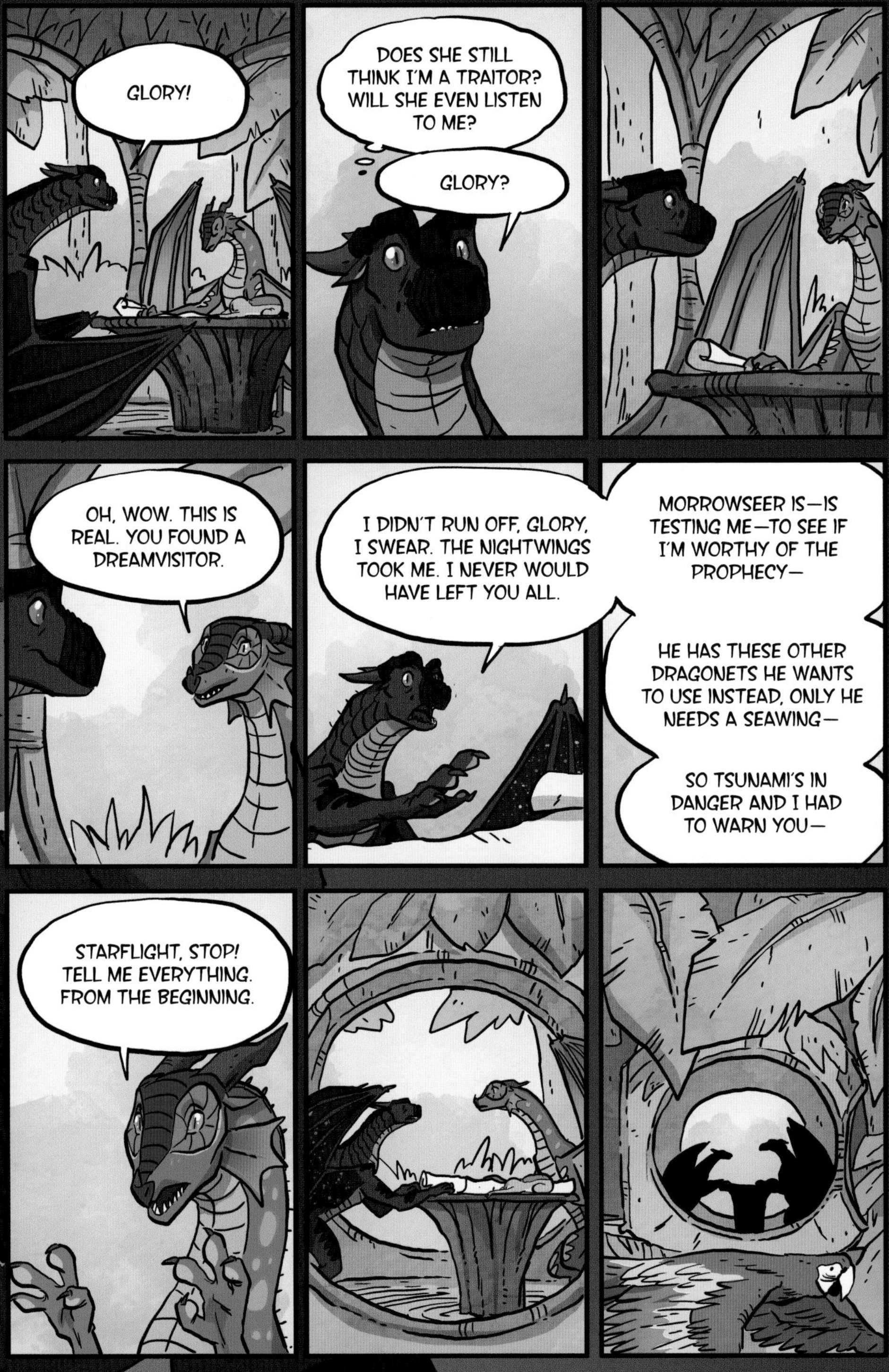
GLORY!
DOES SHE STILL THINK I'M A TRAITOR? WILL SHE EVEN LISTEN TO ME?
GLORY?
OH, WOW. THIS IS REAL. YOU FOUND A DREAMVISITOR.
I DIDN'T RUN OFF, GLORY, I SWEAR. THE NIGHTWINGS TOOK ME. I NEVER WOULD HAVE LEFT YOU ALL.
MORROWSEER IS—IS TESTING ME—TO SEE IF I'M WORTHY OF THE PROPHECY—
HE HAS THESE OTHER DRAGONETS HE WANTS TO USE INSTEAD, ONLY HE NEEDS A SEAWING—
SO TSUNAMI'S IN DANGER AND I HAD TO WARN YOU—
STARFLIGHT, STOP! TELL ME EVERYTHING. FROM THE BEGINNING.

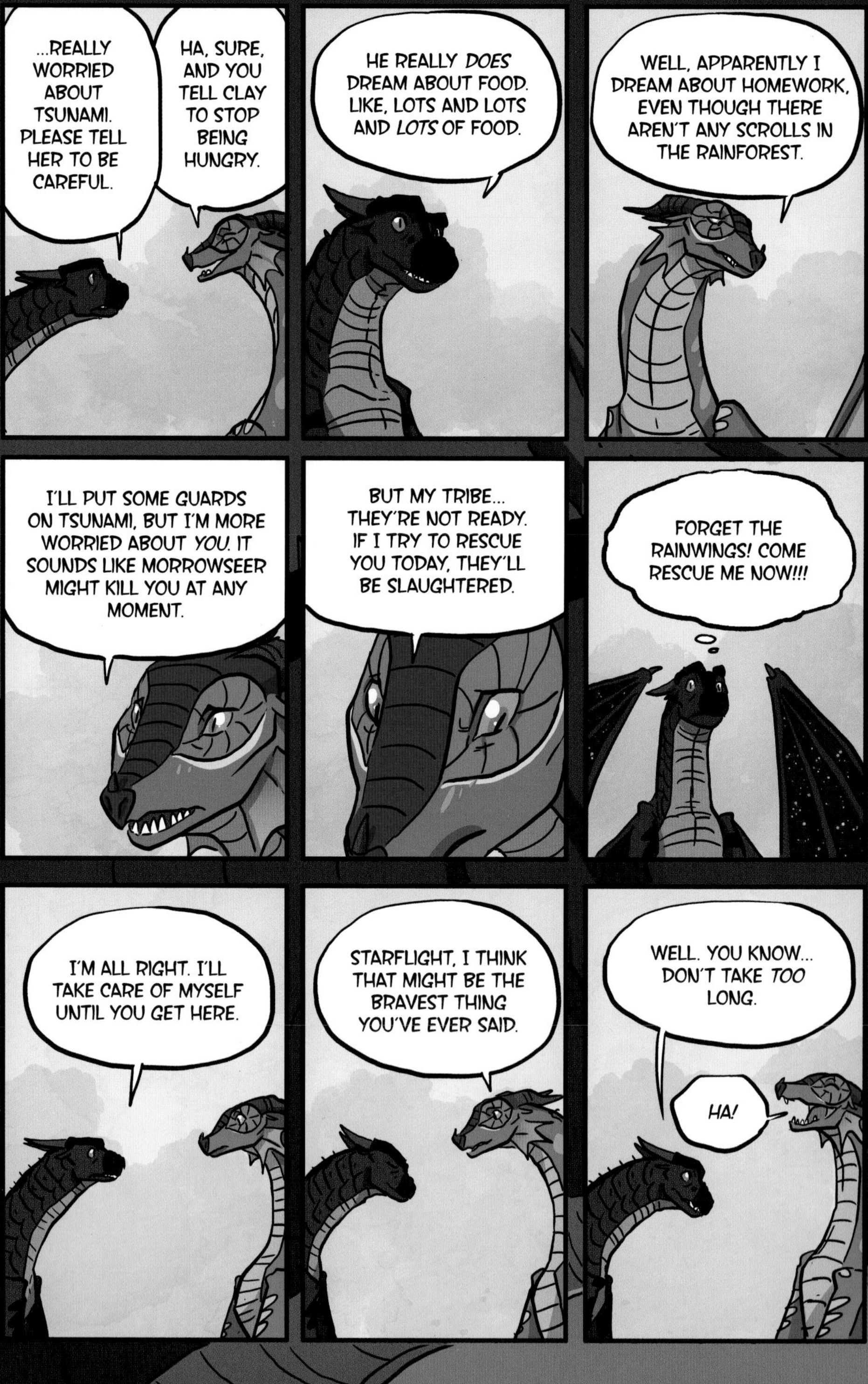
...REALLY WORRIED ABOUT TSUNAMI. PLEASE TELL HER TO BE CAREFUL.
HA, SURE, AND YOU TELL CLAY TO STOP BEING HUNGRY.
HE REALLY *DOES* DREAM ABOUT FOOD. LIKE, LOTS AND LOTS AND *LOTS* OF FOOD.
WELL, APPARENTLY I DREAM ABOUT HOMEWORK, EVEN THOUGH THERE AREN'T ANY SCROLLS IN THE RAINFOREST.
I'LL PUT SOME GUARDS ON TSUNAMI, BUT I'M MORE WORRIED ABOUT *YOU*. IT SOUNDS LIKE MORROWSEER MIGHT KILL YOU AT ANY MOMENT.
BUT MY TRIBE... THEY'RE NOT READY. IF I TRY TO RESCUE YOU TODAY, THEY'LL BE SLAUGHTERED.
FORGET THE RAINWINGS! COME RESCUE ME NOW!!!
I'M ALL RIGHT. I'LL TAKE CARE OF MYSELF UNTIL YOU GET HERE.
STARFLIGHT, I THINK THAT MIGHT BE THE BRAVEST THING YOU'VE EVER SAID.
WELL. YOU KNOW... DON'T TAKE *TOO* LONG.
HA!

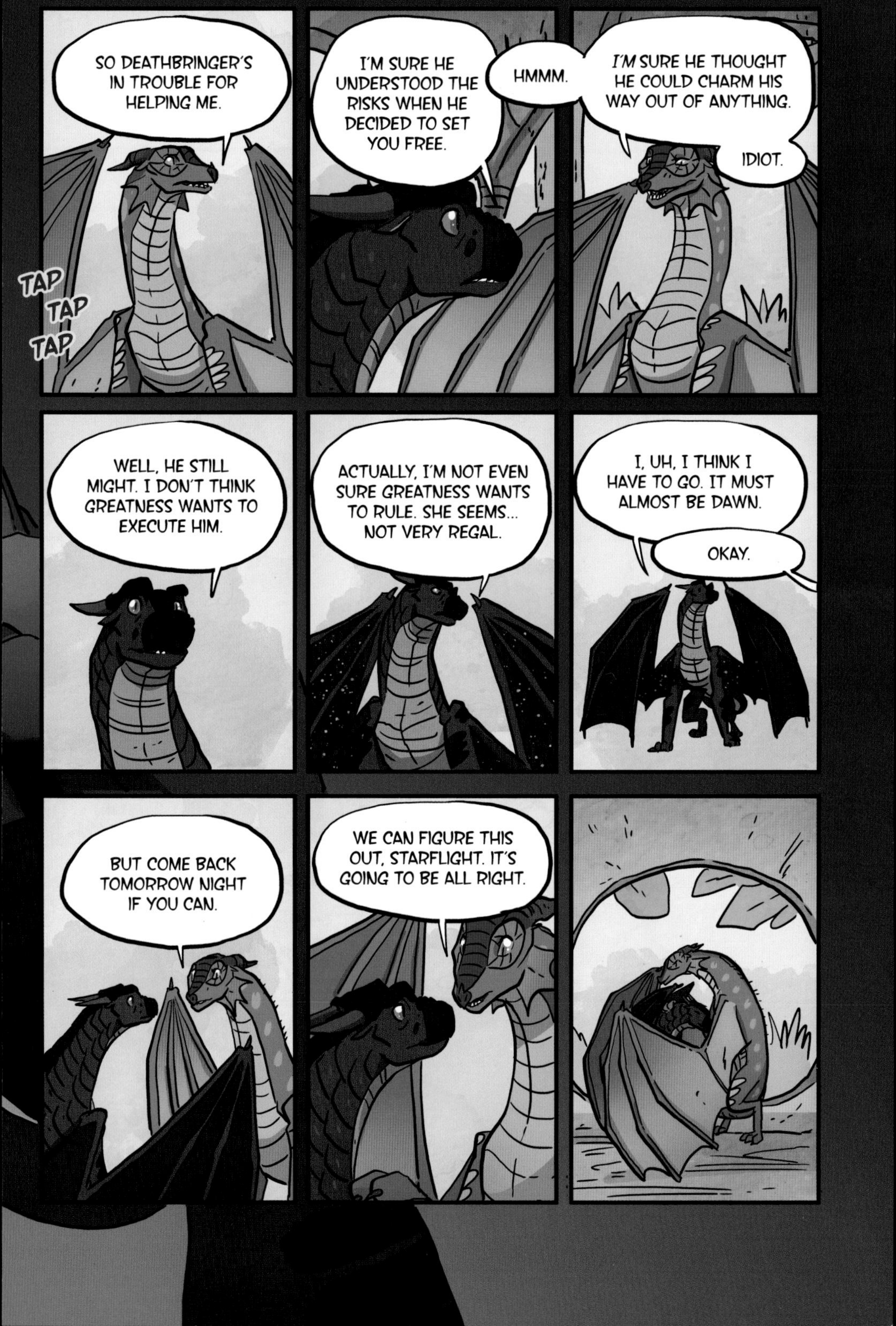
SO DEATHBRINGER'S IN TROUBLE FOR HELPING ME.
TAP TAP TAP
I'M SURE HE UNDERSTOOD THE RISKS WHEN HE DECIDED TO SET YOU FREE.
HMMM.
I'M SURE HE THOUGHT HE COULD CHARM HIS WAY OUT OF ANYTHING.
IDIOT.
WELL, HE STILL MIGHT. I DON'T THINK GREATNESS WANTS TO EXECUTE HIM.
ACTUALLY, I'M NOT EVEN SURE GREATNESS WANTS TO RULE. SHE SEEMS... NOT VERY REGAL.
I, UH, I THINK I HAVE TO GO. IT MUST ALMOST BE DAWN.
OKAY.
BUT COME BACK TOMORROW NIGHT IF YOU CAN.
WE CAN FIGURE THIS OUT, STARFLIGHT. IT'S GOING TO BE ALL RIGHT.

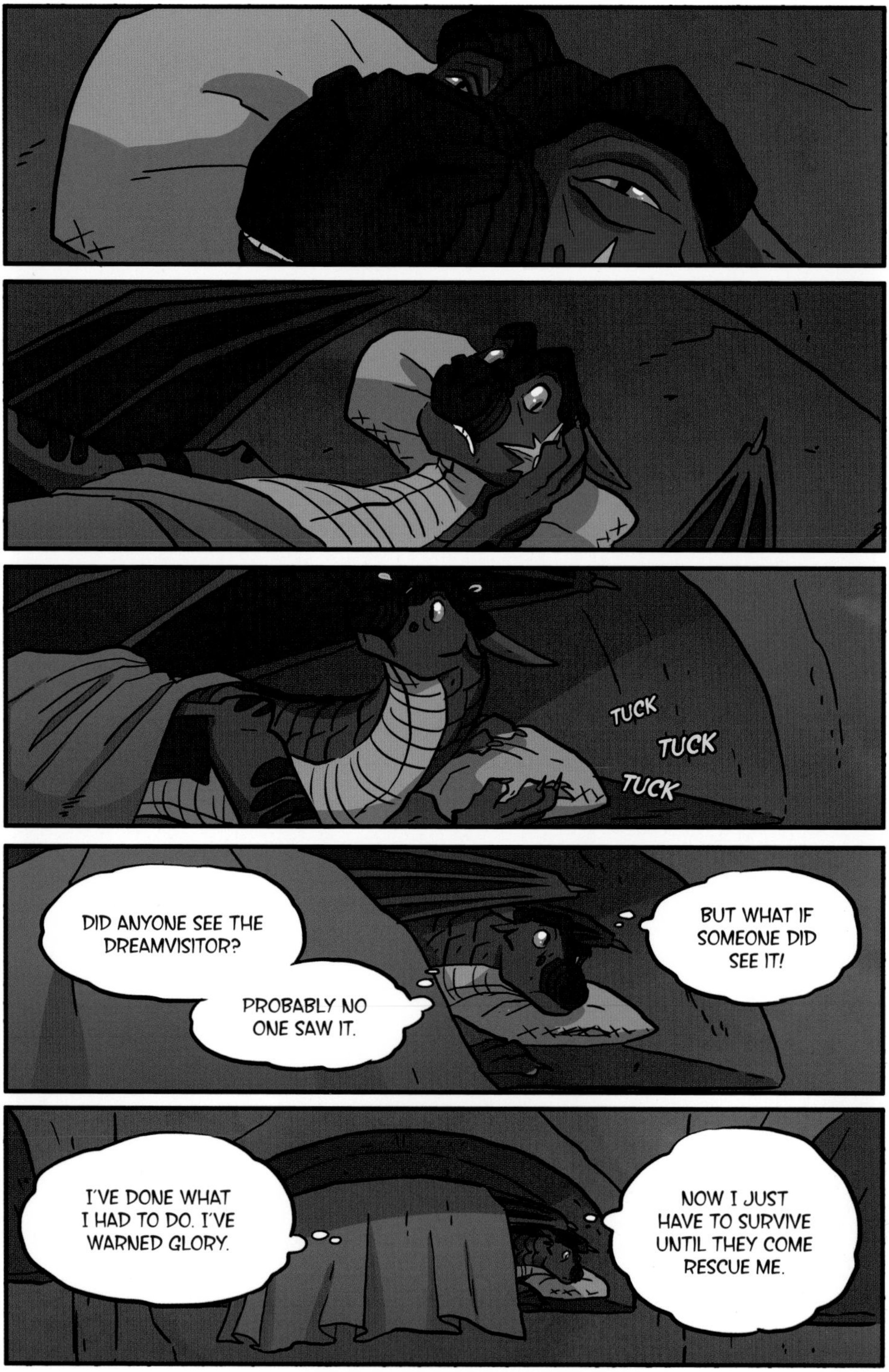
TUCK
TUCK
TUCK
DID ANYONE SEE THE DREAMVISITOR?
PROBABLY NO ONE SAW IT.
BUT WHAT IF SOMEONE DID SEE IT!
I'VE DONE WHAT I HAD TO DO. I'VE WARNED GLORY.
NOW I JUST HAVE TO SURVIVE UNTIL THEY COME RESCUE ME.

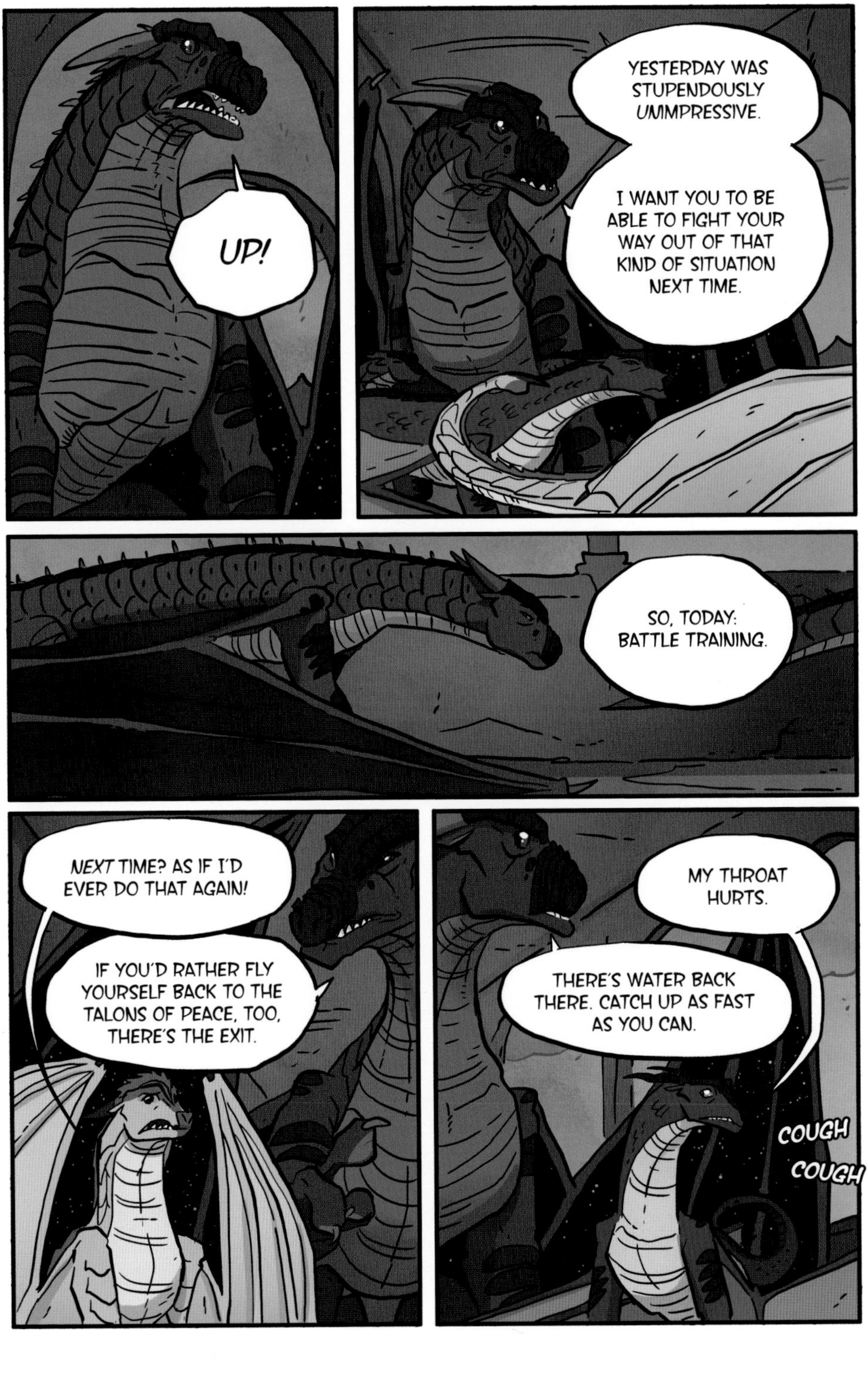
UP!
YESTERDAY WAS STUPENDOUSLY UNIMPRESSIVE.
I WANT YOU TO BE ABLE TO FIGHT YOUR WAY OUT OF THAT KIND OF SITUATION NEXT TIME.
SO, TODAY: BATTLE TRAINING.
NEXT TIME? AS IF I'D EVER DO THAT AGAIN!
IF YOU'D RATHER FLY YOURSELF BACK TO THE TALONS OF PEACE, TOO, THERE'S THE EXIT.
MY THROAT HURTS.
THERE'S WATER BACK THERE. CATCH UP AS FAST AS YOU CAN.
COUGH
COUGH

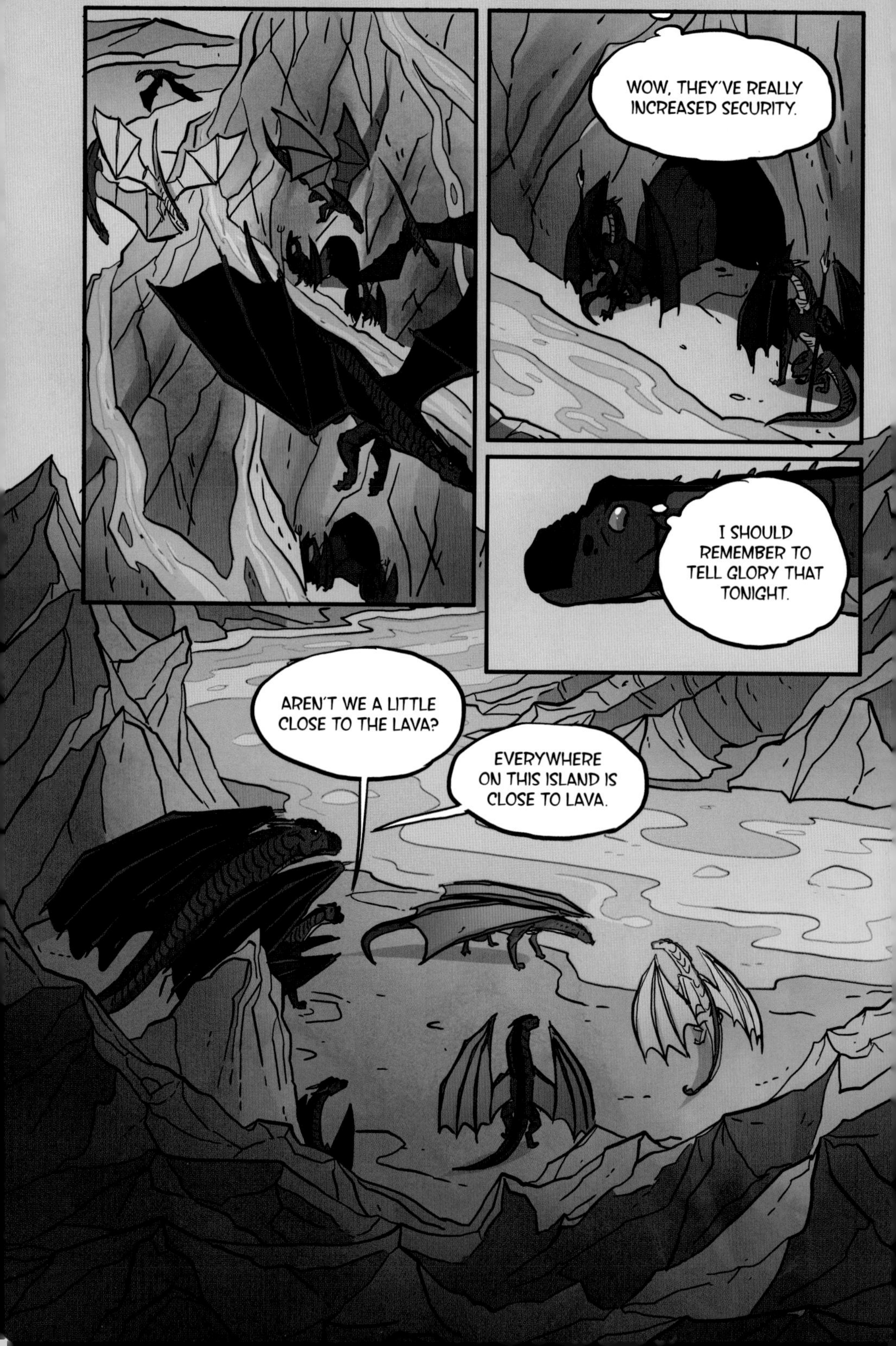
WOW, THEY'VE REALLY INCREASED SECURITY.
I SHOULD REMEMBER TO TELL GLORY THAT TONIGHT.
AREN'T WE A LITTLE CLOSE TO THE LAVA?
EVERYWHERE ON THIS ISLAND IS CLOSE TO LAVA.

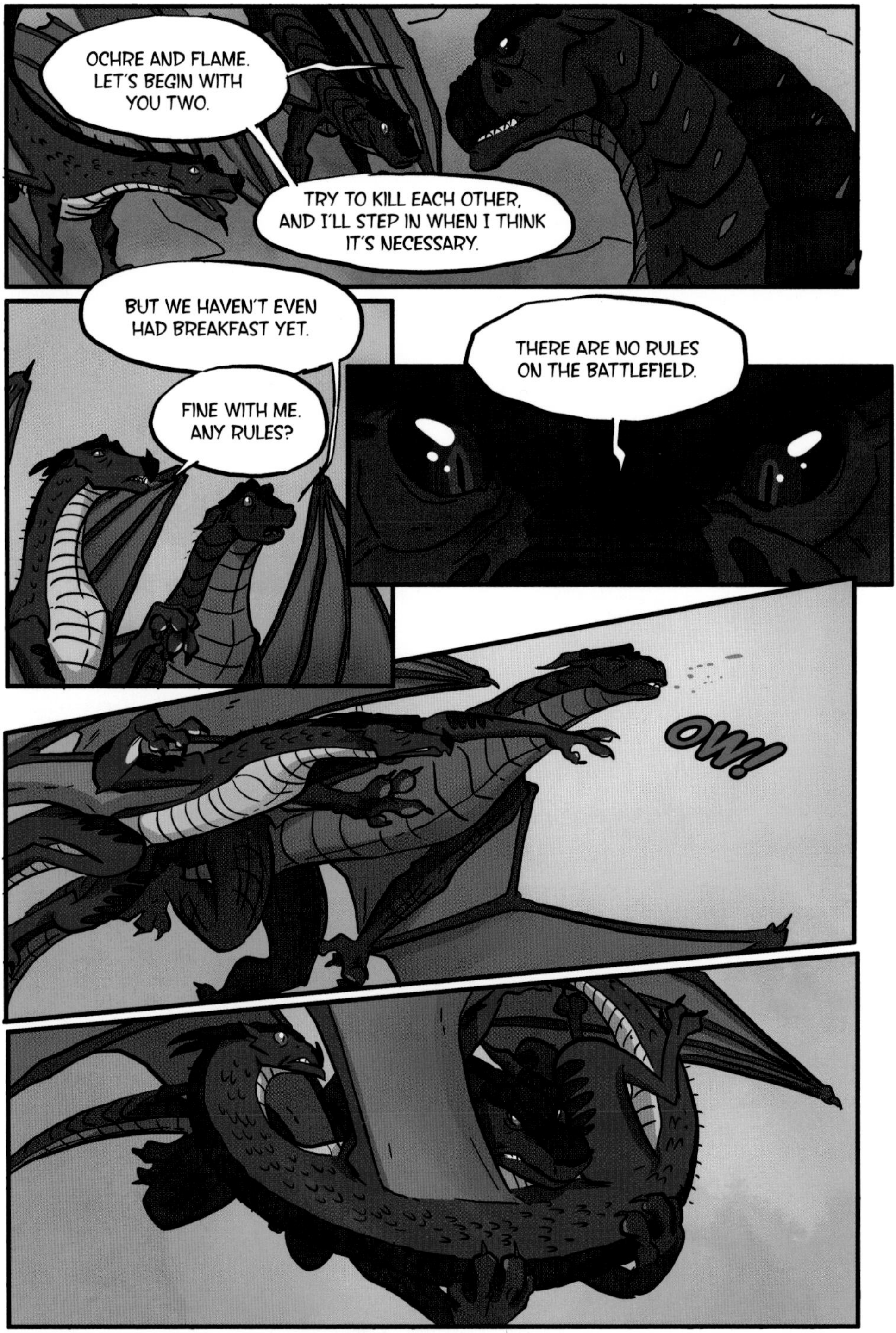
OCHRE AND FLAME. LET'S BEGIN WITH YOU TWO.
TRY TO KILL EACH OTHER, AND I'LL STEP IN WHEN I THINK IT'S NECESSARY.
BUT WE HAVEN'T EVEN HAD BREAKFAST YET.
FINE WITH ME. ANY RULES?
THERE ARE NO RULES ON THE BATTLEFIELD.
OW!!

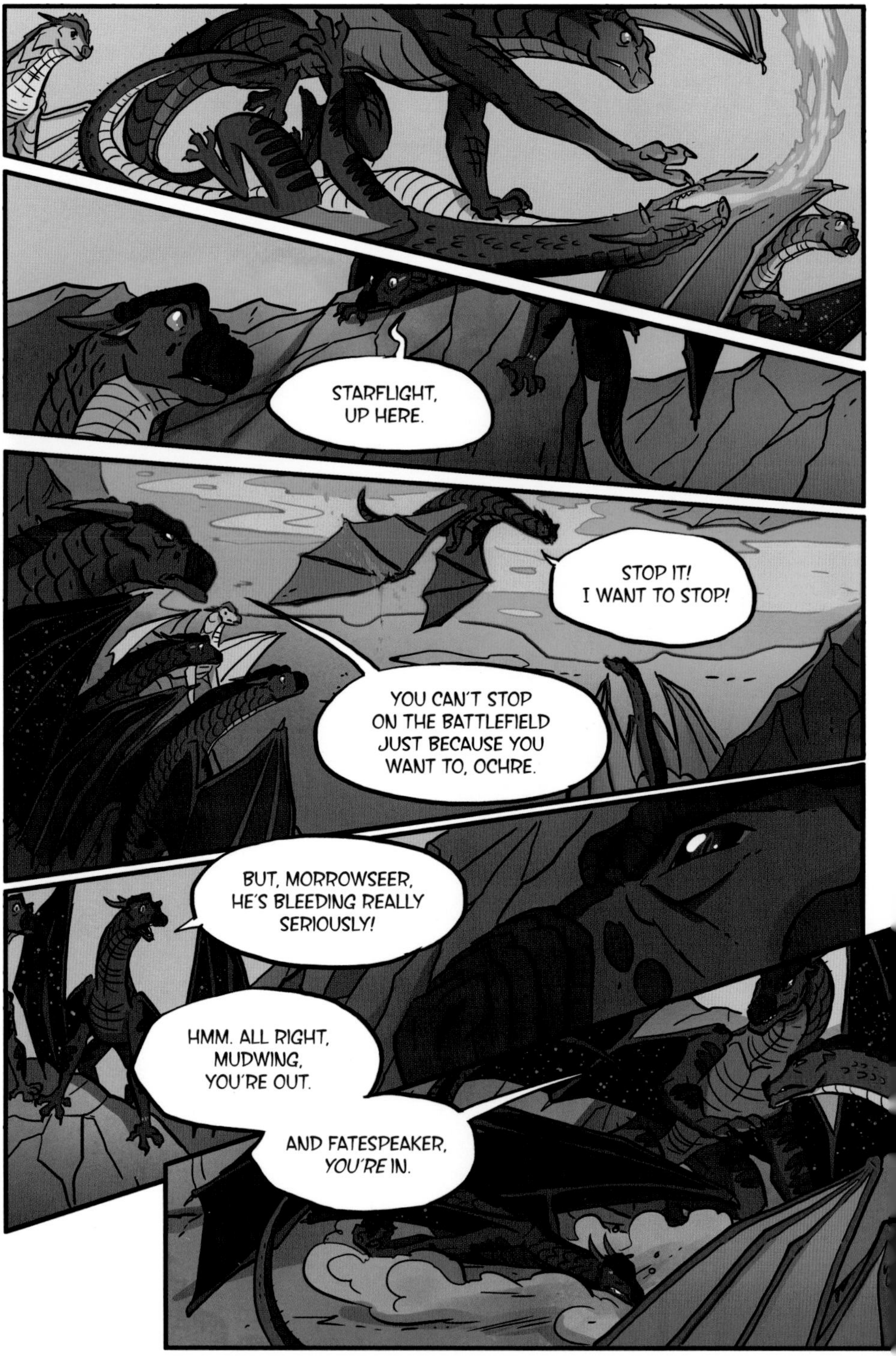
STARFLIGHT, UP HERE.
STOP IT! I WANT TO STOP!
YOU CAN'T STOP ON THE BATTLEFIELD JUST BECAUSE YOU WANT TO, OCHRE.
BUT, MORROWSEER, HE'S BLEEDING REALLY SERIOUSLY!
HMM. ALL RIGHT, MUDWING, YOU'RE OUT.
AND FATESPEAKER, *YOU'RE* IN.

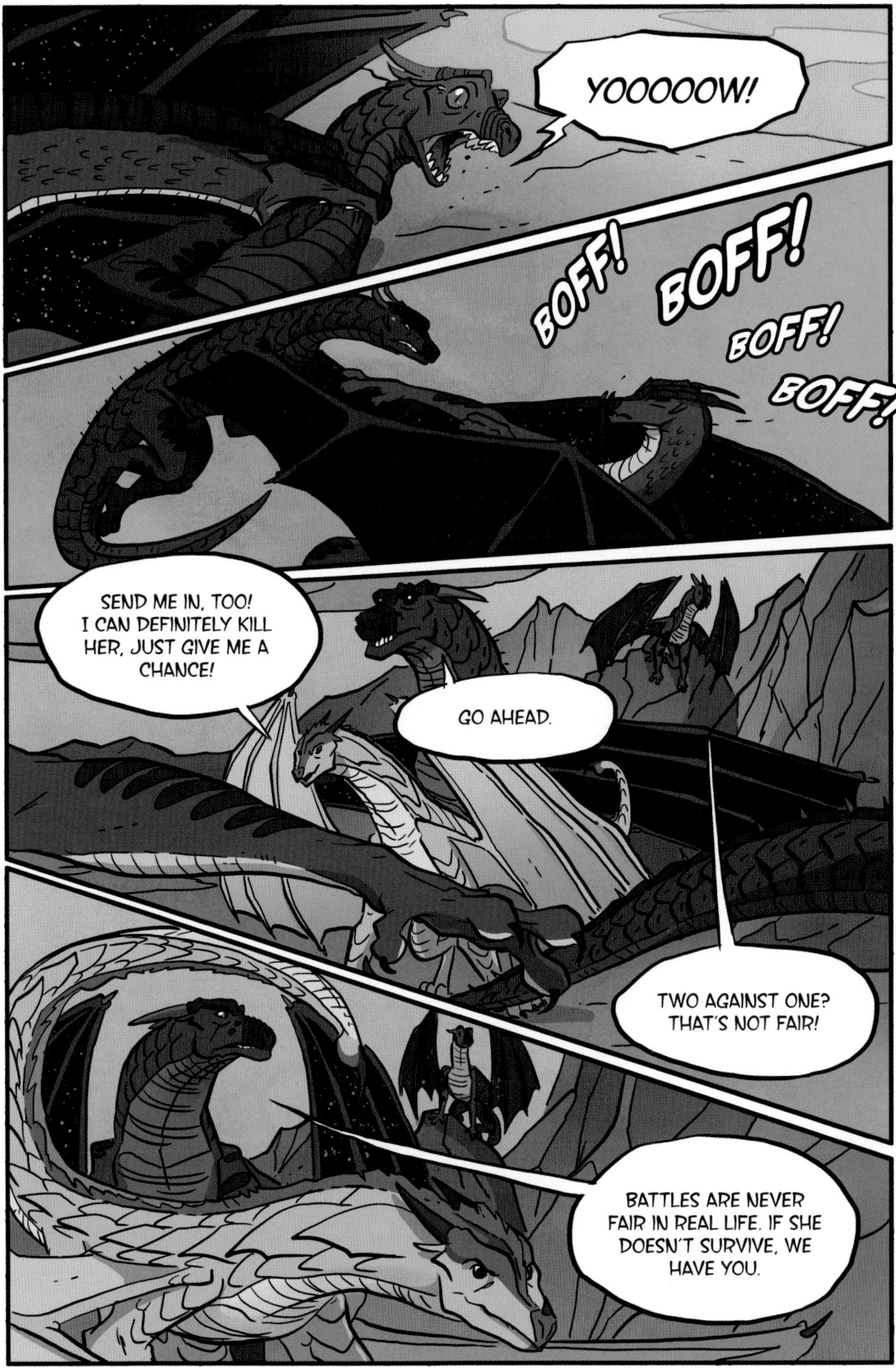
YOOOOOW!
BOFF! BOFF! BOFF! BOFF!
SEND ME IN, TOO! I CAN DEFINITELY KILL HER, JUST GIVE ME A CHANCE!
GO AHEAD.
TWO AGAINST ONE? THAT'S NOT FAIR!
BATTLES ARE NEVER FAIR IN REAL LIFE. IF SHE DOESN'T SURVIVE, WE HAVE YOU.

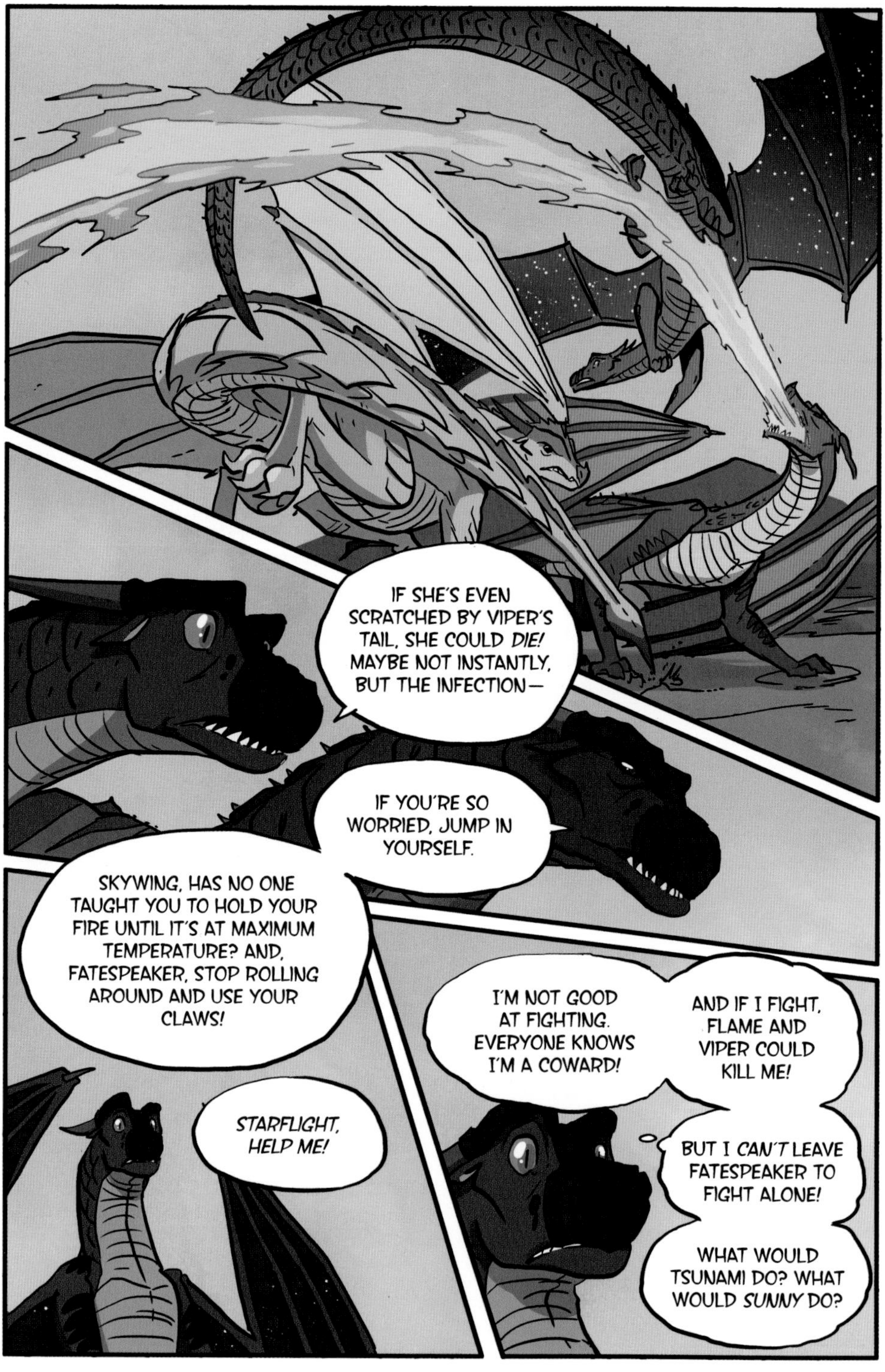
IF SHE'S EVEN SCRATCHED BY VIPER'S TAIL, SHE COULD *DIE!* MAYBE NOT INSTANTLY, BUT THE INFECTION—
IF YOU'RE SO WORRIED, JUMP IN YOURSELF.
SKYWING, HAS NO ONE TAUGHT YOU TO HOLD YOUR FIRE UNTIL IT'S AT MAXIMUM TEMPERATURE? AND, FATESPEAKER, STOP ROLLING AROUND AND USE YOUR CLAWS!
STARFLIGHT, HELP ME!
I'M NOT GOOD AT FIGHTING. EVERYONE KNOWS I'M A COWARD!
AND IF I FIGHT, FLAME AND VIPER COULD KILL ME!
BUT I *CAN'T* LEAVE FATESPEAKER TO FIGHT ALONE!
WHAT WOULD TSUNAMI DO? WHAT WOULD *SUNNY* DO?

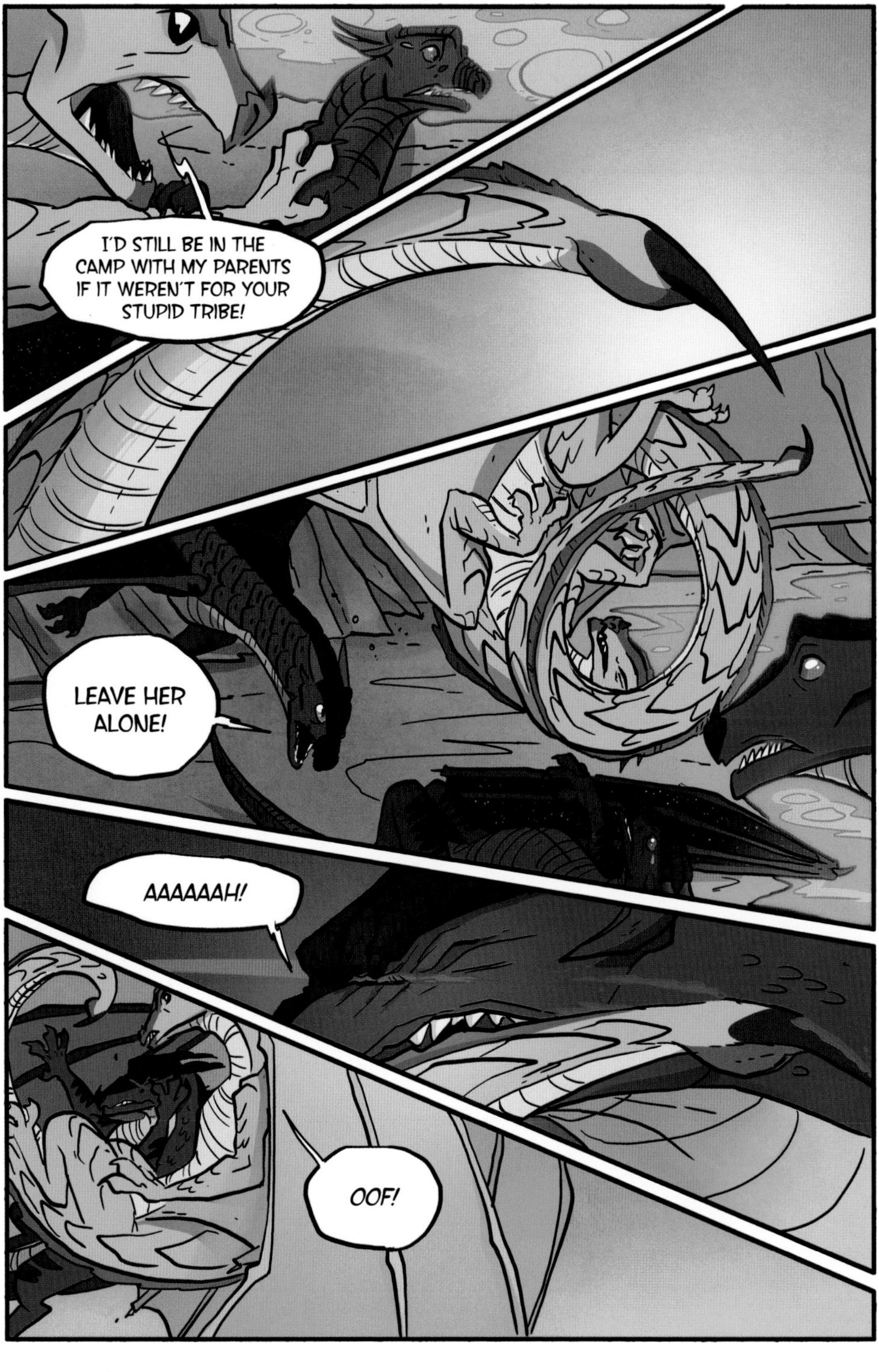
I'D STILL BE IN THE CAMP WITH MY PARENTS IF IT WEREN'T FOR YOUR STUPID TRIBE!
LEAVE HER ALONE!
AAAAAAH!
OOF!

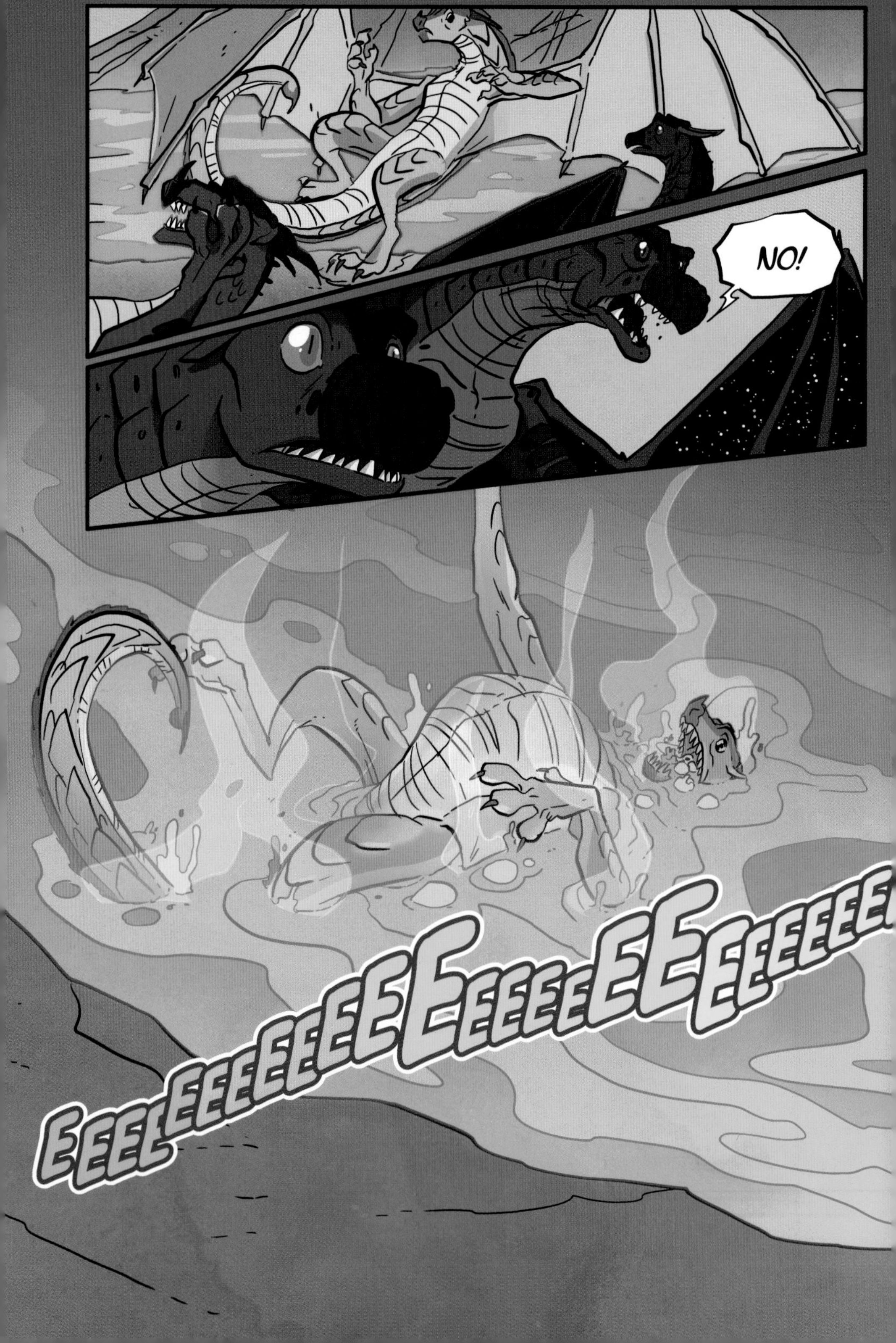

NO!
EEEEEEEEEEEEEEEEEEEEEEEEEEEEEE

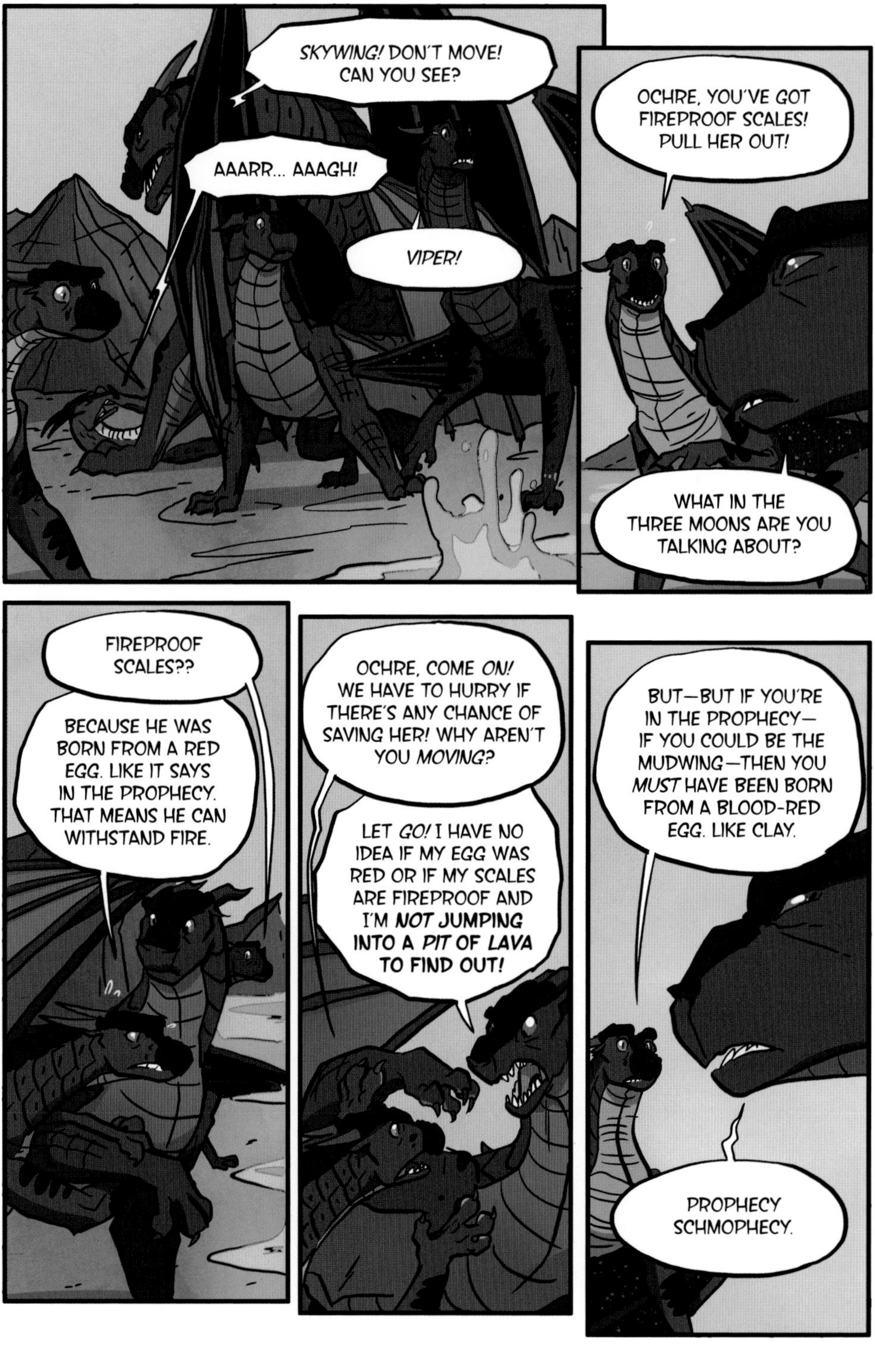

SKYWING! DON'T MOVE! CAN YOU SEE?
AAARR... AAAGH!
VIPER!
OCHRE, YOU'VE GOT FIREPROOF SCALES! PULL HER OUT!
WHAT IN THE THREE MOONS ARE YOU TALKING ABOUT?
FIREPROOF SCALES??
BECAUSE HE WAS BORN FROM A RED EGG. LIKE IT SAYS IN THE PROPHECY. THAT MEANS HE CAN WITHSTAND FIRE.
OCHRE, COME *ON!* WE HAVE TO HURRY IF THERE'S ANY CHANCE OF SAVING HER! WHY AREN'T YOU *MOVING?*
LET *GO!* I HAVE NO IDEA IF MY EGG WAS RED OR IF MY SCALES ARE FIREPROOF AND I'M **NOT JUMPING INTO A *PIT* OF *LAVA* TO FIND OUT!**
BUT—BUT IF YOU'RE IN THE PROPHECY—IF YOU COULD BE THE MUDWING—THEN YOU *MUST* HAVE BEEN BORN FROM A BLOOD-RED EGG. LIKE CLAY.
PROPHECY SCHMOPHECY.

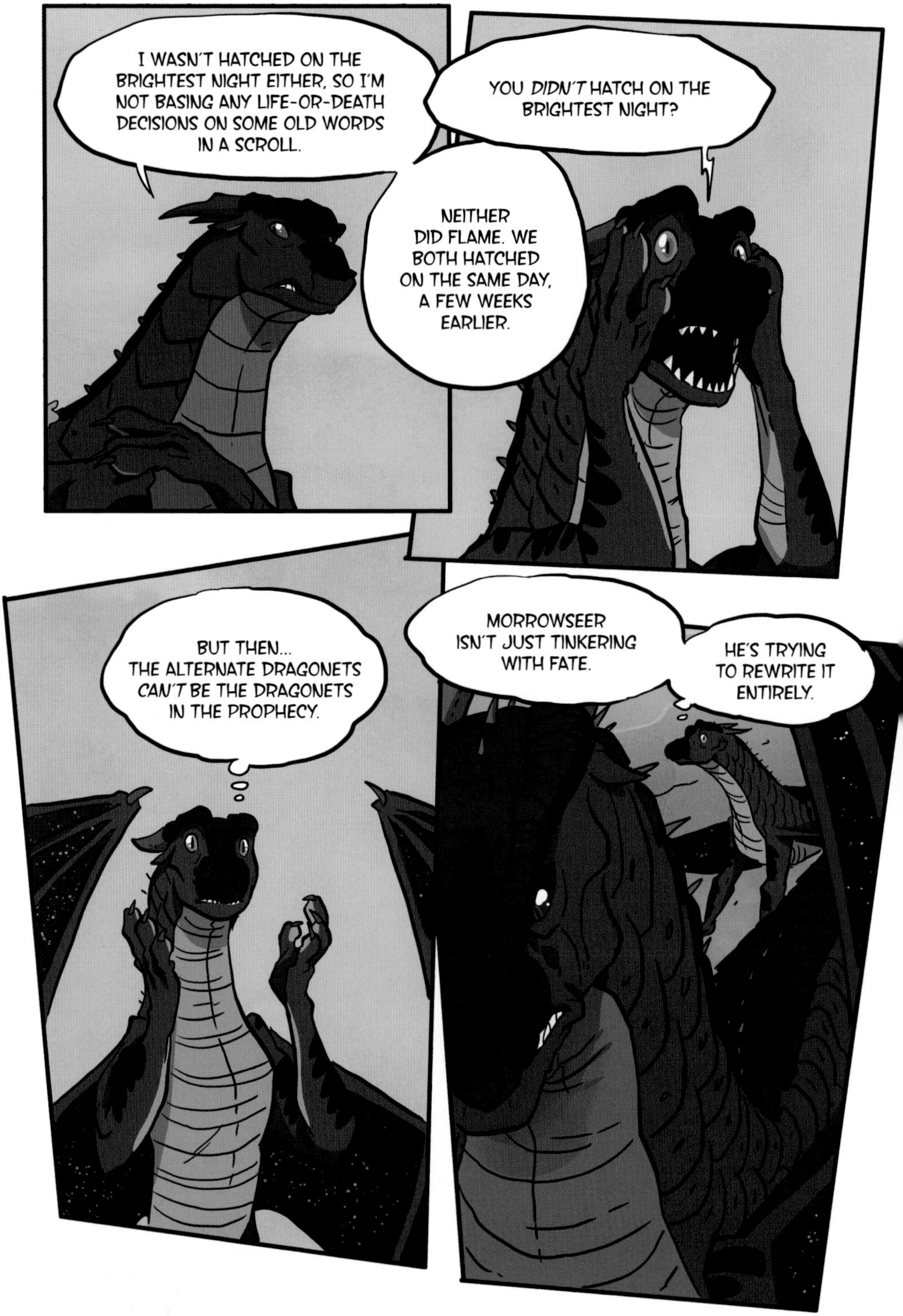
I WASN'T HATCHED ON THE BRIGHTEST NIGHT EITHER, SO I'M NOT BASING ANY LIFE-OR-DEATH DECISIONS ON SOME OLD WORDS IN A SCROLL.
YOU *DIDN'T* HATCH ON THE BRIGHTEST NIGHT?
NEITHER DID FLAME. WE BOTH HATCHED ON THE SAME DAY, A FEW WEEKS EARLIER.
BUT THEN... THE ALTERNATE DRAGONETS *CAN'T* BE THE DRAGONETS IN THE PROPHECY.
MORROWSEER ISN'T JUST TINKERING WITH FATE.
HE'S TRYING TO REWRITE IT ENTIRELY.

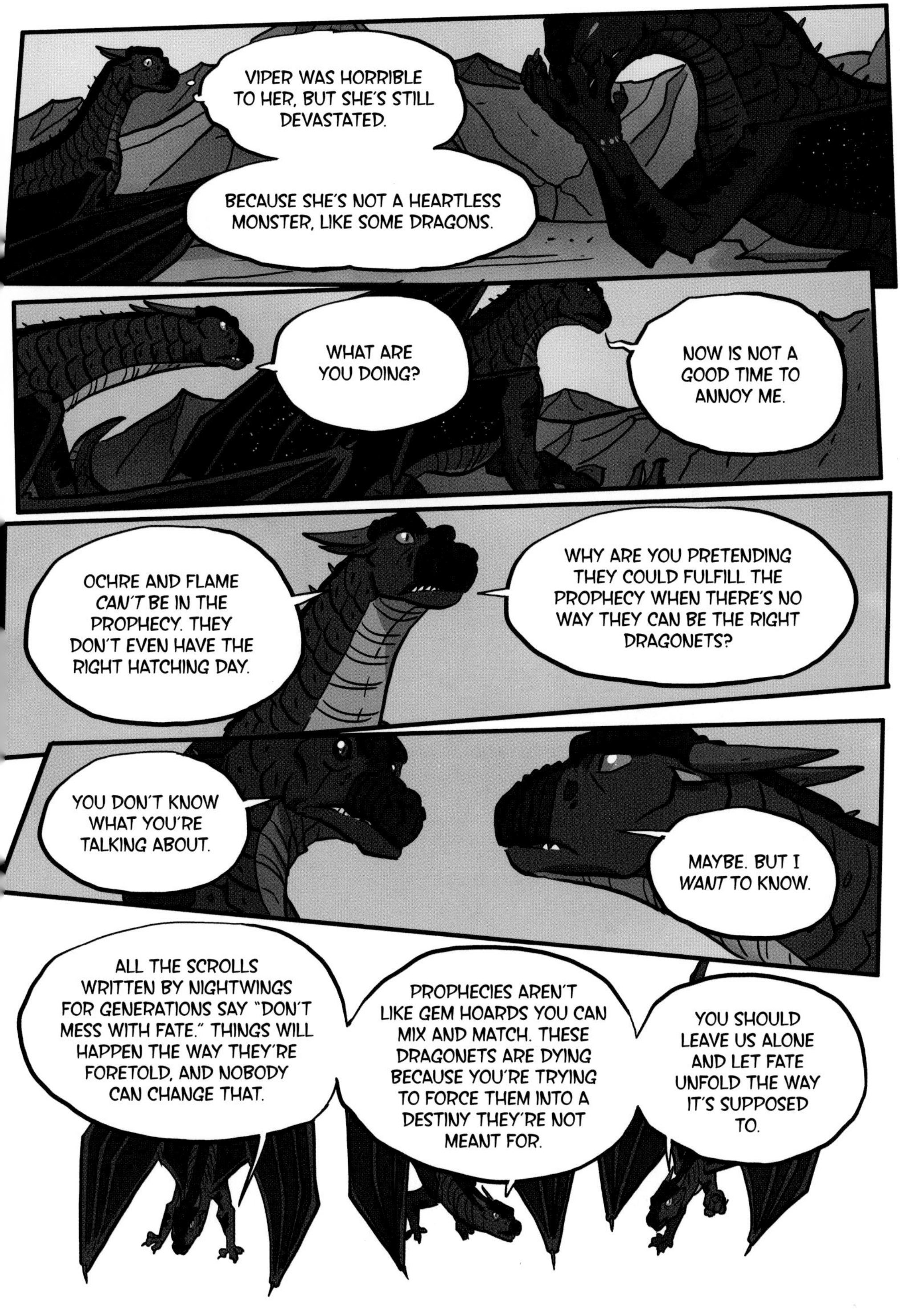
VIPER WAS HORRIBLE TO HER, BUT SHE'S STILL DEVASTATED.
BECAUSE SHE'S NOT A HEARTLESS MONSTER, LIKE SOME DRAGONS.
WHAT ARE YOU DOING?
NOW IS NOT A GOOD TIME TO ANNOY ME.
OCHRE AND FLAME *CAN'T* BE IN THE PROPHECY. THEY DON'T EVEN HAVE THE RIGHT HATCHING DAY.
WHY ARE YOU PRETENDING THEY COULD FULFILL THE PROPHECY WHEN THERE'S NO WAY THEY CAN BE THE RIGHT DRAGONETS?
YOU DON'T KNOW WHAT YOU'RE TALKING ABOUT.
MAYBE. BUT I *WANT* TO KNOW.
ALL THE SCROLLS WRITTEN BY NIGHTWINGS FOR GENERATIONS SAY "DON'T MESS WITH FATE." THINGS WILL HAPPEN THE WAY THEY'RE FORETOLD, AND NOBODY CAN CHANGE THAT.
PROPHECIES AREN'T LIKE GEM HOARDS YOU CAN MIX AND MATCH. THESE DRAGONETS ARE DYING BECAUSE YOU'RE TRYING TO FORCE THEM INTO A DESTINY THEY'RE NOT MEANT FOR.
YOU SHOULD LEAVE US ALONE AND LET FATE UNFOLD THE WAY IT'S SUPPOSED TO.

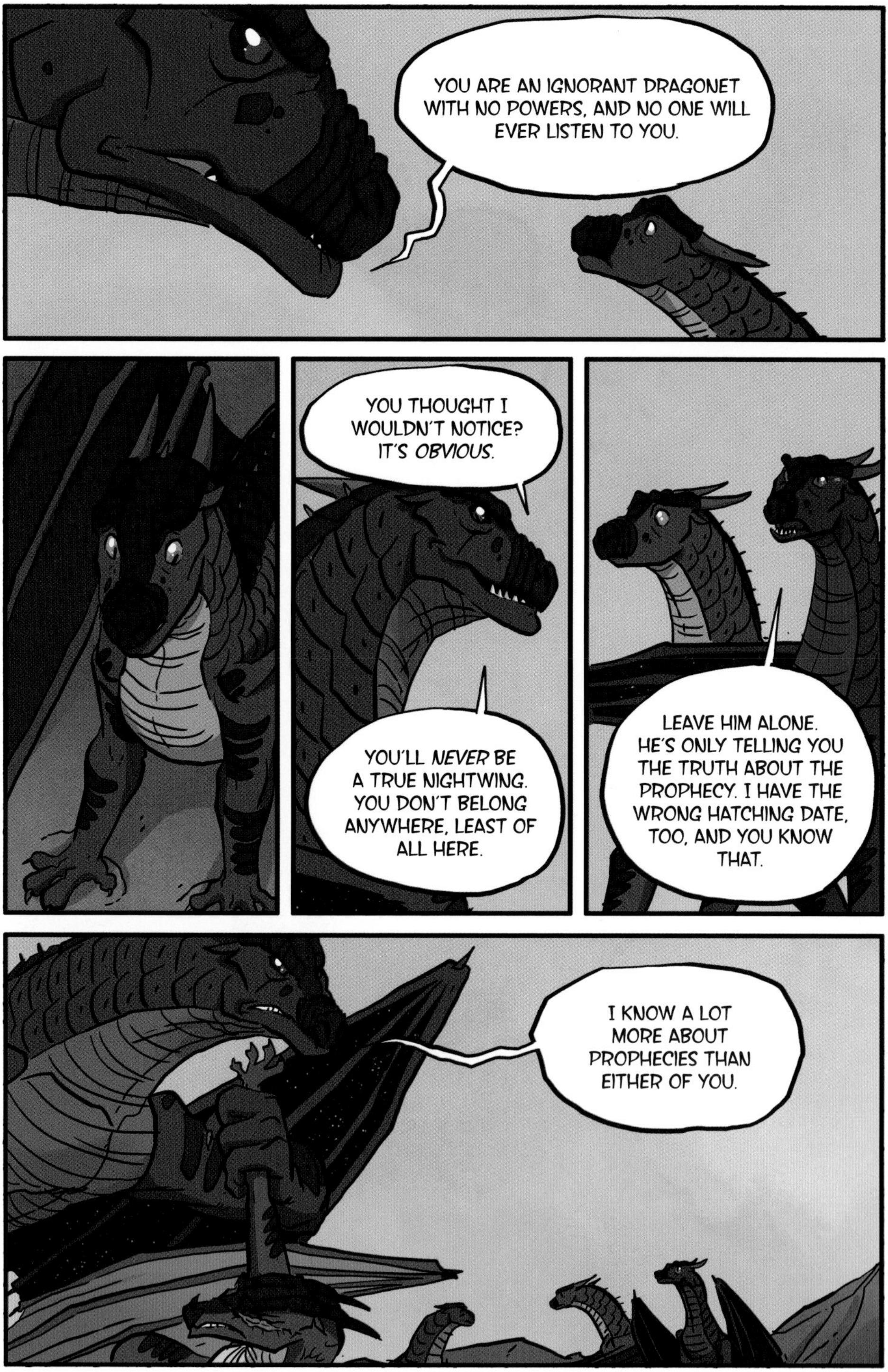
YOU ARE AN IGNORANT DRAGONET WITH NO POWERS, AND NO ONE WILL EVER LISTEN TO YOU.
YOU THOUGHT I WOULDN'T NOTICE? IT'S *OBVIOUS*.
YOU'LL *NEVER* BE A TRUE NIGHTWING. YOU DON'T BELONG ANYWHERE, LEAST OF ALL HERE.
LEAVE HIM ALONE. HE'S ONLY TELLING YOU THE TRUTH ABOUT THE PROPHECY. I HAVE THE WRONG HATCHING DATE, TOO, AND YOU KNOW THAT.
I KNOW A LOT MORE ABOUT PROPHECIES THAN EITHER OF YOU.

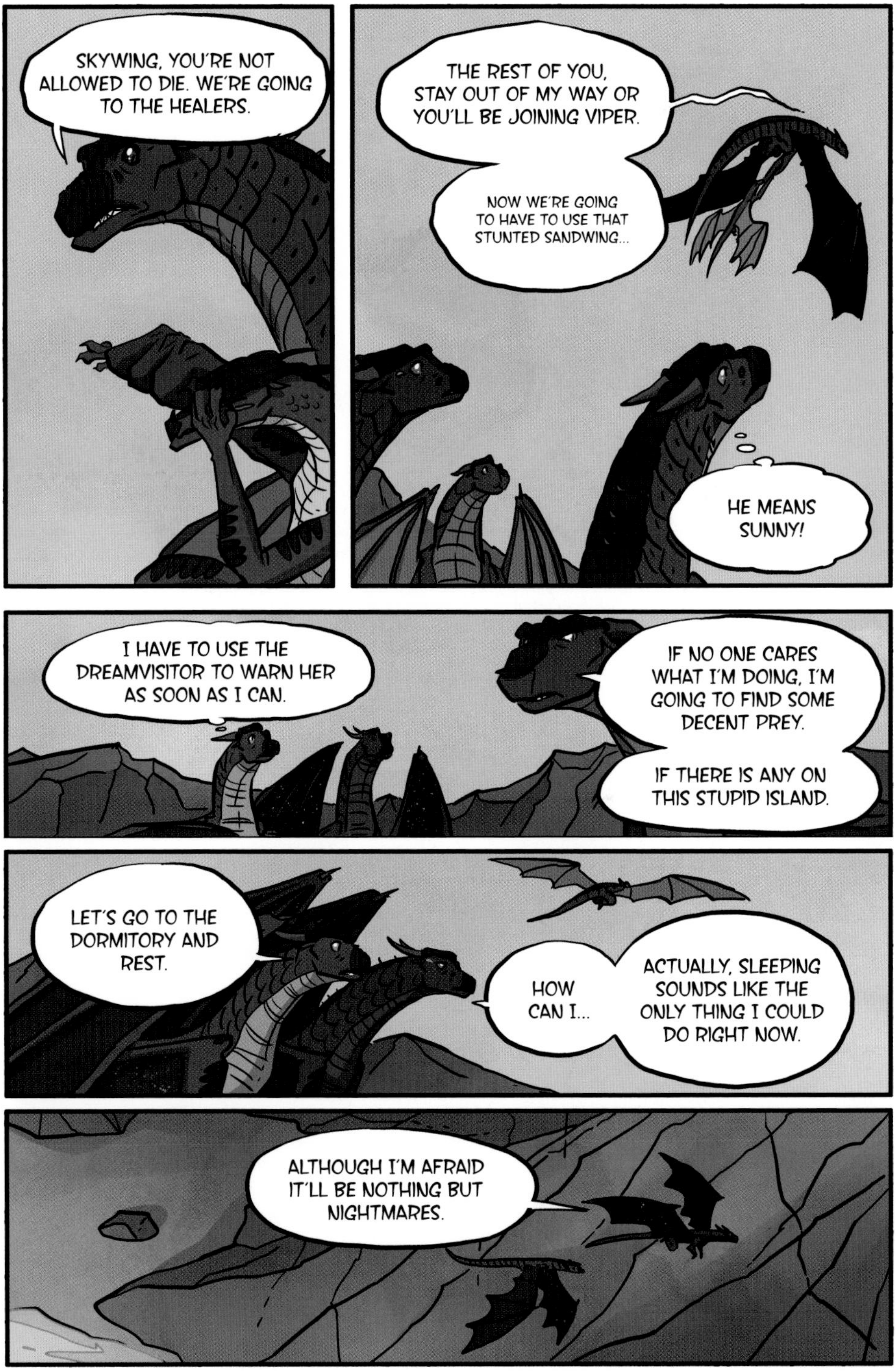
SKYWING, YOU'RE NOT ALLOWED TO DIE. WE'RE GOING TO THE HEALERS.
THE REST OF YOU, STAY OUT OF MY WAY OR YOU'LL BE JOINING VIPER.
NOW WE'RE GOING TO HAVE TO USE THAT STUNTED SANDWING...
HE MEANS SUNNY!
I HAVE TO USE THE DREAMVISITOR TO WARN HER AS SOON AS I CAN.
IF NO ONE CARES WHAT I'M DOING, I'M GOING TO FIND SOME DECENT PREY.
IF THERE IS ANY ON THIS STUPID ISLAND.
LET'S GO TO THE DORMITORY AND REST.
HOW CAN I...
ACTUALLY, SLEEPING SOUNDS LIKE THE ONLY THING I COULD DO RIGHT NOW.
ALTHOUGH I'M AFRAID IT'LL BE NOTHING BUT NIGHTMARES.

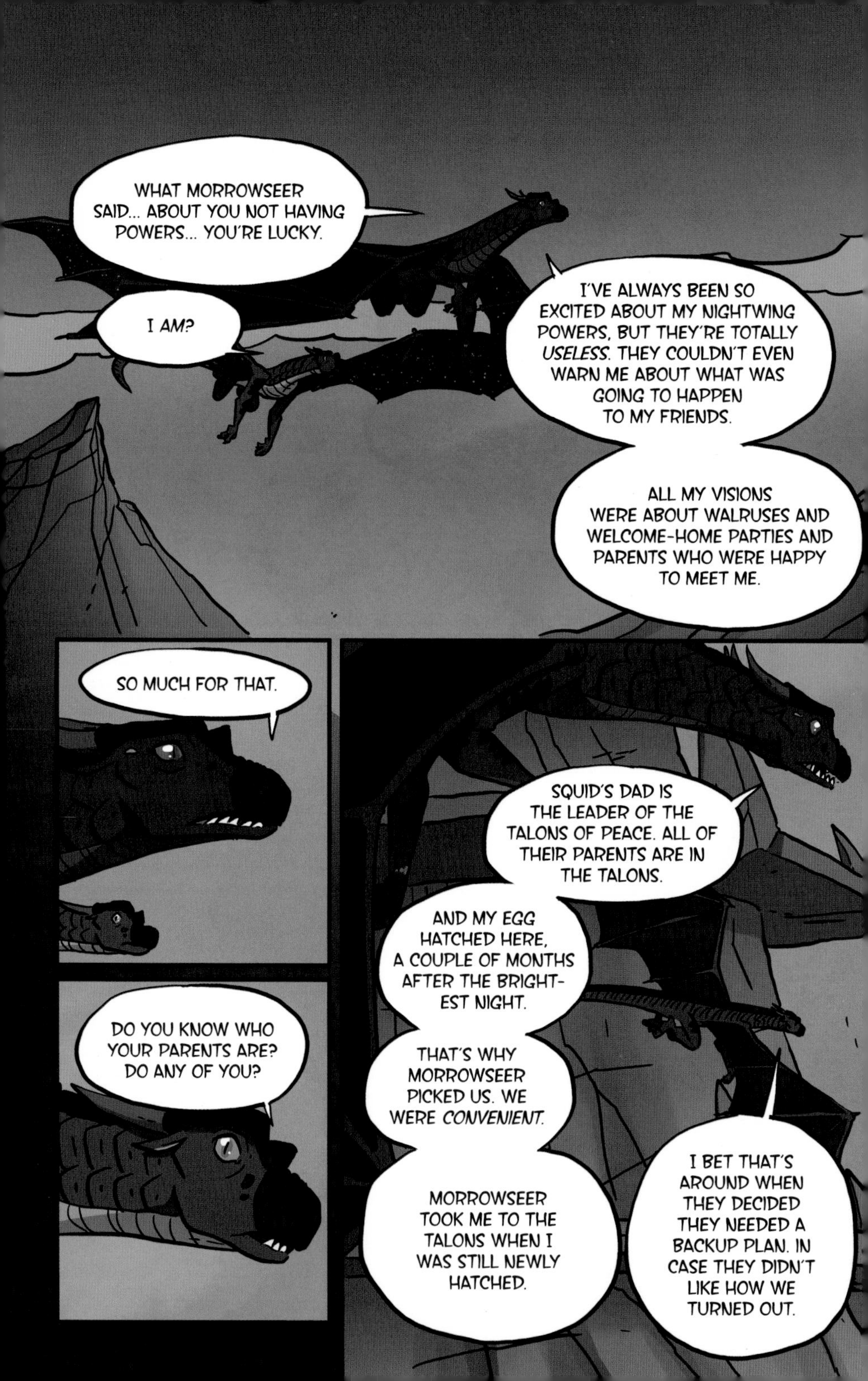
WHAT MORROWSEER SAID... ABOUT YOU NOT HAVING POWERS... YOU'RE LUCKY.
I AM?
I'VE ALWAYS BEEN SO EXCITED ABOUT MY NIGHTWING POWERS, BUT THEY'RE TOTALLY *USELESS*. THEY COULDN'T EVEN WARN ME ABOUT WHAT WAS GOING TO HAPPEN TO MY FRIENDS.
ALL MY VISIONS WERE ABOUT WALRUSES AND WELCOME-HOME PARTIES AND PARENTS WHO WERE HAPPY TO MEET ME.
SO MUCH FOR THAT.
DO YOU KNOW WHO YOUR PARENTS ARE? DO ANY OF YOU?
SQUID'S DAD IS THE LEADER OF THE TALONS OF PEACE. ALL OF THEIR PARENTS ARE IN THE TALONS.
AND MY EGG HATCHED HERE, A COUPLE OF MONTHS AFTER THE BRIGHTEST NIGHT.
THAT'S WHY MORROWSEER PICKED US. WE WERE *CONVENIENT*.
MORROWSEER TOOK ME TO THE TALONS WHEN I WAS STILL NEWLY HATCHED.
I BET THAT'S AROUND WHEN THEY DECIDED THEY NEEDED A BACKUP PLAN. IN CASE THEY DIDN'T LIKE HOW WE TURNED OUT.

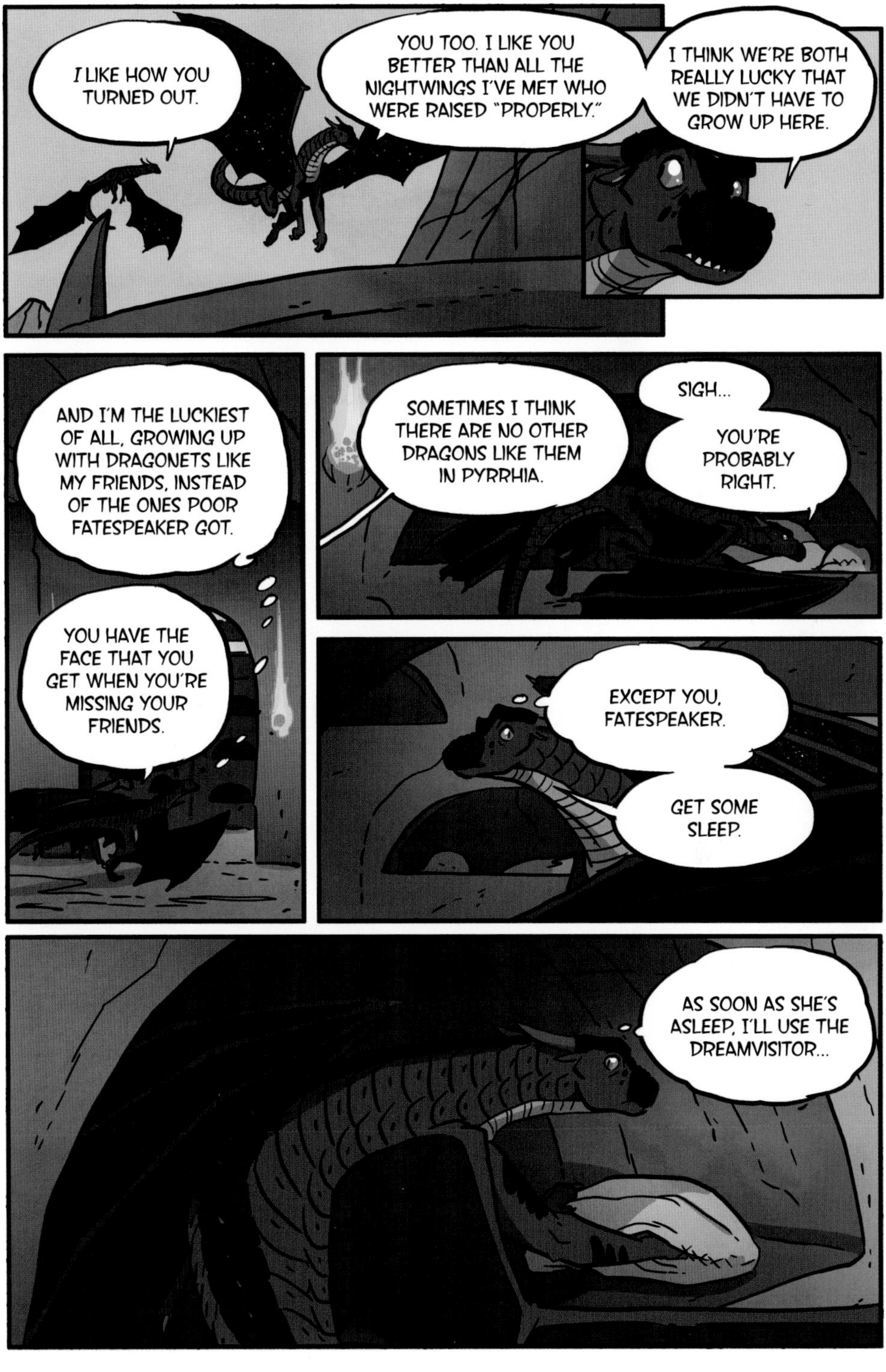
I LIKE HOW YOU TURNED OUT.
YOU TOO. I LIKE YOU BETTER THAN ALL THE NIGHTWINGS I'VE MET WHO WERE RAISED "PROPERLY."
I THINK WE'RE BOTH REALLY LUCKY THAT WE DIDN'T HAVE TO GROW UP HERE.
AND I'M THE LUCKIEST OF ALL, GROWING UP WITH DRAGONETS LIKE MY FRIENDS, INSTEAD OF THE ONES POOR FATESPEAKER GOT.
YOU HAVE THE FACE THAT YOU GET WHEN YOU'RE MISSING YOUR FRIENDS.
SOMETIMES I THINK THERE ARE NO OTHER DRAGONS LIKE THEM IN PYRRHIA.
SIGH...
YOU'RE PROBABLY RIGHT.
EXCEPT YOU, FATESPEAKER.
GET SOME SLEEP.
AS SOON AS SHE'S ASLEEP, I'LL USE THE DREAMVISITOR...

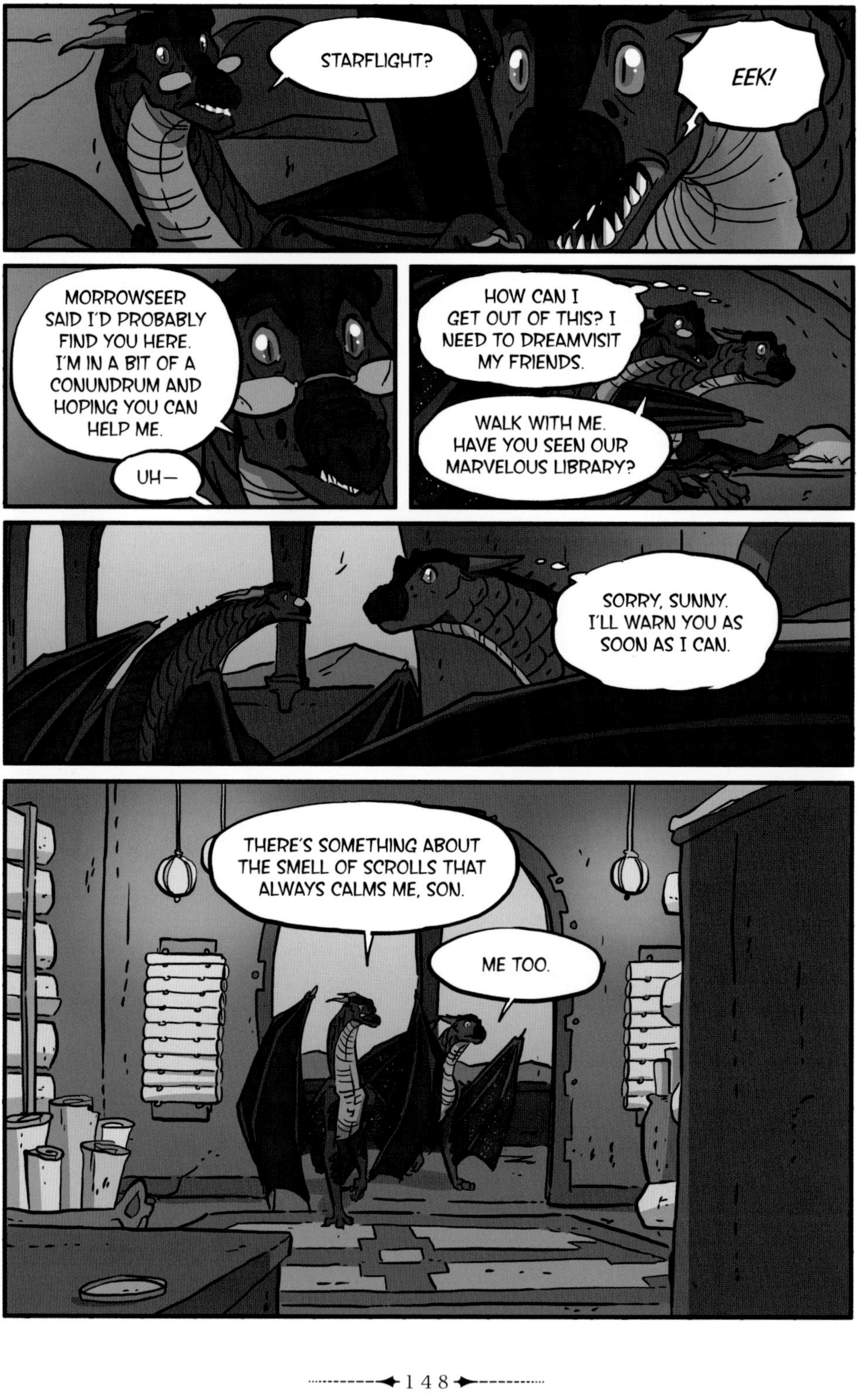
STARFLIGHT?
EEK!
MORROWSEER SAID I'D PROBABLY FIND YOU HERE. I'M IN A BIT OF A CONUNDRUM AND HOPING YOU CAN HELP ME.
UH—
HOW CAN I GET OUT OF THIS? I NEED TO DREAMVISIT MY FRIENDS.
WALK WITH ME. HAVE YOU SEEN OUR MARVELOUS LIBRARY?
SORRY, SUNNY. I'LL WARN YOU AS SOON AS I CAN.
THERE'S SOMETHING ABOUT THE SMELL OF SCROLLS THAT ALWAYS CALMS ME, SON.
ME TOO.

MEDICAL RECORDS, MEDICAL RECORDS.

HELP ME BRAINSTORM. THE QUEEN IS VERY ANGRY ABOUT WHAT HAPPENED TO THE SKYWING DRAGONET. I'M AFRAID HE'LL BE DEAD BY MORNING IF WE CAN'T COUNTERACT THE SANDWING POISON.

WHICH IS APPARENTLY *MY* RESPONSIBILITY FOR SOME REASON, AS IF I'M NOT ALREADY SWAMPED TRYING TO PRODUCE VENOM-PROOF HELMETS FOR THE ENTIRE NIGHTWING TRIBE IN TWO DAYS USING ONLY MY INSUFFICIENTLY TESTED PROTOTYPE, WHICH THE QUEEN SAYS WILL SIMPLY HAVE TO DO FOR NOW.

WAIT. DID YOU SAY TWO DAYS?

IN CASE WE DECIDE TO ATTACK. I TOLD THEM MY RESEARCH IS INCOMPLETE AND I CAN'T GUARANTEE IT WILL GO SMOOTHLY.

THE PROBLEM IS I'VE NEVER *STUDIED* SANDWING VENOM. BUT IF IT'S ANYTHING LIKE RAINWING VENOM, THERE'S NOTHING THAT CAN COUNTERACT IT.

HE HASN'T FIGURED OUT THAT A RELATIVE'S VENOM IS THE ANTIDOTE FOR RAINWING VENOM?

IF ALL THE RAINWINGS MANAGED TO KEEP THAT SECRET, MAYBE THEY'RE TOUGHER AND SMARTER THAN ANYONE THINKS.

NIGHTWINGS KEEP THEMSELVES ISOLATED TO SEEM MORE POWERFUL, BUT IT MEANS THEY'RE CUT OFF FROM SO MUCH KNOWLEDGE. IF THEY DIDN'T FEEL SO SUPERIOR TO OTHER DRAGONS, MAYBE THEY'D LEARN SOMETHING NEW.

UNLIKELY... TRIED THAT ON RAINWING VENOM, DIDN'T WORK...

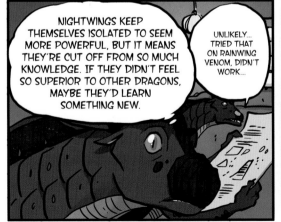

NONE NEARBY... DOUBTFUL...

FOR NIGHTWING *EYES ONLY!*

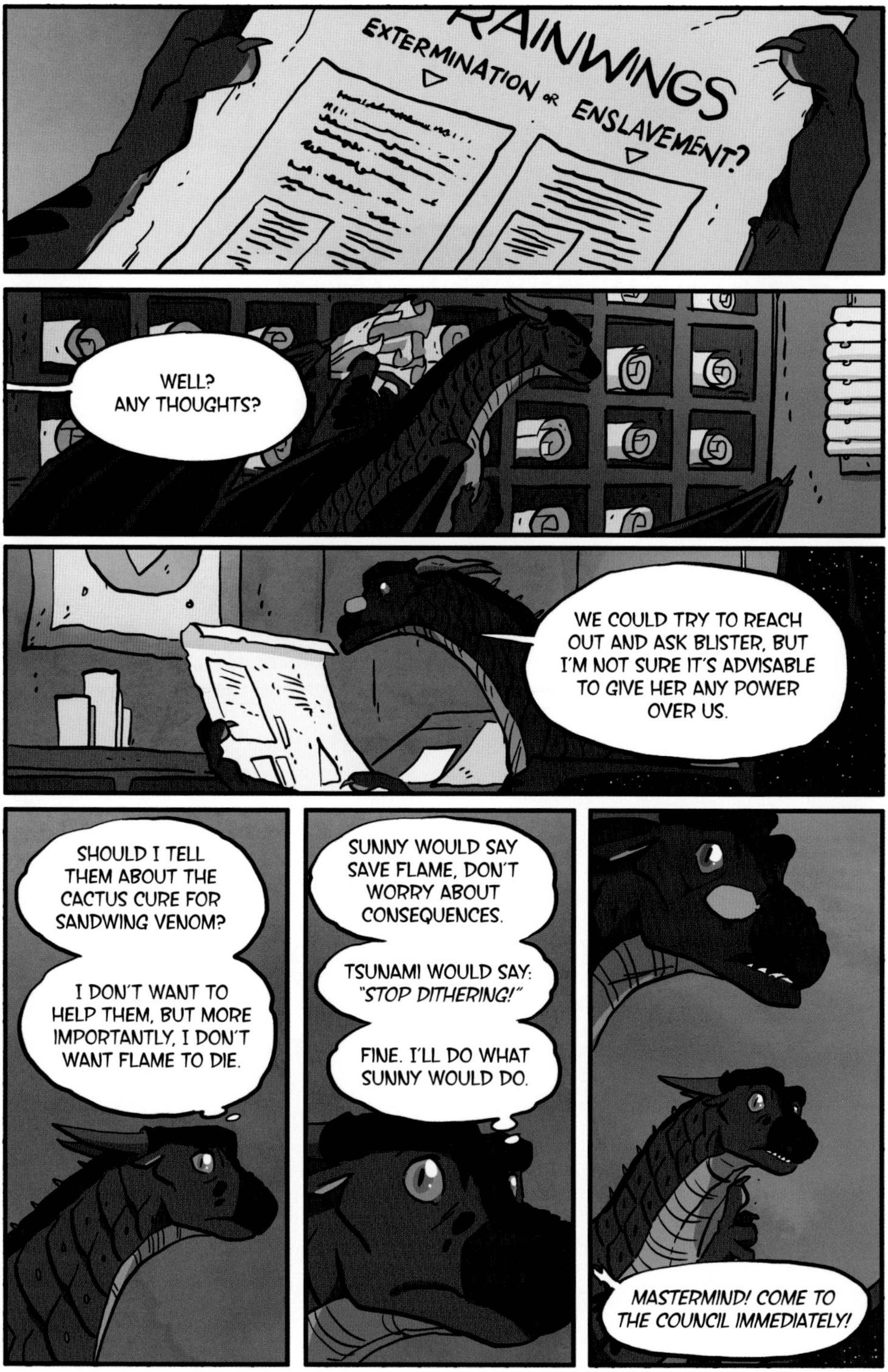
RAINWINGS
EXTERMINATION OR ENSLAVEMENT?
WELL? ANY THOUGHTS?
WE COULD TRY TO REACH OUT AND ASK BLISTER, BUT I'M NOT SURE IT'S ADVISABLE TO GIVE HER ANY POWER OVER US.
SHOULD I TELL THEM ABOUT THE CACTUS CURE FOR SANDWING VENOM?
I DON'T WANT TO HELP THEM, BUT MORE IMPORTANTLY, I DON'T WANT FLAME TO DIE.
SUNNY WOULD SAY SAVE FLAME, DON'T WORRY ABOUT CONSEQUENCES.
TSUNAMI WOULD SAY: *"STOP DITHERING!"*
FINE. I'LL DO WHAT SUNNY WOULD DO.
MASTERMIND! COME TO THE COUNCIL IMMEDIATELY!

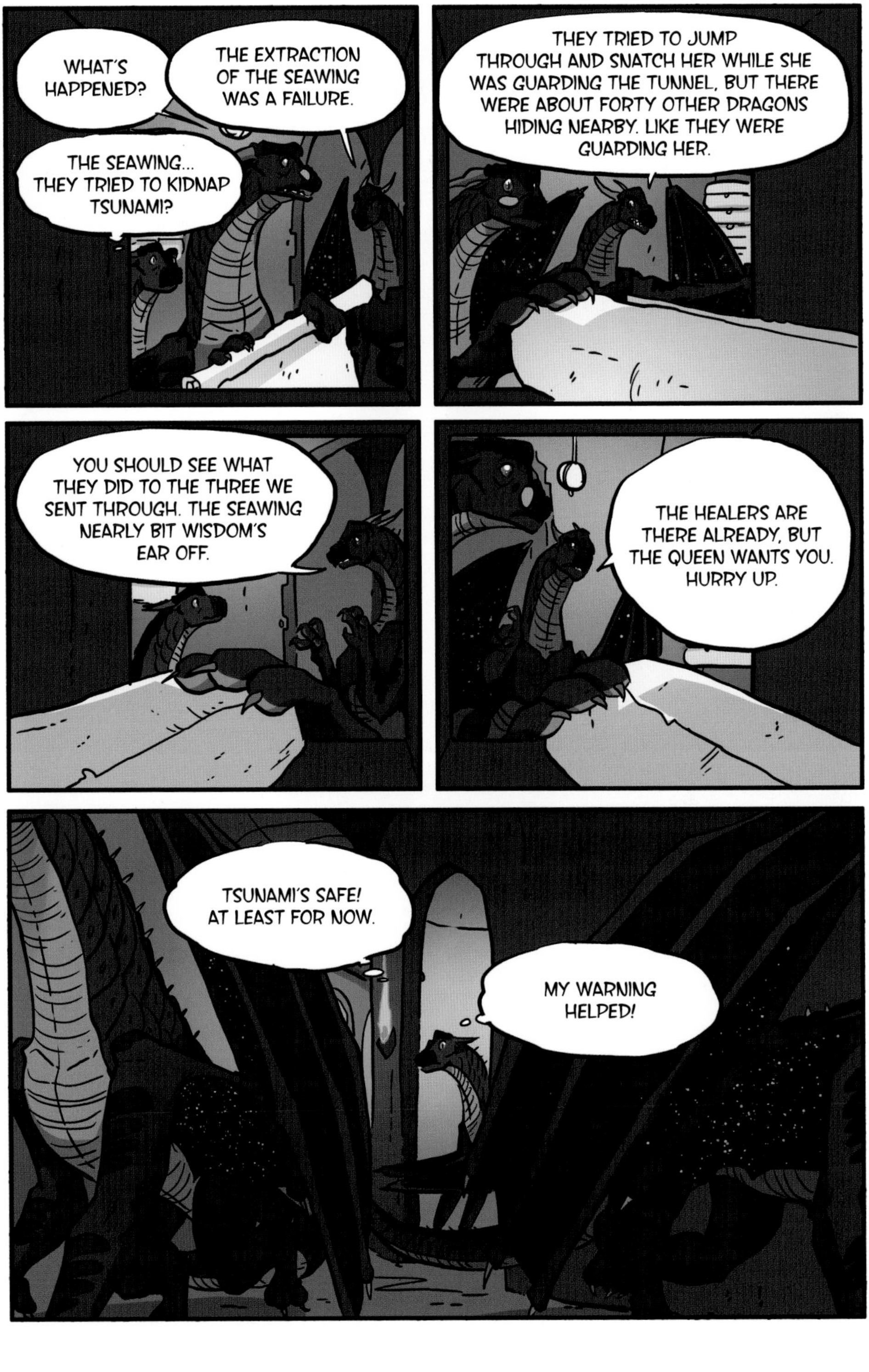
WHAT'S HAPPENED?
THE EXTRACTION OF THE SEAWING WAS A FAILURE.
THE SEAWING... THEY TRIED TO KIDNAP TSUNAMI?
THEY TRIED TO JUMP THROUGH AND SNATCH HER WHILE SHE WAS GUARDING THE TUNNEL, BUT THERE WERE ABOUT FORTY OTHER DRAGONS HIDING NEARBY. LIKE THEY WERE GUARDING HER.
YOU SHOULD SEE WHAT THEY DID TO THE THREE WE SENT THROUGH. THE SEAWING NEARLY BIT WISDOM'S EAR OFF.
THE HEALERS ARE THERE ALREADY, BUT THE QUEEN WANTS YOU. HURRY UP.
TSUNAMI'S SAFE! AT LEAST FOR NOW.
MY WARNING HELPED!

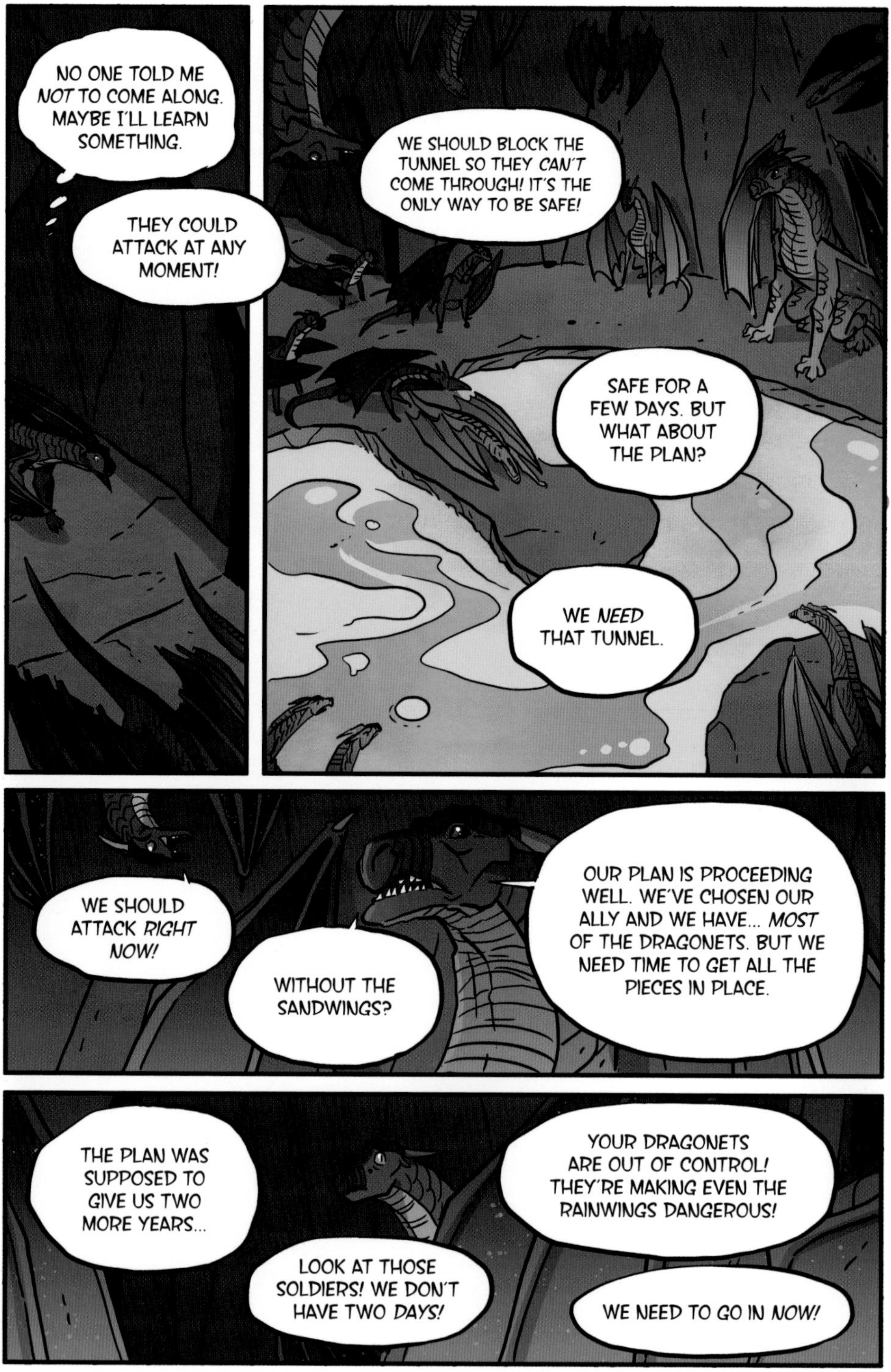
NO ONE TOLD ME *NOT* TO COME ALONG. MAYBE I'LL LEARN SOMETHING.
THEY COULD ATTACK AT ANY MOMENT!
WE SHOULD BLOCK THE TUNNEL SO THEY *CAN'T* COME THROUGH! IT'S THE ONLY WAY TO BE SAFE!
SAFE FOR A FEW DAYS. BUT WHAT ABOUT THE PLAN?
WE *NEED* THAT TUNNEL.
WE SHOULD ATTACK *RIGHT NOW!*
WITHOUT THE SANDWINGS?
OUR PLAN IS PROCEEDING WELL. WE'VE CHOSEN OUR ALLY AND WE HAVE... *MOST* OF THE DRAGONETS. BUT WE NEED TIME TO GET ALL THE PIECES IN PLACE.
THE PLAN WAS SUPPOSED TO GIVE US TWO MORE YEARS...
YOUR DRAGONETS ARE OUT OF CONTROL! THEY'RE MAKING EVEN THE RAINWINGS DANGEROUS!
LOOK AT THOSE SOLDIERS! WE DON'T HAVE TWO *DAYS!*
WE NEED TO GO IN *NOW!*

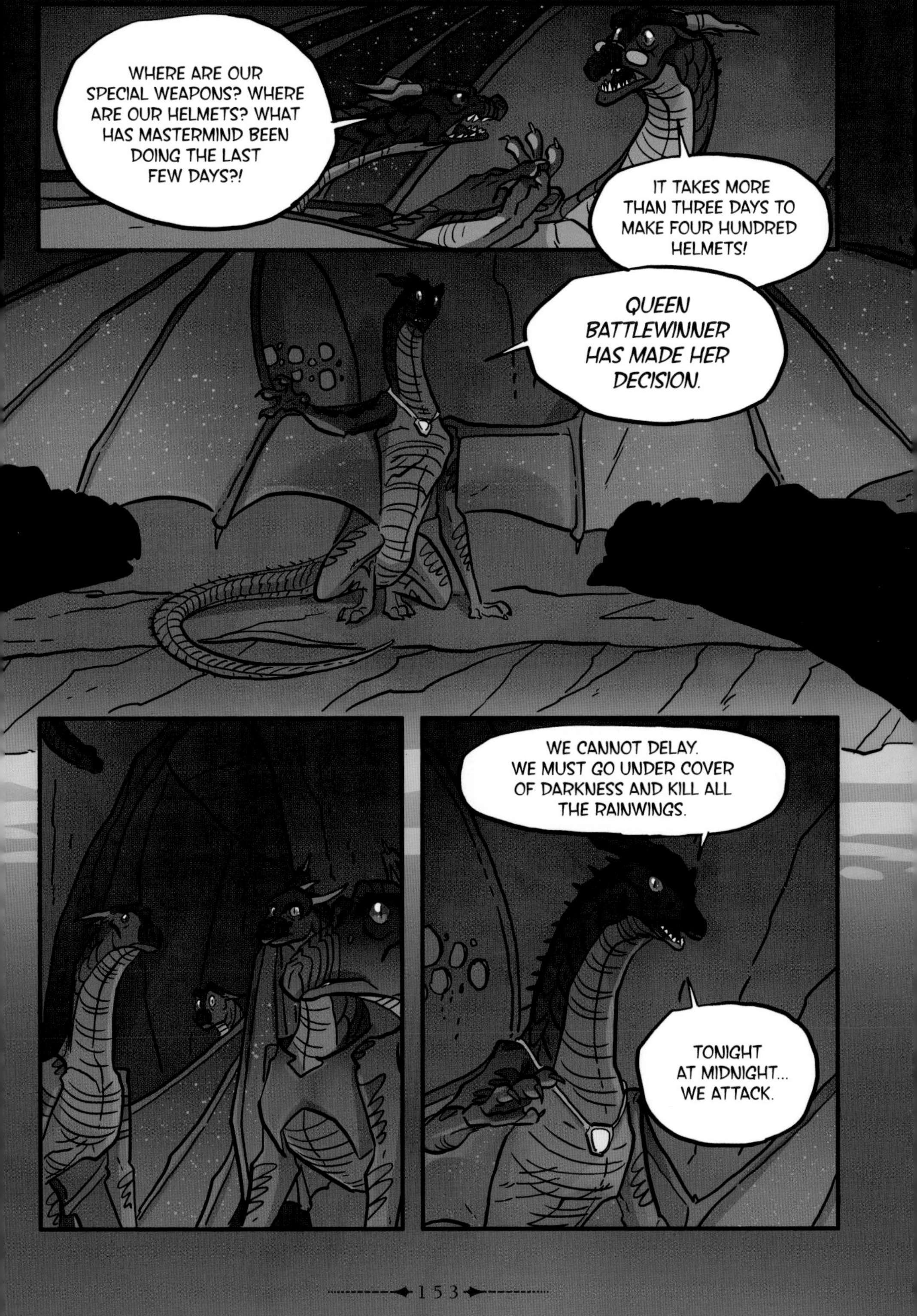

WHERE ARE OUR SPECIAL WEAPONS? WHERE ARE OUR HELMETS? WHAT HAS MASTERMIND BEEN DOING THE LAST FEW DAYS?!
IT TAKES MORE THAN THREE DAYS TO MAKE FOUR HUNDRED HELMETS!
QUEEN BATTLEWINNER HAS MADE HER DECISION.
WE CANNOT DELAY. WE MUST GO UNDER COVER OF DARKNESS AND KILL ALL THE RAINWINGS.
TONIGHT AT MIDNIGHT... WE ATTACK.

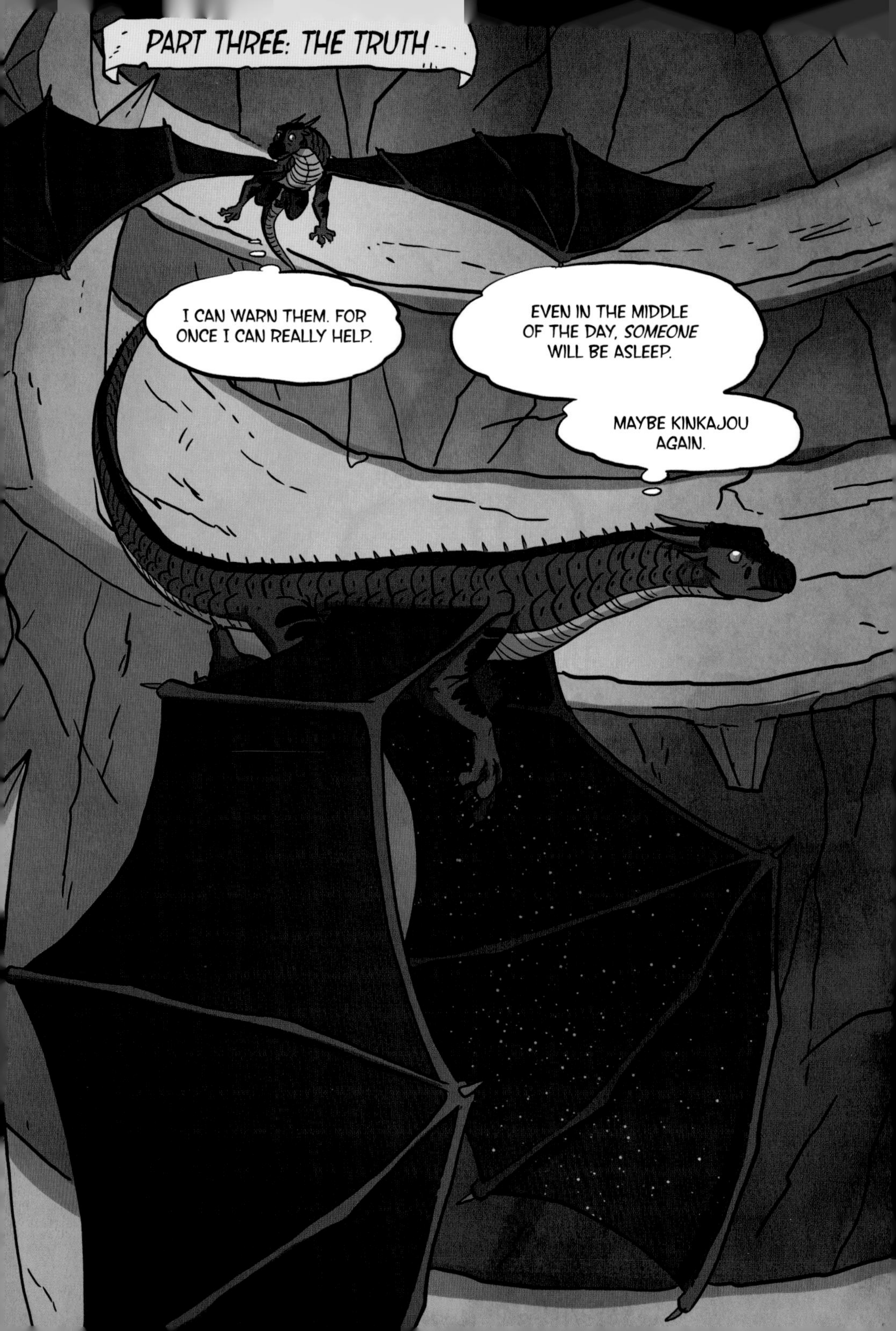
PART THREE: THE TRUTH
I CAN WARN THEM. FOR ONCE I CAN REALLY HELP.
EVEN IN THE MIDDLE OF THE DAY, *SOMEONE* WILL BE ASLEEP.
MAYBE KINKAJOU AGAIN.

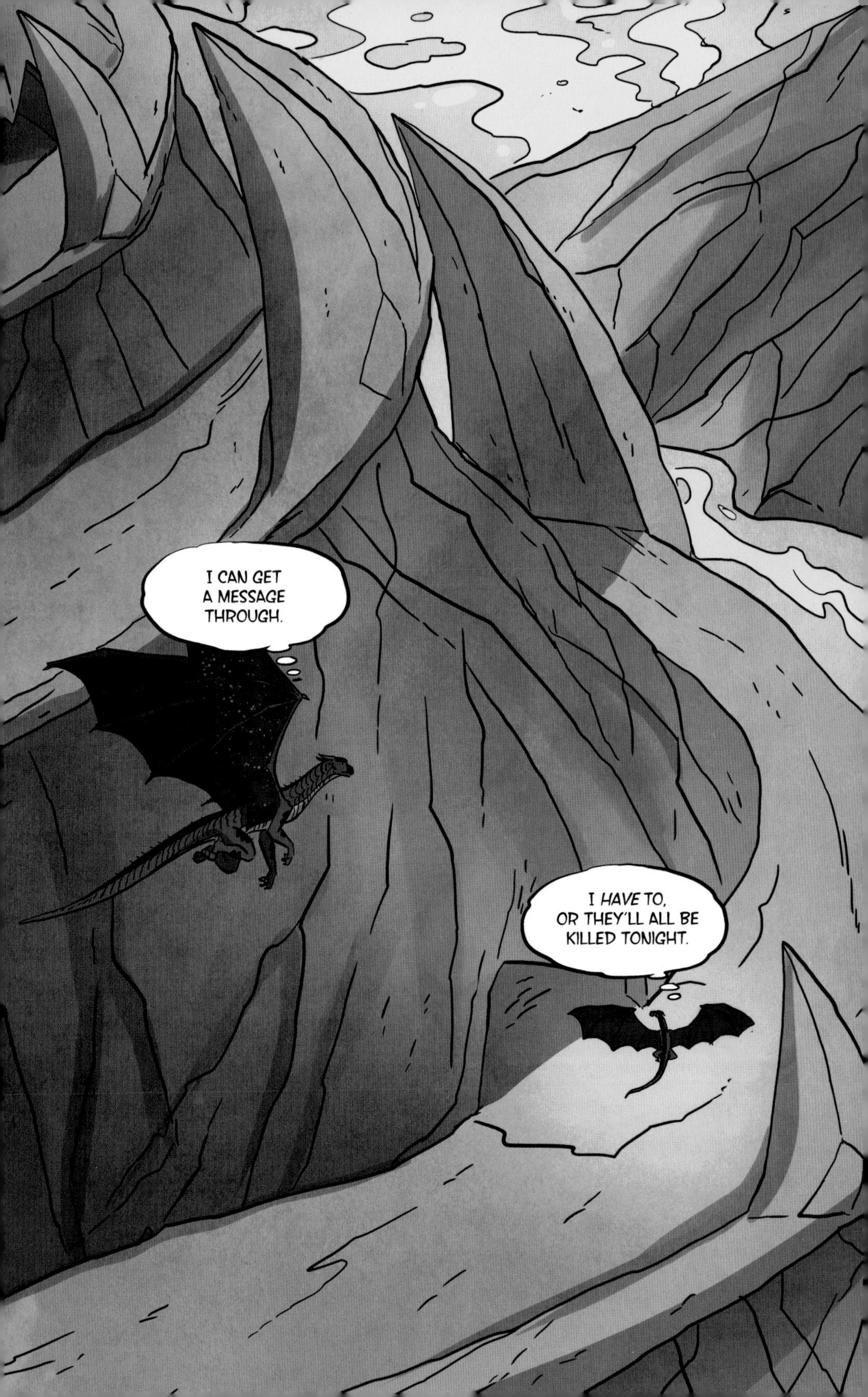
I CAN GET A MESSAGE THROUGH.
I *HAVE* TO, OR THEY'LL ALL BE KILLED TONIGHT.

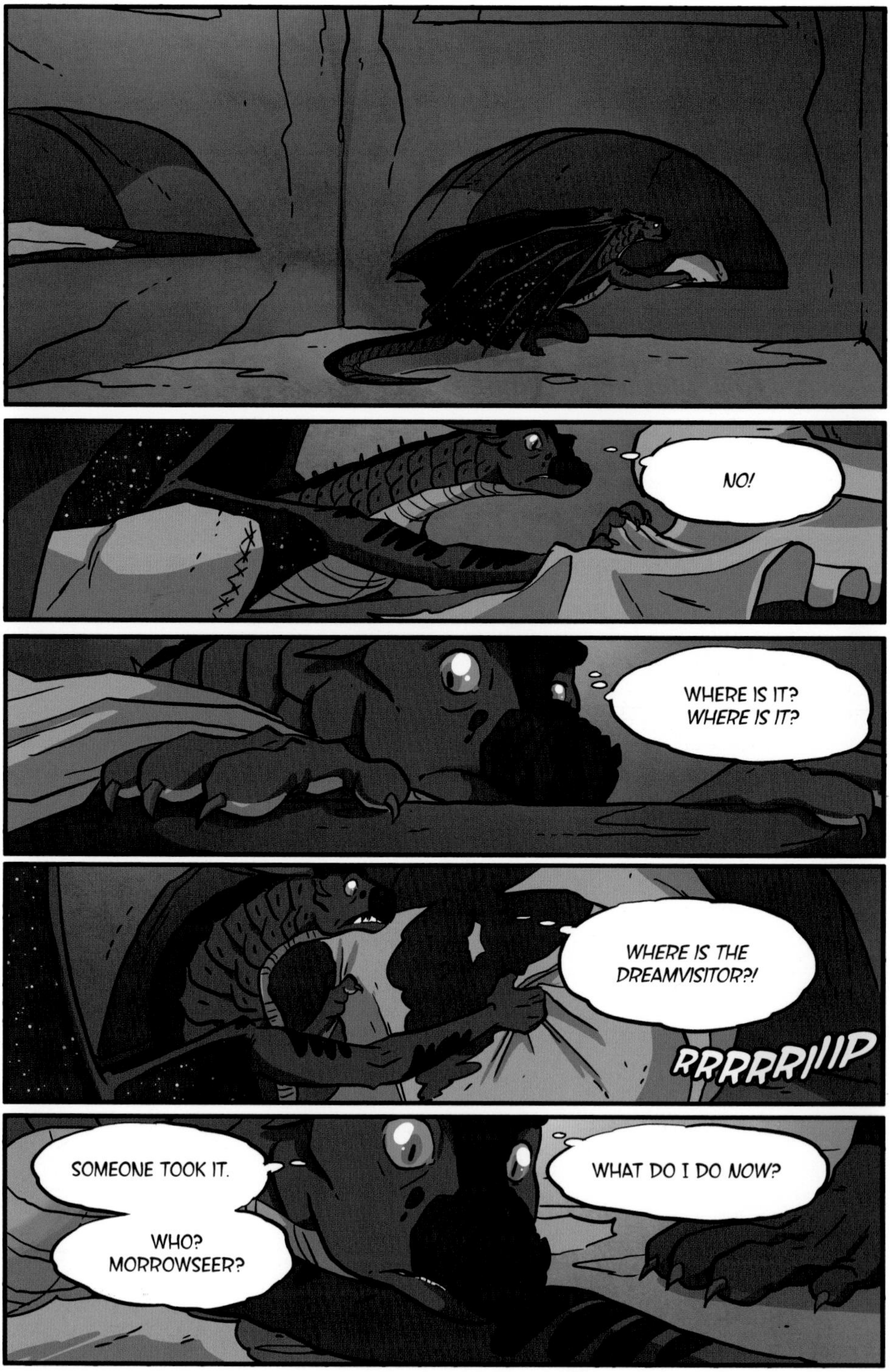
NO!
WHERE IS IT?
WHERE IS IT?
WHERE IS THE DREAMVISITOR?!
RRRRRIIIP
SOMEONE TOOK IT.
WHO? MORROWSEER?
WHAT DO I DO NOW?

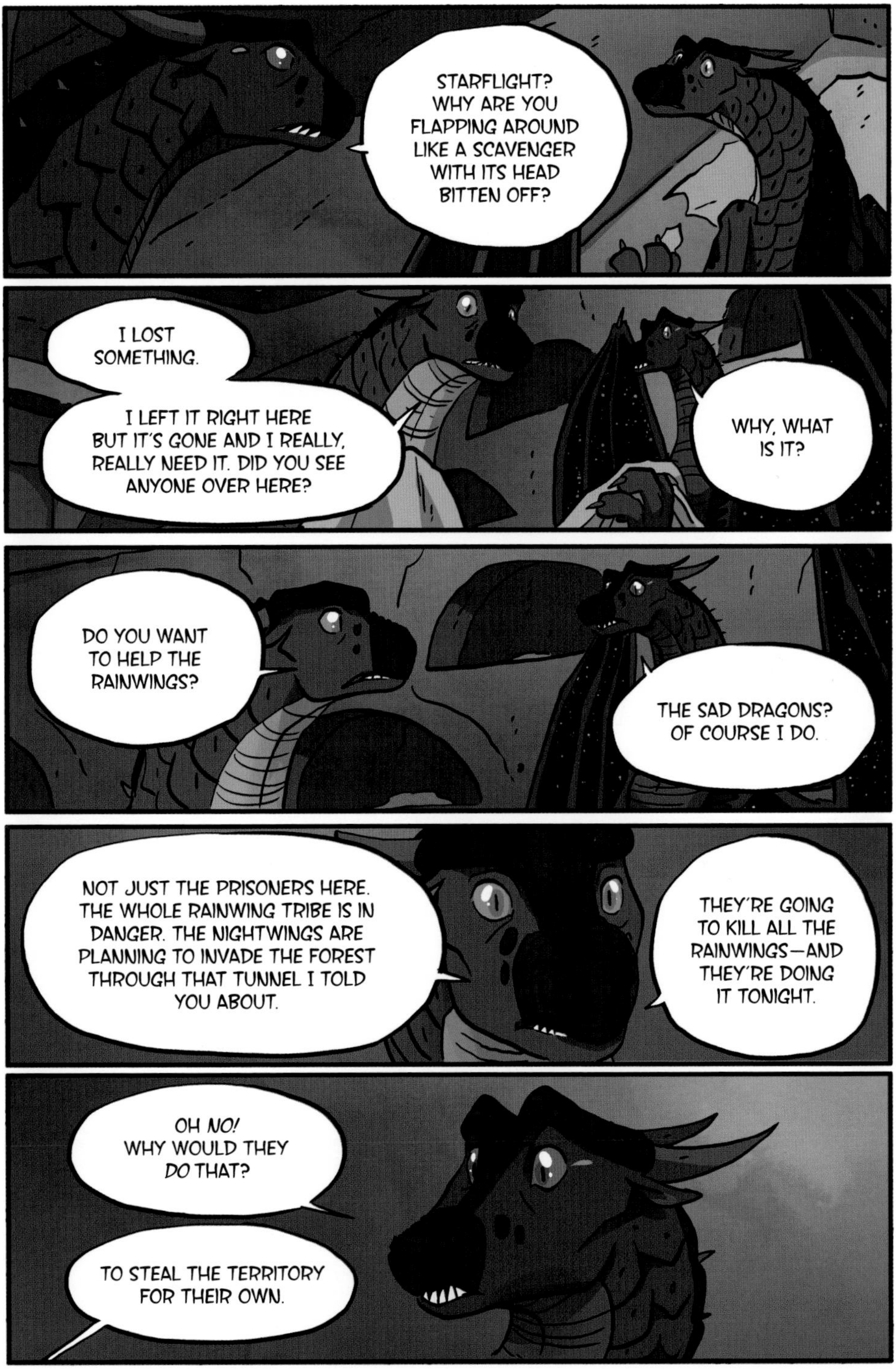
STARFLIGHT? WHY ARE YOU FLAPPING AROUND LIKE A SCAVENGER WITH ITS HEAD BITTEN OFF?
I LOST SOMETHING.
I LEFT IT RIGHT HERE BUT IT'S GONE AND I REALLY, REALLY NEED IT. DID YOU SEE ANYONE OVER HERE?
WHY, WHAT IS IT?
DO YOU WANT TO HELP THE RAINWINGS?
THE SAD DRAGONS? OF COURSE I DO.
NOT JUST THE PRISONERS HERE. THE WHOLE RAINWING TRIBE IS IN DANGER. THE NIGHTWINGS ARE PLANNING TO INVADE THE FOREST THROUGH THAT TUNNEL I TOLD YOU ABOUT.
THEY'RE GOING TO KILL ALL THE RAINWINGS—AND THEY'RE DOING IT TONIGHT.
OH *NO!* WHY WOULD THEY *DO* THAT?
TO STEAL THE TERRITORY FOR THEIR OWN.

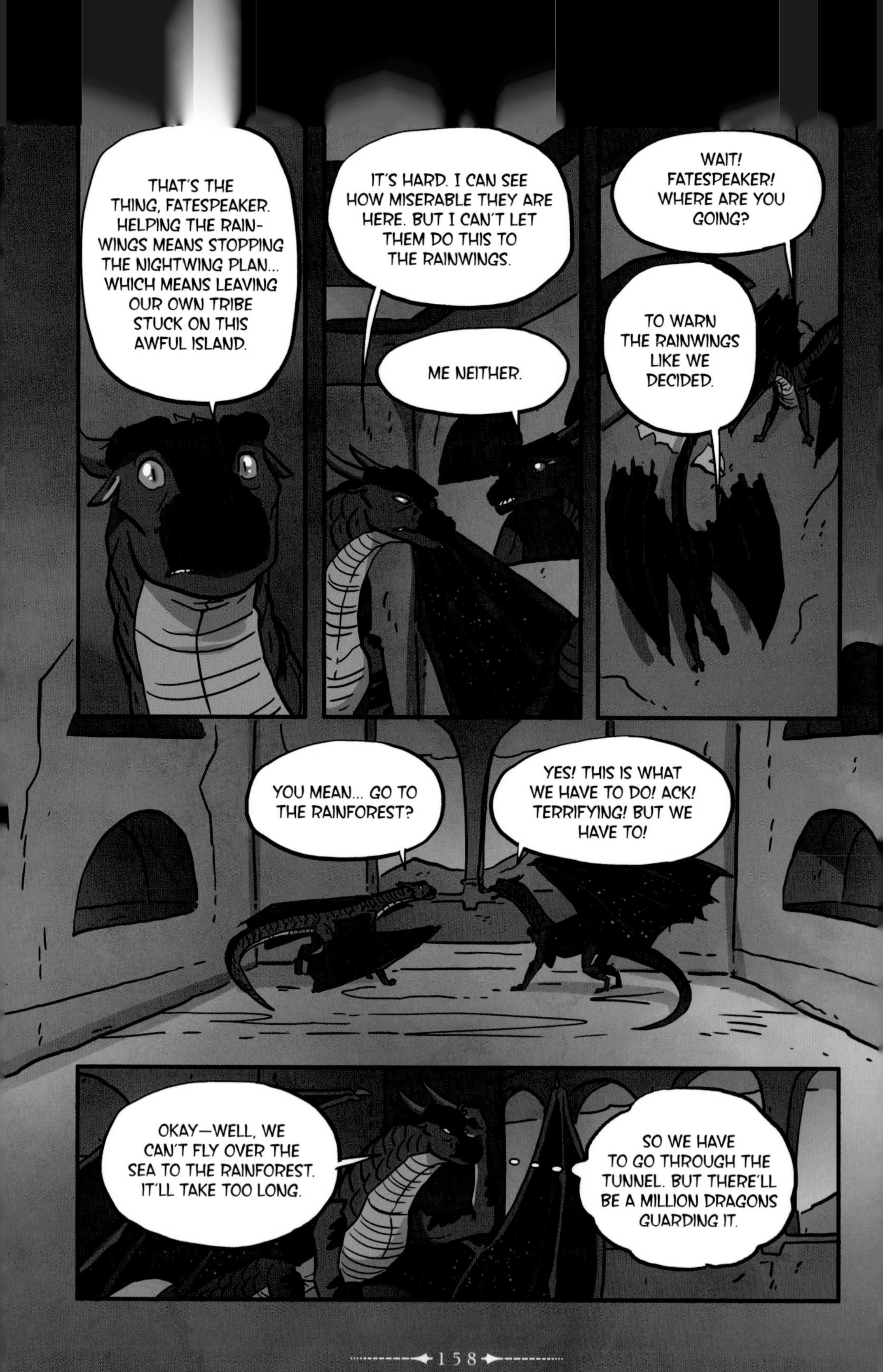
THAT'S THE THING, FATESPEAKER. HELPING THE RAIN-WINGS MEANS STOPPING THE NIGHTWING PLAN... WHICH MEANS LEAVING OUR OWN TRIBE STUCK ON THIS AWFUL ISLAND.
IT'S HARD. I CAN SEE HOW MISERABLE THEY ARE HERE. BUT I CAN'T LET THEM DO THIS TO THE RAINWINGS.
ME NEITHER.
WAIT! FATESPEAKER! WHERE ARE YOU GOING?
TO WARN THE RAINWINGS LIKE WE DECIDED.
YOU MEAN... GO TO THE RAINFOREST?
YES! THIS IS WHAT WE HAVE TO DO! ACK! TERRIFYING! BUT WE HAVE TO!
OKAY—WELL, WE CAN'T FLY OVER THE SEA TO THE RAINFOREST. IT'LL TAKE TOO LONG.
SO WE HAVE TO GO THROUGH THE TUNNEL. BUT THERE'LL BE A MILLION DRAGONS GUARDING IT.

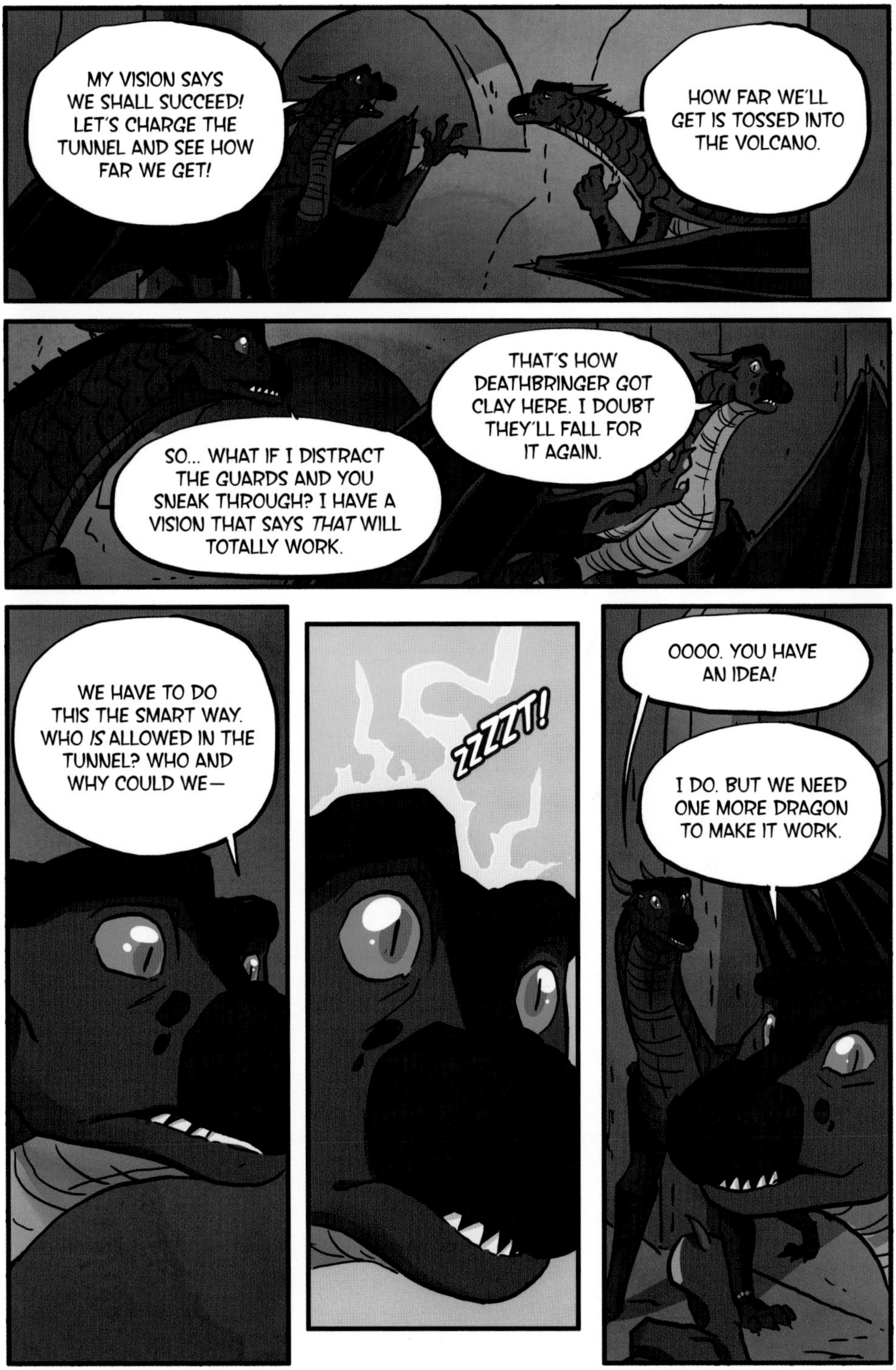
MY VISION SAYS WE SHALL SUCCEED! LET'S CHARGE THE TUNNEL AND SEE HOW FAR WE GET!
HOW FAR WE'LL GET IS TOSSED INTO THE VOLCANO.
THAT'S HOW DEATHBRINGER GOT CLAY HERE. I DOUBT THEY'LL FALL FOR IT AGAIN.
SO... WHAT IF I DISTRACT THE GUARDS AND YOU SNEAK THROUGH? I HAVE A VISION THAT SAYS *THAT* WILL TOTALLY WORK.
WE HAVE TO DO THIS THE SMART WAY. WHO *IS* ALLOWED IN THE TUNNEL? WHO AND WHY COULD WE—
zZZZT!
OOOO. YOU HAVE AN IDEA!
I DO. BUT WE NEED ONE MORE DRAGON TO MAKE IT WORK.

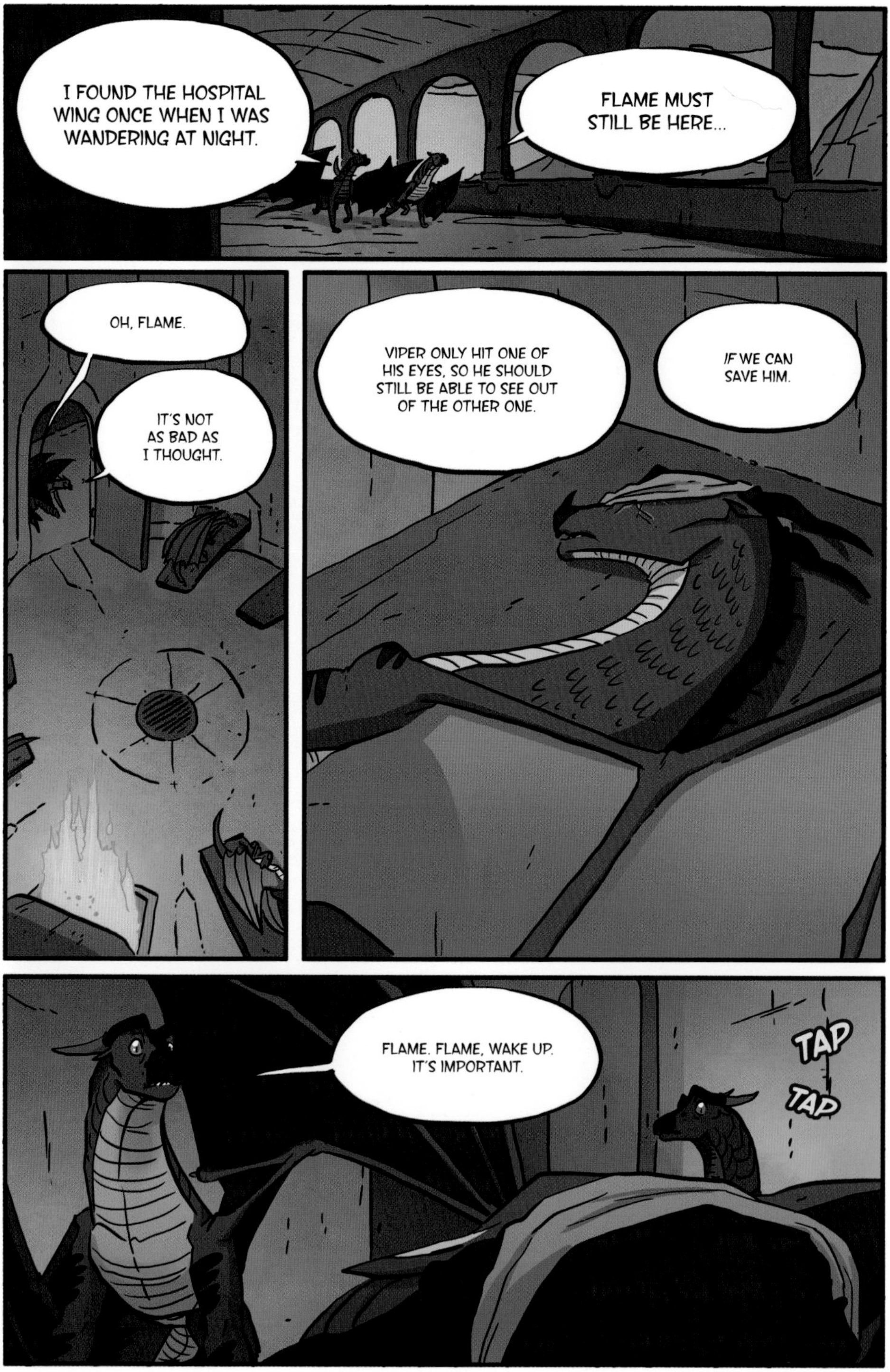
I FOUND THE HOSPITAL WING ONCE WHEN I WAS WANDERING AT NIGHT.
FLAME MUST STILL BE HERE...
OH, FLAME.
IT'S NOT AS BAD AS I THOUGHT.
VIPER ONLY HIT ONE OF HIS EYES, SO HE SHOULD STILL BE ABLE TO SEE OUT OF THE OTHER ONE.
IF WE CAN SAVE HIM.
FLAME. FLAME, WAKE UP. IT'S IMPORTANT.
TAP
TAP

UNNNNGGGHHHHHHHHH.

FLAME, YOU HAVE TO COME WITH US.

WE CAN SAVE YOU, BUT IT'LL ONLY WORK IF WE GO *NOW*.

WHY WOULD *YOU* SAVE *ME*?

BECAUSE YOU'RE MY FRIEND AND IT'S THE RIGHT THING TO DO.

HRRMPH.

ALSO BECAUSE WE CAN USE YOUR TRAGIC FACE TO GET OFF THIS ISLAND.

THAT SOUNDS LIKE A REAL REASON.

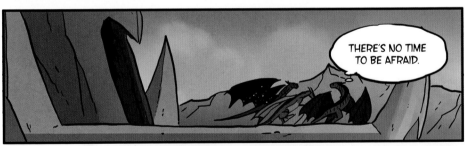

THERE'S NO TIME TO BE AFRAID.

THIS IS THE ONLY THING YOU CAN DO, STARFLIGHT. AND YOU *MUST* DO IT.

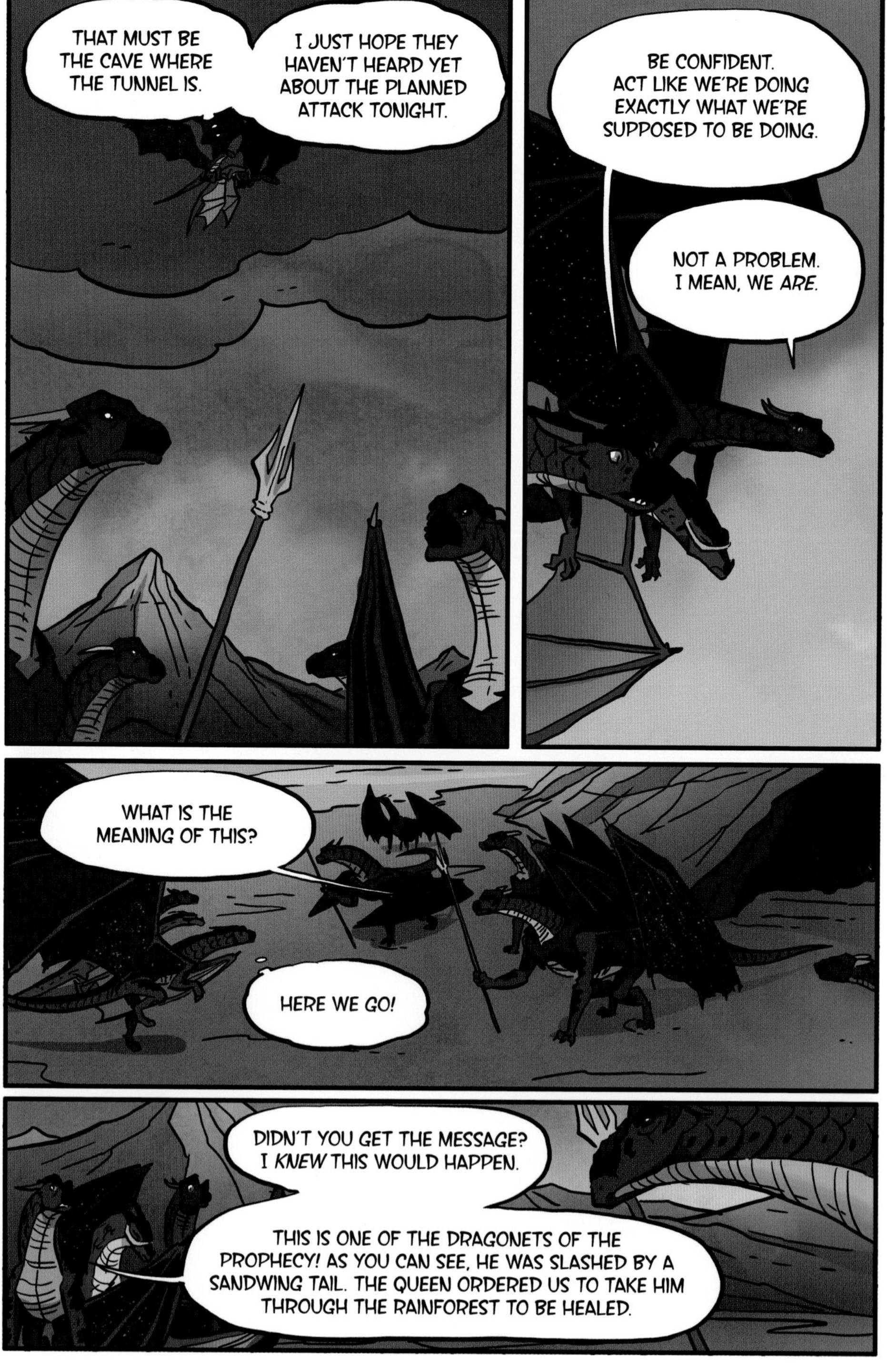
THAT MUST BE THE CAVE WHERE THE TUNNEL IS.
I JUST HOPE THEY HAVEN'T HEARD YET ABOUT THE PLANNED ATTACK TONIGHT.
BE CONFIDENT. ACT LIKE WE'RE DOING EXACTLY WHAT WE'RE SUPPOSED TO BE DOING.
NOT A PROBLEM. I MEAN, WE *ARE*.
WHAT IS THE MEANING OF THIS?
HERE WE GO!
DIDN'T YOU GET THE MESSAGE? I *KNEW* THIS WOULD HAPPEN.
THIS IS ONE OF THE DRAGONETS OF THE PROPHECY! AS YOU CAN SEE, HE WAS SLASHED BY A SANDWING TAIL. THE QUEEN ORDERED US TO TAKE HIM THROUGH THE RAINFOREST TO BE HEALED.

UH-HUH. WHY WOULD SHE SEND *YOU*?

SHE SAID I'M THE ONLY NIGHTWING WHO CAN DO IT, BECAUSE THE RAIN-WINGS THINK I'M ON *THEIR* SIDE.

I'LL HAVE TO VERIFY THIS ORDER.

OF *COURSE* YOU DO. I *TOLD* THEM TO SEND A MESSENGER AHEAD OF US.

BUT NO ONE LISTENS TO ME. NOW THE SKYWING'S GOING TO *DIE* BECAUSE WE'RE DELAYED! THE QUEEN IS GOING TO BE *FURIOUS!*

GASP!

OOF!

EW!

NO! HE CAN'T DIE! HE'S THE *ONLY* SKYWING WE'VE GOT! IF HE DIES, THAT MEANS NO *PROPHECY*, NO *PLAN*, NO *RAINFOREST HOME* FOR OUR TRIBE!

BUT THIS SOLDIER IS RIGHT, HE DOES HAVE TO VERIFY THE ORDER. WHY, WE MIGHT—WE MIGHT—

WELL... I DON'T KNOW.

WAIT, WHAT *ARE* YOU WORRIED WE'LL DO?

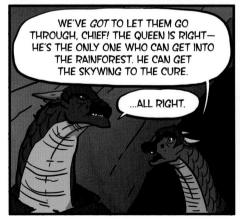

WE'VE *GOT* TO LET THEM GO THROUGH, CHIEF! THE QUEEN IS RIGHT— HE'S THE ONLY ONE WHO CAN GET INTO THE RAINFOREST. HE CAN GET THE SKYWING TO THE CURE.

...ALL RIGHT.

BUT NO FUNNY BUSINESS. FIX THE SKYWING AND COME BACK.

WE'LL BE BACK BY NIGHTFALL.

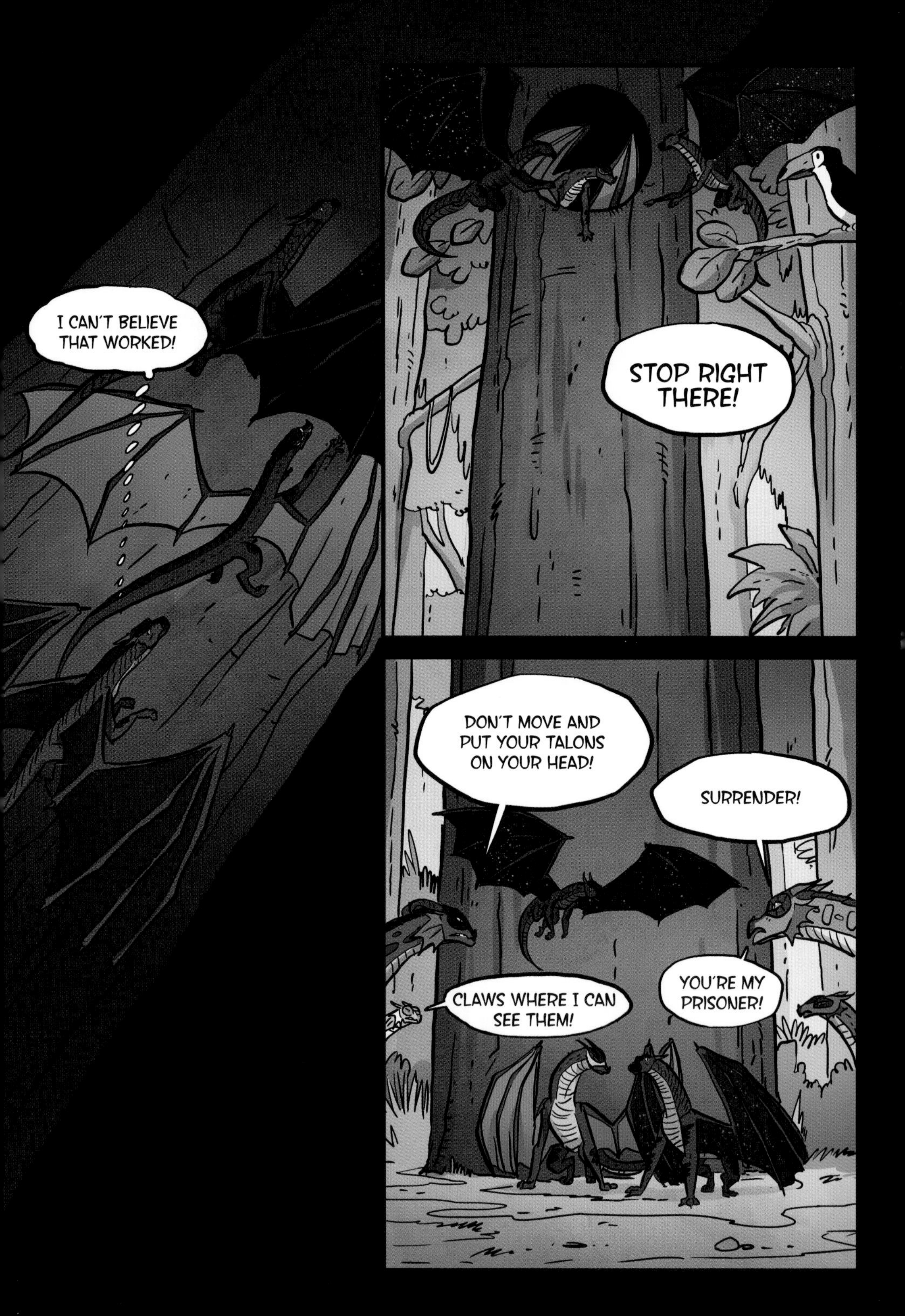
I CAN'T BELIEVE THAT WORKED!
STOP RIGHT THERE!
DON'T MOVE AND PUT YOUR TALONS ON YOUR HEAD!
SURRENDER!
CLAWS WHERE I CAN SEE THEM!
YOU'RE MY PRISONER!

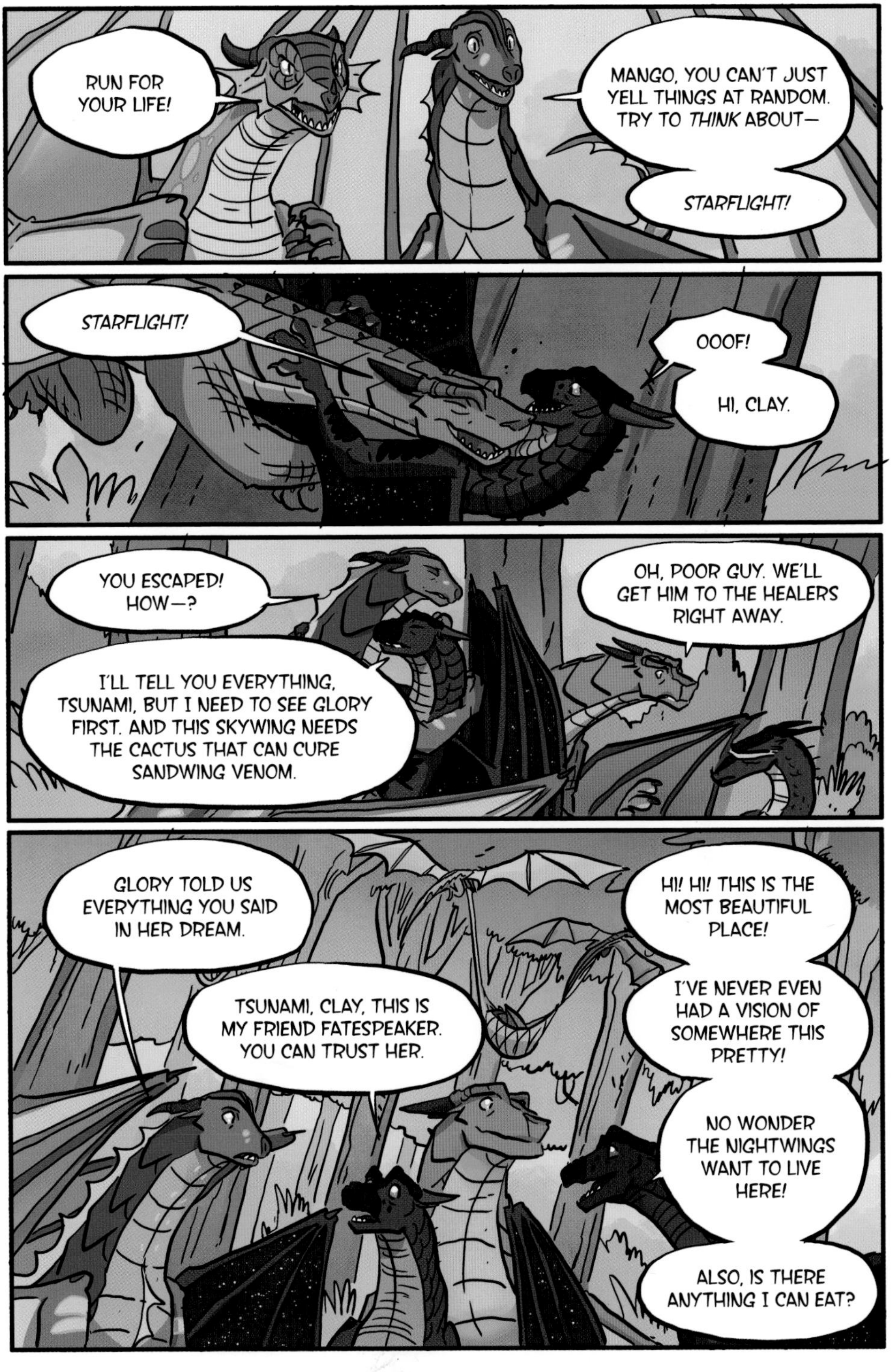
RUN FOR YOUR LIFE!
MANGO, YOU CAN'T JUST YELL THINGS AT RANDOM. TRY TO *THINK* ABOUT—
STARFLIGHT!
STARFLIGHT!
OOOF!
HI, CLAY.
YOU ESCAPED! HOW—?
I'LL TELL YOU EVERYTHING, TSUNAMI, BUT I NEED TO SEE GLORY FIRST. AND THIS SKYWING NEEDS THE CACTUS THAT CAN CURE SANDWING VENOM.
OH, POOR GUY. WE'LL GET HIM TO THE HEALERS RIGHT AWAY.
GLORY TOLD US EVERYTHING YOU SAID IN HER DREAM.
TSUNAMI, CLAY, THIS IS MY FRIEND FATESPEAKER. YOU CAN TRUST HER.
HI! HI! THIS IS THE MOST BEAUTIFUL PLACE!
I'VE NEVER EVEN HAD A VISION OF SOMEWHERE THIS PRETTY!
NO WONDER THE NIGHTWINGS WANT TO LIVE HERE!
ALSO, IS THERE ANYTHING I CAN EAT?

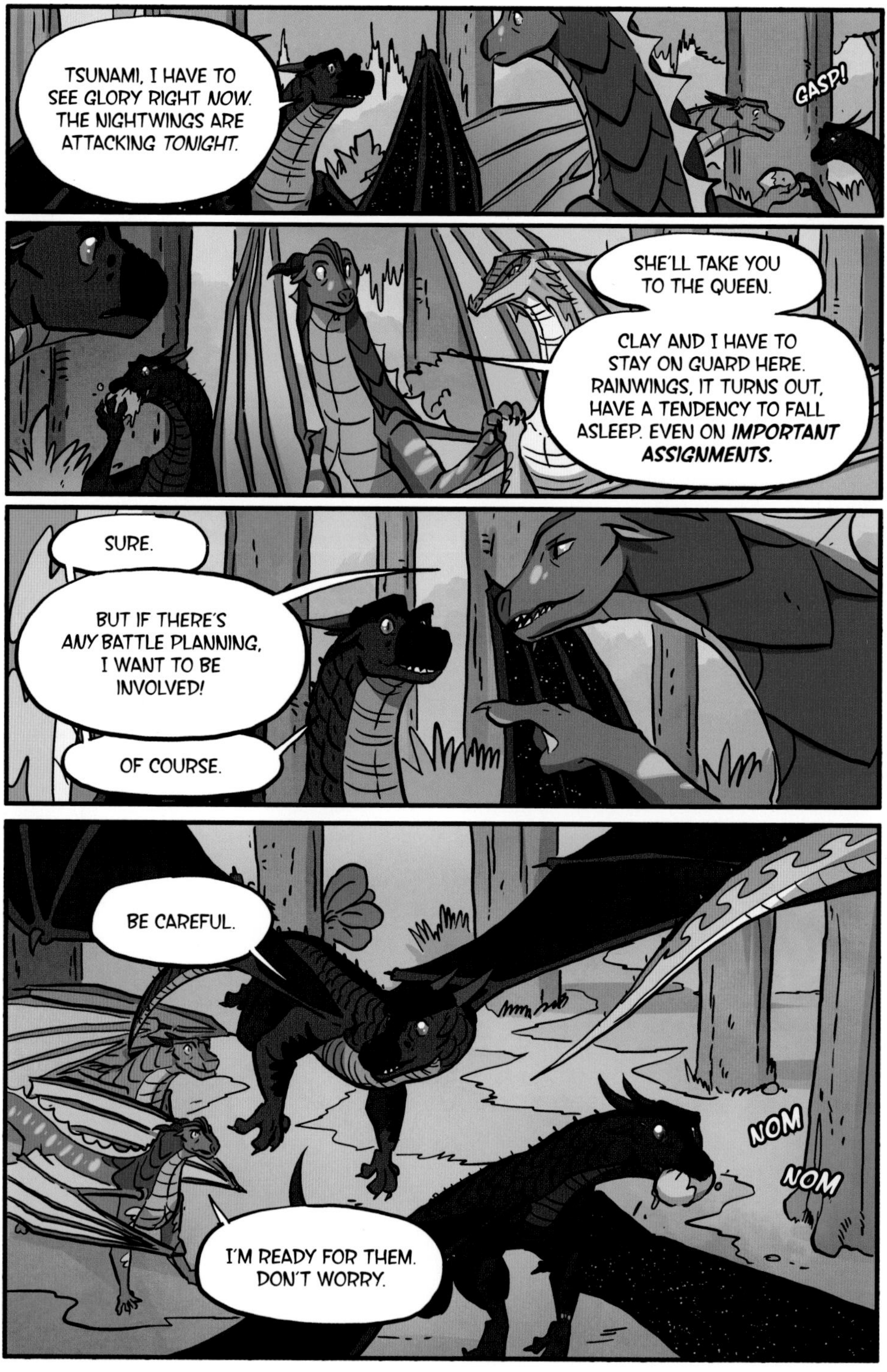
TSUNAMI, I HAVE TO SEE GLORY RIGHT *NOW*. THE NIGHTWINGS ARE ATTACKING *TONIGHT*.
GASP!
SHE'LL TAKE YOU TO THE QUEEN.
CLAY AND I HAVE TO STAY ON GUARD HERE. RAINWINGS, IT TURNS OUT, HAVE A TENDENCY TO FALL ASLEEP. EVEN ON ***IMPORTANT ASSIGNMENTS.***
SURE.
BUT IF THERE'S *ANY* BATTLE PLANNING, I WANT TO BE INVOLVED!
OF COURSE.
BE CAREFUL.
NOM
NOM
I'M READY FOR THEM. DON'T WORRY.

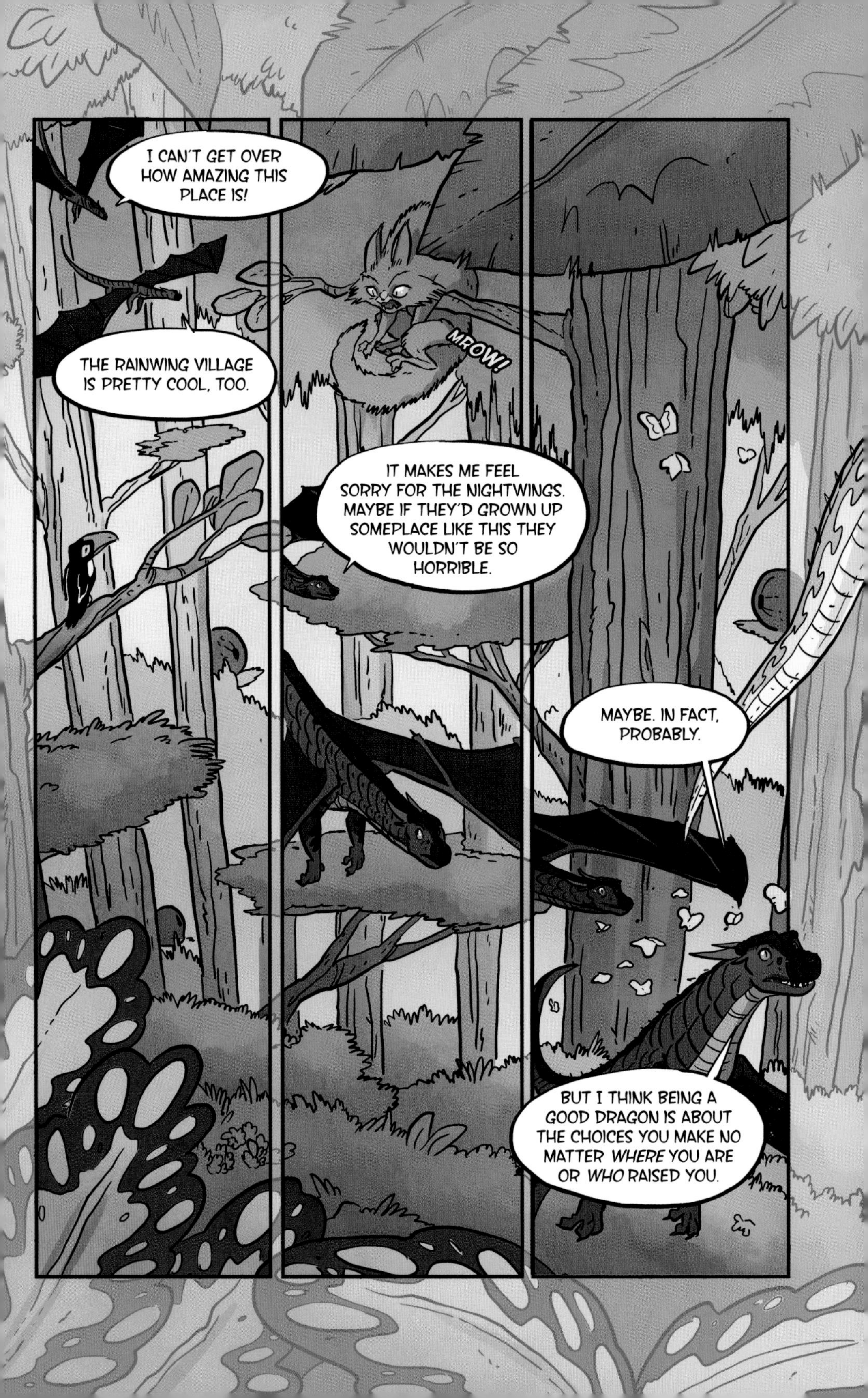
I CAN'T GET OVER HOW AMAZING THIS PLACE IS!
THE RAINWING VILLAGE IS PRETTY COOL, TOO.
MROW!
IT MAKES ME FEEL SORRY FOR THE NIGHTWINGS. MAYBE IF THEY'D GROWN UP SOMEPLACE LIKE THIS THEY WOULDN'T BE SO HORRIBLE.
MAYBE. IN FACT, PROBABLY.
BUT I THINK BEING A GOOD DRAGON IS ABOUT THE CHOICES YOU MAKE NO MATTER *WHERE* YOU ARE OR *WHO* RAISED YOU.

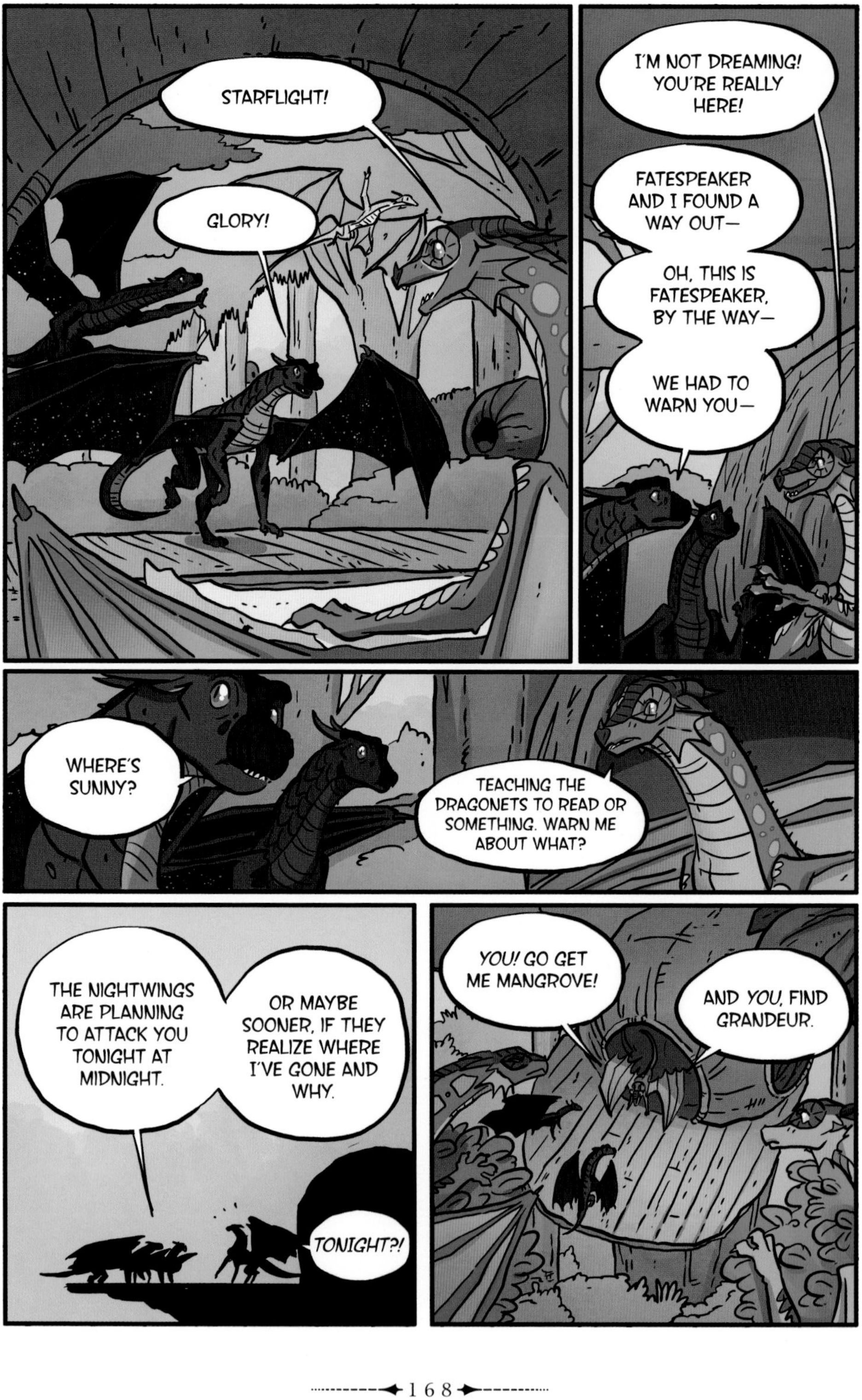
STARFLIGHT!
GLORY!
I'M NOT DREAMING! YOU'RE REALLY HERE!
FATESPEAKER AND I FOUND A WAY OUT—
OH, THIS IS FATESPEAKER, BY THE WAY—
WE HAD TO WARN YOU—
WHERE'S SUNNY?
TEACHING THE DRAGONETS TO READ OR SOMETHING. WARN ME ABOUT WHAT?
THE NIGHTWINGS ARE PLANNING TO ATTACK YOU TONIGHT AT MIDNIGHT.
OR MAYBE SOONER, IF THEY REALIZE WHERE I'VE GONE AND WHY.
TONIGHT?!
YOU! GO GET ME MANGROVE!
AND *YOU*, FIND GRANDEUR.

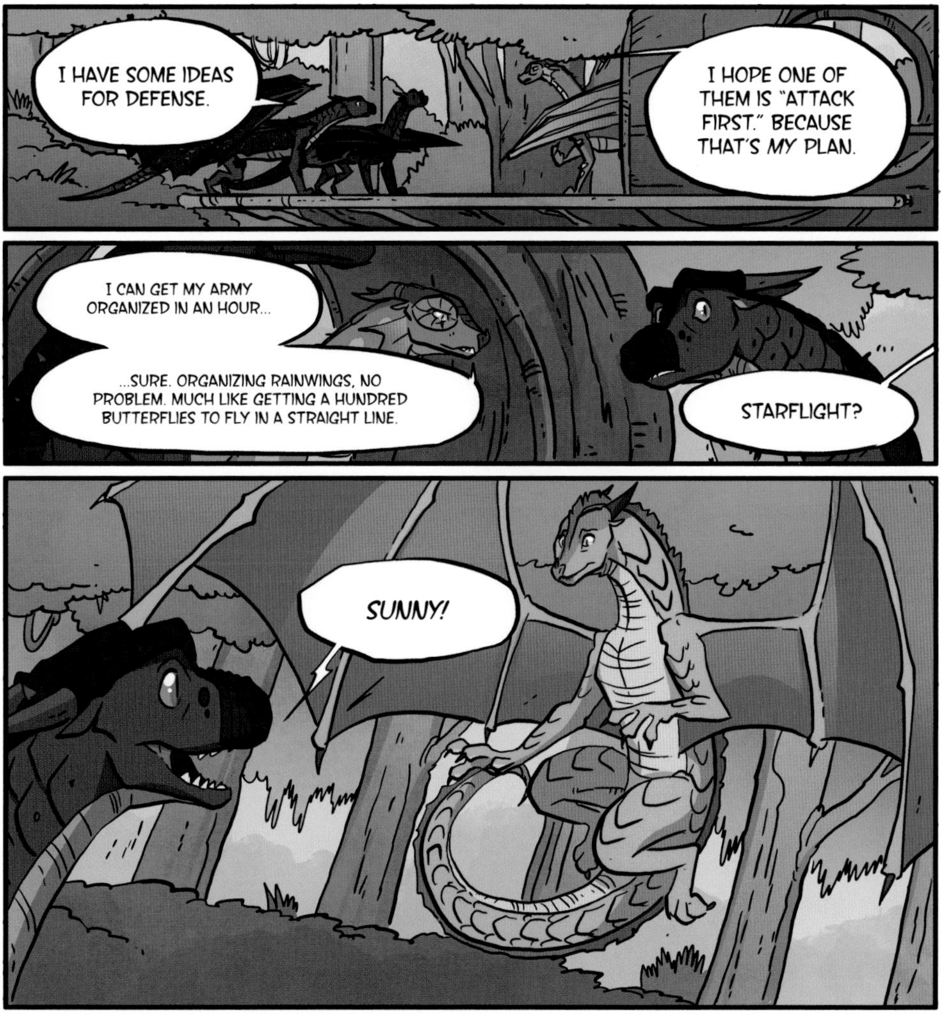
I HAVE SOME IDEAS FOR DEFENSE.
I HOPE ONE OF THEM IS "ATTACK FIRST." BECAUSE THAT'S *MY* PLAN.
I CAN GET MY ARMY ORGANIZED IN AN HOUR...
...SURE. ORGANIZING RAINWINGS, NO PROBLEM. MUCH LIKE GETTING A HUNDRED BUTTERFLIES TO FLY IN A STRAIGHT LINE.
STARFLIGHT?
SUNNY!

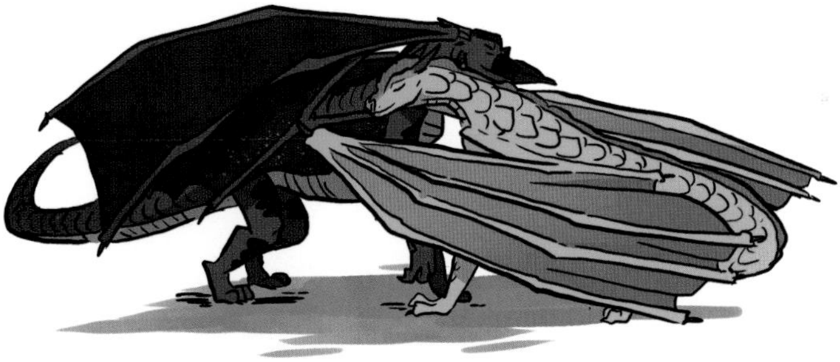

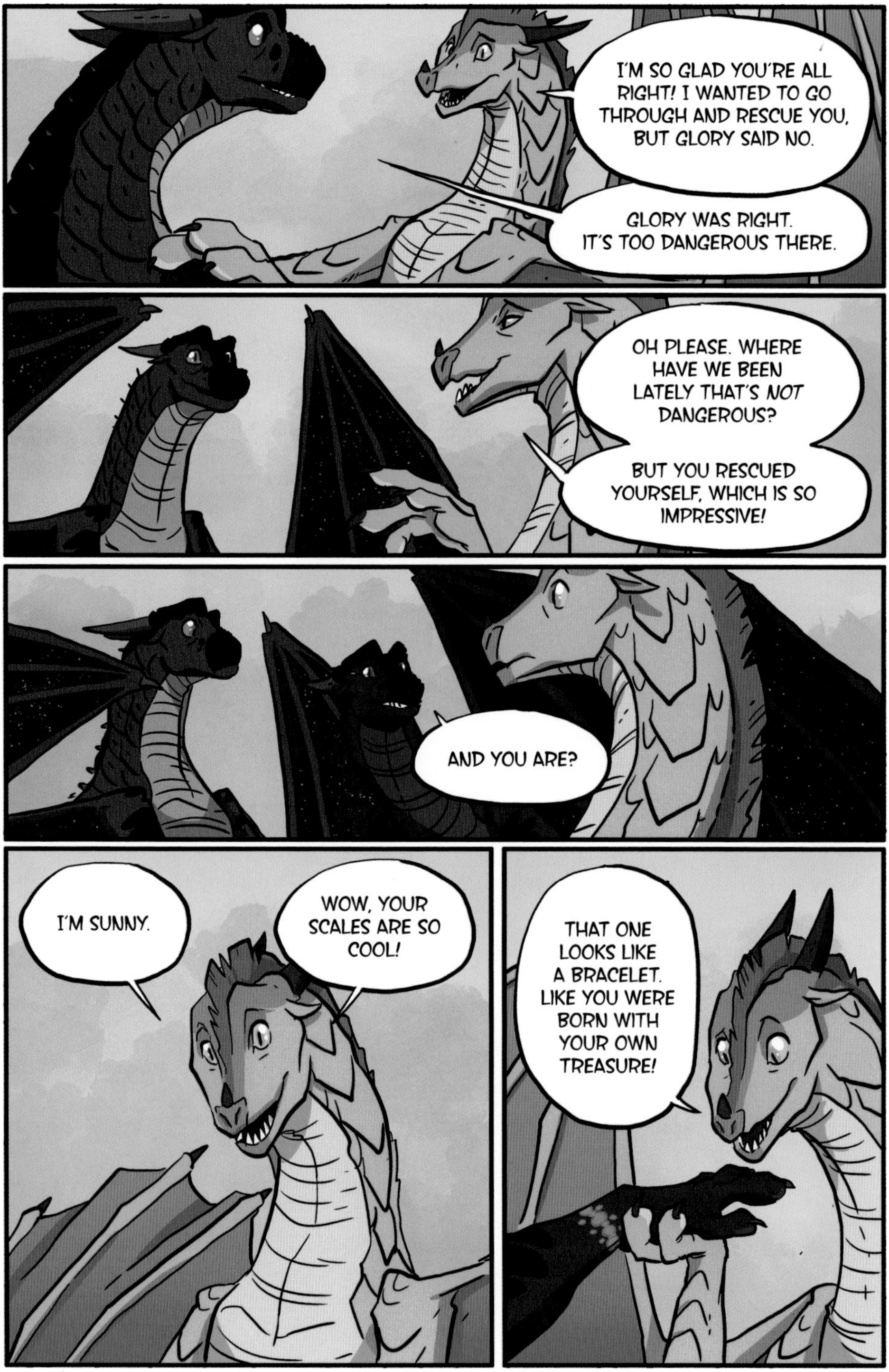
I'M SO GLAD YOU'RE ALL RIGHT! I WANTED TO GO THROUGH AND RESCUE YOU, BUT GLORY SAID NO.
GLORY WAS RIGHT. IT'S TOO DANGEROUS THERE.
OH PLEASE. WHERE HAVE WE BEEN LATELY THAT'S *NOT* DANGEROUS?
BUT YOU RESCUED YOURSELF, WHICH IS SO IMPRESSIVE!
AND YOU ARE?
I'M SUNNY.
WOW, YOUR SCALES ARE SO COOL!
THAT ONE LOOKS LIKE A BRACELET. LIKE YOU WERE BORN WITH YOUR OWN TREASURE!

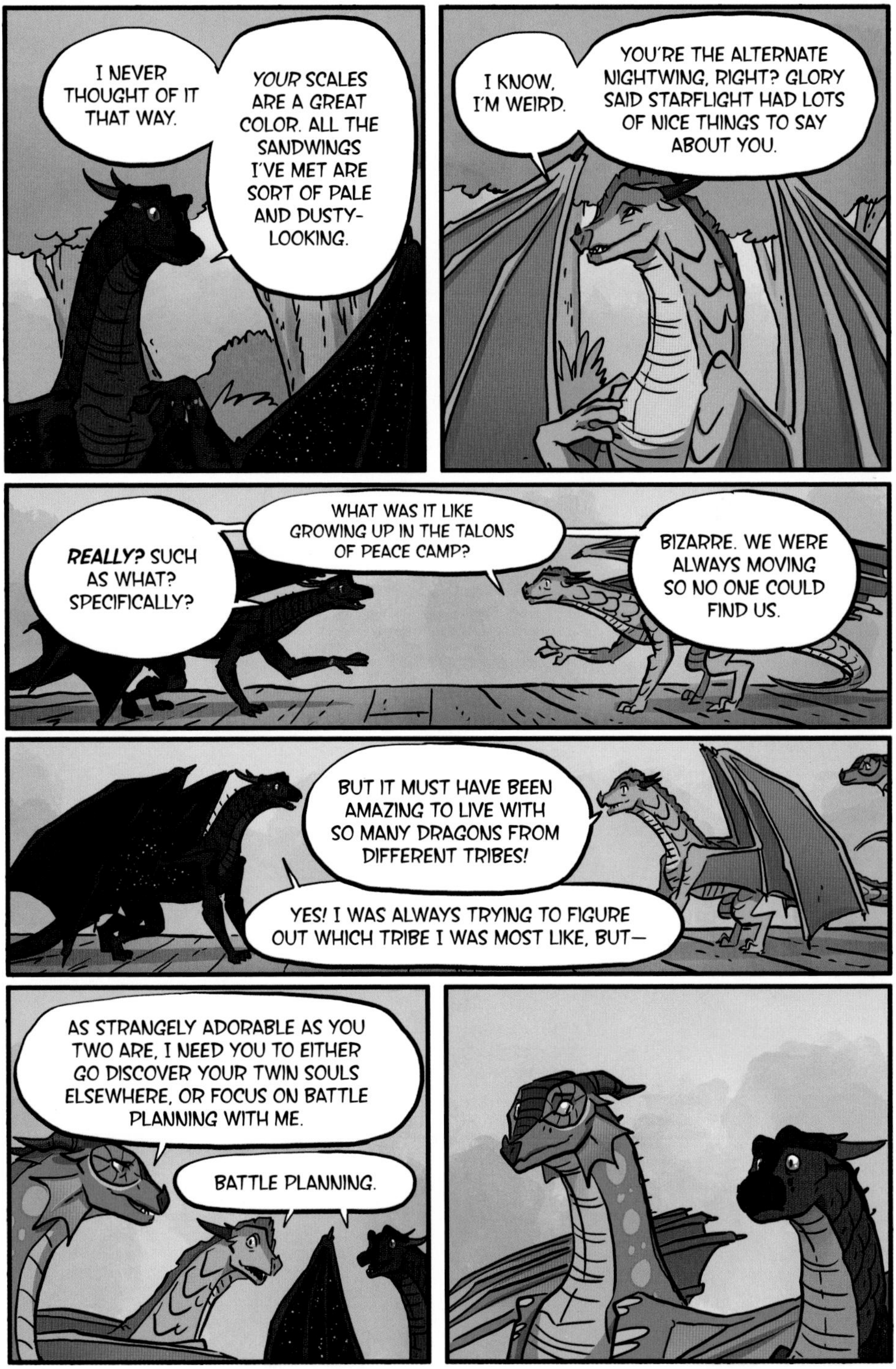
I NEVER THOUGHT OF IT THAT WAY.
YOUR SCALES ARE A GREAT COLOR. ALL THE SANDWINGS I'VE MET ARE SORT OF PALE AND DUSTY-LOOKING.
I KNOW, I'M WEIRD.
YOU'RE THE ALTERNATE NIGHTWING, RIGHT? GLORY SAID STARFLIGHT HAD LOTS OF NICE THINGS TO SAY ABOUT YOU.
REALLY? SUCH AS WHAT? SPECIFICALLY?
WHAT WAS IT LIKE GROWING UP IN THE TALONS OF PEACE CAMP?
BIZARRE. WE WERE ALWAYS MOVING SO NO ONE COULD FIND US.
BUT IT MUST HAVE BEEN AMAZING TO LIVE WITH SO MANY DRAGONS FROM DIFFERENT TRIBES!
YES! I WAS ALWAYS TRYING TO FIGURE OUT WHICH TRIBE I WAS MOST LIKE, BUT—
AS STRANGELY ADORABLE AS YOU TWO ARE, I NEED YOU TO EITHER GO DISCOVER YOUR TWIN SOULS ELSEWHERE, OR FOCUS ON BATTLE PLANNING WITH ME.
BATTLE PLANNING.

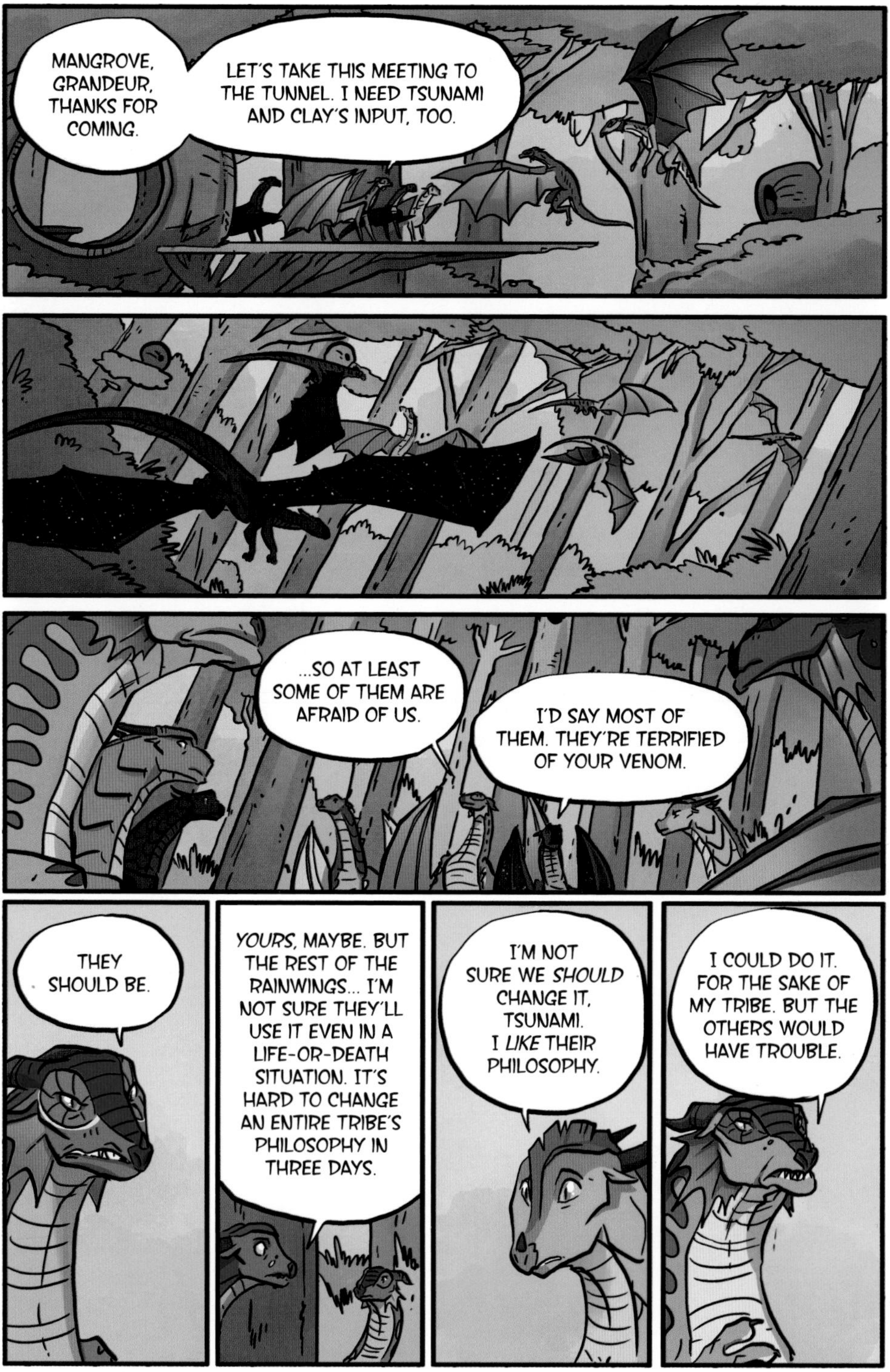

MANGROVE, GRANDEUR, THANKS FOR COMING.
LET'S TAKE THIS MEETING TO THE TUNNEL. I NEED TSUNAMI AND CLAY'S INPUT, TOO.
...SO AT LEAST SOME OF THEM ARE AFRAID OF US.
I'D SAY MOST OF THEM. THEY'RE TERRIFIED OF YOUR VENOM.
THEY SHOULD BE.
YOURS, MAYBE. BUT THE REST OF THE RAINWINGS... I'M NOT SURE THEY'LL USE IT EVEN IN A LIFE-OR-DEATH SITUATION. IT'S HARD TO CHANGE AN ENTIRE TRIBE'S PHILOSOPHY IN THREE DAYS.
I'M NOT SURE WE *SHOULD* CHANGE IT, TSUNAMI. I *LIKE* THEIR PHILOSOPHY.
I COULD DO IT. FOR THE SAKE OF MY TRIBE. BUT THE OTHERS WOULD HAVE TROUBLE.

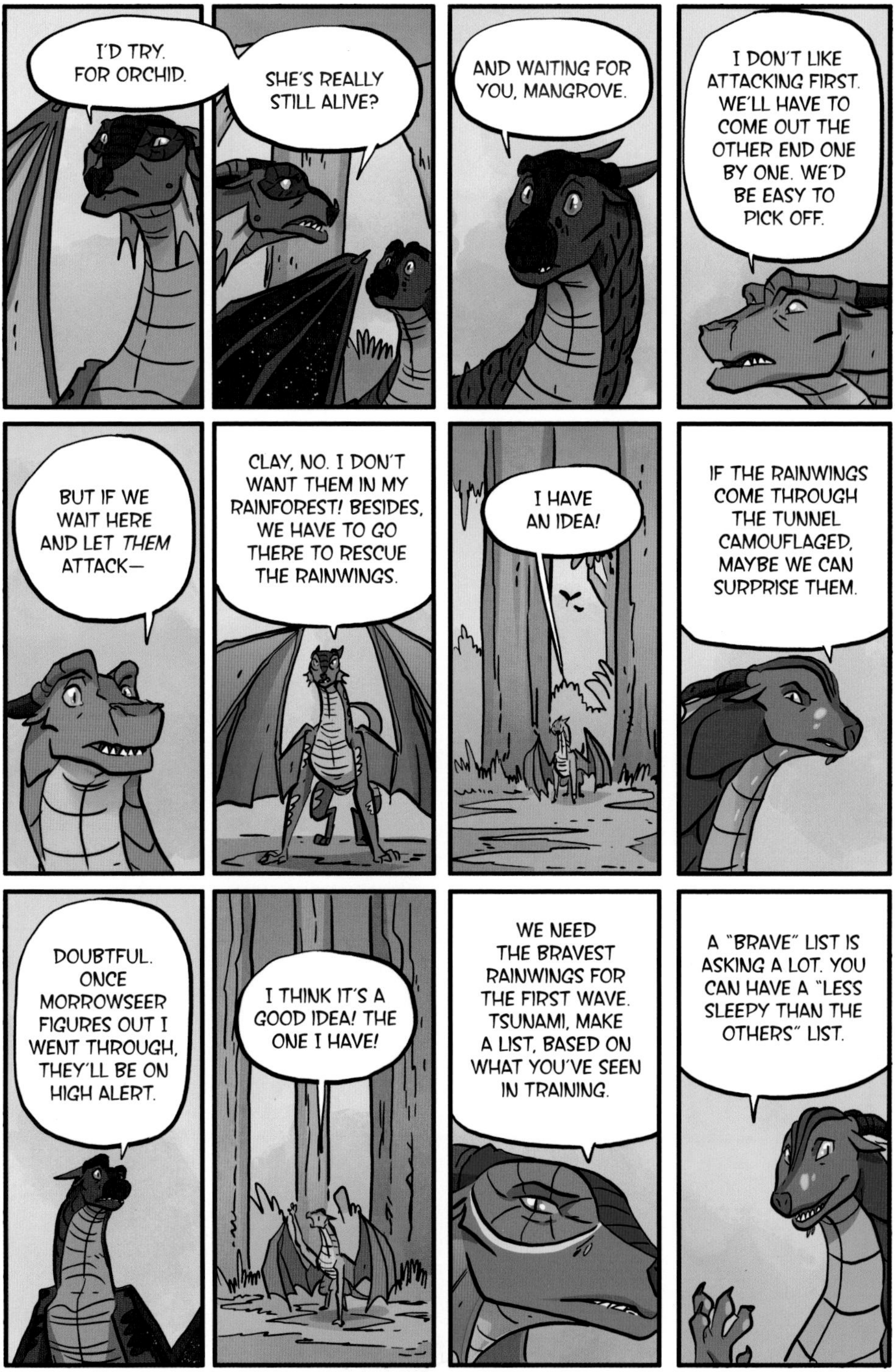
I'D TRY. FOR ORCHID.
SHE'S REALLY STILL ALIVE?
AND WAITING FOR YOU, MANGROVE.
I DON'T LIKE ATTACKING FIRST. WE'LL HAVE TO COME OUT THE OTHER END ONE BY ONE. WE'D BE EASY TO PICK OFF.
BUT IF WE WAIT HERE AND LET *THEM* ATTACK—
CLAY, NO. I DON'T WANT THEM IN MY RAINFOREST! BESIDES, WE HAVE TO GO THERE TO RESCUE THE RAINWINGS.
I HAVE AN IDEA!
IF THE RAINWINGS COME THROUGH THE TUNNEL CAMOUFLAGED, MAYBE WE CAN SURPRISE THEM.
DOUBTFUL. ONCE MORROWSEER FIGURES OUT I WENT THROUGH, THEY'LL BE ON HIGH ALERT.
I THINK IT'S A GOOD IDEA! THE ONE I HAVE!
WE NEED THE BRAVEST RAINWINGS FOR THE FIRST WAVE. TSUNAMI, MAKE A LIST, BASED ON WHAT YOU'VE SEEN IN TRAINING.
A "BRAVE" LIST IS ASKING A LOT. YOU CAN HAVE A "LESS SLEEPY THAN THE OTHERS" LIST.

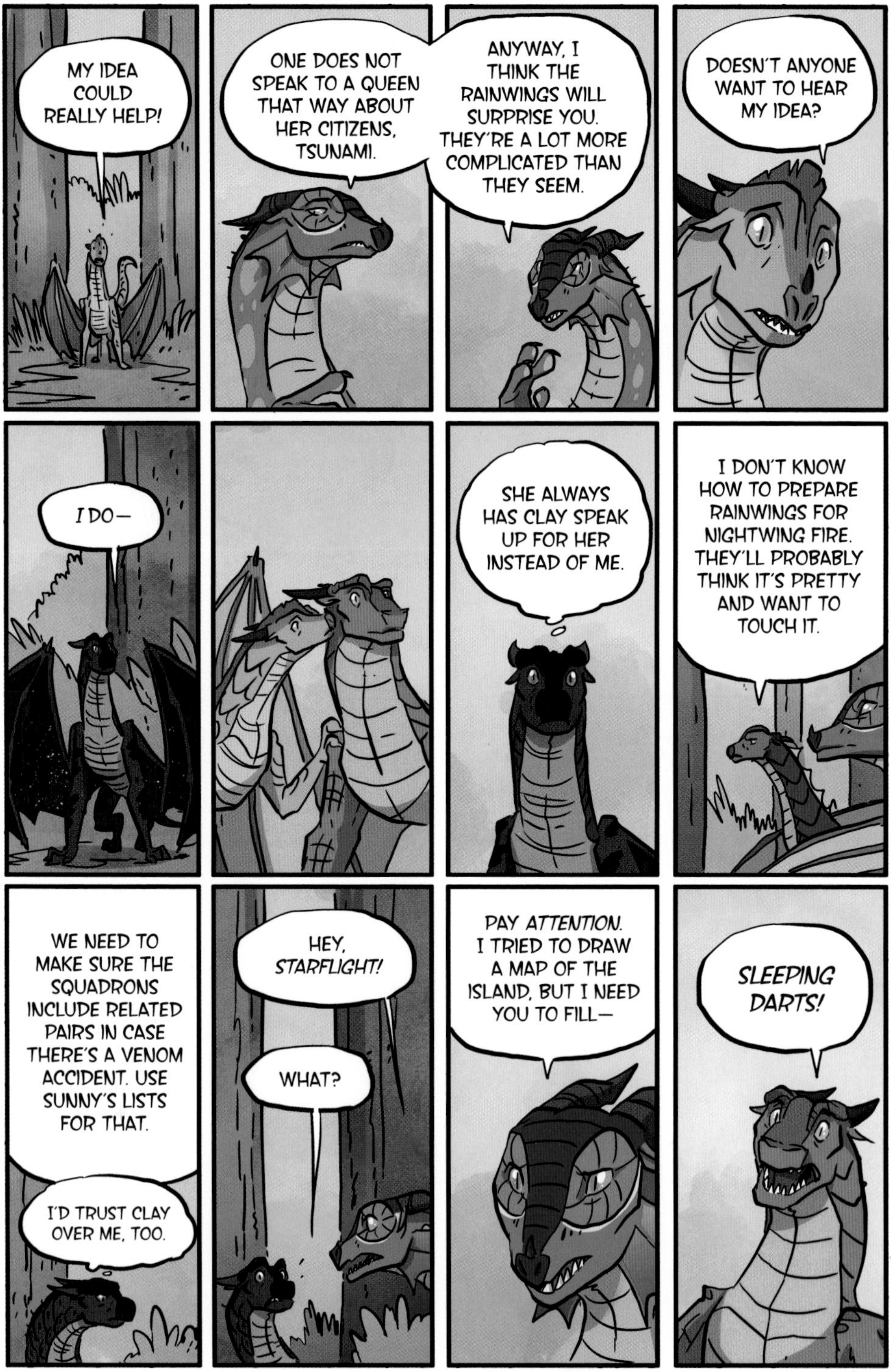
MY IDEA COULD REALLY HELP!
ONE DOES NOT SPEAK TO A QUEEN THAT WAY ABOUT HER CITIZENS, TSUNAMI.
ANYWAY, I THINK THE RAINWINGS WILL SURPRISE YOU. THEY'RE A LOT MORE COMPLICATED THAN THEY SEEM.
DOESN'T ANYONE WANT TO HEAR MY IDEA?
I DO—
SHE ALWAYS HAS CLAY SPEAK UP FOR HER INSTEAD OF ME.
I DON'T KNOW HOW TO PREPARE RAINWINGS FOR NIGHTWING FIRE. THEY'LL PROBABLY THINK IT'S PRETTY AND WANT TO TOUCH IT.
WE NEED TO MAKE SURE THE SQUADRONS INCLUDE RELATED PAIRS IN CASE THERE'S A VENOM ACCIDENT. USE SUNNY'S LISTS FOR THAT.
I'D TRUST CLAY OVER ME, TOO.
HEY, *STARFLIGHT!*
WHAT?
PAY *ATTENTION.* I TRIED TO DRAW A MAP OF THE ISLAND, BUT I NEED YOU TO FILL—
SLEEPING DARTS!

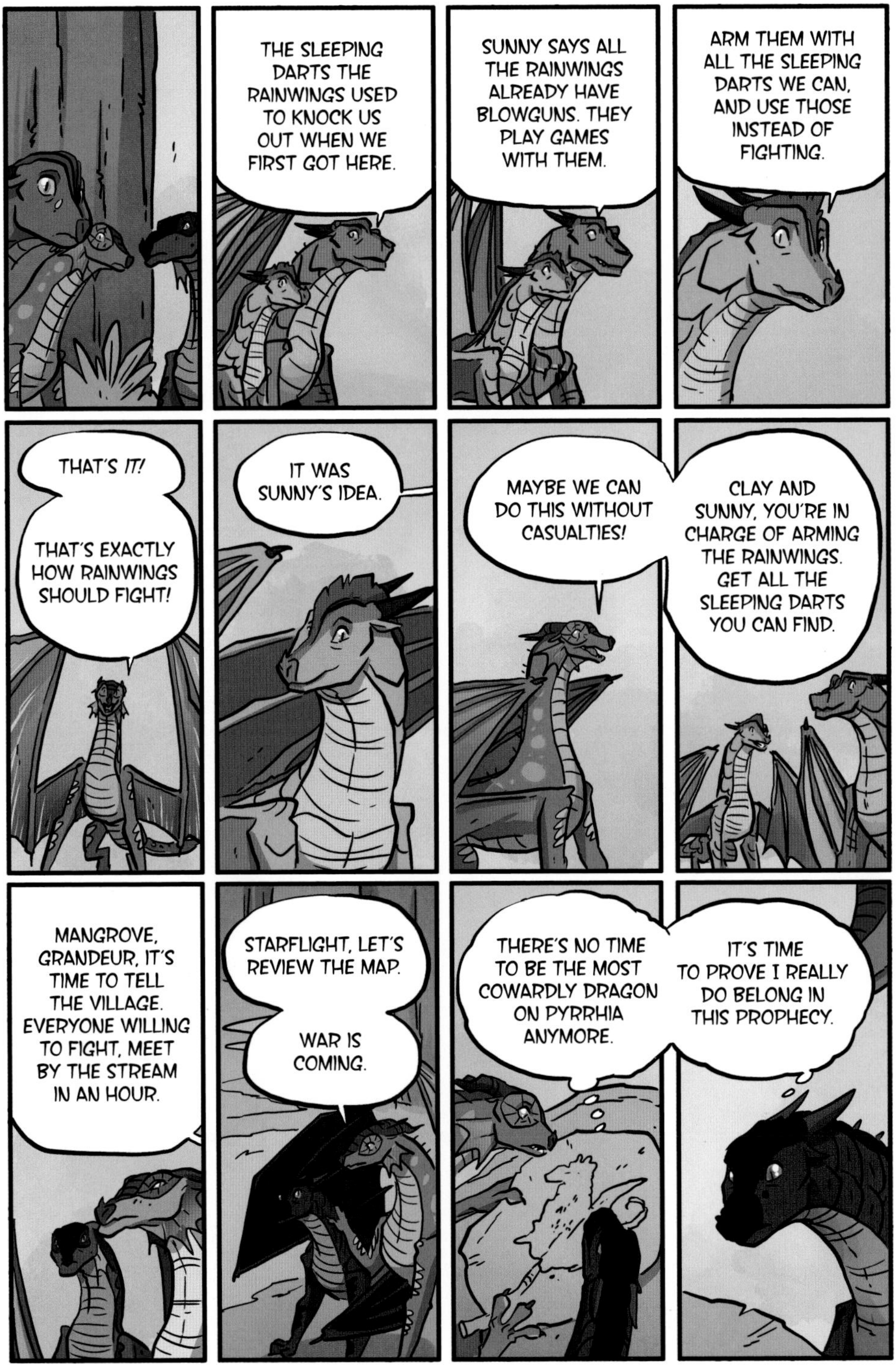

THE SLEEPING DARTS THE RAINWINGS USED TO KNOCK US OUT WHEN WE FIRST GOT HERE.
SUNNY SAYS ALL THE RAINWINGS ALREADY HAVE BLOWGUNS. THEY PLAY GAMES WITH THEM.
ARM THEM WITH ALL THE SLEEPING DARTS WE CAN, AND USE THOSE INSTEAD OF FIGHTING.
THAT'S *IT!*
THAT'S EXACTLY HOW RAINWINGS SHOULD FIGHT!
IT WAS SUNNY'S IDEA.
MAYBE WE CAN DO THIS WITHOUT CASUALTIES!
CLAY AND SUNNY, YOU'RE IN CHARGE OF ARMING THE RAINWINGS. GET ALL THE SLEEPING DARTS YOU CAN FIND.
MANGROVE, GRANDEUR, IT'S TIME TO TELL THE VILLAGE. EVERYONE WILLING TO FIGHT, MEET BY THE STREAM IN AN HOUR.
STARFLIGHT, LET'S REVIEW THE MAP.
WAR IS COMING.
THERE'S NO TIME TO BE THE MOST COWARDLY DRAGON ON PYRRHIA ANYMORE.
IT'S TIME TO PROVE I REALLY DO BELONG IN THIS PROPHECY.

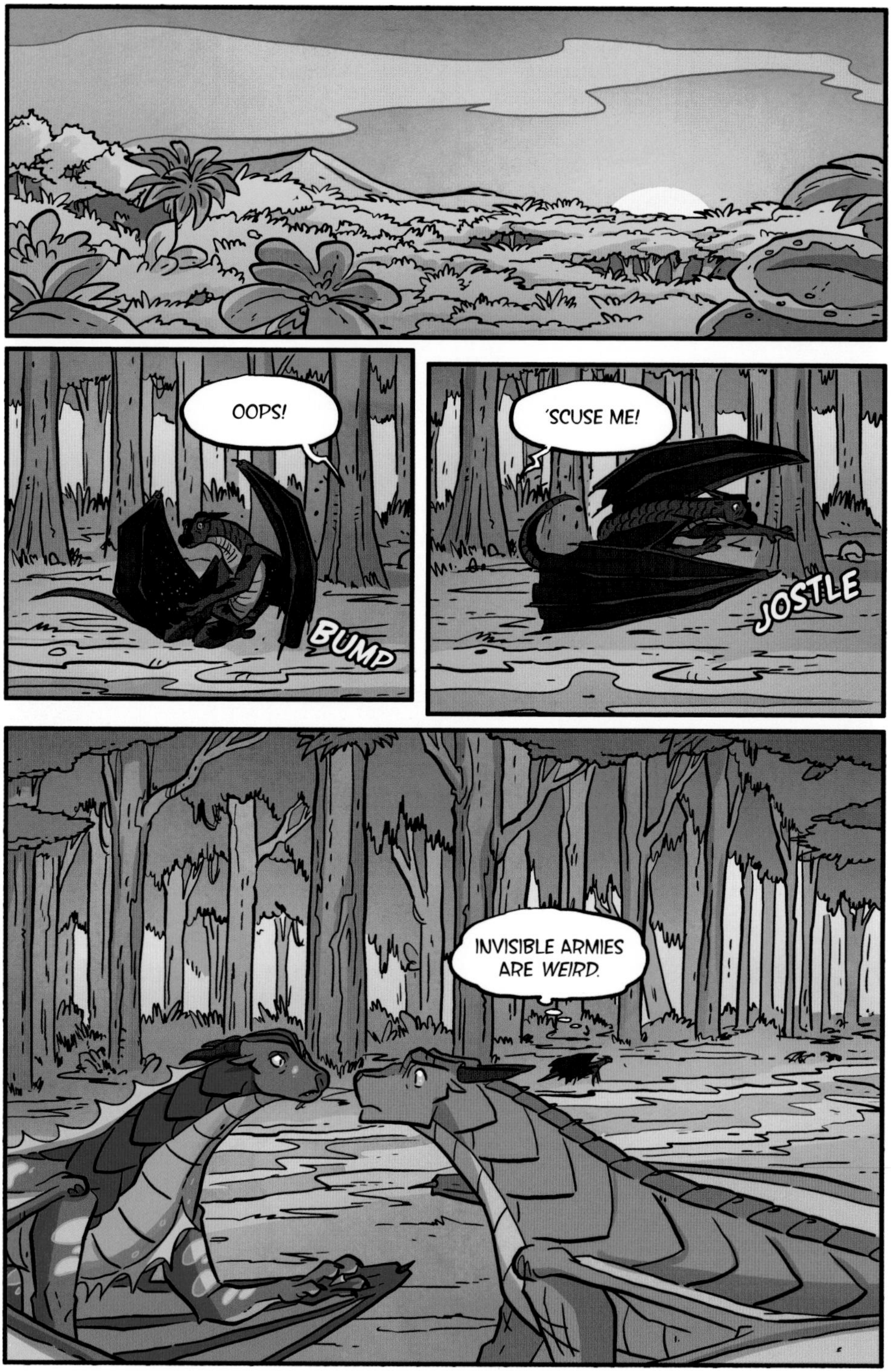
OOPS!
BUMP
'SCUSE ME!
JOSTLE
INVISIBLE ARMIES ARE WEIRD.

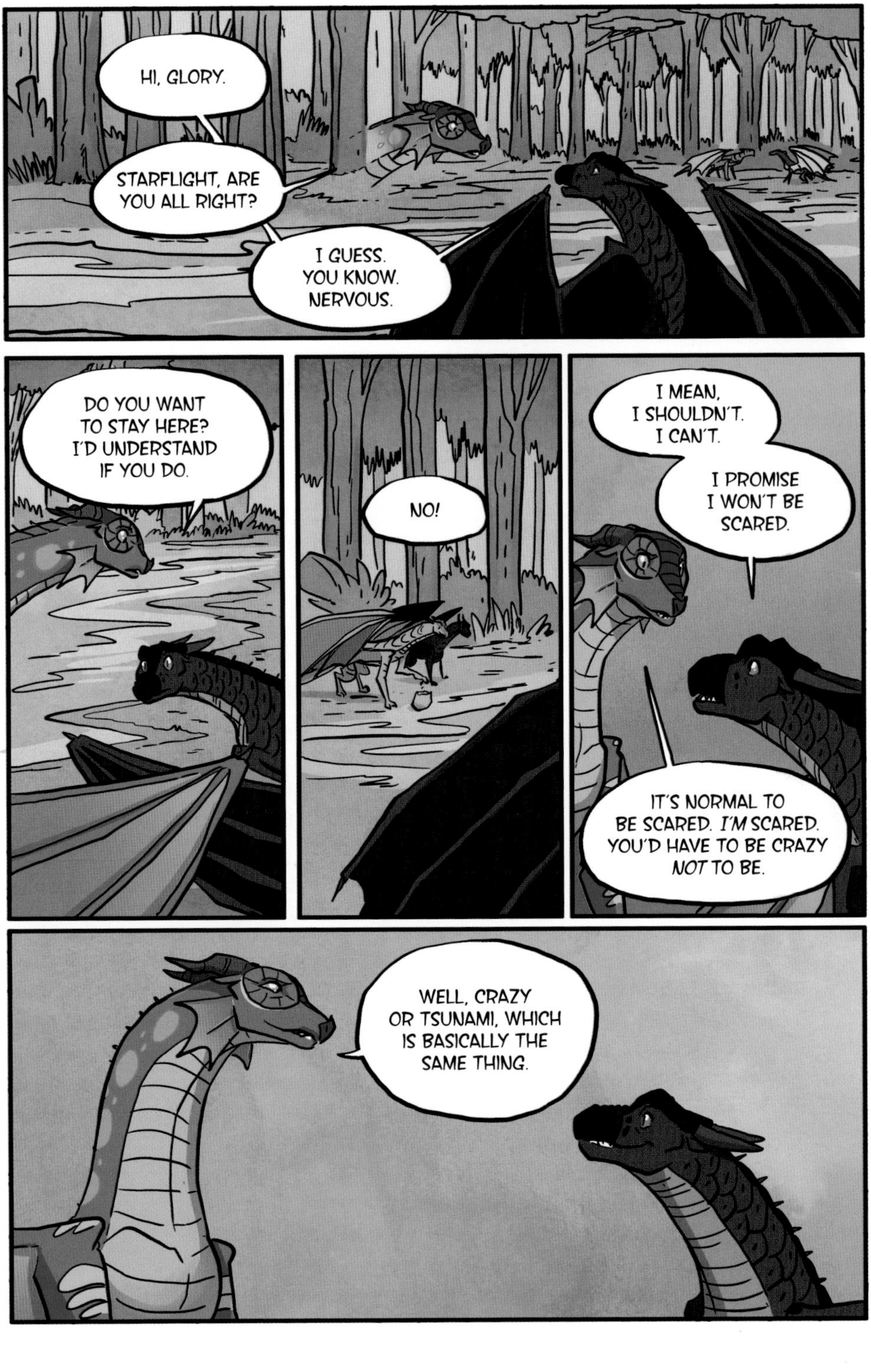
HI, GLORY.
STARFLIGHT, ARE YOU ALL RIGHT?
I GUESS. YOU KNOW. NERVOUS.
DO YOU WANT TO STAY HERE? I'D UNDERSTAND IF YOU DO.
NO!
I MEAN, I SHOULDN'T. I CAN'T.
I PROMISE I WON'T BE SCARED.
IT'S NORMAL TO BE SCARED. *I'M* SCARED. YOU'D HAVE TO BE CRAZY *NOT* TO BE.
WELL, CRAZY OR TSUNAMI, WHICH IS BASICALLY THE SAME THING.

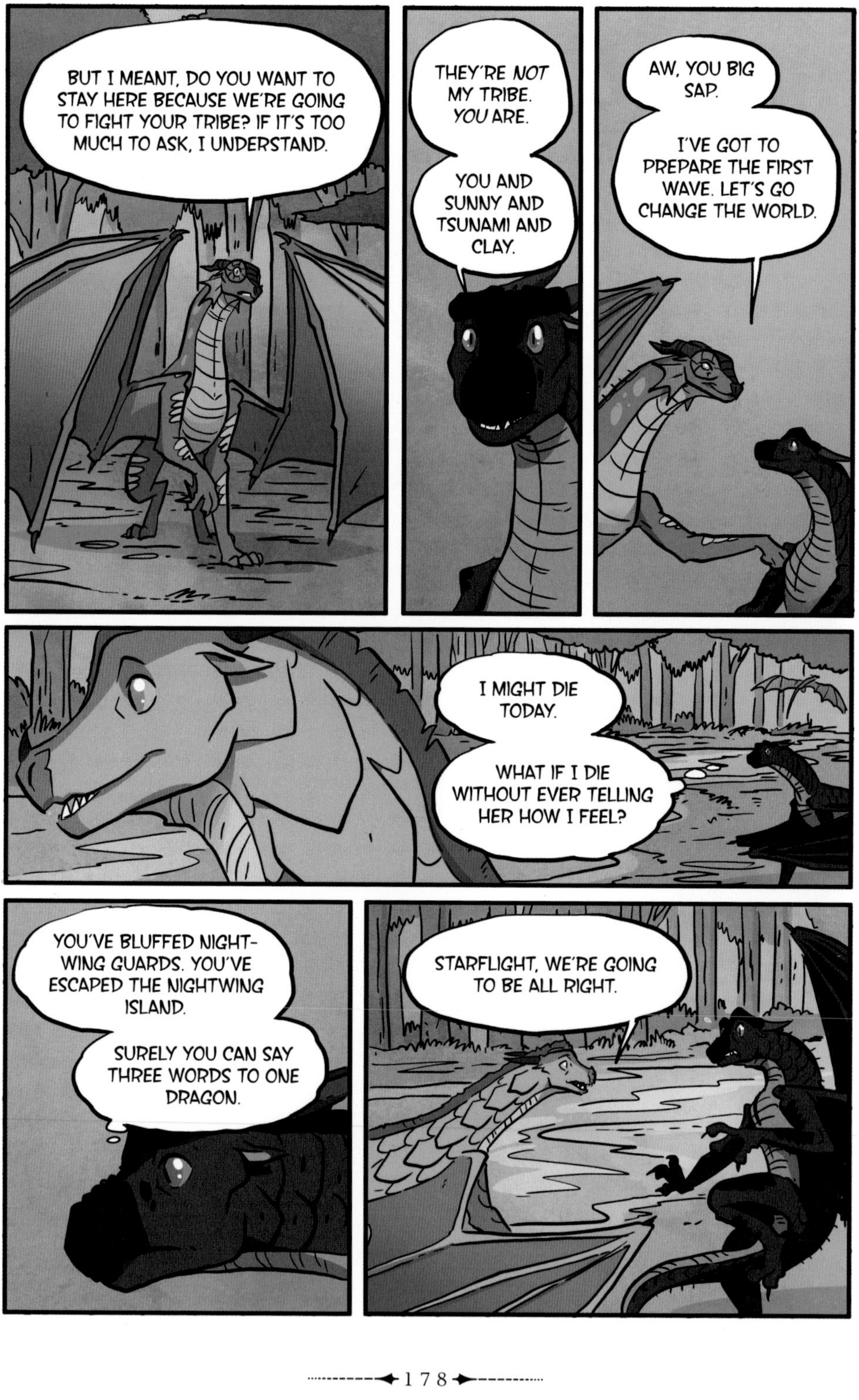
BUT I MEANT, DO YOU WANT TO STAY HERE BECAUSE WE'RE GOING TO FIGHT YOUR TRIBE? IF IT'S TOO MUCH TO ASK, I UNDERSTAND.
THEY'RE *NOT* MY TRIBE. *YOU* ARE.
YOU AND SUNNY AND TSUNAMI AND CLAY.
AW, YOU BIG SAP.
I'VE GOT TO PREPARE THE FIRST WAVE. LET'S GO CHANGE THE WORLD.
I MIGHT DIE TODAY.
WHAT IF I DIE WITHOUT EVER TELLING HER HOW I FEEL?
YOU'VE BLUFFED NIGHT-WING GUARDS. YOU'VE ESCAPED THE NIGHTWING ISLAND.
SURELY YOU CAN SAY THREE WORDS TO ONE DRAGON.
STARFLIGHT, WE'RE GOING TO BE ALL RIGHT.

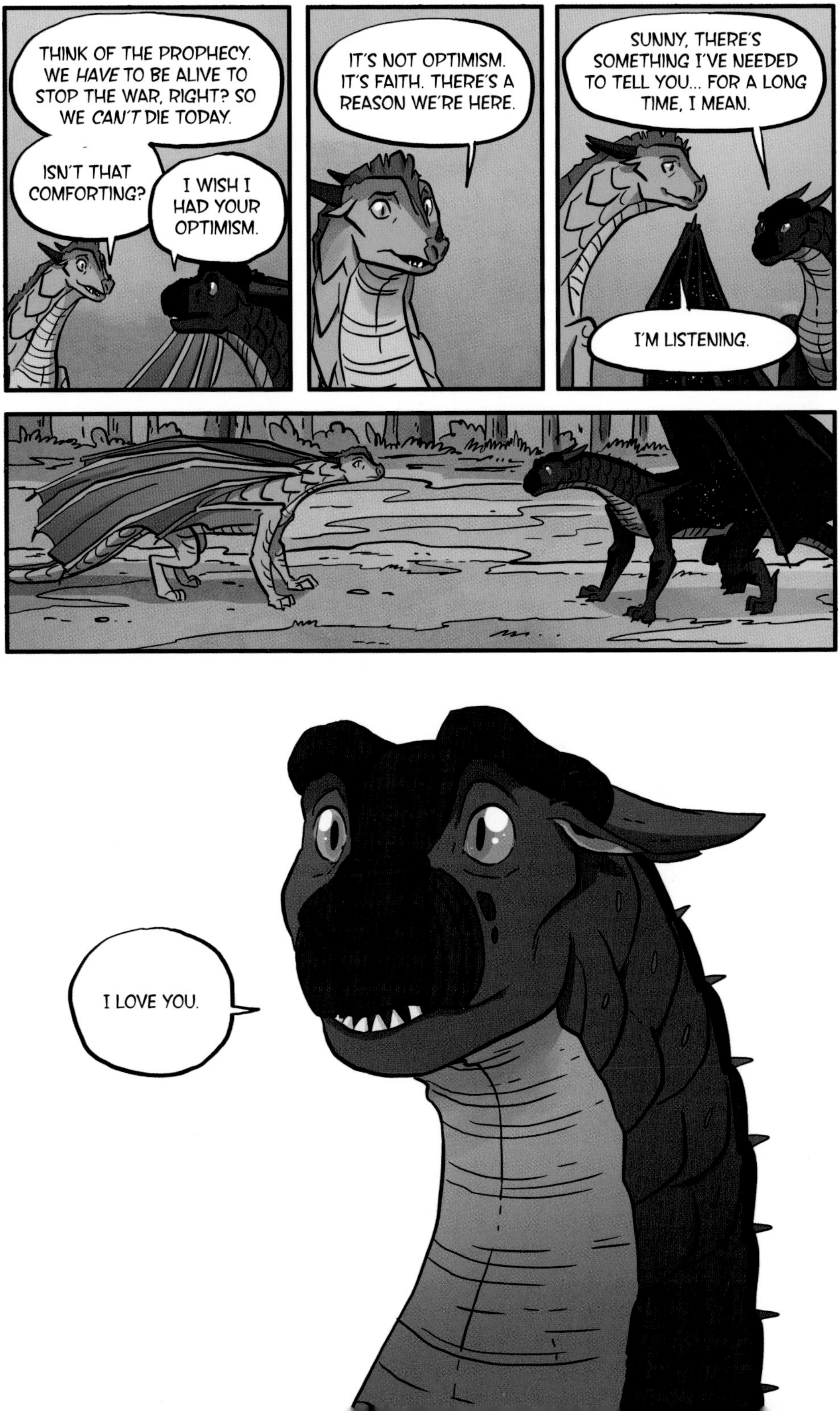
THINK OF THE PROPHECY. WE *HAVE* TO BE ALIVE TO STOP THE WAR, RIGHT? SO WE *CAN'T* DIE TODAY.
ISN'T THAT COMFORTING?
I WISH I HAD YOUR OPTIMISM.
IT'S NOT OPTIMISM. IT'S FAITH. THERE'S A REASON WE'RE HERE.
SUNNY, THERE'S SOMETHING I'VE NEEDED TO TELL YOU... FOR A LONG TIME, I MEAN.
I'M LISTENING.
I LOVE YOU.

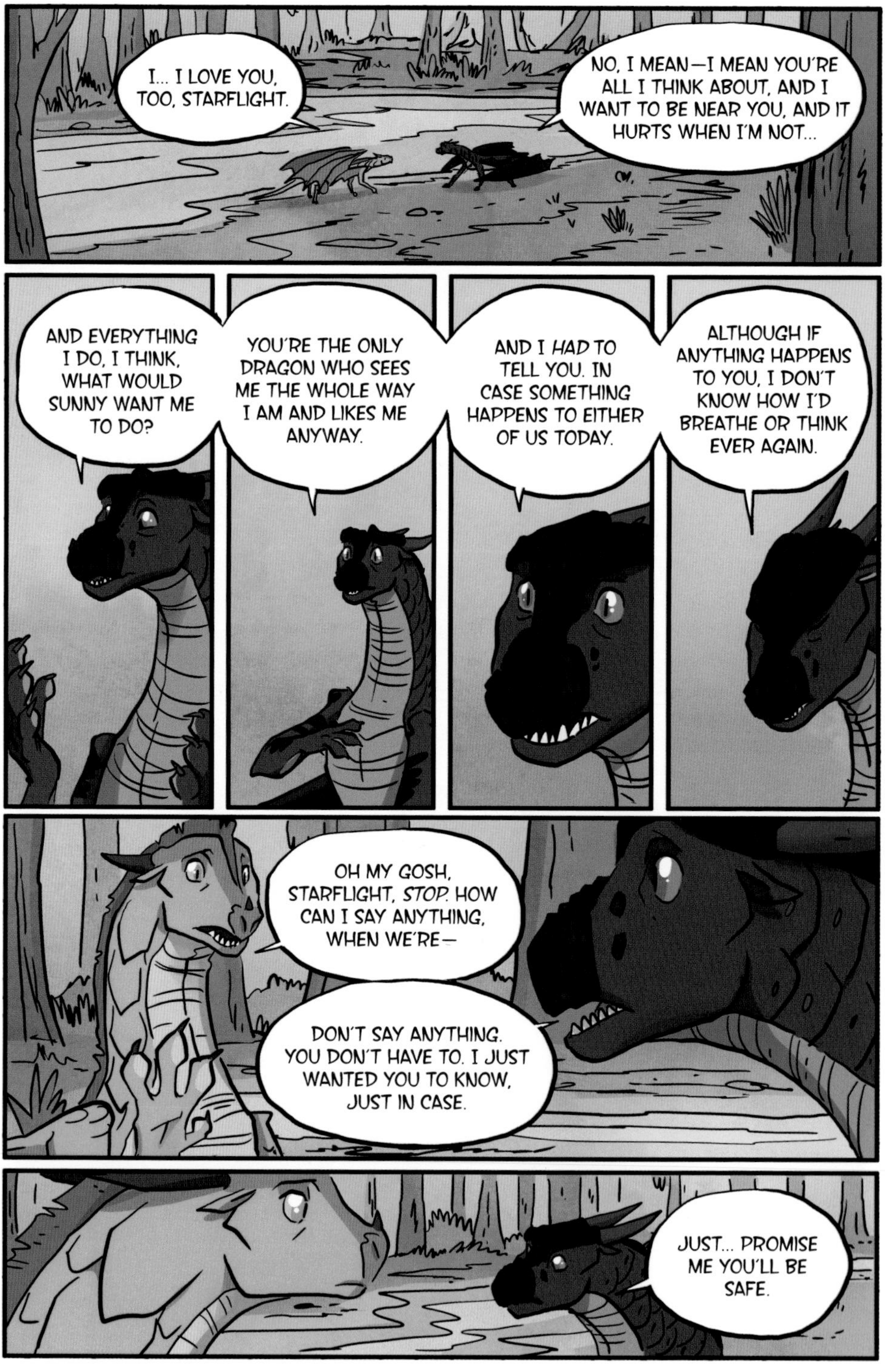
I... I LOVE YOU, TOO, STARFLIGHT.
NO, I MEAN—I MEAN YOU'RE ALL I THINK ABOUT, AND I WANT TO BE NEAR YOU, AND IT HURTS WHEN I'M NOT...
AND EVERYTHING I DO, I THINK, WHAT WOULD SUNNY WANT ME TO DO?
YOU'RE THE ONLY DRAGON WHO SEES ME THE WHOLE WAY I AM AND LIKES ME ANYWAY.
AND I *HAD* TO TELL YOU. IN CASE SOMETHING HAPPENS TO EITHER OF US TODAY.
ALTHOUGH IF ANYTHING HAPPENS TO YOU, I DON'T KNOW HOW I'D BREATHE OR THINK EVER AGAIN.
OH MY GOSH, STARFLIGHT, *STOP.* HOW CAN I SAY ANYTHING, WHEN WE'RE—
DON'T SAY ANYTHING. YOU DON'T HAVE TO. I JUST WANTED YOU TO KNOW, JUST IN CASE.
JUST... PROMISE ME YOU'LL BE SAFE.

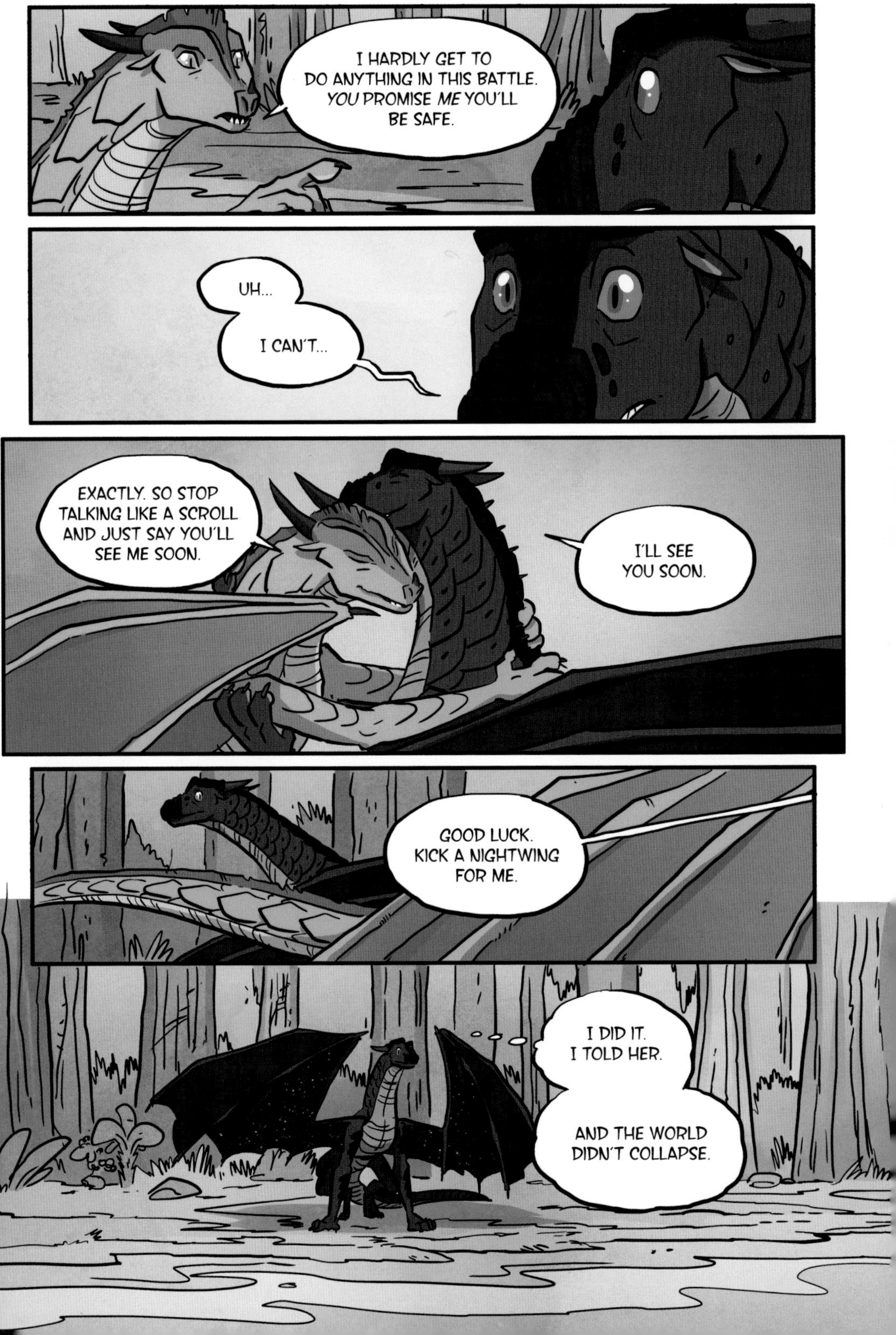
I HARDLY GET TO DO ANYTHING IN THIS BATTLE. *YOU* PROMISE *ME* YOU'LL BE SAFE.
UH...
I CAN'T...
EXACTLY. SO STOP TALKING LIKE A SCROLL AND JUST SAY YOU'LL SEE ME SOON.
I'LL SEE YOU SOON.
GOOD LUCK. KICK A NIGHTWING FOR ME.
I DID IT. I TOLD HER.
AND THE WORLD DIDN'T COLLAPSE.

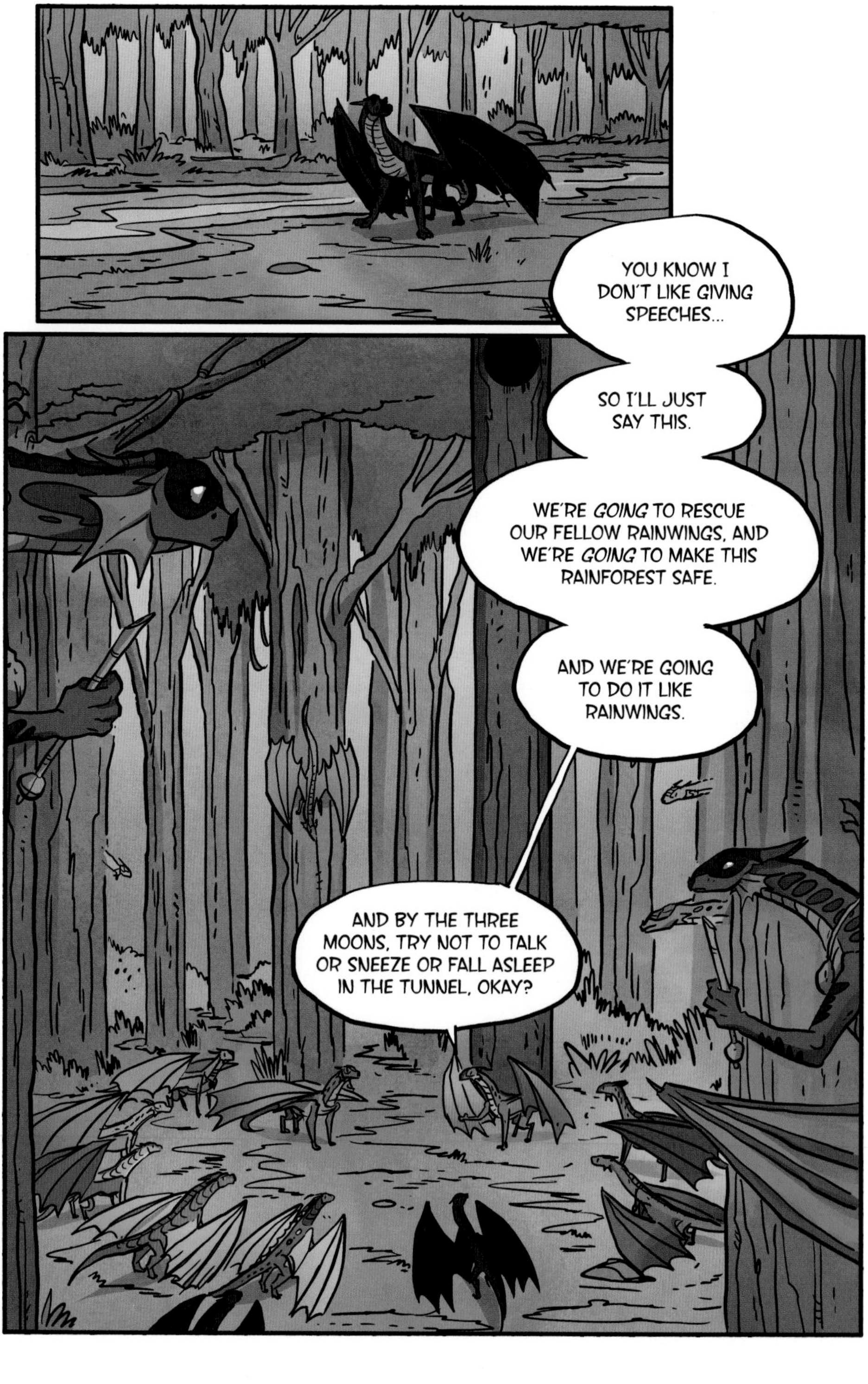
YOU KNOW I DON'T LIKE GIVING SPEECHES...
SO I'LL JUST SAY THIS.
WE'RE *GOING* TO RESCUE OUR FELLOW RAINWINGS, AND WE'RE *GOING* TO MAKE THIS RAINFOREST SAFE.
AND WE'RE GOING TO DO IT LIKE RAINWINGS.
AND BY THE THREE MOONS, TRY NOT TO TALK OR SNEEZE OR FALL ASLEEP IN THE TUNNEL, OKAY?

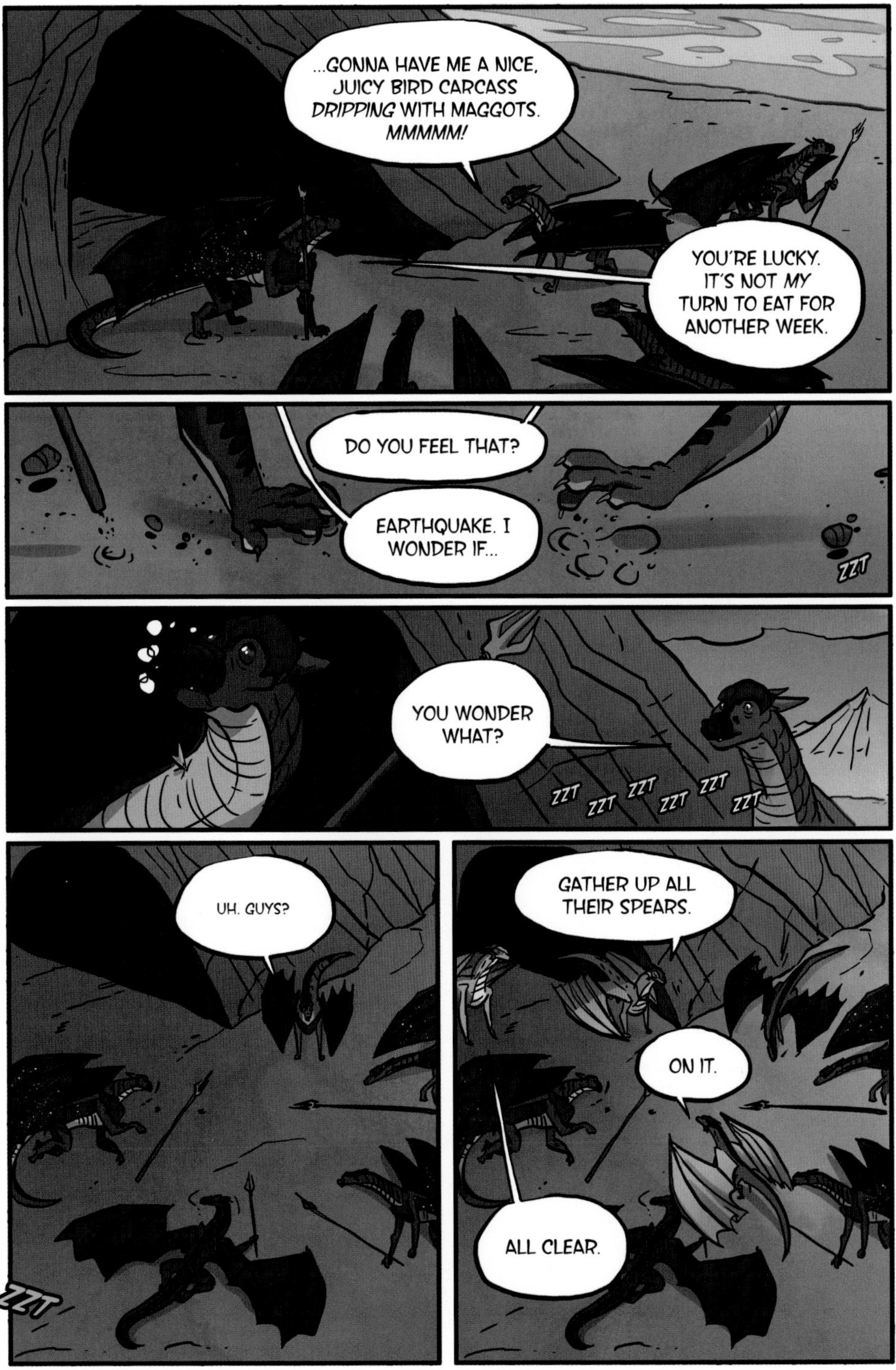
...GONNA HAVE ME A NICE, JUICY BIRD CARCASS *DRIPPING* WITH MAGGOTS. *MMMMM!*
YOU'RE LUCKY. IT'S NOT *MY* TURN TO EAT FOR ANOTHER WEEK.
DO YOU FEEL THAT?
EARTHQUAKE. I WONDER IF...
ZZT
YOU WONDER WHAT?
ZZT ZZT ZZT ZZT ZZT ZZT
UH. GUYS?
ZZT
GATHER UP ALL THEIR SPEARS.
ON IT.
ALL CLEAR.

WHAT A NIGHTMARE.

HOW CAN ANYONE LIVE HERE?

CARRY THIS, STARFLIGHT. IF I HOLD IT, IT'LL LOOK LIKE IT'S FLYING AROUND BY ITSELF.

RIGHT.

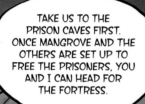

TAKE US TO THE PRISON CAVES FIRST. ONCE MANGROVE AND THE OTHERS ARE SET UP TO FREE THE PRISONERS, YOU AND I CAN HEAD FOR THE FORTRESS.

BUT THAT'S THE MOST DANGEROUS PART. YOU CAN SEND SOMEONE ELSE FOR SPLENDOR.

I'M NOT GOING TO BE THE KIND OF QUEEN WHO SENDS DRAGONS INTO DANGER I'M NOT WILLING TO FACE MYSELF.

AND EVEN IF I SEND SOMEONE FOR SPLENDOR, I CAN'T SEND ANYONE ELSE TO FACE BATTLEWINNER.

BATTLEWINNER? IS THAT A GOOD IDEA?

WEREN'T *YOU* THE ONE WHO SUGGESTED DIPLOMACY?

THAT WAS BEFORE I KNEW ANYTHING ABOUT THE NIGHTWINGS.

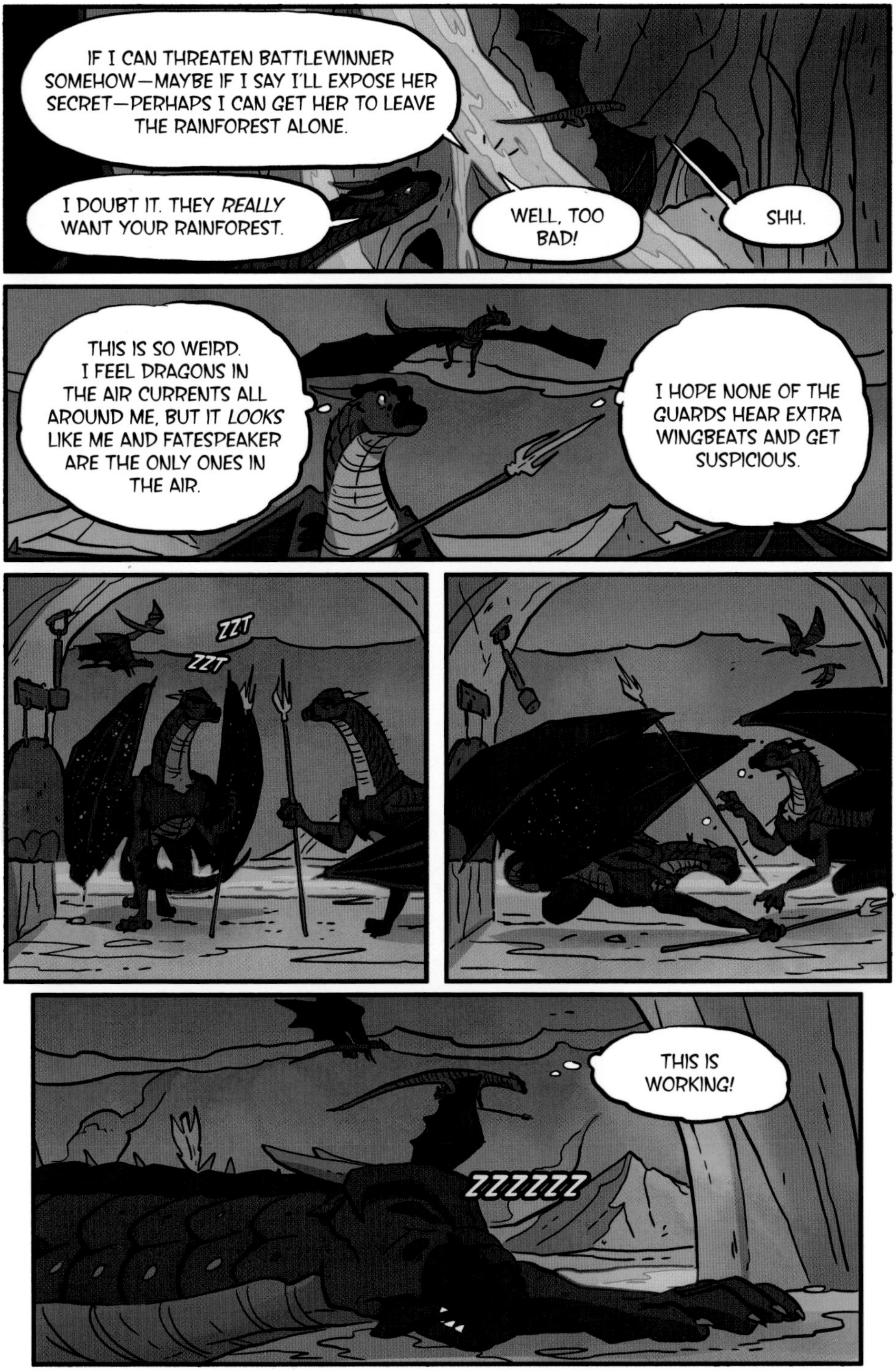
IF I CAN THREATEN BATTLEWINNER SOMEHOW—MAYBE IF I SAY I'LL EXPOSE HER SECRET—PERHAPS I CAN GET HER TO LEAVE THE RAINFOREST ALONE.
I DOUBT IT. THEY *REALLY* WANT YOUR RAINFOREST.
WELL, TOO BAD!
SHH.
THIS IS SO WEIRD. I FEEL DRAGONS IN THE AIR CURRENTS ALL AROUND ME, BUT IT *LOOKS* LIKE ME AND FATESPEAKER ARE THE ONLY ONES IN THE AIR.
I HOPE NONE OF THE GUARDS HEAR EXTRA WINGBEATS AND GET SUSPICIOUS.
ZZT
ZZT
THIS IS WORKING!
ZZZZZZ

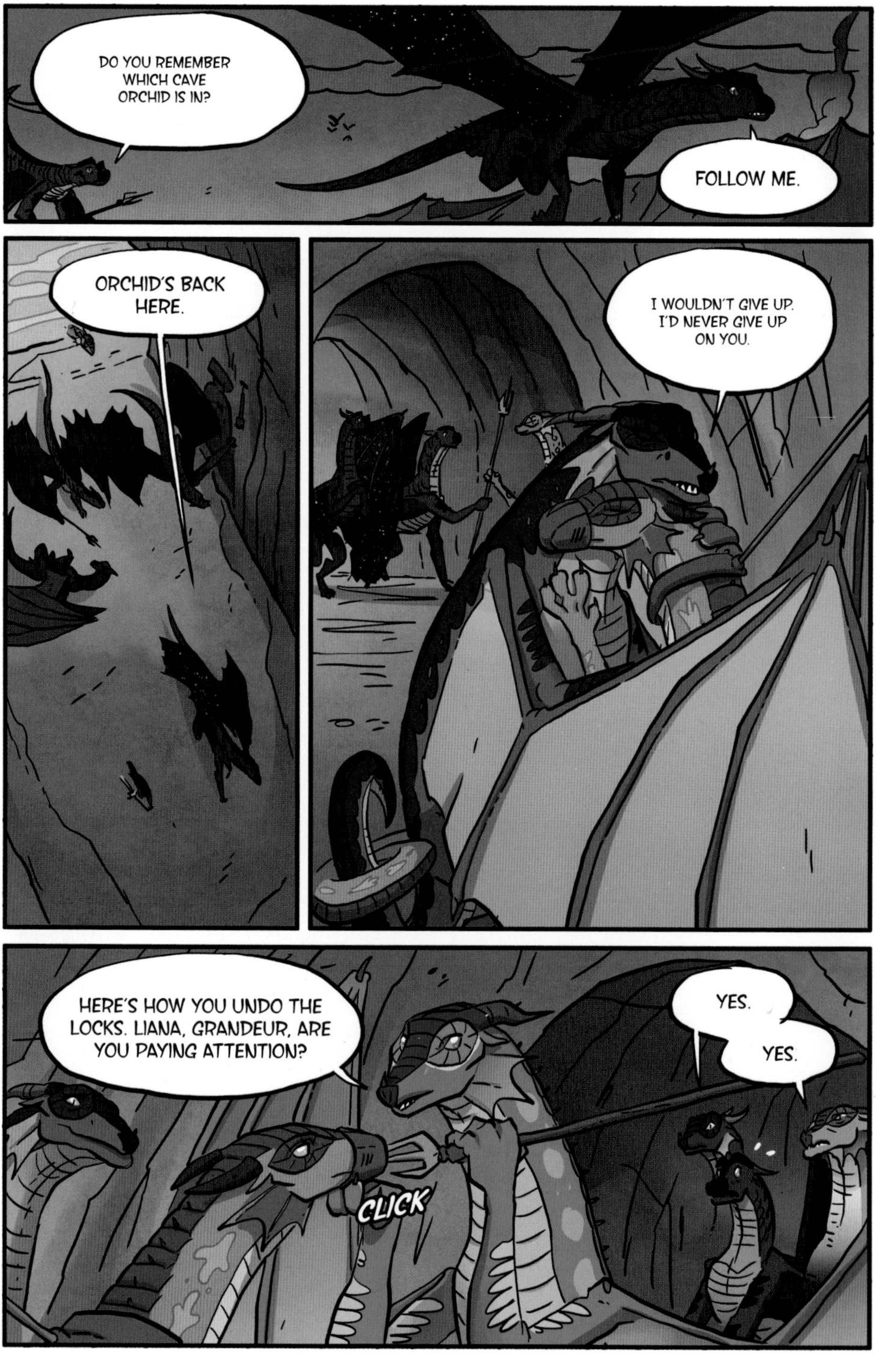
DO YOU REMEMBER WHICH CAVE ORCHID IS IN?
FOLLOW ME.
ORCHID'S BACK HERE.
I WOULDN'T GIVE UP. I'D NEVER GIVE UP ON YOU.
HERE'S HOW YOU UNDO THE LOCKS. LIANA, GRANDEUR, ARE YOU PAYING ATTENTION?
YES.
YES.
CLICK

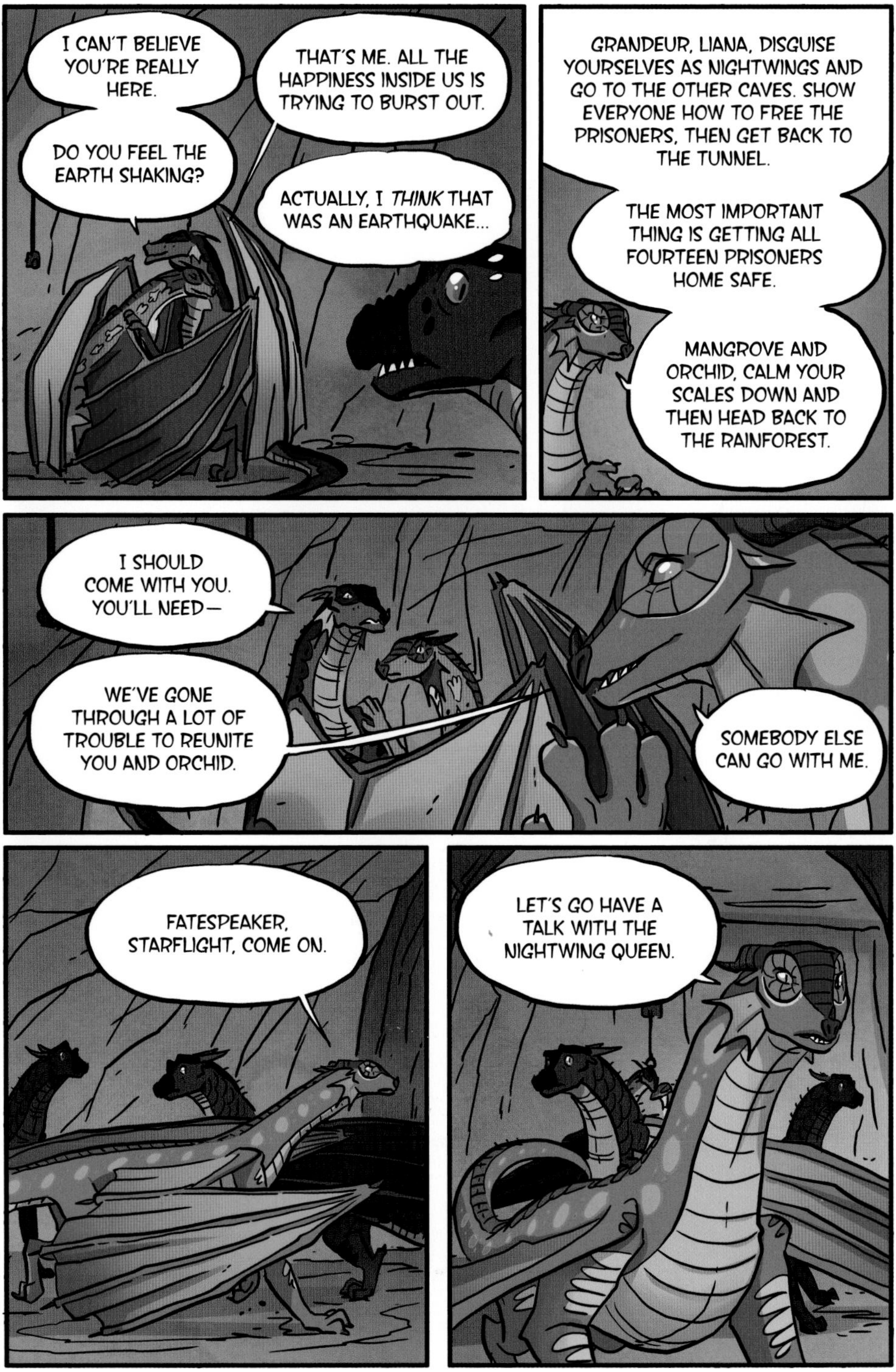
I CAN'T BELIEVE YOU'RE REALLY HERE.
DO YOU FEEL THE EARTH SHAKING?
THAT'S ME. ALL THE HAPPINESS INSIDE US IS TRYING TO BURST OUT.
ACTUALLY, I *THINK* THAT WAS AN EARTHQUAKE...
GRANDEUR, LIANA, DISGUISE YOURSELVES AS NIGHTWINGS AND GO TO THE OTHER CAVES. SHOW EVERYONE HOW TO FREE THE PRISONERS, THEN GET BACK TO THE TUNNEL.
THE MOST IMPORTANT THING IS GETTING ALL FOURTEEN PRISONERS HOME SAFE.
MANGROVE AND ORCHID, CALM YOUR SCALES DOWN AND THEN HEAD BACK TO THE RAINFOREST.
I SHOULD COME WITH YOU. YOU'LL NEED—
WE'VE GONE THROUGH A LOT OF TROUBLE TO REUNITE YOU AND ORCHID.
SOMEBODY ELSE CAN GO WITH ME.
FATESPEAKER, STARFLIGHT, COME ON.
LET'S GO HAVE A TALK WITH THE NIGHTWING QUEEN.

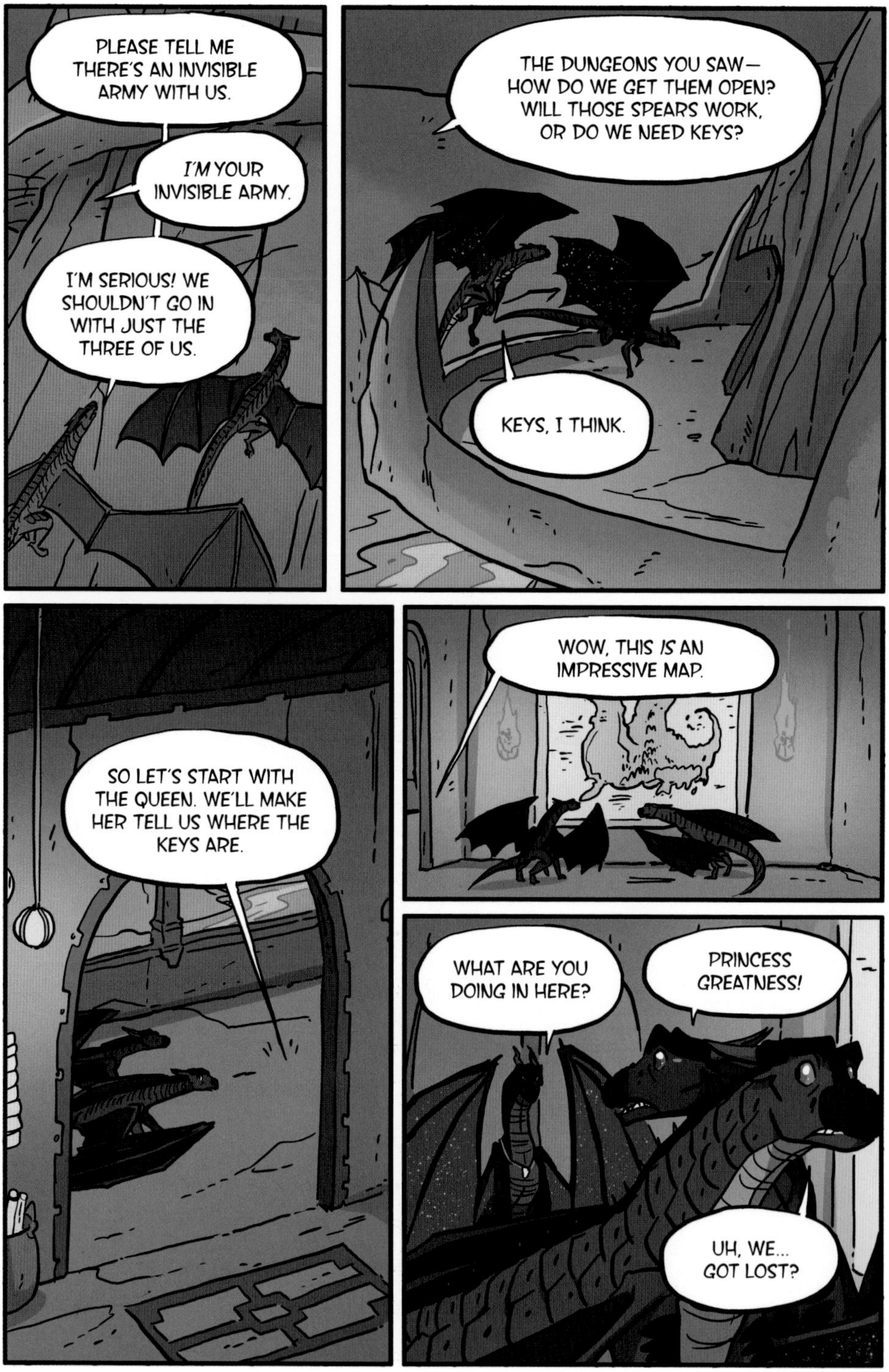
PLEASE TELL ME THERE'S AN INVISIBLE ARMY WITH US.
I'M YOUR INVISIBLE ARMY.
I'M SERIOUS! WE SHOULDN'T GO IN WITH JUST THE THREE OF US.
THE DUNGEONS YOU SAW— HOW DO WE GET THEM OPEN? WILL THOSE SPEARS WORK, OR DO WE NEED KEYS?
KEYS, I THINK.
SO LET'S START WITH THE QUEEN. WE'LL MAKE HER TELL US WHERE THE KEYS ARE.
WOW, THIS *IS* AN IMPRESSIVE MAP.
WHAT ARE YOU DOING IN HERE?
PRINCESS GREATNESS!
UH, WE... GOT LOST?

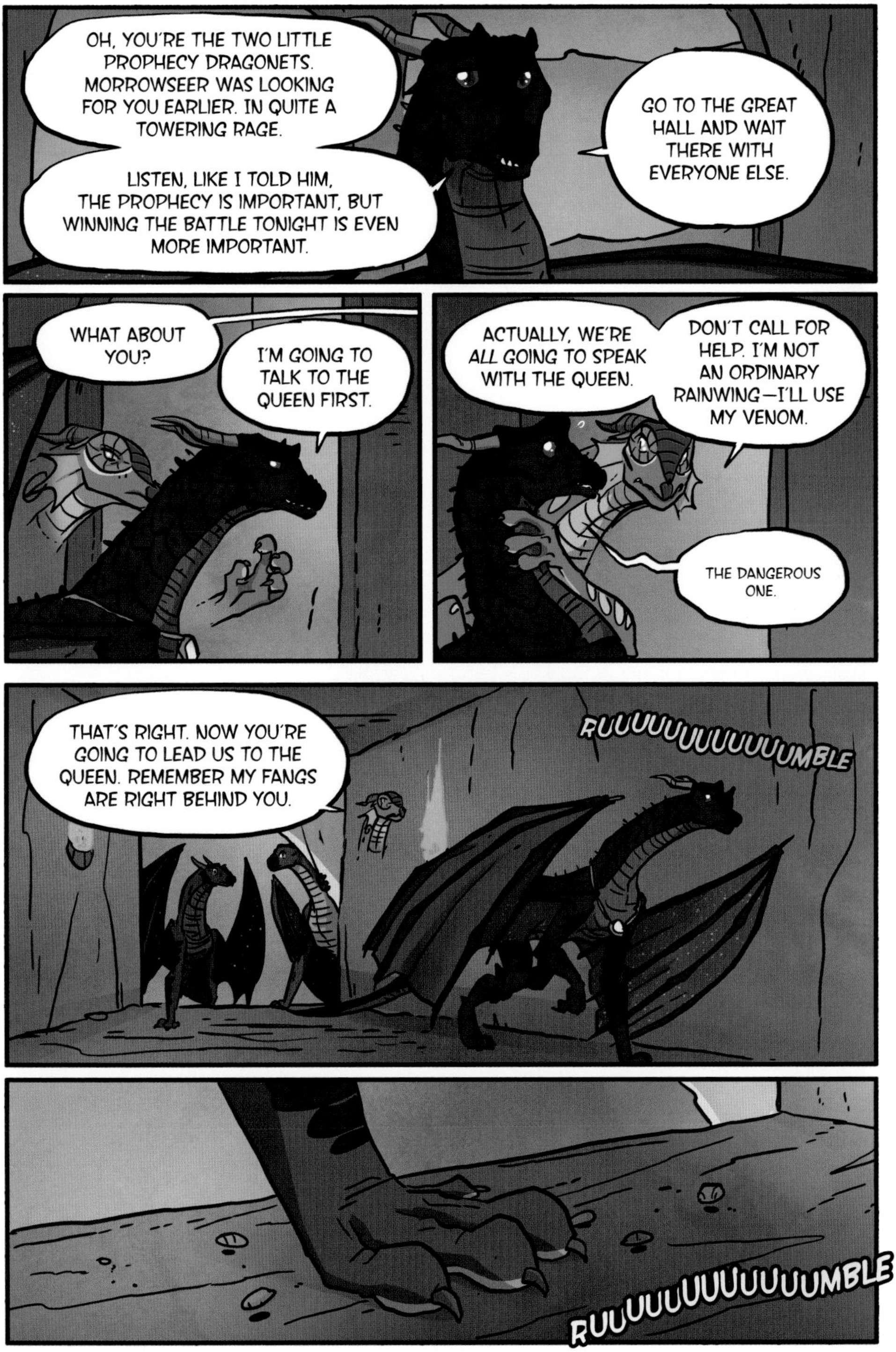
OH, YOU'RE THE TWO LITTLE PROPHECY DRAGONETS. MORROWSEER WAS LOOKING FOR YOU EARLIER. IN QUITE A TOWERING RAGE.
LISTEN, LIKE I TOLD HIM, THE PROPHECY IS IMPORTANT, BUT WINNING THE BATTLE TONIGHT IS EVEN MORE IMPORTANT.
GO TO THE GREAT HALL AND WAIT THERE WITH EVERYONE ELSE.
WHAT ABOUT YOU?
I'M GOING TO TALK TO THE QUEEN FIRST.
ACTUALLY, WE'RE *ALL* GOING TO SPEAK WITH THE QUEEN.
DON'T CALL FOR HELP. I'M NOT AN ORDINARY RAINWING—I'LL USE MY VENOM.
THE DANGEROUS ONE.
THAT'S RIGHT. NOW YOU'RE GOING TO LEAD US TO THE QUEEN. REMEMBER MY FANGS ARE RIGHT BEHIND YOU.
RUUUUUUUUUUUUMBLE
RUUUUUUUUUUUUMBLE

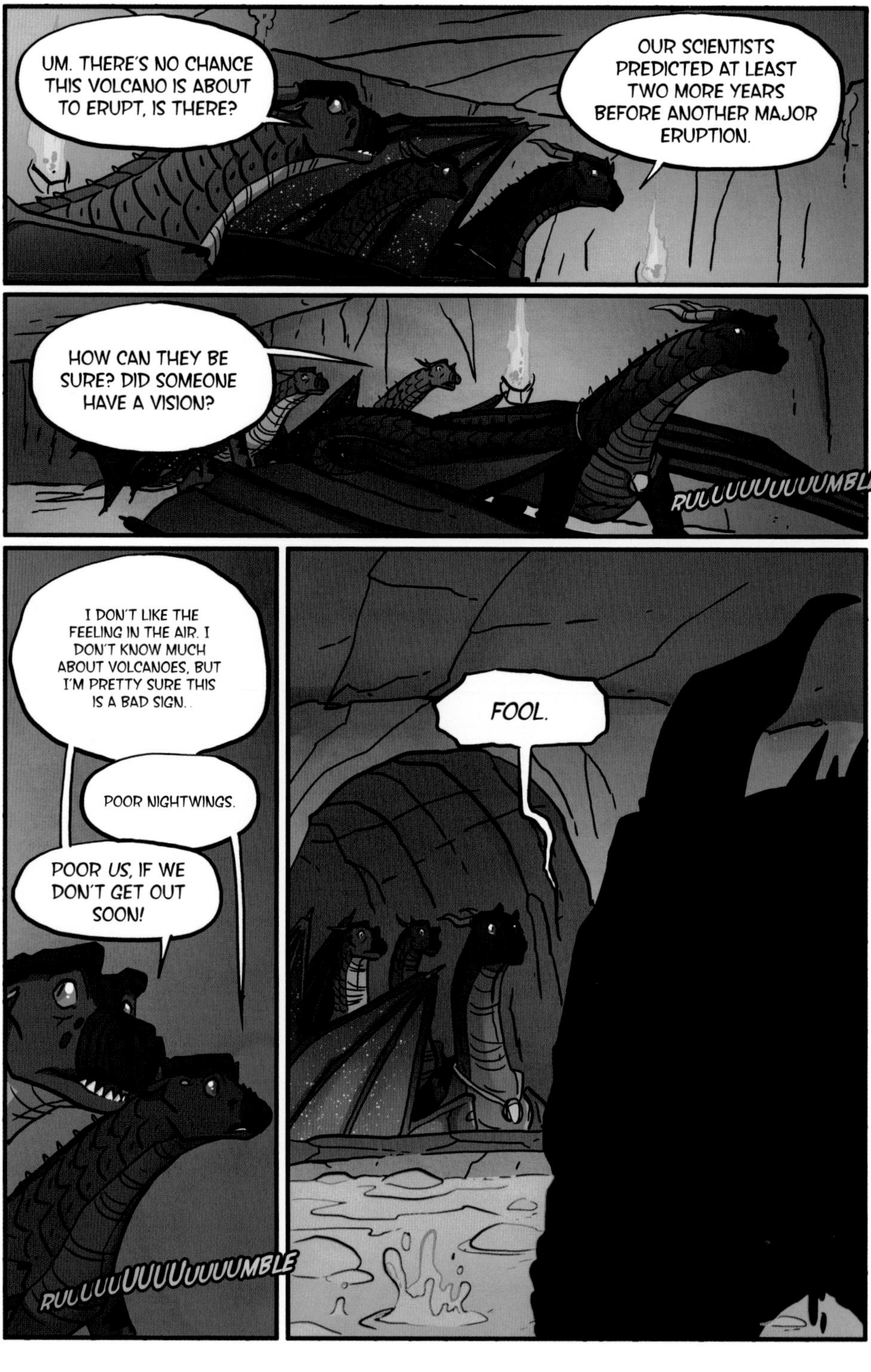
UM. THERE'S NO CHANCE THIS VOLCANO IS ABOUT TO ERUPT, IS THERE?
OUR SCIENTISTS PREDICTED AT LEAST TWO MORE YEARS BEFORE ANOTHER MAJOR ERUPTION.
HOW CAN THEY BE SURE? DID SOMEONE HAVE A VISION?
RULUUUUUUUUMBLE
I DON'T LIKE THE FEELING IN THE AIR. I DON'T KNOW MUCH ABOUT VOLCANOES, BUT I'M PRETTY SURE THIS IS A BAD SIGN...
POOR NIGHTWINGS.
POOR US, IF WE DON'T GET OUT SOON!
RULUUUUUUUUUUUMBLE
FOOL.

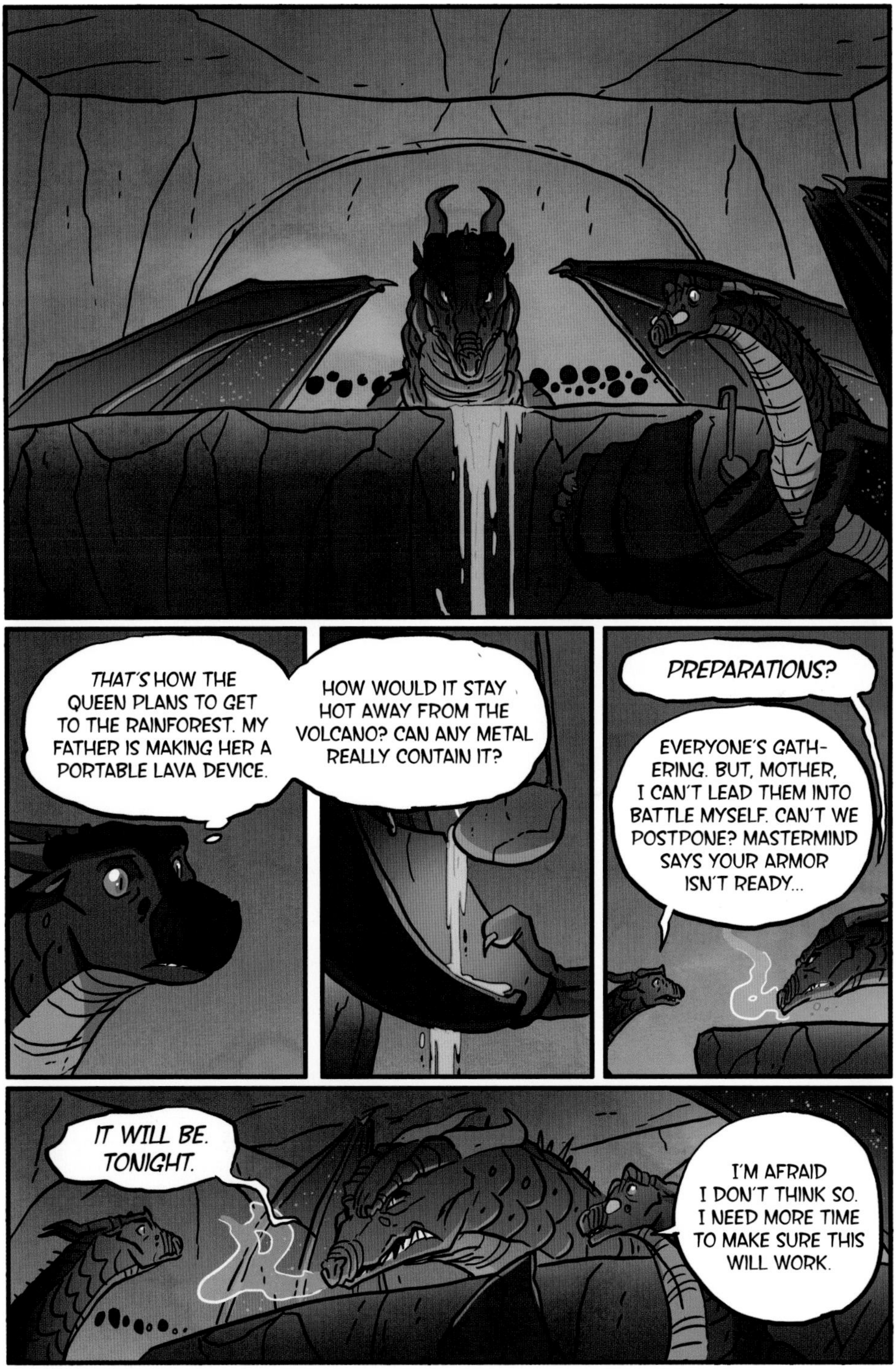
THAT'S HOW THE QUEEN PLANS TO GET TO THE RAINFOREST. MY FATHER IS MAKING HER A PORTABLE LAVA DEVICE.
HOW WOULD IT STAY HOT AWAY FROM THE VOLCANO? CAN ANY METAL REALLY CONTAIN IT?
PREPARATIONS?
EVERYONE'S GATHERING. BUT, MOTHER, I CAN'T LEAD THEM INTO BATTLE MYSELF. CAN'T WE POSTPONE? MASTERMIND SAYS YOUR ARMOR ISN'T READY...
IT WILL BE. TONIGHT.
I'M AFRAID I DON'T THINK SO. I NEED MORE TIME TO MAKE SURE THIS WILL WORK.

TONIGHT, MASTERMIND. I CAN'T TRUST **HER** TO RUN THE INVASION.

YOU *SHOULDN'T!* I DON'T KNOW WHAT TO DO. SO I WAS COMING TO ASK YOU, AND THEN—

THEN SHE RAN INTO ME.

AND YOU ARE?

QUEEN GLORY OF THE RAINWINGS. I'VE COME TO GIVE YOU ONE CHANCE TO END THIS WAR BEFORE WE DESTROY YOU.

FUNNY.

IF YOU THINK AN ICEWING ATTACK IS HARD TO LIVE WITH, TRY RAINWING VENOM. YOUR LAVA BATH WON'T HELP WITH THAT.

HIISSSSSSSSSSSSSSSSSSS

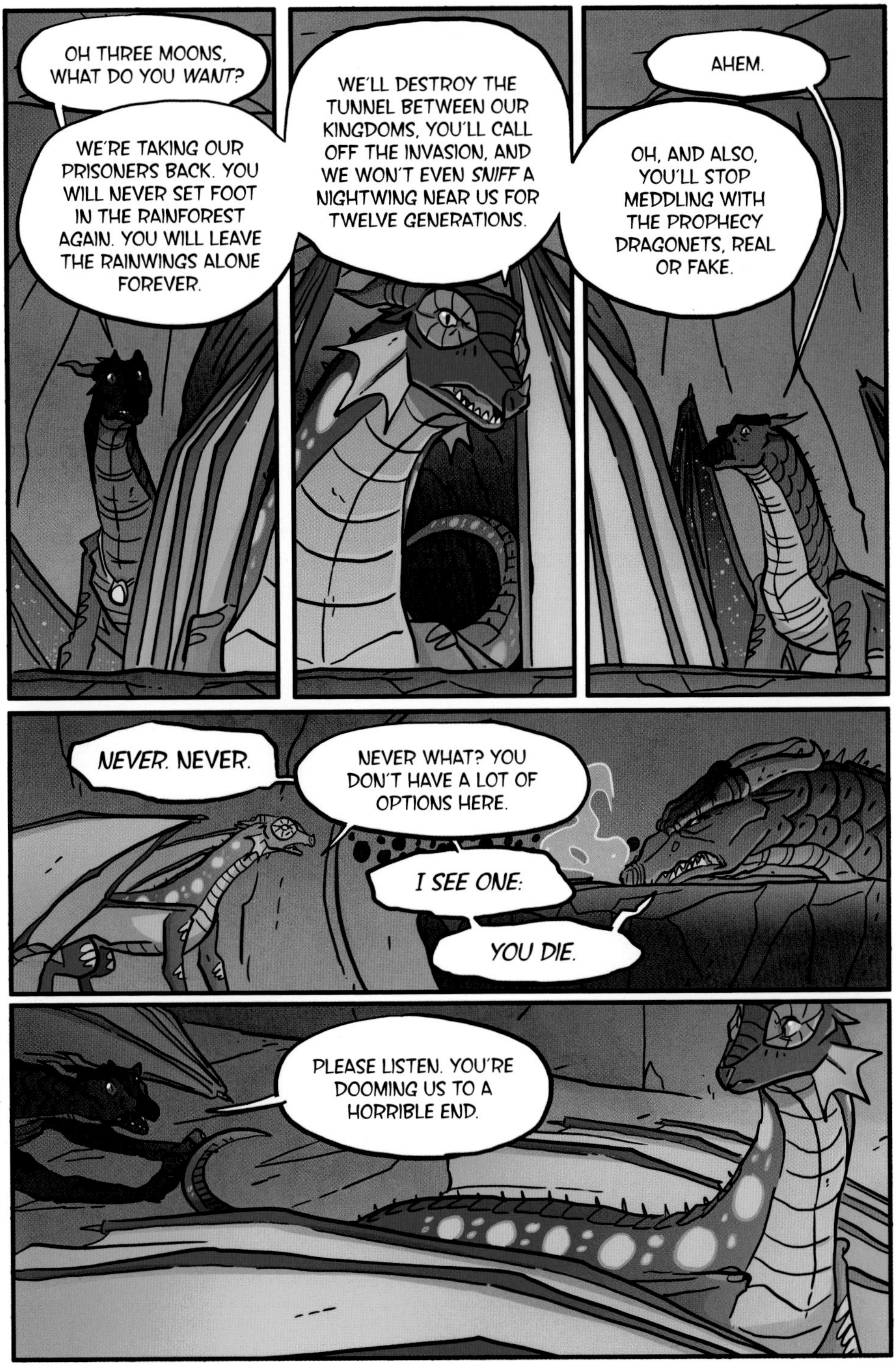

OH THREE MOONS, WHAT DO YOU *WANT?*
WE'RE TAKING OUR PRISONERS BACK. YOU WILL NEVER SET FOOT IN THE RAINFOREST AGAIN. YOU WILL LEAVE THE RAINWINGS ALONE FOREVER.
WE'LL DESTROY THE TUNNEL BETWEEN OUR KINGDOMS, YOU'LL CALL OFF THE INVASION, AND WE WON'T EVEN *SNIFF* A NIGHTWING NEAR US FOR TWELVE GENERATIONS.
AHEM.
OH, AND ALSO, YOU'LL STOP MEDDLING WITH THE PROPHECY DRAGONETS, REAL OR FAKE.
NEVER. NEVER.
NEVER WHAT? YOU DON'T HAVE A LOT OF OPTIONS HERE.
I SEE ONE:
YOU DIE.
PLEASE LISTEN. YOU'RE DOOMING US TO A HORRIBLE END.

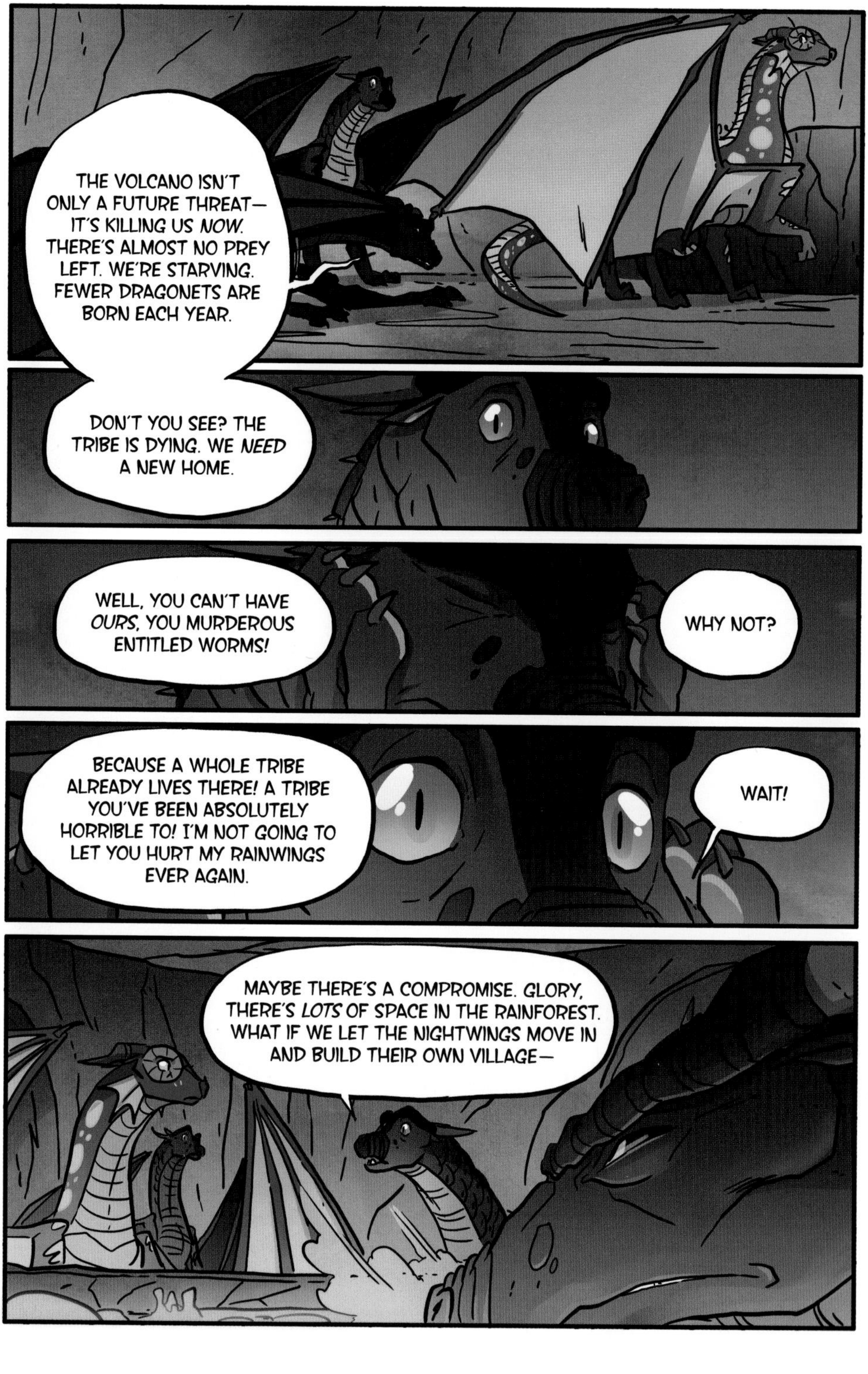
THE VOLCANO ISN'T ONLY A FUTURE THREAT— IT'S KILLING US *NOW*. THERE'S ALMOST NO PREY LEFT. WE'RE STARVING. FEWER DRAGONETS ARE BORN EACH YEAR.
DON'T YOU SEE? THE TRIBE IS DYING. WE *NEED* A NEW HOME.
WELL, YOU CAN'T HAVE *OURS*, YOU MURDEROUS ENTITLED WORMS!
WHY NOT?
BECAUSE A WHOLE TRIBE ALREADY LIVES THERE! A TRIBE YOU'VE BEEN ABSOLUTELY HORRIBLE TO! I'M NOT GOING TO LET YOU HURT MY RAINWINGS EVER AGAIN.
WAIT!
MAYBE THERE'S A COMPROMISE. GLORY, THERE'S *LOTS* OF SPACE IN THE RAINFOREST. WHAT IF WE LET THE NIGHTWINGS MOVE IN AND BUILD THEIR OWN VILLAGE—

BUT *ONLY* IF THEY ALL SWEAR TO ACCEPT *YOU* AS THEIR NEW QUEEN.

WHAT?

A NEW HOME FOR THE NIGHTWINGS, SAFE AND PEACEFUL, AND ALL THEY HAVE TO DO IS GIVE UP THEIR CRUELTY AND VIOLENCE AND OBEY YOU.

HMM.

NEVER!

MOTHER, IT SOUNDS LIKE A GOOD PLAN TO ME.

YOU'RE A PATHETIC HEIR.

RUUUUUUUUUUUUUUUUUUUUUMBLE

I KNOW I AM. BEING QUEEN IS AWFUL.

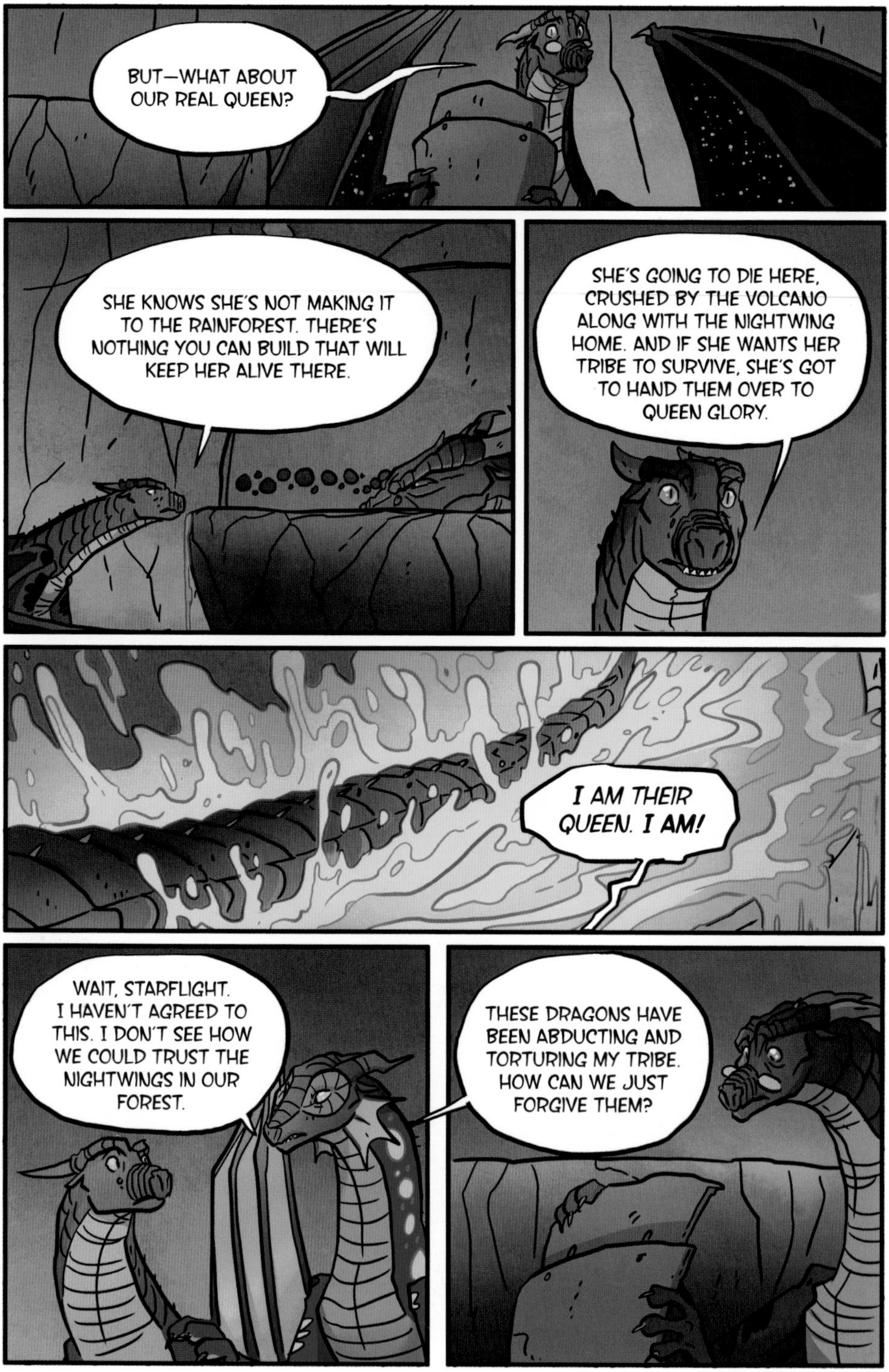
BUT—WHAT ABOUT OUR REAL QUEEN?
SHE KNOWS SHE'S NOT MAKING IT TO THE RAINFOREST. THERE'S NOTHING YOU CAN BUILD THAT WILL KEEP HER ALIVE THERE.
SHE'S GOING TO DIE HERE, CRUSHED BY THE VOLCANO ALONG WITH THE NIGHTWING HOME. AND IF SHE WANTS HER TRIBE TO SURVIVE, SHE'S GOT TO HAND THEM OVER TO QUEEN GLORY.
I AM THEIR QUEEN. I AM!
WAIT, STARFLIGHT. I HAVEN'T AGREED TO THIS. I DON'T SEE HOW WE COULD TRUST THE NIGHTWINGS IN OUR FOREST.
THESE DRAGONS HAVE BEEN ABDUCTING AND TORTURING MY TRIBE. HOW CAN WE JUST FORGIVE THEM?

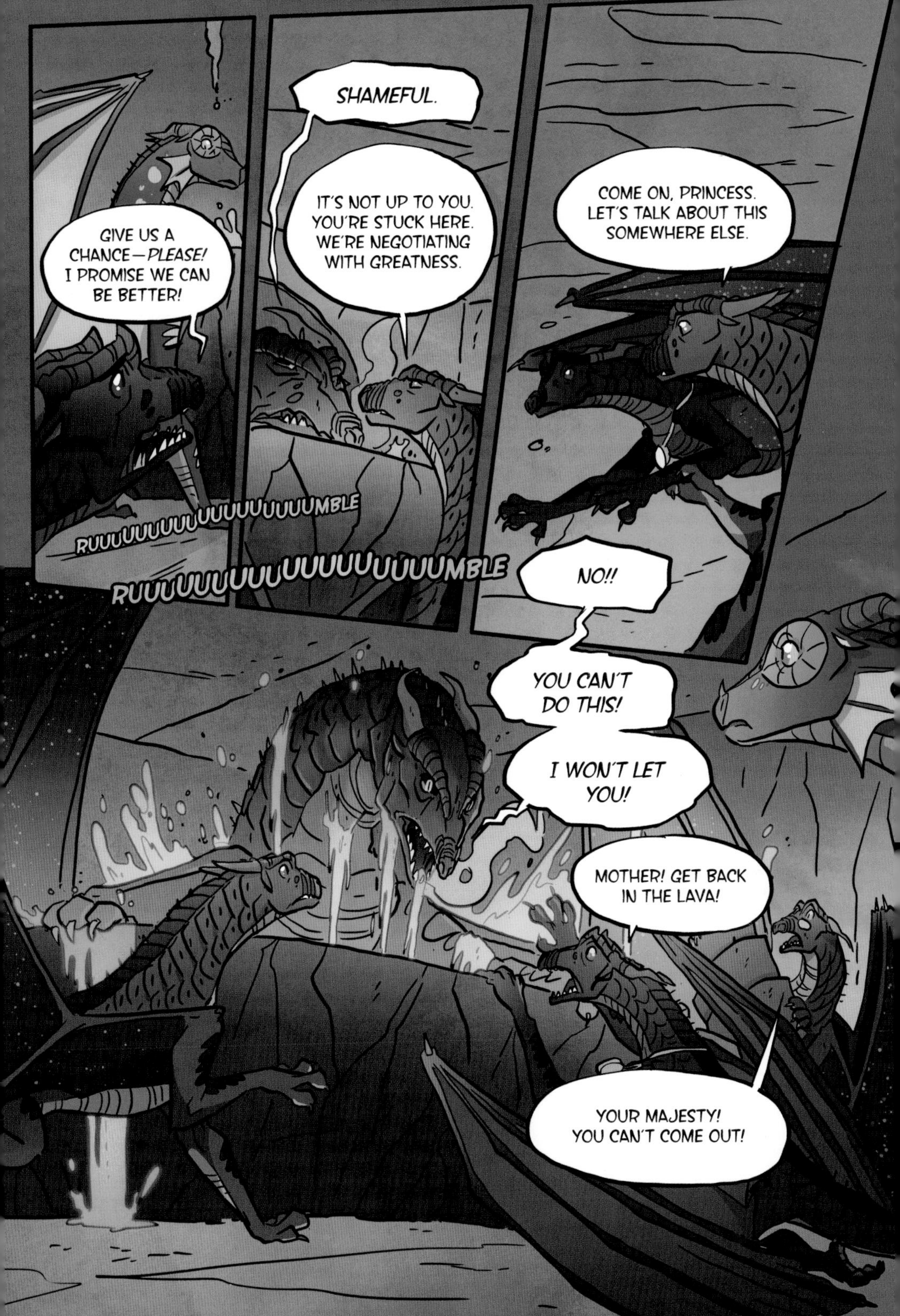
GIVE US A CHANCE—*PLEASE!* I PROMISE WE CAN BE BETTER!
SHAMEFUL.
IT'S NOT UP TO YOU. YOU'RE STUCK HERE. WE'RE NEGOTIATING WITH GREATNESS.
COME ON, PRINCESS. LET'S TALK ABOUT THIS SOMEWHERE ELSE.
RUUUUUUUUUUUUUUUUUMBLE
RUUUUUUUUUUUUUUUUUUMBLE
NO!!
YOU CAN'T DO THIS!
I WON'T LET YOU!
MOTHER! GET BACK IN THE LAVA!
YOUR MAJESTY! YOU CAN'T COME OUT!

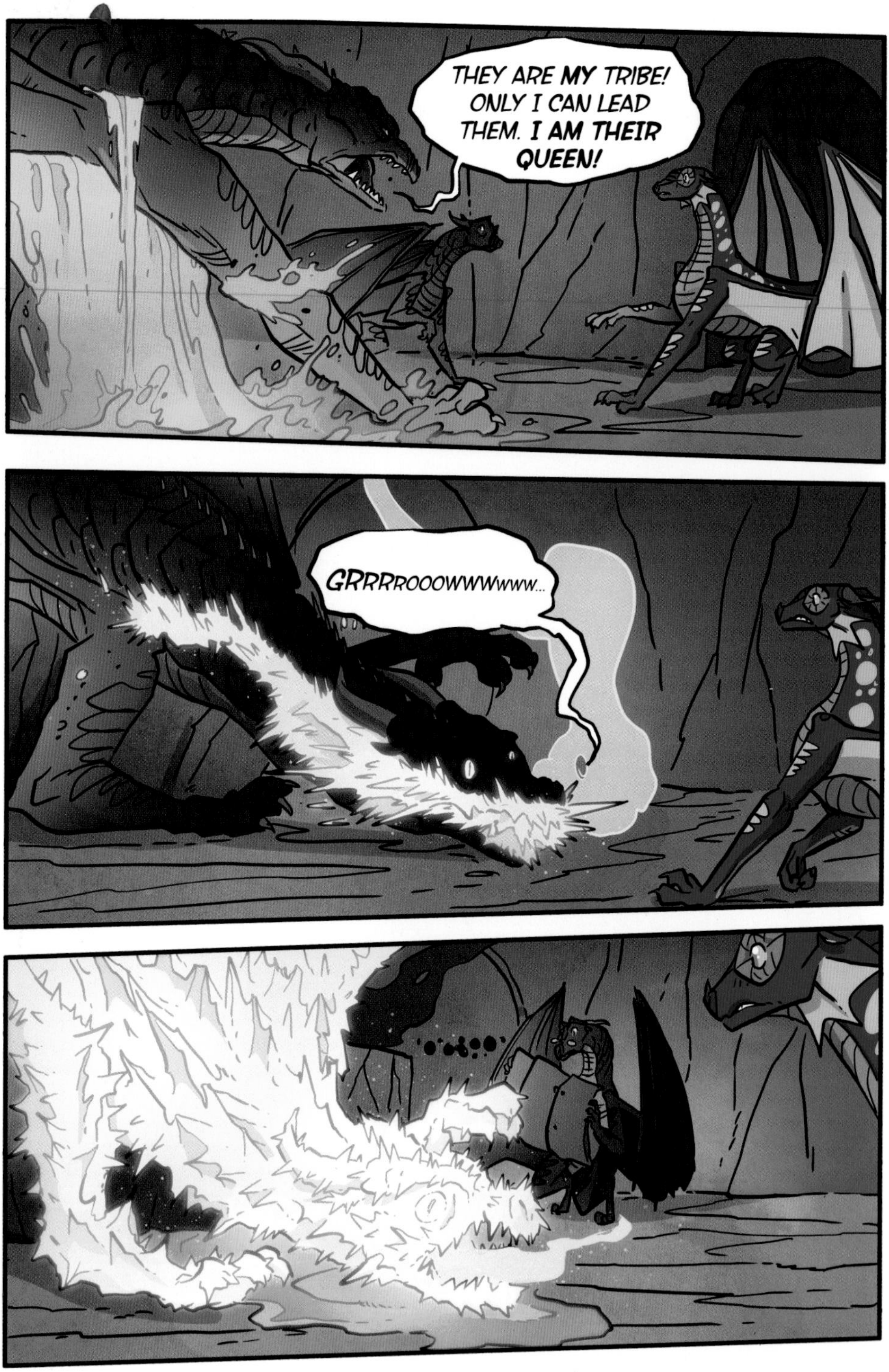
THEY ARE MY TRIBE! ONLY I CAN LEAD THEM. I AM THEIR QUEEN!
GRRRROOOWWWWWW...

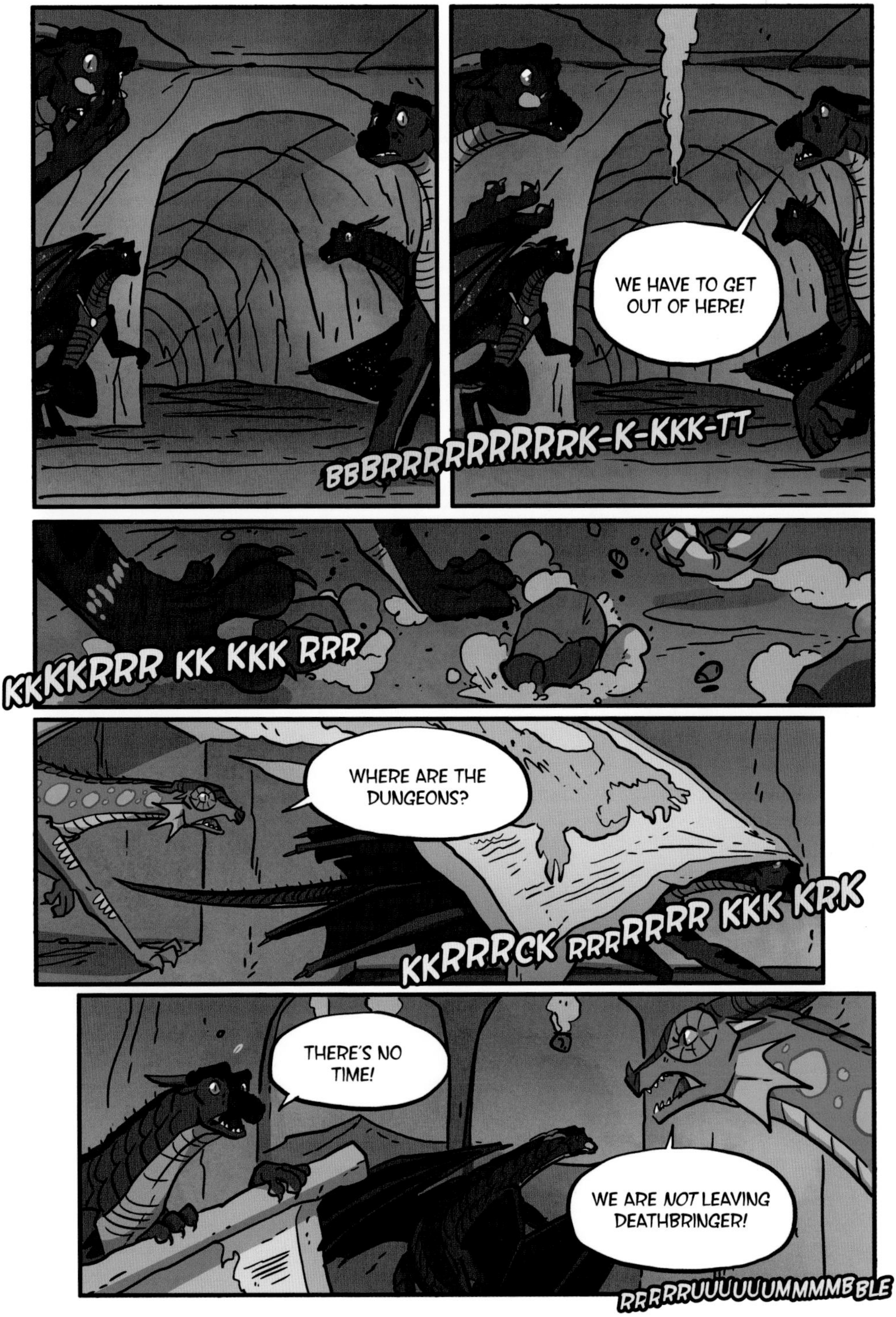
WE HAVE TO GET OUT OF HERE!
BBBRRRRRRRRRK-K-KKK-TT
KKKKRRR KK KKK RRR
WHERE ARE THE DUNGEONS?
KKRRRCK RRRRRRR KKK KRK
THERE'S NO TIME!
WE ARE *NOT* LEAVING DEATHBRINGER!
RRRRRUUUUUMMMMBBLE

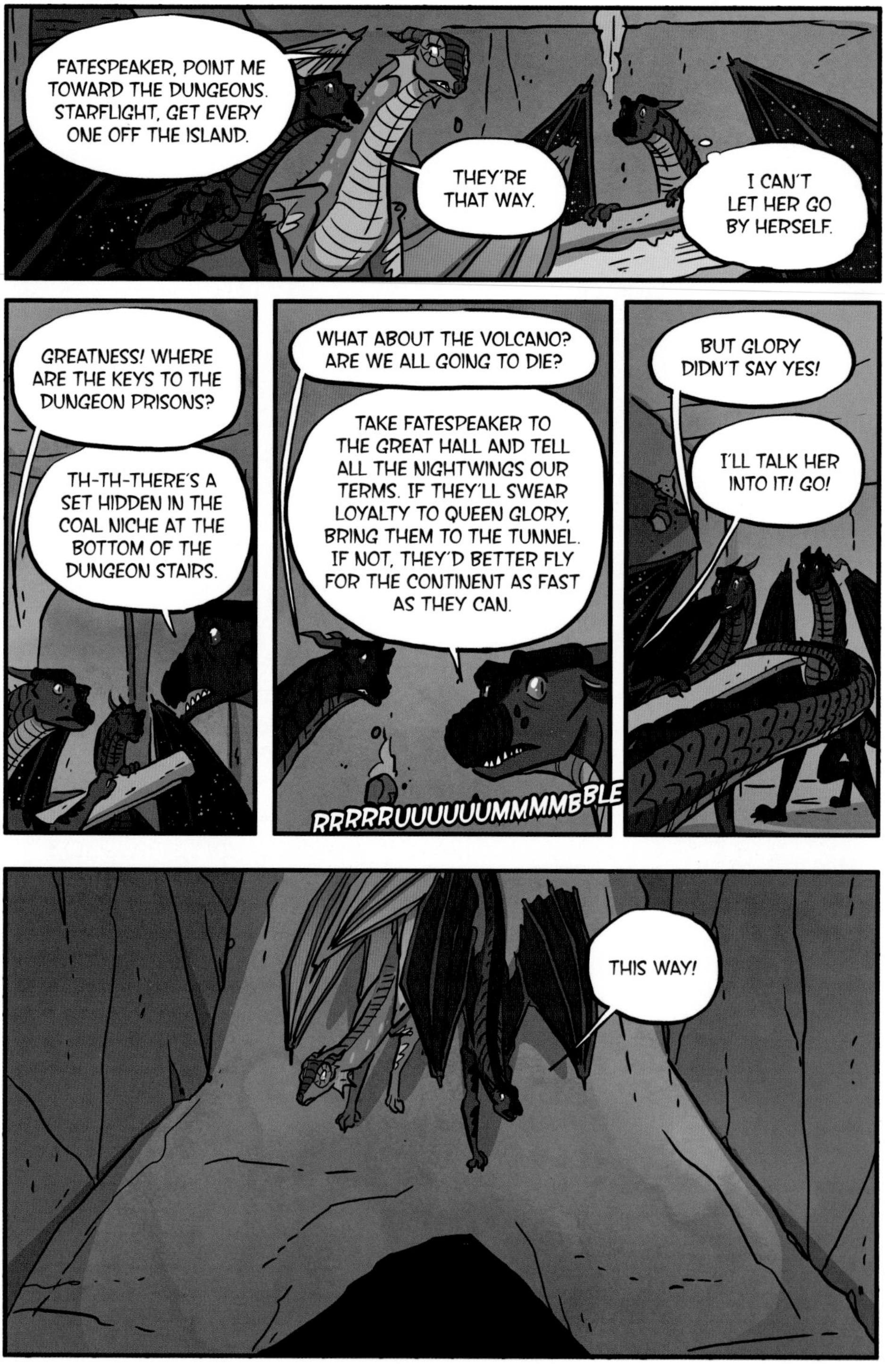

FATESPEAKER, POINT ME TOWARD THE DUNGEONS. STARFLIGHT, GET EVERY ONE OFF THE ISLAND.
THEY'RE THAT WAY.
I CAN'T LET HER GO BY HERSELF.
GREATNESS! WHERE ARE THE KEYS TO THE DUNGEON PRISONS?
TH-TH-THERE'S A SET HIDDEN IN THE COAL NICHE AT THE BOTTOM OF THE DUNGEON STAIRS.
WHAT ABOUT THE VOLCANO? ARE WE ALL GOING TO DIE?
TAKE FATESPEAKER TO THE GREAT HALL AND TELL ALL THE NIGHTWINGS OUR TERMS. IF THEY'LL SWEAR LOYALTY TO QUEEN GLORY, BRING THEM TO THE TUNNEL. IF NOT, THEY'D BETTER FLY FOR THE CONTINENT AS FAST AS THEY CAN.
RRRRRUUUUUUMMMMBBLE
BUT GLORY DIDN'T SAY YES!
I'LL TALK HER INTO IT! GO!
THIS WAY!

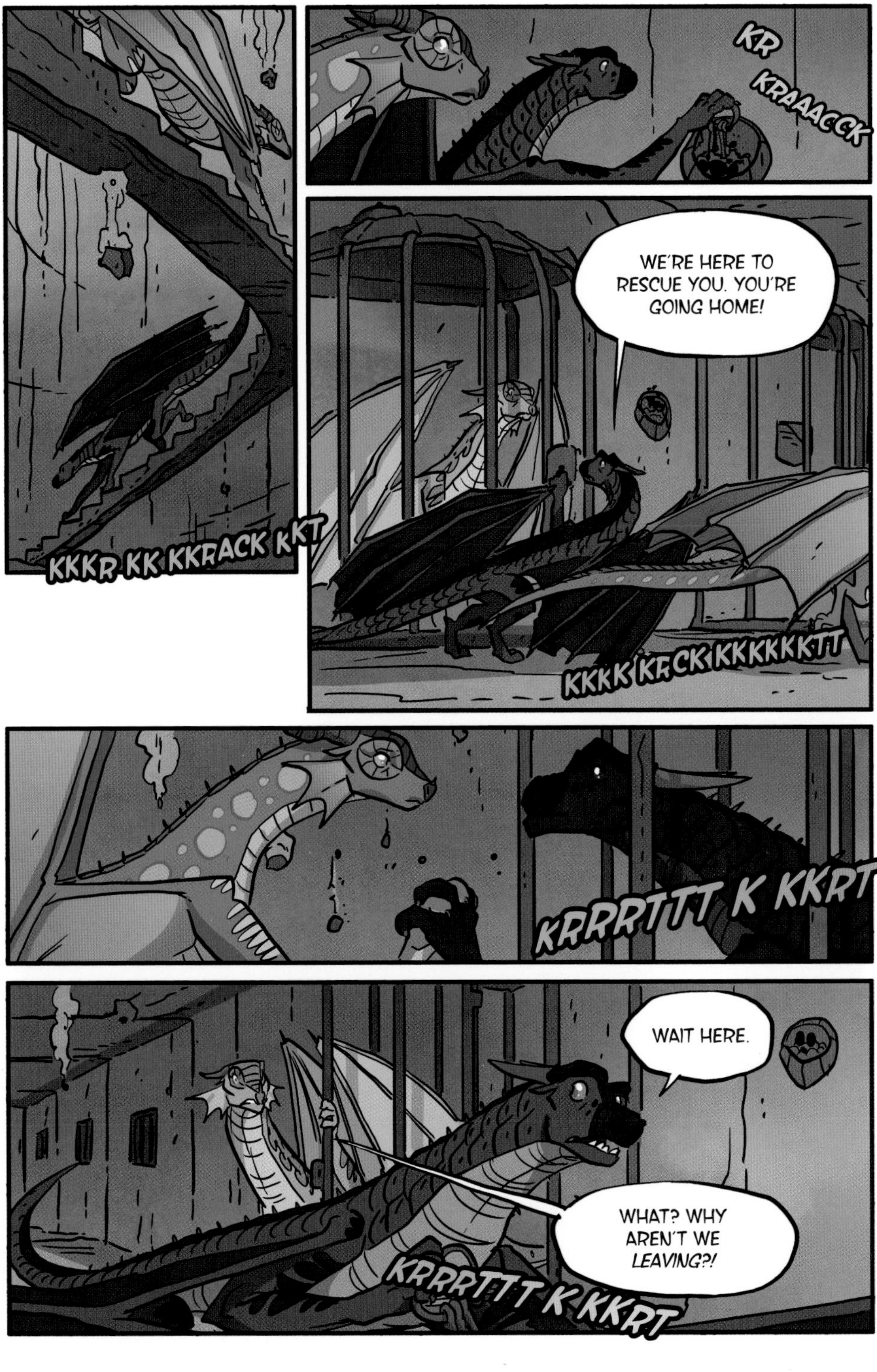
KKKR KK KKRACK KKT
KR
KRAAACCK
WE'RE HERE TO RESCUE YOU. YOU'RE GOING HOME!
KKKK KRCK KKKKKKTT
KRRRTTT K KKRT
WAIT HERE.
WHAT? WHY AREN'T WE *LEAVING?!*
KRRRTTT K KKRT

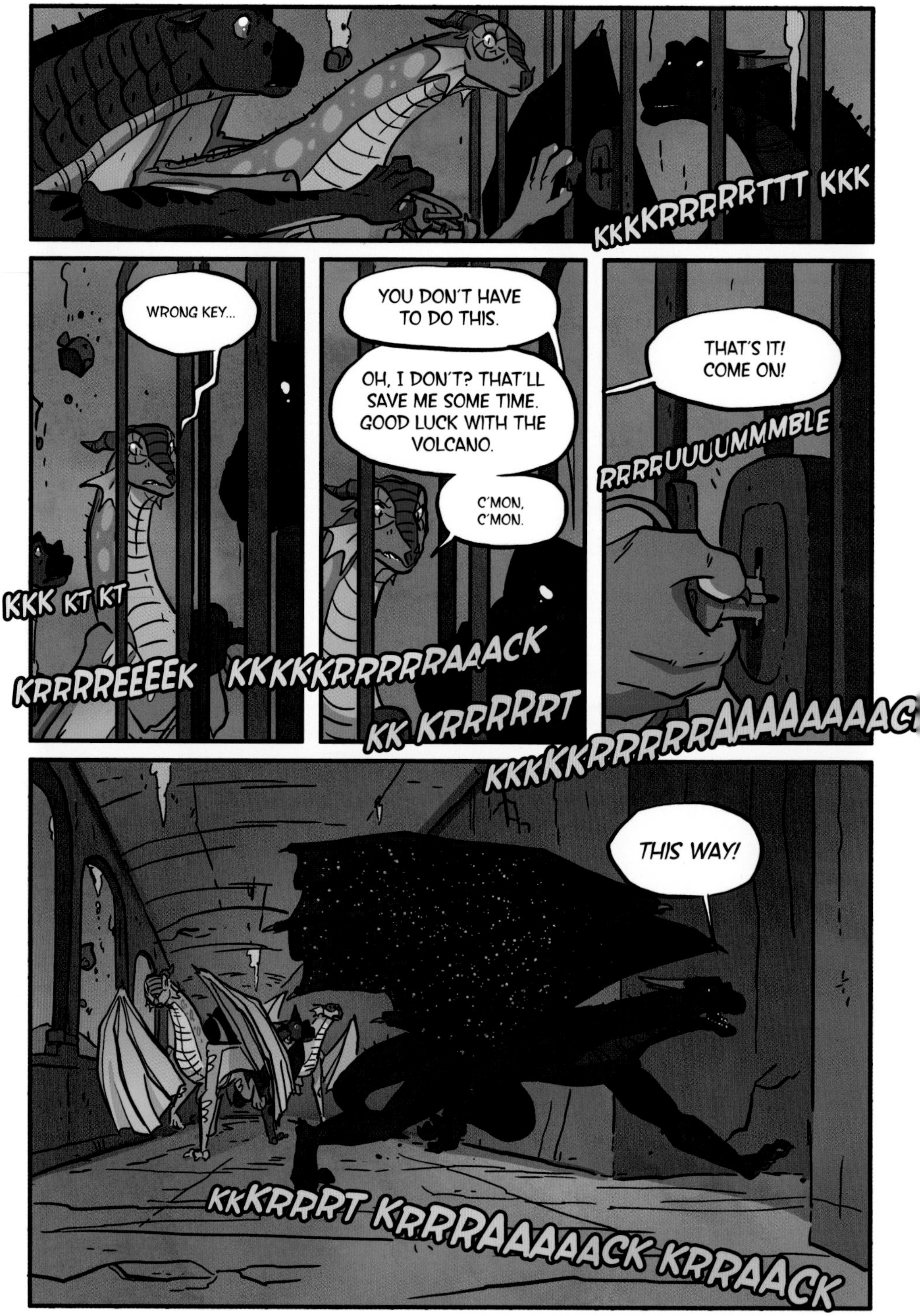
KKKKRRRRRTTT KKK
WRONG KEY...
KKK KT KT
KRRRREEEEK
YOU DON'T HAVE TO DO THIS.
OH, I DON'T? THAT'LL SAVE ME SOME TIME. GOOD LUCK WITH THE VOLCANO.
C'MON, C'MON.
KKKKKRRRRRRAAACK
KK KRRRRRT
THAT'S IT! COME ON!
RRRRUUUUMMMBLE
KKKKKRRRRRRAAAAAAAAG
THIS WAY!
KKKRRRT KRRRAAAAAACK KRRAACK

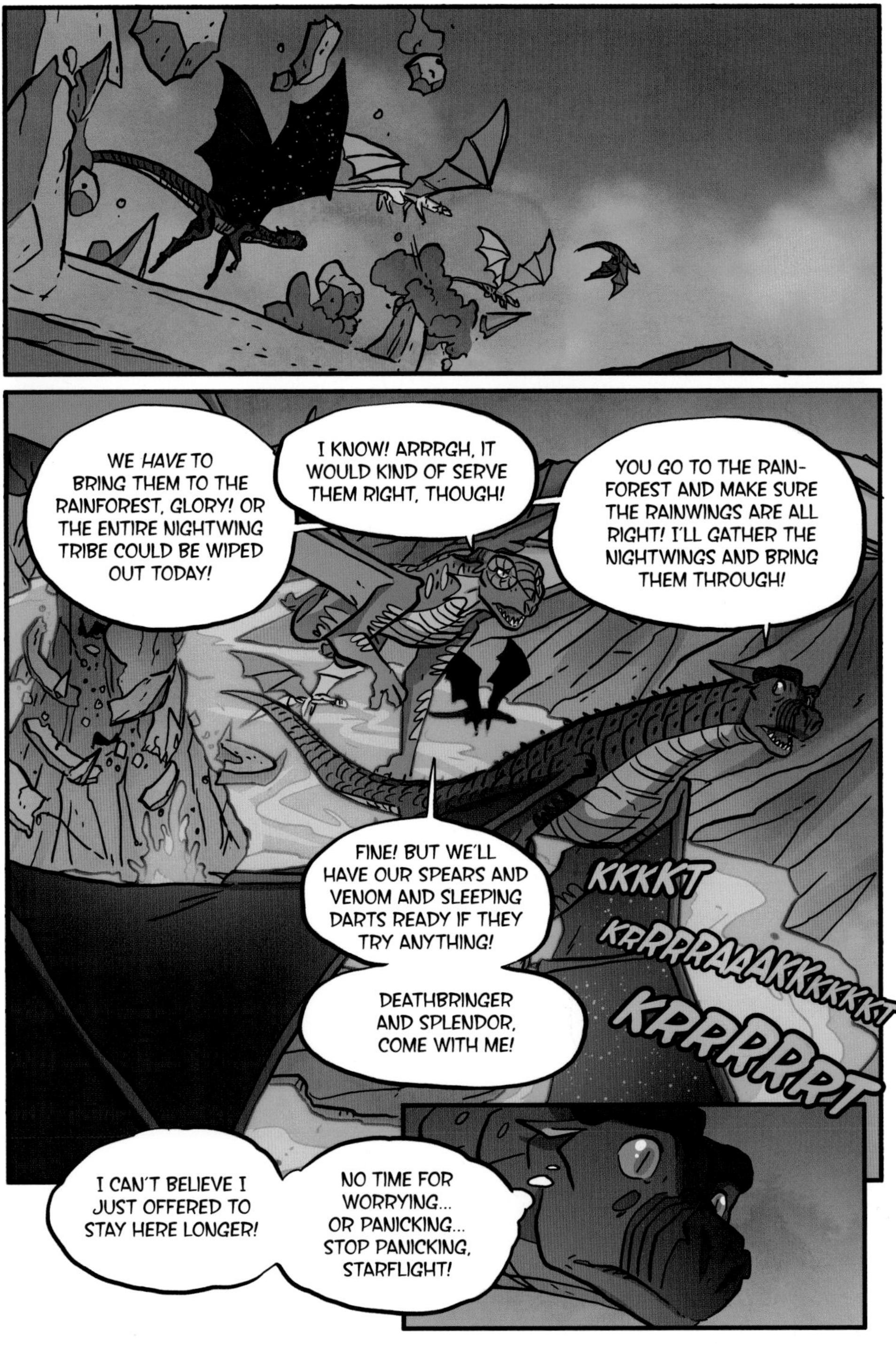
WE *HAVE* TO BRING THEM TO THE RAINFOREST, GLORY! OR THE ENTIRE NIGHTWING TRIBE COULD BE WIPED OUT TODAY!
I KNOW! ARRRGH, IT WOULD KIND OF SERVE THEM RIGHT, THOUGH!
YOU GO TO THE RAIN-FOREST AND MAKE SURE THE RAINWINGS ARE ALL RIGHT! I'LL GATHER THE NIGHTWINGS AND BRING THEM THROUGH!
FINE! BUT WE'LL HAVE OUR SPEARS AND VENOM AND SLEEPING DARTS READY IF THEY TRY ANYTHING!
DEATHBRINGER AND SPLENDOR, COME WITH ME!
KKKKT
KRRRRAAAKKKKKKT
KRRRRRRT
I CAN'T BELIEVE I JUST OFFERED TO STAY HERE LONGER!
NO TIME FOR WORRYING... OR PANICKING... STOP PANICKING, STARFLIGHT!

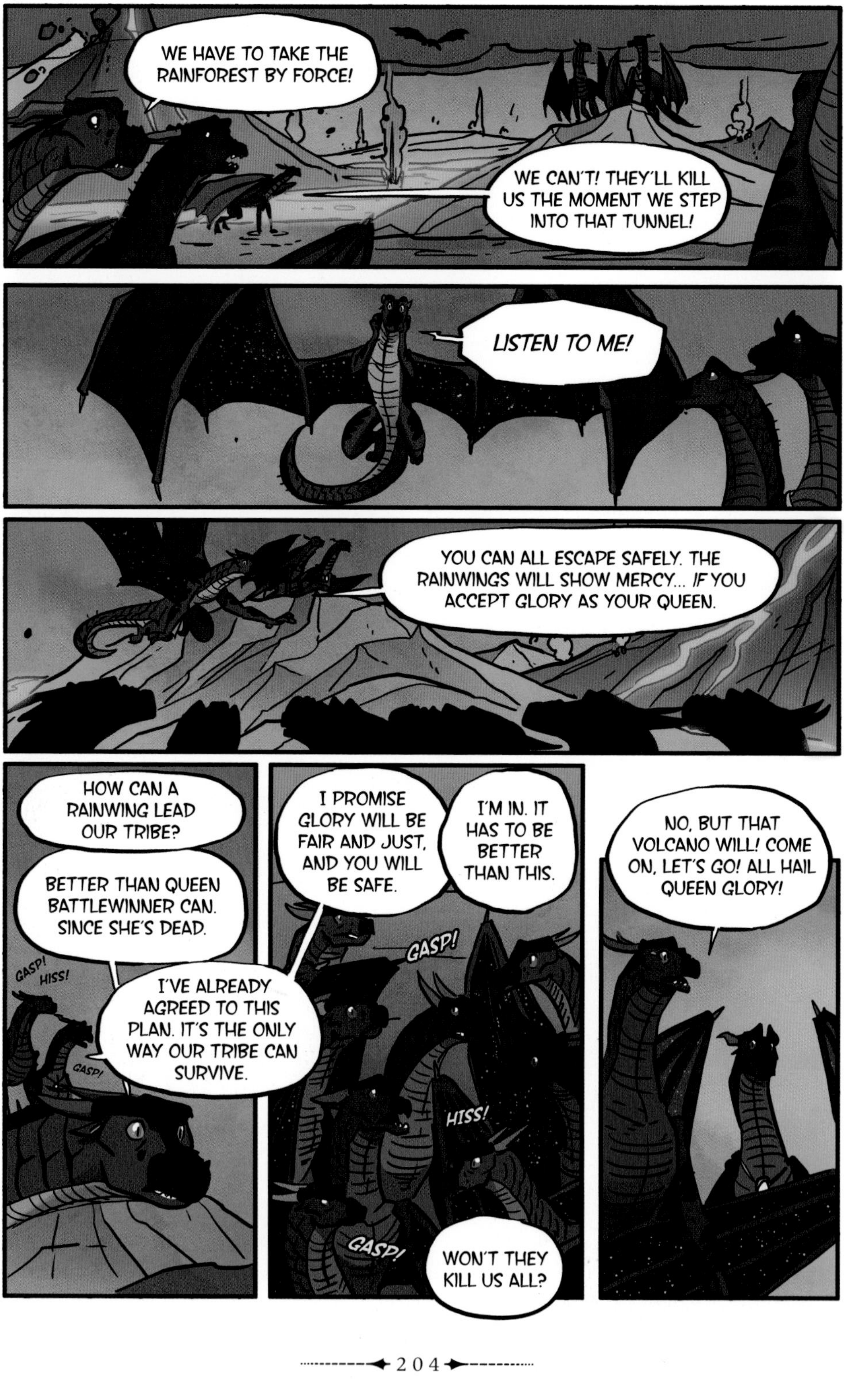
WE HAVE TO TAKE THE RAINFOREST BY FORCE!
WE CAN'T! THEY'LL KILL US THE MOMENT WE STEP INTO THAT TUNNEL!
LISTEN TO ME!
YOU CAN ALL ESCAPE SAFELY. THE RAINWINGS WILL SHOW MERCY... *IF* YOU ACCEPT GLORY AS YOUR QUEEN.
HOW CAN A RAINWING LEAD OUR TRIBE?
BETTER THAN QUEEN BATTLEWINNER CAN. SINCE SHE'S DEAD.
GASP!
HISS!
GASP!
I'VE ALREADY AGREED TO THIS PLAN. IT'S THE ONLY WAY OUR TRIBE CAN SURVIVE.
I PROMISE GLORY WILL BE FAIR AND JUST, AND YOU WILL BE SAFE.
I'M IN. IT HAS TO BE BETTER THAN THIS.
GASP!
HISS!
GASP!
WON'T THEY KILL US ALL?
NO, BUT THAT VOLCANO WILL! COME ON, LET'S GO! ALL HAIL QUEEN GLORY!

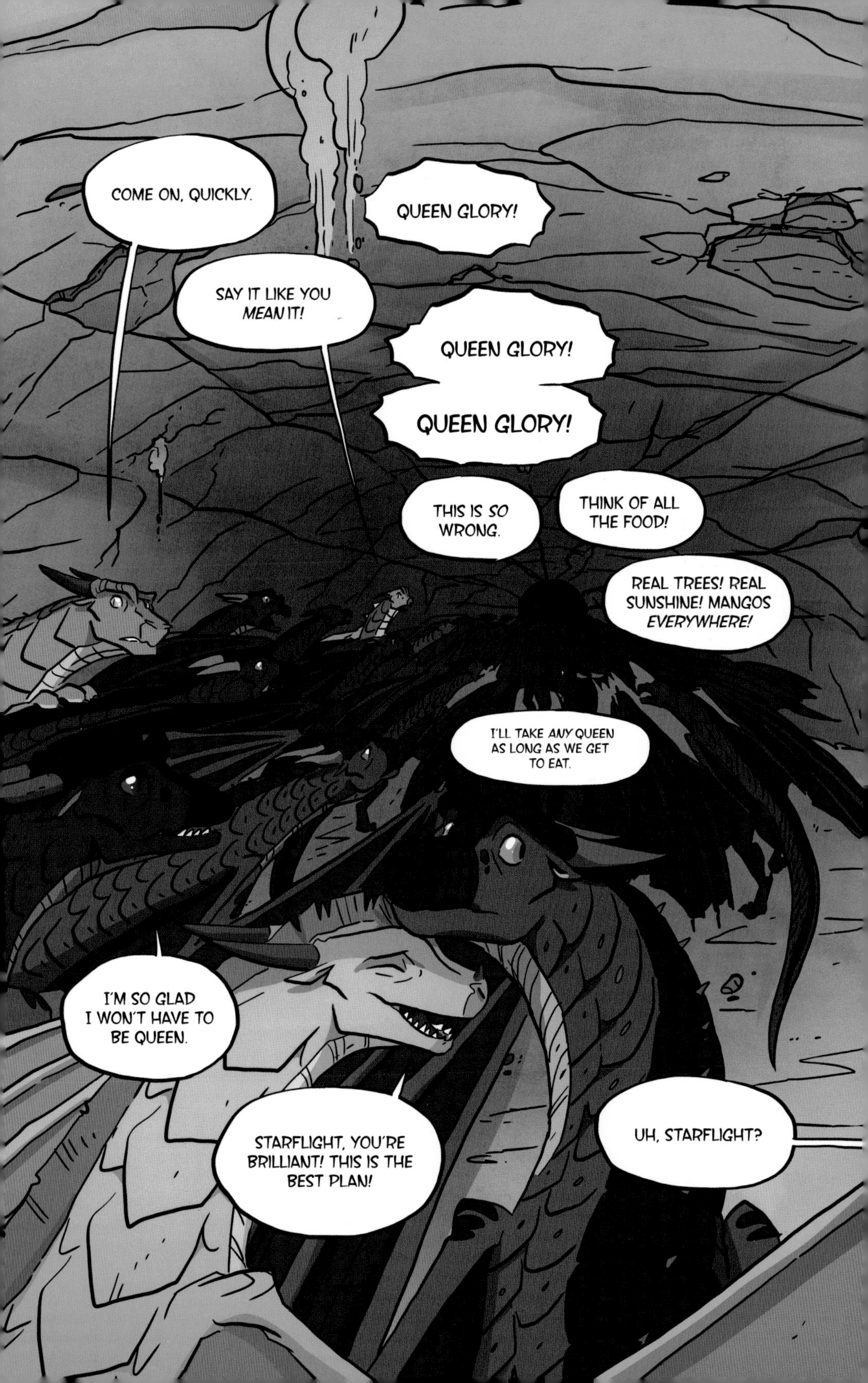
COME ON, QUICKLY.
QUEEN GLORY!
SAY IT LIKE YOU *MEAN* IT!
QUEEN GLORY!
QUEEN GLORY!
THIS IS *SO* WRONG.
THINK OF ALL THE FOOD!
REAL TREES! REAL SUNSHINE! MANGOS *EVERYWHERE!*
I'LL TAKE *ANY* QUEEN AS LONG AS WE GET TO EAT.
I'M SO GLAD I WON'T HAVE TO BE QUEEN.
STARFLIGHT, YOU'RE BRILLIANT! THIS IS THE BEST PLAN!
UH, STARFLIGHT?

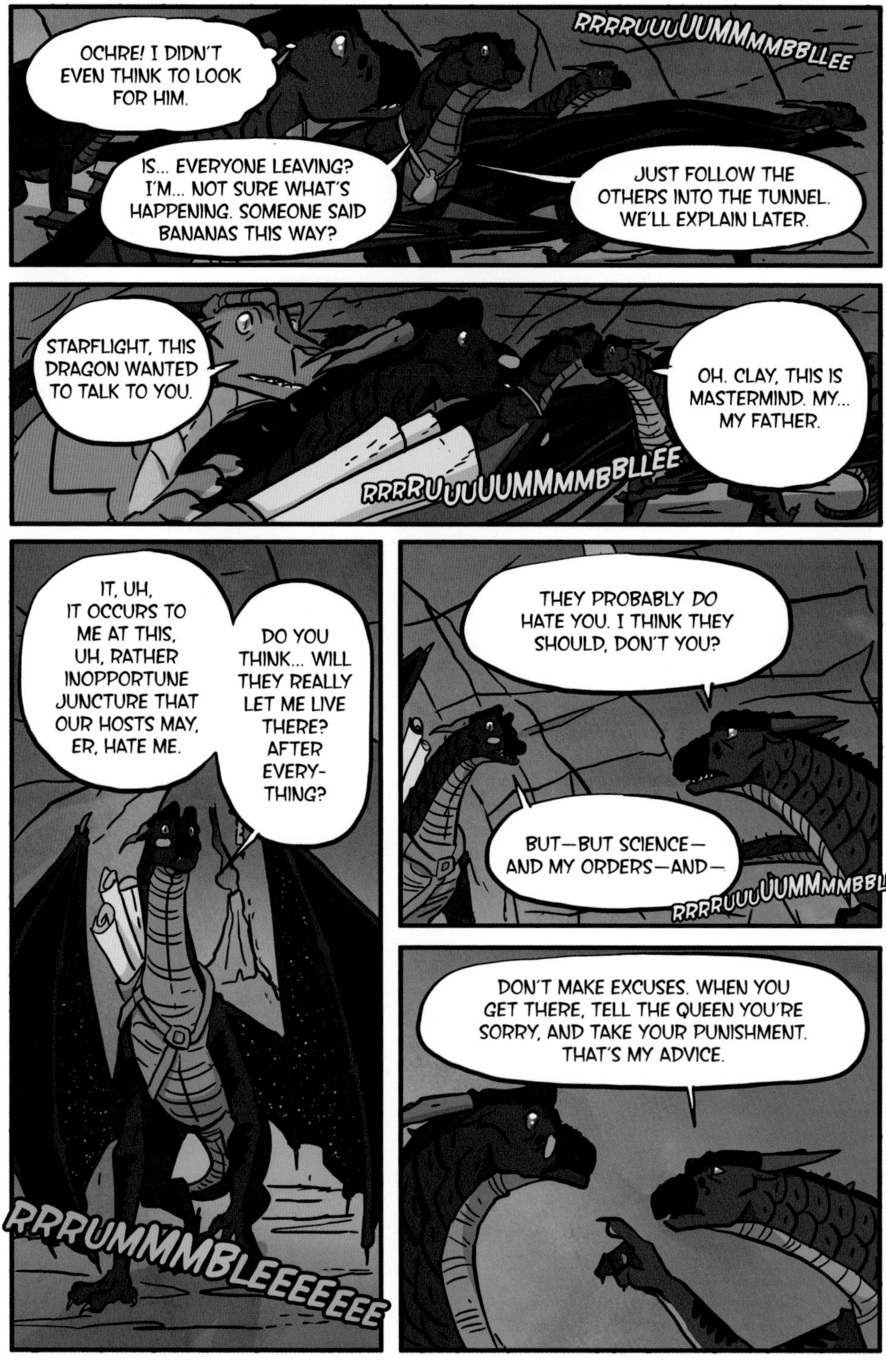
RRRRUUUUUMMMMBBLLEE
OCHRE! I DIDN'T EVEN THINK TO LOOK FOR HIM.
IS... EVERYONE LEAVING? I'M... NOT SURE WHAT'S HAPPENING. SOMEONE SAID BANANAS THIS WAY?
JUST FOLLOW THE OTHERS INTO THE TUNNEL. WE'LL EXPLAIN LATER.
STARFLIGHT, THIS DRAGON WANTED TO TALK TO YOU.
OH. CLAY, THIS IS MASTERMIND. MY... MY FATHER.
RRRRUUUUUMMMMBBLLEE
IT, UH, IT OCCURS TO ME AT THIS, UH, RATHER INOPPORTUNE JUNCTURE THAT OUR HOSTS MAY, ER, HATE ME.
DO YOU THINK... WILL THEY REALLY LET ME LIVE THERE? AFTER EVERY-THING?
RRRUMMMMBLEEEEEEE
THEY PROBABLY DO HATE YOU. I THINK THEY SHOULD, DON'T YOU?
BUT—BUT SCIENCE—AND MY ORDERS—AND—
RRRRUUUUUMMMMBBLLEE
DON'T MAKE EXCUSES. WHEN YOU GET THERE, TELL THE QUEEN YOU'RE SORRY, AND TAKE YOUR PUNISHMENT. THAT'S MY ADVICE.

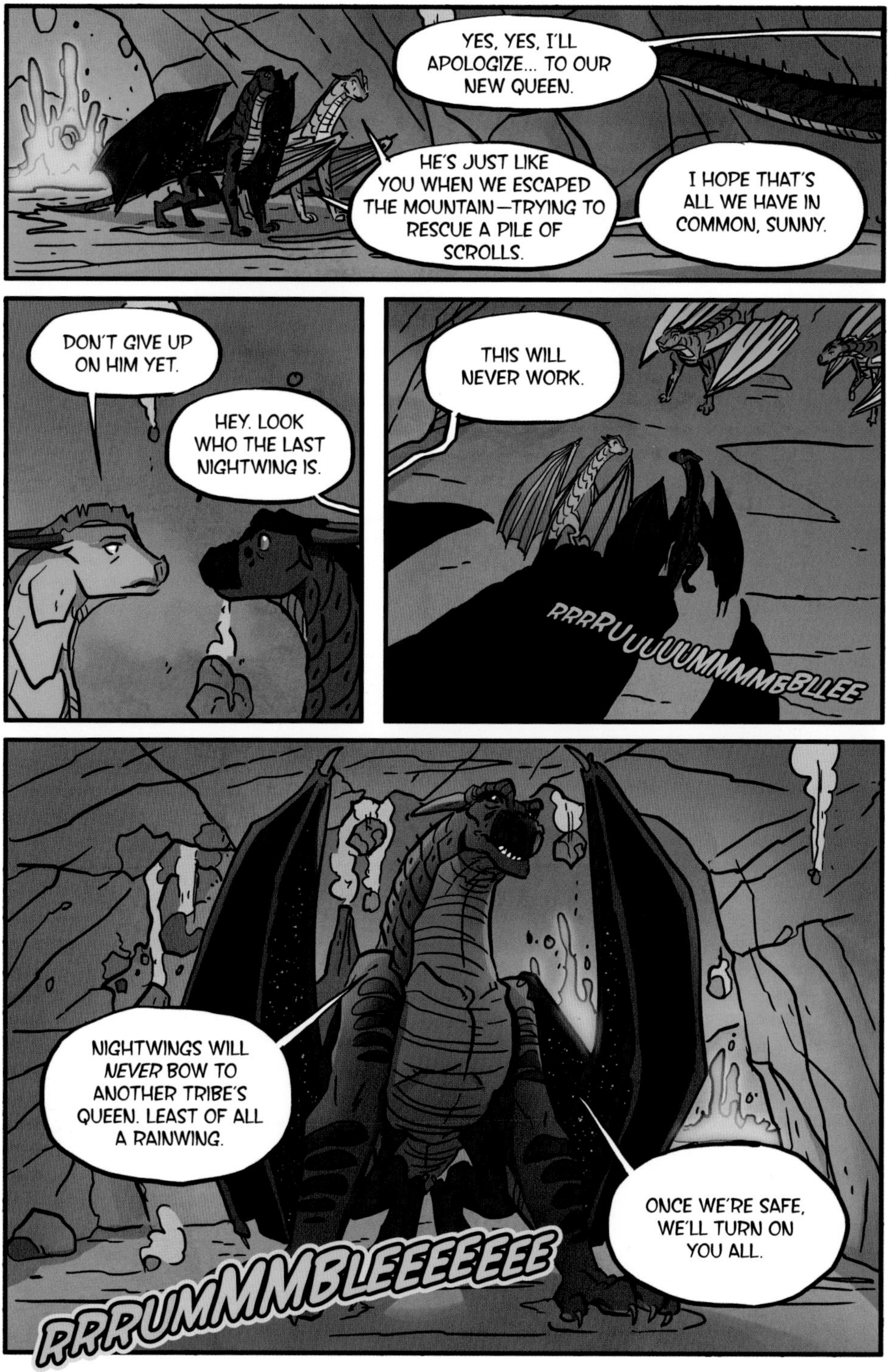
YES, YES, I'LL APOLOGIZE... TO OUR NEW QUEEN.
HE'S JUST LIKE YOU WHEN WE ESCAPED THE MOUNTAIN—TRYING TO RESCUE A PILE OF SCROLLS.
I HOPE THAT'S ALL WE HAVE IN COMMON, SUNNY.
DON'T GIVE UP ON HIM YET.
HEY. LOOK WHO THE LAST NIGHTWING IS.
THIS WILL NEVER WORK.
RRRRUUUUUMMMMBLLEE
NIGHTWINGS WILL *NEVER* BOW TO ANOTHER TRIBE'S QUEEN. LEAST OF ALL A RAINWING.
ONCE WE'RE SAFE, WE'LL TURN ON YOU ALL.
RRRUMMMBLEEEEEEE

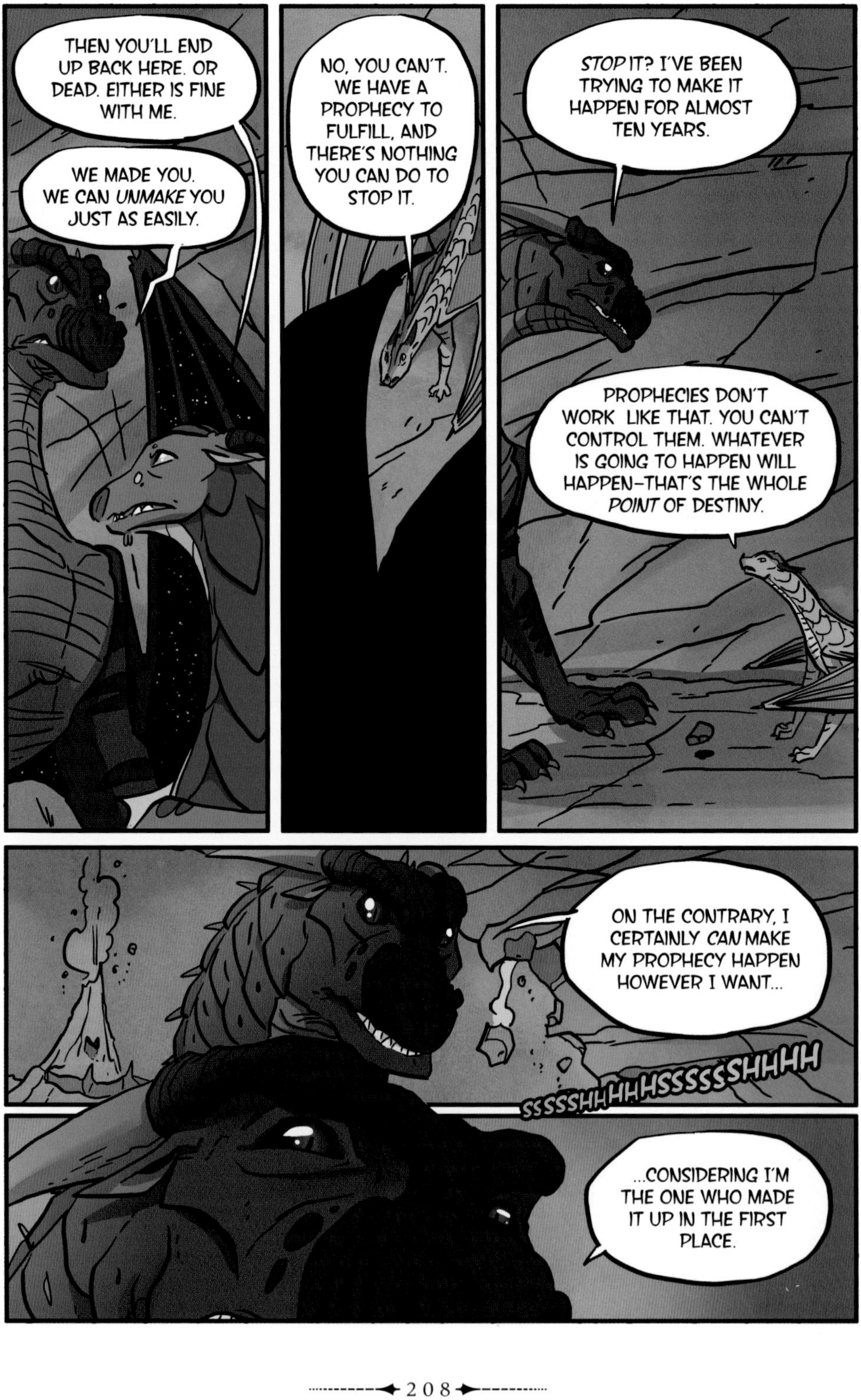
THEN YOU'LL END UP BACK HERE. OR DEAD. EITHER IS FINE WITH ME.
WE MADE YOU. WE CAN *UNMAKE* YOU JUST AS EASILY.
NO, YOU CAN'T. WE HAVE A PROPHECY TO FULFILL, AND THERE'S NOTHING YOU CAN DO TO STOP IT.
STOP IT? I'VE BEEN TRYING TO MAKE IT HAPPEN FOR ALMOST TEN YEARS.
PROPHECIES DON'T WORK LIKE THAT. YOU CAN'T CONTROL THEM. WHATEVER IS GOING TO HAPPEN WILL HAPPEN—THAT'S THE WHOLE *POINT* OF DESTINY.
ON THE CONTRARY, I CERTAINLY *CAN* MAKE MY PROPHECY HAPPEN HOWEVER I WANT...
SSSSSHHHHHSSSSSSHHHH
...CONSIDERING I'M THE ONE WHO MADE IT UP IN THE FIRST PLACE.

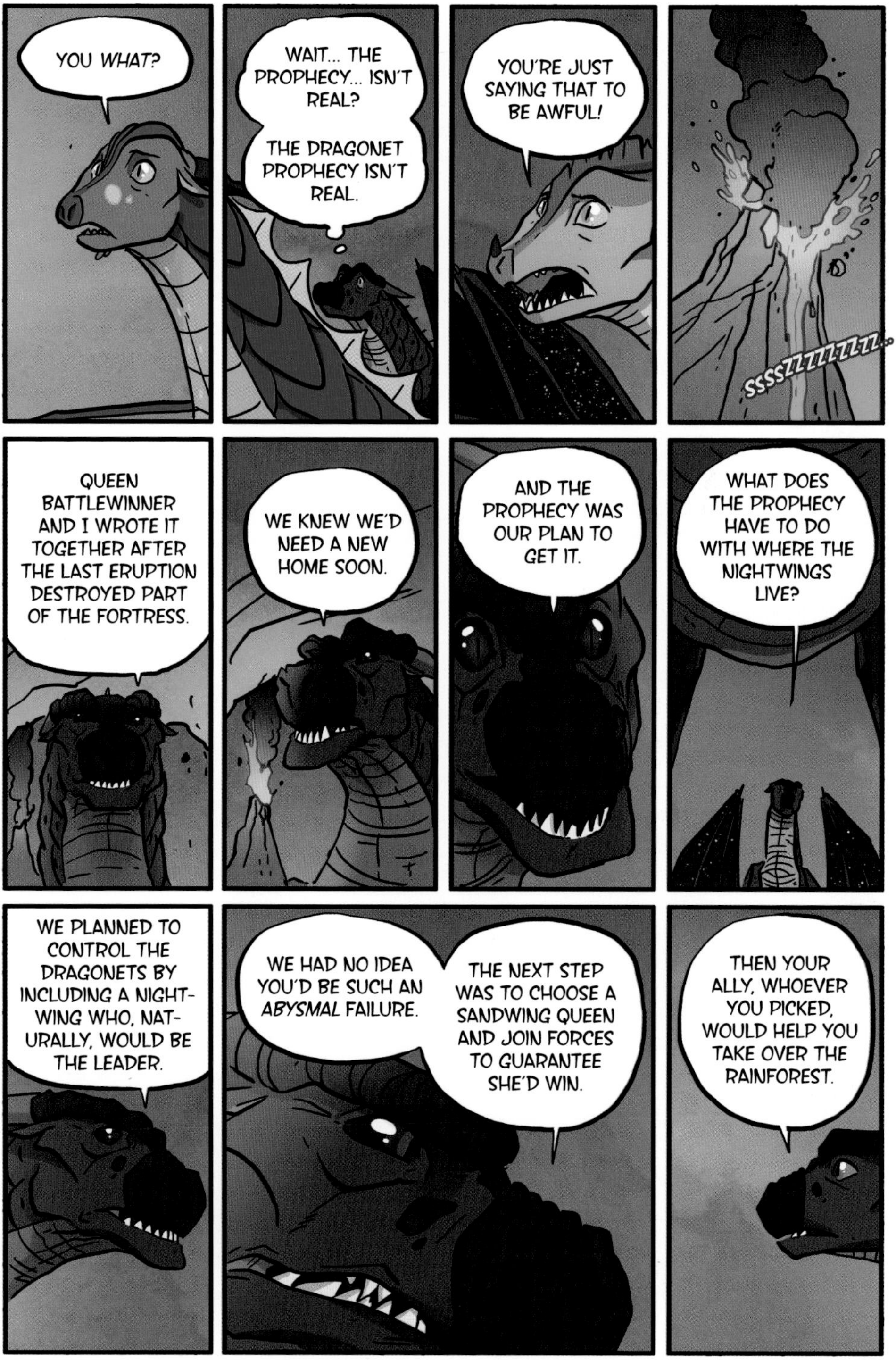

YOU WHAT?
WAIT... THE PROPHECY... ISN'T REAL?
THE DRAGONET PROPHECY ISN'T REAL.
YOU'RE JUST SAYING THAT TO BE AWFUL!
SSSSZZZZZZZZZ...
QUEEN BATTLEWINNER AND I WROTE IT TOGETHER AFTER THE LAST ERUPTION DESTROYED PART OF THE FORTRESS.
WE KNEW WE'D NEED A NEW HOME SOON.
AND THE PROPHECY WAS OUR PLAN TO GET IT.
WHAT DOES THE PROPHECY HAVE TO DO WITH WHERE THE NIGHTWINGS LIVE?
WE PLANNED TO CONTROL THE DRAGONETS BY INCLUDING A NIGHT-WING WHO, NAT-URALLY, WOULD BE THE LEADER.
WE HAD NO IDEA YOU'D BE SUCH AN *ABYSMAL* FAILURE.
THE NEXT STEP WAS TO CHOOSE A SANDWING QUEEN AND JOIN FORCES TO GUARANTEE SHE'D WIN.
THEN YOUR ALLY, WHOEVER YOU PICKED, WOULD HELP YOU TAKE OVER THE RAINFOREST.

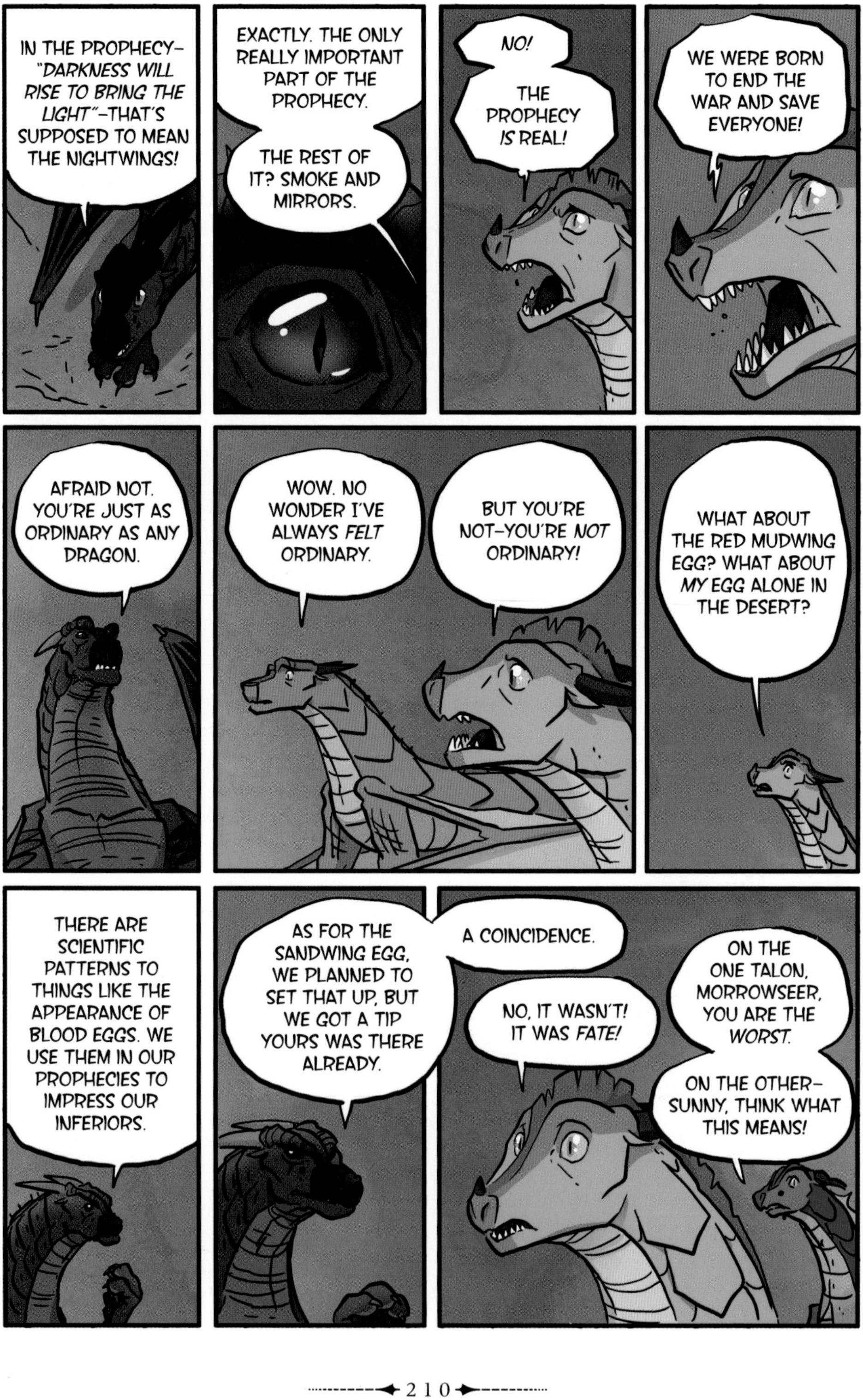
IN THE PROPHECY– "*DARKNESS WILL RISE TO BRING THE LIGHT*"–THAT'S SUPPOSED TO MEAN THE NIGHTWINGS!
EXACTLY. THE ONLY REALLY IMPORTANT PART OF THE PROPHECY.
THE REST OF IT? SMOKE AND MIRRORS.
NO!
THE PROPHECY *IS* REAL!
WE WERE BORN TO END THE WAR AND SAVE EVERYONE!
AFRAID NOT. YOU'RE JUST AS ORDINARY AS ANY DRAGON.
WOW. NO WONDER I'VE ALWAYS *FELT* ORDINARY.
BUT YOU'RE NOT–YOU'RE *NOT* ORDINARY!
WHAT ABOUT THE RED MUDWING EGG? WHAT ABOUT *MY* EGG ALONE IN THE DESERT?
THERE ARE SCIENTIFIC PATTERNS TO THINGS LIKE THE APPEARANCE OF BLOOD EGGS. WE USE THEM IN OUR PROPHECIES TO IMPRESS OUR INFERIORS.
AS FOR THE SANDWING EGG, WE PLANNED TO SET THAT UP, BUT WE GOT A TIP YOURS WAS THERE ALREADY.
A COINCIDENCE.
NO, IT WASN'T! IT WAS *FATE!*
ON THE ONE TALON, MORROWSEER, YOU ARE THE *WORST*.
ON THE OTHER– SUNNY, THINK WHAT THIS MEANS!

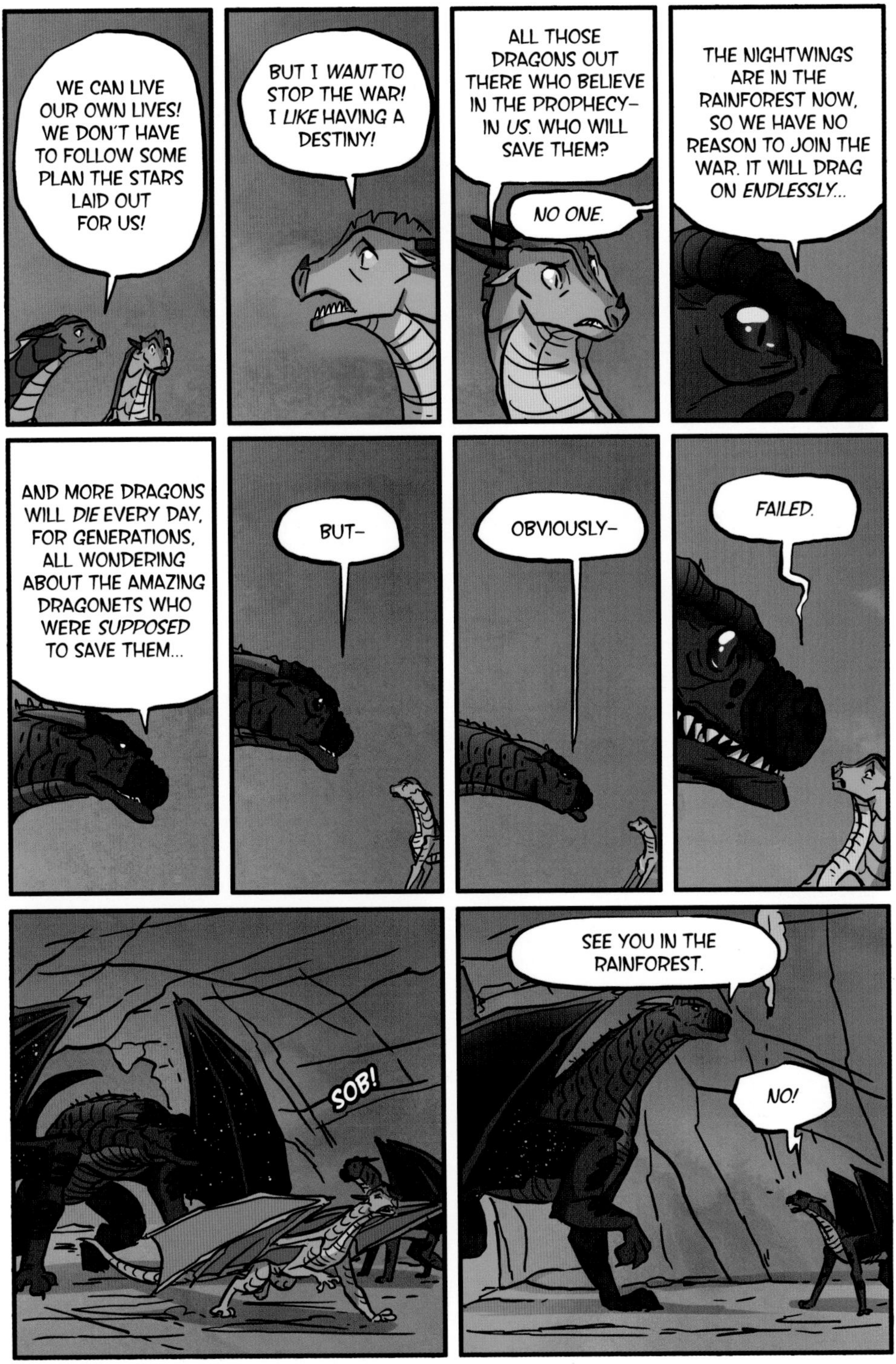
WE CAN LIVE OUR OWN LIVES! WE DON'T HAVE TO FOLLOW SOME PLAN THE STARS LAID OUT FOR US!
BUT I *WANT* TO STOP THE WAR! I *LIKE* HAVING A DESTINY!
ALL THOSE DRAGONS OUT THERE WHO BELIEVE IN THE PROPHECY– IN *US*. WHO WILL SAVE THEM?
NO ONE.
THE NIGHTWINGS ARE IN THE RAINFOREST NOW, SO WE HAVE NO REASON TO JOIN THE WAR. IT WILL DRAG ON *ENDLESSLY*...
AND MORE DRAGONS WILL *DIE* EVERY DAY, FOR GENERATIONS, ALL WONDERING ABOUT THE AMAZING DRAGONETS WHO WERE *SUPPOSED* TO SAVE THEM...
BUT–
OBVIOUSLY–
FAILED.
SOB!
SEE YOU IN THE RAINFOREST.
NO!

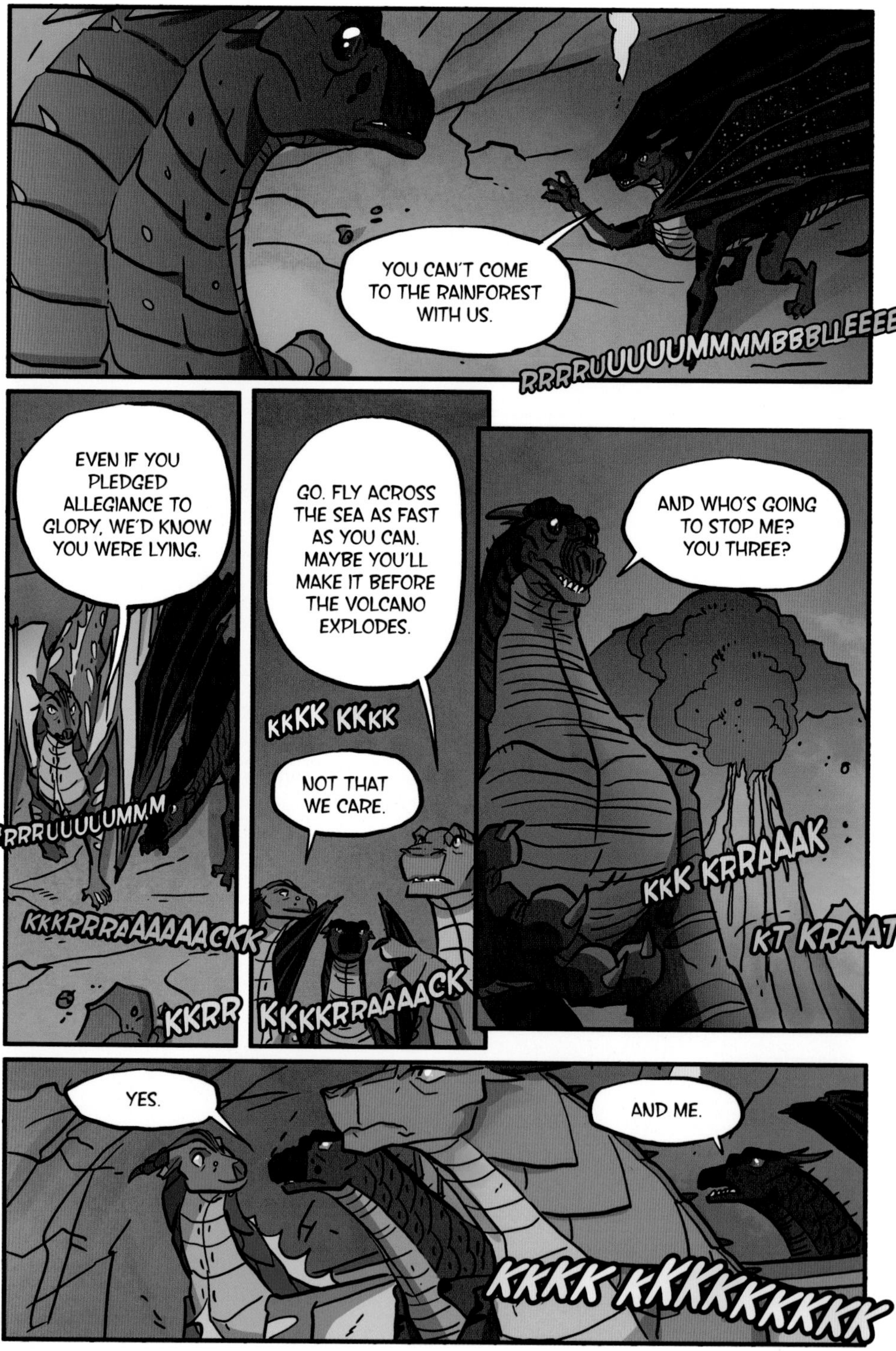
YOU CAN'T COME TO THE RAINFOREST WITH US.
RRRRUUUUUMMMMBBBLLEEEE
EVEN IF YOU PLEDGED ALLEGIANCE TO GLORY, WE'D KNOW YOU WERE LYING.
RRRRRUUUUUMMM
KKKRRRAAAAAACKK
KKRR
GO. FLY ACROSS THE SEA AS FAST AS YOU CAN. MAYBE YOU'LL MAKE IT BEFORE THE VOLCANO EXPLODES.
KKKK KKKK
NOT THAT WE CARE.
KKKKRRAAAACK
AND WHO'S GOING TO STOP ME? YOU THREE?
KKK KRRAAAK
KT KRAAT
YES.
AND ME.
KKKK KKKKKKKKK

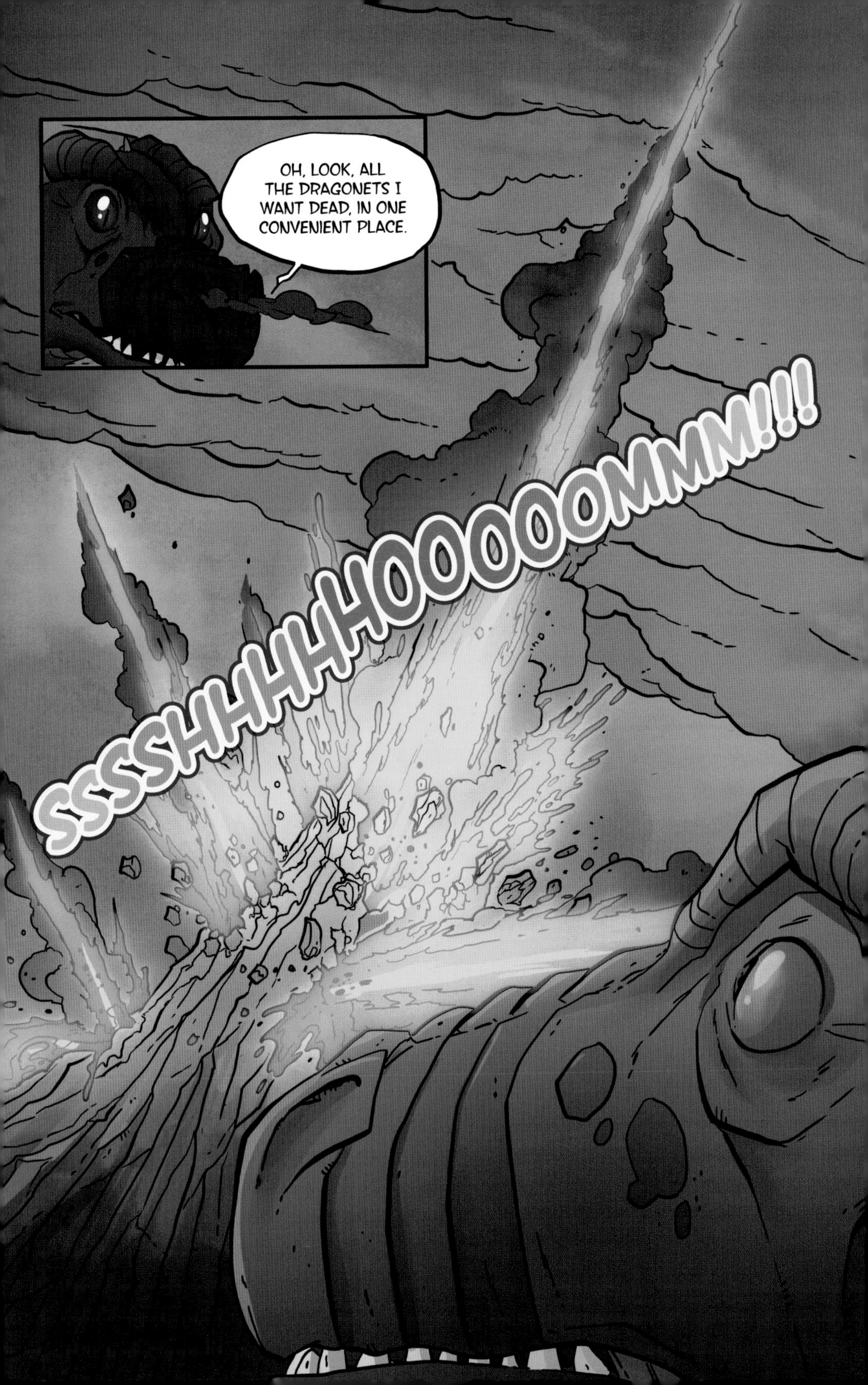
OH, LOOK, ALL THE DRAGONETS I WANT DEAD, IN ONE CONVENIENT PLACE.
SSSSHHHHHOOOOOOMMMM!!!

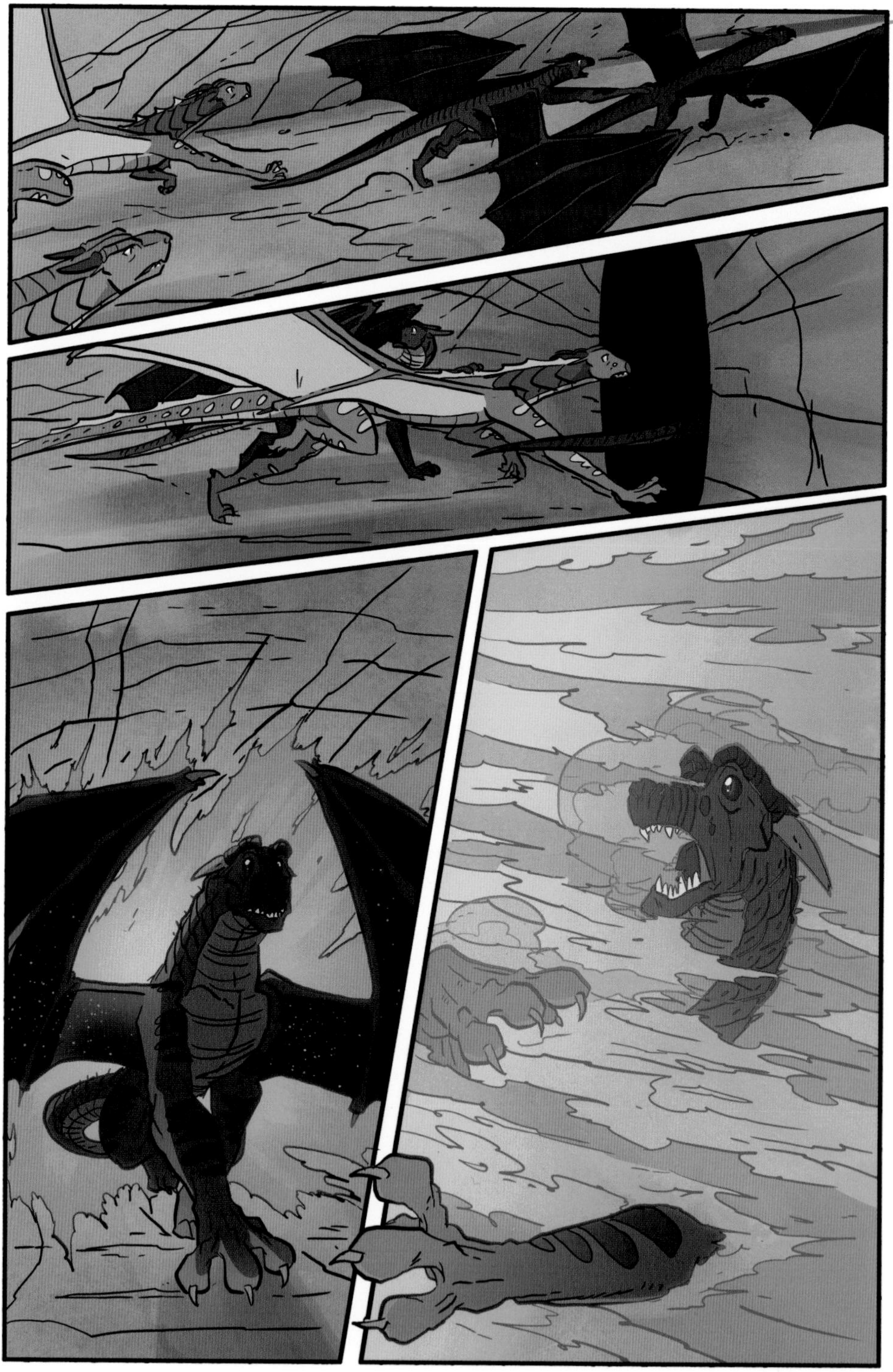

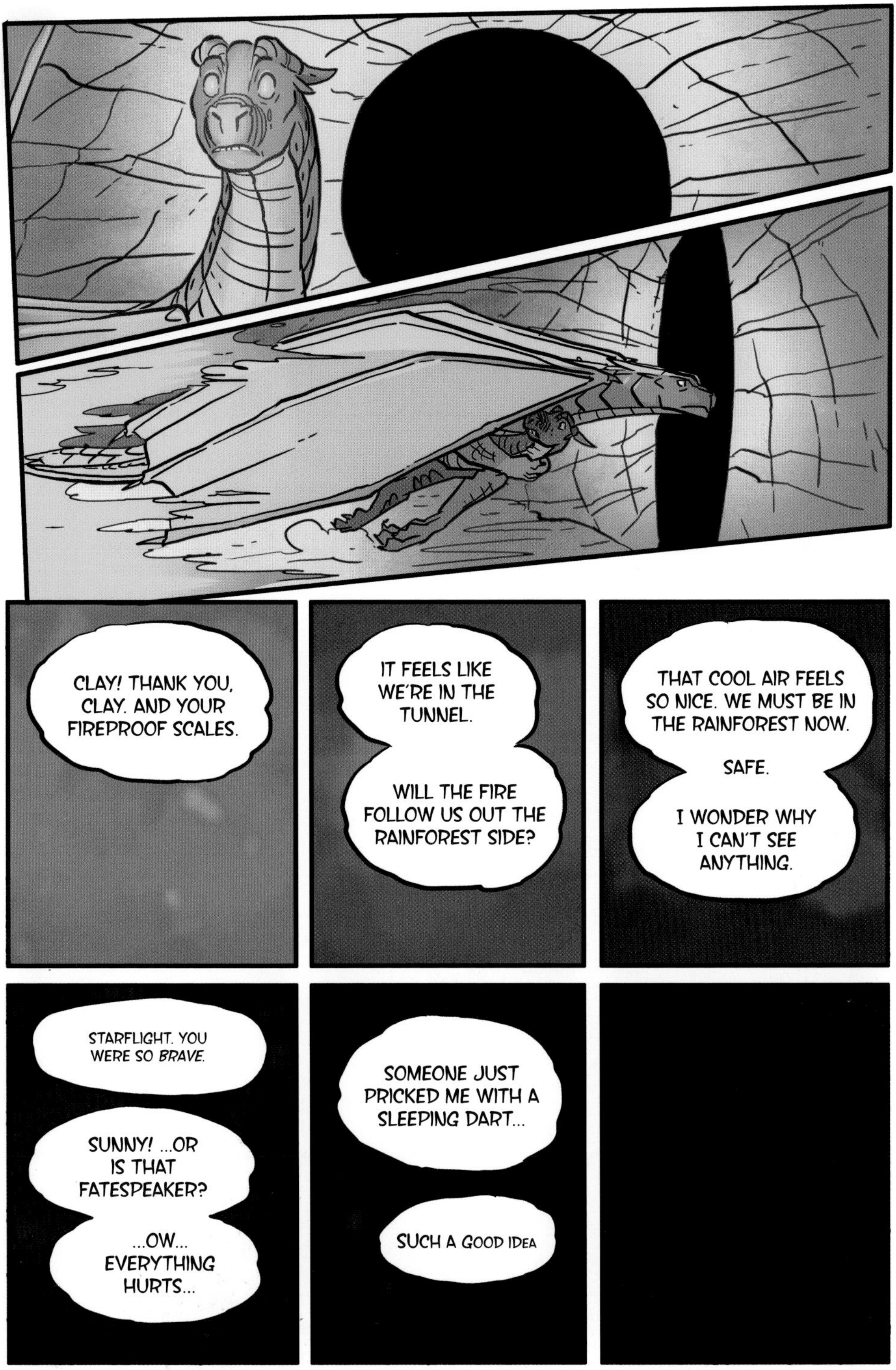
CLAY! THANK YOU, CLAY. AND YOUR FIREPROOF SCALES.
IT FEELS LIKE WE'RE IN THE TUNNEL.
WILL THE FIRE FOLLOW US OUT THE RAINFOREST SIDE?
THAT COOL AIR FEELS SO NICE. WE MUST BE IN THE RAINFOREST NOW.
SAFE.
I WONDER WHY I CAN'T SEE ANYTHING.
STARFLIGHT. YOU WERE SO *BRAVE*.
SUNNY! ...OR IS THAT FATESPEAKER?
...OW... EVERYTHING HURTS...
SOMEONE JUST PRICKED ME WITH A SLEEPING DART...
SUCH A GOOD IDEA

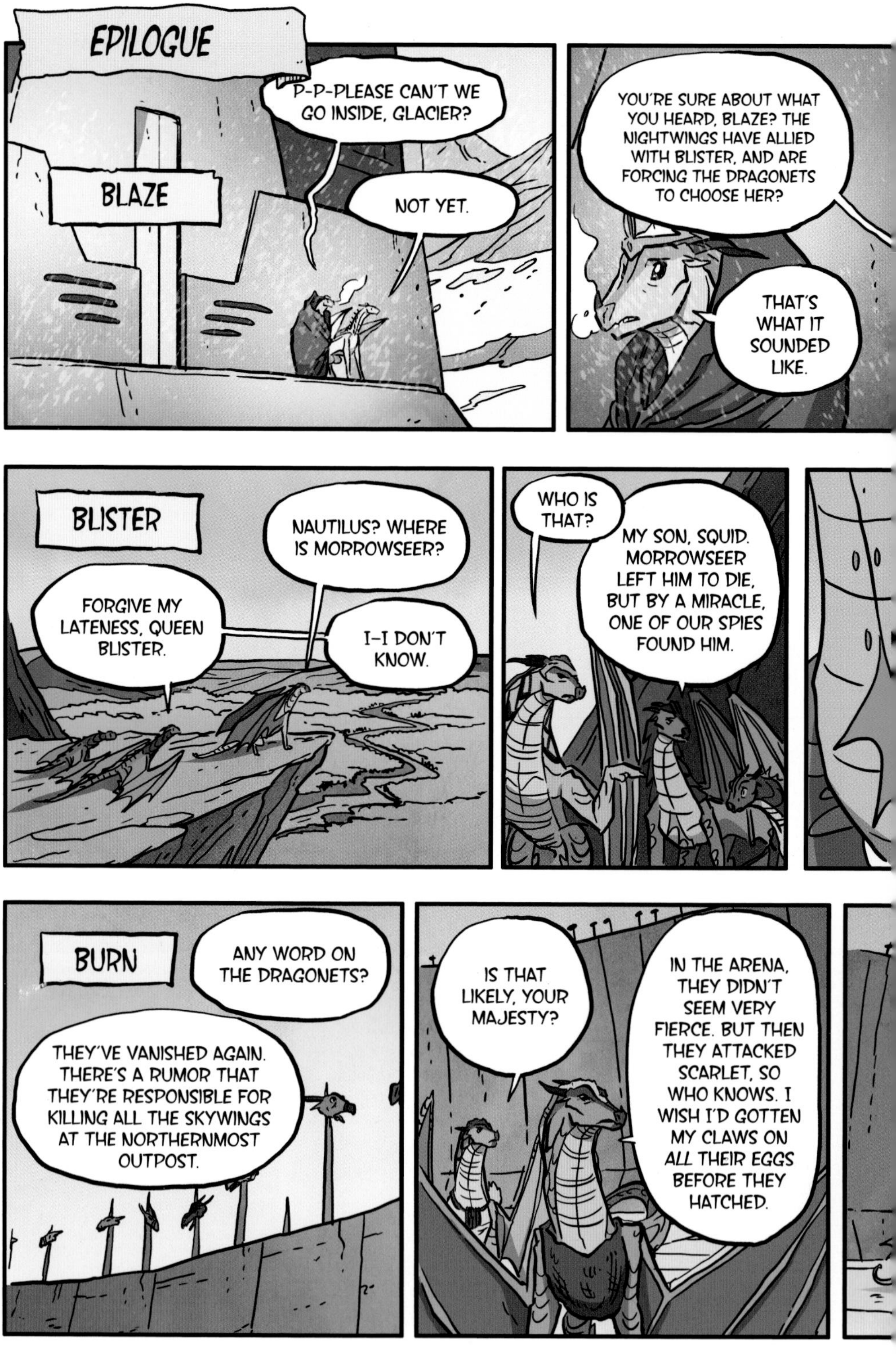
EPILOGUE
BLAZE
P-P-PLEASE CAN'T WE GO INSIDE, GLACIER?
NOT YET.
YOU'RE SURE ABOUT WHAT YOU HEARD, BLAZE? THE NIGHTWINGS HAVE ALLIED WITH BLISTER, AND ARE FORCING THE DRAGONETS TO CHOOSE HER?
THAT'S WHAT IT SOUNDED LIKE.
BLISTER
NAUTILUS? WHERE IS MORROWSEER?
FORGIVE MY LATENESS, QUEEN BLISTER.
I-I DON'T KNOW.
WHO IS THAT?
MY SON, SQUID. MORROWSEER LEFT HIM TO DIE, BUT BY A MIRACLE, ONE OF OUR SPIES FOUND HIM.
BURN
ANY WORD ON THE DRAGONETS?
THEY'VE VANISHED AGAIN. THERE'S A RUMOR THAT THEY'RE RESPONSIBLE FOR KILLING ALL THE SKYWINGS AT THE NORTHERNMOST OUTPOST.
IS THAT LIKELY, YOUR MAJESTY?
IN THE ARENA, THEY DIDN'T SEEM VERY FIERCE. BUT THEN THEY ATTACKED SCARLET, SO WHO KNOWS. I WISH I'D GOTTEN MY CLAWS ON ALL THEIR EGGS BEFORE THEY HATCHED.

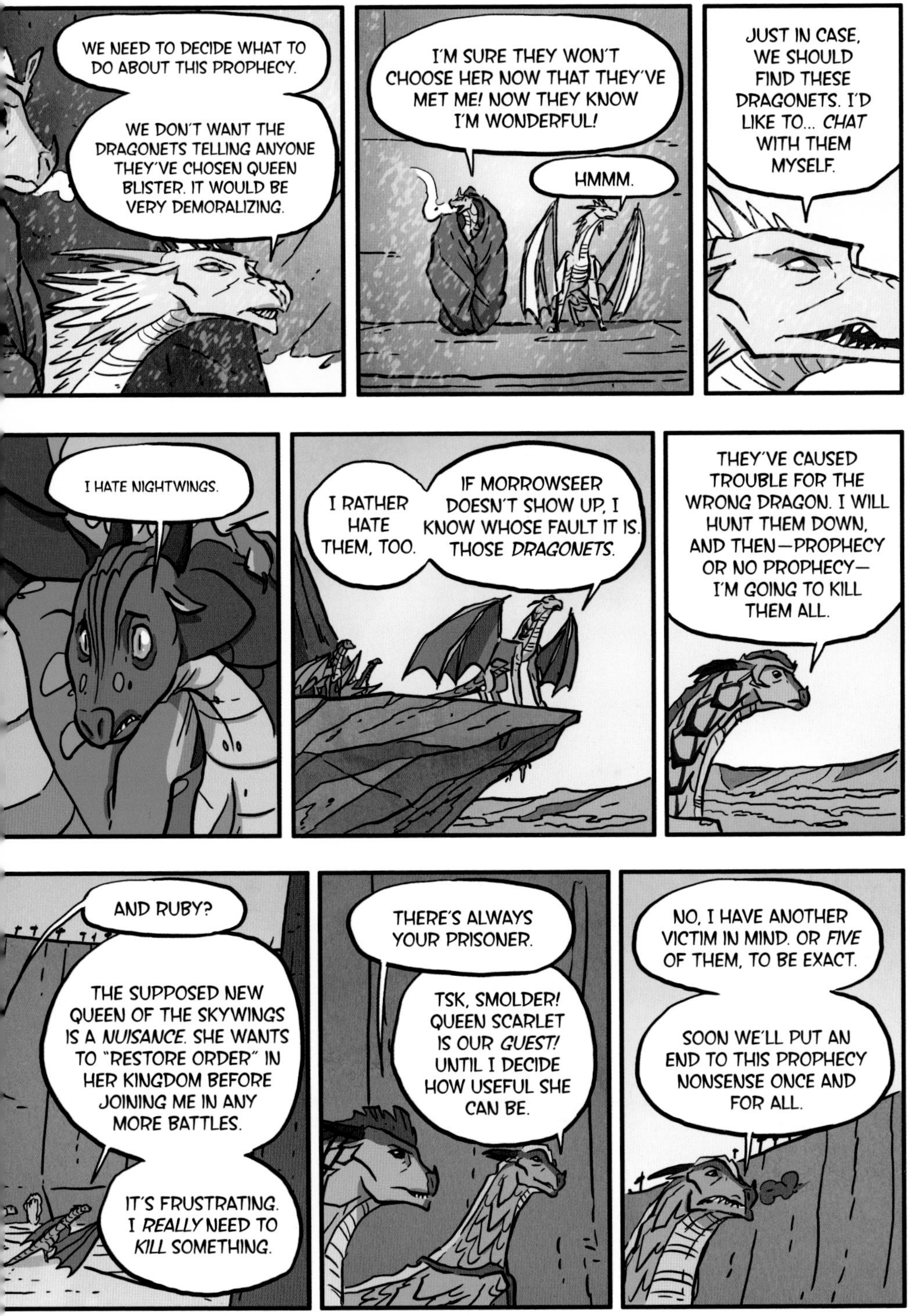
WE NEED TO DECIDE WHAT TO DO ABOUT THIS PROPHECY.
WE DON'T WANT THE DRAGONETS TELLING ANYONE THEY'VE CHOSEN QUEEN BLISTER. IT WOULD BE VERY DEMORALIZING.
I'M SURE THEY WON'T CHOOSE HER NOW THAT THEY'VE MET ME! NOW THEY KNOW I'M WONDERFUL!
HMMM.
JUST IN CASE, WE SHOULD FIND THESE DRAGONETS. I'D LIKE TO... *CHAT* WITH THEM MYSELF.
I HATE NIGHTWINGS.
I RATHER HATE THEM, TOO.
IF MORROWSEER DOESN'T SHOW UP, I KNOW WHOSE FAULT IT IS. THOSE *DRAGONETS*.
THEY'VE CAUSED TROUBLE FOR THE WRONG DRAGON. I WILL HUNT THEM DOWN, AND THEN—PROPHECY OR NO PROPHECY—I'M GOING TO KILL THEM ALL.
AND RUBY?
THE SUPPOSED NEW QUEEN OF THE SKYWINGS IS A *NUISANCE*. SHE WANTS TO "RESTORE ORDER" IN HER KINGDOM BEFORE JOINING ME IN ANY MORE BATTLES.
IT'S FRUSTRATING. I *REALLY* NEED TO *KILL* SOMETHING.
THERE'S ALWAYS YOUR PRISONER.
TSK, SMOLDER! QUEEN SCARLET IS OUR *GUEST!* UNTIL I DECIDE HOW USEFUL SHE CAN BE.
NO, I HAVE ANOTHER VICTIM IN MIND. OR *FIVE* OF THEM, TO BE EXACT.
SOON WE'LL PUT AN END TO THIS PROPHECY NONSENSE ONCE AND FOR ALL.

TUI T. SUTHERLAND is the author of the #1 *New York Times* and *USA Today* bestselling Wings of Fire series, the Menagerie trilogy, and the Pet Trouble series, as well as a contributing author to the bestselling Spirit Animals and Seekers series (as part of the Erin Hunter team). In 2009, she was a two-day champion on *Jeopardy!* She lives in Massachusetts with her wonderful husband, two awesome sons, and two very patient dogs. To learn more about Tui's books, visit her online at www.tuibooks.com.

BARRY DEUTSCH is an award-winning cartoonist and the creator of the Hereville series of graphic novels, about yet another troll-fighting 11-year-old Orthodox Jewish girl. He lives in Portland, Oregon, with a variable number of cats and fish.

MIKE HOLMES has drawn for the series Secret Coders, Adventure Time, and Bravest Warriors. He created the comic strip True Story, the art project *Mikenesses*, and his work can be seen in *MAD* Magazine. He lives in Philadelphia with his wife Meredith and son Oscar, along with Heidi the dog and Ella the cat.

MAARTA LAIHO spends her days and nights as a comic colorist, where her work includes the comics series Lumberjanes, Adventure Time, and The Mighty Zodiac. When she's not doing that, she can be found hoarding houseplants and talking to her cat. She lives in the woods of Maine.